D105885B

THE
CASTLE
CROSS
THE
MAGNET
CARTER

THE CASTLE CROSS THE MAGNET CARTER

A Novel

Kia Corthron

Seven Stories Press

New York ❖ Oakland

SAYVILLE LIBRARY

Copyright © 2016 by Kia Corthron

A SEVEN STORIES PRESS FIRST EDITION

All rights reserved. No part of this book may be reproduced, stored in a retrieval system, or transmitted in any form or by any means, including mechanical, electronic, photocopying, recording, or otherwise, without the prior written permission of the publisher.

Excerpt from *The Story of My Life* by Hellen Keller. Used by permission, W. W. Norton & Co., 2003 [originally 1903], New York.
Excerpt from *Madeline* by Ludwig Bemelmans, copyright 1939 by Ludwig Bemelmans; copyright renewed © 1967 by Madeleine Bemelmans and Barbara Bemelmans Marciano. Used by permission of Viking Books, an imprint of Penguin Publishing Group, a division of Penguin Random House LLC.
Excerpt from *Pittsburgh Courier* archives, January 31, 1942, James G. Thompson, Letter to the Editor.
Excerpt from *Invisible Man* by Ralph Ellison, used by permission, Penguin Random House LLC.
Excerpt from *Helen Keller: Her Socialist Years* by Philip S. Foner, used with permission from International Publishers Co., Inc., New York.
Excerpt from *A Farewell to Arms* by Ernest Hemingway, copyright 1929 by Charles Scribner's Sons. Copyright renewed 1957 by Ernest Hemingway. Used with permission of Scribner, a division of Simon & Schuster, Inc.

Seven Stories Press
140 Watts Street
New York, NY 10013
sevenstories.com

Library of Congress Cataloging-in-Publication Data

Corthron, Kia.
  The castle cross the magnet carter : a novel / by Kia Corthron. -- Seven Stories Press first edition.
     pages ; cm
  ISBN 978-1-60980-657-6 (hardback)
  1. Brothers--Fiction. 2. African Americans--Fiction. 3. United States--Race relations--Fiction. I. Title.
  PS3553.O724C37 2016
  813'.54--dc23
                              2015029672

Printed in the United States of America

9 8 7 6 5 4 3 2 1

In memory of my parents
Shirley Elaine Beckwith Corthron
and James Leroye Corthron

1941–42
PRAYER RIDGE

RANDALL

I

I got the world.

My family and the trees, the library, picture shows, history and geography and Nathaniel Hawthorne and Longfellow and in the advanced class Mr. Faulkner. I got Prayer Ridge and Lefferd County and the state of Alabama and the United States of America. I got the future: college, law school, med school. Or businessman, choices. And ocean liners to Europe, China: all waiting.

B.J.'s world is smaller. The family, and the trees. Some days it's smaller still, all inside himself. He's my little brother. He's eighteen. I'm thirteen.

I sit with him on the rug between our twin beds. *A*'s a fist, B.J., see? And *B*'s four fingers up. And let's see, *C*, you just cup your hand like *C*, see? Then *D* oh wait. *S* is the fist, *A*'s *sort* of a fist but thumb points up. Then *E*— wait, that's trickier. Shoot, I missed *D*. Guess if I were a better teacher, I'd've learned em myself before trying to teach him but I'm short on time, algebra exam tomorrow. I come across the drawings at the front of this book I borrowed from the school library, the "Manual-Finger Alphabet." The book is *The Story of My Life* by Miss Helen Keller, which she wrote while still at Radcliffe. Barely anything been translated into Braille back then, yet Helen at fourteen knew Latin, devouring books in German and French and I don't mean "See Jack run." Grown-up books, literature!

> *A few verses of Omar Khayyám's poetry have just been read to me, and I feel as if I had spent the last half-hour in a magnificent sepulcher. Yes, it is a tomb in which hope, joy and the power of acting nobly lie buried. Every beautiful description, every deep thought glides insensibly into the same mournful chant of the brevity of life, of the slow decay and dissolution of all earthly things.*

Essay she wrote, and only a freshman! Well here's my point: If Helen

Keller could do all that in a world of total darkness and silence, why can't B.J. read when all he is is deaf?

Next day I breeze through the test, $3y + 34 = 2y + 89$ easy, finish five minutes early and turn it over in the avoidance of copycats which provokes a few glares in my general direction. Late September, the year barely begun but my reputation's long been sealed: smartest in the class which is not exactly the golden path to eighth-grade popularity. Lunch I always eat alone which is fine—gives me good time to think. And today what crosses my mind: How'm I supposed to teach B.J. letters when he can't hear the sound they make, words when he doesn't understand what language is? Suddenly this whole teaching thing seems way too big, I better just return that Helen Keller book. Then again Helen had her breakthrough, right? Didn't her teacher help her into the social world? Then again Helen was toddling, already a vocabulary when the sickness stole her senses, so was it that foundation of speech what sprungboard her into communal consciousness? I sip my milk pondering it all as Earl Mattingly pulls my seat out from under me, sticky white all over my shirt, my ass on the floor and half the school laughing.

When I get home the book is not top drawer of my dresser where I know damn well I left it, where the hell? Now B.J. at the doorway holding it, looking at me all eager for the next drill. I take lesson time down to the kitchen, ginger snaps my mother baked, and usually B.J.'d indulge with me but today too raring to learn. Or play, a game to him, like it was to Miss Keller at first.

Two Saturdays back he threw a fit. My mother: "This mighta been cute when you were a baby, but it is not cute anymore," like he would have any idea, like her trying to reason with a cat. He only pulls that stuff when my father's not home because Pa'd take the belt to him, "I don't care how big you are," though long ago he'd stopped whooping me and Benja. B.J.'s tantrum all about I wasn't taking him to the park with me. Used to every couple weeks but then, July, there we are, the blanket all laid out, food my mother made for us and I saw em. Kids from my class, coming out the woods and spy B.J. and me. Even with the distance I can make out their smirks.

So lately when I go to the park I go alone, and here's B.J. home by himself, nobody to play with, and this I think is related to how he's such an attentive student now: got his playmate back. I dip cookie into milk and say the letters real exaggerated as I hand-show em. He's all delighted with cross-fingers *R*, and when I accidentally confuse *G* for *Q* he looks in the book and corrects me. *I* I show him, *J*. He stares at *J*, making that hook with his pinkie over and over, then he big-time catches me unawares. *B* he spells and speaks it, pretty distorted but not out of the ballpark, then *J*, then points to himself. I smile. He figured that out without me telling him, my big little brother B.J. got his Helen-eureka fast. I spell him the rest of the family: Mother, Father, Benja, Randall and, smart again, he knows with the last one to point to me. When the lesson's over I close the book. He snatches it and takes it back with him to our room. Oh Lord, how'm I gonna explain to him it's borrowed and due back less than a week?

The next day's Friday and by some miracle Mrs. Goodman's already checked the algebra tests, and I'm pleased and unsurprised at my big fat A though perturbed her nitpicking brought me down to 96 even if it's still the class high. When I get home B.J. and Ma are all into it. She doesn't understand what kind of game he's playing with his hands, with her hands, is beside herself with his frustrated conniptions. I give her the news flash: B.J.'s spelling "Mother." She gets this dazed look like she can't hardly believe it, and B.J. looks at me grinning, spelling "Randall" over and over so fast, faster even than fourth-period Madame Everhart's spoken French so takes me till the third time before I get it.

Mr. Roosevelt said, "I tell the American people solemnly that the United States will never survive as a happy and fertile oasis of liberty surrounded by a cruel desert of dictatorship."

He's the only person I ever heard was for it.

Reverend Pitsfield to the congregation: "A hundred and seventeen thousand Americans lost in the Great War, now they think they gonna drag us into *another*?"

My parents: "We barely makin it with this New Deal, now Roosevelt threatenin to give us a *raw* deal."

U.S. History Mr. Holcomb: "You know how many soldiers Japan's got? Million and a half! You know how many soldiers Germany's got? *Three* million! You know how many we got? A hundred twenty *thousand*, they'd *pulverize* us! Just eked ourselves outa the Depression, what we got to think about is giving every family bread before we ever ask them to give their sons. Isolationism!"

And then Pearl Harbor. And then half of last year's high school football team headed to Europe or the Pacific whilst the Evanses in pj's unwrapping presents. Benja gets some nice stationery which was what she wanted, plus a jewelry box, B.J. gets three big coloring books and crayons. Watching him rip them open in the sleepy fog of predawn Christmas, I take a rare step back, seeing my family. My blond mother, hair just past her shoulders. My reddish pa, spose I got my strawberry blondness from the both of them. My very blond sister with the thick wavy hair falling a few inches below her shoulders, and B.J., that darker sandy blond color to him. And tall as hell, already looking down at Pa and Pa's tall, and B.J. doesn't seem ready to stop growing. Later in the day, while the rest of us running around past him living our lives, he just sits quietly shading in Santa and those elves.

What I get is binoculars which is not what I wanted but I know better than to show a speck of disappointment. All smiles, "Thank you," and anyhow I have since come up with a plan. In the park in the woods there's this particular oak. I figured out every knob and hole so I'm to the top no time, and from there you can see everything, the picnickers and revelers in the open fields out to the left, and just below to the right you got the clearing, this very clandestine space where once I spied a couple teenagers making out, thinking nobody watching. I couldn't quite catch all that was going on so my spyglasses'll definitely enhance my treetop eye view.

What I wanted: a War to End All Wars Sopwith model, which I saw in the window of Gephart's Athletic Gear and Footwear, 98¢. Real rubber tires and leather seat, tan body and the gold parallel wings with the targets on the top wing, red circle inside white circle inside blue circle. The colors is England, not America, the Sopwith Camel was a British flyer. (Have to say, I did always wonder why in the heck a fighter plane would be decorated with targets.) I'd hinted about it on more than one occasion to my mother, but I guess with her having served in the War to End All Wars that didn't, she couldn't wrap her mind around my wanting a part of it for my personal amusement.

She was a nurse in France, 1918. She knew my father before, from growing up, but those days to her he weren't nothing more than the landscape. Then off to Europe they both go, fairy-tale castles and blitzkriegs and come back, he offered her the ring.

Walking home from church Sunday before Christmas, she told us her prayer: "That this war be over quick, the boys and girls brought home." (The pastor led the prayer for the "boys in uniform" but my mother lets people know "Not all of us girls came back neither.") She goes on: "And I thank You Lord my children are all spared: my oldest deaf, my middle a girl, my youngest too young." Only Benja and me with her. Pa's technically Baptist like us but never was much of a churchgoer, and B.J. no longer. When we were younger, B.J.'d sit in the pew singing even while the kids made fun, till one Sunday the choir director turned around from the loft, not to chew out those brats but staring right at B.J., finger to her lips. Back home he cried, and she held him, Ma reading from the nursery rhyme book he loved, staring at the pictures, staring at her moving lips. That was B.J.'s last day in church, and took two years and a change of choir directors for my mother and sister and me to go back.

Ma and her sisters trade off the holidays, and it's my mother's turn for Christmas. Pa is no drunk but holidays with company he might tie-on with his brother-in-laws. This year he's smashed before dinner, glowering at my cousin Ty. Ty's twenty-two, works at the sawmill with my father, and Pa goes, "The chicken pox! The goddamned chicken pox." When that subject comes up, the extended family know it's time to grab their coats. So nobody left to eat dinner enough for an army but us, turkey and mashed potatoes and sweet potatoes we got for the duration.

On the 29th my father decides to check the temperature. "What's for supper?" from his soft chair as my mother passes by with the dirty laundry she just collected. I'm sitting on the floor by the tree, my mind all in *The Sun Also Rises* which I have a report due on after New Year's, but now I look up. Ma stops, glares at him, moves on through. Thus he knows the degree's still below freezing and goes back to his newspaper.

JAPANESE LAND ON SUMATRA
MORE TROUBLE IN PACIFIC AFTER HONG KONG CHRISTMAS DAY SURRENDER TO AXIS

"I guess we'll be havin turkey till Valentine's Day," says Benja on her way through the room, hurling a meaningful glance at my father who pretends he doesn't see her, and I remember this years-ago Christmas Eve, me five and Benja eight and B.J. ten, and Benja comes to the boys' room so my father can tell us the manger tale. Benja and I liked when my father told stories, and B.J. liked it most of all. All through it he'd be bouncing, uttering sounds he couldn't hear and that made no sense to us. My father paid him as much mind as the furniture, my father's narrating eyes fixed on Benja and me.

"Come ere." I'd just gone back to my American Lit assignment, but now I put the book down and walk over to him, sit cross-legged by his chair. I know by the tone of "Come ere" he plans to talk longer than I'd like to stand. "I tell you about bein in the infirmary in France when the influenza went flyin through?" Now the Christmas music loud from the kitchen radio, my mother making a point that for the time being my father's voice is still off-limits to her ears.

"Veterans always wanna talk about the bunkers. Oh I got the bunker stories, like when me an my buddies three days, no food, no water, the bombin all aroun. I probably already told you that one."

"I think so." Hundreds of times.

"People wanna romanticize it, the bombs burstin in air. But how about jus the sickness? What, less honorable a boy leave his house an home, go other side a the world to fight for freedom an die a the flu? Robbie's fever through the roof. And there mutterin the times a his life he remember the girl he leff behind, last fight with his daddy, flunkin the math test." Pa chuckles. "That his right leg below the knee been blowed off seem to slip his mind while he countin off his life's miseries." In the hallway beyond us Benja flies past, a direct trajectory to the front door. "Where you think *you* goin?"

She stops, stands at the living room entrance, arms crossed. "Party."

"What the hell kinda party?"

"Sherry's birthday."

"Not before supper."

"Food at the party. Frankfurters." *Bang! bang! bang!* from the kitchen. My mother stomping. Calling B.J.

"You can eat a real supper right here first."

"At Sherry's they're done eatin turkey." Her eyes ice.

My father gives her brazenness a good look before he says it. "*No.*" B.J. bounding down the steps.

"It's a supper party!"

"It's a hot dog party. You'll eat supper here."

"I'll be full when I get there! Know how rude it is to go to a party and not eat?"

"I *should* say no to the whole damn thing. An I know you jus goin to see that boy, piece a trash."

They bicker, and I think on how my father tells his Great War stories frequently and my mother tells hers never, even with the picture of her in navy nurse's uniform stuck on their bedroom vanity mirror. But once I overheard one. Fifth grade, I threw up in social studies and they sent me home. My mother wasn't here, B.J. wasn't here so I go up, fall asleep on my bed. Something wakes me. I creep out of my room, top of the steps where I look down but they don't see me, Ma wailing and Mrs. Watkins speaking comfort from the other chair cross the room, and B.J. not knowing what's going on bawling in sympathy, making his deaf sounds, patting her, soothing her.

"It woulda been my first baby!"

"I know. I know."

"I done it. I kilt it. Throwin myself down them steps."

"What was you sposed to do? Not married."

"Coulda give it up for adoption!"

"Waaaah! Waaaah!" B.J.'s sympathy wails.

"That's jus why I say women shouldn't go into the military."

"I was a nurse! I saved lives!"

"And what's your payback? How many of em? A woman can't fight off *one* man, let alone—How many of em? You wouldn'ta even knowed who was the father."

"They made me. I didn't want it."

"I know."

"They made me! I didn't want it!"

"Baby made from that much meanness, it don't need to be out in the world."

"I was a sergeant. One of the privates salutes me before."

"Waaaah!"

"Saluted me an laughed. Then he done it."

"That thing had to die. One way or the other."

"Wa'n't a thing! A baby! I kilt it! Wa'n't a thing!"

"One way or the other."

"That boy died." My father's words snap me back to the present. His eyes far away. "From flu! He woulda got along fine on the one leg, he hadn't caught the bug in the infirmary. I met him two days before he passed. 'How old?' I go. Him: 'Eighteen.' Then, hour before he expire, cleanin up his sins nick a time he confesses. 'Sorry, I lied before. Fifteen.'"

My mother comes walking through with B.J. Smiling, touching his face. "Good boy." He grins back. "Take out the trash, he do it without a fight. Mow the lawn, flip the mattress. Anything you ask, he's the good one." They're gone, upstairs.

Pa snaps his paper back to reading level, disappearing behind it, so I know story hour's drawn to a close. I go back and pick up Mr. Hemingway and *his* Great War. The bookmark fell out when my father summoned me so I have to flip through to find my place.

Who's the good one. *I* do what I'm asked, and *I* never throw tantrums. But we all know B.J.'s her favorite. Mostly I'm not resentful. And what she just said was no cut to me anyway, I know it was aimed at my father who she's still mad at about Christmas dinner.

"So *what* he do his chores when he told." I look up, see my father's folded his paper on his lap, his eyes on me. Take a sec fore I realize he's referring to B.J. "*That* we coulda got from a trained seal."

3

She sits one desk ahead of me, inches away, whisper-giggling to Suzanne Willetts. "Miss Laherty," says Mr. Holcomb, "could you please in your own words explain to the class the concept of the Magna Carta?" Wish I could help her out, slip it in her ear: *England, 1215. Prior to this, if the king didn't like your looks he could have you beheaded, all his whim. Now justice for everybody, something new and radical.* But no way could we get away with it, and anyway, despite her going all agape, something about Margaret Laherty always seems to charm the teachers from being too hard on her. I've known her since first grade. Red-brown hair halfway down her back, think you call that auburn. When the lunch bell rings, she gathers her books, walks out slapping Suzanne on the back, some powerful private joke. Margaret's eyes big and brown. Twinkly.

I stay behind. Sitting alone to catch up on some biology *growl.* Smell it: egg-olive sandwich and cheddar corn muffin, baked apple *growl.* I drink my tin cup of water, trying to appease my roaring empty stomach. Concentrate: Blue eyes can only make blue eyes, but brown-eyed recessives can make brown *and* one out of four blue, plus earlobes! Genes dictate whether yours're hanging free or attached to your neck *GROWL.*

Fourth grade when the Works Progress Administration started school lunch, I was all in favor. But its novelty's definitely worn off. I asked my mother about packing. "We are not poor country bumpkins, I think we can afford a nickel for hot dinner, penny for the milk." I started to argue and she, "And *that* is *that.*" I can't tell her first day back after Christmas Danny Rice pitching his peas at me, amusing half the school. Sitting alone not bothering nobody and still the humiliation, finally I make it *all* alone: empty classroom. I don't like deceiving my mother but tell her the truth she'll send me back there, cafeteria *No.* So the six cents a day I save: my model Sopwith.

Feel somebody.

Henry Lee Taylor. How long he been standing there, the doorway? Dark-hair runt, even shorter than me. "My electric train's so big my pa had to make a special room in the basement for it." Till then I didn't know he could speak, we share three classes but he never raises his hand. Little as he is, there's a crackle in his voice, well on its way down to tenor.

After school I stand before Henry Lee's impressive train set, laid on a table three feet off the ground. The track winds in and out of tunnels, through mountains. Each car's about ten inches long, four high, two and a half wide. Smoke puffs from the engine. Forty-three cars, passenger and freight. Trees and houses and the post office and the fire department and the butcher's and the school and the hospital, *ding ding!* at the street crossing, autos waiting as the safety poles come down, as a traffic light stays red while the train passes, this happens three times and it could happen another hundred far as I'm concerned! But Henry Lee's already bored. He sets a Packard on the tracks at the crossing.

"This is Milly and Jack in the tenth grade. He puts his tongue in her mouth, she's all for it. Uh-oh!" Henry Lee makes the crossing bells go off. "Oh my God! Jack, pull your pants up! Milly, get your bra on!" The warning poles falling. "Hurry! Hurry!" The poles down. Henry Lee's voice jumps an octave. "Oh my God, Jack! What're we gonna *do*, Jack!" Henry Lee hits the switch to turn on the train, headed straight for the car. Henry Lee as Milly lets out a piercing scream. The train crashes into the car, dragging it a few inches before knocking it aside. It lands right side up. Henry Lee, disappointed with nature's choice, picks up the vehicle, snaps his wrist and flings it, allowing it to flip over and over, Milly and Jack screaming the entire time. Again it lands upright. Henry Lee grunts and flicks it with his finger. Finally it falls upturned, hood on the ground. Satisfied, Henry Lee allows a moment of silence before "Whoosh!" Sweeping his hands, indicating the car has burst into flames. A dramatic pause later, he is respectfully grave: "Tragedy."

"Henry Lee." Someone calling from the top of the stairs. "Your mama told me to remind you to make up your bed fore she gets home."

"I *know*!" Furious, like she just nagged him about this ten times, though until this moment I had no idea we weren't alone in his house. The footsteps above moving away. Henry Lee is looking at his train and not at me. "Jesus. What's the point a *hav*in a goddamn maid *I* gotta do her job for her?" Then he jumps up, vanishing into the mysterious darkness on the other side of the basement. I'm thinking I better get going. Already been here half an hour, my mother will *not* be pleased I took a detour coming home without telling her. Henry Lee reappears with a pack. "You smoke?" Twice at my cousin Buppie's last summer. We were out back, and he handed me one he'd snuck.

The first Camel got me sick. The second got me sicker. I see what Henry Lee's got and I'm betting on Luckies.

"My pa thinks I'll be a lawyer like him." Smoke gracefully escapes Henry Lee's nose. Here he seems to carry some expertise, unlike academics where he's average at best. If I get a 97, he might get a 72. "Well my pa's in for a big surprise cuz I'm hopping the trains. He might as well get used to it: his only son's gonna be a pro hobo." Henry Lee chuckles and taps his cigarette. Henry Lee and the room are spinning.

The door above us opens. "Henry Lee, your mama'll be home in fifteen minutes."

"Dammit!" He says it loud, but the maid has already walked away.

"Henry Lee." Sour in my mouth.

"All my worldly possessions in a bandanna tied to a stick. Hoppin top a one freight car to the next."

"Henry Lee, I'm gonna be sick."

"Not here." He ascends the stairs, and I follow. Walking through the kitchen, Henry Lee says nothing to the maid at the ironing board. A colored boy older than us sits at the table doing homework. "Who's your friend?" the maid says, eyes on her work. The colored boy looks up.

"Randall!" As if it were the stupidest question.

"Well Randall can't see your room till it's straight, you know that."

"He's going to the *bathroom*!"

"Alright."

Compared to the mess I made last summer with the Camels, I only throw up a little now so Lucky Strikes must be my brand. Wash my face. I shake my hands dry, afraid to touch the towels all spic n span. They're burgundy, matching the toilet cover and rug and bringing out the touch of burgundy in the wallpaper.

I walk down to the kitchen. "You wanna glass of milk?" Her eyes still on the sheets she's pressing.

"No thank you."

She and the boy look up. Like manners is some anomaly in these parts. My mother was a maid before I was born, and she always said if we ever had one, she'd treat her with the respect she never got. But maids were never in our budget.

"Water?"

"Okay."

She gets a glass from a cabinet, holds it under the spigot. "Randall?" I nod, taking the tumbler. "I'm Mrs. Lawrence. This is my son Roger."

"I'm *finished!*" Henry Lee's entrance, all singsong. Mrs. Lawrence and Roger go back to their previous activities.

"Don't you wanna inspect my bed?"

"Your mama can do that." She sprays Niagara starch.

"I got a new freight car, Roger. Coal." Roger looks at Henry Lee, then at his mother. She shakes out a clean pillowcase.

"For a minute. Then finish your homework." Henry Lee apparently does his homework later. If he does it. Now he flies down the steps. I follow, Roger sauntering behind affecting well the nonchalance.

"Look at this. Shiny like real coal." Henry Lee picks up the tiny pieces, lets them fall through his fingers. Roger nods, observing with remote interest. "Hey, Roger, you just missed a very tragic accident. You wanna see a very tragic accident?"

"I better get goin, Henry Lee." As I speak it, we all hear a car pulling into the driveway overhead.

"Wait a minute." If Henry Lee has heard me, he makes no indication of it, bounding up the steps.

"That means he didn't finish making up his bed, now trying to do it before his mama see it." Roger's eyes have drifted from the train to my schoolbooks.

"I have to go anyway." I don't want to risk meeting Henry Lee's mother and her holding me up, suddenly excruciatingly aware of what I'll be in for at home: my own mother's worry fury, augmented by the minute.

"How come this says *9*?" Henry Lee holds up my algebra book. "Aren't you in the eighth like Henry Lee?"

"Yeah, but I tested high for math."

"I'm in ninth."

"Fourteen?" He nods, opening the book. I might've guessed fifteen. He's had the growth spurt I've been longing for.

"Nineteen forty?" He's looking at the copyright page. "Last year! Pshew, colored school, our books from the twenties." He picks up my big fat lit. "Nineteen forty-one!"

"I gotta go."

"*Ethan Frome.*" He has opened it to the contents. "'The Raven.' 'The

Legend of Sleepy Hollow.'" I gently put my hand on the book, my last polite warning.

"Next time I'll rent it."

I stare at him.

"Nickel for any book you let me borrow. But you gotta let me keep it a whole hour."

"Roger! Come on up, finish your studies." Roger looks up the stairs, toward his mother's voice. Then back at me. I slowly nod, not sure I believe him. He heads up the steps.

"You rent Henry Lee's books from him?"

Roger turns around. "Nope."

"How come?"

"Report card time, Henry Lee always looking for the excuse. Me holding the books he needs? pshew! When he goes searching for the blame, no chance it gonna be me."

"Hah!" Henry Lee grinning, running down the stairs past Roger. "She just wanted to know what I wanted for supper cuz she's on her way to the market. That still gimme a half-hour fore I gotta make that stupid bed."

"Roger!" The tone of a mother's final warning. Roger quickly exits up and out to the kitchen. Henry Lee seems to take no notice of the fact that I'm standing holding my books, obviously about to leave. He stares wistfully up the stairs. And Roger barely giving him the time of day.

"I gotta go, Henry Lee."

He turns back to the train, flips the switch on, motor humming. "I bet she goes, *I'm Mrs. Lawrence,*" his mocking not even close to her real voice. He doesn't look up at me. "Always tryin to pull that crap. She's a goddamn colored maid, call her Sally." The engine puffs smoke twice and makes a *whoo-hoo!* before disappearing around the bend.

4

Moby Dick. The Great Gatsby. The Grapes of Wrath, Leaves of Grass, Our Town, too many choices! Got here early for the best pick, even before B.J. awake. The public library's book sale to support the war effort, and sixty-four cents jiggling my pocket.

She went through the roof after I came home late from Henry Lee's Tuesday, but I could see her soften when I said why. It surprised me, her obviously so glad I finally have a friend. Thought I'd spared her that aching truth: her miserable, outcast son.

So grounded only a day, and Thursday after school I'm back at Henry Lee's with permission. Entering through his kitchen, "Hi *Sally*." He sneers it, nudging me.

"Hello, Henry Lee." Stirring the stew on the stove, her back to us.

"And Randall," Henry Lee acknowledges.

Roger at the table looks up from his books. His mother, "Good afternoon, Randall."

"Hi." Avoidance of direct address.

"There's some cookies for yaw." Henry Lee takes the saucer without offering any gratitude, and I follow him to the basement.

He has a fancy new freight car filled with automobiles to transport: Packards and Caddies, steering wheels and doors that open and shut. "Here's a Buick Roadmaster Convertible Phaeton. You can hold it."

Instead I inspect the new LaSalle. "You got all this yesterday? Since I was here?" Henry Lee shrugs. "Your birthday?"

"No. Does it have to be *your* birthday to get a present?" Yes, birthday or Christmas but I don't say it, and now Roger's footsteps on the stairs. "Hey Roger, wanna see my new automobile transport car? Here's a Packard Super Eight One-Eighty Convertible Coupe. And thisn's a Cadillac Dee-luxe Touring Sedan."

But Roger's looking at me. "I see your books?" I'd dumped them other side of the room. I nod, and he takes a cookie, strolls over.

Henry Lee's lecturing me on the cars and I lean back, tipped on the hind legs of my chair munching my oatmeal raisin. Feeling kingly, and Henry Lee says something to make me laugh. Glance over and notice Roger and my geography gone. Nickel on top of my remaining texts.

"Roger here every day?"

"I don't know what's going on with *Roger*. Used to be he just pop by every once in a while. He got some cracka dawn job movin fruit crates at Farley's and he gotta clean up at night too, then Sally complainin she never sees him so sometimes he'd come by after school to please her. Like Tuesday. But then he came Wednesday *and* today. I had the impression he was disappointed you weren't here yesterday. Guess you two are in love with each other."

When it comes time for me to leave, I get this sick feeling climbing the stairs. What if Roger's no longer in the kitchen? What if he went home with my book—stole it, or just packed it with his own, forgot he had it? Then I think no, I could tell Henry Lee's mom who would get on Roger's mom who would get on Roger. But what if Roger claimed he never had it? Then I could spill the beans on our deal. But what if people didn't believe me? Oh they'd believe me. Colored word against mine? But then what would they think about the deal?

No worries, Roger's there in the kitchen alone studying my geography. He looks up at me, then at the clock, and hands me the tome.

"Germany sure changed the maps. Even since your copyright."

"What if it hadn't been a whole hour? You already paid up front."

"Then it'd be the last time you and I did business."

So today, between all those missed lunches plus Roger geography Thursday and lit Friday, I feel all Rockefeller at the library sale. Still have my Sopwith goals, but for the war effort I can part with a little change. Seems I'm the only kid here, like they all got better stuff to do Saturday.

Pile of miscellaneous. Cookbooks. An old Latin primer. *Scouting for Boys: The Boy Scout Scheme. What It Is! What It Is Not!* which I flip through: memories. Fourth grade I'm on a Boy Scout camping weekend, and Willie Joe Arnold in the sixth says he's ready to give up Scouts for the Junior Klan, and Jack Matthews in the fifth goes, "Why not both?" and Willie Joe goes, "One uniform's enough." Willie Joe of the multitudinous badges could rub two sticks together and make the spark in a flash, and now he ties a stick perpendicular to another, rubs the intersection with a third stick, and when it's fast alit he puts the burning cross in the ground which we all awe-admired till it fast gone to ashes. Then we got into a discussion about lynching which I'm completely against. The way I feel if somebody commits a crime he deserves to be tried by a jury of his peers and let justice reign. Magna Carta to the Fifth Amendment. And Sixth.

Then I spy it. *A Handbook of the Sign Language of the Deaf: Prepared Especially for Ministers, Sunday School Workers, Theological Students and Friends of the Deaf* by J. W. Michaels. Back in the fall I'd had it in mind to renew that Helen Keller book for B.J., but after I had to wrestle him all over our room to wrench it out of his hands, that little volume was staying at school. It killed him, pouting for days.

The other thing. Yesterday Henry Lee complained about having to go to Selma today, some big affair for his great-grandfather's ninetieth. But next Saturday he promised it'd be just us two, doing what we pleased. Like he assumes what I really want to do is reserve Saturday to be his friend. I guess I sorta do. Meanwhile I can tell B.J.'s getting agitated, losing after-school me to Henry Lee. I don't even wanna think about what's gonna happen when he finds out I'll be gone all day Saturdays too, so this library peace offering only cost me a nickel.

I walk in, my brother all red-eyed. I been gone barely an hour, what? He wake *up* bawling, not seeing me? I hold up the book, and suddenly his face light up like Christmas. We fix ourselves jam sandwiches and go to our room, sit on the throw rug. Skip the manual alphabet which we know, and head straight to the hand words: *there's* where you make language. "Mother," "Father," "Brother," "Sister," "Eat," "Sleep," "Thank you," "Home." That last one B.J. latches onto. "You," pointing at me, "home." He signs it and says it in his deaf way, and I nod and say the same thing about him, Yes, we're both home, and he shakes his head cuz what he's trying to say is You *stay* home, his communication is quite clear, and yet like a jerk I keep smiling and faking misunderstanding.

5

Basketballs: right hand, left hand, low, high, round the back. Fifty pubescent boys in gray tees and navy shorts scurrying. Drills may be tedious but are mercifully minus the anxiety of captains picking teams for a game, the prayer I not be the *very* last chosen. Still, PE's an automatic A just for showing up, so I try not to take it too much to heart that when the teachers are screaming, it's about fifty-fifty I'm the object of their vexation.

"Look alive, look alive!" Mr. Shane orders no one in particular.

Right after gym is lunch, which means something since Henry Lee come along. That first week we were getting to know each other, he beckoned me to follow him, through the locker room to the old rusted fire escape, no longer in use. He opened his green and yellow Karo syrup tin. Slices of frankfurter in beans with barbecue sauce! White cake with pink icing! Henry Lee ate his cake first. "Best thing about lunch in school is no mother around tellin you food before dessert." While he has never shared his sweets, he's always been generous with the regular food, barely touching it himself. Afterward he would take out his Luckies so we started calling the old fire escape The Old Smoke Escape. I am eagerly anticipating this ritual when *bang!* A heavy thud to the back of the noggin, shaking my brain around my skull. I'm on my knees and now see the seven other boys of my drill circle staring at me and grinning.

"Jenkins!"

"Sorry, Mr. Shane," says Bruce Jenkins, "but I passed it to him, and I guess his head was somewheres else."

Mr. Shane considers me momentarily, then shakes his head: hopeless cause. I have a headache. I pay very close attention now but the ball does not come, the smirking boys faking as if they're passing it to me then tossing it to anyone but me. I catch on, but I know the moment I let on I'm aware, the ball *will* come, and violently, so I delight them by hopping every time I'm looked at, a puppet awaiting the pull of my strings.

Someone taps my shoulder from behind. I'm certain it's a trick, and I keep my eyes in the circle. Then I hear, "The principal said to fetch you." Such a serious missive I can't ignore, turning to find a fully dressed kid from fifth or sixth handing me the note. Then I see the terror in his eyes and he ducks, protecting himself from the ball banging hard into the back of my head.

When I get to the outer office where the secretary's desk is, Lucille Furman is already sitting there in her gym clothes so she also must've just been excused from PE. The girls' gym is in the basement directly under the boys'. Lucille is smart and fat. She puts her hands on her substantial thighs, as if trying to conceal them. She's probably one of the few people who dreads gym more than me.

"Come on in." Mr. Westerly's noncommittal smile.

I have never been in Mr. Westerly's office before. Diplomas on the wall— college, graduate school. A photograph of him talking with three boys at a Bunsen burner from his high school biology teacher days. "You two may know that St. Mary's competes in debate with other Catholic schools all over Alabama, and then regionally. Unfortunately our local public school system has no such competition."

Mr. Westerly pauses here. Lucille and I stare.

"However. St. Mary's has asked us if this year we would like to challenge them in a practice meet before they go on to their official contest with St. John's, up near Birmingham. So! You are both outstanding students. I'd like you to represent our school as the debate team."

Lucille and I look at each other. Never before had our names and "school team" been in the same sentence.

"If you're interested, we'll set up an empty classroom for you to pre- pare with each other. Mr. Hickory will be your coach. Some days he will be with you, other times you will have independent study on your own. By virtue of your high academic achievements, you've earned our trust. The meet will take place on Friday, February 20th, three weeks from tomorrow. And I see here you both happen to have PE at the same time. I'm thinking you can be excused for debate practice during that period. If you don't mind?"

"I think you oughta do her," says Henry Lee on The Old Smoke Escape between puffs.

"*What?*"

"He said some days they'll leave you alone. All alone."

"To practice debate. Sure, we're really gonna make it when Mr. Hickory can just walk in any second!"

"Just suggestin. Opportunity. You definitely better be practicin the missionary though. Put her on top, one wrong move and you're smithereens, I'd be readin your eulogy. 'Obviously,' I'd say, 'he died satisfied.'" He attempts a smoke ring and chokes.

"I don't think I'm gonna come here anymore." I bite the boiled egg he gave me. He loves chicken salad so he'd asked his mother to pack two sandwiches, claiming to want seconds, and thus we each had our own meal. "I don't wanna get caught."

"You been comin here three weeks. How come, all the sudden?"

"I don't know. Maybe they're looking at me more closely now."

"Oh yeah, the star debater." He stubs out his cigarette and unwraps a stick of Wrigley's in case a teacher were to get too close to his breath. Mr. Westerly said our meet might not be official to St. Mary's, but far as he's concerned if we win, he's ordering two trophies from Gephart's Athletic Gear and Footwear.

"Well," says Henry Lee, chewing, who usually offers me a stick but today doesn't, "no Old Smoke Escape, no lunch."

"We could have lunch somewheres else."

"No!" Once in a while Henry Lee'd do that, get loud, kind of squeal. I shut up and hope he follows suit, me all paranoid like the principal gonna bust in on us, spying, making sure I'm worthy. Henry Lee brushes crumbs down into the shaft. Pigeons flock to the feast.

After school I go straight home, not stopping by Henry Lee's. My mother is thrilled by the news. She's all for me going to college. Not anywheres in our budget but she's thinking like I'm thinking, that being chosen for this debate thing's on track toward my earning a scholarship. Few months ago she and my father got into it, him feeling like eighth grade was plenty for me, he could get me on at the mill full-time after that, and her refusing, insisting I graduate secondary. He thinks high school's okay for Benja, for girls and their frivolous pursuits, just husband-shopping anyway.

Taking advantage of her rush of pride, I fib. "We're gonna be practicing during lunchtime so I'll need to start packing."

It works without a hitch. I'd been feeling guilty about banking the daily six cents she'd been giving me for lunch so the falsehood actually eases my conscience. But then, though I don't ask for it and even argue against it, she's adamant on giving me the penny for milk, which in spite of my shame has to go directly to the Sopwith fund as I refuse ever to set foot in that blamed cafeteria again.

Monday Lucille and I sit in an empty English classroom.

Resolved, that the territory of Hawaii should be granted statehood.

Though we are both clear on the topic, she felt it didn't hurt to write it on the blackboard. We knew nothing about the rules of debate until Friday, when Mr. Hickory from social studies spelled it out. We are given the topic in advance for rugged preparation. In some competitions teams must be ready to defend either side, but we have been assigned to specifically argue the affirmative. We sit several rows away from each other, though Lucille, closer to the front, has turned her desk around to face me for when we need to discuss. Thick volumes are opened before us. For the sake of the meet, extraordinary library privileges have been bestowed upon us: no limits on the number of materials, permission to check out reference books not usually available for circulation.

It's assumed that Hawai'i was originally settled by Polynesians around fifteen hundred years ago. British explorer James Cook was the first documented white man on the islands, in 1778. There was fighting among the chiefs, and King Kamehameha came out on top. By the time Kamehameha III took the throne when he was nine, the missionaries had flooded in and a lot of Hawai'i had gone Christian which the king was conflicted about. When unmarried Kamehameha V died childless, the next king was elected. So was the one after that supposed to be, except the election was disputed, leading to riots, and in come the U.S. and Brits to quell the unrest, and in 1887 the king is coerced to sign the Constitution of the Kingdom of Hawai'i stripping away much of his regal authority and now only the wealthy could vote which was mostly white foreigners Lucille's got cleavage.

Slumped over her books, writing intensely. The white lace on her pink blouse is delicate, her shirt is loose and some of the fabric falls forward her breasts, Lucille's round soft breasts softballs, *basket*balls her eyes snap up! glowering. I quickly go back to 1893, the U.S. overthrow of the Republic of Hawai'i.

"There's this picture of the palace," I say at supper. "The king used to live in it, when they used to spell 'Hawai'i' with a backwards apostrophe, called an *okina*."

"That a fact? It still there?" My mother so charmed about the whole thing. My father keeps his eyes on his pork and beans, pops the remaining half of a buttered biscuit into his mouth. Ma'll be there, I think, I'll look out in the debate audience, see her. Where will Pa be? Corner of my eye, I see B.J. scowling at me from across the table, undoubtedly related to my scarcity around here for weeks, only destined to get worse with the debate research.

"It became the capitol building of the Republic, and then of the Territory." The water flying through the air. I'm sputtering.

"Boy!" My father stands, turning on him, furious.

"B.J.!" Then my mother hand-spells and speaks: "Bad boy! Bad boy!" She is not fast with her fingers, but even through my choking, I am impressed as she has obviously practiced. She pounds my back. The coughing spell over, I wipe my drenched face. B.J. emptied his whole goddamn glass on me! Benja making sure I see the laughter in her eyes while hiding it from Ma and Pa. B.J. starts crying and I wanna slug him. *I* should be crying!

"She's already had it anyway," says Henry Lee, gazing at his trains Friday night. "She could give you lessons."

I stare at him. *"Lucille?"*

"Yep*per*." He places his automobiles in position. Henry Lee has decided to double his casualties by having two cars at once getting stuck on the railroad tracks, crossing from opposite directions.

"You don't know anything about Lucille."

"I know she gets it from her father. You been peekin down her shirt?" In Train World a man I've never seen before walks a terrier. There's a new fruit stand, a happy man with a thick mustache tending it, two women carrying full bags of groceries. Does Henry Lee get new toys every single day of the year?

"That's Alice May Turner, not at all to be confused with Lucille Furman." Alice May the class slut whose dad had her first. Everyone made fun but I felt bad for her. She didn't come back to school this year, left town to have a baby according to the grapevine.

"Both of em."

"How do you *know*?"

"*Every*one knows. Okay, that car's Jack feelin up Millie, and this other one just gets stalled. Jack's like, 'What gives?' Millie: 'What *are* you, a

Peepin Tom?' She yells this to the other car, this other couple." Henry Lee thinks hard about the casting of this new pair. Lightbulb. "Earl Mattingly and Margaret Laherty!"

"What!"

"Usually this is *their* spot, so they're surprised to see Millie and Jack who approached from south side a the tracks."

"Whaddya *mean*, 'their spot,' I thought you said the car stalled!"

"Yeah, but that's not very realistic. 'We're not the Peepin Toms,' Earl Mattingly says. '*You* are!' Then the guys get out. Jack throws the first punch, sendin Earl fallin against his car, nose spewin blood. The girls are screamin! '*Oh Earl! Oh Earl!*'" Henry Lee's penchant for giving his people stupid voices seems to have run amok with his newest creations. "Uh-oh." Henry Lee starts the train in the distance. "Unbeknownst to them—"

"Stop it."

"You son of a bitch," which is Earl, followed by a weird cacophony Henry Lee rather impressively creates with the boys fighting and the girls screaming.

"STOP IT!" I turn the train off, only aware afterward that this is the first time I've touched the control button because Henry Lee has never invited me to.

"*Who toldju to touch my train?*" That squeal again.

"Not real people."

"That was gonna be a perfect crash!"

"Not real people."

Henry Lee stares at the couples, his face pouty. "Okay, not real people. After I finish this out, no more real people."

"*Not* finishing it out."

"I gotta finish what I started!"

"Then I'm going home." I walk over to get my books.

"*Okay*, I won't crash em!"

I stare at him from a distance. "She's not. With him." He looks up. "She's not doing it with anybody."

"Margaret Laherty." Sneering. "And you get your great knowledge from?"

"I just know."

"You like her."

"No!"

"Good, cuz I think she prefers boys won't strain her neck to look down on during the slow dances."

"She's not even two inches taller!"

"Her and Earl Mattingly ain't no fiction. Slippin the tongue, I seen em back of the football field last—"

"So *what*? I don't like her!"

Henry Lee is pulling the red truck out of the fire station. "Oh boy, what a tragedy. The fire is *raging.* The fire truck gets stuck at the railroad crossing, quick decision: Do they let all the people die in the burning building, or do they take the chance of beating the train and saving all the people? Oh boy!" He starts setting it up.

I want to leave. But leaving he knows he got to me. So I sit through a few more heartbreaking disasters, then tell him I need to go home, get some Hawai'i reading in. He waves bye without looking up. When I get to the top of the stairs, I'm surprised to see a folded piece of paper with my name on the seat of a corner chair.

25¢ for 2 Cities til Mon after school?

Concealed under the message are five nickels.

"Roger stopped by quick on his way to work, left that note for you." Sally entering, going straight to the sink and opening the doors underneath.

"Thank you."

"Remember to close the basement door behind you so the cold don't escape up here." She takes out floor cleaner and goes back into the other rooms.

I pocket the coins, flip the paper over and write "Roger," then place it on the chair seat atop my copy of *A Tale of Two Cities*. I go to the basement door to shut it, and glancing down I see Henry Lee has set up the two cars on the crossing again, the approaching train now too close for me to stop it. "'I love you Margaret!' and then '*I love you, Earl!*'" in Henry Lee's girliest voice, and those are Margaret Laherty's tragic last words.

6

In the living room, my father in his soft chair reads the paper while I look over my debate notes. 1898: America appropriates the islands of Hawaii (it was suggested by Mr. Hickory that I lose the backwards apostrophe), and same year in the Spanish–American we win Puerto Rico in the Atlantic and coulda also gained Cuba except we didn't want their debt (so mainly just started keeping a naval base there on Guantanamo Bay). Then in the Pacific America scores Guam and the Philippines, collecting all these archipelagoes sharing a sea with Japan, well we'd already been knocking on Japan's door, trying to make some annexation headway since the middle of the nineteenth, but Japan didn't seem like any intention of budging—

"Set em up, boy."

I drop my notes and run to get the board. It's Saturday afternoon. School can wait.

"I'm a chess man in a checkers town." He's said it before. Chess is one of the few activities where my father and I find common ground. Certainly not athletic pursuits, where he excelled throughout high school (despite his grumblings that they were four wasted years when he could have been pulling a paycheck) while I find all manner of balls suspicious. Certainly not hunting, something he hasn't done in years, but in the days he did he must have intuited it would only highlight in his son some new embarrassment for him, and thus he never asked me to come along.

"When I was your age"—I was eight at the time—"I seen somethin bout some foreign chess championship in the paper. Asked an asked, nobody knew nothin bout the game. Roun that time Prayer Ridge just built the public library, I went to see what was what an lo an behold. Checked out the book, took a piece a paper an cut out my own pawns an rooks an bishops, put em on a checkerboard an taught myself. Played against myself, which is a good way to learn. My challenger exactly good as I was, an the better I got, so did he." Then he gave me my first lesson.

He's been patient over the years, working me up to worthy. Barely a word passing between us. "Chess is a thinkin game, not a talkin one." Beyond our very first two bouts where he let me win to build up my confidence and encourage me to keep playing him, I have never succeeded in landing a victory. Now I make a nice L with my knight, and a millisecond after I remove my fingers he slant-slides his bishop right to that square, click, snatching my warrior up.

"Why'd you wait for me?" Something I'd always wondered. "Why'n't you teach Ma or B.J. or Benja?"

"They don't like chess, they prefer rummy." He always called rummy a women's game, though occasionally he'd play it with my mother to have something to do with her.

"What about B.J.?"

"I wantchu to rethink where you jus moved that rook." In some ways he still casts himself as his own opponent.

In the third endgame I stare at his king, incredibly in my rook's direct path. I look up at him. He grins. "Congratulations. You jus become my equal." He winks. "I think your first win deserves some ice cream." This is almost more father-son camaraderie in one day than I can stand, and I grab my sweater fast before he changes his mind. Strolling out on the sidewalk Pa lectures me about the moves in the first two matches, where I went wrong, and I turn around to see B.J. staring down at us from our bedroom window. We've scarcely seen each other since the water glass incident last week. That night I'd taken a chocolate chip cookie up to our room, turned out the light and got in bed quick, trying to beat him so we wouldn't have to communicate. I heard him coming up a few minutes later. Under the covers I munched, knowing he couldn't hear it, feigning sleep. When he walked in, he could have turned on the light to be mean but he didn't. Got into his pajamas and into bed. Something felt out of whack. I sneaked a peek. Usually he lies down and is instantly asleep, but he was sitting up, staring into space. His breathing heavier than usual, slow and even.

It's just a little stand on the corner. There's a low cement wall nearby and we sit, me licking chocolate, Pa with his vanilla. He starts talking about his previous attempts to bring out the athlete in me, and for some reason this usual source of irritation to him he now finds sociably funny. "I'd pitch that damn ball an you'd whip the air, *hard* swingin." His tongue all white. "You'd give that bat the dirtiest look, like you all made some pact an the bastard didn't hold up his end a the bargain." We're laughing. "No worries, boy. After you graduate this spring an I get you on at the mill, ain't nobody there gonna be askin boutcher battin average." My fingers suddenly clutching hard, the cone goes crack. Now a toddler screaming and hollering, empty cone in his hand, his entire strawberry scoop on the ground at his feet. "Didn't I tell you to stop holdin it like that?" asks his mother. "Didn't I?"

The next Saturday, only six days till debate, my father wakes me. "Get dressed," he whispers. I look at the clock—12:40, the house dark. I'd been in bed since ten. B.J., oblivious to noise, sleeps through Pa's disturbance. Ma, early riser, usually also likes to turn in by ten, except Friday and Saturdays when she waits up for Benja to make her eleven curfew. I hop out of bed and grab the clothes I just slipped out of two and a half hours ago.

In the kitchen he rummages through the icebox. Pops a chicken leg into his mouth, "Want one?" his consonants swallowed by the drumstick. A duffel flung over his shoulder.

It's a long walk. They're looking at gasoline rations for the spring, but the rubber rations already here and Pa's taking extra care with his truck tires: no waste. We carry lanterns to see once we get to the edge of town where there's no streetlights, and I think of how dark it must be in the cities on the West Coast where the war blackouts are in effect. I munch on a wing while Pa twirls a toothpick round his mouth. He doesn't talk which is fine by me, I'm not yet in the wakened world. My father doesn't do things like this, clandestine, so these steps, these moments feel real and not. After an hour we're at the foot of Lowden's Mountain and hit the steep incline, then halfway up veer off to a path in the woods. I see a flash, hear a crackle, smell it: Fire! I turn to Pa, my eyes, mouth wide, but he just keeps walking in the direction of the flames.

As we come closer, into a clearing, I'm relieved to see the inferno is contained. The forest is not on fire. It's only one large burning cross. About forty people, mostly or all men, mill about in Klan robes.

"Shit," my father says. "Never knowed em to start on time before. Wanted you to see em light it." Out of the duffel he pulls his own uniform, slips it on. "Let's go."

As we approach, I see that all eyes are fixed on a man near the cross, screaming a tirade.

"And who are they!"

"The niggers!" comes the reply. Like the responsive readings in church, but here more passion to it.

"The niggers. They get hired on fore a white man cuz a nigger'll work for peanuts! The few of em willin to work at all."

My father waves to three men standing near us. They look at him, look at me. One I know is Mr. Wright who works with my father because of the man's missing two right-hand fingers that got cut off at the mill. One I know is Mr. Stewart because he always clears his throat about once a minute. The third has to be Mr. O'Brien because Mr. Wright and Mr. Stewart and Mr. O'Brien bowl together and shoot pool together and sip Coca-Cola together in front of the Woolworth's. None of em acknowledges us.

"Go over there," my father says soft, indicating a clump of trees beyond the clearing.

From my vantage point I can hear and see all, even better from this more secluded spot since no one's paying any attention to me so I feel less rude staring.

"And who tells the niggers what to do?"

"The Jews!"

"I was strollin down the street the other day," says the orator, now speaking in a more cordial anecdotal tone that allows me to recognize him as Reverend Pitsfield, "arm in arm with my wife who bared my four children who bared my fourteen grandchildren." Some of the men laugh, apparently the ones who go to our church and know Reverend Pitsfield brings to every sermon a brief census of his progeny. He never seems aware that we've heard it a thousand times though because now, like in church, he appears momentarily startled, trying to figure out the joke. "An this nigger come by, couldn'ta been more n twenty-five, an passes right by us. Steada steppin off the sidewalk, he passes right by my wife, she swore he near brushed up against her!"

Stars. The blazing cross diminished a heap of them, but still hundreds sparkling. There's peace where I am, part of the goings-on and separate from them at the same time. I don't understand everything being said by the reverend or the audience, some of it in secret code.

My parents rarely argue, least not in front of us, but a year ago there was a major ruckus on laundry day when my mother threw my father's Klan robe in with the colors and turned it pink. "It oughtn'ta *been* in the goddamn machine *no* way!" I was in my bedroom and could hear him hollering from the kitchen. "Delicate. *Han* wash!" (His current robe is a replacement.) Just how accidental the accident was is debatable, given that my mother has always thought of my father's Ku Kluxing as silliness. She's told us when she was a kid her best girlfriend was colored, though naturally they parted ways once they got to high school. Both grew up to be maids, then my mother joined the navy. "What?" she'd asked Pa once as he was fixing his truck. "Yaw scared the coloreds in this town plannin some big revolt?" He grunted, then stuck his head back under the hood.

At one point a kid in a robe, looking not much older than I am, turns around to stare at me, and I stare back, then his daddy next to him puts his hand on the boy's shoulder, and the kid turns back around to face the speaker. Reverend Pitfield's speech threatens to be long as his sermons, but in the middle of a sentence the cross suddenly breaks, falls over. The men cheer, and in a show of cooperation that touches me, begin to pass ready pails of water to douse out the conflagration, like volunteer firemen called to quell a campfire gone wild. When there is little left but glowing embers, my father waves at me, and we head on home.

At some point, he takes a detour further into the woods. "Pa?" He ignores me. Looking for something.

"Ah! Wa'n't sure I'd find it in the dark."

A big old tree, all these carvings in the bark. When he speaks, his voice carries the quiet of reverence. "Happen aroun aught-three. Since I come in with the century that make me three, too little to remember but my pa tole me. That nigger workin Whitacre's farm violated this white girl, nineteen an married with a child. The whole town took after him: Dr. Brinkley who'd just pulled out my brother's appendix, Mr. Peterson the district attorney, Judge Healey, Reverend Longwood, most a the farmers and most a the merchants, the girl's family naturally though for some reason their name I can't recall, all together, all hands on. The culprit took to runnin but they snagged him quick. Beat him, burned him, dragged him aroun, back of a cart. Practically dead by the time they slipped the noose round his neck. All the while to the end, 'I didn't do it, I didn't do it.' 'Did he?' I asked your granpaw. 'Sure he did,' answered my pa, 'an if he didn't was a lesson to any of em thought maybe they might sometime.' When it was over, Mayor Rook looked at the pack of all of em an said, 'Yaw behaved like honorable men tonight. I'm privileged to be amongst ya.' This was the tree. You fine your granpaw?"

A dizzying maze of carved initials but not hard to locate the imprint of my deceased elder, given name Ebenezer. Big, like John Hancock on the Declaration of Independence: Ɛ.Ɛ.

Still a ways to trek down the mountainside, and not until long after we're back on flat ground does he speak again. "You're thirteen, baptized in the church this year. This is parta growin up too." I'm looking at the Big Dipper. And there, that star with a slight orangey tint. Mars.

"They were cautious. Not about you bein a boy, you mighta noticed a handful there bout your age. What was bothersome was you without a robe which clearly identified me, and the meetin speakin all sortsa inner sanctum things, they wonder do I take it all serious, what a secret society is. Well how you make decisions about what you wanna do, you don't firs taste it? I ain't forcin you into nothin." I wonder if Grand Wizard Pitsfield gets on Pa for never being in church. Or do they call it Grand Dragon? "So whatcha think?"

"It was nice." It was, though I imagine if that cross toppling hadn't interrupted the reverend and I'd've had to stand for another hour of his discourse, the charm might have worn off.

My father shrugs. "I ain't forcin you into nothin." Some rustling off to the left but before my light catches it I'm hurled, flying, deer hooves on me on my chest, Pa yelling slapping its rump, its head turns its antler cut my face and it's gone, vanished into the forest.

"You al*right,* boy? You al*right*?"

"Uh-huh." I touch my forehead, look at my fingertips. Blood.

"We'll get you patched up at home. Goddamn dumb buck!"

My father tells me to sit in the kitchen while he brings down bandages and antiseptic. If he'd brought me up to the bathroom medicine cabinet, we would have wakened my mother who would have flown into hysterics at the sight of my wound and blamed my father for his foolish Klan business. In the light of day and with the gash properly dressed, he must figure her panic will be somewhat abated. The grandfather in the living room dongs—4:15.

"Pa, you said you don't wanna force me into anything." The ointment he dabs on my forehead stings and I flinch. "I was thinking. Maybe I'll go to high school next year. I can always get on at the mill later, but I was thinking. Maybe I'll finish school, get my diploma." He takes my hand and puts it on the bandage to hold it in place while he tears the tape with his teeth.

"We musta surprised it," he says. "People think deer all gentle, nothin but prey. Well ain't nothin more dangerous than prey on the defense." He pats me on the arm and gently leads me up the steps to tiptoe past his and my mother's room before he brings me back to my bed. Feel like my head just touched the pillow when it's time to get up for Sunday school. And only when Ma lets out a yelp at breakfast, her hand over her mouth staring at sleepy me and reminding me of the compress on my forehead, do I know for sure it wasn't all a dream.

"Immediately prior to the crash of '29, Hawaii's commercial growth was staggering. Given its exceptional strategic position, most demonstrably evidenced by the catastrophic events of December 7th, we can expect the territory will benefit profoundly by the influx of capital related to the military industry, propelling it well on the road to full economic recovery, perhaps even eclipsing its astonishing pre-Depression record. And with increased taxes reflecting statehood, Hawaii's economic prosperity would result in prosperity for all of us."

Lucille stands center stage behind the lectern, opening with our affirmative constructive speech. On this Friday the 20th, the day for which we have been priming and cramming, she assumes the economic angle she has prepared, and I sit on the auditorium stage once again astounded by her eloquence which, in front of an audience, seems to have surpassed even her extraordinary fluency in our practice sessions with Mr. Hickory. Lucille, who I had previously thought of as awkward if not cold and defensive, masterfully rose to the debate challenge, which is as much about maintaining a dignified and composed manner as it is about presenting astute arguments. She is smartly dressed in a crisp white blouse and navy jacket and skirt cutting just below the knee, brown penny loafers. I wear my brown Sunday suit, my sole good outfit. This morning my mother had fussed over my hair to an annoying degree. Megan Riley and Nick Fiore of St. Mary's wear their school uniforms. The four of us are attired exactly as we were when our photograph was taken in the county library Tuesday after school. The picture appeared in yesterday's paper with an invitation to the public. Apparently, we were told, this gender equality is rare in debate competition, when more often than not both teams are wholly male.

There are nearly fifty people in the audience, the spectators somewhat spaced apart. Most of the small crowd I can identify, though the announcement in the paper did seem to bring in a handful of unattached onlookers. My mother is there, and Benja, excused by the high school for this special event. There's Mr. Westerly and Mr. Hickory, and Mrs. Flanagan the cafeteria cook. Lucille's, Megan's, and Nick's parents and a slew of St. Mary's faculty. For them, this is the all-important match that will indicate the parochial facility's prowess in official competition. For us, our faculty and our families, this is the all-important match. My stung ego regarding the sparse crowd is quickly trounced by relief, an assuaging of my trembling stage fright, only for it to return with a vengeance when five minutes before start time half the school comes flooding through the doors, belatedly excused from classes to pack the place.

When I got home from the photo session, I changed out of my good clothes and came down to the kitchen, where my beaming mother surprised me with a slice of chocolate cake and milk. I sat and ate, her across the table, and gradually she broached the subject. What did I think about B.J. coming with her to the debate competition?

"*No.*"

"He'll behave himself. If I tell him to be quiet."

"You don't know for sure."

"I do. If I *really* tell him. He'd be so proud to see his little brother up there on—"

"He'll act up! Or he'll get loud! He'll get loud when I stand to speak, cheering me or something! And then I'll get all nervous, I'll lose my train of thought and then I'll—"

"*Okay!*" She gently gestured for me to sit back down. "Okay," she repeated. B.J. entered and spelled "cake" to my mother, a polite request, and she cut him a piece.

"At this time of crisis in our nation," Megan Riley at the lectern, "it is vital that we pull together. We have grimly observed the countries of Europe falling one by one to Hitler's fascistic metastasis of the continent. But it is imperative that our own borders are secure before we fight to protect those of our allies, and that security is achieved through our solidarity as citizens of a unified democracy. The integrity of such a cohesive front is highly compromised by the anti-American sentiments of Communism. Given the rumored crimson tint of the territory of Hawaii's notorious International Longshore and Warehouse Union, one can only imagine the sort of Soviet party-line politics the *state* of Hawaii would bring to Capitol Hill."

I had only heard the word "union" once in my house. When I was in second grade I came home from school to find my father having some quiet tête-à-tête with Mr. Wright from the mill. They were in the living room, and I'd come in through the kitchen, stopping in the doorway. They never noticed me.

"Nex they say Strike," said my father. "An then the company bring in the scabs, and there I am out of a job."

"He's gone," said Mr. Wright. "Nobody asked for no union, nobody sent for no union man, he went back up North where he come from."

"Five in my family, I got five mouths to feed. They come down here whippin it up, playin, it ain't no game to *us*."

"The niggers up near Birmingham goin red. You hear that? Communist organizin amongst the damn darkie sharecroppers *before* the Yankee trash come. Lazy black asses thinkin they oughta be paid like a white man."

"I heard they already been han-pickin the scabs. Just in case."

"No worry, he done packed up an gone. After we give him a little talk-in-to." Mr. Wright punched his right fist into his left palm, like I'd seen in a gangster picture show Benja snuck me into. The gesture looked funny with those two fingers Mr. Wright lost at the mill, and I covered my mouth lest the giggles give me away.

At the lectern I gaze at the audience, briefly but, as instructed by Mr. Hickory, enough to indicate I have taken in each and every one of them. I inhale silently and deeply.

"There has been much concern expressed by those opposed to Hawaiian statehood that two senators representing the sparsely populated Pacific archipelago would confer disproportionate, and thus unfair, federal polit-ical power to the infant state. These presumptions are based on some Hol-lywood image of remote, secluded islands. Hardly. Hawaii's population according to the 1940 census was four hundred twenty-three thousand, more inhabitants than Vermont, Wyoming, Delaware, and Nevada." From three-quarters near the back I notice someone has raised his hand in a V for Victory sign for me, and I smile to myself, seeing it's Henry Lee.

After Sunday school this week I went over to his house just for an hour. I knew the rest of the week I'd be too busy, between regular homework and the final crucial preparations for the debate. But Henry Lee had mentioned Sally would be taking Tuesday off for some funeral and had traded with her regular Sunday off, and that Roger always liked to spend Sundays with his mother, so I calculated Roger's presence should add up to an extra nickel. All the debate excitement had not caused me to forsake my Sopwith ambition.

I knocked on the kitchen door. When no one answered I walked in. No Sally, no Roger. Down to the basement.

I stopped still in my tracks. There was Roger playing trains with Henry Lee. And not in Roger's usual half-aloof way. *Really* playing, though never exactly looking at his playmate.

"It's the tragedy of the century," Henry Lee said.

"A tornado," said Roger, "is approaching this sleepy town. They hear tell of it wreaking destruction in the next state, but these unsuspecting villagers don't worry. This settlement is in a valley surrounded by mountains, Whoever heard of a tornado jumping a mountain? They laugh and pray for all the prairie dwellers in the twister's path and go to bed. Except for the night owls, students up studying, those people driving around in their cars—"

"Tonguin," Henry Lee inserted, demonstrating with rapid gymnastics of his own tongue.

"The last chance for these naïve citizens to take their families on a pleasant leisurely evening drive-around before the rations outlaw sightseeing."

"Hookers! Streetwalkers!"

"Others are alone in their cars, just speculating about life. Looking for the Milky Way. Or thinking one day they'll build a rocket to the moon, they'll walk on the moon which is cold and soft and peaceful."

"But back to the tragedy."

"It would appear nothing could interfere with this idyllic night. But lo, danger lurks in the distance. Even the train thinks it's safe, it'd pull over usually, hold off until the minor storm passed—"

"Wait a minute."

Roger looked up.

"What're you talkin about? the train. The tornado is *not* knockin over the train. The train's expensive, she'd *kill* me. The tornado can mess with the cars and the people but nothin touches the Southern Railway."

"After I graduate I'm hopping the trains."

"Me too!" Henry Lee seemed delighted to find this element of kindred spirit in Roger. Neither of them had yet looked in my direction but I knew damn well they were aware I was standing there.

"I'm gonna be on the bum, out to San Francisco. I'll dip my feet in the bay. I'll drive the city bus."

"They won't let a colored drive the bus."

"They'll let *me*. Then on up to Seattle. And cross over: Vancouver."

"They let colored in Canada?"

"*Yes!*" As if it were the most moronic question ever, but Henry Lee seemed to take no offense.

"I'ma hop the trains too. Maybe we can hop em together. I can go to Canada. Bonn jore."

"*West* Canada! They don't speak French in the West!"

"Roger." His mother calling from the top of the steps.

"Ma'am?"

"Think it's about time you started your homework."

Roger sighed, and for the first time his eyes rested directly on me. I held several books in my hand, ready for rental. I had lugged them to Sunday school and back just for this moment. He stood and gloomily ascended the stairs, passing right by me without comment. The door above closed behind him.

"Jesus!" Henry Lee slammed a fire truck down, still not looking at me. "He don't like to *always* be the student. The minute he havin any fun: *Roger!*" I was wholly undecided whether at the moment I hated Roger or Henry Lee more.

"You got the cards?" I suddenly wanted to whip Henry Lee's ass in twenty-one. We had both grown a bit tired of the trains as of late, though he sure seemed to have been having a jolly ole time with Roger. We sat on the floor. We never played for money. Henry Lee had suggested it many times. I told him my mother wouldn't let me, gambling she considered a sin. For truth, I was just suspicious Henry Lee would cheat.

"You goin to college?" he suddenly asked. I nodded though it seemed doubtful.

"Not me. I'm hoppin the trains."

"Hit me." By this point, he must have glimpsed the bandage on my head from the deer attack, but far be it from him to have acknowledged it.

"Unless I could go to college with Roger." His face brightened. "Yeah, I could go to a colored school. How hard could it be to graduate from there? And they couldn't cry cuz their son didn't get the damn degree. Wouldn't they love it! Now *that*'d be worth it, look on their faces. Their only child: proud graduate a Sambo U!"

"The U.S. has various protectorates," affirms Nick Fiore, "and any one of these could apply for statehood. But there is one major liability that distinguishes Hawaii, a domain bringing together multiple cultures owing to the immigrant plantation workers. Nearly forty percent of Hawaii's inhabitants are of Japanese descent. *Forty percent!* It could be argued that Pearl Harbor was such an easy target because the Japanese most likely had spies that had traveled there, *legally*, many times."

I think of how our flat maps, U.S. to the left and Japan to the right, make it seem like we are the world apart, when all you have to do is fold it and see Japan practically kisses Hawaii. I think about when I came downstairs this morning in my suit, passing my father hidden behind his newspaper, the headline:

JAPANESE CONTAINMENT
PRESIDENT SIGNS EXECUTIVE ORDER 9066

My mother chatted away in the kitchen, oiling my hair. Pa could have traded with somebody to get off today, but apparently he chose not to. For all I know he might have already had the day off and traded to make sure he was *on*. Then I heard the front door open and close, him gone to the mill for the day.

"Where's B.J. gonna be?"

"Takin him over to Aunt Pearlie's. She's makin her apple crumb pie he likes, he won't even need to know anything went on." She pats my hair. "Okay, you're done. Lemme fix you a plate."

"I don't think I can eat."

"You *better* eat. Your pa give up both his bacon strips so you could have four." I stared at her. She smiled. "He said you'll be the one needin the energy today."

"My full name," our opponent continues, "is Nicostrato Giovanni Fiore. A mouthful." The audience laughs, and he smiles. "My parents came here from Naples, the land of our current enemy. But as you can see, I have fully assimilated. My brother Ludo volunteered for the army, flew overseas two days ago. We are not certain where he is right now. He could very well wind up killing a distant cousin. This war is a catastrophe, but not one of our making. It is the brainchild of a few mad despots-in-arms, namely Hitler, Hirohito, and Mussolini. But my brother, my parents, my entire family. We are Americans. We have happily dived into the Melting Pot.

"I'm not so sure this melting process has progressed so well with our Japanese immigrants isolated on islands so far out in the Pacific, not much closer to San Diego than to Tokyo." Apropos of nothing other than that the opposing team has the floor, Henry Lee crosses his eyes and twirls his tongue, which old physical science Mrs. Thatcherall spies, and in the interest of good sportsmanship she flicks Henry Lee twice sharply in the temple.

On Sunday when I came up from Henry Lee's basement and into the kitchen, Roger was poring over his own books. I relished the look of disappointment on his face when he'd see that I'm leaving already, that he blew his chance to look over my texts. I shut the basement door behind me, and he looked up. Gazed at me before he spoke.

"Did anyone ever ask the *first* Hawaiians if they wanted to be Americans?" I stared. I hadn't ever mentioned anything about the debate to him. Did Henry Lee? "The ones the Americans originally stole the islands from?"

When it's time for my rebuttal, I stand on the podium. I had worked through lunch, too nervous to eat the tuna sandwich my mother packed. I'm guessing no one else is prepared to argue with the news that just hit the papers today. I take a moment to look out at the audience. My mother and sister smile wide at me, and I am suddenly overcome with a terrible regret that my brother is not sitting there with them. This just might be the finest moment of my life and, because of my own stubbornness, he missed it. He would've been quiet if Ma had told him to. He would have been so *happy* to see me up here. Why do I always have to be such a creep?

"My opponent has made mention of the melting pot theory, assimilation into the culture of the United States. He has hypothesized that while his family, of Italian background, has evolved into full-blooded Americans, that this same conversion is not possible for, or is of no interest to, the Hawaiian Japanese. Mr. Fiore's family is part of Prayer Ridge, Alabama, a town of few newcomers, most families here for generations. I wonder if Mr. Fiore's family would have melted so quickly if they were living in New York City, where there are other options, Little Italy right around the corner.

"But we are talking about the Japanese. Yesterday President Roosevelt signed Executive Order 9066. The legalese is nearly incomprehensible, but the newspaper editors have spelled it out: Americans of Japanese descent are to be sent to internment camps. Japanese families who have been here for generations will not be exempt. Families of people now serving America in the armed forces will not be exempt. With regard to my opponent's concern that the Japanese have not properly assimilated into the larger American society, it would appear their forced segregation from the rest of America would be a monumental deterrent to such a process.

"Although President Roosevelt's order lacks specificity with regard to these 'military areas,' the newspapers have interpreted it well. To be sure, there recently have been internments of residents of German ancestry, of Italian ancestry, but these detainees made up a minuscule percentage of their ethnic population, and were mostly noncitizens. This belated decree affecting the Japanese is much more far-reaching. Whole neighborhoods will vanish, the camps filled with mothers, old men, children. So it would seem those who melt into the pot most seamlessly do not appear to be those who *think* American, but rather who *look* American. Like the Founding Fathers, none of whom, to my knowledge, were Japanese, or African, or Cherokee.

"So we as a democratic nation, vastly different from Hitler's regime, we demand that eligible Hawaiians serve in the war, and simultaneously may force over a third of the Hawaiian population into confinement. And all Hawaii has asked of us is statehood. That in addition to the undertaking of all the attendant responsibilities of being American, many of which have already been thrust upon them, they might also enjoy the *privileges* of being one of these United States, to vote and to be represented. Don't we owe them that much?"

I feel ecstatic in my surprise attack, stunned by my own impeccable articulation. The audience stares, gaping, and for a brief insane moment I wonder if I'll get a standing ovation. Then, as some of the mouths close and the stares transform into glares, I am hurled into the terrible reality that I've just lost Prayer Ridge the debate.

When it's all over, there's some kid from the yearbook to take our picture. Mr. Hickory behind with his hands on Lucille's right shoulder and my left. Why didn't the idiot snap the shot *before* the debate, when we were all nervous smiles? Of course Megan and Nick and the St. Mary's gang are laughing, beaming. Mr. Westerly appears, and I look to him for some small comfort, but he seems almost to scowl at me, then congratulates Lucille on a good job. Mr. Hickory is shaking hands with St. Mary's and waves

Lucille and me over to do the same. Nick and Megan are kind, trying to be ungloating winners. One of their nun teachers, an old woman, gives me dirty looks. A young nun smiles brightly at me. Mr. Hickory is giving Lucille some encouraging conciliatory words. He turns to me but before he can say anything, the principal calls him over, and he indicates for me to wait until he returns. Where's my mother?

"That was great!" It's some kid, maybe a couple of years older. Dark hair, tall, wiry. "I didn't understand half of what yaw said, but you sure sounded smart!" He offers his hand. "I'm Francis Veter. I used to go here, graduated sixt grade few years ago." We shake. "I saw your picture in the paper and I came. I must say I am thoroughly impressed!" Everybody in the St. Mary's circle is praying now. Gratitude. Wonder if they'd be praying if God had lost it for them.

Lucille's parents are comforting her. She wipes her eyes, trying to do everything not to burst into tears but it's coming. She hasn't even looked at me since my rebuttal. Her mother is also heavy, her father tall and comparably slim. The way she is with him, I'm sure Henry Lee made up that whole thing about the two of them.

"Hey Randall." I turn around. Francis Veter is still standing there. "I saw you. Before." He winks, like some secret between us. I have no idea what he's talking about.

I look over at Mr. Westerly who seems to be ranting to Mr. Hickory. They steal glances at me. When Mr. Westerly notices I am looking back, he turns away. I head fast for the exit.

The air out on the football field is chilly but I barely notice, bawling on the sidelines thirty minutes straight. In the distance some boys running cross-country. Monday I could have been some kind of school hero but instead I'll once again be the dunce. None of them gave a damn about the debate but they'll use it, just another excuse to get me, act like they hate me, like they're so disappointed about the blamed competition but for truth they'll love it, all the more reason to pull my chair out from under me, to flick at my ears when the teacher's back's turned flick my ears till they're blood red, my face blood red and I'll pretend it doesn't bother me I'll shoot myself, I should just shoot myself, my father hasn't hunted in ages but still gotta be bullets in that shotgun I could go into Pa's work shed and get that shotgun and blow my brains out *blam* and I am soothed by the image, my brains and blood splattered all over the walls. There's one of my eyes, there a piece of my nose. I'm peering close to figure out if that pink spot is from my tongue or my lip when I see Mr. Hickory walking toward me with the young nun.

"Randall! I thought I told you to wait for me." But he's all smiles.

"I liked your speeches today, Randall," the young nun says, also glowing.

"Randall, this is Sister Gabriel. Math teacher."

"And I really, *really* liked your rebuttal." She holds out her hand, and we shake. "Excellent work."

"It sure was."

"If *I* were the judge, I guess I would have had to vote against my own school." With that, Sister Gabriel leaves.

"That *was* some rebuttal, Mr. Evans."

I look at him. I don't know what to say. I'm afraid anything I say might turn on the sobs again.

"Listen. People don't wanna hear what you said. *I* didn't wanna hear what you said. But if the panel voted fair, who made the stronger case and not just who said the safe things, you young man would have *easily* given St. Mary's their first loss of the season." He touches my arm, giving it a warm squeeze. "I sure hope you're considering law school."

Nobody's home except my father grousing about no supper on the stove. "Probably took him out for ice cream to make up for leavin him all day," he mutters. He's likely right. Aunt Pearlie's got nine kids most still living at home, plenty enough to keep B.J. busy, and yet he still would have felt abandoned by us. Pa doesn't bother to ask how the debate went.

I go up and change out of my good clothes. Before running off to tend to B.J. they could have at least left a note for me: *Good job.* A few days ago she asked me how to say *I love you* in the sign language. She was enchanted when I showed her, immediately running off to show him. After a while I went to stand at the living room doorway, observing them. They were doing it back and forth, mother and firstborn son, him mimicking her, but he was confused: What is love? She tried to show him, holding her heart, showing her heart beating. Finally she held him and kissed him many times, silly and affectionate. He was thrilled and at last seemed to comprehend. Eventually she turned to sign *I love you* to me. An afterthought.

I hear them all coming in downstairs, B.J.'s voice, Ma and Benja laughing and talking, ignoring my father's grouchiness. I wash my face several times, trying to erase all evidence of my blubbering, of the day. When I'm through I stare in the mirror. *Sure hope you're considering law school.* I heard this episode of *Perry Mason* on the radio a few weeks ago. Once again he proved the case, shocking everyone in the courtroom into a collective gasp.

I come down to the living room and there they all are, Ma, Benja, B.J. Grinning at me. B.J. holds it. The trophy from Gephart's. I know Mr. Westerly wasn't planning on purchasing it until after the debate, and depending upon its outcome, so my family must have gone on and ordered it ahead of time, making it ready regardless.

RANDALL EVANS
BEST SPEECH
PRAYER RIDGE DEBATE COMPETITION
FEB. 20, 1942

8

B.J. sits on the ground with our cousin Deb Ellen, him teaching her. He wanted to show her the sign words, and she always liked playing with him. She turned thirteen Wednesday, but they waited till today, Saturday, 14th of March, to celebrate her birthday in the park. Bright spring sun, and over on the colored side I see some girls skipping two ropes at once. The frankfurters and potato salad done, now Ma helps Aunt Pearlie set up the picnic table for the cake and ice cream.

"You ready to call the troops over?" my mother asks her sister and best friend. Aunt Pearlie is two years my mother's senior. "I notice I got one soldier's mouth a-waterin right here." She winks at me, wearing the red rose brooch I got her for her own March birthday last week. Well there went the Sopwith savings—start over.

Aunt Pearlie's a great baker. The cake is moist, the icing dream creamy.

"It ain't gonna be like this for your birthday," Aunt Pearlie warns Chris-Joe who's ten, the baby of the family. "They sayin the sugar rations gonna hit startin May. You might get a cake an you might not."

"Aw," grumbles Chris-Joe, demonstrating how it is never too early to whine.

"It's delicious," says my mother.

"Ice cream too," says Aunt Pearlie. "People with a sweet tooth sure gonna feel the sacrifice. Guess you be havin a string bean birthday."

"*Aw!*"

She smiles at her youngest. "I hid a little sugar away. It oughta still be good come July the twenty-sixt."

"Least with the victory gardens we never be short on vegetables," my mother says. "My peas been really tasty, an now I got some nice cabbage. That an a little pork's a meal."

"You ain't gettin your wish," Buppie, who's fourteen, informs Deb Ellen.

"You don't even know what my wish was."

"It's the rations. Applies to birthday wishes too."

"Oh you're a regular Jack Benny."

"I'm knittin him some socks," Aunt Pearlie tells my mother. "His letters, he's always complainin bout his cold feet. You think they'll let him wear em? Or they say he just gotta stick to the army socks."

"I'm sure they'll let him wear em."

Jack is eighteen, Aunt Pearlie's second oldest boy, in France.

"Got up early, felt like I had so much to do. Harry called, said he just had the news on, talkin bout the West Coast blackouts. Harry said he didn't really believe we need to keep lights out for fear of enemy planes targetin us, said he thinks it's just the government wantin to keep us reminded we're at war." Like my parents, Uncle Harry had served in the Great War and was of the opinion that entitled him to criticize the government whenever he damn well pleased.

"I don't know if that's true," my mother says. Then shrugs. "Even if it is, keepin us reminded we're at war seems plenty good reason to me."

"I don't wanna be reminded!" wails Chris-Joe. "I want my cake!" His ma pops him in the lips.

"Toldja I saved some sugar but keep it up, it'll go to Artie Ray's birthday September. Hear me?"

"B.J.'s teachin me the sign language, Aunt Bobbie," says Deb Ellen.

"I saw," says my mother.

"He learnt me some words. An the letters. An with the letters he learnt me, I learnt *him* a couple words." Around the table are Ma and Benja, B.J. and me, and Aunt Pearlie and her brood: Lily who's got to be twenty now and her husband Pete John and their toddler girl, Lily holding the newborn baby and Lily's big and pregnant again. Then Todd Joseph seventeen, Lee Frankie sixteen, Artie Ray going on fifteen, Buppie fourteen, Deb Ellen newly thirteen, and Chris-Joe almost eleven. The three absentees are Ty the firstborn, working at the mill, Jack in the service, and Uncle Harry who got some wartime weapons job in Birmingham and now stays most of the time with his brother and family there. Pa calls Aunt Pearlie The Baby Machine, not when my mother's around. He also calls the whole family The Hillbillies, which isn't exactly fair since they live in the valley like us.

"Benja, you heard back from your soldier?" asks Aunt Pearlie. Over at the Methodist church some lady headed up this letter-writing campaign, soldiers with nobody to write to them. Benja signed up fast.

"Not yet. I wrote eleven days ago."

"Be patient. Sometimes a while fore I hear from Jack, but jus when I start to worry a letter always comes."

After dessert, evening's settling so Deb Ellen and company pull out the sparklers. I don't know how they smuggled them in, what with all the rations, but those Joneses always seem to have their ways. As soon as B.J. sees them he starts agitating Ma to go home. She tries to tell him the mini combustibles gonna be taken to the other side of the field but he doesn't care, he wants to leave. He's always been terrified of even the tiniest firecrackers. Finally she gives up, and stands to kiss Aunt Pearlie and all those nieces and nephews goodbye. Todd Joseph and Lee Frankie take the cue to also stand, both got the early shift at the mill tomorrow. Lily stays at the picnic table to talk with her mother and give the baby a bottle, while Lily's husband Pete John tosses a big ball with their little girl, and I and the other cousins go off with our handheld pyrotechnics. There are a dozen in the box and five of us. Two apiece and the birthday girl will get a third. A lingering mystery over who gets the final one. "Draw sticks?" I suggest. No one answers. I've noticed this with Aunt Pearlie's kids, on occasion ignoring me. Maybe not deliberately rude, but like some unspoken agreement between them not to discuss that final sparkler yet, something they all understand instinctively and for which I have to play catch-up.

The five of us ignite the first round, which we all find satisfying, if over way too soon. Then Deb Ellen slips off into the woods to pee, and with only boys left the conversation naturally turns to sex.

"Who *you* doin?" asks Buppie.

"Margaret Laherty." The first girl who came to mind. Well, after Lucille, but they all surely saw her picture in the paper with me for the debates, and I am *not* setting myself up for the rest of the evening or the rest of my life filled with Randall-and-Fatty jokes. The only other girl I thought of was Lily who I've always had a cousin crush on, but I'm sure not going to mention that to her brothers. As if they don't already know. I pray they don't remember Margaret Laherty from elementary. None of the boys are in school anymore except Chris-Joe the baby, couple years behind Margaret and me. The others all stopped after sixth, working odd jobs around town. Ty had got on at the sawmill when he was twelve, and by a very close call nearly wound up with a three-finger hand like Mr. Wright. After that Aunt Pearlie put her foot down to Uncle Harry, none of them goes into the mill till they're sixteen.

"Oh yeah?" Buppie wears a pleased smirk in response to my choice in women, and I am thus relieved in my certainty that he has no idea who

SAYVILLE LIBRARY

Margaret Laherty is or he would have most assuredly let out a big laugh over my imagining she would ever give me the time of day.

As Deb Ellen returns, lightning bugs start blinking. "Hey!" She dashes back to our picnic table. Artie Ray lights a cigarette and doesn't share it.

"Well," he says, "we sure were glad your pa didn't come. Otherwise we'd have to hide the booze." They all crack up. A reference to the embarrassment last Christmas when my father's behavior incited the mass exodus of extended family before dinner. Deb Ellen returns with a big jar, grass in the bottom and holes in the lid. She begins running around, collecting fireflies.

"You excited about high school?" Chris-Joe asks me.

I shrug. "Guess so." They apparently haven't heard from Aunt Pearlie that Pa's of a dissenting opinion on the matter.

"He thinks he's goin to high school." Buppie smirking at his little brother.

"Ma said I can!" Chris-Joe says.

"No Jones ever went past the sixt," Buppie remarks.

"Ty didn't go past third, and Pa didn't go at all," says Artie Ray. "Pa signed on at the mill when he was ten. Ty didn't till he was twelve so Pa used to call him 'the princess.'" Buppie snickers.

"Benja's in the tenth?" Chris-Joe.

"Eleventh."

"All of em!" Chris-Joe in a bitter pout, stomping off a few yards away. "All of Aunt Bobbie's kids goin to twelfth!" I never before thought of my family as so erudite.

"Not B.J.," Artie Ray reminds him.

"He doesn't count!" Chris-Joe throws a stone, barely missing Artie Ray. Artie Ray stands, a warning. "Hey boy."

"Lily was engaged at sixteen," says Buppie, "married at seventeen, a ma at eighteen. Now she's a ma twice over goin on three."

"I'm a uncle!" says Chris-Joe, suddenly over his angry spell and coming back to our throng.

"I'm a aunt," says Deb Ellen, "but I sure ain't gonna be no ma. Yaw can have all the kids ya want."

"You keep up your tomboy ways," says Artie Ray, "ain't no man gonna wantcha."

"Then I sure will keep up my tomboy ways."

"I want another sparkler," says Chris-Joe.

"In a while," says Buppie.

"Why?"

"Cuz we're *savin* em! *Savorin* em! You use it up now, then cryin the blues cuz they're gone already." Chris-Joe starts bawling. "Oh you definitely ain't the one gettin that third sparkler." Chris-Joe starts howling. "Shut *up!*"

"I was over there today," says Artie Ray. "She got a letter from Jack."

Chris-Joe instantly stops crying and Deb Ellen, that quick already holding a menagerie of a good twenty fireflies, turns sharply toward Buppie. "Where?"

"Lily's, where'dja think?"

They all stare at him.

"Well don't you even wanna know what he had to say?"

"I do!" says Chris-Joe.

"He said France is a dog pit, and the food tastes like dog shit."

"He didn't say that word!" Chris-Joe.

"He sure did. He wouldn'ta wrote that to Ma but he wrote it to Lily. He said they marched seventeen miles nonstop, then creepin in the trenches, moved ten yards over three days. Cold an half the time pourin, he signed up fearin he might get shot an die but now thinks what gonna earn him the Purple Heart is new-monia. Love, Jack."

"He didn't say love to the family?"

"I mean 'Love to the family. Jack.'" Chris-Joe is relieved.

Deb Ellen's eyes narrow. "You made that up."

"His words, not mine."

"'Love, Jack. I mean, Love to the family, Jack.'" Her eyes rolling.

"Okay, he didn't say 'love to the family.' I jus said that cuz it's what *he* wanted to hear." Meaning Chris-Joe, who now confirms this with "Aw!"

"I'm joinin the army," says Buppie.

"I'm joinin the army!" says Chris-Joe. "If I get my growth spurt next year I'll pass for fifteen."

"Lookin fifteen'll do you no good, fool," says Buppie. "Fifteen-year-olds get in for lookin *eighteen.*"

"They let anybody in," says Artie Ray.

"Not the army, I'ma be a *flyer!*" Chris-Joe starts racing around, his arms outstretched: plane. Artie Ray looks at Deb Ellen, her eyes still hard on him.

"Whatta ya blamin *me* for? I didn't tell Jack to write to Lily steada us."

"You made the whole goddamn thing up."

"You know the way Ma and Lily can get into it." Artie Ray looks at the picnic table in the distance. "Both of em actin like butter wouldn't melt in their mouths now, but one wrong word. Jack prolly thinks he better write to Lily separately since he never knows when her and Ma's gonna fall out, stop speakin."

"He could write to each of us," Deb Ellen says.

"To eight of us?" the boys say in unison. Chris-Joe adds, "Plus *Ma?* Plus *Pa?*"

"He only writes to Lily separate cuz she's in a separate household." Artie Ray.

"I gotta go to the woods!" Chris-Joe hops away, holding himself.

"An cuz Lily's his favorite sister." Deb Ellen flashes a glare at Artie Ray.

"Oh he's jus foolin on ya," says Buppie, "don't bite the bait." From over on the colored side, another birthday happening: singing and the lit cake.

"Come on," Artie Ray says, "let's light up the sparklers."

"I'm not ready yet," Deb Ellen retorts.

"Then guess you'll miss out."

"I GET TWO MORE!"

"I get mine! I get mine!" Chris-Joe running out of the woods, still pulling up his pants.

"Jesus! Don'tchu see a girl lookin atcha?" asks Buppie.

"Nope." Chris-Joe grins at Deb Ellen, who slugs him. He starts wailing.

"Oh Christ," says Buppie.

"Well long as he's blubberin, I'll take his sparkler too." Artie Ray moves toward the box.

"No!" Chris-Joe grabs his sparkler, lights it, smiling through his tears. As the four of us watch the shimmering in the boy's hands, Deb Ellen, still sulky, gives each of her brothers the evil eye, her irises shining in fury. I have never seen her cry. She's an athlete, the talent and the drive, skinning her knees and elbows and ignoring the blood to keep the ball in play. The only other time I have glimpsed this look in her was the night before Jack left, when Aunt Pearlie threw him that going-away dinner. He was in a bedroom, some intimate farewell time with Lily and her daughter, his godchild. I was coming back from the bathroom and overheard the private episode, stopping myself short, caught between trying not to pass by the doorway lest it appear I was

eavesdropping and being stuck in a spot where I couldn't help but eavesdrop. Deb Ellen had just barged in, grabbing Jack and now trying to pull him off the bed, wanting him to throw a football with her. He was patient, telling her to give him a few minutes, and when she wouldn't stop he finally snapped at her to let go and leave him and Lily and the little girl alone. With her and Lily the only girls, I'd noticed moments with Deb Ellen vying for the attention, especially from Jack, no question her favorite brother. With his definitive reprimand, she'd stomped out, and saw me near the door.

And as if this memory simultaneously comes back to Deb Ellen, her gaze now settles on me. Quiet me, here in the middle of some major Jones family dispute that I don't even wholly understand. Maybe to her my silence comes off as superior. My heart skips a beat.

"It wa'n't Ty's fault." Even with her staring right at me it takes a moment before I realize I'm the one she's addressing.

"What?"

"Your pa. He mighta picked that Christmas fight with Ty, but Ty ain't to blame."

"Deb Ellen," warns Artie Ray.

Oh yeah, Pa bringing up the chicken pox, the damn taboo. But something ominous in Artie Ray's tone. Well whatever this little drama is, I want it to be done and over with. Fix my eyes on her. "If you got something to say, say it."

She shrugs, looks away. "Maybe I don't." She's not toying with me so much as just realized she stepped into a dangerous room she isn't sure she wants to enter. She goes to the sparklers box. "Hah! I'm gonna light my other two *together*!" She strikes the fire. The double-flash is impressive.

"Yaw can fight among yourselves over that damn last sparkler." I turn to leave.

"You know they weren't married long before B.J. born." I turn around. Artie Ray.

"*So?* The way I hear it tell your ma an pa wa'n't married long fore Ty popped out neither." My cousins make me lose my grammar.

"Yeah, the difference is Ty was still my pa's." I start to charge him. "Your pa liked Ty!" I stop short. They all stare at him, Deb Ellen no longer paying attention to the live torch in her hand. "My brother was three before your ma an pa got hitched, so still in the courtin stage, your pa prolly tryin to impress your ma, bein all friendly with her sister's baby." He stops. I wait. All of them staring back at me, my breath coming faster.

"So B.J. gets borned," Deb Ellen taking it up, "an my ma an Grammaw at the hospital, gettin ready to bring him an your ma home. An your pa volunteers to babysit Ty, he's four then, waitin for all the women to come back with the new baby. But Ty, he has the chicken pox. An they bring baby B.J. home, an then baby B.J. gets the chicken pox." And she stops.

"Yeah, *and*? Everybody knows that, *God*. Wasn't anybody's fault, the spots hadn't shown up on Ty yet, they didn't know he was sick. Pa. I know Pa blames Ty sometimes, like at Christmas, that's not right, I guess he's just upset and—"

They glance at each other.

"What!"

"Your pa knew about the chicken pox," says Artie Ray. "Ty remembers. He went playin in the mud, and your pa give him a bath. He saw the spots on Ty's chest. Ty remembers. Uncle Ben goes, 'What's all this?' an Ty goes, 'Itch! Itch!'"

"Lucky B.J. jus got deaf," chimes in Deb Ellen. "Chicken pox coulda *kilt* a baby," stating the blamed obvious. I look at their faces. Is this a *joke*? You never know with the damn dimwitted Joneses.

"So, wait a minute. You're trying to tell me my father *on purpose* got B.J. infected." They stare. "And why in the hell would he wanna do that."

I'm regretful soon as the question's passed my lips.

"You ever wonder." Artie Ray all careful. "You ever wonder how come the engagement lass three years? Why it take your ma so long, ready herself for husband an babies?"

Truthfully I never thought about that before but sure won't let on. Not that it matters: Joneses got the scent of the bloodhound, teeth of the Doberman.

"Wa'n't her fault." Oh Deb Ellen trying to be soothing now? "Everyone knows what happens to women in the navy."

"Morons!" I'm laughing loud. "You're saying my mother got pregnant with B.J. in the service."

They stare.

"The war was over 1918! B.J. was born 1923! What, you think she carried him around five years?" They stare. "WHAT!"

"Somethin happened in the navy," Artie Ray ventures.

"I know! I *know* what happened, I know. She miscarried. She lost that baby, I know!"

"It wa'n't her fault," assures Artie Ray. "They made her—"

"I KNOW!" They thought they were telling me something I wasn't aware of and they were wrong, end of discussion, relief. So why do I feel sick?

"Then you know about their honeymoon?" Buppie finally adding his voice. They all glare at him, as if this was going too far, yet I know wherever the hell we're going, we were headed there from the beginning.

"They drove to New Orleans," he continues. "Fancy schmancy."

"I think I know where my parents' honeymoon was!" Though thinking back, if I ever brought it up, they never seemed to want to talk about it.

"She seen em." Artie Ray regaining his voice. "Your ma seen em, the two of em."

Buzzing in my ear. Cheeks hot.

"Two from the horde done it to her back in the navy. They seen her in New Orleans: déjà vu. You might understan the awkwardness, everybody reckonizin everybody. She *tried* to avoid em—"

"YOU DON'T KNOW SHIT, ARTIE RAY! Who *told* you? *Some trash you heard on the street!*" A boy-scream's unusual, and the family thirty yards away looks over at us.

"Your ma tole my ma," Artie Ray says carefully, "and my ma tole Lily. Not till she was grown, she asked about B.J. once. An Lily tole me. Sure you wanna hear?"

"It wa'n't her fault." Deb Ellen jumping in, trying to snatch the punch line. If I hear her say that one more time—"They were like, 'We had her first!' Two against one, your poor pa couldn't fight em off."

But Artie Ray steals it back. "An after they knocked him weak, there's your poor ma. One holds your daddy down while the other—"

I seize the jar of lightning bugs, lift it high over my head, slam it down, *crash*! The fireflies escape, a contained yet spectacular moment of panicked flittering lights that renders all those Joneses to silence. Deb Ellen is particularly mesmerized, and I imagine in the future she'll want to crash every firefly collection. I storm away. Behind me, "Don't blame your pa! He jus feels bad, I bet. That's why he's sore on Ty, he can't help it." Shut up, Deb Ellen, before I come back and cut your goddamn tongue out. "An don't blame B.J.! He can't help where he come from! Wa'n't *his* fault—" and I hear one of her brothers slap her, then some kind of screaming skirmish.

You have to walk pretty far into the woods to come to the clearing, the clandestine space where I once spotted that groping high school couple in full view of my perch at the oak top, and in the pitch-black it takes me longer to find it but I do. Lie on my back. No moon and a million stars. If I look straight at one place and not think not think then the fireflies also become big yellow stars, shooting stars, and I decide to start making wishes. And though I know my life is wanting in a thousand ways, at this very moment I can't come up with one damn thing worthwhile to wish for.

9

Autobiography

I was born April 14, 1928, the year before the Crash. My brother Benjamin, Jr. ("B.J.") was going on five then, and my sister Benja was three. They were both named after my father. My mother gave me her first initial: "R" for Roberta, though everyone calls her "Bobbie" so it sounds like my family is four "B"s and an "R."

I have three vivid memories from before I could walk. One was when I was in my crib and my mother had a stuffed bunny, playing with me.

The second was when I crawled over to Benja who was combing her blond doll's hair, and I tried to grab my sister's doll, and she was pulling it from me and finally she smacked me and I began to cry. Then my mother came in and smacked my sister and my sister began to cry, and my mother gave the doll to me. The next day I looked for the doll but my mother told me the doll moved away from us because the doll was so sad that we kept fighting over her. I cried but my sister didn't cry, and I didn't understand why my sister wasn't crying. Years later I asked Benja if my mother had fibbed, if she had really just told my sister to keep the doll in her room hidden away from me. "Yes!" Benja exclaimed. She seemed impressed that I had figured this out, and more impressed that I even remembered it. She laughed very hard for several minutes.

The third vivid memory is my brother B.J. carrying me around and me watching the world go by in his arms, because my house and my yard felt like the whole world. In the yard he put me on the tricycle and pushed me and let me go, and I fell off backwards into the soft grass, and I remember how scary it was, how it happened fast, and suddenly I was on my back looking up at the sky. I wasn't hurt but I cried, and my mother came out and yelled at my brother but he couldn't hear her because my brother is deaf. And she picked me up, and he cried and cried, and little as I was I knew he wasn't crying because she yelled at him but because she had taken me away from him. I screamed louder and louder which made her keep me from him, but ironically I was crying because I wanted to be back with my brother, so the more she kept me from him, the harder I screamed, a vicious cycle.

When Miss Dawson assigned us to write our autobiographies (and even I joined in with that collective class moan), she said we needn't cover everything, that it's better to hit a few highlights and be specific than try to go through our entire lives quick and general. This would be a start.

I finish my homework at the kitchen table, then come up to my room where I stop in the doorway. B.J. on his bed studying Benja's latest *National Geographic*. Not flipping pages, like someone just looking at the pictures. He seems to be reading. But he *can't* be reading, he can't read. Now he starts hand-spelling, his lips moving like he's having a discussion with his hand about some article. As I step into the room he looks up, but seems to see through me, his hands still moving, his mind on Africa and elephants or Asia and tigers. He turns back to the magazine.

Occasionally Henry Lee and I fall out, or I just get bored with his stupid trains, and I'm back with B.J.'s sign lessons. My brother should snub me for always making him last resort but instead he's perpetually happy-happy when I come around. My mother and sister have learned a few words but, beyond the basics, nobody but me's persevered with the language, and my brother and I have gradually begun to have real conversations. Even in my most neglectful days of distraction by school or Henry Lee, B.J. always makes sure we hand-talk a little in bed before turning out the light. Now I gentle slip the magazine from his fingers and take out something new: pen and paper.

Under my tutelage, B.J. writes *B.J.* and *Mother* and *Randall* and *Benja* and *Father* and *pen* and *paper* and *Randall writes* and *I write.* His letters are large and crooked like a first grader's, but legible.

I teach him a game. Take out some marbles. This sky blue one you may *borrow*, this red one you may *keep.* A few minutes later I take back the borrowed marbles, but when he tries to return the others I refuse. He loves games, and he loves new words, so he throws no tantrums about me taking back the borroweds and is delighted when he comes to understand the concept of borrowing, which happens fast. Meanwhile I start teaching him days. I show him our calendar, and I draw one up for him. Every morning I point out the date. By the third day he points it out to me before I can show him. Prior to this he comprehended a week intuitively: five days Benja and I spend at school, followed by a day at home, followed by a part-day at home after Sunday school—but now he has it on paper, a chart seven squares across that makes his instinct concrete. Combining the lessons of borrowing and of days, I show him a book I'd borrowed *today*, and let him see on his calendar that exactly one week later I return that book and have now borrowed another. After all this I feel he's ready as he'll ever be. So Saturday the 21st of March, start of spring, I take him: first trip to the public library.

Soon's we walk in B.J.'s mouth flies open, awestruck at the hundreds of volumes. I take him to the children's section. There aren't a lot for him. Most on the kids' shelves are chapter books beyond his level, Hardy Boys, Nancy Drew. But on his own he finds *Mike Mulligan and His Steam Shovel.* Some of the children stare at him, coming up on nineteen perusing the picture books. B.J. takes no notice. He's often stared at, and I wonder now if he really isn't aware or if, over the years, he's built some kind of wall between himself and the gapers. I'm infuriated by adults who exercise such a rude lack of self-control, and while I'm somewhat forgiving of little kids on their own, if a parent comes near they'd better correct their wild brats quick or get the nasty look from me.

As B.J. turns his pages, I consider my task done and start to move to the adult section for my own book. But my brother wants to know what

"Mulligan" is. I tell him it's the character's last name. He seems confused. Like our last name is Evans. He stares at me, and I realize until now he never knew he had two names.

When I think we're ready to check out, B.J. points out that he has noticed people with more than one book. I give him a limit of two, and he leaves with *Mike Mulligan* and *Madeline*. At home I read them to him once, signing them, then I run off to Henry Lee's for a while. When I return he can read them by himself.

A week later I'm apprehensive. How will the returning go? But he happily lets go of *Mike Mulligan* and replaces it with *The Poky Little Puppy*. *Madeline* he renews. The next week he does the same, replacing *Puppy* with *Curious George* and re-renewing *Madeline*. The librarian tells me he will have to return *Madeline* next time so others can borrow it, and though he isn't pleased, he does so minus theatrics. The week after he returns *The Little Engine That Could*, he notices that *Madeline* has not been checked out over the last week, so he decides he has now earned the right to have it again. At the circulation desk the librarian purses her lips but says nothing, and B.J. happily leaves with his favorite. *Madeline* is in rhyme, and I wonder how he can appreciate it without hearing the cadence. What's it sound like in his head? Some nights before bedtime, especially if B.J. has had a hard day, I read the book aloud while signing it to him, and he signs with me and calms down.

The supper dishes washed, my mother goes to sit on the edge of the back porch to smoke and think. Late April, the sun mighty warm already, preparing for the coming dog days. At the kitchen table my head's into the Louisiana Purchase. My father sits in his living room soft chair reading the paper. Although I'm supposedly not to be disturbed, I'm the only person remotely within earshot of him, and he's compelled to comment on the most interesting tidbits aloud. "Hey. There's a team in the nigger leagues called the New York *Black* Yankees." He chuckles to himself. Truthfully he dismisses *all* professional baseball and football as Northern hogwash since, with the exception of St. Louis, no teams are south of Washington, D.C., and St. Louis isn't exactly Dixie. His loyalties remain with the school outfits: University of Alabama, Lefferd County High. Country music has been playing softly from our bedroom upstairs, and now it gets louder.

I think about going out to my mother. This is the time she might talk.

Doing the housework, she's too busy. This quiet time, her head's in a different place. The music gets louder still.

"Turn that down, boy!" My father bangs loud on the wall. B.J. gets the message, and the music goes out. He likes it loud. Full volume he can put his hand on the radio and feel the vibrations. I walk out to sit with my mother. She says nothing, which means I'm not bothering her, I'm welcome to stay. For a while we don't speak. She would be fine to keep it that way though she'll tolerate my breaking the silence, we both know I didn't come out here because I wanted *not* to talk. Still, when she decides her breather is over, she'll get up and go back inside, this window of opportunity is not necessarily a wide one. Where to start. Do I *want* to start? Ma, you never talk about nursing in the navy, what was that like? You know why Pa always seems so hard on B.J.? You and me and Pa's and Benja's earlobes all hang loose, B.J.'s is attached, wonder why.

What I say is, "How come B.J. fears the firecrackers?"

She takes a puff, her eyes fixed somewhere in the distance. "Kids. He was a little thing, six or seven. They never played with him, but guess they lured him out this one day, actin like some game." She taps ashes into the ashtray she holds. "Put firecrackers on his shoulders. He didn't know what firecrackers was, he thought they was his friends. Set em off." She spits out a bit of cigarette paper. "I was worried soon's I'd noticed he'd disappeared. The other kids never liked him before, so he had no call to run off with any of em. I was worried cuz I couldn't just holler his name an bring him back like with yaw." She closes her eyes. "Heard him long before I seen him. Runnin home hysterical, you never noticed that little brown colorin, his neck an shoulder? 'Tweren't no birthmark." Sighs. "I took him around a while, pointin out this kid or that, this house? That one? Wantin him to tell me who done it. He kep holdin up three fingers, three boys. I assumed they was boys. But either he didn't wanna give em up, or they was strangers from outa town cuz he never pointed out no one. I prayed they was strangers. Hated to think he was so desperate for friends, he knew who the devils was an—" She looks up at the sun, wipes her brow. I wait, but she just keeps staring skyward.

"How did he get outside by himself?"

"Your pa was watchin him. I had to go to the doctor. With you, I think. Still a baby, you got some cough. Pretty rare I left him home with your pa." She chuckles. "There was one other time, I can't remember why now. He was a toddler. I come home an *all* his bottled milk gone. I said, 'Ben, you don't jus give it to him every time he hollers! Drink all that milk, make him sick!' Which musta been what happened, I could see his little puffy eyes, cried hisself to sleep." She stamps out her butt. "You wanna go fetch your ma a nice cole glass a ice tea?"

I pour two glasses. The music from upstairs has come on low again. When I go back outside my mother has moved a few inches to lean her back comfortably against the pillar. She smiles lazily at me. I hand her the glass and sit opposite her, sipping from mine. The ice gives me a headache.

"Deb Ellen goes everybody knows what happens to women in the navy."

I am stunned I said it. My mother also, staring at me. Then she shakes her head, looking elsewhere.

"Deb Ellen is an ignorant girl." She sips. "You two are skippin down different paths. She'll be married an a ma fore you know it, prolly not in that order. You goin to college. Cousins now but grown-up, you be like strangers, stickin with your own tribes. Be lucky *we* ever see ya again." I think she's teasing with the last remark. Then I see she's not.

"I'll always come back! My family!" Not necessarily the extended part.

Her eyes sad but she smiles. "I hope so."

I take another sip. *You goin to college.*

"Mr. Hickory thinks maybe I should be a lawyer."

"He does?" Now she *is* smiling. "Whatta *you* think?"

I'm trying to be serious but can't help but smile myself. "A lawyer could be good." The radio music blasting.

"God*dammit*, boy!" My father barging up the steps.

"Blessed are the peacemakers," my mother says before going inside. In advance of the coming mêlée, I step into the kitchen just quick enough to snatch my history book, then run out to sit way over under the elm at the end of the yard where I'll hear nothing but the birds.

When I return three-quarters of an hour later, my mother is making cookie batter and humming. B.J. waits close to her, expectant and happy. From his reddened eyes, I can tell there was quite a row before the intervention of the diplomat. "I suddenly got the bakin urge." She tears off a piece of dough for B.J., who eats it like a dog she's feeding. She tears off another piece, sets it in front of me. I stare at it. I'm nearly an eighth-grade graduate. I'm too big for dough, I'm not some pet eating uncooked food. She doesn't look up from flattening the raw pastry with her rolling pin when she says, "I'm gonna have to have a talk with Pearlie. Seem like Deb Ellen know a lot more than she oughta, her age."

"Maaaa," entreats B.J., so she tears him off another piece. He eats it and smacks his lips loud and rolls his eyes all goofy, and she laughs so hard she practically falls over the chair. I smile, chewing on my own dough.

When the treats are hot and fresh out of the oven, my mother asks me to take a couple up to Benja, who's writing a letter to her assigned soldier. I knock. I know my sister's in there but she doesn't answer. "Benja?" I crack it open.

She's crying. I remember seeing her cry when she was little and I littler, but how many years has that been? She sits at her desk looking down at some letters, several internationally postmarked envelopes, and a bunch of stationery sheets balled up. "Shut the door, shut the door!" I quickly obey.

"I write, 'You stay well and you bomb those Jerries.' He writes," she snatches up a letter, "'The Jerries are a little far from here. I'm in the Philippines. And I'm in the infantry. It's a little hard to drop bombs from the ground.' I write, 'Oh yeah! I knew you were in the Pacific, sorry! Well, you get those Japs.' He writes, 'Well if you've read a newspaper anytime lately, you might have noticed the Japs are pretty much getting us,' what am I sposed to say? Whatever it is, it's wrong! So I write, 'Well okay you hurry home then.' And today I get, 'The fastest way be step on a mine, home no legs in a wheelchair, or hit by a grenade, home in a very small box' I *hate* him! Every other girl got a soldier so grateful for a pen pal, and I get—" She wipes her face. "Tomorrow I'm askin Mrs. Nedermeier for a new one." She balls up the letter she was writing, then picks up another blank airmail sheet and goes to her drawer, taking out a dime. "You write it."

I stare blank at her.

"Tell him goodbye from me. I don't think it's right to just stop—" She catches her breath. "Tell him goodbye."

"You could—"

"*No!* I don't care if it's two damn words, I can't bear writin him no more. I don't care your handwritin's different from mine, you write it and I'll sign it. And I'm not signin it 'Benja,' I'm signin it 'Benja K. Evans.' And not 'Kaye' my name, 'K' my initial. Formal. Take it back to your room. Ten cents for your trouble."

In the name of officialdom, I print.

Dear Private Adly,

I am saddened to realize that my letters, which were
intended as a comfort to you, have instead become
a source of irritation. I apologize if I have in any way
offended you. It is probably best if our correspondence
ends with this letter. I wish you all safety and Godspeed.

I open my bank. With the quarter I got for my fourteenth birthday precisely one week ago, and now the dime: $1.02.

The next day after school, I roll it gingerly along the table, the rubber tires smooth. Thank God the Sopwith was already in Gephart's before the rubber rations!

"Where'dju get the money for that aeroplane?" she wants to know, worry on her face. What, she think I stole it? I ever stole before? No!

"I dunno. Some chores I did around school. Cleaning desks." She looks at me suspicious, walks away. B.J. coming in wanting to touch it, I hand-tell him, Wash your hands! Then he comes back, picking it up, Gently! Gently!

The day after's Saturday, and I'm all ready to show my flyer to Henry Lee. But my mother, "Get him outa here! He's all in my hair." Laundry day and B.J.'s driving her nuts, following her around. Also I detect a hint of blackmail: she won't check in with the principal about my alleged lucrative desk-cleaning position if I take B.J. and give her a rest to do her chores.

Roger's mom, usually all busy, is staring right at us when we come in the kitchen, like she sensed something new.

"This your brother?" I nod. "He got a name?"

"B.J." I spell out "Sally" for him.

"Whatchu doin?"

"Spelled your name."

"That a fact?" The first time I've ever seen her smile. She pulls down the cookie jar. "Show me."

I speak as I spell it: M – R – S – L – A – W – R – E – N – C – E.

She continues smiling, then says, "That ain't what you spelled before," and turns back to wiping off the stove.

I'm thinking Henry Lee'll be weird about having B.J. there, and I'm pretty much looking forward to it.

"Hi," I say coming down the stairs. Henry Lee, having heard the second set of footsteps, looks up, frowns. "This is B.J." To B.J. I sign: Henry Lee.

Henry Lee studies him several moments before speaking. "You like the trains?" He pushes the button to set it running. B.J.'s surprised face is all glee. Henry Lee goes on a long lecture, the fascinating world of his diesel caravan, despite knowing damn well my brother doesn't understand a word. Maybe Henry Lee likes that: no interruptions.

"This garage door slides up for the fire engine to come barrelin out. Here's the coal car. Look like real coal, right? Don't touch. This safety stick really goes down when the train approaches the street crossin, *don't touch!*"

I sit staring at them, brand-new Sopwith Camel model in my hand which Henry Lee doesn't even seem to take notice of. Finally he sits back and lets B.J. observe in peace, my brother's face all wonder. "I never met a dummy before."

"Don't call him that."

"Lemme see it." I'm so relieved Henry Lee has finally shown interest, I hand my flyer over instantly, completely forgetting I'd meant to hold back a bit. How long had I been coming here before he let me work his train? He inspects the Camel from different angles. I figure as we play I could ease into asking him could I put one of his little people in the pilot's seat, he's got so many little people, and maybe he'd let me keep the guy under the promise I bring the model over often for him to play with, but I barely have time to flash these thoughts through my mind before he hands back my aeroplane, seeming already bored with it.

"I wasn't being mean. Before 'dummy' got to be an insult, it just meant somebody who couldn't talk."

"I think I know that."

"So."

"So he can talk."

"Can he?" Henry Lee looks at B.J. with new interest, and I know I just slipped up. The train goes into the tunnel and comes out the other side, and B.J. laughs out loud. Apparently it's his favorite part.

"I mean, it sounds a little funny. He can't hear, so he doesn't know what the words are supposed to sound like, and he doesn't know what *he* sounds like, so—"

"Make him say somethin."

My stomach tight. "What?"

Henry Lee has not taken his eyes off my brother. He walks to him, leans into his face, and with great exaggeration enunciates "train." B.J. glances at him, but cannot transfer his attention from the moving passenger and freight cars, so Henry Lee turns it off. B.J. opens his mouth to protest, and I fear a tantrum might be coming, but Henry Lee points to the locomotive again and says, "*Train.*" B.J. stares at him. Henry Lee picks up his Packard. "*Auto.*" He points to himself. "*Henry.*"

B.J. looks at Henry Lee, a little smile turning the corners of my brother's mouth. Suddenly Henry Lee claps his hands violently in B.J.'s face. "SPEAK!"

B.J. and I are both startled. Then I hand-tell him: Say my name.

He looks at me, then at Henry Lee. B.J. is no longer smiling.

"*SPEAK!*" Henry Lee's eyes wild.

"Ran ul."

Henry Lee looks at him, confused.

"That was 'Randall.'"

"*Randall?*"

"I *told* you it wasn't gonna sound exactly—"

"No no. Say it again." B.J. is confused. Henry Lee purses his lips, acting as if it is a struggle for him to say it: "Ran ul."

My eyes flash at Henry Lee.

"Ran ul," he says again, in B.J.'s face.

"Stop that."

"Ran ul," says B.J. *My breathing.*

"Ran ul," says Henry Lee.

"Henry Lee."

"Ran ul," says B.J.

"Ran ul," says Henry Lee.

"Ran ul," says B.J.

"Ran ul!" Henry Lee is bigger, he jumps excitedly.

"Ran ul!" B.J. imitates Henry Lee's actions.

"Ran ul! Ran ul! Ran ul!" they chant together. They are communicating. Here he's making fun of B.J., but B.J. seems to be enjoying himself. They *both* seem to be enjoying themselves, sharing something. I'd like to kill Henry Lee.

In the midst of the chant, Henry Lee falls out laughing. B.J. also laughs. His laugh is not a hearing laugh. It's too abrupt and too harsh and too loud.

Henry Lee suddenly sits up, his smile now a smirk. "It's all a terrible tragedy," he says, and spends the next several minutes setting up the doomed teenage lovers in their car. When he turns on the train, B.J. is enchanted again. But as the reality of the approaching catastrophe dawns on him, he is increasingly horrified. At the last possible moment, he puts his hands on the track, stalling the train.

"What are you *do*ing!" Henry Lee slaps B.J.'s hands away. The train makes a few abnormal sounds, then chugs on. Now the engine is so close, there's only one way to save the lives of the promiscuous dolls: B.J. shoves the engine from the side, the whole train crashing off the track and onto the floor, four feet below. Henry Lee screams.

"WHAT DID YOU *DO?*"

Henry Lee puts the train back on the track, the switch flipped on. The engine hovers in place and does not move. Henry Lee goes on a tirade, screaming and waving his arms. The situation with the train is certainly dire, but even tantrum-prone B.J. is stunned by Henry Lee's hysterics, as am I. Finally Roger's mother opens the door above us. "What's goin on down there?"

"That *dummy* ruined my train!" He swerves around to face me. "Don't you bring him here no more! Don't you *never* bring him here no more!"

"Oh." I hear Roger's mother shut the door to go back to work, as if her question was just idle curiosity.

"*SALLY!*"

A few moments later the door opens. "Yes."

"THEY RUINED MY TRAIN!"

"Hm. Well I guess your mama an daddy'll have to get it fixed."

"THERE'S NO FIXIN IT! THERE'S NO FIXIN IT!" He is stomping up the steps, then turns back to scream at me. "YOU'RE PAYIN FOR IT!"

As soon as Henry Lee is gone, B.J. turns to the train control box but I quickly jump up to put my hand on his hand, signing, Henry Lee says no. B.J. signs, I want train. I sign, No, Henry Lee says no. B.J. signs, Henry Lee pansy. I giggle. I'm sure he has little idea of what the word means, apparently part of the new vocabulary Deb Ellen imparted to him at the park. Still, I'm pondering Henry Lee's threat. Where could I get the money to pay for his train? I gaze at my Sopwith miserably.

Roger comes down the steps with two oatmeal cookies. "My mama said to give these to yaw." His eyes fall on my plane. "Lemme see it."

I hand it to him. He smiles a bit as he delicately touches it, bestowing to me the gratification I didn't get from Henry Lee. He gives it back. "My mother said I should introduce myself to your brother."

I sign to B.J.

"What's that?"

"The sign language. I said, This is Roger. This is my brother B.J." Roger nods to B.J. B.J. smiles at Roger. I get my cards.

"Twenty-one?"

"Okay."

I indicate for B.J. to join us. The three of us sit on the floor as I shuffle.

"You can't take history today. I have a test Wednesday."

"Takin nothin." Roger checks out his hand.

"What?"

"Found this boy. Ninth grader at the white high school, loan me his books for free."

I stare at him. "Why would he loan you for free?"

"I don't know. We're friends. Hit me."

"*I'm* your friend!" It just popped out. Roger stares. I swallow. I suddenly feel like a heel, selling knowledge and here a better person just offered it, no strings. "You can borrow my books for free if you want."

He shrugs. "I'm already doin it with this boy now. Plus he likes to study all summer. I like to study all summer. Hit me." B.J. suddenly guffaws.

"Guess he got a good hand."

"He just does that sometimes." B.J. looks at me. His smile is sweet. He signs: Sally Roger nigers. Deb Ellen definitely increased his lexicon. She never could spell.

"What's that?" Roger asks. "Hit me."

"He says he likes you and your mom," which is true.

The next day I don't go to Henry Lee's after Sunday school, and in the afternoon he and his mother come a-knocking. Just the mystery of her, being around so rare, made her scary. What the train needs is an eighty-five-cent part, which I'm sure Henry Lee's folks can easily afford but it's the principle. My mother is confused and worried, my father glowering at them, and to a lesser degree at me. B.J. nearby, fascinated by it all. My voice trembles, and I tell the truth. When Mrs. Taylor finds out about Henry Lee's "accidents" with all his new cars she bought, also risking the train, she tries to contain her fury, apologizing for having bothered us and making it clear both that she will take care of any repairs herself and that Henry Lee will be dealt with properly when she gets him home. He shoots me deadly glares on his way out. My father asks why I spend time with that "pansy" anyway, the second time in two days I'd heard the term with respect to my playmate, then he goes upstairs without waiting for an answer. I wonder if this is the end for Henry Lee and me. Hardly an ideal friendship, but it was the one and only I had.

That night I realize now that B.J. can read, I better stop just leaving anything open for him to see. I'm flipping through his sign language book and on the inside back cover, a blank page, I see what he'd written in brown crayon. My "dummy" brother is a damn sure rapid learner, having translated my cursive, even as he and I'd only been working in print.

autobiography

chiken make bj deaf ma love bj benja love bj randall love bj carry baby tricycle fall baby cry pa no love sally roger debellen bj want milk bottle pa drink all bj milk drink all baby bj milk bottle bj no milk hungry baby hungry firework bad henrylee bad pa no love i love brother randall randall

Though the jury's still out on whether my education will continue past this June, I join about half the eighth graders who sign up for High School Visitation Day, a preview for the fall. Lefferd County High is the only public secondary in the county (not counting the colored school and private St. Mary's) and therefore large, nearly eight hundred students, the freshman class graduates of the six county grammar schools. It's only four blocks from my home but I leave early, nervous I may have trouble finding the auditorium. No worry: there are plenty of well-marked signs. In the lobby are four tables: A–E, F–K, L–R, and S–Z.

"Last name?" a woman asks. I am given a handwritten index card.

EVANS, RANDALL

9:00	Chemistry	Mrs. Feldman	Rm 203
10:00	Euclidean Geometry	Mr. Thoms	Rm 104
11:00	PE	Lionel/Franks	Gym
12:00	LUNCH		Cafeteria
12:30	Latin I	Miss Collins	Rm 230
1:30	English 9	Mr. Schneider	Rm 210
2:30	U.S. History	Mr. Porter	Rm 111

There are only a handful of us early birds, our number by degrees swelling as the time ticks closer to the 8:30 bell. I sit quietly in my Sunday suit, my hair slicked back like on debate day, my mother seeming just as excited by this new academic adventure. And gradually I become aware of something amiss. No one is poking fun at me. The kids from the other schools don't know me and anyway everyone is too frightened, no longer on sure footing. I see Margaret Laherty two rows ahead. She's flanked by best friend Suzanne Willetts and second best friend Doris Nivens, and Margaret tries to whisper to Suzanne, but they're both too anxious to converse for more than a few syllables. The bell rings and we all fall to silent attention as Mr. O'Hare, the principal, crosses the stage. He turns to face the standing star-spangled, his right arm outstretched toward the banner, palm down. We know the drill and scramble to rise with the same gesture, turning palm up on cue with "to the Flag." (Henry Lee claims the government's gonna change it because it looks like the Nazi and Fascist salutes, but I doubt that: tradition.)

> *One nation,*
> *Indivisible,*
> *With liberty and justice for all.*

The principal utters a few words of welcome, followed by admonitions regarding the mature behavior he expects from high school students. As we stare, tense and alert, he briefs us, *too* brief, on the complicated building layout, even rooms in one wing, odd in another apparently miles away, and we have just five minutes to get from any one class to the next. He is in the middle of explaining that it is Team Appreciation Day, when all athletes show school pride by wearing their uniforms, when the bell rings. "Good luck!" and his smirk implies we'll need it.

Sprinting to make it to my odd-winged first class on time! "Don't run in the halls!" barks a teacher old enough to be my grandmother.

I walk through the door just as the bell rings. There are three empty seats in the back, two at the end of one row and one at the end of the adjacent. In front of this sole seat sits a small girl looking as stressed as I am, obviously also an eighth-grade visitor. I take the desk beside her. While catching my breath, I glance around the room and notice the glass tubes and spheres that make me think of a real scientific laboratory. On the wall is a poster, a strange chart where iron is abbreviated "Fe" and silver "Ag."

Mrs. Feldman, sitting behind the counter at the front of the classroom, is a good generation older than my parents. She peers over her spectacles suspiciously. Her students are dead silent, uneasy, a chemistry book opened to the appropriate page on each desk. After an interminable stillness, she speaks. "Chapter Eight."

The shuffling of pages is a welcome relief from the tension of the hush, but even this is too much for Mrs. Feldman. *"Quietly!"*

Margaret Laherty comes rushing into the class, flustered and confused, desperately searching for a seat.

"Excuse me."

Margaret is too disoriented to hear.

"Excuse me."

Margaret stops, terrified.

"Can you please tell me the time?"

"I'm sorry, I got lost—"

"I asked you to please tell me the time."

Margaret stares, frozen.

"Do you *know* how to tell the time?"

Margaret glances at the clock in the corner. "Nine-oh-three."

"And do you know what time this class starts?"

"Nine o' clock. I'm sorry. I'm one of the eighth-grade visitors, and—"

"Yes. And by the time you get to high school, I hope you will have learned that class start time is a requirement, not a suggestion."

I can't remember the last time a teacher ever yelled at Margaret Laherty! I'm sure I've never before seen her looking like she wanted to cry. She sits in the empty desk right behind me, and my heart beats fast.

As the lecturer begins snapping random questions, a girl with thick dull dark hair hanging just below her shoulders, heavy black-framed glasses, and a smattering of acne keeps raising her hand, but eagle-eye Feldman appears selectively blind, ignoring the poor girl, while calling on the clearly unprepared students, eighth-grade visitors mercifully exempted. I'd like to explore chemistry further but wonder if there might be another instructor who teaches it. Or are *all* high school teachers this menacing? Eventually Mrs. Feldman is pacing behind the counter, a melodrama of waving her arms, shouting at all her bump-on-a-log students until she swerves around to finally face the girl with her hand up.

"We are all aware *you* know the answer, Emily, you *always* know the answer!"

Emily, stunned and crestfallen, lowers her hand. A snicker briefly escapes another student, and Mrs. Feldman instantly jerks around to identify the source, but there is no sign of a culprit among the panicked students with averted eyes.

"You see? Yaw's laziness has gotten me so frustrated, I screamed at my star student." She opens her desk and pulls out papers. "Friday's test, if you'll recall, had a possible one hundred plus a five-point bonus. Emily Creitzer?" Emily's wide eyes stare at Mrs. Feldman. "One hundred five, perfect score. The class curve starts at one hundred."

Not even Mrs. Feldman's terrorist tactics can suppress the groans.

"That's not a curve!"

"You're lucky I didn't start the curve at a hundred and five. The rest of you can pick up your tests on the way out."

Right on cue, the bell rings. Emily gathers up her books slowly, looking down, avoiding the glares shot in her direction. I turn around to try to make quick small talk with Margaret, "What are your other classes?" hoping more of ours overlap. But she's already gone, no doubt getting a head start to ensure she's not late to second period.

The eighth-grade seats in Euclidean Geometry have been pushed to the very back against the wall with a space between us and the last row of regular students. There are three visitors here already, two boys and a girl, none of whom I know.

"Everybody ready?" asks Mr. Thoms, passing out papers. "Upside down, upside down." After each of the regular students has a sheet, Mr. Thoms picks up a few papers from a different pile and moves to the back of the room, placing one on each of our desks. "Keep your test paper upside down till I say Go."

Test?

"But we're—" an eighth grader starts.

"*Sh.*" Mr. Thoms stares at the clock. When the second hand reaches the twelve: "Go!"

Everyone flips their tests from the blank back to the front. I see now that while the regular students have an exam, we have been given a puzzle.

Eighth-Graders, Crack the Code!
KXGPZQX,
JXK HSXVFQXJ!

A few minutes later, I'm the first to solve it.

WELCOME,
NEW FRESHMEN!

Afterward I look around the room, observing the high schoolers racking their brains. I wonder what Roger's classes at the colored school are like. He told me he was the second smartest next to some girl, which I'm guessing is the truth, otherwise why not just say he's the smartest? Yet here he was, until recently renting books from somebody a grade behind him. He says they sing a different national anthem. I wish there was a Colored School Visitation Day. Like an exchange—they visit ours and we see theirs.

I'm startled to notice Mr. Thoms hovering over my desk. He sees my work, still the only one to have solved the riddle, and gives me the A-OK, touching thumb and forefinger. Does Roger's school have proms? Does he go to them? Does he ever get grades so high to mess up the curve for everyone else? Do dumber coloreds hate the smarter coloreds? But Roger's tall. Roger's tall and good-looking and that's why Henry Lee likes him. And Henry Lee's no "funny boy." Everybody likes good-looking people, just the way the world is.

The gym is way over on the other side of the odd wing, but I make it there on time, not that I'm looking forward to PE. But turns out since we eighth graders obviously didn't pack any gym clothes, we are not expected to participate. Mr. Lionel hands the nine visiting boys two decks. We split into groups and play blackjack and rummy and watch the high school boys run laps till their insides burst. My group is me and four boys I don't know who call me "Stretch" and it's a good-natured tease, not a taunt.

The five of us go to lunch together. We point out the high school girls we want and will surely get next year. Bradley picks a cheerleader in her uniform for Team Appreciation Day, but William John knows for a fact that she's a senior and won't be around in the fall. Bradley shrugs. "Her loss." She is sitting with other cheerleaders and, to my surprise, Earl Mattingly, who I haven't seen all day, comes up to the pack of short-skirted Oxford-wearing girls and sits among them. The tall black-haired boy is enthusiastically welcomed. He has already been picked for next year's junior varsity football team, skipping right over the freshman squad, a feat unheard of. Now Bradley asks about my schedule for the rest of the day. When I mention English with Mr. Schneider, Nathan says, "I had him. He's funny! Hope he tells you about the tiger."

"Shut up!" says Jay Andrew. "You'll give it away!"

Across the cafeteria I see Emily Creitzer sitting alone, doing homework. Every few minutes, she pushes her glasses back up her nose. I wonder if the book she's working out of is chemistry. I wonder if she would tell me what kind of experiments students get to do with all those tubes and spheres if I asked her.

"Oooh is that your girlfriend?" asks Bradley, who has followed my gaze.

"She's pretty," says Nathan, because she is not. We all laugh.

Jay Andrew laments that the teacher he had for Trigonometry, Mr. Lenox, wouldn't be around next year. "Enlisting into the army soon as school's over."

On the other side of the lunchroom, I notice Margaret Laherty and Suzanne Willetts, talking quietly and looking unhappy, like they're both having a really bad day. Margaret glances several times at Earl Mattingly, but never walks over to speak to him. He seems to be having a terrific time and never looks in her direction.

"I got one," I say. "When Snow White went to the ladies' doctor, what did they find?"

My quartet of an audience eagerly awaits.

"Seven dents." My friends explode in laughter. Henry Lee told me that one, and I also laughed even though I didn't quite understand it, then nor now.

On the way to Latin I, I spot Henry Lee walking in the other direction. We have not spoken since the train episode, but as today feels like an entirely different plane of existence, I wave to him as if nothing happened. He doesn't see me, focused on finding his next class.

Miss Collins is a young, pretty woman with black hair styled in a bob. She studies her teacher's manual as the students file in. Behind her a map is rolled down, entitled "Latin Countries of the Roman Empire." The only student I recognize in the class is Emily Creitzer. When the late bell rings and all are seated, Miss Collins pulls the map, causing it to roll itself up. Behind it, written on the blackboard, is

I have laryngitis. May I have a student
volunteer lead the class today?

Emily's hand is up like a shot. A few others also raise their hands, but Miss Collins's warm eyes are on Emily. The teacher tips her forehead slightly in the girl's direction. A few soft frustrated sighs from the other students as Emily struts to the front of the class.

Teacher Emily asks the students to take out their homework and instructs some to recite conjugations, others to write conjugations on the board. She is an unexpectedly confident and encouraging teacher. "Good try, Amy Jane, but that would be the stem if it were a *first* conjugation verb. This is a *third*." Miss Collins seems to be smiling at Emily the entire class time. Finally she goes to the board, startling Emily by the interruption, and writes, "How do we thank Emily?" and the better students reply *"Gratias tibi ago"* while the other students look blank. The bell rings. Some of the kids go up to Emily to compliment her on how she handled the class, making no effort to hide their surprise at her success. With every admiring phrase, Emily smiles graciously. "I *want* to be a teacher!"

When I enter Mr. Schneider's English, there's a line of six students, among them Bradley's cheerleader, waiting for the teacher to sign their yearbooks, which he does quickly and with a flair. Mr. Schneider is tall and well built with sandy hair. There are no open seats in the back. I'm the first eighth grader here, so I stand near the rear, and four subsequent visitors take my cue, including Suzanne Willetts, out-of-step and abandoned by her old self-assurance. I'm stunned when she nervously smiles at me in recognition before turning away to stare at the floor. "Hold on," Mr. Schneider says to the visiting students. On the board is written

The Merchant of Venice

Portia	Shylock
The quality of mercy	I am a Jew

I notice that for the third time today I am sharing a class with Emily Creitzer. At her seat she looks down into her already opened textbook, clearly having lost the ebullience of the Latin class just last period.

The late bell rings. Mr. Schneider says, "Find a seat," and we realize we are to insert ourselves among the regular students in the handful of open desks available. I can feel the trepidation of my fellow eighth graders, something I felt myself this morning, but now I confidently find a chair. The others follow suit, except for Suzanne, who seems frozen before a firing squad. Out of the familiarity of always being in a huddled group at Prayer Ridge, she seems at a loss.

"Repeat: find a seat," says Mr. Schneider, amused but not unkind. Giggling in the class. Suzanne, red-faced, sits in the only chair now available, having to walk to the front.

"Who's Portia?" Half of the regular students raise their hands. "Who's a Jew?" Laughter as the remaining regular students raise their hands. "Shuffle! Jews here." He indicates the desks on the right side of the room. "Gentiles here." Some of the students look confused. "If you're not a Jew, you're a Gentile."

They trade seats, clearly an exciting change of pace.

"Mr. Johnson."

The boy called upon stands and recites.

"I am a Jew. Hath not a Jew eyes? Hath not a Jew hands, organs, dimensions, senses, affections, passions; fed with the same food, hurt with the same weapons, heal'd by the same means—"

"Go back."

The boy frowns, befuddled.

"Miss Fitzgerald." Mr. Schneider is looking at another Jew. "What did he miss?"

"Subject to the same diseases."

"Aw!" Johnson, who wears a football jersey, smacks his forehead with the palm of his right hand. Titters in the class. I've seen him play, the tight end Eric Johnson, going to a couple of games with my father to keep him company. He begins again, reciting in a singsong monotone, this time getting through to the end: "And if you wrong us, do we not revenge? If we are like you in the rest, we will resemble you in that. The villany you teach me, I will execute, and it shall go hard but I will better the instruction."

"You skipped a few lines but we'll get back to that," says Mr. Schneider. "What's it mean?"

The class is silent, perhaps unaware they were expected to comprehend the words as well as memorize them.

"I don't know," Johnson shrugs. "He's a Jew."

"A Christian wouldn't ask for a pound of flesh," calls out Bradley's cheerleader, sitting smack in the middle of the class. Another cheerleader sits next to her.

"That's not what Shylock is saying," says Mr. Schneider. "I wanna know what Shylock is saying with the speech."

"That Christians and Jews are the same," says Cheerleader No. 2.

"Correctamundo!" says Mr. Schneider, and the class chuckles.

"I know what he's sayin," says Cheerleader No. 1. "I'm sayin I disagree."

"He's sayin he's doin what the Christians taught him, and now they'll understand it cuz it's bein done to them," says a girl from the Gentile side. I'm surprised to see Emily Creitzer with her face down, trying not to be called upon. Didn't she do the assignment?

"Exactly! Now. What's Portia got to say about all this pound of flesh business?"

A moment of hesitation from the Gentile side, then a boy raises his hand.

"Mr. James."

The boy stands.

"The quality of mercy is not strain'd, / It droppeth as the gentle rain from heaven / Upon the place beneath: it is twice blest; / It blesseth him that gives and him that takes—"

The boy is stuck. After a more than acceptable silence, Mr. Schneider calls for help. "Gentiles?"

Most of the Gentiles, but not Emily, say in unison: "*'Tis mightiest in the mightiest!*"

"'Tis mightiest in the mightiest!" The James boy goes on. "It becomes / The throned monarch better than his crown—" His eyes scanning the ceiling for the next word. When the silence goes on too long, Mr. Schneider glances at Emily, a vague smile on his face.

"Miss Creitzer."

Emily looks up, eyes wide.

"I'm sure *you* can recite 'the quality of mercy.'"

Emily stands. She looks down at her desk.

"The quality of mercy is not strain'd, / It droppeth as the gentle rain from heaven—"

"Stop muttering, Miss Creitzer, we need to *hear* it."

Emily takes a breath, looks up, and speaks.

> *The quality of mercy is not strain'd,*
> *It droppeth as the gentle rain from heaven*
> *Upon the place beneath: it is twice blest;*
> *It blesseth him that gives and him that takes:*
> *'Tis mightiest in the mightiest: it becomes*
> *The throned monarch better than his crown;*

His sceptre shows the force of temporal power,
The attribute to awe and majesty,
Wherein doth sit the dread and fear of kings;
But mercy is above this sceptred sway;
It is enthroned in the hearts of kings,
It is an attribute to God himself;
And earthly power doth then show likest God's
When mercy seasons justice.

There is a silence. I cannot take my eyes off Emily. Even through her fright, she has given her words meaning, seeming to actually *understand* what Shakespeare is saying, what *she* is saying, so we understand.

"In contemporary English?"

Emily stares wildly.

"What have you just said?"

"It has to do with. She's asking—"

"Who?"

"Portia. Portia's asking the merchant to not. To have compassion, *leniency,* not to hurt Antonio—"

"'Hurt'?"

"To shave off the pound of flesh, she's asking the merchant—"

"And the merchant is?"

Emily seems utterly confused. Mr. Schneider sighs. "Is the merchant a Gentile?"

"The Jew! The Jew! Portia is asking the Jew if he will please be gentle with Antonio—"

"Who's Antonio?"

"The debtor. Antonio is the debtor who borrowed three thousand ducats from Shylock, the Jew—"

"What's a ducat?"

Emily frantically searches Mr. Schneider's face for the answer, then looks down at her desk shaking. The random snickers from the students don't surprise me, but the smile on Mr. Schneider's face is unsettling.

"I don't know. Money."

Mr. Schneider turns to the rest of the class. As if for the thousandth time: "What do we do when we come to a word we don't know?"

In unison: "Look it up."

"The gold ducat was currency, a coin used throughout Europe from the twelfth century up until just before the Great War. At the end of its usage it was worth a little more than two dollars, the silver ducat about half that amount. Continue."

"So. So Antonio was wealthy with ships but he didn't have cash, and his friend Bassanio needed three thousand ducats to travel to Belmont and woo Portia. So Antonio borrowed from Shylock, and Shylock hated Antonio for being a Christian and for making fun of him being a Jew so he said if Antonio didn't pay back the debt on time he would exact a pound of his flesh and Antonio said okay so Bassanio wooed Portia but when it came time to pay back the debt Antonio's ships were at sea so he couldn't pay and Shylock who was even madder because his daughter eloped with a Christian and some of Shylock's money so Shylock comes to collect the pound of flesh and Portia dresses up like a learn'ed lawyer man and says 'the quality of mercy' asking Shylock to save Antonio's life which Shylock refuses until Portia points out that Shylock can only take Antonio's flesh not his blood so they win."

We all erupt in outrageous laughter. Emily is utterly confused, apparently unaware of how long it has been since she has taken a breath.

Last spring, I was flipping through Benja's old seventh-grade yearbook. She was always protective of the current volume, not allowing any unauthorized personnel to handle it, and I was definitely unauthorized, but as soon as the new issue came out twelve months later, she could be oddly cavalier about the previous year's once-sacred tome. I noticed my seventh-grade earth science teacher Mr. Reilly had signed her book. "To a sweet girl and good student." I remarked upon it.

"*Everyone* liked Mr. Reilly." She continued looking into her mirror, pinning up her hair in curls for the night.

I didn't say anything, and though my eyes remained on his picture, I could tell in the silence she had looked up.

"Except. He did have a habit a pickin on kids that kids already picked on. At the time I thought it was kinda funny. We all liked him better for it. But now. I don't know. I guess he was kind of a jerk."

I turned to my sister, sticking a bobby pin in, not looking at me. It was the closest we ever came to addressing our very different social standings.

"Thus," Mr. Schneider picks up, "Portia's speech is about?"

Poor Emily had thought the torture was over, having started to sit, but now she is snapped back on her feet. "Excuse me?"

"What is Portia asking of Shylock?"

"Leniency." He stares at her. Her voice quieter, pleading: "Leniency?"

Mr. Schneider continues to stare, and Emily seems close to bursting into tears. Then the teacher laughs incredulously. "Miss Creitzer! What is the speech about?"

Emily is a deer in headlights. Mr. Schneider sighs.

"What's the first line of the speech?"

"The quality of mercy is not—"

"The quality of what?"

"Mercy."

"Of *what*?"

"*Mercy.*"

"Of *what*?"

"*Mercy! Mercy! Mercy!*"

Emily's entire body is shaking. The class is silent. Mr. Schneider appears momentarily uncomfortable.

"They're killin Jews!"

All turn to Cheerleader No. 2.

"In Germany! The Axis!"

"And where did you hear that, Miss Hanson?"

"I heard. My mother said—"

"There is a segregation of German Jews from German Gentiles. That's all we know for certain. Anything else is conjecture." Everyone stares at Mr. Schneider. He laughs. "I'm *not* supporting the Axis! What I'm saying is we can't just blanket assume one hundred percent of *everything* going on in Germany is wrong. Who here would want colored kids coming to this school?"

No one raises a hand.

"Then I think we can all understand the concept and necessity of separation. Miss Hanson. You are a Jew."

She stands and recites. Letter perfect. Mr. Schneider smiles at the cute cheerleader. "Excellent."

Miss Hanson turns pink and sits. In what appears to be an afterthought,

Mr. Schneider turns to Emily, who finally felt it was safe to sit as Miss Hanson had begun her speech. "Excellent, Miss Creitzer." Then he turns to the class at large. "How's about a little riddle?"

"Yes!"

"What has four legs and one arm?"

No one knows.

"A very happy tiger."

A roar of laughter, and the bell.

"Read page 185, Sonnet 52!" A few students line up to get Mr. Schneider's John Hancock in their yearbooks.

I have the hang of it now and get to my last class downstairs and on the other side of the school three minutes early. After the late bell rings, Mr. Porter, a tall, bulky man in his fifties, pulls down a map. Taped over it is a nineteenth-century political cartoon. The immediate foreground image is what appears to be a combination Sambo/ape creature leisurely lying back with his legs crossed, mindless eyes in the clouds. Everyone laughs. On closer inspection, we see a hardworking white farmer chopping wood, another pushing a plow as he comes home to his family. In the other corner, a sketch of the U.S. Capitol Building with this etched into it:

FREEDOM

AND

NO WORK.

and the headline over the entire drawing:

THE FREEDMAN'S BUREAU!

AN AGENCY TO KEEP THE **NEGRO** IN IDLENESS
AT THE **EXPENSE** OF THE WHITE MAN.
TWICE VETOED BY THE **PRESIDENT**, AND MADE A LAW BY **CONGRESS**.
SUPPORT CONGRESS & YOU SUPPORT THE NEGRO.
SUSTAIN THE PRESIDENT & YOU SUPPORT THE WHITE MAN.

"Welcome to Reconstruction," says Mr. Porter, and the class cracks up again.

From there on out, things are less entertaining with the instructor lecturing and writing notes on the board that the students copy. He quickly skims over Reconstruction, which he intermittently refers to as the "Hard Times"—the postwar decade and a half reconfiguring the Confederacy which meant, among other things, some former slaves and free coloreds were elected to government seats—and moves on to the Gilded Age, which he seems markedly more enthusiastic about. He speaks of economic prosperity and of America's new wealth and capitalist leadership in the world, of Rockefeller and Vanderbilt and Carnegie and Morgan, the better students shaking their hands to bring life back to them before resuming the rapid note taking, and near the end of the hour a sudden thought crosses Mr. Porter's mind. "Who coined the term 'Gilded Age'?"

Silence. Students search their notes but the answer is not there. Tentatively, I raise my hand.

"Ah! An eighth-grade visitor thinks he has the answer. Mr. . . . ?"

"Randall."

"Mr. Randall!"

"Well, Evans. Randall Evans."

"Mr. Randall Evans!" The class giggles. "Can you tell the class who coined the term 'The Gilded Age'?"

"Mark Twain."

"Correct! I guess you come from a pretty smart grammar school."

"No, I read it on my own." Some students now turn to look at me, the attitude behind their expressions unclear.

"You read it *on your own*?" Mr. Porter is clearly rubbing me in their faces. Usually this would mortify me, but today I kind of like it.

"It was the title of the book Mr. Twain wrote with Mr. Charles Dudley Warner, *The Gilded Age: A Tale of Today*. They were being sarcastic about the ostentation of the era." With the last sentence Mr. Porter is suddenly no longer smiling. He stares at me openmouthed, as do several of the students, and the bell rings. I smile and exit. Dismissal.

I wanna run! On the steps outside the school I see my boys, Bradley and William John and Nathan and Jay Andrew. I wave. "See yaw next year!" Somebody besides Henry Lee. Variety!

I wait until all the students are out, all the buses gone, quiet. I run. I gotta run! Around the even wing and the odd, around the auditorium and the gym. When I fly by the field, I see Emily in the distance alone, sitting on the bleachers, her books on the seat beside her. She clutches her yearbook. I do another lap, and these are big laps, each a good quarter-mile, and I'm running *fast,* and when I come back around she's still there. I get faster, faster, earlier I'd snickered at those poor dolts in PE doing sprints while me and my boys sat laying down our aces, but now I could beat em all! Faster! When I come around again, Emily still clutches her yearbook, but this time she's sobbing, her whole body heaving. Why's she crying? Oh she must've glimpsed her own picture in the yearbook. Haha! My boys'd love it if I told that one! Oh boo hoo, Emily. I pass her faster, faster.

On the next lap I slow down. I didn't even buy a damn yearbook this spring, waste of money. After last year's went into the garbage, along with all the clever sentiments from my classmates.

> *Randall Evans, walking museum,*
> *Such a smidge we barely see him*
> *His dummy brother's his only friend*
> *Though his sister's rack's a dividend.*

When I see Emily around the bend I'll say something to her. How much I liked her *quality of mercy.* I wonder if at Roger's school the kids get mean in yearbooks. Can colored schools afford yearbooks? Walking slow now, I turn the curve, I'll talk to Emily. But Emily's gone.

I know tomorrow will be regular. Margaret Laherty'll be the same, Suzanne Willetts. We'll all be back home at Prayer Ridge School, and Margaret and Suzanne'll be happy and grateful and I'll wanna be here.

But tomorrow's hours away. Today! Today I sweat and I start up fast again as the teachers exit the building, then the janitors, I sweat in the low sun running, running.

11

I was all primed for life to go back to normal once I returned to Prayer Ridge School following High School Visitation Day. I was *not* prepared for just how much more normal things could get. If I had any doubts that my wondrous seven hours at Lefferd County High was all in my imagination, that in an odd parallel reality I was the confident one and Margaret Laherty and Suzanne Willetts the awkward outcasts, the proof of my marvelous Tuesday is confirmed by the extra layer of payback cruelty Suzanne has in store for me upon our homecoming Wednesday. For the rest of the week it seems I'm having my chair pulled out from under me three or four times a day, Suzanne never the direct culprit but invariably in the vicinity and always laughing the loudest. Once she nudged Margaret Laherty, trying to get her to join in the fun, and Margaret did vaguely smile but then got up and left. On Friday I'm pushed into the mud during track and field, forcing me to take a shower, something I otherwise wouldn't dare do. When I look down, I see someone's put all my clothes under the water with me, and I go to my geography exam soaking wet. I hope things might calm down over the weekend, but on Monday I'm shoved into the mud again, and I come out of the shower wrapped in my towel to discover someone has stolen all my clothes. As I bawl, Mr. Shane screams at my gym locker partner, who swears he was not the guilty party, though admits that against the rules he'd given out our padlock combination to way too many of his friends to name them all. For the rest of the day, I'm attired in an old football uniform two sizes too large, making me almost as big a laughingstock as had I'd gone to class naked. At the end of the day, I go to my hall locker, QUARTERBACK ironically carved into its wood, and find my apparel lying in front of it, filthy and torn. At home, I throw up numerous times which provides legitimate excuse for me to be absent the next day, but the day after my mother, who gathers something awful happened at school but can't get me to speak about it, insists I go. Mercifully the worst seems to have fizzled away now, either because Mr. Shane's fury had put the vultures on the alert or because they'd simply tired of torturing me for the present.

On Friday comes a note during civics, last period. What could the principal want with me now?

"Congratulations, Mr. Evans. You've been chosen to be class valedictorian."

Mr. Westerly goes on to explain that it had been very close between me and my debate partner Lucille, but she had blown it that time in seventh grade when she got caught after more than two weeks faking women's troubles to get out of PE, dropping her to a C for the class, her only non-A on record and something I heard she had sobbed over. Confidentially the principal informs me, even if Lucille and I had tied he would have given the honor to me, feeling that, especially in a time of war, it would be proper to have a young man deliver the valedictory address. I stare at him, dumbfounded, as I had the impression Mr. Westerly would hold my infamous debate rebuttal against me forever. Well frankly, neither this meeting offering me the honor nor his handshake at the end of it is quite as enthusiastic as it should be, but no matter. I can't wait to tell Ma!

The dismissal bell rings then, and as I am gathering my books at my locker, Henry Lee comes up to me, the first time since the whole train incident almost a month ago, and casually mentions he has some sitting man from his train set he no longer needs who would probably fit well into my Sopwith pilot's seat, I could stop by now and look at it if I wanted. I hadn't even mentioned my yearnings for a pilot to Henry Lee! And this sudden easing into reconciliation. Well who else did he have to play with? It occurs to me for the first time that, before I arrived on the scene, Henry Lee as an only child with perpetually busy parents had *no one,* not even anybody at home. It didn't take any words from Sally for her to have made clear nanny was not in her job description, and Roger. I always wondered why Henry Lee never considered that Roger might have been more friendly had Henry Lee been more respectful, or at least polite, to Roger's mother.

When we walk into the kitchen, Roger is at the table doing homework as usual. He looks up, obviously surprised to see me after all this time, and nearabout smiles. In the basement, Henry Lee hands me his sitting man, which turns out to be a sitting woman, wood with red lipstick and yellow hair. "Oh yeah," he says, though I'm sure he didn't really forget. It does look like she might fit in my plane. "Call her Amelia," says Henry Lee. "She can do transatlantic crossins and have accidents," then he looks away embarrassed, maybe about bringing up the accident issue which had gotten him into trouble and led to the rupture in our friendship, or maybe about his careless reference to that lady who disappeared over the Pacific four years back, or both. Henry Lee's trying to be nice. Whether this is temporary I don't know, but for the moment I'm glad to be here, aware now how much I'd missed my playmate the last few weeks. Still, I decide for the future I'll keep his whiny bossiness in check, he's going to *earn* my friendship. He pulls out a board game I didn't know he had. "Chess?" He had gotten it some Christmas but no one ever taught him how to play. We sit on the floor, and I tell him rook goes straight and bishop goes diagonal and no one mentions the silent train tracks: elephant in the room.

When I come back up the steps, I notice Roger's bent over the same chemistry textbook used by the students at my high school visitation. He sees I'm interested and lets me flip through it.

"How's he study if you have his books?"

Roger makes this secret smile. "We got a system." In his notebook, he has worked out some pretty elaborate chemistry equations, and this not even his official homework. There's that thing teachers say, He's got a good head on his shoulders but he doesn't apply himself. That's Henry Lee. Roger has a good head and applies himself through the stratosphere.

Earl Mattingly just doesn't have a good head.

"What's the difference if you come in a little low, Evans?" the star athlete asks me. "You're gonna pass anyway. It's not gonna affect your grade, the standards are pass/fail."

"We might go to States if Earl's on the team next year, Randall," chimes in Margaret Laherty, sounding more and more like some housewife desperate to keep her man. Rumor has it that at the end of High School Visitation Day, Earl walked one of the freshman cheerleaders home. "But he's gotta pass the standards!" Margaret goes on. "Won't you please help us?"

The last week of May, days before graduation, is "the standards," tests you have to pass to get beyond eighth grade. It might be said that Earl's good looks and athletic inclination have been his downfall, as they have stood in the way of any motivation to toil outside the football field, since his eminence there has charmed everyone into finding a way to make all else somehow work out. Unfortunately, the standards go directly to the state board for evaluation where nobody's going to know or care whether you can kick a field goal from forty yards. If Earl doesn't pass the standards, he doesn't go on to ninth grade, and his days of secondary school athletic glory are over before they have begun. In a town where high school football is king, it's suddenly as if our community's entire hope for the future precariously rests on Earl's abilities in long division. There's a curve of some kind with the standards, but the system is complicated. All Earl knows is that the lower the highest score, the better for him.

Friday morning, I bring in my Sopwith, put it in my locker. Amelia did fit, and after school I'll stop by Henry Lee's, to celebrate the last day of school except for graduation exercises and to sigh relief that the standards are over with. The halls are quiet, the rest of the school having an end-of-year party way off in the cafeteria so they won't disturb the exam takers. I head to the test room early and pray.

Earl Mattingly walks in and sits right next to me. He gives me a nod. It's bad enough he and Margaret have asked me to take some humiliating fall from grace in the name of school spirit. Does he expect I will let him *copy* from my test? Mrs. Vaughn from home ec has been designated to moderate our exam, the thirty of us assigned to this room, and from the time she says "Go," I keep my paper covered.

I finish early, turning my test over to deter any wandering eyes. Cuz guess what, Earl and Margaret? I did my damn one hundred percent best.

I lean back in my chair. When I reflect on it, it really hasn't been such a terrible year. Sure, the daily taunts and periodic bouts of pure torment. But there was glory too, Lucille and I will forever be the *first* Prayer Ridge debaters. We didn't win but it was an honor being selected, and Mr. Hickory certainly made it clear my contribution was outstanding. And then came that very flattering note from St. Mary's addressed to Mr. Westerly saying that, as competition progressed, their team was so indebted to Prayer Ridge who had proven among their most formidable foes, and who they hoped would consider continuing this relationship into the future. When Lucille and I were called into the office for Mr. Westerly to read aloud that missive, with Mr. Hickory beaming, even the principal seemed pleased, though I imagine next year at the outset he'll strongly advise the team to avoid certain subject matter. Mr. Hickory handed Lucille and me each a copy of the letter of gratitude he had typewritten himself, with the special feel of an original since we each had our own unique Mr. Hickory typographical corrections. For the first time since the debate, Lucille smiled at me.

This was also the year of my first best friend, if you don't count cousin friends when I was smaller, and a teenage best friend is something extraordinary if intermittently annoying. It was the year I taught my brother to communicate, to converse and to read. The year I was chosen to be valedictorian of my graduating eighth-grade class of ninety-three students. After the exams I'll go to Mr. Westerly and to school librarian and speech advisor Mrs. Braden with my drafted oration, the culmination of much exertion over the previous two weeks since the principal gave me the good news, for any editorial suggestions that I may incorporate before graduation Wednesday. And this was the year I had a spectacular day as a preview to high school. I still don't know for sure what the coming September will bring. I sometimes see myself walking home from the mill at fifteen, coughing up sawdust like my father. If nothing else, I can remember Visitation Day, I can say I only had one day of high school but it sure was a splendid one.

And now I notice that my eyes, the thoughts behind them miles away, have inadvertently landed on Earl Mattingly's exam. Earl Mattingly also has noticed, and is glaring at me, and I look from him to Mrs. Vaughn at the front, who is staring at me a bit stunned, and I turn back to Earl, where behind his piercing eyes, I detect something like pleasure.

"I *wasn't* copying! Why would I copy offa him? My marks are higher!"

We are in the office: Earl, me, Mrs. Vaughn, Mr. Westerly.

"All I know is I looked up an your eyes were on my paper. Weren't that the rules? Eyes on your own paper?" Earl turns to Mrs. Vaughn.

"Those were the rules." She is steadfast yet not wholly confident. She has no character history on which to base her judgments. She's the home ec teacher. She doesn't know the boys.

"I didn't look at his paper!"

"Your eyes were right on it." Earl's dark irises hard on me.

"Not seeing it! I didn't. I finished my exam early, I was thinking about something else! I didn't know my eyes. You saw my paper was turned over, I was thinking about something else!"

"I said *very clearly*, 'Eyes on your own paper.'"

"Yeah!"

"I know! I'm sorry! It was an accident, I'm sorry! But I didn't. My paper was upside down! I was done!"

"Well I wouldn't know about that cuz *I* kept *my* eyes on my own *paper*!"

"It *was* upside down! I was done! I was *done*!" I stare at tense, silent Mr. Westerly, my shining eyes begging him to intercede. He *knows* my grades. He knows *Earl's* grades. Mrs. Vaughn and Earl also stare at the principal.

Then I remember how everyone just loves Earl, and a cry I hadn't antici-pated escapes my lips.

"Well." Mr. Westerly clears his throat. "What Randall says is true. Given his grades, and given Earl's, it's difficult to imagine that Randall copied from Earl. Randall, as a matter of fact, has been chosen as valedictorian of the class." Mrs. Vaughn looks at me, surprised. It's doubtful she keeps up with the valedic-tory business since the honor is never bestowed upon someone based on her expertise at opening a near-empty cupboard and whipping up a grand dinner for eight. "We will turn in the standards to the board as they are. If Earl's and Randall's scores are close, we will reinvestigate the matter. But if Randall's score is significantly higher, the scores will stand and will average into the curve." Earl groans, slamming back in his chair, arms crossed. I finally breathe.

But Earl would never so easily back down from a fight. "The *rule* was—"

"I'm getting to that." Mr. Westerly's eyes are on me. "Randall. I am of the opinion that you've told the truth, that Earl perhaps mistook your wandering mind for cheating. However, rules are rules, and they are not to be suspended to allow for daydreaming. Peeking at another student's test, whether inadvertent or not, is a serious offense. And not becoming of a val-edictorian of our school." He leans forward. "I hope you have not already wasted too many hours with the speech."

Apparently Earl couldn't fathom just how devastating Mr. Westerly's words were to me, that the athlete had already exponentially exacted his revenge, because when I return to my hall locker—how he had gotten my combination I'll never know—my War to End All Wars Sopwith model aeroplane inside is smashed, demolished, a wheel among the tiny bits. My Amelia, like *the* Amelia, missing.

I have a plan. I have a plan and if I had any qualms about it, the universe confirms my decision: when I get home from school the house is empty—no deterrents. My father at work, my mother having left a note.

Lily had the baby. Be back around 6. ITS A GIRL!

And no B.J., no Benja. Guess they all went to meet their new cousin. I go to the closet and I find the sheet, I twist the sheet I make the noose.

I consider the pretension. I could jump off a building instead, except nothing's higher than two stories around here, best I'd do is break my leg. I could throw myself into the river but it's twenty miles away, I'd have to walk or hitchhike to it, plus I'm a pretty good swimmer so it would take a lot of will not to. Not to.

I don't want Ma to find me. Maybe I should leave a note for Benja. "Could you come into my room for a minute please?" Yeah, then I'd go down in history as the creep who did that to his sister. Anyway be just like her to holler through the wall, "No!" and go on painting her fingernails as my body swayed until supper when my mother would yell and yell for me until she lost her patience and came up herself. I know it's selfish but. I'm *not* going to the mill next year! And what if Pa *did* let me go to high school? How do I really know it wouldn't be just four more years of *this*?

I need a note! Can't just leave my family with nothing.

> I love my family.
> The kids at school are

Uh-uh. Why give them the power, thinking *they* pushed me over the edge? Rip it up.

> I love my family.
> This has nothing to do with them.

Not good. They'll be home soon, I'm pressed for time but I take a breath. I put in all that effort for the debates, for the valedictory speech, the least I owe my family is this last bit of care. It needn't be long, but it has to be right.

And I realize my struggle is in trying to find a reason. My family will want a reason. But it's too complicated, a suicide note the size of the Bible. Miss Dawson's favorite composition word: "Simplify."

> This is the hardest thing I have ever done.
> Because I love love love love my family.
> I will miss you all very much.

Okay. No other business. I move my desk chair to my closet, remove the hanging clothes from the bar. For once I'm relieved I'm short so when I knock the chair out from under me, there will be a few inches between my outstretched toes and the floor: no turning back.

I stand on the seat, noose around my neck. Close my eyes. Next week is B.J.'s birthday. It won't be a happy one for him. Don't think don't think, get through this you'll never have to worry about another thing. I stand on the chair backwards, facing out into the room, keep my left foot down but not too much weight, lift my right foot, place it on the chairback to push, take a breath I *push*

"RAN UL!"

My eyes snap open. Where did he come from? Gaping wild, his entire body trembling.

"RAN UL!"

We stare at each other, frozen. Then he snatches *Madeline* lying on his made bed, *Madeline* which he checked out of the library the umpteenth time. He sits cross-legged in front of my chair, and through his sobs he begins to read.

> *In an old house in Paris*
> *that was covered with vines*
> *lived twelve little girls in two straight lines.*
> *In two straight lines they broke their bread*
> *and brushed their teeth*
> *and went to bed.*

With his right hand, he clutches my left ankle tight, his face down in the book. His voice, his horror coupled with his deafness, is wildly distorted, yet through it all he evinces a certain forced calm, and I'm feeling gradually soothed, for the first time hearing what the rhyme must sound like in his mind. Late in the tale, I gently slip the noose up and off, and I step down from the chair, and by the time he gets to

> *and that's all there is—*
> *there isn't any more*

B.J. and I are sitting on the floor cross-legged next to each other, the book shared between our laps, me wordlessly listening to my big brother telling me a story, marveling at the exquisite vividly colored illustrations catapulting Paris right into the bedroom of two sons of America.

12

*We live in a time of war. As we eighth-grade graduates walk
down the steps of Prayer Ridge School for the last time, weighing heavily on all our minds are our servicemen, the brave men
and women fighting in Europe and the Pacific in the name of
freedom for the world, and for all of us back home in America.*

When I say "and women" I look right at my mother the veteran and watch
her beaming smile become incredibly brighter. My speech advisor Mrs.
Braden said women were understood as part of the generic "servicemen,"
that adding the phrase meant clutter for an already too-long sentence.
Women, she said, was not a necessary word. I said it was.

It's quite warm this morning in early June, the sun high and bright over the
temporary amphitheater. Many church fans rapidly flutter in the audience. For
this outdoor ceremony I work hard at projecting my voice, and I am heard.

Mr. Hickory intervened. I don't know what was said between him and Mr.
Westerly, and I heard their voices had become progressively louder, but the
Monday following my attempted suicide, I was again summoned by the principal
who revoked his previous decision. I, and no one but me, would deliver the valedictory address. Doubtless also related to Mr. Hickory's intercession, the principal
made a point of introducing Prayer Ridge's inaugural debate team, and Lucille
gave a short speech before mine. It felt to me only fair, her one and only slipup
being that PE incident, and I was nearly as happy to hear about her oration as she.

*We are all praying this Second World War will be over swiftly.
Still, for ever how long it takes, we as a country vow that in this
struggle against tyranny, we will emerge victorious. We are not
in this conflict by any foolish aggression on our part, but rather
because we were forced into it. And now we will not come out of
it until we bring about democracy for all those who have been op-
pressed by totalitarianism. Emma Lazarus wrote a poem called
"The New Colossus," which famously begins, "Give me your tired,
your poor, your huddled masses yearning to breathe free." Emma
Lazarus also said, "Until we are all free, we are none of us free."*

My mother and sister in white gloves and hat, Ma wearing a navy dress with white polka dots, Benja a white dress with navy polka dots. Benja's idea. They bought the material and pattern together, each sewing the other's.

My sister got another pen pal soldier, somebody from right here in Prayer Ridge, whose mother died in childbirth when he was five, and whose father died of polio a few years back. He was thirteen then, he and his siblings divvied up among relatives, he sent to a depraved farmer uncle who worked him and beat him like a slave. This soldier, Aaron Sprigg, was ever grateful for Benja's letters, and she has proven herself an enthusiastic correspondent. She prays for his safety.

B.J. wears a gray suit, pale blue shirt, blue tie. We told him over and over the function would be long, that if he came he'd have to be still and quiet. He signed it and signed it and after he finally started speaking it, "I come! I come!" my mother said, "Then get dressed." He sits next to her.

And, astonishingly, wearing the only good outfit he owns, the black suit he reserves for funerals, my father sits between my mother and Benja. I had to leave the house earlier than my family today, so I had no idea he would be here until I looked out from the stage. Thank the Lord I glimpsed him before things started, before I was called to the lectern, because at the sight of him I almost burst out weeping.

> *Young though we may be, we at Prayer Ridge School are not removed from the tragedy of war. There are those among us already who have older brothers who will not come back. Matthew Donovan. Jeffrey Willetts.*

Suzanne Willetts behind me breaks into huge sobs. Her family just received the news four days ago. A funeral yesterday, a graduation today. Despite our differences, hearing her grief I must rally the utmost effort not to cry myself. Many in the audience lose the battle, putting down fans and picking up hankies.

Last night Pa said it, direct as he ever would be: "I hope after you graduate the twelfth grade they still got openins at the mill." And he left the room. I closed my eyes, releasing a breath I didn't know I'd been holding for months.

B.J. grins and signs, My brother My brother My brother. When I thank my family in my speech I smile and, though no one but my mother and siblings will understand, I sign for all to see: B.J. He mentioned nothing to the rest of the family about the noose in our bedroom. He never would.

After the ceremony I'm stunned to finally meet Henry Lee's father. "At long last, the famous Randall Evans!" He shakes my hand warmly and even gives me a quick embrace.

In the afternoon, we picnic at the park as do several other graduates with their families. My father tends steaks and burgers on the grill, such a feast implying this is a milestone indeed. My mother was almost in tears this morning, her cake skimpy from the rations, but I told her about Henry Lee's mother's recent experiments with baking, how I had gotten stuck having to eat a big slice of rock-hard coffee cake she'd made, and how much better to have just a little of my own mother's scrumptious devil's food. I think Ma knew I'd exaggerated the Mrs. Taylor story a little, but still she laughed gratefully and tousled my hair.

The sun has slipped behind gray clouds, the humid threat of rain. B.J. and I sit on a blanket in the grass playing rummy. He keeps score, an arithmetic lesson I'm giving him. His penmanship is much improved, as well as his English syntax. Yesterday when I got home from Henry Lee's after school there was a note in his handwriting.

Ma and I gone to the market for eggs.

B.J. wins 545–410 and wants another hand. But I'm tired of sitting still. In the old days my quitting would have been cause for a major tantrum, but B.J.'s demeanor seems to have become increasingly calmer in conjunction with his access to communication. Benja, who has been surprisingly amiable all day, comes over to take my place. She points at our brother and good-naturedly hand-spells "Dead meat."

Mr. Wright and Mr. Stewart and Mr. O'Brien, Pa's secret society buddies, come over to talk privately with him. Mr. O'Brien wears a suit because his daughter Renna also graduated from the eighth grade today. Renna won no awards. She barely passed. But Mr. O'Brien was there to hear them call her name and to whistle and cheer, despite the fact that everyone was asked to withhold applause until after all the graduates had been recognized. Mr. Wright and Mr. Stewart have no graduating children today so are dressed casually. I grab a pickled egg from the bowl my mother just set on the table and head for the woods. My Christmas binoculars hang around my neck. Bird watching.

The truth is I never used the spyglasses as I thought I would—to peek at lovers in the woods, to see if that one glimpse I accidentally captured so long ago might be repeated. While I had no problem glancing from afar, the idea of zooming in with the binocs seemed to have a particular moral corruptness about it.

I find my favorite oak and scale it. She'll shoot me for getting my good suit dirty but at least I avoid tearing the fabric. The moment I reach the top, the clouds part, and the sun beams down, and I interpret the perfect synchronization of my summit with this solar emergence as a very good sign for my future. I tilt my face back to soak up all the rays, eyes closed, and I remember my mother saying that I may be leaving Deb Ellen and Buppie behind, that I will find my own tribe among the other college-educated. As I lower my face, I look down to the left, where I just came from. Through my binoculars, I see my mother talking to Aunt Pearlie. I'm glad she's here, my favorite aunt, and glad she left her unruly brood behind. I see B.J. tallying up the score from the last rummy hand and Benja shuffling for the next. I see my father flipping the meat while his Klux chums continue their talk. I take off the magnifiers and turn to the right.

Oh my Lord. A young couple in the clearing. I smile. They don't appear to be touching though. Just sitting up on a blanket, books lying around them. Still, something close about it: intimate. With the naked eye, I can't distinguish their faces.

There's something odd about the scene, even from a distance. I believe my eyes are playing tricks on me and I rub them, and then I look through the binoculars again. No invasion of privacy since they aren't doing anything, I reason. The lenses are out of focus, but even in the first blurry glimpse I can see what felt amiss. That which couldn't have been what I thought, was.

Black and white.

I twist the lenses clear as I can. And when I peer through my handset again, my mouth slowly opens wide.

Emily Creitzer from High School Visitation Day. And Roger.

So this is the "boy" Roger said was loaning him books. But it doesn't feel like loaning so much as...*sharing*. I was with Emily half that day, and even in the Latin class where she got to teach, I never saw her look so happy. And

Roger? I didn't know it was in him to smile like this. They look at their schoolbooks and they talk and they smile.

And then they kiss.

I take down my spyglasses, look away! Oh my God. Something flutters my stomach *oh my God*! Oh my God maybe. Maybe I didn't see it. I must've mistook it. Maybe she was whispering something to him. But why even be sitting that close? And why whisper here alone with no one else around, and *why are they alone together with no one else around*? I take a breath, bring the binoculars back to my eyes. The metal trembles in my hands.

They just seem to be talking now. But who laughs that much doing homework?

And they kiss again. His black lips against her pink.

And she opens three buttons of her blouse, and he touches her there.

I snatch the lenses away breathing breathing oh my *God*! This is not just some vicarious lust, wrong as that is, white man with a colored streetwalker. This is. This is a black *male* and white *female* oh my God. Oh my *God*!

I *hate* them! They're both smart, they *know* better! All I have to do . . . All I have to do . . .

I could right now. Yell for my father. And for Mr. Wright and Mr. Stewart and Mr. O'Brien, they'd be here quick. Course Roger and Emily'd hear my shouting and run, get away. Or I could quietly slip off the tree, get Pa and them and bring em all back for a surprise greeting, give Roger and Emily what's what. All on me. To make what's what come about, set it all in motion.

They kiss again! I feel sick, Jesus! Didn't Sally ever teach Roger *anything*? I know she did! I was never clamoring for the white robe, I'm not! But there's decency, there's— Why would Roger and Emily *do* something like this? Disgusting! And if they had no sense of respectability themselves, then they know damn well everyone else does, how in the hell can they just flaunt it, antagonize all of white society? Idiots! *Trash*! Through my binoculars, I look to my left now, the four of them, my father and his Klan cronies, Mr. Wright fanning his hat in front of him to cool off, clumsy with his three fingers. One whistle I could send for them, one move. Would make my father proud. Now B.J. stands looking around, no doubt for me.

A crow soars overhead, low and cawing loud, moving from the park out to the woods, coaxing us all to look up. Ma and Aunt Pearlie and B.J.

and Benja and Pa and Mr. Wright and Mr. Stewart and Mr. O'Brien raise their eyes a moment before I raise my eyes, a moment before Roger and Emily raise their eyes, and there we are. For five seconds, all eleven of us seeing exactly the same.

B.J.

autobiography

chiken make bj deaf ma love bj benja love bj randall
love bj carry baby tricycle fall baby cry pa no love sally
roger debellen bj want milk bottle pa drink all bj milk
drink all baby bj milk bottle bj no milk hungry baby hungry
firework bad henrylee bad pa no love i love brother randall
randall elephant mother elephant baby i like the music loud
cake bake batter pa read paper the smallest one was
madeline she was not afraid of mice she loved winter snow
and ice benja deal the cards mother dress blue henrylee
train fall no milk rations what is curious randall what is
george randall what is city randall monkey monkey national
geographic.
Ma hands say clean your room.
The library is many many book.
I show father deaf spell he not like slap me slap me

43
+36
79

It was hot today mother made lemonade I drink three
glass.

I read the secret of the old clock long. Randall said I
should read Hardy Boys but I like Nancy. What is will
I say Nancy is searching for the will. Randall say will
is death sometime I understand death sometime my
understand fly away.

Dead deaf not same.

Every night dream Randall hang from the rope. Then I
wake keep my eyes on him until he wake and brush his
teeth he stay stay.

1941–42
HUMBLE

I got nine lives!

You ain't got no nine lives, cat got nine lives. Dwight don't even look up. Dwight always drawrin.

I'm a cat! I'm a cat! I'm a cat! Meow. Hahahaha!

Shut up.

Whatchu drawrin?

He don't answer. I go over. He settin on our bed. He settin on our bed drawrin.

He got wings! That man got wings!

It's Icarus, Dwight say. Dwight good at drawrin! Look! Fingernails!

Who's Icarist?

A myth.

Huh?

A made-up story.

Who's Icarist?

Thought he could fly to the sun.

Aw! He nekked!

You don't see no private parts, do ya.

I don't see no *close*.

Dwight stop talkin. He prolly done talkin. He use to talk but he don't talk much no more now he's in the sixt.

I got nine lives. I got nine lives. I got nine lives.

Shut *up*.

Everbody got lives. Two lives. I seen em.

Whatchu talkin about?

I see yours right now. One there. An one there.

Now Dwight look up.

Stop doin that with your eyes.

I ain't!

Mama said stop doin that with your eyes.

I ain't! They do it all by emself!

That's cuz you cross-eyed.

I'm cross-eyeded! I'm cross-eyeded!

Stop jumpin!

I whisper: I'm cross-eyed.

But sometime you make it happen on purpose an Mama said stop it.

I run out the room I hop down the steps.

I'm a cat! I'm a cat! I'm a cat! I hop like a bunny down the steps. I'm a bunny cat! Hahahaha!

Settle down, say Mama.

I'm a cat! I got nine lives!

Cat don't got nine lives, that's a myth.

A made-up story!

Very good! She doin Miss Idie's ironin. Sheets an pillacase, white! white! white! white!

You got the spring fever, she say.

I ain't sick!

I mean you're excited. The sun.

Yes! The spring fever! The spring fever!

Settle *down* or go outside.

I fly out! I fly to the sun like Icarist! Sun on my head, the birds tweet tweet. I skip to Colored Street. Colored Street's two streets over, most everbody colored. The street sign say Oak Street. We live on Mixed Street. My mama say Mixed Street useta be all white, then some colored move in, then some more colored move in, then no more colored move in for a while, till us. So now all the colored on Mixed Street is the old people an us. Mixed Street is Rock Hill Road, we at 124 Rock Hill Road, Humble, Maryland!

Ooooooh, Jeanine's cat got babies! Bea Ann an Donny an Emma Jean standin aroun. Donny an Emma Jean an Jeanine an me same class, Miss McAfee's firs grade. Bea Ann in the second. Jeanine live at 113 Colored Street. Haha! 113 Oak Street.

Want one? Jeanine say to me.

Yes!

Bea Ann cryin. My mama say No cats, no cats.

Jeanine say to me, Your mama let you have a kitty?

Yes! (It ain't exackly The Truth. The Truth: I don't know!)

No cats, Bea Ann cryin.

Emma Jean claim the black. Donny claim the blacknwhite.

You claim em now, says Jeanine, but they too little to lee their mama. You come back an get em when they six weeks, June the fith.

June the *fith*? But it only April the twenty-fourth! I can't wait till June the fith!

You'll wait if you wannem.

Her uncle gonna drownd em! Bea Ann cryin. Her uncle take em down to the crick!

Only if I don't give em all away. He say enough strays roun here.

I point at the tannie. That a girl or boy?

Boy. You can't even touch em, the mama smell the human, she won't touch em no more. That why you gotta wait six weeks. The mama need to nurse em.

I look at the mama, she also a tannie like my baby kitty. I see her walk on two feet, smilin, wear her nurse cap, red crost on it.

I fly back to Mixed Street. Birds chirp chirp. I know what I gonna name my tannie. Parker. It just come to me. Parker. Donny an Emma Jean an Jeanine an me in the same class but I'm the smartest! I'm the smartest, firs grade!

Dwight on the front porch with Roof. Cracker Jacks.

Where you get them Cracker Jacks?

They stare at me, chew. They don't say nothin.

You better not a stole em!

You better mine your own business you know what's good for you, say Dwight. Roof say nothin, chew. Roof's white, his family live at 137 Rock Hill Road. His shirt dirty. Always his shirt dirty, always his family dirty. Mama come out the back with Miss Idie laundry basket.

I'm a cat! I'm a cat! Hop to her.

I gotta go to work, jumpin bean.

Jeanine's mama cat got cat kittens, I wanna kitten!

Who got kittens?

We turn to the big bushes. Ole Miss Onnie's voice from the other side.

Who cat got kittens?

Miss Onnie scare me! I look fearful to my mama.

He said Mae Webber's little girl's cat over on Colored Street, Miss Onnie.

Jeanine! I whisper.

Oh. Better not be nunna *my* cats.

Jeanine her name! I whisper.

I fixed all them lately-come females, better not be any of em carryin no packages. Then Miss Onnie voice gone.

Move, Mama say, I gotta go to work.

Can I have a tannie? Little tannie kitty?

She sigh. We barely feedin you an Dwight, how we gonna feed a cat? Then she walkin to work.

Go up to our mulberry tree, I eat the berries. My hans purple. I done sat in the mulberries, oooh, my pants purple, she gonna smack me!

Back to the front porch, Dwight playin jacks with Roof. The red ball *bounce, bounce.*

Dwight, teach me jacks!

Scoot, Dwight say. *Bounce.*

I go over to Miss Idie's. Her street white like Miss Idie. Humble is mostly white people. Mostly mostly mostly white people. One time I say to Mama, How come Daddy don't work close by, come home every day? She say the glass factory, the tire factory, the textile factory, the paper mill, brewery— them jobs go to white first. Lass hired firs fired. Porters he knew is steady for colored.

I go in Miss Idie's back door. My mama part-time. She cookin for Miss Idie, chicken soup. Whatchu followin me aroun for? Inside, pretty day like today.

Is that the little gentleman? Miss Idie real ole, she kinda blind.

Yes, Miss Idie, my mother say. She won't never say Yes, ma'am.

Well I think I got a little somethin for him. Miss Idie like my visits. I follow her an she hold out a chocolate ball. My eyes crost an there's two hans an two chocolate balls.

Thank you! It sweet an gooey.

Alone with my mama Miss Idie kitchen she say, Why there purple on them pants? You settin under that mulberry tree again? Didn't I tell you—

Out the door! I see the butterfly flutter flutter. The church bell dong one dong, that mean dinner! Mama be home for dinner, she only Miss Idie's part-time. Dwight already at the table eatin his butter an tomata sanwich. I set down pick up mine, tomatas out my mama's garden!

Mama, I love tomatas outcher garden! We have em for supper too?

She nod, she settin at the sewin machine, her eyes on Dwight's trousers.

Mama, which butter an tomata sanwich you wamme eat? Hahahaha!

But she don't laugh. I didn't mean to make her sad!

We been savin. You gonna have your eyeglasses before second grade, baby.

Afternoon I lie in my yard, close my eyes, warm sun. Smell. Spring! I got nine lives. I got me an Mama an Dwight an Daddy, that's one. I got Colored Street, I got school, that's three. I got the mulberry tree by myself, that's four, the more lives you got, the longer you live, I live old like Mesusalah! I got Sunday school, an I got regular school. Six.

In bed in the dark. Already took my bath, now Dwight taken his. Sometime I get scared till Dwight come to bed, but tonight the moon full, I see from the glow from the window.

Dwight come in clean from his Saturday night bath, get on his side a the bed, pull the covers over him. He don't even speak, he don't even say good night!

I say, Dwight. You teach me jacks? He prolly say no, he prolly jus ignore me.

But Dwight pop right up, he get the jacks an ball!

Whisper, he say, or she tell us back to bed. Then he show me. Bounce, pick up one. Bounce, pick up two. Bounce,

Pick up three! I get it I get it!

Whisper!

Boys? We hear her call, we quiet like dead. When it's safe he start up again, but this time no soun, he move his lips. I stare at his lips. Bounce, pick up four.

DWIGHT

You don't hurry up we'll miss the cartoon!

Now Eliot flyin out the house, catchin up with me. Big grin like usual, all sunshine.

Yaw goin to the pictures? Roof comin up behind. What's playin?

Tarzan. What else.

I like Tarzan! Eliot hoppin. There be cartoons before Tarzan?

Ten school days leff till summer, says Roof. How boutchu?

We *in* the same county. Same schedule.

I'm gettin the Perfect Attendance certificate! Eliot tells Roof since I already heard it a thousand times.

Somebody movin into Cooper's, Roof says. No socks an the hole in his loafer so big practically his entire little toe on the ground.

How you know?

I heard. Anyhow somebody took the For Sale sign down. Didn't ya notice?

I'm the only one in firs grade gettin the Perfect Attendance certificate!

Maybe not. Still got ten days to go, maybe you miss one of em, Roof tell him.

No I won't.

Maybe you get sick.

I won't!

Well *I'm* feelin sick. Roof starts coughin an sticks his coughin mouth right in Eliot's face.

Stop it, Roof!

We'll see if you go to school Monday now.

I *will*!

There's a long line at the thee-ater, teenagers an little kids for the matinee.

Why's everbody here? Roof complainin. Not a cloud in the sky, why ain't they outside playin?

Why ain't we? say I.

After we buy our tickets, Roof turns to me. I don't even gotta ask, I can tell by the smirk on his face what about to come out his mouth.

Well, guess I'll see yaw after the show.

Roof goes on in while Eliot follows me aroun to the alley entrance. Colored entrance. Some days Roof'll come with me, set with the coloreds in the peanut gallery but today he decided to be a punk. At the concessions Eliot gets Good & Plenty, I get Turkish taffy.

Bout seventy thousand steps to the firs balcony. Eliot's pantin, restin. I'm sighin an holdin my breath, pretendin like I don't even feel it, meanwhile my heart beatin 800 miles per hour.

Can't we set *here*? He ask me that same damn question every time.

You see any colored people here? When he catches his breath, we trudge on up to Balcony Two.

Plenty a white seats down below but colored section practically full already.

I wanna touch the ceilin, Dwight!

We go up to the back row. I lift him, his palm on the ceilin, whole face smilin. I'm too old for this. But I like it, I touch it too. Me an Eliot, giants.

Dwight.

Me an Eliot look. Richard. Two years older, fourteen. Tall. Slim. Also an artist, Miss Dixon the art teacher always beamin at his work too. Kimmie an Talia in tow, still pickin their seats.

Hey.

You wanna come over to Talia's? Kimmie asks. We're gonna play Criss-Crosswords, then maybe go to the graveyard.

Hm. Well I got Eliot.

I can go too!

No you can't. Plus we come here with Roof, so.

Talia scrunches her nose, hearin Roof. The lights go out, an they scuttle down to fronta the balcony.

The Looney Tunes is a blacknwhite, Joe Glow the Firefly. The firefly is pure-dee cartoon, a little guy lookin a lot like Jiminy Cricket from that Pinocchio lass year, an carryin a lantern which is his light. But the rest a the picture. The shadows. More like a realistic sketch than a comic. An the perspective. How huge each eyelash a the sleepin man the lightnin bug walks on. The earthquake jus from the man twitchin his face. The avalanche come down on him when he open a Morton salt, who coulda *thought*a all that?

When the Tarzan come on, I only half pay attention. Thinkin bout

Richard an em, hardly ever do I play with. The inconvenience, Richard four miles away. Kimmie an Talia right over on Colored Street but they're girls, an Talia kind of a snooty one. Still I ain't forgot Roof abandonin me for the white seats, maybe I *will* leave with Richard. Drop Eliot off at home, catch up.

Eliot's choking. I bang him on the back. Some of his Good & Plenty gone down the wrong way. Second his throat's clear, he start shakin em out again like to eat some more. I snatch em away.

Hey!

Take a rest, fool!

After a while I give em back, my whisper stern: *Eat slow.*

When the lights come up I'm lookin for Richard an company but they're already gone. Outside me an Eliot see Roof waitin for us.

That was the best one yet!

Yeah! Eliot agreein with him.

Those Africans. You sure can see the whites a their eyes.

Yeah! says Eliot gigglin his head off.

Wooga wooga. I look at Roof. Ain't nobody in that picture said Wooga wooga but he sayin it now, like all Africans talk like that. At our house Eliot runs up on the porch yellin Mama, I saved a Good & Plenty for you!

She come out. Oh hello Roof.

Hi Miss Claris.

How long your mama got now? Month?

Three weeks she say.

Well, lemme know she need anything.

We walk up an acrost the street to Roof's. You get candy? he asks all hopeful.

I already ate it.

Oh.

It was jus taffy. I say this knowin he love taffy. Wooga wooga.

The gutter hangin off Roof's porch roof, some board in a second floor winda replacin the glass somebody kicked through. There's this flat wood dog out front with **The Bart n's** on it, one a the little kids musta picked off the O. I thinka Roof's backyard as the magic garden, so fulla junk we jus stroll through till we come acrost somethin interestin.

Who's doll head's that?

I dunno. Tisa's. Or Cath Cath's.

Here's how it goes. Roof, twelve like me. Then Tisa ten, Joellen eight, Beaver seven, Cath Cath five, Lucy Deucy two.

Where'd it come from? Where'dja get all these toys?

I dunno. Some Christian. They was pretty beat up already when she give em to us outa her bin. Hey you think your daddy let us get on the trains again?

I shrug. That only happen the wunst.

So? Maybe it happen again.

He be home Tuesday, I can ask him. I try pullin up the doll head but it's connected to a body buried I don't know how deep. Then I spy the treasure. Box a colored chalk, fresh. How them Bartons just toss off perfectly good chalk not use it? I take the steps up to Roof's back porch, start sketchin. Roof's back porch i'nt a real wood porch, just a square a see-ment at the top a the see-ment steps an leadin to the back door. I'm not there a minute before Lucy Deucy come slammin the door open, starin at me. Thumb in her mouth.

Get back in there, says her brother.

No! She come out, dirty an all. I start to help her down the steps but she snatch herself away, goin down backwards.

What I heard was they was movin in this Saturday, says Roof, rollin a ole tire. To Cooper's.

Oh. I keep sketchin. Then I look up. They got kids?

Heard they do. Most a Roof's yard's jus dirt. Now Lucy Deucy crawlin around, pullin up what little grass there is.

Roof lookin at my work. Hey, that's that lightnin bug from the cartoon.

I make two of em, one blacknwhite like what we seen, the other color. I make decisions on the palette.

I wanna do a club.

Lass week you said no coloreds in your club.

That was a different club.

The total membership a that White Only club from lass week was you an your sisters till they quit at supper time.

This is a different club!

Giggle giggle. Lucy Deucy laughin, buryin her head in the hangin laundry sheets.

This one's the Tarzan Club. No! The Train Club. I can be the engineer an you can be the porter.

How about *I* be the engineer an *you* be the porter?

Okay, he says. Picks up a piece a glass an pricks his finger.

I ain't doin blood brothers with you no more, Roof, you got a different club every week, my fingers is sore.

This one'll last.

A winda opens from the second floor. It's Tisa. She steps right out on the roof over that extended firs floor back room, walks down to the ledge, hangs off a few seconds, then drops to the ground. Like a circus every day at Roof's!

I wanna be in the club, Tisa says, standin on the ground like that five-foot fall wa'n't even fazin.

Nope. Only open to peoples seen the inside of a train. You ain't.

She turns to me. I can be parta the club, Dwight?

I shrug. His club, I say. There's pink, an pastels ain't so common in jus ten pieces a chalk.

Lucy Deucy chokes for a second on grass she jus ate. Roof goes over an I think he gonna smack her back like I done Eliot but instead he give her a hard smack on her behine. She screamin.

How many times you told not to eat grass? he says, grabbin her under her arms an bringin her up the steps. Miss Ray Anne opens up the door.

What's goin on? Oh hi Dwight honey.

Eatin grass again, says Roof, handin his sister to his mother.

Miss Ray Anne's skinny as a beanpole cep for that great big belly she's carryin another three weeks.

How many times you been told? Miss Ray Anne sets Lucy Deucy on the floor inside, now hollerin her head off.

That's nice, Dwight. Tarzan an Jane an the lightnin bugs. Miss Ray Anne admirin my work, like she don't even hear Lucy Deucy.

Thank you.

You sure are an artist. You know that girl plays Jane's only sixteen years old? Then she goes back in, steppin right over howlin Lucy. Lucy wails a while longer settin inside a the door, then gets up to go upstairs still shriekin.

I'll do spit brothers, I offer.

Okay. We both know spit ain't strong a bond as blood but it's far as I'm goin today. We spit on our palms, shake.

This club is exclusive, says Roof, catchin Tisa out the corner of his eye.

Only people seen the baggage car on the train get in. I don't look up from my work but sense her givin him the glare.

Blacks can get in too, he go on, if ya got the right qualifications.

What did you call me?

Colored.

I got my own club, says Tisa, settin on a half-buried tire. Exclusive. I know she don't even know the word.

Like we wanna be a part of some girls' club.

You can't but Dwight can. We meet by the dock every Thursday. It's called the Swimmers Club.

I look up. Roof snaps hard eyes at his sister. The door opens, Miss Ray Anne holdin Lucy Deucy who unbelievably ain't decreased her holler volume one iota.

Who dipped this soup out an only ate half? Her eyes on Tisa. Tisa groans, stomps back inside. When the door's shut an it's half-quiet Roof walks over to the fence, leans his back against it. I sure am lookin forward to the seventh a June, he says.

Sixt, I correct. That's the lass day.

Seventh. The sixt she gonna warm my behine wunst she sees my report card. He take off his shoes an wade in a mud puddle. I flunk every test, he say, but always I pass. D-minus D-minus D-minus. Cuz what teacher gonna write F an sentence herself to another year a me? He find this little wood fishin rod an start fishin in his puddle. So sixt, last day a school be hell. But seventh. That be starta *my* freedom.

Finish my sketch. Can I keep this chalk? If yaw ain't gonna use it.

We're gonna use it.

It was stuck in the groun for the wind an the rain.

We're gonna use it.

I throw the whole dang box back down in the yard. Then come down myself. Couple Budweiser bottles, few bricks. Baby bike half buried in the dirt, takes some muscle to pull it out. Roof kickin aroun his puddle. This water here's plenty deep enough for me, he says.

Roof's scared a the water, Roof can't swim. I ride aroun on the little bike, my knees high in the air like some circus clown.

Hey. Think I got a bite, says Roof, an liffs his fishin rod out, a little metal part magnetized to a filthy pink fish an a filthy blue fish, the catch a the day.

Here come the train! Here come the train!

Through the mountains, roun the bend. Humble got lotsa mountains, Humble in the valley mountains all roun, someday I climb them Apple-lay-shun Mountains! He wavin the flag! The man wavin the flag, Mama!

I know. She lookin down the railroad tracks, her lips turn up to smile. If ain't no peoples gettin on the train, the man don't wave the flag. If the man don't wave the flag, the train don't stop in Humble! Them days we hope Daddy can get to the winda, wave at us while the train roll past. But the man wavin the flag! Hoppin, Mama hole my han tight for fear I run out in the tracks, I won't!

Train slow, slow. Stop. Mama an me look up an down, where they get off?

There he is! There's my daddy let the peoples off! I try to run but Mama hole my han tight. It almost nine at night but sometime she let me come see Daddy. He put down the step, they step down, he take their suitcase, hole it for em they step down. When the peoples all off he turn aroun, grin at me an Mama, we come hug tight! Then his grin fall down. Where's Dwight?

I hollered for him. Off with Roof prolly. He be here Friday.

Daddy always happy! happy! see me an Mama. But always the happy lose somethin he don't see Dwight. *We* here, Daddy! *We* here!

My daddy train porter the Capitol Limited, New York go to Worshinton go to Chicago Chicago back to Worshinton back to New York, train stop in Humble on the way! Twenty-one hours goin to Chicago, then he gotta stay there all day till nex train goin back to New York, then he gotta spend the night till nex train back to Chicago, sometime six days past fore I see my daddy! Goin to Chicago he stop in Humble right fore bedtime but comin back *from* Chicago happen 5:30 in the mornin, Mama don't wanna wake us so we can only see him sometime comin but she get up see him comin *an* goin.

Dark when we get home. Dwight better be there or he in trouble!

Where was you? I hollered for you when we went to see your daddy.

Dwight shrug. Roof's. I don't know. He settin at the kitchen table drawrin.

Well I tole him you gonna see him goin on Friday.

He shadin in his drawrin, say nothin. She smack his arm.

What!

You heard me.

I heardja! I'll be there Friday!

Don't gimme no lip! He sigh.

In bed Dwight sleep, I listen to the rain. Dwight useta wanna go every time Daddy goin through town. He don't see the sad Daddy get, *We* here, Daddy! The rain harder, make me gotta pee! I don't like walkin to the bathroom in the dark by myself! Dwight. Dwight!

What.

I gotta pee!

He mad but get outa bed come with me. One time he wouldn't an I got so scared to go by myself I didn't. He hit me an I started cryin, an she mad at him, Why's he cryin? an I think Dwight gonna get in trouble but when she find out I'm cryin cuz Dwight hit me cuz I peed the bed then *she* hit me! How old are you, boy? She tell him he don't never have to go with me but he say Yeah, an *I'm* the one have to sleep in the wet bed with him, so after that he always come with me if I wake up gotta go.

Relief! But I gotta run cuz soon's I'm done Dwight headed back to the bed, even fore I pull up my underpants! He do that on purpose!

Why you play with Roof when you pose to come see Daddy? You useta come all the time see Daddy with me an Mama! His back to me, he say, Cuz I ain't a big baby like you. I say, I'ma tell Mama an Daddy you said that. He don't say nothin but I know his eyes goin all rolly, even in the dark.

I dream I got a new playfriend we climb the trees. She's dirty, she's Roof's little sister that died, I don't know her name. When I wake up I don't tell no one bout my dream. Mama say I gotta be nice to Roof cuz his little sister died. But she say don't never say nothin to Roof bout his sister but sometime I wonder bout his sister. Whatta *you* starin at? Roof say. Button my lip! I say an run off. There's other dirty white families Mama call em white trash but one time me an Mama alone in the kitchen an I call Roof's dirty white family white trash an Mama slap my arm.

Here come the train! My mama hole me tight while my daddy the porter help the peoples off the train, take their suitcases for em. He turn aroun to us. He look tired, tired. The porters got very long shiffs, Mama say, they get very short rests. He come to Mama an me smilin an then he raise his face an his face got the worry. Where's Dwight?

Mama surprised. He was jus here—

Dwight come out the train station, done bought a red hot cimmamon ball, suckin on it. I notice he didn't buy none for nobody else!

Boy, whatchu doin in there! your daddy's train pullin up.

Dwight look at her, but mostly his eyes on Daddy. Daddy oughta whoop him good, fronta all these peoples. He prolly think he's too big for that. Hahaha!

But Daddy don't look like he gonna whoop him. Come ere son, say Daddy. Dwight do an Daddy give that miscreant the warmest hug of all. I seen miscreant on Dwight's vocabulary list. Miss McAfee said you learn a vocabulary word by usin it in a sentence so I jus did.

DWIGHT

There's us an nex to us is Miss Onnie an nex to Miss Onnie Cooper's. Coopers was this ole white couple, spry when I was little, later feeble, later dead. For a few months after some grown man granson from Virginia'd show up occasionally, an eventually For Sale out front.

Train Club last about two days. Then I suggest the Architeck Club, which Roof ain't a speck impressed on till I commence siftin through his well-stocked junkyard an start erectin my tower with what I find, now he all interest. Hey Dwight, how bout some planks from this ole cart for the castle? How bout wheels from this toy wagon, how bout this doll head for a gargoyle? I say tower, Roof say castle, we meanin the same. Yet all the time our mind on Cooper's, findin excuses to walk down the street an glance over, but no move-ins never show up.

Then Thursday after school. Day before lass day, big fat movin truck an two white men struggling with a couch up the eight porch steps. The white school jus three blocks away so Roof always beat me home, Roof already there grinnin at me.

Toldja, he say. We set on Mr. White's brick wall, it stand about a foot an a half off the groun. Mr. White's colored, Mr. White's a ole drunk lives direckly crost from Cooper's, he don't mind we set here, our front-row eye view.

Now the movin men pullin twin beds out the trunk. See? says Roof, like I ever disputed him on whether there was kids in the move-in family. We haven't yet seen anybody from the move-in family. Jus the movin truck which is enormous, and the movin men which is several. Next: piano. Not the big black gran kind like in the Ginger n Freds. Just a regular brown but me an Roof sure ain't seen nothin like it cep school.

They're rich, Roof says, all awe.

An art! The movin men's liftin big flat things wrapped in cloth, an one a the cloths slips off an I see these ain't framed family photographs, these is paintings! An a big heavy heavy desk with carvins all meticulous, a black wastebasket hand-painted Japanese ladies!

Roof!

His mother. He grumblin, Cuz I didn't take the garbage out.

Roof! She got a powerful holler, even with her stomach overflowin with baby.

What!

Come take the garbage out like I toldja!

Roof all sarcasm: Like our kitchen, you really can tell the difference between what's garbage an what ain't. But he goes.

Vanity. Two a the men holdin the bottom the drawers removed, one walkin sideways with the meer. Accidentally the meer bang gainst the hangin porch swing. The hangin porch swing was the Coopers', come with the house. It's a scratch maybe, no tragedy, but the front door fly open an a white lady pop out, Please be careful!

Hi.

I give a start! Didn't see this white boy standin before me. Look to be bout my age. Blond.

Where you live?

I point.

You like backgammon?

What's backgammon?

You like checkers?

I nod.

Backgammon's like checkers, except smarter. Come ere. I'll graduate you.

He walk ahead, leadin me right into his house, right through the front door while the movers is negotiatin the queen-size headboard. Follow him upstairs.

This is my room. I look aroun. Still bare cept a twin bed with nekked mattresses, little dresser.

This whole room yours? You don't gotta share?

My sister got her own room.

He lay out the board an the checkers a backgammon an we set on the floor. A little studyin to remember the setup patterns but besides that I catch on quick. He wins two games an we deep in the third.

Carl!

I figure it's the same white lady tole the movers Please be careful. I look at the boy. He don't look up.

Carl!

His eyes don't budge from studyin his nex move, like he's deaf to the woman. Maybe she's callin his brother? He got a brother?

Her footsteps comin up the stairs. When she reach the top, Carl! Didn't you hear me oh! Hello!

Even though she yellin at him, her voice all soff, smilin.

Hi.

Carl, you didn't tell me you had a friend.

I guess you got the hang of this goddamn game cuz this time you goddamn gonna win, an with that he make the suicide move which he got no choice to do. My eyes pop out my head! This boy cussin in fronta his *mama*?

What's your friend's name, Carl? Sweet as roses.

I don't know, he says, lookin at me. What's your name, friend?

Dwight.

Well Dwight, I just went out and got a few groceries. Would you like an apple? And some milk?

Yes, please.

Carl?

You plannin on movin today or tomorrow, *Dwight*?

We on the fifth game, him wantin to make up for losin the lass two, when she comes up with two glasses a milk an two apples sliced up pretty on two saucers, like tea with the queen.

You're learning from the best, she says. Carl was runner-up to his school's backgammon champion.

He cheated! Carl snaps.

I'm Mrs. Talley.

Thank you, Mrs. Talley, an I take a delicious sip to demonstrate my appreciation.

Then Carl turns to her for the firs time, smilin. Thank you, Mom.

Now she smiles big. Well I'll leave you two boys alone, an she turns an leaves.

Should I shut the door so we're not disturbed again? Carl asks while she still most definitely in earshot. Before I can answer he stans an slams the door so hard I hear somethin fall an crash downstairs. Carl rolls. Doubles! He snaps his fingers, happy-skippin his men roun the board as I wait for Mrs. Talley to come stompin back up the steps an scream at him. But all I hear's the sound of a broom sweepin below an though I stay till my suppertime I never see her rest a the day.

Whatchu cryin for?

I stop. There Miss Onnie, where she come from? Starin at me, big blue eyes steel eyes.

I *ast* you a question, boy. Settin on the curve blubberin.

Now I blubberin loud. Jeanine uncle gonna drownd Parker!

She look at me hard.

My kitten! Bea Ann say Jeanine don't give em all away before June the fith, Jeanine uncle gonna take em to the crick, drownd em! An my mama won't lemme take Parker! An today June the fith!

Stop that bawlin!

I stop it but I got the hiccups.

Bring it here.

Lookin at her.

Bring the damn thing here. If it ain't diseased, I'll take it.

I run! Miss Onnie savin Parker's life! Miss Onnie the nicest white lady I know! There's Jeanine!

What?

Miss Onnie savin Parker's life!

Huh?

Miss Onnie say if tannie kitten ain't diseased, she take him!

He ain't diseased.

She take him!

Jeanine go inside her house. Somethin smell nice smell warm from her kitchen. She come back out with Parker.

Parker! Take him in my arms, he gettin big! Miss Onnie savin Parker's life so your uncle don't drownd him!

Uh-uh. He was gonna take the whole nest but we give all the rest of em away. This the only one leff. Mama said the kitten all big, like a real person now, Uncle Ramonlee don't got the heart. You wanna brownie?

Me an Jeanine at Jeanine's kitchen table, brownies all warm.

I ain't goin, says Uncle Ramonlee. Damn white man's war.

Well maybe it ain't gonna happen, says Jeanine's mama.

Oh it gonna happen.

Well maybe they won't call you.

Oh they gonna call me. Nineteen, why won't they call me? All them white boys gonna need some colored service, whip up the slop for em, kitchen. Not me.

Miss Onnie! Miss Onnie! I got the cat, here's Parker!

Miss Onnie feedin her cats in her yard, all wantin the milk, all wantin the scraps. Mama say Miss Onnie got seventy-leventy cats!

Lemme see.

Miss Onnie take Parker, she look him over head to toe.

Okay. I got my girls fixed anyhow, he won't be botherin em.

She drop Parker in with the rest. He fightin for the food. Them big cats won't let him in!

Miss Onnie, he gonna starve! Look, the big cats won't let him get no food!

He ain't gonna starve. Miss Onnie use her foot, push big cats out the way. Parker eat some. Then she let big cats back.

I don't think he got enough, Miss Onnie.

Mine your business, little boy. Look at all them cats. Think I don't know how to raise cats? Then she go to another dish, push big cats out the way so a little blacknwhite get a taste. I know how to care for the runt.

Eliot! My mama callin.

What's the new family like?

We in the kitchen, supper. Mama wanna know all bout the new white family movin in, askin Dwight.

I don't know. They okay.

Tomarra's lass day, Mama. Then summer vacation!

I know. She answer me but eyes still on Dwight.

Where they from?

Ohio.

They got kids?

Yeah. Boy my age. Carl. He got a sister. Forget her name.

What kinda work the daddy do?

I don't know! I jus met em today!

Don't get smart.

I got my cat, Mama! I got Parker!

Now she turn to me. Didn't I tell you no cats?

Miss Onnie say she take care a him for me!

Oh. Ain't Miss Onnie already got seventy-leventy cats?

Ring. Mama get the phone.

How come he move here today when he posed to be in school? I say.

Where he moved from they already finished school. Don't you go grillin me too.

I stop grillin Dwight, eat my macaroni an cheese. I love macaroni an cheese!

Mama come back. Why your teacher wanna see me tomarra?

I wait for Dwight to answer, sometime he in trouble with his schoolwork! Then see him an her's lookin at me.

I don't know. Maybe cuz I'm gettin the Perfect Attendance certificate!

That didn't sound like what it was.

I peer through the bushes, I see all them cats but I can't find Parker. Then I see him, bring him to our yard. Mama ain't in the kitchen, I run in, get a bitta milk, lay it out our back porch for Parker. Nex mornin fore lass day a school I do the same: Parker's breakfass. School half-day, then dismissal, all the kids gone but me. Me an Mama standin at Miss McAfee's desk: cryin! cryin!

Stop that cryin, boy! You did it.

I didn't mean to do it!

Now how you didn't mean to color in your schoolbooks.

Jus one! Jus the readin book! I forgot I did it! I didn't mean to!

Well, Miss McAfee says. Miss McAfee look like Marian Anderson, smile like Marian Anderson cep today I see no teeth. Well. You have been the best behaved boy in the class all year, Eliot. I must say I'm surprised at you.

Miss McAfee surprised at me! She only say that to the bad kids! I'm cryin!

Stop that. Mama smack my arm. It don't hurt my arm but it hurt my feelins. I try stop cryin.

How much the damage gonna cost us, Miss McAfee? Worry her face. I almost start cryin again! I know we ain't got no money!

Well, say Miss McAfee. Since this is your first infraction. The teachers still have to be at school two more days. I want you to write one hundred times I shall not vandalize school property. Say it?

I shall not vandalize school property.

I've written it here for you. Now you copy it a hundred times, alright? You know what vandalize means? You know what property means?

I get it from the contest.

Context. But now she smile.

I'll use it in a sentence, that way I learn it. When you vandalize somebody's property, you hurt their feelins.

Very good. You'll bring your paper back to me tomorrow?

Yes.

How much the damage gonna cost us, Miss McAfee?

Miss McAfee shake her head, like we don't gotta pay. Then she open her desk an pull out the certificate. Congratulations on perfect attendance, Eliot.

I try smile but my eyes still wet. On Miss McAfee's desk the book open for us to see, the pages I vandalized. Dick an Jane runnin with Spot the Dog. I took a brown crayon an colored in Dick an Jane.

So I'll see you tomorrow, Eliot.

Yes.

She turn to my mother. He never says Yes ma'am.

Yes ma'am was from the slave days, say Mama. I told him I ever heard him say it, I'd smack him.

When we outside Mama look at my certificate, look at my report card. In the firs grade they don't give A-B-C-D but everything Miss McAfee write is high an lass thing she say

> Eliot is a superior student, of extraordinary curiosity and ability. It has been a delight to have had such a fast learner in my classroom. I could hardly keep up with him!

Mama smile at my report card at my certificate. What kinda special cake I should bake for these? Chocolate?

I wa'n't expectin *that*!

I set at the kitchen table, write it over an over while she mix the batter. She look at my work. Them *P*'s startin to get sloppy.

Too many *P*'s in property! My arm tired!

Okay, you take a little arm rest till I say.

Okay! I stand, gonna find Parker.

Stay right there.

I set, sigh.

If you hadn't turned Dick an Jane colored, you wouldn't have homework after the lass day a school. But her mouth turn up like to smile.

In come Dwight.

Where you been?

Carl's.

Where's your report card?

Huh. Huh, where'd I put that?

Find it.

He do, an from the look on her face I know Dwight ain't gettin no special cake tonight. She taken him upstairs but firs she look to me: Your break's over.

28. I shall not vandalize school property.

After supper I lay out Parker's supper milk, by nex mornin breakfass he expectin it, waitin for me! Then me an Mama walk my homework to Miss McAfee an she smile, ack like nothin bad never happened. She say, Have a good summer, Eliot! Don't stop your reading! I say, Yes, Miss McAfee! Mama think ma'am is slave talk, even though Miss McAfee colored Mama say Don't never say ma'am but still respeck your elders: Yes, not Yeah.

Mama gone to Miss Idie's part-time, I layin out Parker's milk meal an here come Dwight.

Better not let Mama catch you givin milk to that tabby. Fan your behine.

Miss Onnie got too many cats. Parker don't get enough!

He get enough. Miss Onnie's voice from behine the bushes. Dwight take off! I wanna take off but lee Parker fend hisself?

Come ere, Yella Cat. I see her feet through the bushes but bushes high, Miss Onnie ain't tall enough see over the top. Yella Cat, why she call Parker that? Yella ain't a name! An he a tannie!

Like it hang in the air, high over my head. Water sailin over them hedges, floatin below the clouds, then it fall. *Splash!* Parker scream an run, I run cry into my house. Everything happen fass! When Mama get home see me all wet I cry, I tell her how Miss Onnie threw the water over the bushes drownd me! Mama march me over there, *bang bang* Miss Onnie door. When Miss Onnie come, my Mama tongue flyin, han on her hip.

Miss Onnie say I *told* that boy I take care a my cats. I don't appreciate him lead em off, sneak feedin em milk at *your* house.

My mama look down at me. *What* milk?

Home I get the whippin. She take a switch! I cry an cry. You think we got money for milk wasted on cats? Then she say go tell Miss Onnie I ain't gonna do that no more. I try wipe my face go over. My behine don't hurt cuz Mama don't never hit hard but I always forget that while she doin it.

Where all the cats? Miss Onnie's yard usually fulla cats, now I see none. Then I find em. They all inside Miss Onnie's house at the windas lookin out. There's Parker. They all lookin out, backa the yard. Their mouths movin, they cryin to get out! But it kinda look like they singin to get out, they in the cat choir!

There Miss Onnie backa the yard, throwin bread crumbs to the birds. The birds everywhere.

Miss Onnie, how come you locked all them cats up inside?

She don't look at me, jus tossin the crumbs. Birds gotta eat too, she say. An shouldn't have to worry they *get* et in the process. She got a lotta bread crumbs. The more she throw, the more birds come.

I help?

She open her bread crumb bag bigger. I put my han in. Me an Miss Onnie feedin the birds!

Sorry I fed Parker when you said no, Miss Onnie. I won't do that no more. Tear in my eye.

She tossin.

I said I'd take care a that cat, you ack like I's a liar. I'm seventy-three never tole no lies, my mama name me Honesty. I stuck by it.

You play badminton?

Nope, but Carl show me how to set up the net, his backyard. Half-day, lass day a school. I beat him off the bat, 21–16. Nex game he givin me all manner a criticism on my serve, my swing. Still I win, 21–14. He pretty mad game three. Jumps way ahead, 17–11. Then I start closin in. 17–12. 17–13. 17–14. 17–15.

I'm thirsty, he say. You want some iced tea? An he drop his racket like game over an go into his house. At the door he turn: Comin?

I follow into his kitchen. We settin at the table drinkin, then some skinny teenage girl come in, hair light brown, darker n Carl's blond. Short pigtails. Walk right by us like she ain't surprised at all to see some colored boy, stranger in her house. She go straight to the icebox.

I just made that iced tea! You drank it all?

Carl smile an shrug.

How many glasses you have?

Carl still smilin, sayin nothin. I raise a finger.

One. Maybe *you* had one, but *he* drank the rest of the pitcher before you got here. She slams the icebox door an walks out mad into the other rooms.

You got sisters?

I shake my head.

God blessed you.

I got a little brother.

My piano lesson's getting ready to start. Haven't even unpacked and already she got a damn piano teacher coming over. You play?

I shake my head.

Come on, an he throw half his ice tea down the sink, then walk out for me to follow.

The firs-floor room with the piano ain't livin or dinin, an extra room they call the family room. He's good. Somethin classical, somethin boogie woogie. He's fast! Doorbell.

There she is, you gotta go. Come over later, I'll help you with that serve.

Ain't lookin forward to it but gotta go home sometime. Ain't carried nothin from school but my report card an it I slip under a front porch slat, then I slip in through the back porch. But there she is, cross arms waitin for me. Eliot settin at the kitchen table writin somethin all teary.

Where's your report card?

Huh. Huh, where'd I put that?

Find it.

An after I do: Why you get that D?

No point lyin. I tell her we had to do a report on *Civil Disobedience* and a report on Benjamin Banneker an I didn't do neither. I don't tell her Mr. Darcy specially mad I didn't turn in Benjamin Banneker when we go to Benjamin Banneker School.

Now, summer vacation, she homeworkin me.

Civil Disobedience
By Henry David Thoreau

That's as far as I get when I look up out my window, see Carl tightnin his net. I'm back fore she get home from workin Miss Idie's so how she find out I don't know, but there she stand: *Badminton? Badminton?!*

Her whippins most n genrally's just a few smacks on the butt, they wouldn't hurt much if it weren't for my refusin to cry so she hit harder, it sting on the skin but sting harder on the inside, both us all the tears. So nex day I figure I go to the liebary, take the report seriouser.

Civil Disobedience
By Henry David Thoreau

In Civil Disobedience, Henry David Thoreau says prison is "the only house in a slave State in which a free man can abide with honor." Henry David Thoreau was very very mad about slavery and about war against Mexico. Henry David Thoreau was all for not paying taxes to support an injust government and went to jail for it. Henry David Thoreau wrote "Law never made men a whit more just; and, by means of their respect for it, even the well-disposed are daily made the agents of injustice." Law began with the Magna Carta.

Mr. Darcy liked quotes, an quotes adds words. Ninety-five. Ninety-six if you count "well-disposed" as two, one oh two if you count the title an "By Henry David Thoreau." Mr. Darcy wanted the reports to be four hundred but my mother don't know that. We had a separate lesson about the Magna Carta so thought I'd throw that in. I show it to her. You can do better than this for Benjamin Banneker. But I don't have to start that till tomarra.

Wanna sell lemonade?

We go into the kitchen, his mother stirrin up the pitcher. She look up at me an smile. Hi Dwight. I filled the pitcher, plus two glasses extra for you boys now.

We gotta make a sign, Carl says. We go up to his room, he pull out colored pencils an paper, write LEMONADE 2¢, neat enough. I gotta go to the bathroom, he says, an by the time he come back the LEMONADE 2¢ sign also feature a mouthwaterin pitcherful with ice an lemons, a flyin cow jumpin over a smilin man in the moon.

What's that got to do with lemonade?

Customers will be drawn to the picture. Attract em. Then we sell.

That's wonderful, Dwight! says Mrs. Talley, walkin by with a basket a laundry. You have artistic talent. But I'm sure you've been told that before.

Too much, says Carl, an takes another piece a paper to redo his minimalist design in three seconds flat, bringin it out with us no further discussion.

Drunk Mr. White takes a cup, an Miss Onnie on her way to D'Angelo's for eggs an butter, an Miss Priscilla an Miss Pauline out on their daily walk, the two elderly white sisters up the street always lived together. Carl asks me about each a our customers, but I hardly get out a sentence fore he's announcin his own opinions, none of em good. It ain't that he don't like em exackly. He jus find em all funny, an not the kind a funny he'd tell em to their face.

Then comes Roof. He stand right in fronta our table.

Hi. All he say, look at me.

Hi. This is Carl. This is Roof.

Hello, say Carl smilin all polite so I know for sure he gonna badmouth Roof soon's his back's turned.

Where you been? Roof asks me.

Inside mostly. Punishment. My report card.

Roof looks at Carl, then back at me.

I woulda come up but I figured you was on punishment too. You tole me your report card was gonna be worse even n mine.

I already got beat for that, an he glances at Carl again, then walks away.

He your friend?

Uh-huh. Sometimes.

Roof?

Rufus.

Oh. I don't wanna talk about Roof no more an I guess Carl gets this cuz he drop the subject, start goin on about Miss Priscilla an Miss Pauline's funny lookin stockins again.

When we up to thirty we call it a day, an I take him to D'Angelo's. The penny-anny, Tootsie Rolls an Cracker Jacks an nigger babies an still fifteen to pocket. But Carl claim since it's his mama's lemon an sugar invested into it an his mama made it, he think it more n fair he keep ten an allow me a nickel. Then we do some badminton. He win the firs two an when the third get to be 19–13 my favor he suddenly remember he gotta clean his room, collect the rackets an head inside.

That's a forfeit, I say. My win.

If it makes you proud to win by default, then sure, your victory, he say, shuttin the door behind him.

Nex day I'm settin on our front porch slidin chair not slidin, weighin the pro n con a Carl when here come Roof. I look over an he's there, bottom a my porch steps lookin up at me. You wanna treasure hunt? he ask.

The Messengill house couple blocks over is a piece a junk, broken windas an big holes in the floorboards, trashed out, whatever furniture leff stole long ago. Wunst I fell through the rotted-out steps goin up to the second floor. The Messengills was said to be rich, so the thing was to find treasure amongst the junk. What flies in the face a this wealth theory is the house is small, no mansion for sure, but then people comes back with it was only one a the Messengills' houses. The only thing we ever come out with is a broken piece a chandelier or ole boot, which of course is wholly valuable.

Okay, I answer. Maybe.

Maybe?

Yeah, okay. I glance toward Carl's house an Roof follows my look. What's he like?

Carl? Oh he's great. Taught me backgammon. You ever play back-gammon? Like checkers but more complicated. Strategy. He's got a nice board.

How old is he?

Our age! Guess he'll be at your school in the fall. Badminton too! I helped him set the net up in his yard. See it? Now I start slidin in the slidin chair. His mother's nice too, always bringin us snacks.

So I got this idea. That ole fireplace, front room a Messengills. Them loose bricks. Remember? Where else treasure be buried?

That lemonade stand, we cleaned up! Spent most on the penny-anny, but the leftovers we split.

I show Roof my nickel. Roof's eyes get slitty.

You should hear him play the piano! Every time I go over there his mother makes us snacks. Lemonade, or apples an milk.

You already said that.

Yeah well. Just I was thinkin a showin him the path down to the crick today. So that might be a conflict with us an Messengills.

Roof stare at me.

Well, I guess me an Carl could go to the crick tomarra. I prolly should go down, let him know not to expect me today. By this point his mama prolly come to expect me too! Every day Carl want me there!

His mama don't mind niggers in her house?

I stop rockin. Me an Roof's eyes glued.

You should see his house. Clean! I didn't know white people could be so clean!

How Roof get the speed, come flyin up the porch an sock me off that slidin chair fore I know it? We rollin down the steps, blind punchin, both us bleedin noses, thank God my mother workin at Miss Idie's, not home.

Stop that, hoodlums! Somewhere in the distance I hear Miss Onnie's voice but everything outside Roof's eyes Roof's fists some other world far away. Then us splashed, ice water!

Toldja go on home, boy! Miss Onnie with her flower pitcher. We done broke part, blinkin. An *you*. Oughta be ashamed, right on your mama's porch steps! Me an Roof run our separate ways, an even though nobody in the house but me I hold in my bawlin till I get to the bathroom, closed door.

Where you get that scab under your nose? she ask, home from work.

Fell.

I fixed my own sanwich, Mama, Eliot says. Butter n bread. I love butter n bread!

In bed that night he wide awake.

Dwight, what's the Magnet Carter?

I frown. What?

Mama leff your paper out on the kitchen table you said the Magnet Carter.

Can you read? I said the *Magna Carta*. It's how justice started. England, 1215.

I like Magnet Carter better! I like a big ole horseshoe magnet! I hold it up at the train tracks an Daddy's train come flyin to me, I hold it up bring Daddy home! Hahaha!

I roll over away from him. All wound up, I can tell he gonna be chatterin, long night.

Whatcha mean justice?

What?

Whatcha mean justice? The Magna Carter?

Carta. Justice means fair law for everybody.

He chew on that a while and I pray he slip on to sleep. Then he say, I like that! I like the Magnet Carter! Then he lookin out the winda, stars.

Twinkle Twinkle Little Star. How I wonder what you are. You know what it sound the same like, Dwight? *Baa Baa Black Sheep Have you any wool? Yes sir Yes sir Three bags full.* You know what else it sound the same like, Dwight? *A B C D E F G, H I J K LMNOP* You can put em all together! *Twinkle Twinkle Little Star, Yes Sir Yes Sir Three bags full. Q R S, T U V* hahahaha! Or you can say *A B C D E F G, Yes sir Yes sir Three bags full. Up above the world so high* hahahaha! Or you can say *Baa Baa Black Sheep Have you any wool? Yes sir* I mean *LMN* I mean. I mean. *Baa Baa Black*

SHUT UP!

Okay.

Then he hummin it!

I'm a kill you!

An I'ma tell Mama Miss Onnie tole me you didn't get that nose scab from fallin.

Suddenly I'm on toppa him, my hands clutchin his arms hard gainst the bed, my face in his face. An all I can say: *Don't*.

He go screamin an cryin to Mama. I sigh, wait for her to come flyin in here yell at me but she don't. He don't come back neither. Maybe she let him sleep with her tonight. Still I stick to my side in case he come, never do I feel right takin over the whole bed.

A Pullman Porter is a very honorable position for a colored man, says Mr. Talley jus before he serves. Do you know the history of the Pullman Porters?

Oh God, says Carl, an whacks the birdie over the net back at his daddy.

Get used to it, Dwight, says smilin Mrs. Talley, carryin a chair in each hand from the kitchen. Mr. Talley's a history teacher so *every*thing for my children becomes a history lesson. Right? she asks her children.

Darnit! says Christina, who slammed the birdie into the net. Only today did I finally figure out Carl's sister's name. We're playin doubles, Christina an their dad agains me an Carl. Christina's fifteen.

The Pullman Company transported Abraham Lincoln's body. His coffin.

Twelve serving fourteen, says Carl.

In recognition of that historical milestone, Mr. George Pullman committed to providing employment on his luxury trains for our newly freed slaves.

Suh-*lam*! says Carl an laughs, his father lookin down, birdie at his feet.

Would you all like some cinnamon rolls with your iced tea? asks Mrs. Talley. I just baked some.

I think that hit the net, says Christina.

It did *not* hit the net, says Carl.

Don't worry, says Mr. Talley, winkin at his daughter. We'll get em.

Thirteen serving fourteen, says Carl.

Oh! and I'll slice that watermelon, says Mrs. Talley an heads back in the house.

Hey, says Carl to me, do they call your daddy *George*? All smirky.

No, says his dad, they got rid of that. Terrible practice!

The union, I say.

Yes, says Mr. Talley, all in some kinda reluctant thought.

Out! says Christina.

Dammit! says Carl.

My serve, says Christina, goin after the birdie.

Yes, the Brotherhood of Sleeping Car Porters. They did some good things for the porters, but you've gotta be careful. That darn A. Philip Randolph!

Fourteen serving twelve, says Christina.

Thirteen! says Carl.

Came out of the National Negro Congress, says Mr. Talley. Know what the National Negro Congress was?

Fourteen serving thirteen, says Christina.

Communists, says Mr. Talley.

Dwight's friends with the white trash up the street, says Carl. My eyes snap to him.

Aaaah! growls Carl, even though he made me miss the birdie.

Don't say white trash, says his father.

Fifteen serving thirteen, says Christina. In official play, fifteen's game.

We said we're playing to twenty!

Lucky for you, his sister retorts an serves.

Aaaaah!

Sixteen serving thirteen.

Who's Dwight's friends? asks their father.

Up across the street, that broken-down fence broken spout, who else's yard's fulla garbage? *Aaaah!* Carl throws down his racket.

Temper, says Mr. Talley.

Seventeen serving thirteen, says Christina.

Well I'm sure they can't help it, says Mr. Talley.

They can't help being dirty? says Carl.

They can't help being poor.

Cuz all poor people are dirty?

Sorry, I say.

Aaaah! says Carl.

Eighteen serving thirteen, says Christina.

Dwight's friend's name's Porch.

Roof. Rufus. Sorry.

Aaaah!

Nineteen serving thirteen. Game point.

Carl! Craig! Mrs. Talley callin from the back door. Could one of you strong men help me with this table? It's a little heavy.

You stepped over the serving line! says Carl.

What serving line? says Christina.

You were practically on the net!

I was not! And there's no serving line, you can't make up rules halfway through!

She's right about that, says their father, but for future reference don't get any closer than the edge of the clothesline.

Do-over, says Carl.

No!

She was practically on the net!

Alright! For the little booby baby I'll do it over. Nineteen serving thirteen, *game point.*

Out! says Carl.

It was *not* out!

On the line is out.

What line?

From now on, says Mr. Talley, the rosebush will be out.

Do-over, says Carl.

I'm not doing another do-over!

Look at me! says Mrs. Talley, her left hand holdin a wood table that looks heavy, balanced on her head, her right hand holdin a plate a cinnamon rolls. Now I know why the African ladies do it this way!

Settin on my bed I shade my sketch: me, Carl, Carl's father, an Carl's sister playin badminton, Carl jus hit it at his dad an his dad runnin for it, Carl's mother settin a apple pie on a picnic table. The apple pie an picnic table is poetic license. Everybody smilin DicknJane.

Daddy's home! Daddy's home! Eliot hoppin, statin the obvious. At supper Daddy says, I got a special guest comin in three days.

You be back three days? Eliot all grins.

Yeah, but then I work a couple weeks straight. Switched my days off special for this special guest. He be comin on the train with me, somebody real famous.

Who! Eliot practically fall off his chair.

A surprise.

Is it Gary Cooper?

It ain't a movie star, says Daddy, nippin it in the bud before Eliot start a string a movie star guesses. Eliot look confused, like how can you be famous you ain't a movie star?

Dwight finished his last report. It's a real nice one. She smilin at me. I wanna hear it! Daddy say.

After supper, them on the couch, Eliot on the floor, me standin.

Benjamin Banneker wrote six farmer's almanacs every year from 1792 to 1797. These almanacs were unique because they didn't just predict the weather. They also had essays, which I will subsequently report on.

Benjamin Banneker was born in 1731 in our state of Maryland in what became known as Ellicott's Mills and what is now Ellicott City. Benjamin's English grandmother married her African slave Banna Ka which gradually got changed to Banneker. Then their mixed daughter married her African slave, and from them came Benjamin. His grandmother taught him to read and he went to a Quaker school for a time, but mostly he taught himself. He borrowed a pocket watch and after he studied the inside of it he carved wood to make all the pieces just like the pocket watch and he built a clock from the wood that chimed every hour. He was 22 when he finished the clock and it worked four decades until it was destroyed in a house fire right after he died which might or might not a been accidental.

Benjamin Banneker was a farmer. He was also a mathematician and a scientist and an astronomer. He was hired to be part of a group that surveyed the land that became Washington D.C. He used his astronomical work for this, figuring out the position of the earth by the way the stars looked. A letter in the Georgetown Weekly Ledger about Benjamin said his "abilities, as a surveyor, and as an astronomer, clearly prove that Mr. Jefferson's concluding that race of men were void of mental endowments, was without foundation."

Benjamin Banneker was for peace. In his 1793 almanac he included "A Plan of a Peace-office for the United States" which was written by Benjamin Rush who was a founding father of the United States. What the plan called for was a Secretary of Peace.

Benjamin Banneker was against slavery. He and Thomas Jefferson disagreed about this, and wrote letters to each other arguing about it, which Benjamin Banneker published in his almanac.

White people and colored people respected Benjamin Banneker and his high intelligence. Benjamin Banneker was proud to be a Negro man, he was proud of his color. He wrote "I am of the African race, and in the colour which is natural to them of the deepest dye; and it is under a sense of the most profound gratitude to the Supreme Ruler of the Universe."

Many times through it Daddy sayin I didn't know that, I didn't know that, an now both lookin at me all proud.

In bed Eliot says, What did Benjamin Banneker invent? I say he weren't an inventor, he studied things. The stars, an the weather. An he built a clock outa wood! Eliot say. Yep. An he knew the eclipse! Yep. An he figured out the land by lookin at the sky! Yep. Benjamin Banneker was smart! Eliot say, then we play I Spy. I don't do I Spy much no more, baby game, but wunst in a while. Make him happy. Then he's yawnin. I hear his sleep breathin, I stare at the stars, the same stars Benjamin Banneker used to lay out Worshinton D.C. way back, way back

I'm standin in the tower Roof an me made in the Architeck Club. It ain't that I'm small, it's that the tower got big, life-size, castle like Roof says. I'm way up at the top lookin out. An Carl's lookin out from one floor below me all smug, he don't notice I'm just above. It's like ancient times, green fields, but over yonder there's Eliot wavin at me from Colored Street, in my dream Colored Street's down there even in the meadows a Medieval an there in the middle a Colored Street cross from Eliot's this little church but Eliot's lookin the other way, his back's to the church. An I'm tryin to figure how to get Eliot up in the tower but he seem content fine on Colored, Eliot grinnin wavin holdin a white book with white raised letters on the cover: THE MAGNET CARTER, I see him from my castle cross Colored, an down on the groun direckly below the castle there's Roof, he wanna cross the moat to the castle but he can't swim, an I'm rackin my brain how to get Eliot in the castle how to get Roof in the castle when suddenly there's fire, the cross on the church grew huge an caught afire but Eliot don't see it, Eliot smilin up at me, then Carl from the floor below turn an glance up like he knew I was there all along, an speak: Badminton?

Nex mornin I look out my bedroom winda. Cloudin over. Carl up already. All that gray in the sky, he takin down the net fore it get wet. I do my chores quick—make my bed, pull the garden weeds—then pack marbles in my pocket. Or maybe backgammon again.

But outside I follow a ole instinct an turn leff steada right an fore I know it I'm standin fronta Roof's. I don't gotta knock on his door cuz he already lookin out at me from the second floor, his bedroom winda. From inside I hear a newborn baby hollerin.

Treasure hunt?

He stare at me a long time fore he answer.

Can't. Punishment.

Oh. How come?

I was swingin on my bedroom door an knocked it off the hinges.

Oh. Roll a thunder. If I run I can beat the big rain gettin to Carl's. Maybe we can bring Monopoly out on Carl's front porch, watch the downpourin. Carl started teachin me Monopoly but we had to quit fore the end. This time *I'm* banker.

Like Roof seen my mind wanderin to Carl's, he say Maybe treasure hunt tomorra? Somethin catch in his voice. His nose still got the scab from the fight.

Wanna play marbles? I can bring em up to you.

Roof's eyes get a startle. Much as I love his yard, most an genrally I ain't up for the obstacle course a his house, me an Roof always play outdoors or inside my house, never his. The raindrops start fallin big, hard.

Okay, he says just as it fass come to a crashin shower, an I rush in an step over Joellen's skate an Beaver's broken fire truck an some folded clean clothes an tossed-about dirty clothes as I scale the stairs up to the boys' room, Roof's an Beaver's on the left.

Here come the train! We see Daddy come off 5:30 a.m. train! Usually tired from work but today he smile big. Brung a man behind him. Tall man! Tall man!

This is my wife Claris. An this is Dwight. An this is Eliot. This is Mr. A. Philip Randolph.

Dwight's mouth fly open. He musta hearda Mr. A. Philip Randolph. Mr. A. Philip Randolph famous!

Where's Mr. A. Philip Randolph?

Worshin. Restin. He be down for supper. You wanna hop a little lighter, jumpin bean? She put extra sugar sauce on the bake chicken!

How long Mr. A. Philip Randolph stay with us?

Call him Mr. Randolph. Jus one night.

Aw!

How come he here?

Me an her look up. Dwight standin door a the kitchen.

There's a man in New York, Mr. Tompkins. Retired porter. Mr. Tompkins let the end-a-the-line porters sleep a few hours, his place, he don't charge much, then they get up, go back to work. When they awake, he tell em they got to unionize. Your daddy not sure at first, Daddy an me talk. Then Daddy helpin Mr. Tompkins, tellin the porters unionize. Mr. Tompkins preciate it, Mr. Tompkins ole an tired. Very brave a your daddy. He coulda got fired, almost did. Mr. Tompkins know Mr. Randolph an tell Mr. Randolph boutcher daddy. Your daddy meet Mr. Randolph, *big* union organizer, why your daddy all day taken him to meet the Humble porters. Right now Mr. Randolph got other work to be done, your daddy wanna be a part. He invite Mr. Randolph take his rest stop on his way to Worshinton here.

Dwight mutter mutter.

What's that?

Funny coincidence, he tell her. Mr. *Randolph's* name jus come up couple days back.

I can tell she don't like how he say *Randolph* so before she jump on him I jump in with my questions: Mama! What's unionize? What's organize?

But it ain't quick enough cuz in walk Daddy. When can I tell Mr. Randolph supper be ready?

Now, if *he* ready.

He's ready. Stop that jumpin boy, knock the plates off the shelves.

I stop. Daddy go get Mr. Randolph.

Set the table, she say.

Mama put the food on while Dwight put the plates an glasses on while I put the forks on. I can't put the plates an glasses on cuz she afraid I drop it break it on accident, but one time Dwight dropped one on accident!

Everything is delicious, Mr. Randolph say.

Thank you, Mama say. Supper is bake chicken an string beans an corn puddin. I love bake chicken! I love string beans! I love corn puddin!

You boys know who Mr. Randolph is? Daddy ask.

I look at Mama. She tole us but I didn't understand! Daddy come in, I didn't get to ask my questions!

He organized the Brotherhood of Sleeping Car Porters. My union!

You a porter, Mr. Randolph? I ask.

No, though my brother was for a spell. I organized the porters. I wanted the organization to be called the International Brotherhood of Sleeping Car Porters and Maids. The maids *are* represented, but I wanted the women represented in the title too. I got outvoted.

What's organize?

Bringin people together, Daddy say. For a union. Their rights.

What's a union?

Dwight sigh.

Stop playin with your corn puddin, she tell Dwight.

A union is an organization of workers, say Mr. Randolph, so they can fight collectively for their rights. Collectively. Together.

Before Mr. Randolph came along colored on the train paid half what the whites was, we expected to make up the rest in tips or starve. Had to arrive *five hours* before shiffs to prepare the train, an you don't get paid till the shiff starts. Porters made to double-out, work double shiffs, no rests! Sneakin sleep on a table, in the baggage car, I remember!

Set up straight, Dwight, she say.

Porters had to buy their own cleanin supplies! Shoeshine wax! Soap! Mr. Randolph hadn'ta come along, they still be callin me George!

George? But your name Lon, Daddy!

I know!

Hahahaha!

Hahahaha! my daddy grin, laugh right back at me!

That was before my time, say Mr. Randolph. White men started it. The Society for the Prevention of Calling Sleeping Car Porters George. Gag at first. Then no gag.

All the members named George! say Daddy.

Some prestigious members, say Mr. Randolph. Senator Walter F. George of Georgia.

Senator George a Georgia say No George! Hahahaha! Daddy smile at my joke.

England's King George the Fith!

Hahahaha!

George Herman Ruth Junior!

Hahahaha!

Also known as Babe Ruth!

I stop laughin, stare at Mr. Randolph, my mouth hang open. Dwight look up.

Daddy say, Time Mr. Randolph an the union done, we up to a hundred seventy-five dollars a month, work cut down to ten-hour days, six-day weeks!

A hunnert seventy-five dollars! I say.

Firs colored union to bargain with a major corporation! Daddy say. Firs colored union get a charter with the American Federation a Labor!

Semi-charter, say Mr. Randolph. Don't get me started on the crackers in labor.

Mr. Randolph, you think the New Deal been good to colored people?

Yes, ma'am, I do.

Mama, he said ma'am. She slap me under the table. It don't hurt.

Out of the New Deal came the National Labor Relations Board. The Wagner Act, outlawing those bogus unions created by the company, and providing for *autonomous* unions: labor bargaining with capital. All that helped Negroes. Still, we could go further. The National Negro Congress.

Of which you was president.

You know my biography well, ma'am. Yes, I was the first president.

Communists.

Everyone turn to Dwight.

They *are*!

I can tell Mama an Daddy both wanna smack him but they ain't closed enough.

Yes. Many of them were *white* Communists, and the white bothered me a lot more than the red. Don't get me wrong. I believe there are plenty of good white people in the world. I also believe Negroes can, and should, fight for themselves.

Ain't *you* a Communist?

Who told you that! she snap.

Carl's dad.

Daddy confused. New neighbors, she say, eyes rollin. White.

Ain't chu?

Let it alone, boy. My daddy's tone.

I'm a socialist, Dwight. I participate in the struggle for righteousness, for poor people in general and poor Negroes in particular. I am not a Communist, as I believe capitalism should not be abolished but rather reaped for the communal good of all, allocated fairly, no ostentatiously rich, no desperately poor. I am not a Communist because I believe in decision making more generally shared rather than the distribution of wealth coordinated by a small coterie of individuals at the top. Still, there is much overlap between communism and socialism, and at first I had no problem working with the Communists who essentially put together the Negro National Congress. However, I have often been confused by the efforts of Communists, most notably by white Communists. They supported the Scottsboro Boys, a very just and worthy cause, but then quickly abandoned their honorable militancy against fascism the moment the Soviet Union signed its Non-Aggression Pact with Germany. Of course they reversed that decision following the Nazi invasion of the USSR, but this fickle mentality of When-the-Soviets-say-jump-we-ask-how-high I find troubling, and frustrating, and most importantly extremely counterproductive toward our goals of justice for all.

Now Dwight's mouth hang open! All the questions I got to remember to ask! Who the Scottsboro Boys? What is fascism? What is counterproductive? How come Mr. Randolph say Dwight an he ain't said *my* name wunst!

Speaking of German aggression. Mr. Randolph turn to Mama an Daddy. You both know why I'm headed to Washington.

Yes, the march, but please tell us more, Mr. Randolph. Slicin her bake chicken.

The March on Washington for Jobs and Equal Participation in National Defense.

You know what kinda jobs out there, the war mobilization? Daddy sayin to her. Weldin? Rivetin? An they been keepin colored out!

We want those jobs for colored men and women. That's what the marchers will demand.

We in a war? I thought we wa'n't in a war.

Not yet son, Daddy say to me. But soon. Probly soon, an Daddy sigh.

Lon an I have discussed this, and we will certainly be there for the March on Worshinton, Mr. Randolph. *And* our children.

We goin to Worshinton? I say.

Three-hundred-dollar-a-month jobs! say Daddy.

Mama's mouth open. Three hundred dollar???

I'm meeting with the president Tuesday. The president does not want the march to take place. Up to him, but I'll need some guarantees for Negro jobs then. Executive order guarantees.

All four of us mouth wide open. *President Roosevelt!*

We goin to Worshinton? I say.

Mr. Randolph says depends on the president, Daddy say. We might.

I'm grinnin! I never been to Worshinton! I hardly been any place but Humble. Cep walk over the bridge to Mann's Addition, West Virginia. Cep Latchmore, Pennsylvania, where Aunt Beck live.

They got a plant right in Boddimore! Daddy say.

We've already chartered trains, buses. We're expecting a hundred thousand.

A hundred thousand! Mama an Daddy say.

If the president doesn't wise up. The committee at the top is all Negro, the March on Washington Movement. *All* black.

My friend Jeanine's Uncle Raymonlee say it's a white man's war.

Mr. Randolph look at me. Your friend's uncle is very wise, Eliot.

Eliot! He know my name!

And not the first Negro of that opinion. So much work to do at home, our *own* freedom, why should we be running across the ocean fighting for some European's? But I believe if we are resourceful we can use this war, since our national participation in it seems inevitable, we can use this war to stipulate our rights as Negroes. Mr. Randolph take a bite a chicken, all thoughtful. I am a pacifist. I maintain all conflicts can and should be resolved through negotiation. But if we *must* fight, if Negroes *must* serve in the military, then our recruits are owed the opportunity to show their mettle and be respected as combat soldiers.

We can fight good as them white boys!

That's right, son. Two seconds Dwight ack decent an Daddy smilin all over him.

We *can,* say Mr. Randolph to Dwight. At Tuskegee they're training Negro men to fly right now.

Negro pilots? Dwight's face all wonder.

Negro pilots! Still. It's a segregated military, that has *not* changed. Well, one thing at a time. For now, the march will focus on jobs. After twelve years of Depression if there is suddenly money in war manufacturing for American workers, we as Negro American workers are owed our share.

What's a pacifiss?

Peace, Eliot. I believe in peace. There are people who believe in war as the means and peace as the end, people who believe in guns for peacekeeping, but I believe in peace. Period.

Me too! I'm a pacifiss too, Mr. Randolph!

You *are?*

No war no war.

No war no war, my mama join in, smilin at me. Then she go on: Jus the war buildup. Jobs!

I trust in Mr. Gandhi. *Satyagraha.* Civil disobedience.

Henry David Thoreau went to jail for civil disobedience. You ever been to jail?

He ain't no jailbird! I swing at Dwight, but my fist miss.

I have, Dwight, but never for long. Sedition. For exercising my freedom of speech at a time of war, I was arrested in Cleveland, but I was quickly released thanks to the racism of the Cleveland judge. He didn't think Negroes were smart enough to think up all that complicated radicalism! Mr. Randolph almost fall out his chair laughin!

I wish you was my granddaddy, Mr. Randolph! You smart! Hahahaha!

I'm nobody's granddaddy, Eliot. I never had children.

You never had children!

No. But I have a wife Lucille that I love very very much.

Mr. Randolph. I heard tell you were once a great Shakespearean actor.

Mr. Randolph look surprised. You *do* know my biography, ma'am! He smile, bite a corn puddin. Well. Long time ago.

Actor? say Dwight, like hopeful.

Mr. Randolph turn to him. You like Shakespeare?

In bed in the dark I go You know what's in Worshinton? Monument! Capitol!

No kiddin. Dwight's back turned away.

We might see President Roosevelt. We surely see President Roosevelt, he live in Worshinton too! Maybe we see a Worshinton Black Senator! Daddy likes em. He likes Henry Spearman on third base, he says he's a good hitter. I am a Jew I am a Jew. Hahaha! You like Mr. Randolph's speech? That's nice he done that Shakespeare for us. Hahaha! What's a Jew?

Shut up an go to sleep!

Hunnert thousand in Worshinton! I try to whisper but it a loud whisper. Hunnert thousand a us! Hahahaha!

For a second I think Dwight gone on to sleep. Then he make a funny voice. Mr. Randolph, what's a union? Mr. Randolph, what's a pacifist? Mr. Randolph, you smart! I wish you was my granddaddy! Sycophant.

What you call me?

Look it up.

Mornin! I can't wait to go to Worshinton! Starin up at Mr. Randolph, lather all over his face, twirl his blade in the water.

Gonna happen, Mr. Randolph say to the mirror, unless President Roosevelt smartens up. We'll call the whole thing off if he just make an executive order, fair hiring. Mr. Randolph mow the razor up his neck, smooth, smooth.

I seen Worshinton crostin the Potomac. And Worshinton D.C. set right *on* the Potomac. Hahaha! Humble set on the Potomac too. Hahahaha!

Gonna happen unless the president gets wise. Then he smile down at me. I'm an organizer, Eliot. I help pull people together, get our rights so the capitalist boss doesn't slave em, so the government doesn't slave em. Slavery's over. Justice.

We put Mr. Randolph on the train to Worshinton an he wave an we wave, smilin! Then we walk home quiet, four of us quiet. I feel sad. I wish Mr. Randolph move into our guess room, live there every day.

The afternoon Dwight come in the livin room, I throw the dictionary at his head.

Ow!

I ain't no syncopant!

He walk out to the kitchen laughin to hisself.

Afternoon I go to my room get my wood robot. A hunnert thousand Negroes, I tell him. Robey can't hardly believe it! Mr. Randolph say Negroes should fight for ourself, Mr. Randolph say we get our rights! I walk Robey over the bed, over the dresser, by the wase-basket. In the wase-basket is jus one piece a paper balled up, paper from Dwight's sketchpad. Dwight don't never throw out his sketchpapers! Dwight drawr good, he don't never make mistakes!

It's him an Carl an Carl's family playin badminton. *Now* I see the mistake! Dwight drawr Carl's family white like he shoulda, then musta forgot an drawr hisself white too.

DWIGHT

You like Shakespeare?

I never read no Shakespeare, that don't happen till high school. But I nod, I don't know why. In the livin room Mr. Randolph says I am a Jew and winter a discontent an then he's Othello, a colored man, that one I really wanna understand but even though he give a quick summary a the story it's hard to figure outa context. Middle a the night everybody sleep, I get up to pee. I creep past the guestroom so I don't wake Mr. Randolph, his door cracked. Walkin back I see he ain't even in the bed. Tiptoe downstairs. He on the front porch, settin on the slidin seat. I go to the door. I try bein unnoticeable but he see me through the screen.

You couldn't sleep either, Dwight?

I look at him, cat got my tongue.

Sit with me.

We slide gentle.

Tell me what you know about the night sky.

There's the Big Dipper. An there's the Little Dipper, leads to the North Star.

You know the significance of the North Star?

Slaves followed it north.

Mm hm. First star you see in the night's a bright one: Venus. Gone now. But there's Mars. And Orion's Belt. Pleiades, the Seven Sisters. Do you know the story of Orion and the Pleiades sisters?

I shake my head.

Greek mythology claims Orion the Hunter caught a glimpse of the seven sisters and pursued them for seven years.

He catch em?

The god Zeus turned them into pigeons, then put them there in the sky. When Orion died, he was placed right behind, forever chasing them. Mr. Randolph breathes in air. I like summer nights in the country. No crickets in New York.

How you know about Pleiades? And Shakespeare? College?

I went to the Cookman Institute, an esteemed high school for Negroes in my home state of Florida. Latin, Greek, philosophy, forensics, French, science, music, literature.

What's forensics?

Debate. In my family's home we had few books, but good ones. Dickens, Keats, Austen, Charles Darwin, Frederick Douglass. I was my class valedictorian and still not so strong a student as my older brother James Junior. My father was an AME minister, he made sure we knew about the African Hanibal who fought the Romans, about Denmark Vesey, Toussaint L'Ouverture, Nat Turner. I read from Paul Laurence Dunbar, from home and school I had a first-rate education.

Whadju learn in college?

I never went to college.

Guess my mouth pop open cuz Mr. Randolph smile.

Wanted to. But not much opportunities for Negroes back then. So after high school I worked. Sold insurance a while. Worked in a grocery store. Drove a truck. Pushed a wheelbarrow full of fertilizer.

Why you not a actor no more?

Well. My parents were religious people. They didn't think it was proper.

A cricket all loud. Under the slidin chair?

And I think I had a different calling. I transferred my booming actor's voice to public speaking. When I was young, I'd soapbox in New York City, speaking about our oppression as Negroes, how the poor would rise up. The Irish police would want to harass me. When I'd see them coming out the corner of my eye, I'd make a quick detour in my speech. *See how the British imperialists have been treating the Irish!* And they'd turn right around, leave me alone!

Miss Onnie's wind chimes tingle.

I believe it was meant to be, my path in life. The greatest gift, pearl of wisdom my father gave to my brother and me: You must be concerned about things that are far more constructive and far more valuable to mankind and to all people than just making money.

Then Mr. Randolph turn to me.

You want to go to college?

I look at him. I look down.

Things are different now. Not the same barriers as in my day.

I shrug. I don't like school much. My parents. They wamme to go.

Uh-huh.

I don't like school much.

What do you like?

Flash fronta my face, quick his hand snatch it. Open his fist. Firefly strollin his palm his finger.

I seen this Looney Tunes at the pictures. All from a lightnin bug's point a view. Steada his light attached, he carried it, lantern. I laugh, tired. Mr. Randolph turnin his hand so the firefly keep walkin.

When I was growing up, some of the other boys would pull out the lights. You do that?

I shake my head. But shamed to say I seen Roof do it all the time, never stopped him.

Good, say Mr. Randolph. Something that sits on your hand so peaceful, doesn't bite, doesn't sting. Just brings beauty. Light. Why would anyone want to make violence against the light?

You think we're goin to war? For sure?

He gazin at the bug, small smile like he ain't heard me. Then: Yes.

You think Hitler likes *Merchant a Venice*?

He looks at me, then back at the bug. I don't know, son. And the light flies away. He set back. These mountains. You're lucky, having them with you all the time, part of you. Even in the night you feel their presence. Majestic.

Can I show you somethin?

I tiptoe an nobody wakes. Under the bed, pull it out. Eliot's eyelids flutter but he stay sleep. Back down to Mr. Randolph, show it to him. Mama ironin. Daddy on the train in his uniform. Eliot an his cat. Bugs Bunny an Barney Google, Orphan Annie an Roof an Carl, Miss Onnie an Eliot, Mr. D'Angelo in his store, the New York Black Yankees, Franklin, an Eleanor, an Benjamin Banneker, an self-portrait: me drawin. Sketches an sketches I show Mr. Randolph, I don't genrally show em to nobody. I ain't embarrassed. I jus don't think no one besides my family so interested. Mr. Randolph look through em, studyin each one, sayin nothin. When he's finished he hand em back to me.

Art school, he say.

Actin is an art, I say, but you give it up for public speakin. Higher callin.

I said *different* calling, not higher. Everyone finds their own way.

Kitchen light nex door.

Your neighbor's an early riser.

Miss Onnie. She's old.

Sometimes I visit the Metropolitan Museum in New York. I see Rembrandt and Leonardo and Manet and Renoir, the ancient Greeks and ancient Egyptians and even ancient sub-Saharans, miles and miles of jam-packed galleries. It's big—I haven't seen it all. Still. Several trips and us I haven't found yet. American Negroes. That's a big gap.

Now Miss Onnie open her side door an hundreds a cats rushin out. I look down an there's Parker on our porch, standin on his hine legs, beret on his head, palette an brush, paintin on his easel. Oh hi, Dwight, he say. Eliot up yet?

Dwight.

I snap awake!

Maybe you better go on up to bed.

I gather up my sketchins, draggin.

I sure do like your drawings.

Okay, I say, an pull myself up the steps. Mr. Randolph is gone two days fore I think back to that sleepy moment. Was he askin to keep a drawin?

I already done the sketch a me an Mr. Randolph on the middle a the night porch same day he left. He wrote down his address on the pad in the kitchen. I draw a copy a my drawin for my own keepin, then take out the money I got for cuttin ole Miss Priscilla and Miss Pauline's grass an buy a three-cent stamp. Send the original to him.

I get the hang a Carl's *Monopoly* over the nex couple weeks, clean him out one day leavin him scowlin. Come home, think I'll draw me dressed like the *Monopoly* money man, top hat an cane, when I see a postcard my side a the bed. I never get mail. On the front is this white palace. I wonder is it the White House or do the King a England live there? But flip it over, at the bottom left the printed letterin says THE METROPOLITAN MUSEUM OF ART [THE MET], NEW YORK CITY. On the right side is my name an address an a stamp. On the left-side top, neat and small: *Thank You!* A.P.R. An under it this crude pencil sketch of a lightnin bug smilin at me, carryin his own light.

ELIOT

Windy! Sunday school this mornin, wind almost blow me an Dwight away! Mama say it like March but today June the 22nd, outside chilly, inside chillier! Mama holdin me in her chair in the blanket. Dwight on the floor in the blanket, studyin the funnies. Color funnies!

I think Miss Onnie like me better now. I useta think she didn't like me.

She set in her ways, say Mama. I like Mama in her lazy moods.

I thought maybe she didn't like me cuz I'm colored.

Dwight look at me funny.

Why wouldn't she like you cuz you colored? Mama say.

Cuz don't some white people don't like—

Dwight rollin on the floor.

What!

Miss Onnie *is* colored, my mama say.

She look white!

Well she ain't.

Her eyes cole blue. When I was settin on the curve cryin—

Curb, say Dwight.

I think Miss Onnie a nice white lady! Save Parker's life after she seen me settin on the curve cryin—

Cur*b*!

She's not white. She jus got a lotta white in her.

Whatcha mean? I ask Mama that, in my head I see all these little white people walkin aroun inside Miss Onnie.

White people come before her. I bet some of her white male ancestors didn't come by invitation neither.

I can tell Dwight sigh a little, then go back to drawrin. I frown, gonna ask Mama what she mean again, but she rip it in the bud: An that's all you need to know on that subject.

The wind *Whoosh! Whoosh!* Dwight flip to The Yella Kid, got his sketch paper sketchin The Yella Kid. Why on't he bring *me* some a the funnies?

Miss Onnie same like The Yella Kid? Dwight find that funny too, *Shut up, Dwight!*

Don't say that, my mother say to me.

I wanna read Annie!

When I'm done.

He gonna take all day drawrin!

He only had the funnies a little while, he ain't gonna take all day drawin. Right?

Right, Dwight say, an don't even look up at her! He ain't respeckful!

Well look like he *is*! I'm jus tryin to rip it in the bud!

Nip, an Dwight laugh like the funniest thing ever, like *he* the smart one. On my report card Miss McAfee wrote It has been a delight to have had such a fast learner in my classroom, nobody wrote that for *him*! I start to say somethin else but Mama rip it in the bud: You gonna get your turn, an she snuggle me warmer.

Tray's The Yella Kid! Hahahaha!

Don't talk like that boutcher cousin, stop callin people yella. She quiet a while. Then she say, Don't say nothin. But I heard when Miss Onnie was young she was pretty, an light enough to pass. She got the offers for dates an even offers for marriage from the white men, but all she refused. Coulda past on over to white never look back, but liked her own people too much.

I never hearda *pass* before excep like I pass firs grade, but I think I got it from the contest. *Whoosh!* the wind comin through the cracks under the doors. Mama hole me tighter. Dwight, you need another blanket?

Nah.

When she did marry her husband, he a real dark man. I heard wunst they was visitin Boddimore on a trip, he jus enlisted in the army an wearin his uniform, an walkin down the street some white men surround em. They didn't think colored should be soldiers anyway, an him there with a white woman. Threatenin to lynch him.

Now Dwight look up.

They grabbed him an her screamin *I'm colored!* Lucky she got a colored voice, it spared her husband. I heard they never went back to Boddimore.

What war Miss Onnie's husbin a soldier in, Mama?

I don't know, she say, holdin me warm. One of em.

We gonna have a war?

Hm. Might be.

Daddy gotta go to the war?

No, your daddy too ole, she answer Dwight. Too young for the other war, too ole for this one.

Too young for the other war, too ole for this one, my daddy jus right! Hahaha! When I get to read Annie, Dwight?

Wonder how Daddy Warbucks got all rich? Dwight ask me, I know he bein smart. *War*. Bucks.

Your daddy thirteen, too young but his brother gone. Uncle Leeroy in Harlem then, parta the Harlem Hellfighters dontchu say that word. The Three Sixty-ninth. Good soldiers, earned the medals. *An* good musicians, Uncle Leeroy play the clarinet, the Hellfighters had a jazz band. The French dancin, happy, French didn't know nothin bout jazz. Till then!

Mama, what's lynch?

She look at me. Dwight don't look up but he stop sketchin, he was shadin but I hear him stop. Time tick-tick I think she ain't gonna answer. I hope she tell me, Miss McAfee say you learn a vocabulary word by usin it in a sentence.

Killin colored people. When white people kill colored people, they don't need a reason. Kill em jus cuz they colored.

Firs I wanna laugh, I think she kiddin. Then I see she not. I stare at her. I turn to Dwight, he don't look up but he don't drawr, his face all serious. Then I'm cryin, cryin, I can't stop, I don't know why I'm cryin! I don't understand what she say but I feel sad! Sad! Mama hole me. Dwight get up an leave. I don't know why Dwight get up an leave but I don't think it's meanness.

Mama gotta go make supper. Dwight leff the funnies behine, mine! I see the funnies, but in my magination I see me in the mansion, me an Annie an Daddy Warbucks but Annie's colored. Her hair already look colored, hahaha! An Daddy Warbucks colored, then in come the soldiers, the Three Sixty-ninth, nobody shootin, jus marchin an playin the jazz toot-toot. Then they salute me, an I salute em back! Then I'm singin! I'm the boogie woogie bugle boy a Company B!

DWIGHT

Carl gone off to camp three weeks which he says he does every July. Firs day he's gone I wanna go to Roof's but I feel funny cuz prolly been a week since I seen him. I had it in my mind to split my time even, Carl an Roof, but it seem more n more I jus started headin toward Carl's every day by habit. I figure if I set out my front porch on the slidin chair Roof come by eventually, either walk by ignorin me mad, or come up say hi, either way I'll know what's what. Nex door Eliot playin with Parker, Miss Onnie come to her door talkin to him, I sketch it. Wavy lines for Miss Onnie's gray hair, gettin loose from her bun an fallin like a white woman's.

Guess Carl ain't aroun for you to play with.

I look up.

He gone to camp.

We stare.

So I ain't good enough play with even when Carl ain't here?

I look down at my pad. I jus wanted to get some drawin in, I say. In the lower right I jot my name even though I ain't finished yet even though most an genrally I forget signin off anyways. It don't look so neat so I erase, write it over. *That* don't look so neat so I erase, write it over.

You don't play with me if Carl's here, you don't even come over say let's three play together.

You don't like him!

Roof look down at Carl's house without thinkin, scowl at Carl's house. What I don't say is also Carl don't like Roof, which is the real reason I don't suggest threesomes. An Carl all tricky, he jus might act all for it, then we three get together an don't know what happen. Thirdly, I got my Carl life, I got my Roof life, think they work better apart. I don't play badminton with Roof, but I ain't never taken Carl to Messengill's neither, which for truth me an Roof still ain't made it to this summer.

Messengill's?

Like Roof got so loss in how much he hate Carl, eyes glued in Carl's house's direction he forgot about me till I ask that question. His eyes snap back.

Now it *is* a treasure hunt to actually find anything, it all been pretty much cleared out. What's leff mostly is rubble filled with the remnants a some recent teenage rendezvous: beer bottles, cigarette packs. A box a matches with a few left inside. We go for the fireplace like Roof wanted, but the couple loose bricks don't lead to much. We separate, scurryin through the trash. I find some mug, look like it was stole from a bar. A little Cracker Jacks magnifiyin glass, that I definitely hold onto. Four pennies.

A crash an Roof screamin. I run to the nex room.

Hole in the rotten floor, he gone right through to the basement. I didn't know Messengill's had a basement.

Roof!

Nothin.

Roof!

Oh God. Oh God, Roof's dead. Or knocked out God. I gotta get somebody. I gotta run home get his mother, get my mother oh God.

Roof! My tears.

Snickerin. I peer into the darkness.

Roof! He laughin out loud. Idiot! I'm kickin crap into the hole, on his dumb head I hope.

Okay, stop! I see his han aroun the hole, then he pull hisself up, head an shoulders visible. I did fall through, but it ain't deep. Just a shallow drop, five feet. Tryin to lift his foot up. I think a offerin my assistance, then don't.

Then the rotten floor aroun the hole give way again an he fall back down. Now *I'm* laughin.

Dammit!

Here, gimme your han.

Wait. Wait a minute. Hey pass me down that matchbox.

How come?

Jus do it!

I hand it to him. I hear the snap, then: glow.

Holy smokes!

What!

Holy smokes!

I jump down through.

What Roof lit was a ole rusty lantern, still workable, thrillin enough. But what it lit up. Mural. Oil paintin completely coverin a wall. *The Vitruvian*

Man nex to God reachin out to Adam from the Sisteen nex to *David*. Like exact replicas, though course *David* was sculpture. Replicas except these all dark-complected. Brown-skinned.

Geeminee, that's a lotta ding-dongs! Roof crackin up.

How'd he get down here? I ask.

Who?

Who ya think. Painter. Then we fine the real entrance, little square door lead up to the ole kitchen. Take some effort to push it open but we manage, all our strength together. Now see the problem: the artist done hid the doorway, covered with bricks, moss. We climb out.

Wait, says Roof.

What?

Gettin that lantern.

Leave it.

You lost it? That's the best treasure this place ever coughed up!

And what about when he comes back?

Who?

I give him a look.

Dang, al*right!*

An don't come back later by yourself to get it.

You're not my boss.

Don't.

You're not my boss.

Midday so me an Roof go home to eat. Mama left out boiled egg slices for a sanwich. I remember when I was little we never had nothin called lunch, if I happen to say I'm hungry between breakfass an supper Mama try to fine me somethin, nothin formal. Then school lunch start the habit, she try. Roof I know for sure jus goin home to scavenge, an he might or might not come up with somethin. All them Bartons is beanpole skinny.

You're puttin your filthy hands on that bread? Go worsh yourself, boy!

I worsh up in the bathroom, lookin out at the high summer sun. After dinner be hours fore I got to be back, supper.

Over the crick bridge, through downtown, along the railroad tracks, up the hill. Hour hike to the outskirts. I thinka when Richard miss the school bus, havin to walk them four miles.

By the time I get there the clouds rollin in, wind pickin up. I ain't never been to Richard's place before but I know the way—Follow Ole Mill Road till it stops: woods.

There's a wood house and there's a little wood house. Couple little girls jumpin rope in the dirt, no grass. They stop, look at me. Richard was first, then five sisters after.

Richard aroun?

One of em speak, look about eight. Think that one's Jojo, Josephine. He in his studio.

Studio?

She point to the little house. I walk over. Tap tap.

Richard swing it open, mad face. I guess that was for his little sisters disturbin him cuz when he sees it's me he break a smile. Hey Dwight.

Hey Richard.

Whatchu doin over here?

Jus walkin.

Oh.

His little sisters starin.

You wanna throw a baseball?

Your sister said you got a studio?

Oh yeah. Come on in.

It ain't huge but bigger n it appear from outside. Pictures everywhere. I start takin it all in, slow, an Richard go back to paintin, let me experience his gallery. A few pencils but mostly oils, still lifes an landscapes an people, his sisters, that must be his mama, his daddy. Apple on a table, a boy's big left han foreground clutchin the apple, the boy's face peekin over the table but mostly hid behind the apple so all we see's right eye, right ear, temple, hair.

Self-portrait?

Uh-huh. Little smile on Richard, seemin to enjoy my tour. From his easel he can see out the winda at his sisters. What he's workin on's two girls skippin rope.

Where you get oils?

We got relatives in Pittsburgh. Near em this ole lady, live by herself. Miss Tootie. She own a general store for years, save up all her life, now all she do is paint. Her mother was a little girl slave, her granmother remember slavery well. Miss Tootie got flowers in her paintins, slaves in her paintins, she see I got the knack, whenever we visit, she gimme the oil paint, brushes.

How you rate a studio?

This my granmother's house, she use to keep chickens. The Depression come an she didn't no more, then she died. Nothin in the coop but cobwebs for years, I asked my mama could I. She said long as my chores done first.

I look at his sisters outside. I look at the easel. Not at all naturalistic, but better. Still early on but already I see he captured their essence: joy.

You like it?

I ain't one to oblige anybody fishin for a compliment. These paintins is *good,* he *got*ta know it. So I'm all set to shrug, They okay, but when I turn see his face I catch the tension, like my opinion mean a lot an he ain't exactly sure what it be.

Yeah, I say. I like em.

I see the relief.

None of em look like what I seen at Messengill's.

His mouth pop open a minute. Then he close it, smile. How you know?

Who else aroun here good at art? Who else gonna make David colored?

He crack up.

How come?

He shrug. Good to copy ole masters, ya learn somethin. They'll tell ya that in seventh grade art.

I mean, how come you paint it there when you got yourself a whole studio here?

He stop smilin. Some things I don't think my mama want me to paint.

Oh. His sisters outside: Miss Mary Mack Mack Mack. The wind whippin.

I seen these, art book in school. How you remember the details?

He look at me. Then he loosen a couple floorboards, pull out a big ole art book.

Stole it?

No!

Why you hidin it?

Miss Tootie give it to me. He shrugs. Didn't know if my mama'd understand it all. Hans it to me. It's heavy, so I set on the floor with it on my cross legs, lookin at every page.

I stop at a bunch a people dressed like Shakespeare times. Action: talkin, plannin. There's darkness at the ceilin, an a lotta dark on the people, though a little light captures their faces. Only woman in the paintin is lit ridiculous bright, gazin at a man dressed in gold.

Rembrandt, says Richard. *The Night Watch.*

I turn. *Mona Lisa* an *Starry Night* an Degas' an Matisse's dancers. Nex chapter I stop in my tracks. All them people! An rifles, an determination. In the middle a lady stands strong, her own rifle, serious face, her two black eyebrows seem like one long one. *Ballad of the Revolution* by Diego Rivera. Take me a while fore I can pull my eyes away for nex section: sculpture. *Venus de Milo. The Thinker.*

David.

Details: curl a his hair, curve a his brow, sharpness a the nose. Smooth chin, an the right hand at firs seemin graceful an lazy but no. Somethin deliberate. The right fingers gentle indent the thigh. The lines a the torso. An somethin. Somethin below the torso.

You sure been lookin at *David* long, says Richard. I jump, didn't know he come right nex to me. Little smile his face. You know David had a friend? Jonathan? From under his bed, Richard pull out another of his own paintins. Two brown men in loincloths lookin at each other, somethin sly, somethin tender. On the top's one caption: 2 Samuel 1:26, on the bottom's another: 1 Samuel 20:30.

Now Richard back to David, Richard's fingers delicate grazin David's private parts. How Michelangelo make us see how beautiful it all is unrobed? I can't take my eyes off Richard's fingers caressin the page an I think I oughta move my leff knee away from Richard but it don't move, my knee stay right there warm against his knee his face so close I feel his breath also warm *very warm*

Richard, I needja ta—

His mother at the door! Richard's face snap up mouth pop wide, eyes wide, stare at her. And then her eyes lower: the book. Richard slam it shut.

What's that?

Art.

Open it.

Art book, Mama—

Open it.

He open it to Gauguin, *Still Life with Apples, a Pear, and a Ceramic Portrait Jug.*

That ain't whatchu had before.

Mama—

Show me whatchu had before.

Richard slow open it to *David*. She look at it, her eyes twitchin. Then she turn pages. As it happens, pretty much every entry in the vicinity a *David* be a nude. The little girls musta gone in the house, wind harsh, day sky turn dark.

Her face whip up lookin at me, like finally noticin I'm here.

Who *you*?

Dwight. I live—

You give this to him?

No! I look at Richard, Richard look at the floor. No!

You a Campbell?

I nod.

Yeah, I see your daddy's eyes. Maybe I oughta tell your mama. Up here with my son lookin at this nasty book. An she take a swing with that heavy book, whack Richard's shoulder. Nasty! Why you wanna look at this? Smack him upside his head, *Boy!* She tear out a page. Nasty! Throw open the winda, hurl out the page into the wind. Nasty! Tear out another, let it soar. Nasty! Nasty boy! Then she notice Richard's paintin with the loincloth men.

I fly outa there, the trees all a blur. Look back only wunst, I see crumbled pages a art flyin through the air, then half a Richard's paintin, Jonathan torn away from David.

The rain start hard, soaked long before I get home. Set on my porch a minute, catchin my breath. I ain't ready yet to go inside. Then I am, up to the bathroom, dry my hands, my hair. I bring the Bible out to the porch. David son a Jesse speakin to Jonathan son a Saul.

I am distressed for thee, my brother Jonathan: very pleasant hast thou been unto me: thy love to me was wonderful, passing the love of women. (2 Samuel 1:26)

Then Saul's anger was kindled against Jonathan, and he said unto him, Thou son of the perverse rebellious woman, do not I know that thou hast chosen the son of Jesse to thine own con-

fusion, and unto the confusion of thy mother's nakedness? (1
Samuel 20:30)

Along come Roof.

I got a idea. That was *you*. Painted that wall. Messengill's. An actin like you ain't never seen it before.

I stare at him.

Them paintins was colored people! Who else colored can draw that good?

Roof stand starin at me in the downpourin sheets like he don't even notice the wet.

But I don't take credit I ain't earned. I look down at the Bible an close it.

Wa'n't me, I say. Oils ain't my medium.

You wanna school a dog, you need a bone.

Then Uncle Ramonlee demonstrate. Hole out that chicken bone, beagle puppy run for it, *No!* Set! Fetch! Roll over! Shake my han! Play dead! Puppy do good, she get the bone! She don't do good, no bone. She learn quick! Me and Jeanine clappin! Uncle Ramonlee pet that puppy, her tail wag fass. Uncle Ramonlee pick her up, that puppy lick his face!

I like your puppy, Uncle Ramonlee! He ain't my uncle, he ain't even twenty yet but I don't know what else to call him cep what Jeanine call him. He on't care.

Uncle Ramonlee got her from out on the farms, say Jeanine. Her mama had a litter: nine babies!

What's the puppy's name, Uncle Ramonlee?

Althea, say Jeanine, like Althea Gibson. You know her?

Uh-uh.

She colored an won the tennis! Jeanine tell me.

Althea love you, Uncle Ramonlee!

He ain't lookin at me, but he smile. Well. You can train em with a kick or you can train em with a kiss. Now he laughin, Althea's tongue ticklin his nose!

Walkin back to Mixed Street, I fine a nickel!

Ding ding!

Well, what can I do for you, Eliot?

(I see the penny anny candy. I like some penny anny candy! But not today, not today.)

Mr. D'Angelo, what kinda fish I buy with a nickel?

Right fore I pay for my fish he answer the phone. Dangelo's? He always do that, Dangelo's when everbody else say *Dee* Angelo's!

July sun hot! Ps ps ps ps. Parker. Ps ps ps ps.

There he come through the bushes! My eyes crost, two Parkers! Hahaha!

You wanna school a cat, you need a fish.

Set, Parker. Set. No, like this. I push his behine down. Set. Set! Good, Parker! have some fish. You gotta pet em too, let em know they done good.

Shake! Shake my han, Parker. Come on, liff your paw. Liff your paw! *Good*, Parker.

You gotta have patience. You gotta love the cat. You can't train no cat outa meanness.

Okay, roll over. Rooooooooooll over. See what I done to ya? Now you try it by yourself. Roll over. Parker. Rooooooooooll over. Here, I'll help ya again. Rooooooooooll hahahaha! Parker roll over right on toppa me! Ya gotta love the cat!

On Colored Street Uncle Ramonlee outside on Jeanine's back door stoop readin the paper, Althea in his lap. Althea see me, she come greetin, *Yap yap!*

Uncle Ramonlee, I keep tryin to train Parker but he won't mine!

A long while, then Uncle Ramonlee lower his paper, like he jus heard me, Althea: *Yap yap!* I wait for Uncle Ramonlee say somethin, his eyes on me but I think he already thinkin bout somethin else.

I said I'm trainin Parker my cat with kisses not kicks, but he don't do nothin! He won't roll over! He won't shake my han! He play dead, but he do that all the time anyway even if I don't tell him to!

Cuz he a cat.

Huh?

He's a *cat,* he don't follow orders. Dogs follow orders, an he lift up his paper to read again.

AMERICAN TROOPS GARRISON ICELAND
US MARINES REPLACE BRITS AND CANADIANS

Thought we weren't in no war.

Huh?

I point at them headlines.

It's defensive. Defendin Iceland. We still neutral. Then he look back in the paper again, say low: For now.

Oh. Now Uncle Ramonlee readin the paper, but not. I never seen Uncle Ramonlee look sad before, I cheer him up.

Uncle Ramonlee, you save Althea so she don't get drownd!

It take a second, then he hear me.

Huh?

You saved Althea!

He stare like I'm Mars.

Weren't they gonna drownd that puppy litter like you almost drownd Parker's kitty litter?

I didn't drown no kittens!

Now we starin at each other. I say nothin else, scared! say nothin else.

Then he soff. Well. Guess I thought about it, world don't need no more stray cats. Changed my mine. What right *I* got? Decide they die.

Hi Eliot! Jeanine at her back door.

Hi Jeanine!

Uncle Ramonlee, can me an Eliot play with Althea?

He let us play with Althea! Rollin an runnin, *yap yap!* Then Uncle Ramonlee yell time for her to eat. He feed her, pet her, but still his face like no feelin. Then he pick her up, she lick his face. Althea love Uncle Ramonlee! Parker love me! I love Parker! even if he don't mine. Well, I might try train him again, but if he don't wanna, that's okay. What right *I* got?

Then Uncle Ramonlee lay the paper on the groun and set Althea right on **AMERICAN TROOPS GARRISON ICELAND**. Uh-oh, whisper Jeanine to me, potty trainin, Althea gotta do her business. An Uncle Ramonlee set back down on the stoop, light a cigarette, lookin toward the mountains but I can tell he seein farther, farther.

DWIGHT

The Dusk Club meets every evenin jus fore sunset. The Architeck Club tower was dismantled an rebuilt an now the dusk ritual is for each of us to find one thing to add to the new tower. Tonight Roof puts in some raggedy black shoe, I uncover a milk bottle not even cracked. This is our third Dusk Club meetin three consecutive nights, makin it one of our longest runnin organizations. After incorporatin the items we stand, close-eyed, reapin the power a the tower when we hear Who's funeral?

Daddy! Roof run up to Mr. John. I don't see him that often cuz most an genrally he get home from work after I gotta go home, which is now, dark.

Hold on, say Mr. John before Roof touch him, lemme clean up.

Mr. John filthy, the blackness all over. He work the Marion coal mines, ten miles west. Twist on the outside spigot, pick up the hose an worshin hisself down. How you, Dwight?

Fine.

Lemme do it, Daddy!

I gotta go home, Roof. Walkin out I see Roof grabbin the hose, sprayin his dad, grinnin.

My whole family out on the front porch. Mama an Daddy slidin on the slidin chair, Eliot on Daddy's lap, all of em laughin at somethin.

Dwight! Come on, we goin for ice cream! He bouncin on Daddy's lap.

Your daddy's lass day, figure we walk down to the cone stand. Send him off.

Come on, Dwight, waitin for you! Eliot's excitement makin the slidin chair go bumpy. Usually that get on their nerves but tonight everybody smilin.

Eliot say chocolate, Mama an Daddy strawberry. I say vanilla, then Daddy say You a big boy now. You want somethin a little more substantial?

I look at em. I ain't never had nothin but a cone before.

For *tonight*, she say, clarifyin extravagance ain't gonna become no habit.

Hot fudge sundae?

We gotta wait a little cuz the picnic table already got the Wiley twins, Marco an Mokie an their parents. They wave. We wave back. Take your time, Daddy tell em, though with ice cream meltin ain't like we can hold on forever. They nod gratitude but I can see their mama sayin Come on every time Mokie or Marco take a breath between licks.

We can set there, say Eliot. There's five other picnic tables, two of em all empty.

That's for the white people, say Mama.

The white people's on the other three, say Eliot. Can't we use one a them two they ain't usin no way? None of us say nothin.

When Marco an Mokie's family gone an we seated, Daddy say, I might not be comin home often as I was from the trains.

Why? say Eliot. The fudge on my white ice cream make me thinka snow-cap mountains. Rockies, I seen pictures in a book. Green grass summer down below an snow way up in the sky. We got mountains all aroun Humble but Appa-layshuns ain't high enough, if they snow-cap it only cuz it's winter.

Depend on when I can get a ride home from Boddamore, Daddy tell Eliot. The train stop right in Humble, I could get on get off. Don't work that way, new job. *Defense* job.

How come Uncle Brice can't bring you back? say Eliot.

I'm *stay*in with Uncle Brice but he ain't got a car. Ridin down with Charlie Harmon but don't know when Charlie comin back. We start the same firs day but might not have off the same days. An the gas rations, Charlie ain't so much to spare no way. But my off days. When I get the two in a row wunst a month, I'll find somebody, gimme a ride.

Wunst a *month?* We only see you twelve times a year?

You good with your arithmetic, Daddy say an kiss Eliot.

You can't ride the train home no more?

Train comes from D.C., it don't go through Boddimore, say Mama.

Then why you gotta do the new job?

More money, Daddy tell him.

So?

We need it Eliot, she say. In the valley a the snow-cap mountain a my sundae runs a river, blacknwhite stripe. When I push on the mountain more runoff, the river risin.

I'll call every week.

How come you can't call every day?

Expensive, she tell him.

Thought you makin more money?

Can't throw it all away, long-distance. He say it soff, patient.

Why not?

Eliot, she say.

The cherry roll down the mountain slow, slow. I push it back up, it roll down again. I'm Sisyphus, push it up, down it roll.

You alright, son?

Startled! My father's han touchin my arm. Everyone starin at me.

Yeah, I say. I see I ain't tasted nothin in a while so I take a spoonful. Uh-huh, I say. Three white tables open now, I notice Eliot's friend Jeanine in line lookin at us, standin with her mother an uncle an I know we ain't got much longer to be settin here. They'll say Take your time an like the Wileys, polite we won't.

Daddy gone two an a half weeks. Every day Eliot: When he comin home? When he comin home?

I finish my chores, go knockin on Roof's, bring a baseball to toss. He come to the door. Looky what I found.

We set on his front porch steps. It's a ole photo, these little boy miners, white boys lookin black, raccoon eyes. He points to a little little guy, second to the right.

My daddy. He was eight when he started in the mines.

Wheredja find it?

Their top drawer. The new baby starts screamin its head off. I forget if it's a he or a she.

Think I wanna go out to Marion today.

Okay, I say. Then we look up. Lucy Deucy out on the dang porch roof!

I bring the ball back home. There's a letter my side a the bed. Mr. Randolph lass month, now this: I ain't never had so much mail!

Dear Dwight,
  Last night we had a big campfire and marshmallows. I like swimming and tetherball but I could live without archery. The guys in my cabin are okay but my counselor's a prick. I had five pancakes for breakfast. Don't even try to write me back because it takes days, I'll be home before I ever get it. When I get back we'll

take down the badminton net and set up the volleyball, which is more heavy duty. My parents said they'd get me volleyball if I went to camp without complaints this year so I earned it. When I first get back I have to go out to dinner with them, so we'll have to wait for volleyball till my second day. In volleyball you have to win by two.

Your friend,

Carl

Roof an me set on the side a Turtle Gap Road, him barefoot like always for summer. The charity shoes his family gets free for school he say hurts his toes.

I'm gonna be one of em.

Who?

The boys. Daddy's picture.

What're you talkin about?

Mines. Daddy said I can do it when I'm thirteen.

No you can't.

Says who?

Laws against it.

My daddy was in the mines when he was eight.

That was before. Kids can't do it no more. Child labor, we read about it at school.

A car comin our direction. We stand, stick our thumbs out. It pass us by. We set.

Still happens.

What?

Kids! The mines!

Then they're against the law.

Then I guess they are.

Big bird flyin overhead, we look. My daddy taught me how to reckonize big preyin birds. They don't flap. They soar.

How about you an that stupid lemonade stand?

That's different.

How's it different?

It ain't a real job! It's somethin kids do. Like you don't know. It ain't dangerous, it ain't legally labor.

Labor schnabor.

A car full of a white family goin by the other direction. We stand, stick our thumbs out. They peer at us, judgment, before the car disappear. Like we skippin school or somethin. In the summer! Or maybe white an colored ain't sposed to be playin together. Or maybe they ain't never seen no hitch-hikers before. Maybe I shoulda asked em that. Hey! ain'tchu never seen no hitchhikers before?

My daddy said I can. When I'm thirteen.

Whatta ya wanna do *that* for?

Money! He pick up a stone, hurl it way out over the fields crost the road. Daddy ain't forcin. He say it up to me, whatever I wanna do. Like I'm really gonna say, You know Daddy think I'd rather stay in school, I do so well there. He hurls another stone. Whatta yaw do in *your* school?

Whatta ya think. Same thing ya do in your school.

Why, you *been* to my school? Car. We stand. The man hit the accelerator goin past, like he afraid we might jump in while his car's in motion or some-thin. We set.

English, history, math, science, gym. Sound familiar?

But don't you all read colored books?

What?

Books colored people writ!

I don't know!

I just imagined they be easier. Like I'd prolly get A's at your school. Unless they in some colored language white people don't understand.

My glarin eyes turn to him slow.

Guess you be in classes with Carl come the fall.

Now he turn to me.

Like you ain't had enough troubles! Carl's smart, the teachers wonderin why he get a hundred same test you barely scratch a D!

The white school's *big*, okay? Prolly not even see *Carl*. I *wish* I went to a teeny tiny little school like yours. What kinda competition, just a coupla coloreds.

Got a letter from him today.

Who?

Carl! He said he's havin a good time at camp. He said him an me'll set up for volleyball in his yard when he gets back. Your friend, Carl.

Volleyball's a girl's game.

Not really. He says they have these *huge* breakfasts. Camp. He goes there every summer. It's in Pennsylvania. All he had to do was not complain about camp an his parents buy him volleyball! Not that there's anything to complain about camp far as *I* see cuz—

Roof make this big ole grunt, stands an kicks dirt way high up in the air. A pickup comin. I stand. It stop, some white farmer lady drivin, overalls. She give us the nod an we hop in back. Rare we get in the mind to go to Marion but whenever we do ain't never not got a ride yet. Facin each other mad in the truck bed, we don't say nothin the longest time. Then I see his mouth fall open. I turn aroun. The county fair! In for the week. We can't see much but the tents, the Ferris wheel! We'll beg our mothers an still prolly not get the money to go, so this close as we ever gonna come.

By the time we get to Marion we're speakin again. We slap on the rear winda a the cab just before the edge a town. The driver drop us off, we wave our thanks an she drive on. Walk about a mile. Gradually we start seein the tracks for the boxcars filled with coal. Built into a hillside's the square entrance, WOODBURY MINE. Even though we waited till afternoon to come out, we still a good two hours early, so explore the woods a while. When we see the sun gettin lower we try findin our way back, then panic, neither a us sayin but both thinkin we lost an nobody we know know where we are to come look for us. Then we hear a coal car in the distance an follow the sound.

There they come. The colored and the white men all blackface, some minstrel show but the performers lookin all exhaustion.

You got a smoke?

We turn aroun. He don't look more n ten, smaller n us.

No, not today, say Roof.

The white boy jus stare, like it take him a while to understand. Then he walk away. Roof's eyes stuck on him.

See?

You don't smoke.

I'm talkin bout his age!

Only one. It ain't like in your daddy's day.

Never said it *was* like in my daddy's day. All I said was if I want I can go in thirteen, no one stoppin me.

Crash of a coal car gainst another one.

Out he come. Mr. John's body look bent, crooked, his face all pain, Mr. John a daddy already look like a great-granddaddy. But when Roof call he pipe up seein us, break into a grin. Seven men an a boy give Mr. John a nickel each an hop into the bed a the pickup, he ridin em back to town.

We in the cab, up high lookin down, Roof nex to his daddy, I get the winda. The truck dirty but it ain't quite got the clutter a Roof's yard. Roof goin on about the farmer lady driver an ridin her truck bed, makin it all some big holy adventure. When we get to the fair Roof fall quiet, not wantin to miss it while we pass. Then Mr. John slow down, stop. Get out an talk with the passengers behind. Me an Roof look at each other, say nothin, hopin. Then five men an the boy gets out, walkin the lass two miles in. Mr. John back in behine the wheel, hand us a dime apiece.

The two what's leff don't mind waitin for yaw to get a Ferris wheel an a cotton candy. Come right back. To Roof: Don't tell your mama. Then Mr. John have a big coughin fit.

You comin, Daddy? Roof so excited, tryin not to hop in his seat.

Look at me. Mr. John raise his hans to show all the black, more coal shakin from him onto the car seat. He light a cigarette an we scramble out.

We happy arguin the pros n cons a cotton candy firs to take on the ride with us or Ferris wheel firs to eat cotton candy in the truck drive back. Option Two win out.

Humble an environs is mostly white, but it don't take but a minute inside fore I realize this fair seem to be *all* white. Still, I walk straight on through the admission gate, nobody look at me sideways so I guess colored is allowed in. Standin in the Ferris wheel line I wonder I get to the front the man say No colored! My leg shakin a little. But the man runnin the ride don't gimme no bad looks, no crabbier than he is with everybody else. Slam me an Roof in. An it goin. From the groun Ferris wheel don't seem so fass, from the groun Ferris wheel don't seem so high! At firs I pray it be over quick. Then somethin change. High in the sky, lookin down at all those people. For a second I'm in my dream again, top a that castle cross from Colored Street, but this is different. These is all white people I'm high above of. These is the people gets in the places say WHITE ONLY, the places if there be another sign say COLORED you know it gonna be poor quality if the COLORED sign exist at all, well suddenly all those WHITE ONLY white people below my feet lookin small real small.

My cotton candy's blue, Roof's is purple, an we eat it slow the truck ride back, savorin till we gettin out fronta Roof's house.

Hose me down boy, his daddy say, then have another coughin fit. I say bye an walk toward my execution, since dark happened more n a half-hour ago.

Where the hell you been, boy! Missed supper, an you know you sposed to be in by dark! Before I can think what to say, An you *better* not tell me you an Roof hitchhiked to Marion again!

Okay, I won't tell you.

She hole me smack my behind, this time it *do* hurt. Then jus screamin, How many times I gotta tell you! An your daddy called an you missed him, now you got him worried too! Don't think you leavin this house tomarra! Not tomarra, not the nex day, not the nex! An the tears roll down her cheeks like *she* the one got smacked!

In bed turned away from Eliot wipe my face.

Dwight. Wamme getchu a chicken leg?

When I was little an Eliot a baby, Daddy use to talk about Jack an the Beanstalk, punished so he sent to bed without supper. My parents never refuse us food if they got it. But after a whippin who in the mood to eat? Even if I'm starved I say it: I ain't hungry.

Dwight! Telephone!

Drag down the steps.

Hello?

Hi Dad.

I know.

I know.

I know.

I won't.

Okay. Bye.

That all you have to say to your daddy?

I don't even answer, hoppin up the steps fass fore she hear my belly rumblin. He called at one week he called at two weeks, this only halfway into the third week so she musta instigated today's calls after I come home late. He wanna talk so bad he can come home do it in person.

Three days stuck inside. One afternoon I look out my winda, see Mr. Talley pushin the lawn mower round his yard, Christina pullin weeds. He's a teacher so like kids he got summers off. After a while he come over help her with the weedin. Talkin.

Eatin mornin cereal my lass day a prison. Can kids work in the mines?

What? she say. Newspaper open, her face in it.

Kids. Coal mines.

Shake her head. Use to. Not no more. President come out against it couple years ago. She turn the page.

Roof says *he* is. Nex year. Thirteen.

She frowns. He can't. Illegal.

There was one little white kid there, comin out all coal black. It's outa my mouth before I think prolly not a good idea to remind her a that excursion. But she don't get mad. Jus put down the paper, shake her head sad an sigh.

Like he sensed the day I'm granted parole, Roof come knockin.

Jacks?

We done about ten games on my front porch when I see down the street Carl's car pull up. Carl an his dad get out. I forgot this was the day he come home. His mother come out on the porch all excited, her han on her mouth, clappin her hands, chatterin fass but don't dare touch him. Mr. Talley stan with Carl a few minutes, his arm round his son's shoulders, talkin to him. An I'm sprised seein Carl lean his head against his daddy, like affection. *Your turn*, say Roof.

Goin to Roof's that evenin I notice Carl's car gone, their family muss be out for his welcome-home dinner. I gather twigs to put somethin natural in the tower for a change, wonderin with Carl home if this might be the lass night a the Dusk Club. Meanwhile Roof comes up with somethin better n twigs. Tosses his jacks into the air an let em all fall, rainin on the tower, landin where they will.

You boys still out here?

Mr. John. Roof go to his sooty father, turn on the hose an water. I watch em a while, both kinda forgot about me. Nightly father-son ritual, them grinnin like this the firs time they ever done it, the coal rollin off Mr. John, rivers a mud at their feet.

Soon's I walk in the door she say Daddy's on the phone. Eliot hoppin aroun, Lemme talk again! Lemme talk again!

No, Dwight ain't talked to him yet.

Hi Dad.

Dwight! How are *you*?

Okay.

Have a good time with Roof?

It was okay.

Well. I got a couple little presents for you an your brother when I get home.

When's that?

I don't know yet but I sure am tryin hard to fine someone gimme a ride nex week. Nex week be a whole month since I seen my family.

Okay. Here, Eliot wants to talk again.

I gotta pee so run up the steps. Then I worsh my hands, look at my face in the meer. Then I throw water all over my face, wipe it. Look at my face in the meer.

Run down to the livin room where Mama on the phone now.

I gotta talk to Dad, I forgot somethin.

Wait a minute.

I gotta talk to Dad, I *forgot* somethin! She look at me a second, then han me the phone.

Dad! I forget to tell ya. I forgot to tell ya that day me an Roof went to Marion, you shoulda seen how Mr. John smile to see us! Then we rode back with Mr. John an Mr. John give us money an we went to the fair! We had cotton candy. We got on the Ferris wheel! So high up! Then we come back here, every night Roof hoses his daddy down from the mines, every night! An then, an then *Carl*, he been away, camp but he jus got back, his family sure glad to see him! His daddy picked him up from camp, maybe Mr. Talley'll play volleyball with us! He's a teacher, he's aroun *every day*, *all* day in the summers! Oh! An I think Mr. John likes our tower! Roof's an my tower! He sees how we build it, he sees it *every night, every night*!

I feel my mother start to rub my back soft an I snatch away from her, keep turned away from her. It was sposed to be a happy story, so how come the more I talked it the madder I got? Louder?

Stop cryin now son, my father say gentle, I miss you too. An after a few minutes my bawlin finally do subside, an then I hear Daddy's cousin Uncle Brice askin Daddy What's wrong? Here, you want my hanky? An for the firs time I wonder what it muss feel like other side a the receiver.

My mama gone to work an I stand in the pourin. She might smack me but I like the drench, *snap snap* hit the street. I like the smell, runnin! my arms stretch out.

Laughin all by yourself, like somebody crazy. Dwight on the front porch. Mama told him go to D'Angelo's, eggs an milk. Why he gotta come out barefoot, put his shoes on outside the house anyway?

You wanna play somethin? You wanna play mud pies?!

Think I'm a little ole for mud pies.

You wanna play jacks?

I gotta go to the store.

Then you play with me.

Goin to Carl's.

You don't never play with me no more!

He got his shoes on not even answerin, then I hear a cryin. Parker got locked outside Miss Onnie's! He on Miss Onnie's front porch, tryin to get in from the rain. I walk up, Miss Onnie's porch.

Hey you better not go there. Dwight got the terror eyes but I ain't leavin Parker out scared.

Ps ps ps. Parker! Here he come! Ps ps ps ps Miss Onnie's door fly open. I feel Dwight behine me on our porch shot up, standin. I stare at Miss Onnie.

Who toldju get on my porch, boy?

You lock Parker outside, he was cryin!

Aw, Yella Cat, sorry I done at. She tap the doorway with her fingertips for Parker to come but Parker ain't innerested. Miss Onnie frown. Then stay like that, ya high yella thing. She go back inside, shut the door.

I stay on Miss Onnie's porch pettin Parker. I look over at Dwight. Two Dwights. He starin at me. Then he laugh, run through the rain-rain to the store. A lightnin-thunder come: scare Parker! Miss Onnie come back out. I think she gonna yell at me Get off my porch! but she jus set in her rocker rockin gentle.

My mama use to say thunder was the devil beatin his wife. Miss Onnie lookin out at the rain. Then her eyes on me. You believe that? I shake my head. I don't believe that neither. Why they gotta come up with ugly stuff like that? Why your eye doin at?

I'm cross-eyeded.

Oh. Here.

She toss a ball a yarn at me, light blue. I hold it up, the string hangin down. Parker tryin to catch that string. Hahaha! Hahahaha!

Miss Onnie. How come you call Parker high yella?

She suck her teeth like she got kale stuck in em. Jus mean, she say. That's what people'd call me, High yella light enough to pass. Cuz my hair's good too. But I never wanted to pass. I picked my husband cuz he was the darkest thing goin, by luck he jus also happen to be the sweetest.

He die?

Uh-huh.

How he die?

She starin at the rain, I think she forget to answer. Then she say, The army, he was sposed to kill the Indians. The women, babies. He didn't wanna kill no Indians, he didn't mean that when he signed up for the army. So he left. Then the army found him an hung him. She sigh, then peer at me. You like cookies? I nod! She go into her house, come out with the ginger snaps. She holdin a skinny black cat. Some other ones try to get out but she take her foot, push em back in.

I let em out in a minute. You gotta watch out for the runts. She got a dish, give that runt a private feedin. This is Pepper. Name her after my mama. Slave. She an me like twins. She said all the white in me an her come from evilness. She married my daddy blacker n coal, an all my sisters an brothers come out a nice rich color but me. I marry Ronnie hopin he color up my babies but the two I had didn't stick in me past the second month. Then Ronnie gone to the army, then he gone.

It pourin harder! Rain sposed to cool off, not make it humider, she say. She walk over, stick her head over the banister edge. Gettin soaked! Shakin out her hair, the water fly everywhere! Miss Onnie look like a wet dog! Ah, that's better! she say. I come over stick my head out. Both us shakin out our soggy heads, gigglin!

After supper Mama fix us peaches n cream, tell us come out, keep her company on the front porch. We set on the slidin seat, two seats fit two grownups but Mama an us can fit three, I love the slidin seat! Mama in the middle, arms aroun us. Rain rain.

You on Miss Onnie's porch the whole afternoon? Dwight say.

Miss Onnie say I can play with Parker anytime I want! Even our yard.

You *been* playin with him.

Yeah but now I ain't got to sneak.

Cuz you an Miss Onnie *friends.*

We ain't friends!

Stop fightin. But she don't say it mad.

When I was a girl, my mama told us those were the people dancin in the streets. See em? The splash when the hard raindrops hit the pavement, people dancin in the streets. See em?

I look. I see em! I see em! I'm clappin!

Dwight nod. I don't know why he look sad.

Nex day's a flood! Water up near toppa the curve! Curb! I wanna go out play in the flood but Mama say no, flood carry you away. It ain't that high! Then she let Dwight go to Carl's! She watch him, make sure he don't play in the flood, Mama watch me I go find Parker! She still say no!

Then the sun come out hard. Flood gone! I'm sad, then I see Miss Onnie feedin the birds. I run over! I help, Miss Onnie?

Take some crumbs. Me an Miss Onnie feedin the birds!

Dwight! Eliot! Supper!

I come back from Miss Onnie's. Dwight on Carl's porch, him an Carl laughin bout I don't know what.

Dwight! Mama call supper!

Dwight look right at me, then turn back to Carl, *still* laughin. When she swing open the door like to get mad he come off Carl's porch fass, head our way!

I helped Miss Onnie feed the birds!

He suckin his pigs' feet, look at me. Dontcha mean feed the cats?

She also feed the birds. She lock up the cats in her house, throw out the bread crumbs. I suck on my pigs' feet. I love pigs' feet!

Him an Miss Onnie big buddies now.

Well, she say. Nothin wrong with that.

Nothin wrong with it? He's six, only friend he got some crazy ole lady? Pourin hisself ice tea from the pitcher.

Stop sayin crazy, boy.

I say, Lease *my* friend's colored.

The pitcher slip outa Dwight's han. Commotion to clean it up, Mama hollerin but Dwight jus stare at his shirt n pants all wet, like he froze jus starin.

Gettin ready for bed he don't say nothin. I feel like I wanna say, I got friends, I got Jeanine an em, sometime I go over to Colored Street an play but I prefer playin with Parker but I don't say nothin. We in the dark a long time, his eyes stuck on the ceilin.

Then he say, How many colored kids my age *in* this neighborhood? I ain't playin with no Kimmie an Talia. Girls.

There's Marco an Mokie.

This neighborhood.

There's Richard.

Richard's miles away!

There's—

Nobody!

Then Dwight don't say nothin a while. Then he say, Me an Richard don't speak no more.

You tryin to pass?

I don't mean it mean, I jus wondered. Dwight chuckle to hisself. I wait for him say somethin else but he don't say nothin. Somethin keep me all night dreamin then wake, dreamin then wake an every time I'm wake I see Dwight ain't budged, eyes still starin at the ceilin like he tryin to do some arithmetic problem an the answer he hope written up there.

I got a funny feelin. Carl wrote come down day after he get back, we set up the volleyball net but I got a funny feelin like I go to his house, he ack like he don't know what I'm talkin about, all different after three weeks away at camp. Also I really do wanna start dolin out my time more even between Carl an Roof. Maybe I oughta jus stay inside, wait for Carl come to me. But what if he don't?

Sketchin on my bed, almost eleven. Sky grayin over, seem like rainin every day. Maybe Carl at his house wonderin where I am after he wrote the invitation. If I'm goin, better now before the torrent.

Soon as I step out my front door I get shook. There's Carl on his porch lookin down at Roof on the sidewalk below. Engaged in conversation. Now Carl turn my way. Wave, smilin. Roof see me too. I wave not smilin, stroll down, no kinda rush.

The firs day do *not* wear red, Roof's sayin to Carl. That's Humble East, cross town. Rival, you musta heard of em by now. Blue's nice to wear, Humble West blue, or you can wear some other color, jus not red.

Never?

Football days, when there's games, always blue. If ya can. Maybe all your blue's dirty. But not red. You can wear red any day but football days an the firs day.

How're the teachers?

I ain't heard much. Be my firs year secondary too. I did hear pray you don't get ole Miss Englewood, English.

Pick your classes?

Uh-uh, not till ninth. Seventh an eighth they assign sections. All the sudden thunderclap an a streak.

Whoa! says Carl. You all wanna play Monopoly? Indicatin the porch.

Roof look at me a second, like he need my permission. I say nothin. Okay, he say to Carl. Well, I ain't never played it before.

I'll teach ya. I taught Dwight, an Carl goes inside to get the board as the big drops start ploppin. I notice the two of em jus decided it's Monopoly, ain't neither one bothered to wait for my two cents.

On Carl's porch Roof says, He was askin about school. Cuz almost August, an me an him at the same school after Labor Day.

I thought you didn't like him. Lower my voice.

Roof shrugs. Foun a penny in the yard, on my way to D'Angelo's get some bubble gum he stops me, talkin. Roof shrugs again. Guess he okay.

You have a choice of the iron, the thimble, the rocking horse, the purse, the cannon, the hat, or the lantern, Carl comin out says to Roof. I like the sports car, Dwight likes the shoe, and we lost the battleship.

Maybe I wanna be lantern today, I say.

I be the shoe then, says Roof.

We set cross-leg, board in the middle while Carl explains every stupid lass detail to Roof. The worth a each property, land versus the railroads, how to get sent to jail, developments.

Since ya brought it up. We say limit to one hotel, or no limits?

I see Carl's eyes glance to Mediterranean and Baltic. *My* strategy! Buy the cheap land an cover it in prime real estate!

Well, strictly according to the rules, only one. But if we decide to bend the rules—

Let's stick by the rules, I say.

Who wants to be banker? You probably shouldn't since you never played before. Dwight?

This the firs time that question's been put to me. Every other instance Carl jus automatically appoint himself banker. I wanna say No thank you jus to catch him by surprise, but say no now I might never get the question asked again.

After two passin goes for which I give him his two hundred an a lotta property bought, Roof is happy with rollin two trays an ecstatic followin em up with boxcars, thinkin he on a doubles streak, till Carl remines him three doubles is a jail sentence, so then Roof look more serious rollin an rollin an rollin the dice in his hand, prayin not to repeat his good luck which suddenly be bad. I imagined this day different, Carl's firs full day back. Sunny an puttin up the volleyball net an me askin him about camp an what is tetherball an maybe his daddy an sister joinin in to volleyball an his mama bringin out the lemonade. I could ask Carl about camp now but I don't wanna. It was somethin I had in my head to be a conversation between two friends already knowed each other pretty good.

Roof!

His mother hollerin. After all Carl's explanations, we ain't been playin long enough for anybody to buy up a whole lot so them green houses and red hotels Roof been eyein the whole game don't never even come out the box. Roof let go a big groan an despite the monsoon drag his feet all the way up the street to his house.

Carl look at me.

You wanna keep playin?

I shrug.

Wamme teach you piano?

We set on the bench side by side. He liffs the cover. My eyes dancin. All them keys!

Listen to this.

Okay, that's Middle C. I'm gonna teach ya the C Major scale now. It's all white so don't worry about the black now. C D E F G A B and now you're back to C. Listen to this C, now this C. That's an octave.

Why don't it start with A?

Huh?

You jus went by the alphabet, C D E F G A B. Wouldn't it be easier A B C D E F G?

A's not in the middle.

Well maybe it oughta be.

Well it's not. Now play that C Major scale.

Huh?

What I just did. Not so fast! you need to hear every note. Yeah. That's good. Okay, chords. A chord is at least three notes at the same time. See? Try it. *Why'd you hit that black key?*

I like the black keys.

That sounded terrible! You're not ready for the black keys yet, they're sharp.

After supper I think about goin to Roof's but the rain pourin again, how we sposed to do our outdoor tower ritual? Anyhow I already seen Roof today. Carl's.

Nex mornin still drizzly. I knock on Roof's door early. Miss Ray Anne holdin the baby, smilin.

Oh hello there Dwight. Roof ain't up yet.

Could you tell him I be aroun for the Dusk Club if it ain't rainin?

The Dusk Club?

Uh-huh.

Okay.

That was luck. If it'd been Roof he'da wondered why I couldn't play *now*. Though I kinda covered myself there, I could say I gotta do my chores now which wouldn't be a lie cuz I leff the house before my work, now gotta go back hit it. But *after* your chores, he'd surely say nex, an then I'd be stuck. Cuz *after* my chores I planned to go to Carl's. I *do* plan on splittin time between em but I ain't seen Carl in three weeks so we gotta catch up.

The sun suddenly out bright. Takes a while to set up the poles for the volleyball net, his dad comin out to help. When it's ready we play two against one, firs game Mr. Talley on my team, second Mr. Talley versus me an Carl. Mrs. Talley come out with some kinda fruit punch she say she been experimentin with. She happy to see me, she missed me. Then me an Carl one-on-one till supper.

What's tetherball?

Stupid camp game. (I don't say but recall Carl mentionin in his letter he liked it.) Ball tied to a rope, rope tied to top of a pole. You hit it one direction, your opponent hits it back at you. Poor man's volleyball, then he tells me at camp he learned the 1942 volleyball official new rule: touchin the ball anywhere from the knees up is legal.

Sky clouded over again but I can't exactly cancel the Dusk Club cuza overcast. Roof's dirt yard's muddy, which I enjoy. The tower pretty much decimated from the rains, the pieces lyin in a pile roun the foundation so we rebuild from scratch, embracin the opportunity to make it better. It's fun, but tomarra I want more volleyball or another piano lesson. I don't know what I'm gonna say when Roof asks me about tomarra, but he never does. Instead he jus seem grateful I bothered with him at all with Carl back. Walkin home I turn aroun at my house an sprised to see Roof still standin there, lookin at me kinda sad.

Flood! I beg her can I go to Carl's an firs she say no, then she relent but watch me from our porch, make sure I don't stop to play in the water. Like I'm really gonna drown, four-inch deep.

After my piano lesson Carl pull out Criss-Crosswords. Carl got so much indoor stuff rainy days ain't never a disappointment! Mrs. Talley bring us brownies an milk. Carl spells BELCH the same time he does, loud. We both crackin up. Then I take his C and CADET. Then he take my T an TRASH.

I was thinkin of whatshisname up the street. Then he roll over laughin again.

Till that moment I had no idea if maybe Carl felt different about Roof, him actin all cordial that Monopoly day. I start up again too, all contagious, howlin till the tears. Then I try to take the S for JUDAS, J tile's eight points, but Carl says no proper nouns so I pass.

When I knock on Carl's nex day his mother answers. She done sent him to D'Angelo's for eggs, but Come on in, Dwight, you can wait for him in the family room with Mr. Talley.

I'd just as soon wait out on the porch but I do like I'm told. I like Carl's family but without Carl I feel kinda funny.

Listen to this, Dwight, says Mr. Talley. You know it?

He got his phonograph playin. I seen it before but this the firs time it been turned on while I'm here.

Touch it if you want, Mr. Talley says. Gentle, don't make the record skip. You know Jelly Roll Morton?

I hearda him.

Stride piano. The right hand playing the melody while the left brings in the bassline. Rhythm. Morton could play the melody with just his right *thumb!* In the bass he moved in major and minor sixths instead of octaves. New Orleans sound. You hear it in Satchmo. You know Louis Armstrong?

I nod. I think, I didn't imagine colored music be comin outa this record player!

God, I wish Bolden's recordings had survived! Not many were made, the technology wasn't yet in place. His band was the start of it all. Jazz.

Dwight, say Mrs. Talley enterin with her tray, have a cookie?

If the Bartons had a phonograph surely be nothin but country n western comin out of it. An never know when nigger gonna pop outa one a them Barton kids' mouths. I kep waitin for that here, but guess it ain't gonna happen. Whole different brand a white people, like they don't even notice I'm colored. Carl walks in the door. Badminton or volleyball? he say to me.

Walkin home for supper I think maybe better I spend more time at Carl's. Good for me, make me on bess behavior, show em how Negroes can be. Up the street I notice Mr. John's pickup parked, muss be his day off. He don't get many days off. Mr. John an Miss Ray Anne's nice. Still, bein with Roof an his family I sure ain't improvin on myself. I ain't tried at all to be on good behavior there, I jus am what I am.

Some days go by I forget about the Dusk Club, or playin till dark with Carl then too late for the Dusk Club. One evenin Carl an his family go out to some barbecue they was invited to an I use the opportunity to walk up to Roof's. Miss Ray Anne answer the door.

Oh hi, Dwight. Where's Roof?

I step back. I come over here lookin for *him*.

Oh. She look confused. Oh. I *thought* that was odd. Lass couple days he say I'm goin out with *my friend*, I thought Why don't he jus say Dwight? But guess he meant some other friend. I didn't know he had no other friends! She laughs. From inside the house Beaver an Cath Cath start fightin over somethin. Oh I better see what that's about. You come aroun again soon, honey. An she shut the door.

I turn aroun to walk on home, then stop. Go back, take a glance in Roof's backyard. Not a remnant left a the castle we built, cleared away clean like it was never there.

Which way does the *E* point?

Dr. Leibowitz put his big machine over my eyes, it scary! Brush agains my eyelash, what if my eyelash get caught in there!

Mama!

I'm right here, baby. I hear her I don't see her.

Which way do the *E*'s point, Eliot?

I point my finger to the right, to the leff, up, up, leff, down.

Very good. How about now?

Mama!

I'm right here, baby.

When it over Dr. Leibowitz say, Pick out your frames.

I look at Mama. Any color I want?

Any color you want.

There's black! There's brown! There's red-brown! There's light blue! I like light blue!

Try em on, he say.

I try em on, look in the mirror. I want em!

Try another pair, she say.

I can't have em?

I jus want you to try more than one before you make a decision.

I pick a brown pair. I try em on, look in the mirror. I want em!

I come home wearin my black pair. Everything I see only one of. We walk in, I see Dwight one Dwight. He look at me. I think he gonna be mean.

But he smile. They look good, Eliot.

I love my brother!

Week later school start. Mrs. Brent. We hear she strict! She seem strict!

There are things I will *not* tolerate in my classroom. No tardiness. No talking while I'm talking. And no nose picking, *that's* a one-way trip to the principal.

But after a few days she nicer. To *me* she nicer. She like me! I do my work! I'm smart!

Class, what did we learn yesterday about the poetry of Paul Laurence Dunbar? What makes him so distinctive?

My han up!

Eliot?

He write in die-lect *an* standard.

Mrs. Brent smile at me!

Yes, he wrote some poems in the Negro dialect of the time and others in the standard American English. He was as adroit as any white poet writing in the language, but he also had pride in the English of his own people. Now what do you think "adroit" means from the context. Eliot?

He wrote jus as good as the white people!

Very good!

Dwight huggin the covers! I pull em back, he pull em harder! October startin chilly! Dwight still sleep, Saturday he sleep forever!

I hear somethin. Coal truck! Coal truck! Run down the steps!

Mama already top a the basement lookin down. Don't let her see me! They open the basement winda, pour the coal down the shoot! It all loud, she can't even tell I'm right behind her! Coal so pretty, coal smell so good! October 11th, firs coal a the year!

I can tell when they almost finished, coal mountain! I tiptoe away. Mama catch me starin at the coal mountain, she be mad! She fraid I play in the coal mountain, eat the coal mountain like lass year. I ain't! I told her I ain't, promise!

I go through the shortcut bushes find Parker, play with Parker. But I keep thinkin bout it, thinkin bout coal. I come in the kitchen. My mama upstairs. Late mornin, soun like Dwight still ain't up. Quiet, quiet, I run to the basement door! Step down the steps, easy! easy!

Coal! I love the coal, hahaha! I love bein in the coal mountain, toppa the coal mountain! My behine buried in the coal mountain! I'm the queen an the coal mountain my dress! Hahahaha! Coal smell good. Mmm. Coal lick good.

Eliot!

Quiet quiet.

Eliot, I'ma fry some bacon. You want some bacon?

I love bacon! But I ain't hungry. I'm full. I'm full on coal, hee hee hee.

Then I hear her callin outside for me, I run up the steps! Up to the bathroom! I worsh myself worsh myself clean clean clean!

Eliot!

I got dirty outside, Mama, I'm worshin up!

Didn't you hear me callin you?

Uh-uh.

Well hurry up an come on down here.

I walk in the kitchen. Dwight already eatin his bacon, he like it a little soff. I like it crisp! crisp! Dwight take a bite, then stop froze. Starin at me. Mama turn aroun, gasp!

You been in that coal?

Uh-uh! Uh-uh! Dwight whole body shakin. Stop laughin, Dwight!

Why you tellin *him* stop laughin? *You* the one actin silly. An you been eatin it too, aintcha? How many times I gotta tell you not to eat coal? It ain't food, boy!

Stop laughin!

Now smile, she say.

I do. Dwight almost fall off his chair! Mama pull a han meer out the drore, show me. I shoulda brushed my teeth, black black.

Stuck inside all resta the day! I can't even say Night to Parker! Cry myself to sleep, wake up snifflin. The tree branches outside the winda make a shadow dance in our room. When Dwight's not here, I don't like that shadow dance!

Dwight come to bed, I'm bawlin again. Dwight turn away, don't say nothin like he don't hear me like he death or somethin. You act like you don't hear me like you death or somethin, Dwight!

Deaf. He still don't turn look at me!

I had to have my Saturday night bath Saturday day, I couldn't go outside resta the day!

What was you gonna do? Walk aroun filthy?

An no pie! Why I gotta have early bath *an* no pie, *two* punishments! Cruel an unusual!

Eliot! she holler. Stop that cryin an go to sleep!

I put my hans over my mouth, *try* not to cry!

You better stay outa that coal, he whisper.

I can't help it! It shiny! It smell good!

You better stay out.

The wind blow, the tree shadows dancin.

In my dream me an Mama an Dwight *all* buried in the coal mountain, *all* happy tastin the coal mountain, hahahaha!

How many's in your class? She walk me to school early today, before Dwight leave. We stop in D'Angelo's.

Seventeen! Then I get another thought. Seventeen in my class, today *October* seventeen. My birthday! My birthday! I'm glad my birthday's Friday. At school they gonna sing Happy Birthday, if my birthday was Saturday I don't get that!

We color jack o'lanterns. I ain't never seen no jack-o'-lanterns before, I guess the white people make em. Sometime my mama call me punkin. My jack-o'-lantern got three teeth. Enda the day everbody sing Happy Birthday to me! Then Mrs. Brent give everbody a long fat pretzel stick! I love long fat pretzel sticks! Crunch crunch crunch! Then she say, Mrs. Campbell bought us all these pretzel sticks for Eliot's birthday. Tell Eliot thank you for his mother. An everyone thank me for my mother!

Mama! Mama! They all thanked me for my mother Mrs. Campbell for the pretzel sticks! She waitin outside for me.

Did they? She smile, hole my han.

In the kitchen, I look at her makin cake!

I'm seven! I'm seven! I'm seven! I get cake I get ice cream. I get chocolate cake chocolate ice cream Happy Birthday, Eliot! Happy Birthday, Eliot, hahahaha! The telephone ring!

Hello, Mr. Seven!

Hi Daddy!

How it feel, ole man?

I'm bigger!

I know.

When you comin home, Daddy?

Thursday. You wanna hear a joke?

Yes!

Why are fish so smart?

Cuz they wear glasses!

No.

Cuz they read!

Cuz they live in schools.

Oh! Hahaha!

Get it?

Yeah! Cuz they live in schools an read! Hahahaha!

I blow out all the candles! Know what I wished for, Mama? I wished for marbles, an a puppet, an some cars, an a secret. Where you goin!

Studyin with Carl. Dwight got his coat on already!

How you study with Carl? He go to the white school!

We both got the same current events.

My birthday! *My* birthday!

Get offa that chair, she say.

My birthday. I say it softer. He gotta stay.

We both got tests Monday. An tomarra he got company, his uncle comin for the day. We don't study together today, we both flunk.

Liar! She smack my behine. I mean *fibber!*

We gotta know all the capitals a the war.

We ain't in no war!

Just cuz we ain't in it don't mean it ain't there. Dwight lookin at her, not me. I say France, he say Paris. Quiz each other. We gotta study. I sure don't know Luxembourg. I sure don't know Latvia.

Okay, she say.

No! But he already out the door, goin to Carl's. I don't like that Carl! Birthday posed to be four of us. No Daddy, now Dwight gone. Now *Mama* gone!

But she come back. Burlap sack. I look inside.

Eight of em. Eight people on the clothespins, Mama dressed em up! Ole man with the cotton beard. Bride in her gown. Sailor in his sailor suit. Pullman Porter.

I'm makin a puppet story with my clothespin people! Dwight come in front door while I'm settin on the steps makin my story.

Dwight! I ain't mad atcha no more for leavin my birthday.

He walk by, take off his coat like I ain't said nothin!

Dwight! Didn't ya wonder what my secret birthday wish was? It's a secret! I already had the secret even before my birthday, I been holdin my secret since June!

Better not tell or it won't come true. Then he trot pass me upstairs.

I never thoughta that. Good thing I didn't tell!

November, I still keep my secret! Drawr a turkey. My turkey tail feathers is red an blue an yella an green an purple. Donny say, That ain't a turkey, that's a peacock.

I say, Turkey.

He say, Peacock.

Turkey! I slap him!

Boys! say Mrs. Brent.

Hunnert on my spellin test! Firs Friday a December. Hoppin to Dwight, waitin for me bottom a the school steps.

So what? You always get a hunnert your spellin tests.

I spelled police. Know how Emma Jean spelled police? P – O – L – E – E – S. Haha! Know how Donny spelled police? P – L – E – A – S – E. That's *please*, not police! Hahahaha!

Dwight don't say nothin. He don't even tell me shut up.

How you do *your* spellin test?

Seventh grade don't got spellin tests.

Oh. *You* know how to spell police?

Walk faster, it's cold.

Okay. Jeanine say her daddy say it gonna snow tonight. You think it gonna snow tonight? We wake up tomarra, all white. All snowy white everywhere, Saturday!

Walk *faster*.

Okay. Look. I'm jumpin. Hahaha!

Walk right, fool.

I run in my door. I got a hunnert my spellin test!

Lemme see! she say. Then she lookin it over. Dwight go on upstairs.

Dontchu speak?

Hi.

What's the matter?

Nothin.

See. Freight. Honor. License. Police. They ain't easy, they ain't cat an sat!

I know.

You proud a me?

I'm proud a you every day. She lookin up the steps.

I'ma show it to Daddy! Daddy comin home Sunday?

Uh-huh.

I'ma show it to Daddy. Jeanine was the only other one got all hunnert percent every Friday till lass week she spelled anchor wrong an she cried. Wamme spell anchor for ya? Where ya goin?

See what's goin on with your brother.

In bed I go, How come you was sad after school?

He quiet a long time, then he say, George Worshinton Carver.

Who's that?

You don't know who George Worshinton Carver was?

Was he parta The Society for the Prevention of Calling Sleeping Car Porters George? Hahahaha!

Inventor.

But was he a inventor parta The Society for—

No.

He was like Thomas Edison?

Cep George Worshinton Carver's colored.

Colored inventor?

Uh-huh.

What he invent?

All kindsa stuff. From food. He turn food into all kindsa stuff.

How come he made you mad?

He ain't made me mad.

Sad?

He ain't made me sad!

Who did?

Dwight roll over away from me so I know that's all the answers I'm gettin on that subject.

Dwight. I'ma tell ya my secret. I ain't tole nobody else! I been keepin this secret all the way from June. It was my birthday wish secret!

Hmm. That all Dwight say so I know I better talk fass fore he sleep!

I wisht when we go to the March on Worshinton we get to see Mr. Randolph again!

It quiet. Then Dwight roll over on his back, lookin at the ceilin, frown his face. Then he roll again, turn to me, look right at me. Whatta you talkin about?

Mr. Randolph! I wanna see him when we go to Worshinton.

We ain't goin to no Worshinton.

Yes we are! March on Worshinton!

Eliot! That was called off! That was sposed to happen July 1st, that was called off months ago!

My breathin fass fass.

You better not cry. Geeminee, all this time you been thinkin it was still gonna happen?

Why they call it off!

Cuz Mr. Randolph met with President Roosevelt an he told President Roosevelt give colored people the jobs or we gonna march. So President Roosevelt gave colored people the jobs, gave Daddy his job. So we didn't march.

Why President Roosevelt gotta do that!

Dwight laughin to hisself. Go to sleep, boy. I look at the ceilin, sighin. Nothin to do but sigh, sigh, try not to cry.

After a while Dwight say, Got somethin for ya. He turn on the light, make me squint. Pull out the drore, pull out his tablet, tear off a page.

It's me, Dwight drawred me. I'm grinnin, I wear my glasses, I hold my spelling test, A-plus. I like it!

I know Dwight ain't lyin. But maybe he make a mistake? I hope he make a mistake. But I know he think he ain't made no mistake cuz he bein nice, wake up middle a the night an I got all the blankets an he jus curled up tryin to keep warm no covers at all.

Ain't seen Carl a while. Afternoon after firs day we got together. Tole me there's eight sections his school, A through H. He got placed in 7-B, second smartest, week later tole me his dad talked to the principal, moved him up to A. How many sections your school?

One, we all nineteen seventh grade the same class. There ain't that many colored in the county.

For a time still went to his house, him bringin friends home. Most of em were alright, but then talkin bout some teacher from their school or some girl from their school an there I am, mute-dumb.

Middle a September I stop by Roof's. He settin floor a his porch grumblin, She said I gotta do homework first! I gotta write a stupid essay on what's my opinion about Congress just brought back the draft peacetime. He writes somethin, then That's enough for now. Runs into his house to look for his football an I see he ain't got farther than **Rufus Barton, 7-H.** Over the fall, I fine myself spendin more time with Roof. The new friend his mama mentioned turn out to be Zack Rhodes, live up Jake's Hill. Zack's tall for the ninth an Roof's short for the seventh so they sure make a pair. Neither of em has any interest in talkin about school so with them I never feel outside the conversation.

Eliot's glasses all fogged up in the December mornin freeze. Gotta admit he look cute, though sometime I miss the way his eye useta slip in toward his nose. Come on boy, it's cold! He catch up, grinnin. I drop him off with the little kids firs floor an climb on up the stairs, secondary.

Genevieve Watson! What do you know about George Washington Carver?

Miz Carey's short an stout an fast. High voice, twitter like a bird, always seem to be in a good mood. But don't make the mistake a thinkin easy-grader.

Genevieve goes to the fronta the class. She start to read from her report but Miz Carey grab it from her right off.

I didn't ask What did you *write*, I asked What do you *know*.

Genevieve's eyes like saucers.

From what Genevieve recall from her report an what Miz Carey fill in I piece together this. Born jus before Emancipation on the Missouri farm a Moses Carver. Baby George an his mother kidnapped by slave traders, Moses trades a racehorse to get George back, George's mama never found. George an his brother raised by their master an mistress like their own children, no local school take colored so mistress teach em to read an write. Still a kid when he goes to Kansas, closest colored school. College in Iowa. Music an art, accomplished pianist! Then science for his higher degrees, then at Tuskegee forty-seven years teachin colored farmers an conductin scientific experiments.

An abridged list of accomplishments:

> developed crop rotation
> invented over three hundred uses for peanuts, more n a hundred for sweet potatas, soybeans an pecans
> made a member a the Royal Society of Arts in England, which very few Americans ever got invited into
> One a his students was the Crown Prince a Sweden!
> Advised Theodore Roosevelt an Gandhi from India!
> His painting displayed in the 1893 Chicago World's Fair!
> Once speakin before Congress the Southern reps heckled him at firs, but he mesmerize em, his ten minutes extended, then extended, then extended . . .

My han shoot up!
Dwight Campbell!
What was his painting?
A flower. George Washington Carver was a gifted painter, his subjects plants, flowers, landscapes. The painting that had been displayed in the World's Fair was of the *Yucca gloriosa,* a rose. Other questions?
I look aroun. No one say nothin. My han shoot up! Everybody lookin at me, usually I ain't got much to say in school.
Dwight Campbell!
What other kindsa products besides food come from the food?
Paints! Plastics! Cosmetics! Gasoline! Of all his hundreds of inventions, he only patented three.
My face puzzled. But. Then I remember raise my han.
Dwight Campbell!

But couldn't he a been a millionaire? Patented em all?

Yes, he could have. But this is what he said about his discoveries: "God gave them to me, how can I sell them to someone else?"

Percy Moore grunt.

What was that, Percy Moore?

Nothin. *Any*thing, I didn't say *any*thing.

Dwight Campbell!

He still alive?

Yes! Though he is quite up in years now. She gaze at all the notes she wrote on the board. I often think of his poor mama. To be kidnapped away, her babies stolen from her. And on top of this grief, what sort of miseries was she subjected to, her will not her own, her life the ownership and whim of another? Oh the anguish! The despair! Ponder that!

We do.

And the bitter irony. George born one year before emancipation. One year later he and his mama never would have been separated.

Fool.

Hand up, Percy Moore! And if you have something to say, say it loud enough for all to hear.

Percy raise it.

Percy Moore!

He shoulda took the money.

Sold the patents.

Yeah. *Yes.*

Well he didn't. He was not greedy. Other questions?

Percy mutter somethin else to Tobias Proud and Mokie Wiley an Genevieve Watson. Tobias snicker, Mokie frown skeptical, Genevieve's mouth fly open.

What's going on over there?

Nothin, says Percy. Nothin.

The bell rings. Lunch.

Percy Moore. I'd like to speak to you for a moment?

You sure all up under Miz Carey today, Campbell, says Percy in the locker room.

I liked it, I say an shrug, sniff under my arms, hopin after forty minutes a basketball drills I don't stink too much.

Liked what? says Chester Reese from the eighth. Seventh, eighth, an ninth all got gym together.

George Worshinton Carver, says Marco Wiley. His twin Mokie changin his shirt nex to him, them twins share a locker. Clear down the aisle Richard from the ninth dresses. When we picked lockers back in September I know he waited to see where I would go jus so he could pick his far away as possible. He ain't spoke to me wunst this year, not meet my eyes. The girls always hangin on him.

She goes *He was not greedy*, Percy makin fun of Miz Carey's high fasstalk. A lotta the guys get a kick out of it. Percy continue: An I said Yeah well I know what he *was*.

What? says Chester.

A punk. Percy snickers.

What! says Chester.

How *you* know? says Mokie.

I heard stuff.

You heard stuff.

He *got* some man! says Percy. Some other colored scientist, work with him.

You're full of it Moore, says Marco slammin his locker. Then he think better of it, smile. Or maybe it's cuz you seen his picture, want him for yourself. Some of em fallin out laughin. That handlebar mustache, Marco go on. Those big brown eyes.

I look up, almost jump back seein Richard standin near. Listenin, some kinda amusement on his lips.

Say whatcha want, says Percy. I know what I know.

I slam my locker ready to go.

So whaddya think, Campbell? says Percy.

I'm tyin my shoe not lookin at em. I don't like the looks a that bow so I untie it, tie again.

Ast you a question. How's your great Negro hero rate now?

I look at him. I jus learnt about George Worshinton Carver today like the resta yaw. Now how I'm sposed to know bout his personal life.

Percy an Chester crack up. Personal life! says Chester.

That how all the white boys talk? asks Percy. Your *friends*?

Everyone lookin at me, waitin for me to answer. Some of em I see the twinkle in the eye. Richard's face I can't tell. He don't got the smile no more but what he replace it with I ain't sure of.

You wanna know what I think, Percy?

Yeah I do.

Here's what I think. George Worshinton Carver was a gifted artist an genius scientist who invented hundreds a products an revolutionized agriculture. He taught poor colored farmers an he taught Swedish royalty. Three different presidents asked to meet with him which he did. He coulda been a rich man but instead chose to serve humanity, one a the greatest men ever lived in the eyes a colored *an* white but goddamn if it don't take one a his own race to try an bring him down.

Flyin out the locker room I hear everyone cheerin behind me, this is my victory. But victory ain't what I feel. What I feel is when you say somethin but it didn't come out quite right but you not completely sure what went wrong. Duck in the hall bathroom, pantin, pantin the sweat, headache like explodin.

After school Eliot waitin for me on the sidewalk, jumpin like a damn flea, talkin bout some spellin test. Halfway home there's a moment all the sudden I think I'll be sick right on the sidewalk, but it pass.

Set up on my side a the bed, arms huggin my knees.

What's wrong?

She catch me by surprise, standin in the doorway. Figured she be all caught up in Eliot's spellin achievements downstairs.

Nothin.

Somethin. I don't answer an she come set on the bed but still gimme space.

What happened in school today?

My head poundin.

Whadja learn?

I swallow. Talked about Gift a the Magi.

Oh I remember that one. You like it?

It was okay.

What else?

Crackle. Ole house. Mama an Daddy say it's settlin but I don't think houses ever get settled, they constantly changin, livin.

Parts a the heart. Right ventricle, lell ventricle, aorta, posterior vena cava—

Eliot laugh loud from downstairs. Nobody else there but somethin tickle him, livin his own little world.

Whatchu smilin at? she asks.

Eliot. You hear him laughin? Then all the sudden I'm bawlin. Her arm aroun me, pull me close to her. When the cries dry up, I tell her We learnt about George Worshinton Carver.

That interestin?

Uh-huh. Even through the closed winda can hear Miss Onnie yellin at one a her tabbies. Then Eliot runnin, prolly wantin to go outside to her.

The sobs again!

Big baby!

No you ain't. Teenage is a lotta tears. You gonna be a teenager soon.

Then I'm quiet.

People can be mean.

They sure can.

Like, somebody, a real good person, a real special person does good things for mankind an all they can do is say things about him.

Bad things?

I stop. I stare at her. I look down.

Is things always bad cuz people says they is?

The house crackle crackle.

You was little, Eliot a baby. Me an your daddy take yaw to the park, you gotta go, you can't use the bathroom like the little white boys an girls, your daddy gotta take you to the woods an you cryin cuz it ain't that you gotta pee, it's number two an ain't no toilet paper in the woods but that the way it gotta be, goin home right after that cuz you cryin, poop on your leg. That might be the law but that ain't right to me! What other people claims is right an wrong ain't necessarily— She don't finish, she wipe her eye. People gotta stand up for themself. Nobody do it for em.

The wind blow hard, rattle the windas.

Sometime I look at you, sad. Make me sad. Teenager's a funny time, mixed-up time. But then I come up here, cleanin your room an I find your drawins. Then I remember you got somethin dancin bright inside a you. Most people spend their life tryin to find somethin an here my son not quite thirteen already see it. Then I feel okay, I know my son Dwight gonna live a happy life.

Cryin again! She hole me both arms an I think this is it, this moment with my mama. An my little brother downstairs happy an hoppin, I ain't never gettin married! I don't wanna grow up, I want it always to be this, me an Mama an Daddy an Eliot, always together.

Nex mornin I sketch us, my family. Daddy be home Sunday, tomarra! I'll show him my drawin. An I sign it which I don't always do: Dwight Campbell, 12/6/41.

I wake up with a cold—an Daddy comin home Sunday, tomarra! Mama checkin my forehead an bringin me Coke, Daddy come home Sunday mornin bring me a horse! Little wood red horse but the afternoon everything different. She checkin on me, but somethin else worry her face. Daddy too! The radio on all the time.

Monday I feel all better! But it late! Mama I don't wanna miss school, I wanna get the Perfect Attendance certificate again!

Mama smile a little, happy I'm feelin better to run down the steps but still ain't happy like she oughta be!

No school today, she say. An go back to the radio! Her an Daddy an Dwight ears to the radio, President Roosevelt on the radio an this remine me a what Dwight said the other night about the March on Worshinton called off.

Mama! Dwight say we ain't goin to Worshin—
Sh!

I look at em an now I know. All these months I keep a secret inside, figure I don't say nothin it come true. But now I know we ain't goin to Worshinton!

Basement. Usually I'm bad in the coal only wunst a winter but I need it! Bury my legs in it! wipe my face the tears. What Mr. Roosevelt jus said is true so true. This *is* a date live in infamy.

DWIGHT

Christmas afternoon Mama say I run outa the brown sugar, my sweet potatas gonna be a disappointment this year an Daddy say Ain't nothin you cook ever a disappointment love *knock knock*.

Only wunst or twiced before Carl ever been inside my house, now here he come, guess seein how I made out presents-wise. I got clay an toy soldiers an gloves, Eliot got a fire truck an jack-in-the-box an mittens. Carl all polite meetin my daddy firs time, thankin my mama for the cookie, then: Come over see mine.

I suspect Carl's place be floor-to-ceilin Christmas. Instead he only got one but it's big: bike.

Pretty soon hard to get these, says Mr. Talley, touchin the tires. Rationing rubber.

Mrs. Talley gave Mr. Talley a nice chest set which apparently he an Carl been wearin out, so now Carl teaches me. Mr. Talley stands gazin at us sippin his Christmas coffee, which I get a whiff of walkin by, a little like the brewery.

You hear the Japs took Hong Kong today? Mr. Talley asks me. His laugh is big, Santa jolly an somethin else.

Christina says, I learned another carol an she goes into the family room with Mr. Talley followin an we hear from the piano God Rest Ye Merry then Hark the Herald while Mrs. Talley in the kitchen keepin a watch over the dinner preparations while I win firs chest game (Carl: *Beginner's luck!*) an then he beats me game two (Carl: *See?*) an Christina an Mr. Talley walk past us to the kitchen an Mrs. Talley comes out an says, Mr. Talley and Christina are helping themselves to the Christmas cookies, Dwight, you come get some whenever you want, an I say, Thank you, an Carl goes, Come on, an I follow him into the family room.

One two three one two three to me's a waltz an I say so but Carl don't answer, jus keep playin it, eyes on the music. My lessons ended long ago. Carl got bored teachin me, an anyhow after school started I wasn't comin over so regular anymore. The sheet music Carl playin from says Moonlight Sonata. Eventually Mrs. Talley come in quiet quiet, searchin through the drores of a dresser for somethin, eventually start to hum Carl's tune without thinkin which I think is nice. Somethin very holiday come over me an just a moment me an her catchin a smile at each other an a little laugh escape me but it cut off quick when Carl suddenly bang hard on the keys an stop playin. He don't even turn aroun to look at her, all she gets his back. Oh sorry, she mutter, an gone. Now he resume, his fingers sailin the keys. The minutes go by an I'm thinkin it's bout time to leave when she come again, all tiptoe, tray a cookies, two glasses a milk. Firs she han me mine. Thank you, my lips move. All delicate she place the other glass top a the piano above Carl, no soun she make, only the piano like we in a silent movie, Carl's eyes on the music ain't missed a note. She about to go but then can't, drawn to the notes she close her eyes, smile, swayin ever so gentle, an Carl so skilled he keep playin uninterrupted with his left han while his eyes stay on the sheet music while takin his right han off the keys usin it to pick up his full glass a milk an hurl it all in his mother's face. She sputter, make this funny gasp an Carl put the glass down back to playin with both hans, the music never stopped, while the white drippin off his mother's chin and she leave, shuttin the door behind her ever so quiet. I stare at the empty glass, my knee start to shake. Then Carl finishes. Octave with the left hand, triplet figuration with the right, he says. That's Movement 1: *Adagio sostenuto*. Then he proceed on to Movement 2.

□ □

By tradition Roof always invited to my house on my birthday Febyuary second. Ain't seen Carl in a while but seem wrong not to invite him too, he invited me to his in January at the roller rink. I told him I asked my mama an she said no, the roller rink colored gotta bring their own skates an I ain't got none. Carl tole his mama an Mrs. Talley on the phone to the rink to verify it's true an it is, so she call aroun an one a the boys invited had a ole pair he let me borrow an my mama wa'n't happy cuz she wanna boycott the damn rink but she didn't wamme be rude to Carl so I went. Mrs. Talley paid for everbody's entrance an then left an we skated. She said no one had to bring a present though I notice half the boys did. I'm a little embarrassed by mine so relieved Mrs. Talley insist Carl don't open any of em till after he take em home. The skates didn't fit my feet right an gay me blisters but the boys rented the skates got blisters too so that wa'n't nothin.

Roof an Carl, wonder how that be. But by some stroke a luck Carl's sister got a piano recital so Carl gotta decline my birthday.

My mama gimme a new pad an charcoal pencils. I know I'm givin ya nothin you don't already have. But just so's you don't run out.

Thanks, Mama.

We ain't never expected a present from Roof so sprised he hold out somethin. Cartoon cut outa the paper. I know you been collectin em, he say.

Nex day settin on my bed after school, slice a leftover cake. Firs I make the double V like she asked me to. Then I pick up the cartoon Roof gimme. I open my little drore filled with the clippins.

One of em is three Congressmen on a horse. The horse is branded NEW DEAL. The men are singin *Oh, the Old Gray Mare, She Ain't What She Used to Be.* President Roosevelt drives by in a fancy new car which says WIN THE WAR and he tells the men on the New Deal horse *Turn Her Out to Pasture, Boys. We've Got to Get Going.*

There's ones encouragin people to buy war bonds signed Dr. Seuss, an I wonder how a doctor got time also be a cartoonist. This man seem to appear on all of em, this Oriental man with big teeth an big spectacles. One has him an Hitler's faces on Mount Rushmore, their eyes closed, the Oriental man's teeth's so large he doe'n't seem to be able to close his mouth. DON'T LET THEM CARVE **THOSE** FACES ON OUR MOUNTAINS! BUY UNITED STATES SAVINGS BONDS AND STAMPS!

Then there's cartoon clippins nothin to do with the war, like a blond white child in a white outfit nex to a little colored child more tattered. Neither of em looks dirty, yet the white kid says, WHY DOESN'T YOUR MAMMA WASH YOU WITH FAIRY SOAP? There's a colored maid so happy the family she works for has a Tracy sink: *m-m-m-MM! They sure have the <u>Nicest</u> things.* An Topsy Tobacco, the skippin little dark girl with the nappy hair: I IS SO WICKED!

An the Pullman Porter overhearin the white couple upset cuz the lady caught a cold on their honeymoon. The Porter smiles an speaks nothin like my daddy. *Pahdon me, fo' overhearin' yo', but Sal Hepatica does BOTH dose things. It's a min'ral salt laxative and it helps Nature counteract acidity too. Las' trip a doctah tole <u>me</u>.*

What I'm wonderin is how come the colored people an the Japanese people don't look human, or don't *act* human. I don't know who that Japanese man is. It don't look like Emperor Hirohito, it don't look like Prime Minister Tojo, but that white man sure is Hitler. Cartoons sposed to exaggerate the person. But why when the person ain't white all that gets exaggerated's the race?

Dwight!

She can holler up to me but hate if I holler back, I'm sposed to jus drop what I'm doin an come down.

Makin her list. Needja to go to D'Angelo's. Some sugar, butter. I give her the double V I made for the front winda an she smile, gimme a kiss. While she searchin through the cupboards to see if she forgot anything I look at the *Pittsburgh Courier* letter-to-the-editor again, taped on the icebox door.

> *Being an American of dark complexion and some 26 years, these questions flash through my mind: "Should I sacrifice my life to live half American?" "Will things be better for the next generation in the peace to follow?" "Would it be demanding too much to demand full citizenship rights in exchange for the sacrificing of my life." "Is the kind of America I know worth defending?" "Will America be a true and pure democracy after this war?" "Will colored Americans suffer still the indignities that have been heaped upon them in the past?"*
>
> *This may be the wrong time to broach such subjects, but haven't all good things obtained by men been secured through sacrifice during just such times of strife?*
>
> *The "V for Victory" sign is being displayed prominently in all so-called democratic countries which are fighting for victory over aggression, slavery and tyranny. If this V sign means that to those now engaged in this great conflict then let colored Americans adopt the double VV for a double victory; The first V for victory over our enemies from without, the second V for victory over our enemies within. For surely those who perpetrate these ugly prejudices here are seeking to destroy our democratic form of government just as surely as the Axis forces.*

Mrs. D'Angelo's mindin the store. Most an genrally she's friendly as Mr. D'Angelo but today in a little argument at the cash register with a white lady. Figure it might be a few minutes before Mrs. D'Angelo free to ring up my sugar an butter an salt so I flip through the comics.

Dwight! How *are* you, dear?

I look up from *Captain America*.

Hi.

I haven't seen you in ages! I don't think you've been over for a visit since Christmas!

Mm. Well, Carl's birthday.

Yes, we *saw* you then but it wasn't at our *house*. I *love* having you around the family. You *are* one of the family! You've been with us since we moved here, it doesn't feel right not seeing you every day like we used to.

Aw.

Oh! Her eyes closed, hand on her heart. The present you gave Carl. So perfect! The best gift by far! It's hanging over the piano. Framed.

I laugh a little, shift my feet.

But I guess you didn't know! Carl hasn't thanked you. I told him to make sure he thanks all the boys at school but you're not in his school.

I nod, glancin over at Mrs. D'Angelo an the lady, their voices gettin louder. My credit is *good*, the lady say.

I'm so sorry Carl couldn't come to your birthday but I think Christina would just have been devastated if he'd missed her recital.

That's okay.

Well he has your present. When can you come over and get it?

Oh. He didn't have to do that.

Well he did. His first friend in Humble. I hope you'll *always* stay friends.

I try to smile. Hard to look her in the face.

How about Saturday afternoon? I can make you some of my brownies. You like those, don't you?

They're gonna put the Japs on the concentration camps, an I hope all the wops an the krauts go there too! hurls the white lady at Mrs. D'Angelo as she leaves, slammin.

Everybody's in the family room! says Mrs. Talley when I drop by two o'clock Saturday. Soon's I walk in I see it: drawin I made a Carl playin the piano framed an hung over the upright. Carl settin cross-leg on the floor, some kinda mail-order catalog on his thighs. He look up when I walk in, but like his mind distracted go right back to the page.

Which one? says Christina, puttin her leff wrist in fronta me, then her right. Firs I'm confused, then I realize each had its own smell.

That one, I say.

See? she say to Carl an Mr. Talley. Carl don't look up. Mr. Talley been standin starin at me since I walked in, wineglass in his hand, smile on his face.

I hear congratulations are in order, he says.

Yes! Both the boys are teenagers now, says Mrs. Talley. Practically grown up. I'll get the brownies, an she's gone.

On the wall's a world map that wa'n't there lass time I was here. There's red thumbtacks in the U.S., Canada, Britain, France, Australia, New Zealand, an the Soviet Union. There's blue thumbtacks in Germany, Japan, Italy, Poland, Denmark, Holland, Belgium, Norway, France, the Channel Islands, Bulgaria, Yugoslavia, Romania, Hungary, Finland, Estonia, British Somaliland, an the Philippines.

Recent action in the Pacific theater, says Mr. Talley. The Japs captured Manila, Kuala Lumpur. But we're fighting back in the former, or so says the danged yellow press. Whoops. He tries to pour from a wine bottle into his empty glass but the bottle's just as empty.

You drank that whole Chablis Dad, says Christina, holdin a han meer an tryin different lipstick colors.

Look at that map! says Mr. Talley. Ever think you see America red? But between the Soviets as Allies, and Axis Japan gnawing at Red China, well.

Here you go, Dwight. Mrs. Talley enterin with brownies. These have walnuts, these are plain. She puts the plate on a table, then settin on a soff chair, picks up her spectacles an takes some embroiderin she'd been workin on. I don't think I ever seen her settin down before.

Empty, says Mr. Talley, still clutchin the bottle, smilin an lookin at Mrs. Talley.

You've had enough, she says without lookin up.

Edwin enlisted, says Christina, suddenly droppin her meer to look at her mother.

Yes, you've mentioned that, says Mrs. Talley.

I'm going to write him every day. Christina don't wear pigtails no more, graduated to a bob. Carl takes a pen an circles somethin in the catalog.

Carl, do not vandalize my catalog! says Mr. Talley, though there's a little smile on his face, like he oughta be madder but right now he's feelin too good to be.

I'm worried about him, says Christina. He's gonna be a flyer.

I'm thirsty, says Mr. Talley, walkin out with his glass. Carl brings me the catalog.

YOUNG ENGINEERS WANT ERECTOR
SETS FROM HALL OF SCIENCE

~~$15⁰⁰~~ $11⁹⁸

Super Automotive Set
with 110-Volt Motor

Builds over 180 action models. Gear box, wheels, boiler, auto-motive parts for trucks, fire engines, tow cars, cranes, trench diggers. Electric magnet for lifting. No batteries or trans-formers needed. Packed in steel cabinet. Shipping weight, 19 lbs.

79 N 04785...**$11.98**

Edwin's my fiancé, says Christina.

Yes, you've mentioned that, says Mrs. Talley.

Carl takes the page from me an shows it to his mother.

Half-birthday, he says.

She looks over her glasses at it, then back to her work.

We'll see.

It's cheaper than the other one.

We'll see.

Carl turns to me. Monopoly?

Mr. Talley comes in pourin a newly opened wine bottle. Damn krauts, so cocky! Moving into Soviet territory, hey, the Russians just recaptured Kiev, take *that* up your ass, Hitler!

Craig! says Mrs. Talley.

Open season, says Carl, as many hotels as you can afford. My firs roll I get one an a two, put me right on Mediterranean. Dammit! says Carl.

Mary Jo and Seth Landers just got married, says Christina. It meant something to him. Before going overseas. Knowing he had somebody, till death do they part.

Here comes Dwight the slumlord, mutters Carl.

Oh Dwight! We didn't even explain. Since Carl's birthday comes so soon after Christmas, and we're all empty pockets from the holidays, three years ago he very thoughtfully suggested that we celebrate his *half*-birthday. So on January 7th he has his party and friends can give him presents if they like, and on *July* 7th, his *half*-birthday, he gets the presents from the family. Wasn't that smart of him?

I think the adjective you're looking for is greedy, says Christina.

Pig, says Carl.

Alright, says Mrs. Talley.

They're all gonna disappear, says Mr. Talley. One day you'll look around the neighborhood, all the men eighteen to thirties, gone.

Craig's been volunteering at the draft board.

Had to do something. Since I wasn't going to be a fool air raid warden, blowing a goddamn siren. You know who volunteers for *that* job? The assholes.

Craig!

Go straight to jail? Carl throws the card down. How the hell *that* get top of the deck? The game's hardly started!

Oh! I almost forgot your present, Dwight! I'm kinda sorry see her get up to get it. Felt like a whole different Mrs. Talley settin down.

Franklin D. didn't want war in Asia, says Mr. Talley. Sure, he was hoping to go after *Hitler* while the country was screaming isolationism, but two wars at once he didn't figure we could handle. Then, surprise! Pearl Harbor, early Christmas from Hirohito and the rest of the damn yellow Fifth Column.

He's leaving for Florida in a week, says Christina. Edwin. Eglin Air Force Base.

My little brother's friend's uncle got drafted, I say. Lives over on Oak Street. I never say Colored Street to white people.

But white people know what Oak Street is so Christina looks confused. He's colored?

I nod.

I didn't know colored boys fought.

Course they fight, her father tells her. Well, they *serve*. Cooks. Cleaning the latrines.

There's gonna be colored pilots! Trainin em, Tuskegee College. Tennessee.

Colored *pilots*? Christina all agape at me.

Where'd you hear such a thing? asks her father.

Lotsa places.

Oh that must just be a rumor, says Mr. Talley.

Free Parking. Boring! Carl slams his car down there. You know some people play that all the money collected from Chance and Community Chest goes into the middle of the board, then when you land on Free Parking: windfall! It's not strictly according to the rules. But we could play it like that. If you want.

The SS thinks it's unbeatable. Well here come the Yanks! Carl's father raises his glass, toastin.

Double V! I say. Victory over our enemies from without, an victory over our enemies from within!

Hear, hear! says Mr. Talley. Then he frowns, confused.

What the hell's double V? asks Carl.

Colored slogan. I made the Double V, my mother put it in our winda. From this article she cut out, taped to our icebox.

Frigidaire! Carl says. He always calls it that! I don't know if the horse-n-buggy still come to his house but we live in 1942.

Happy birthday! says Mrs. Talley, comin in holdin somethin wrapped.

And what's that other thing you say. Most and generally. He means usually!

We were thinking. Maybe it's time for us to get married too. Edwin and me.

After college, says her mother, eyes on me openin my present.

Well he *wants* to go to college, that bill for soldiers—

After *you* finish college, Mrs. Talley turnin to her.

Oh! Christina all frustration.

Do you like it?

Yes! Thank you! I start flippin through, feelin the slick pages. Never had a art book to call my own.

Well, Carl and I thought you might like it.

I turn to him. Thanks, Carl.

Carl says, What is it?

I need to marry him *soon.* You never know what might happen.

What's the enemies within, Dwight?

I turn to Mr. Talley. Segregation. Lynchin.

I know a little about art, says Mrs. Talley. I had an Art Appreciation class. College. She flips through my book.

Well, says Mr. Talley, that's a little like racing to patch up the roof while the whole house is burning down. We have to get our priorities straight.

If anything ever happened to Edwin, I don't know what I'd do!

The first priority is to make sure next week we aren't all speaking German. Or Japanese. Know how many syllables Japanese takes? Nobody'd get anything done, take you twenty minutes just to say I'm leaving for work, honey-sun! Carl's father cracks up.

I went one year to college, I took an Art Appreciation class. I came to appreciate the Impressionists, Monet, Degas. Do you like the Impressionists, Dwight?

If anything ever happened to Edwin, I'd just want him to know he had someone to call a wife.

You mean a widow, says Mrs. Talley, admirin the chapter on Impressionists. Christina look all shocked, then run cryin out the room. Carl's dice hit the board.

Boxcars! Carl skip his sports car roun the bend.

There was a colored soldier used to cook for us back in '19, France. Stanley. Can't recall now if that was his first name or his last. Loved that guy! He used to say, Lieutenant Talley suh, youse de nicest white man aroun heah, an Ise sho gonna make sho youse gets the biggis hunka meat they is suh. Mr. Talley bustin his insides, the laughter.

Boardwalk! Your ass is grass now, Campbell.

Carl, says his mother.

What kind of meat *is* this, Stanley? I'd ask. De ah-mee meat suh, whatevah dat be. *I*se sho don know, Lieutenant Talley suh! an Mr. Talley laughs so hard he falls back in his chair with his wineglass but careful careful doe'n't spill a drop.

Dwight home?

Nope.

Roof frown.

Okay, tell him I come by.

Mama, where's Dwight?

I don't know. Up Roof's, I guess.

Uh-uh. Roof jus come lookin for him.

I don't know. She settin hand-sewin on my dungarees.

Dwight! Dwight!

Not in our bedroom. Not in mamadaddy's bedroom. Dwight!

I go down the basement steps. He settin on the mountain a coal, cep now it's just a hill a coal. Sketchin.

Dwight! I smile, found him. Didn't you hear me callin?

His eyes look up, not friendly. Whatta you want.

Nothin. Jus lookin for ya.

Why.

Just wondered where you were.

You foun me, now go.

It ain't *your* basement, stay long as I want. An I set on the steps, crost my arms.

He make a big groan, come stompin up the steps right by me.

No privacy! Slammin out the back door.

In bed I say, Dwight, they callin for snow!

Uh-huh.

Your birthday the grounhog seen his shadow. That mean only six weeks leff a winter. An a week pass since your birthday now only *five* weeks leff a winter. Aw! I like winter!

It mean six more *long* weeks a winter.

Oh! Yay! I like winter! I fiddle with my loose tooth. Didja get your birthday wish, Dwight? Whadja wish for?

My business. Ow!

What!

Spring! I know what that mean, another spring come through the mattress, stab Dwight.

Didja wish for snow for your birthday? I hope we get snow! If we get snow, you help me make a snowman?

He sigh.

Didja wish your birthday wa'n't Grounhog's Day? You're a grounhog, Dwight. Hahaha! I'm glad *my* birthday's not Grounhog's Day, glad my birthday a day all by itself. Cep I wish my birthday was Christmas. *Double* the presents! Hahahaha! Then people sing *We wish you a merry Christmas We wish you a merry Christmas We wish you a merry Christmas an Eliot's birthday! Shut up an go to sleep!*

Blizzard! I run down the stairs! Dwight already up eatin oatmeal.

Snow!

She smile tired. Twenty-two inches. No school today. Siddown, you want cinnamon in your oatmeal?

Yes! She put it in front a me, I smell it. I love oatmeal! Dwight finish eatin jus while I start. He go get his gloves an coat.

Wait for me!

He out the door!

Never be able to drag him outa bed this early if it *was* school, she say.

I know. Hahahaha!

She set with her oatmeal. You gettin to be a big boy.

I stop smilin. Wonder what she an Dwight talkin bout fore I get up!

Your brother asked about movin into the guestroom.

My mouth open!

If we have guests, then he go back to your room. But when it's jus the four of us you could each—

No!

She sigh. There ain't no goblins, Eliot.

I stare at her, gettin the shaky lips.

Okay. I asked him if he wouldn't mind waitin till you a little older. Okay?

Okay! I slurp up oatmeal, think I ain't never gettin a little older, hahaha!

On Jake's Hill the big kids with sleds. Dwight an Roof sharin Zack Rhodes'es. I share Jeanine's toboggan. Screamin, flyin down the hill! Every time I go to Dwight he turn away from me. Always he ignore me but today he ignore me *hard*.

Cold! I come home to warm up but fore I go in my house I wonder about Parker. Ain't no cats in Miss Onnie's yard. I knock on her back door.

Her back door the side a her house, facin the side a *our* house *our* back-side porch *our* back-side door. Miss Onnie usually in her kitchen.

She open. Whatchu doin out there in Alaska?

I was lookin for Parker. I look past her, cats everywhere.

Come on in. Yella Cat! she yell. Siddown, he be out direckly. You like cocoa?

Yes!

Prolly lass chance for chocolate fore they rationin it off, she say. Then she pour. Blow it. I said blow it! Wanna burn your tongue off?

Parker come out, hop up on my lap.

Miss Onnie, your house all I hear is mew mew, all I smell is mew mew.

Miss Onnie throw her head back laughin. I didn't even know I made a joke! I'm laughin too!

I go make a snowman our backyard. I can't do it right! Gettin close to dark when she gonna call us to come in, all I got's a hump! Cryin!

Come ere, I'll show ya.

Dwight! He help me! It start lookin like a snowman.

Eliot! Dwight! She on the back porch, got her sweater on but no coat, rubbin her arms, hollerin out to the street.

We're here, Mama!

She turn aroun. Oh. I *like* that snowman!

Can we finish, Mama? I'm jumpin, jumpin!

Okay, long as you stay in the yard. Fifteen more minutes. She shiver, go back inside.

We finish. I wanna get coal for the eyes but Dwight say no. He take his fingers an carve the eyes an the nose an the mouth, it look just like a person!

You know how to make snow angels?

He show me. Lie on the groun, let your arms swish, up down up down. Let your legs swish, apart together apart together. I do what he say, then I get up, see what I done. It look jus like a angel! I love my brother!

Near enda Febyuary, Mama settin at the kitchen table doin arithmetic like she always do near enda the month every month.

Daddy an I think we might have a little surprise for you boys.

What!

If the arithmetic add up. Little surprise.

Helen Brown, what did I just say was the capital of North Dakota?

Helen eyes pop open! She ain't heard Mrs. Brent say the capital a North

Dakota, Helen always fallin asleep! I got to write the date on the calendar on the blackboard today, Tuesday the 3rd a March. Today school feel long cuz Daddy come home from Boddimore yesterday Monday the 2nd a March an goin back tomarra Wednesday the 4th a March, I wanna go home see him now! Dismissal bell! I run out the school, *bang!* My face smashed with snow! Dwight laughin. I run after him! I try to throw the snowballs at him but mine falls apart! Other kids throwin snowballs an runnin. Them twins Marco an Mokie. Jeanine try to throw at her big cousin Cirelle who always wear the pink bows in her hair, then outa nowhere this car come almost hit Jeanine! Everbody stop. White man jump outa the car.

Whatta ya doin! Yellin at Jeanine. Yellin at alla us!

Jeanine stare at him, eyes big. He's ole, he look like forty. His wife settin in the other seat, she don't get out. She don't look at us, she look straight ahead not see us.

All you damn kids, this is a street, not a playground! Didn't anybody never tell ya look up the street before ya step out? He start to get back in his car, sayin Act like you blind.

Act like *you* blind, say Mokie.

Our mouths fly open! Man fly back outa his car, slam the door eyes hard on Mokie, *What did you say?*

An it's a *alley*, not a street, Mokie say. The man move toward Mokie an Mokie take off! We all take off! Little *niggers!* we hear the man say way back there, way back there we run far from him! Runnin, runnin, an when we don't see him no more: laughin!

Mama! Guess what me an Dwight—

But we don't see her in the kitchen an we don't see Daddy. Then we hear them talkin soff, upstairs. I run up. They back in our bedroom.

Mama! Daddy! Guess what—

I stop. Dwight right behine me, stop. There's Mama an Daddy. An two little beds. Dwight's an mine bed gone. Two little twin beds, one by the winda, one by the wall. Me an Dwight look at them beds, look at Mama an Daddy. Mama an Daddy grin. Dwight jump on the one by the winda.

No jumpin, Daddy say. These beds gotta last.

I seen these beds! say Dwight. In the winda, Ryan's Used.

They's the ones, say Mama. Dwight lie down, like to own the bed by the winda.

How come he gets the winda!

You're the one always scared, lookin out at the tree at night. But I don't care. You want this one?

Where's our bed!

Mama lookin at me. Give it away.

To *who*!

Miss Polly Jean. She got all them kids, right? Half of em was sleepin on the floor.

I stare at her.

That bed was fallin apart, the springs comin through. You know we got it when Grammaw died, old.

Then how come you give it to Miss Polly Jean!

Better n em sleepin on the floor.

I want my ole bed! I take to sobbin.

God, say Dwight.

Don't say that, say Mama.

You don't know how lucky you are, Daddy say to me.

I bawl louder. Daddy say, Wamme give ya somethin to cry about?

In the night Mama tuck me in. It's cold without Dwight!

She gimme a extra blanket. Good night. Kissin me.

The lights out, I say, I ain't talkin to you, Dwight. You jus fine without me, I'm jus fine without you.

You oughta punish me like that more often, Dwight say somewhere in the dark. I wanna kick him but he too far away!

School nex day Wednesday Ellen an Helen thank me for the bed. Ellen an Helen Brown's twins. Our mama an daddy say you ever wanna visit overnight, you welcome.

Mama! Ellen an Helen say I can stay overnight! Can I please please!

Mama look at me. Then she on the telephone.

Okay, Miss Polly Jean an Mr. George say you can stay tomorra night. You take the bus home after school with Ellen an Helen an come back nex day. Okay?

Okay!

Now if you go, you can't cry for Mama. You never stayed overnight by yourself away from home before. You gonna be a big boy?

Yes! I won't cry for Mama, I say. But inside I ain't sure!

An you be polite to Miss Polly Jean an Mr. George.

I will!

An don't ask for no seconds! Even if you still hungry.

I nod. Mama never tole me never ask for no seconds before. Sometimes I ask an she say All we gots is firsts today, but she never say I couldn't ask.

Go to my room. Dwight on his bed sketchin. I go see what he's drawrin. He turn away, like to hide it from me! I flop my behine down on his bed.

Get off!

Don't haveta.

He pick me up an drop me on my bed! Then go back to *his* bed!

I'm tellin!

What else is new?

Mama! I bring her. Mama, Dwight threw me off his bed!

Eliot, you don't share a bed anymore. Dwight's bed is *his* space. He can't get on your bed without your permission, you can't get on his bed without his permission.

He threw me crost the room! I slam my behine down on my bed, crost my arms.

Look at them pouty lips, she say. I'ma cut off them lips, have em for supper.

Dwight snicker.

Shut up, Dwight!

Thursday school I try to think about the county seats a Maryland but I keep thinkin bout the school bus! I never rode no bus before.

Bell: school done school done! I come out with Ellen an Helen to go to the bus. There's Mama!

I jus come by to say See ya tomarra. I can't believe I ain't gonna see ya tonight! She hug me. Mama'll miss you.

I'll miss you too, Mama, I gotta get on the bus! I run away from her after Ellen an Helen. They get windas right behine each other. Helen set with their sister Crystal Lee from the fith. I set with Ellen an since I ain't never been on a bus before Ellen trade with me so I get the winda! We drive all the way to Fort Naylor where Ellen an Helen an Crystal Lee Brown daughters a Miss Polly Jean an Mr. George live, all the way to the enda the county. We pass a lotta white schools. We got the only colored school the whole county! Drivin over a hour all the stops, by the time we get to the Browns it's dark. A whole herd a kids get out here, all Browns.

It ain't a far walk to their house. Their house like a playgroun! Kids every-where! Sharon's the oldest, nineteen, on down to the baby, three months ole. Seventeen kids!

Welcome, Eliot. Miss Polly Jean real nice to me, but yellin at all her own kids. Some of em doin homework, some of em runnin wile!

You have very nice eyeglasses, Eliot.

Thank you, Miss Polly Jean.

My kids never needed em. But Ralph Lee in the third grade lie on the floor, got his eyes so close to his readin book his nose practically touch the page. How he read all them kids goin wild aroun him! Their house ain't so messy though, not like Roof's house is messy. But Mama say we can't call Roof trash cuz his little sister died.

At supper the big kids set at the table, us little kids set on the floor, Miss Polly Jean's house ain't very warm but everybody runnin aroun warm it up. But my behine cole on the cole floor.

We got fish sticks. I love fish sticks! Three fish sticks an buttered potatas an peas, I don't even need seconds, firsts is plenty!

Now I see everyone else got one fish stick, the little little kids got a half fish stick. Everone got a little piece a potata but I got a whole half. Some a the littler kids stare at my plate, stare at me.

Wanna see your bed? say Ellen.

In the girls' room her an Helen an Crystal Lee an Perry Ann side by side, Julia May stretched out crost the bottom. Five! When it was me an Dwight's bed was jus two! Sharon sleep downstairs on the couch. Sharon say I need to get married an get outa here. Sharon say I'm nineteen, I need to start my own life. Like that she say it, six times.

Sorry, Eliot, Miss Polly Jean say to me, we ain't got no bed yet for the boys' room. The babies in Miss Polly Jean's room with her. Nine boys includin me on the floor, gettin close for the warm.

Daddy doin the afternoon shiff? Harvey asks.

Yes, say Miss Polly Jean, be back 11:30. Yaw better be sleep by then. Mr. George at the tire factory, Mama tole me. Them jobs opened up for colored since the war.

In the dark I shake from the cold! Shake cuz I miss Mama! I get my hat an coat an still cold, can't hardly sleep from the cold! I feel the tear but I make it stay my eye, it freeze my face! Somebody sneeze. I can't hardly move my arms, we all huddled an still cold! Jimmy Lee, youngest, pee the bed cep ain't no bed, all his brothers *Aw!* Him cryin.

The house get up early early, we gotta be at the bus stop way earlier n me an Dwight even wake up! Nobody mention nothin bout breakfast so I don't neither.

Cold! Dark! We wait a long long time for the bus, our breath big. Some a them Browns holdin their coats shut, the buttons missin.

The mornin bus lot colder n yesterday afternoon! We the firs people on it besides Troy an Mary Jane from the high school. Still see our breath on the bus! Long ride. I get the winda. I see a couple white schools pass by, too bad them Browns can't go nearby to the white school I think yawnin then I'm sleep.

In arithmetic I'm yawnin again. In social studies Mrs. Brent say, What did I just say, Eliot?

I don't know! I stare at her. She do not look pleased.

At recess some a the big kids take over the monkey bars. They playin Japanese Interment Camp. The Japanese is jailed inside the monkey bars, the soldiers is on the outside.

Show me your ID! says Byron Freeman from the eleventh. Hi jaki eks komeenono.

Butch Quarryman from the tenth from inside a the monkey bars cracks up. That ain't no Japanese, fool!

Show me your ID, you Jap! Some a the little kids go cryin to the playgroun teacher the big kids won't let us on the monkey bars.

I need food for my baby, says Janey Wells from the inside. My baby needs some milk.

My baby needs some milk, says Gary Ray Horne from the seventh in a funny voice.

Shoulda thoughta that fore you bombed Pearl Harbor, says Butch Quarryman.

Hey, says Mr. Raleigh comin over, You big kids: off!

In line to go back inside after recess, Jeanine whispers to me, We're nex.

Huh?

Nex they put colored on the concentration camp.

Uh-*uh!*

That's what Uncle Ramonlee said. We set an watch this happen, guess who they comin for nex? Then they drafted him an he gone. Mr. Raleigh go, Second grade! wavin us back in.

Dismissal bell! Glad to go home, *my* bed! Glad to sleep in my own new used bed!

Mama! You come pick me up!

I missed you, I couldn't wait till you got home! How was your overnight visit?

It was okay. Where's Dwight?

I already seen him, told him he could go on ahead if he wanted.

Walkin home, I like holdin Mama's han.

Mama. We gonna get put on a interment camp?

She stop walkin. What?

A interment camp. Like the Japs.

Japa*nese*, don't say Japs!

Like the Japanese.

No. Inter*n*ment camp.

Mama, wanna see my spellin test? Nother hunnert! Always I get a hunnert, haha!

Who said we were gonna get put on internment camps?

The big kids was playin Japanese Internment Camp on the monkey bars, an then Mr. Raleigh told em get off, an then Jeanine tole me her uncle Ramonlee said we's nex then he go off to war.

Don't you play that game!

We *was*n't. The *big* kids was.

Don't you *never* play that game, it's not funny! She shakin my arm!

It gonna happen to us nex?

She let go a me. No, she say. But her face worry worry.

Supper is porknbeans. Porknbeans is hot dogs cut up in bake beans. I love porknbeans! It warm in our kitchen with the stove on. Dwight butter his bread, he don't even look at me.

It warm in our bedroom under the covers! Me an Dwight on our new used beds waitin for Mama come kiss us good night. Our new used beds is fun! Dwight readin his homework, it's Friday! He don't gotta read his homework, he jus don't wanna look at me!

I won't get on your new used bed no more, Dwight.

He look up, his face surprise.

Thank you, he say. Like he really mean it, his eyes shiny like it all important. I don't like sleepin by myself. I liked sleepin with my brother. But Dwight's eyes tell me him likin his alone is bigger n my not likin my alone.

We got room now, Dwight. Look! I make a snow angel on top of my covers for Dwight, an I don't even kick no one doin it.

Second week a May spring comes, sunny an warm. Friday locker room the Wiley twins bring up the idea a pickup baseball Saturday. Richard an Chester say they in. Percy can't, gotta help his dad paintin some houses which make him mad, a few others also got chores an everybody else don't live close enough. Spread the word, says Mokie. An since every colored boy our age settin right here, Spread the word mean to white.

Roof say sure, one a the lass games fore he off to work the mines. (I think, I'll believe that when I see it.) Roof asks Zack who says okay.

Two o'clock we meet, our school playground. Ten of us, so each team get a pitcher, catcher, first base an two outfield, the catcher doublin as ump an sworn to be fair. Since the game was the twins' idea, they get firs dibs to be captains, but course only one of em gonna do it since they always wanna be on the same team. Marco says yes an Mokie forfeits his captaincy to Richard. So Marco picks Mokie, then Richard picks Chester, then Marco picks Brett the white boy live near him an Mokie, then Richard picks Trudie the white tomboy he brought, then Marco picks me, then Richard picks Zack, then Marco picks Kip the white boy live near Chester, then Richard picks Roof.

Richard's a real athlete, an a good sport cuz he says he'll play outfield knowin if he's pitcher every innin jus be three up three down for the other team, which is us. Everybody else is decent players, but with the lack of a full outfield defense by the bottom a the sixt it's twenty-eight us, thirty-three them.

I'm walkin in from the field when I notice through the chain-link behind the batters we got us a fan. Seem like he been there a little while. Lookin content, watchin the innin change, his fingers grippin the wire criss-crossins an then he turn right to me.

Hey Dwight.

Hey Carl.

The moment I spied him I wondered is he sore at me. Here's a neighborhood pickup game I didn't even tell him was goin on. More significant, after that day comin over for my birthday present I ain't been by since. Partly it's about goin our separate ways with our different schools, but also takin up with Carl again mean bein with his family, an while his folks ain't never been nothin but nice to me, I just as soon never again be in close vicinity of his father when his father in close vicinity of a wine bottle.

An anyway nothin never stopped Carl from comin to my house. Why'm *I* always expected? Cuz *he* got the Monopoly? badminton? Or cuz I'm sposed to be all fine aroun white people but he less comfortable, house a Negroes.

All this weighin on my mind yet now it occur to me he don't seem mad at all. Lookin the opposite: smilin, wishin he was playin but not complainin, an I feel guilty. Lean my back gainst the fence, nex to him, me lookin at the game from the inside, him lookin at it from the out.

You goin to camp again this summer?

Yeah. This'll be my last year though. Thirteen. Unless I wanna be a counselor.

Do ya?

Hell no.

Kip gets a triple.

My dad says if the weather stays nice, we can put up the volleyball net next weekend. You should come over.

I look at my glove, inspectin it. Tattered, I had it since fith grade.

I thought. You kinda had your friends from your school now.

Carl frowns, shrugs. They're alright.

Marco brings Kip home an puts himself on second.

There's a girl though.

I turn to him. He looks down, laughs embarrassed.

I think. I think she likes me.

I look at my glove again, yank out some threads. That bring out more threads, yank them out.

What she look like?

Blond. Two braids down to her waist. Freckles. Not too many.

She in your section?

The beginning of the year she was, 7-B. Polly Swift. Always sitting right in front of me, alphabetical. We were just getting to be friends, then three days after school starts my dad gets me moved to 7-A. Carl sighs. Luckily, alphabetical we still see each other in homeroom. Sometimes the library. I didn't even wanna go to 7-A! Bunch of pricks.

Some argument whippin up: ball or strike? My heart flyin, hand in my glove shaky. Me an Carl never mentioned girls lass summer. But so what? Why the subject make my brow sweat?

I haven't told anybody. Those guys from school. You're the only one.

You gonna say somethin to her?

I don't know. He runs his han through his hair, his eyes shiny. I don't know!

Brett slam it toward firs an take off runnin, but firs-base Trudie claim it's a foul. Everybody get into the act now, squabblin. Roof stand up at home, turn aroun to look for me, only other person not in the fight. His eyes narrow when he see who I'm with.

You like any girls at your school?

Deep breath. They're all nice.

I'm sure they're all *nice*. I'm asking about anybody you *like*.

Hey kid.

Me an Carl both turn to Mokie.

Look, we need an impartial ump. You do it?

Carl looks at me. Then he looks at Roof. Then he looks at Mokie.

Sure.

Long innins. In the bottom a the seventh, Roof's on third. Richard slams it into leff field. When Roof sprints home, he rams himself into Carl, knockin the ump over.

Hey! says Carl.

Sorry, says Roof, not hidin his smirk.

Carl pulls up his pant leg. Blood.

Sorry, says Roof, not smilin no more, jus walkin away.

Top a the eighth our team finally pulls ahead. After an unspoken period a probation, Carl the ump comes to be respected an his calls all taken as official cuz his calls all seem to be fair. People seen me talkin to him an were likely waitin to see if he'd show me favoritism, an they seen the way Roof looks at Carl an prolly wondered he show him *anti*favoritism, but when Roof come runnin to my firs base an the ball got to me a moment too late before I tagged him, Carl called it safe like he shoulda. Only Roof still wants to fight some a the calls when nobody else is, an it's startin to get on people's nerves. Comin up on 5 p.m. an we're wantin the dang game over.

When Richard's team takes the field top a the ninth, they're pitchin the ball to each other a few minutes to warm up their catchin in this lass chance to hold us. While they're hurlin it Carl's turned aroun, lookin at us linin up for the bat. Outfielder Trudie throws it to pitcher Chester who throws it to firs baseman Roof who throws it to Zack at home except instead a Zack it zoinks Carl on the backa his head, an he goes down, still.

Everybody runs to Carl. Lyin on his back, arms out like Jesus. You okay? You okay? Then he sets up, rubbin his head. Yeah, I'm okay. Just grazed. He looks a little fuzzy. Sorry, sorry, Roof's sayin, an he looks it, looks scared.

I'm okay, says Carl standin up, shaky.

After a few minutes Carl looks better, an everyone starts goin back to their places. Headin for the field Richard mutters to me, Looks like your white boys is fightin over ya.

What! I swerve to him. Carl's jus two feet away but doe'n't seem like he heard, maybe he's still a little dizzy. Meanwhile Richard jus keep movin like I ain't said nothin, hurls the ball at Chester the pitcher then trots to the out-field. Chester throws it to outfield Trudie, Trudie throws it to Roof. When Roof sends it back to her, his throw's suddenly shy-gentle, apparently not wantin to knock out nobody else.

Bottom a the ninth they're up, one out, forty-four us, forty-two them, Zack on first an Trudie on third, Roof up. I notice Carl take a step back-ward, like just in case Roof swing the bat too wild. Roof lets the firs pitch go by, ball. But when he goes for the second an misses, his swing's so dainty seem like if he *had* hit it it wouldn'ta gone more n three feet.

Let's *go* Barton, says Richard, pickin up on Roof's timidness.

So nex pitch Roof swing hard an it goes sailin over our outfield heads. I sprint after it. Trudie come home, Zack come home which ties it, an seein Roof roundin third I hurl that ball all the way to catcher Brett. My throw is perfect, Brett's catch is perfect, Roof flyin toward him an Carl takes two steps well outa the way a collision. Roof slides, Brett tags him, an then Roof touches home. Our team cheers, only one more out an we hold em at the tie, give us another chance, extra innin. Richard's team groans an then Carl makes the signal.

Safe.

For a few seconds everybody, includin Roof, jus stare at Carl, open mouth. Then my team start screamin the fury an Richard's team applauds, but lookin more puzzled than triumphant. Roof glares at Carl. Carl stares at Roof peaceful, all Buddha. Then Roof slams his bat down an leaves, stompin out the playgroun an I guess stompin all the way home.

I walk back with Carl, wantin to make sure he's okay after that bump on the head. We're quiet a long time, then he says, That's why you haven't been over lately? Cuz I'm white?

I'm startled, then guess he heard somethin a what Richard said.

How come it's always gotta be *your* house? How come you never come to *mine*?

He stops an looks at me, like maybe that never occurred to him. Okay, he says. Okay. Can I bring Monopoly over?

There's a bunch a birds all gathered over a piece a bread on the sidewalk. Carl growls, runnin through em an they fly away in a panic. Soon as we pass, they come back.

I'm pretty nice to that kid, huh? Considering he's never given me anything but a bloody knee and a concussion.

How come you did that? That lass play?

He gets a funny smile on his face. Show you're the bigger person. That's what I was always taught.

I don't think your mother meant for you to cheat.

Who said anything about that bitch? My *father*.

I don't say anything for a minute. I'm thinkin about him actin the bigger person, about him seemin so nice to Roof today when he knows damn well I know how nasty he can be behind Roof's back, an what. He think Roof's too dumb to see it?

What're *you* friends with him for? Tell you what. In school, all he's ever seen with is the trashiest.

An how you judge who's the trashiest?

By how often I overhear nigger thrown around which in their case is about five times a sentence.

I kick a big rock high, later I know my toe be achin but now I don't care. I wanna punch Roof, this jus the culmination of a long day a his crap, but somethin ain't settin right. For one thing, ain't nobody gonna tell me all a Carl's high n mighty 7-A cohorts never occasionally put that word to use in a sentence themself.

Course I'm never around his class. Dummies. But some stuff, can't help but hear in the halls.

It ain't been easy for him.

Why, cuz he's *poor*? Carl spittin the word, like it tastes bad, like there's Roof on the one hand an my family an his on the other. Rockefellers.

His sister died.

What?

It was hot, way I heard it. He was three an she was a year, couldn't hardly catch their breath, their house like a sauna. To cool em off, Miss Ray Anne takes the worshtub out in the yard an fills it up with cool water, put em in it. But somethin happened. Nobody remember what the emergency was but she *had* to go back in the house, just a minute, an when she return the baby drowned. Roof watched her drown. Till his mother got hysterical, he thought the baby layin face down in the water was jus playin.

Jesus.

Roof don't like water. Scared to swim, never learned. Won't even go to the crick.

Carl squints into the sun.

Don't tell no one what I said. Sometime Roof make me mad too but. I don't know.

Last summer you promised you'd take me to the crick.

Okay. I shrug. This summer.

After I drop Carl off at his house I'm about to turn into mine, barely make suppertime, when I see Roof standin in his front yard behind his broke wood fence starin at me. An suddenly I don't know why I said that stuff to Carl. In the moment it seemed like maybe it'd make peace between em. In the moment I felt like Carl tole me about that girl, in the warm weather like lass summer when we was close an guess in the moment maybe I wanted to be friends with Carl again. But why'd I decide to rekindle with Roof's business? An what was I thinkin anyway. Pityin Roof might make Carl like him better? I walk up to Roof's house.

He cheated.

I say nothin.

That lass run. Brett got me out, an Carl called safe.

I know.

He glares at Carl's house.

Bastard! Why's he gotta do what he do? Then he turn to go back inside his house.

Roof.

What.

You hit Carl in the head on purpose?

He thinks.

I can't remember.

I look at him.

I know I hate him. I know I turned aroun fass throwin the ball. I know he went down. Roof stop now, ponderin them three facts, like he ain't sure himself how they all might fit together, then turn aroun again, up on his porch, go inside an shut the door.

Sunday afternoon Mama makin her lass-chance apple pie, what she call it, lass chance fore the ingredients be scarce: flour an the sugar an the butter. The government jus give us the ration book. Me an Eliot watch her, waitin for the dough.

Knock at the back door. Carl holdin the Monopoly board.

Come on in Carl, she says. Would you like some dough?

All the times I been to Carl's his mother offerin the freshly baked brownies or cookies an course firs day since Christmas he come to my place an my mother: Here's a fine pile a raw dough for ya.

Dwight an Eliot like it, she says.

I love dough! Eliot practically bouncin outa his chair.

Okay, says Carl.

She makes more n she needs for her crust so Eliot, Carl an me get nice big balls. I'm bettin Carl's thinkin this must be how the coloreds snack, an if I ain't already embarrassed enough my mama gotta put her arm aroun me an gimme a kiss in fronta him.

I like dough, Carl says. I look to see if he's serious. He seem to be, an he sure eat every lass gooey crumb.

We set on my bed an by the fourth pass go I'm handin over three hundred thirty for landin on his two houses on Atlantic Av.

I used to lick the bowl. Then he quiet, starin at the houses I jus paid rent on. When she'd make a cake.

How come you don't no more?

He rolls. Indiana! Looks like that gives me a complete set on the reds.

Eliot hoppin in.

Whaddya want?

Crayons. Colorin with Mama. He get em out the drore, then hop out the door an down the steps.

I'm gonna talk to her, says Carl. Before the end of the school year.

I stare at him. Your mother?

Polly!

Aaaaaah! By now I know the rent on his Tennessee hotel, start countin out the nine-fifty.

You know who else hops like your brother?

I shrug. My reserves don't look good.

My mother.

I look at him, frownin.

He laughs. My aunt Grace told me. She and my mother never got along. Family reunion my grandmother gave a couple years ago, she tells me about how giving birth to my sister almost killed my mother, she never wanted to go through that again. So twice after when my father planted her up, she'd drink some special tea and hop up and down and eventually the thing roll out, all bloody. *Hop! hop! hop!* Carl hops every time he says it. The first time *hop! hop! hop!* It worked! that baby right down the toilet. Second time, *hop! hop! hop!* Flush! But not me. *Hop! hop! hop!* She tries. *Hop! hop! hop!* Try again. *Hop! hop! hop! Hop! hop! hop! Hop! hop! hop!* I'm stuck like cement. Aunt Grace thought it was a sin what she did to the others, Aunt Grace said she feels children should always know the truth. So when we got home I repeated the truth to my mother. First she tried to lie her way out of it, then the apologies. *Oh Carl I'm so sorry!* Carl playin like he's cryin. *Please forgive me! That was such a long time ago! I'm so happy to have you, I LOVE you!* Oh! and *Please don't tell your father!* Carl snickers.

So that was the end of me licking any bowl that lying bitch's fingers been in. On the other hand. You know that erector set, half-birthday? Looks like I'm getting that *and* an amateur radio kit, Free Parking! He full-blown ecstatic cuz he convinced dumb me to put all the Chance an Community Chest money in the center for whoever land on Free Parking, winner take all.

I'm envious Carl got a granmother to be throwin a reunion. I'm a granparent orphan. All died before I was born or when I was little, the only one I remember's my mama's mama who passed when I was six. At the funeral dinner several ladies separately told my mother how Gran meant the world to em, an afterward I heard Mama whisper to Daddy how when they were young an in trouble Gran helped em out. I had to get older to figure out what *young an in trouble* meant for girls, so what? *That's* what Carl holds gainst his mother? Mrs. Talley's one a the kindest ladies I know, her only fault bein spoilin Carl. An *this* is why? An don't her treatin her son like King Dog only lead to him bitin the han that feeds?

Still I feel a little sorry for Carl. It all honestly seem to bother him. I roll two an a one.

It wa'n't you.

He look up.

Not her fault. Nothin to take personal, jus tryin to get rid of it. She couldn't tell it was you.

Oh you know all about it, huh?

I shrug, waitin to see how mad he gonna get. Then he laugh to himself, some joke I ain't invited into. Roll. Eleven! Land him on Park Place to match up with his previously attained Boardwalk. Looks like you might be in need of a loan soon, Campbell. Trottin his car roun the board, then look up an grin. My interest rate's not *too* high.

Crickets. Stars. I smell the coffee, muss be almost mornin! I hear her on the steps. Dwight! Eliot!

I'm wake! I'm already wake, Mama, you don't have to wake me! Hahaha! Dwight! I say. Time to get up! Our trip! He don't stir but I hear a sigh.

I got toast! I love toast! Where we get a car, Daddy?

You know Mr. Briar from the Chicken Shack? He's my daddy's firs cousin. He couldn't go to the picnic but he loan me his car.

Eat your toast Dwight, Mama say.

I like the car. It smell good! Dwight still wanna ack sleepy-mad but he like the car too, all innerested, the outside an the inside. He behine Mama, I behine Daddy, driver. The sun come up. I count the cows.

How long to Pennsylvania?

Two an a half hours, Daddy tell me but he don't turn aroun, his eyes straight ahead, drivin. To Latchmore, Pennsylvania.

How long's two an a half hours?

Shorter, you take a nap, say Mama.

I can't nap! I can't nap, hahahaha!

Stop hoppin! say Dwight.

Aunt Mae your sister, Mama?

Aunt Mae is Daddy's *aunt*, she answer me. Uncle Mac is her husband.

But we miss the fireworks!

They got fireworks in Latchmore jus like in Humble, she say. But fireworks Fourth a July, today's Decoration Day. An anyway this Fourth a July nobody gettin the fireworks. The war blackouts.

Memorial Day!

She look at me. What?

Mrs. Brent say Decoration Day's Memorial Day.

She frown. When that change?

She say it always been Memorial Day. People jus took to callin it Decoration Day.

How Mr. Briar get gas for the car? Dwight wanna know.

Saved up his rations, say Daddy. He ain't used his car much lately. Times he had to close the Chicken Shack. No jobs, who goin out to eat? But with the war jobs, he say the Chicken Shack profitable again.

Horses! I say, eyes out the winda. After a while Dwight fall asleep. Not me! Car stop, I run!

Get back here, she say, say hi to Aunt Mae, Uncle Mac.

Hi Aunt Mae! Hi Uncle Mac!

Well hello there, Dwight.

I'm not Dwight! I'm Eliot!

Well hello there, Eliot.

I'm happy to see you, Eliot.

I'm happy to see *you*, Aunt Mae, then I run! I spelled aunt right on the spellin test, even if it sound like ant! Dwight already off with the big boys. Uncle Mac Aunt Mae got a big big yard, run run! Toddie's six, me an Toddie pull up the worms after the rain lass night, lass night it rained in Latchmore, Pennsylvania.

You sleepin in the barn?

Yep! I tell Toddie. Then Uncle Buster an Aunt Meggie come with their six. Cousins! Red Light Green Light an Simon Says, I'm a airplane!

I'm a airplane too! say Toddie come up behine me an we laughin an he flappin an hollerin but I say Airplane don't flap, Toddie, birds flap! Airplane wings smooth.

In the kitchen Aunt Beck shuckin corn. Yaw comin to stay with me tonight?

I nod!

Good. You wanna shuck?

I like shuckin!

Aunt Beck. Me an Dwight sleep in the barn tonight?

We'll see. Don't put that cob in the pot yet, you didn't get all the silk out. John Alan, you remember your cousin Eliot?

Sure. Hi, Eliot. John Alan smile, rub my head nice, then out the door.

John Alan's a good boy, say Aunt Beck. Straight A's, goin into tenth grade now. Let's see. I'm your daddy's sister, an John Alan's mama Anna Lee is your daddy an my first cousin, that make Anna Lee your second cousin, that make John Alan your third cousin I *told*ja don't put no corn in the pot still got silk on it.

Toddie starin at me from the door.

You wanna play? she ask.

I nod!

Go.

Me an Toddie out the door! Little stream nearby, me an Toddie off to catch froggies.

I have to pee I have to pee. Toddie say Pee in the brook. No! My mama catch me smack my behine. I run back inside Aunt Mae's Uncle Mac's house, I run upstairs. Two kids in line ahead a me! I don't know them cousins, cousins everywhere! Wonder if cousins from Uncle Mac's side is my cousins? Pee pee pee pee pee pee pee I go in! Nick a time!

When I get out I'm gettin ready go outside look for Toddie but he right there with the other kids lookin at Uncle Sam. Uncle Sam do magic! One a the little kids pick a card, Uncle Sam guess it every time! Now Toddie got a card.

Four a hearts, say Uncle Sam.

What it is! How you *do* that, Cousin Sam? say Toddie. Toddie say Cousin Sam, my mama say Uncle Sam, Mama an Daddy say we gotta say Uncle an Aunt with cousins old enough to be uncle an aunt, we never say Cousin Capital C.

Come ere, Eliot.

Aunt Amy! I run to her! she in somebody's bedroom. Aunt Amy hardly older n a firs cousin. She hug me, pick me up.

Oooh been a long time since I seen you! Look at those glasses! Look how big you gettin!

Seven!

Oh that's practically grown. She have me on her lap on the vanity seat, lookin in the vanity meer, puttin on her makeup. Hummin.

What's that, Aunt Amy?

My lipstick. You wamme put some on you?

No! She laugh. But I kinda do. I kinda wanna see what lipstick look like my lips. It smell good. I kinda wanna see what lipstick taste like.

Whatcha hum-hummin, Aunt Amy?

> *Praise the Lord, we're on a mighty mission*
> *All aboard, we ain't a-goin fishin*
> *Praise the Lord and pass the ammunition*
> *And we'll all stay free*

I like that song! You sure got a lotta makeup, Aunt Amy.

That's cuz I got a lotta money now, workin at the *de*fense plant.

Whatchu do at the *de*fense plant?

Well, I paint the antiaircraft shells. *Big* missiles. Taller n a house!

Taller n a house?! What color you paint em, Aunt Amy?

We paint the tips red. There's orange in there too. Wanna see?

Yes!

She show me her han. It startin to turn orange.

Cheer from the hall! I run out, see what Uncle Sam doin. He pullin a penny from behine their ear, they get to keep the penny!

Me! Me!

He try to do me but he can't fine no penny in my ear! He keep tryin, tryin. I tryin not to cry. Then he say, Oh *this* is the problem. I was lookin for a penny.

Then he pull out somethin silver, an he say, It's a nickel.

Everbody lookin at my nickel! Then somebody yell from downstairs Kickball! All the kids run down. I want to too but I gotta pee again. Nobody in line this time! When I come out everbody gone. I start to go downstairs outside but I hear somebody laughin. I hear boys laughin, I see a bedroom door closed an I hear boys other side of it. I tip, tip. I crack it I peek. Big boys. There's Dwight but he don't see me. He settin nex to our cousin Tray, Tray light-complected. Dwight an the big boys, most of em bigger n Dwight. John Alan's talkin, all the other boys listenin. I humped her I humped her, say Straight-A John Alan. She didn't put up no fight, black n ugly as she was. I hear the boys laughin. I don't know what John Alan's talkin about. Wonder if Dwight know what John Alan's talkin about. Dwight smile but he don't like it I can tell he don't like it. Then all the sudden Dwight lookin right at me. I can't tell what his face is. I think his face is scared an I think other stuff too. I turn, walk back down the hall. I see Uncle Sam in that other bedroom talkin to Aunt Amy. Uncle Sam's fun! I never met Uncle Sam before but when I seen his picture I always thought he was mean. I thought he was mean an white. His picture on the poster, in the magazines, but he look different. That white beard, pointin I WANT YOU FOR THE U.S. ARMY. I hear squealin from outside an remember Kickball. My fourth cousin Louise from high school pitchin for the little kids. I join the team. I kick a double!

Suppertime I get my hot dog, potata salad, Mama's pickled egg, Aunt Mae's porknbeans, corn me an Aunt Beck shucked. The little kids have races. I'm fass!

I win the third race, I win the seventh! Toddie cryin cuz he don't win none, he can't even beat Chee-Chee an she's five an he's six. Then we get watermelon. I love watermelon! Then the big boys an the men playin baseball. Dwight up to bat, Uncle Avery on second. My brother crack the ball hard, him an Uncle Avery run all the way home! Gettin dark now, they hardly see the ball.

Over where the grownups settin, Uncle Sam with a cup in his han. Don't you *go*, boy! he say to Lukey. Lukey's John Alan's big brother.

Already signed up, say Lukey. Basic trainin nex week.

Blame fool! say Uncle Sam.

I'm confused! When Uncle Sam white on the posters, he *want* peoples to sign up, he want YOU.

Bang! Bang! Bang! The fireworks, we havin fireworks after all, fireworks for Memorial Day! I search for em, I hear em don't see em, then somebody snatch me up! Mama snatch me up, Where's Dwight? she say, Where's Dwight? Everbody runnin to the house. There's Daddy! Where's Dwight? Must be twenty little cousins an big people lookin out the front room winda, cousins an big people all over the house all inside. Uncle Sam shootin a pistol in the air! When he start to reload, some man cousins take him down. They knock him down hard an they knock him down more. He wipe his bloody nose. Mama come down the stairs with Dwight, Okay, she say, let's go. Pullin away, I starin out backa the car. Uncle Sam all by hisself, he don't look mad no more, look like he cryin.

We say Aunt Beck's farm but for truth it useta be a farm but the land sole before Aunt Beck move in, she got a house an a barn an a garden. String beans. Cabbage.

Apple pie! It ain't skimpy neither. How Aunt Beck make that big apple pie with the rations? Daddy skip it, stead help hisself to another ear a corn. Sweet this year, say Aunt Beck. That's too much salt, Lon.

Bet you glad you married into this family, say Aunt Beck to Mama. Always a show!

Uncle Sam really shoot that gun?

Quiet, Mama say to me.

Sam fine till he get that liquor in him. Want some coffee with your slice? Not me, Beck, keep me up all night.

Coffee never affected me. Course mostly milk an sugar in my cup. You want a cup, Lon?

I'm fine.

Aunt Beck. Me an Dwight sleep in the barn?

You have to ask your mama an daddy about that. Lon, you gettin butter all down your shirt, you know that corn was sweet enough, it didn't need no butter. Daddy pick up his corn an go out, set alone on the edge a the porch to eat.

Mama, me an Dwight sleep in the barn?

Long as it's okay with your Aunt Beck.

Tiny they named her good, say Aunt Beck. Sam's mama. Not much bigger n a child. I never knew his daddy but musta been a mountain to look at Sam.

Maybe I don't wanna sleep in the barn.

Dwight!

Your brother's jus teasin you. Right? Mama give Dwight a look.

Dwight get a smile. Long as you don't pee the hay.

I don't pee! Not since before firs grade!

Settle down, say Mama.

Nine of us. Well there shoulda been ten. Me, then Patsy, then Sue Ellen, then Avery, then Lon, then Cecelia, then Bootsy, then Will Roy, then Ivy Lynn, then Amy the baby. Then the typhoid took Cece when she was two. But Sam. All he had was him an his mama, him an Aunt Tiny. After *she* gone—

I think Aunt Beck got more to say but she stop right there, now no grownups talk all quiet cep cricket cricket cricket. Daddy on the porch hearin us light a match to smoke.

Winda in the ceilin a the barn: stars. There is no animals in the barn, there is only hay for sleepin. Dwight take out his toy soldiers. I didn't know he brung em, Mama didn't know he brung em or she woulda said No, you'll lose em. We play from the light streamin in from the kitchen.

Dwight. What's humpin?

His eyes lift up hard on me. Say it in fronta Mama an Daddy, your butt be sore a month. Then he back to the soldiers. I knew it was a bad word from the way the big boys was laughin, I think but don't say.

Mama come to the barn door. Go to sleep or come back in the house. Lucky not enough light for her see the soldiers. Then she shut the door, all black black. We lay down we can't see nothin.

There is the moon. I'm wake now, see the moon shine bright through the barn door, what wake me? Barn door open an there stan the man. He stan dark in the door, I see shape a him no face, there is moonlights all aroun him. Dream Man.

You all sleep?

I look at Dwight. I look to Dwight but don't turn my head jus my eyes. I can't see Dwight's face in the dark. He ain't moved but I can't tell if he wake.

You all joinin up?

He wait for us to answer, like it a real question.

Naw, yaw ain't joinin up. Too smart. That dumb boy a Anna Lee's goin in. Why the hell a colored man fight for *this* country?

Snap, flash. He light a cigarette. He puff it he blow it. I see the burn a the cigarette but him still a black shape man.

I been there. Army. France, that other war. I was sixteen. They wouldn't gimme no gun. Cook. But once some bullets come flyin through, cook right nex to me take one through the head coulda been mine. He survived cuz I first-aided him but what kinda damn survival? Discharged him, how's a nigger with half a brain can't hardly speak no more sposed to get a job? He puff.

Nineteen hundred an eighteen. Back home, Humble. Humble sweet Humble, ain't that where yaw live? I was born there too, fore it got all built up. Shoulda burned that bastard uniform but stead I'm wearin it, wearin it proud. Spiffy-lookin are ya? say the white men. Take it off. Take off that goddamn army uniform, who you think *you* are. Better n a regular nigger? If that's whatcha think you made some huge mistake, take it off. I wouldn't. More they said Off, more it stayed on, practically livin in it, eatin in it, not sleepin in it, I kept it clean. Pressed. One time middle a the night here they come. Hollerin, carryin the torches.

KKK? I ask, my eyes wide. I remember Mama an Daddy talkin bout em. I think I see Dwight stir, but now still again.

Sure, some of em. But all in regular clothes, didn't matter, those days most whites Klan or sympathetic to. My mama an me had a fishin dock stuck out into the crick. We slip into the water under the pier, our faces barely peep above, just enough to breathe. Icy water, we open our mouths wide cuz we close em, our teeth chatter so loud it draw attention. Prayin silent in our heads. We hear the cracklin flames.

Daybreak we slip out. House burnt to the groun, to nothin. My mama siftin through the rubble, see what she find. I run over to Mr. Gibson's, two mile away. Mr. Gibson got a boat, take me an my mama outa here, far away, leave damn Humble forever. I get the boat, bring it back to her.

Cricket cricket cricket. I wait. Dream Man gonna finish his story?

There she be. They didn't call my mama Tiny for nothin, half my height. The breeze is gentle but that enough to sway her. Lookin like she asleep, so peaceful. Hangin from that oak.

Uncle Sam puff that cigarette one more time, then he gone. I look to Dwight. Dwight's eyes wide open. Dwight, I whisper. He turn away from me.

Breakfast! Mama call.

Gettin dressed, I had a dream lass night, Dwight. Bout Uncle Sam, wanna hear? Dwight fass in his pants an out the door.

Pick at my fried egg. Eat that, Eliot, Mama say. I never knowed that boy to be picky before. Come on, we gotta get on the road. Aunt Beck say, Lon, what kinda breakfast jus black coffee. I'll fix you an egg. Don't shake your head at *me*.

In the car everbody quiet. Finally Mama say, She's the oldest, Lon. You know she always gotta be the oldest, I didn't think she was bad as lass time. Daddy say nothin.

I speak quiet. Was a dream lass night, Dwight? That was the Dream Man, he wa'n't real. Right?

Yeah, was a dream, now shut up.

In our beds I stare at the nickel from Uncle Sam's magic. Dwight ain't said much a anything since Dream Man which never happened he say. I put my nickel under my pilla.

My dream we on the playgroun at school. There's Japanese families, lot of em all scrunched up locked inside the monkey bars. Walkin all aroun free's the white people kilt Aunt Tiny. Some of em wear their Klan clothes. I'm there but nobody see me. I don't know nunna these people. I never met nobody Japanese before not nobody Chinese, I only seen em on the movie news, all I ever see in real life is colored an white but in the dream I feel like I know the Japanese people like they some cousins but the white people ain't. I stan there thinkin an thinkin how can I get them Japanese cousins outa the bars an put the white people into the bars, scratchin my brain but never do I figure it out.

DWIGHT

Two A's, three B's, two C's, flyin colors for me. One teacher writes *Has a good head on his shoulders if he'd only apply himself* an another teacher writes nex to it *Yes!* Lass day's sunny an hot like it oughta be. We had a half-day an I step out on my porch, stretchin, breathin the summer: freedom.

Up the street Roof standin out in his yard. I don't usually expect to see him till day after lass day, lass day he's always inside, report card punishment.

What's that you're hummin?

In a cavern, In a canyon, Excavatin for a mine, Lived a miner forty-niner an his daughter Clementine. Then he starts hummin it again. That smile.

For real?

For real. *Hm hm hm hm*

When you gonna start?

Tole my daddy I'm ready to go in tomorra, but he say he wamme be a kid one lass week a my life. So week from Monday. *Hm hm hm hm*

Blackface. Like the rest of em.

Sixty-two cent a hour? Sure, I be blackface.

My mouth fly open, calculatin the dollars that add to in a day! I don't say it, try hidin the envy but he caught it, his eyes twinkly.

Oh my darlin, the boss gonna set me an Daddy up same shiffs. So I ride with him every day. *Oh my darlin, hm hm hm hm, hm hm hmm hm hm hm hm*

You waited the whole school year for summer, now throw summer away for the caves. Dark.

Roof jus keep hummin.

An what if you find out it ain't nothin but misery?

Then I know the difference between misery a school an misery a the mines is I get paid.

We stare at each other. I look away firs.

Wanna make a tower?

Can't. I'm on report card punishment. Like it really matter now. Whistlin. She's at the store so thought I come out for a breath. Prolly oughta go back in fore she turn at corner. He lookin the direction she gonna come from. Or maybe not. She didn't yell loud like usual, maybe she ain't gonna big enforce the punishment. Like she see it all a new way now, me a man. He resume the hummin. I turn to leave.

Come tomarra though. I still got nine days a vacation.

Okay. Whaddya wanna do?

He think. Messengill's.

Okay.

Roof! Lucy Deucy callin from a second-floor winda. You fix me a jelly samwich?

Dwight. Sundays. Sundays I have off. You an me, okay? Nobody else. Well maybe Zack if we need three for whatever we doin. But nobody else. Okay?

I'm hungry, Roof! Lucy Deucy got a mess a hair one side in a pigtail, other side hangin loose, wild.

Sundays my only play day here on out, jus you an me. An maybe occasionally Zack. Okay?

Okay.

Roof turn to go back in his house. *Dreadful sorry, Clementine.*

You don't haveta go. She hot-combin her hair.

I *wan*na go.

Okay, she say, puttin on black gloves. When you see Jeanine remember to tell her you sure are sorry bout her uncle.

I never been to a funeral before. It's at Jeanine's house. Mama an me an Aunt Peg-Peg an Uncle Rick in Jeanine's front room an Mama an Aunt Peg-Peg tellin Jeanine's grandmother an Jeanine's aunts an uncles I'm sorry I sure am sorry. Sometimes people breaks out cryin, sometimes they jus look tired. Jeanine's front room packed with people an chairs, some people brung their own chairs.

Can we set up front?

Up front is for the family.

Oh. Hot in here!

Don't complain. I asked you if you wanted to come.

I wanted to come!

Then try n be quiet. Respectful.

This your youngest, Claris? ask a ole lady.

Yes, this is Eliot.

Well hello there, Eliot. How old are you?

Seven.

Seven! Then she set down in fronta us.

Mama. I'm whisperin. What's in that little box?

That's the casket.

I look at her. I look at it.

How it fit him? It don't look big enough fit me!

Don't say that, she say sharp. After a while she whisper but her eyes front, Those are his *remains*.

Please be seated, say Reveren Keyes from our church. Now I see Jeanine an her mother in the front row.

When the inside part done we walkin, ack like a parade to the cemetery. Mama say at a funeral say casket not coffin, cemetery not graveyard, passed on not died. I wanna ask what is remains but I think I better hold that till we back home. At the cemetery they put the little casket in a little hole. Then they cover up the little hole an stick a flag in the dirt. That flag from the goverment, some man behine us say. Naw, say some woman, the undertakers done it, then they argue soft a minute. Then we walk back to Jeanine's house. The chairs been moved up against the walls an a table with all kindsa food in the middle a the room. People's eatin, me an Mama eatin. Then we see Jeanine's mother.

I sure am sorry to hear boutcher brother, say Mama.

Jeanine's mother sigh, nod. Ramonlee was the baby. Then she pinch my cheek. It don't hurt. An how's Mr. Eliot today? Her smilin eyes all glassy.

Fine. Few minutes later I see Jeanine near the door.

Hi Eliot! She all cheery.

Hi Jeanine. Jeanine bein cheery make me wanna be cheery but I make my face sad. I sure am sorry boutcher uncle.

She whisper to me. It ain't my uncle. It's a rabbit.

I look at her, whisper. In the casket?

She nod. How Uncle Ramonlee fit that little box? He jus hidin out, waitin for the war be over to come home. Then Jeanine look up an smile, Hi, Mr. D'Angelo!

As we leavin I hear Jeanine's other uncle say to Jeanine's mother, How'd it happen? He ain't gone nowhere, he hadn't even leff the States!

I know, Jeanine's mother say quiet.

He hadn't even leff the States!

Walkin home I see Liddie waitin for us on the porch. We got relatives! Mama's relatives. Aunt Peg-Peg an Uncle Rick, Liddie an Mitch the baby. They in the guess room. Liddie's six but she only goin into the firs, I'm seven an goin into third cuz my birthday come late, October. Me an Liddie same size, I'm little in my class. Liddie don't go to my school, she go where she live in Bear, West Virginia, but they all come lass night for the funeral today. I wave to Liddie! Liddie, here I come!

Daddy an Uncle Rick in the livin room, talkin bout the war. Daddy jus got back from Boddimore, not in time for Jeanine's Uncle Ramonlee's funeral. Mama an me an Liddie an Aunt Peg-Peg changin Mitch the Baby in the guess room.

I remember babysettin Ramonlee, say Aunt Peg-Peg.

I remember Ramonlee had a big ole crush on you, say Mama. She pull out a ole album, all kindsa pitchers. Picnic. Mama an Aunt Peg-Peg an Jeanine's mama an Uncle Ramonlee look like Dwight's age.

Liddie turn to me, I got a dog. Home.

I got a cat.

Me an Liddie go outside. Parker, I call, Parker. Liddie join in: Parker!

Parker don't come. Liddie say, My school start nex month, September. I say, Me too! Then me an Liddie swing on the tree branch an make the mud pies an eat the mud pies an then we in trouble, we gotta get a bath an No playin! Jus worsh!

Nex day Aunt Peg-Peg an Uncle Rick an Liddie an Mitch the Baby at their car huggin bye to Mama an Daddy an Dwight an me an I feel somethin at my leg. Parker! Aunt Peg-Peg take a picture a me and Liddie and Parker, then they drive off. Playin on the back porch with Parker, Mama in the yard hangin clothes. When she come carryin the wicker basket I say Mama, Jeanine tole me there was a rabbit in that casket. She say her uncle Ramonlee wouldn't fit.

Mama stop, look at me. It's Ramonlee in that box alright, what's left of him. His remains. He got hurt an they had to cut his legs off, then he passed on. But don't go contradictin Jeanine. Nobody can't tell nobody else how to grieve. Then Mama take the basket inside.

Nex day after Sunday school, hot! Parker waitin for me on the porch! I rollin aroun with Parker! We ain't never passin on, Parker! We got nine lives!

Dwight come out on the porch, set on the edge, drop his jacks. I play?

Nope. He drop ball, grab one. Drop ball, grab two.

You wanna pet Parker? I know he gonna say no.

Drop ball, grab three. He look at the sky. You think it gonna rain?

The mornin sunny, then cloud over, sunny, then cloud over. Nope. I say it cuz I know it what he wanna hear. Now Dwight roll Parker on his stomach, tickle him. We both ticklin Parker, it too much! Parker run from us but not far, starin. Then Dwight go back to his jacks an when he miss he say, Your turn. Takin my turn!

You wanna camp in the backyard tonight?

We jus camped in the backyard.

No! That was lass week!

Bounce, pick up three. Maybe.

Maybe! I'm happy about maybe! but I don't say nothin, jinx it. Usually when Dwight say Maybe he mean yes, he jus wanna play like maybe he don't mean yes. Here come Carl.

Hey.

Hey, Dwight say.

Been to D'Angelo's today, say Carl all smiley. He prolly got candy an ain't even offerin to share it with me. Dwight stan like him an Carl got business. Carl pet Parker but pet him backwards. Parker hiss. Carl do it again. Parker sink his teeth in.

Ow!

Who don't know not to rub a cat the wrong way? Dwight laughin a little.

I'll get you for that Tabby, says Carl.

Where you goin? I ask Dwight.

Out, but I spy his trunks peekin over belt loops.

Better not go swimmin, I say. Might rain.

Thought you said it wouldn't, say Dwight, still walkin, not even turnin roun to look at me.

Crazy like your crazy owner Crazy Onnie, I won't forget that Tabby, says Carl.

My cat! I say.

Come *on*. Dwight already out the yard. Carl run to catch up.

I take Dwight's red jacks ball, roll it by my cat. Fetch, Parker! His eyes follow the ball, right to leff. Fetch, Parker! His eyes follow the ball, leff to right.

I'ma follow Dwight. I think I'ma follow Dwight, I know him an Carl gone down by the crick. You stay here, Parker. You stay here, stop followin me, Parker. Stop followin me, hahaha. Now you runnin ahead a me, how you even know I'm goin that way?

I hug my kitty cat! I heard dog is man's bess friend, well cat is boy's bess friend! I got Mama an Daddy an Parker an Dwight. I love my brother even though sometime he mean. There's big kids racin down the street on scooters. Some a the big kids is colored, some a the big kids is white. Early Auguss, school just roun the corner but today everbody fun in the sun like it all go on forever, easy easy.

I won't forget that, Tabby. Carl talk like some gangster movie, Only a dang cat, *Carl*, an you hadn'ta been rubbin it the wrong way it wouldn'ta bothered you. In my head but I don't say it.

Not hard gettin to the water from our side a town, but findin the swimmin place with dock an tire swing's trickier, trek through the woods. The trees is thick an still a scorcher bearin down, wipe my brow. Carl ahead, leadin despite I know the way an he don't. Lass summer I took a dip only the one time, spotted Marco an Mokie headed in the direction so joined em. Outside a that I was either with Roof who don't go for swimmin or with Carl who I placed in some head box with badminton an backgammon, not The Crick.

The heat don't slow down Carl's chatter chatter, how this mornin he heard his sister tell his father bout some ole house the police raided wunst again, teenagers drinkin, smokin. The authorities say the foundation's shaky, say high time tear it down fore it fall in on itself, kill somebody. But here's the mystery: In the basement all these painted wall murals. Obscene things. Negro things.

I pick up a stick, hurl it to the trees. I never took Carl to Messengill's but funny Carl never ventured there hisself. Lookin at it, backa his blond head an somethin come to me: I'm Carl's only friend in the neighborhood. Further, I ain't seen Carl's white school pals in a spell, which make me wonder whether Carl fell out with some of em, or all of em, which make me wonder if at the present I'm Carl's only friend period. Then again in the buddy census who I got outside a Carl an Roof? An Roof seem gone, graduated into the grown-up world a hard labor an little time for anything else cep eatin an sleepin.

Jus me an him Sundays. That's what he say, *demand*, so there I am knockin. Miss Ray Anne: Roof's too tired, Dwight honey, sleepin his day off. We got together that week between school an when he started, but after that like some play played every week, that scene with me knockin an Miss Ray Anne like his receptionist *He ain't in honey* repeat the nex Sunday, an nex. After the fourth I'm sick of it, stop tryin. Ain't seen Roof in near two months, thus back to me-an-Carl every day, lass summer all over again.

Peekin over Carl's hip pocket I spy the toppa his billfold, catch me by surprise since he never seem to carry one before Polly an now Polly an him's bust. For a while all roses, him discoverin she liked him much as he liked her, him smilin goofy an taken to carryin a wallet jus to always have her photograph in reach. Finished out seventh a couple and on into the summer—ice cream parlor, occasional picture show. Then she start to soun funny on the telephone, other times he hear her mother callin Telephone! an then suddenly her mother revise her previous: she ain't home. Come to find out she got her eye on some high school boy, ninth goin into tenth an gainfully employed *behine* the ice cream counter. Wipe that ear-to-ear grin off Carl's face, he back to his regular hot n cold but with Roof excavatin coal who else I got to play with? Well. Not *quite* same as lass summer. Now he come to *my* door. Only fair, an anyhow I just as soon not be no household guest a his these days. Since misery tend to appreciate company I don't even wanna imagine what kinda relay baton his broken heart been passin on to his poor mother.

But mostly we been okay. He gimme tennis lessons at the playgroun in the sun, or carry his Monopoly to my porch in the rain. Yet an still he been askin bout the crick all summer an me puttin him off. I like to keep Carl an his moods in familiar territory which the crick is not. Then yesterday he confrontin: Why you keep dawdlin? An I don't feel like answerin so here we are.

She said some kids from her class got arrested, getting expelled. Carl tossin the words back to me over his shoulder. But about those murals. I don't know. Rumors.

I sigh too low for him to hear. Be sorry to see Messengill's go. On the other han no Roof to explore it with, like it already long history.

Oh geez.

I look up. Carl snappin through the brush to see it better, even while we can view the tree jus fine from where we're standin. Thick trunk, an on it in colored chalk there be ole Barney Google in U.S. army fatigues. Lynched. Hangin over a bubblin brook, still smilin with his goo-goo-googly eyes.

Geez! Humble Maryland's suddenly become the art capital of the world! Carl's lip corners turn up to smile.

You got blood where that cat bit cha.

I'ma get that tabby. Carl pitches a stick. Twirlin fast like a pinwheel before the faint crack, landin in the distance.

There's where the path ends. Here on out keep a watch for these white rags bow-tied on the tree branches. He nod dutiful. I could tell him I can walk the way blindfolded but I don't. Allow him the firs-time adventure a findin the markers.

There's one. He spy a rag tied to an oak limb. Rumble a thunder. It's *hot*! Wipin his brow. Then glance back to me, grin: Blondie.

Hair at my temples always bleached by late summer, which some people finds real startlin an delightful given I'm just as dark-complected as the resta my family. Glimpsin that little sandy edge in the meer make me smile, but Carl don't need to know. Unfortunately the pride flush up too fast, he caught it fore I could turn my mouth scowl-down.

Holy Toledo. Carl detect another chalk sketch off the beaten path. Captain America. Hung.

Now he turn, starin at me straight-on firs time a the stroll, accusation an a smirk. Hopin I'll confess to somethin I'm innocent till proven guilty of. He ain't interested in playin the judge. All he wants is to be in on the joke.

What ever happen to all those white-boy friends you had from school?

He shrug. What's it to you?

Jus seem like you had friends one day, nex not.

I have em. When I want em. Carl hurl a stone. How come you don't have any colored friends?

I do. I mean I get along with em. School. They're jus not as convenient at home.

Guess that's me too. Stuck playing with whoever's convenient, then pitch me a side glance while he swing himself up, lower branch of a tree.

What are you doin?

Taking a break. He start scalin the oak.

We're almost there.

I'm taking a break, it's hot.

I lean against the tree, pinch a piece a my shirt fannin my stomach, an now lass night's dream suddenly in fronta me like real, the night vision been reoccurrin different ways since Decoration Day. Great Aunt Tiny. *Real* tiny, like a doll, rope tied roun her neck. The rope tied to a pole. She jus looked asleep like Uncle Sam said, but now she bein slapped back n forth by white boys. Tetherball.

Hey. I can see the water from here.

I look up at him. Squirrel come out its hole, gimme the wunst-over. Come on up.

I take in the map of it, the secure branches, the ones might snap quick, send me hurtlin. Grab onto a low limb, *slow*. I ain't got Carl's purebred ability, him settin higher n safety far as I can tell. Maybe tree-climbin he perfected at Happy White Boy Camp. I stop at the stablest branch jus below him.

See it?

Not high enough.

Kids swimming. If I had a BB gun. Carl aim with his finger: *Pow*.

Off to the right a oriole appear, settle near that treetop. Peer aroun, measurin up the prospects, fly off.

I told my dad one day you were gonna take me to the crick. He said, The *what*? I said, The *crick*. He said, The *what*? I said, The *water*! He looked completely confused! Then he said, The *creek*! Jones *Creek*!

I poker face, showin nunna my cards. For truth till this moment I'd no idea crick an creek was the same, figured they was jus two different in a line a dictionary same-meanins: 3. Brook. 4. Stream.

Not just you, all the kids in my school call it The Crick. Humble. I'm a hick, I live in a crick.

The tetherball players were the boys I met from Carl's school, cep in the dream they were Carl's campmates. Carl was there, not playin but officiatin. *Violation against the blue team*, he said.

After my sister finishes talking about those filthy Negro pictures in that raggedy old house, my father goes to my mother, You think Dwight might've made those pictures? and my mother goes, Oh come on, Craig, Dwight's not like that. Dwight doesn't make trouble. And I thought, That's for sure. If there's one thing Dwight does *not* make, it's trouble.

Carl's danglin leff shoe just inches above, my arm's reach easy. Just a little yank an there tumble Carl a hundred feet, splat.

I'm goin, an I take the initiative: descent. To prove somethin Carl stay put better part a thirty seconds before movin off his perch.

Just tell me this. On the groun Carl racin to catch up. How many are there?

How many what?

Lynch cartoons. I'd just like to see em all.

I walk faster. Mr. Randolph said he broke the sedition laws jus by speakin his mind about the other war. Could colored chalk sketches be some kind a felony?

Whaddya think? I'm gonna tell somebody? What, you don't trust me?

What difference does it make? You already decided I done it, so leave it.

I wanna hear it from your lips. I wanna know how many more.

What for?

Cuz I've told you stuff about me and you've never said anything to me about you.

I turn aroun. *What* stuff about you?

He stares.

That was only after I said somethin to you firs.

What firs?

About Roof's little sister that drowned.

Yeah, about Roof, and I tell you about my mother, nothing ever comes up about you! Now Carl frown. Why'd you tell me that about Roof anyway?

I don't know. Shrug. Maybe I thought you'd like him better. Stop bein so hard on him.

Carl mullin this over, brow all furrowed like he workin out some brain-tanglin crossword. I turn, walkin on ahead.

Dwight.

I sigh. Stop.

If you thought telling me his deep dark secret might make me cut him some slack. Was there ever a day you thought telling him *my* deep dark secret might make him cut *me* some slack?

Whoosh! flock a blackbirds takin off. We look up. I keep starin, then feel his irises trained on me again, bring my eyes down to meet em.

Three.

His eyebrows raise.

You already found two chalk pictures. One to go.

Scream an a splash. Trees open up an there they are: dock, tire swing, the crick. An now I see the kids Carl spied from high in the leaves. I assumed they was white. Wrong.

Richard's head's just above the water, Kimmie settin on Richard's shoulders. Kimmie: No don't, please don't, strugglin not to laugh an Talia four feet away smilin. Richard smilin, everybody grin, party out there in the middle a the half-a-football-field wide crick. Richard say, One, two, *three!* an flip Kimmie backwards *splash.* Kimmie come back up, Talia Me me me! an now Richard starin at two boys standin on the bank. Or, to be more precise, at the colored boy. Kimmie an Talia stop the horseplay, follow his gaze.

Carl all bright. What are we waiting for. Come on!

Strips down to his trunks, runnin out on the dock *bam bam bam.* Leaps into the tire swing, flies out an plunges hisself the midst a the screamin scramblin colored. Carl resurface, the girls giggle.

Come on, Dwight.

I put my hand side a my face, shadin my eyes from the harsh sunlight. Then I remember the sky done clouded over but can't backtrack now, squint like the rays blindin me. Walk to the dock, take off my shirt, fold it neat. Take off my shorts, fold em neat. Set em all on the enda the wood slats near the bank. Take a step on, *creak.* Take another, ain't no rush, *creak creak.*

Come *on,* Dwight.

Come *on,* Dwight, the girls echoin Carl, yards away but my vision's good, I see what kinda laughter behine their eyes. I leap for the tire.

Sway, sway. No need exertin myself with the sun boilin the world, I pay them no mind. But now feel myself pushin the pendulum, higher, higher, the kids far beneath. Miz Carey brung in a picture a the Empire State Building, world's tallest, opened when I was two. Now I stand at the top a that tower, Carl an Richard an Kimmie an Talia stories an stories below, they speak but I see only lips movin, too far down for me to hear, ants.

GO!

I don't know which a the four spoke but I'm fallin hard, fast, they all squeal an scatter. *Crash!* Underworld, no soun, eight legs leisurely treadin overhead. I won't come up. Lass summer with the twins I held my breath the longest, forty-seven seconds, I'll stay under so long Carl an Richard an Talia an Kimmie'll finally look at each other an shrug, give up an go home. Under the surface I see Richard's studio, an Richard paintin his sisters Richard capturin their bliss, and his self-portrait apple an the eye. Then it's cold an windy an there I am on the floor readin the funnies an Eliot cryin cuz he jus learnt a new word: *lynch.* Now I'm at Carl's an Mrs. Talley holdin the plate a brownies. *These have walnuts. These are plain.*

Yanked up from behine! Strong hands liff me by my underarms, break through.

Jesus! I thought you were drowning, says Carl, my apparent savior.

You okay? asks Kimmie.

Listen to him coughin! says Talia. You tryin to kill yourself?

Just catch your breath, says Kimmie. Relax.

Jesus, says Carl the Hero.

Why'd you take so long to get in the water in the first place? asks Talia.

Okay now? asks Kimmie.

Sprised he get in the water at all, seein colored in it, says Talia. Kimmie hits Talia's arm. What? says Talia. Richard tryin not to smile. Carl look at Talia an Kimmie, then at Richard, then at me.

Here's the game, says Richard. See it?

Hey, where'dja get that? asks Talia. Richard holdin a rock painted bright orange.

I brung it.

Richard's an artist, Kimmie says.

Yeah, this a real masterpiece, says Richard.

I mean other stuff. He can paint you, and you really see yourself.

So's Dwight an artist, says Carl.

Yeah. Dwight's an artist alright, says Richard.

They're *both* artists, says Kimmie. Richard smiles at me, which everyone sees. An somethin else he make in his smile for only me to see, though I ain't clear what it is.

My mother gave Dwight an art book for his birthday. She says Dwight has real talent, real potential.

Carl facin away from me, I'm lookin at his back so hard to tell if he's smilin. An if I did see him smilin not sure I'd know what it mean.

Here's the game, says Richard. I drop the rock. On five, we dive. Got it?

Got it, says Talia, her swimsuit strap slippin down a bit off her right shoulder, an Talia's started developin a bit on her right side. Oh boy.

Richard drops the rock in the water: One. Two. Three. Four. *Five!*

Everyone dives, me a little behine so by the time I'm down, Carl's already back up: I got it! I got it! Now everybody to the surface. Carl holdin the rock now notices Talia's slipped swimsuit, then Talia noticin Carl noticin her swimsuit. Talia let out a little squeak, plunge under to make herself decent.

Now me, goes Carl. One.

Kimmie join in. Two. Three. Four. *Five!* Everyone under. This time I spy the rock quick, but slow to decide whether I wannit. Kimmie snatches it, crash through. I got it! Everybody to the top.

Richard: Let's race. He turn to Carl. You an me. That big rock an back.

Kimmie referee, make sure they both at the startin line even if the startin line's invisible. On your mark. Get set. Go!

Carl's a strong swimmer, natural athlete. But so's Richard, an Carl's thirteen, Richard tall an fifteen. If there was such a thing as buildin up a sweat swimmin, Richard wouldn't even had.

The winner! says Kimmie. Richard barely smile.

Dammit, says Carl.

Awwww, say Kimmie an Talia, like they never heard a kid say it before.

Now you. Richard's eyes on me.

You did good, Carl, Kimmie says. Richard's tall.

*Dam*mit!

Underwater this time. Why's Richard get to make all the rules?

Get in position, Talia says.

I don't think Dwight should have to do it, Kimmie says. Look at him panting, he's still scared from almost drowning.

I'm not pantin.

I'm standing right next to you, all I hear is ha-ah ha-ah ha-ah ha-ah.

Get in position, Carl says. Richard an me at the line. On your mark. Get set. Go!

Down. Everything slow motion. There's noise above the surface but it's some other universe. Richard pulled far ahead an I don't care, Richard already at the rock, me still yards away an here he come approachin on the return, he'll finish without ever havin to come up for air whilst I already surfaced for a quick refuel. The water crystal today, I see him clear like a winda. An think, When he passes I could cheat. Richard so focused on the finish line, I could make a U-turn never bother to touch the dang rock. He'd still win, jus less embarrassin my defeat, what's the difference? But I'm plagued with the curse of integrity, I trudge on the honest path an as we're about to pass I look over an see Richard stock still, starin straight at me. Muss be a good ten feet a distance between us but I see him clear seein *me* clear as he pull down his trunks.

Fly to the surface! coughin, chokin. Carl an Kimmie an Talia stare. Richard surfaces, finish line.

The winner! says Talia.

Now the girls race, says Kimmie.

Dwight didn't even make it to the rock! Talia cracks up.

Sure he did, says Richard. He touched it an was on his way back. Talia looks at me, Richard's lie make her face all frowny confused. Richard look at me an air it is again. Mystery smile.

Relay race! says Talia.

First the girls alone, says Kimmie, then Talia screams.

An there on the bank, starin at us stands a Blackface. Take me a sec to reckonize him.

Ew, says Talia, he's dirtier n usual. Richard giggle, Kimmie tryin not to. Carl smiles.

He got on at the mines.

I think we could guess that, Talia answerin me but her eyes still on the bank.

We *knew* that. People *know* that.

I didn't know that, Talia correctin Kimmie. But I could guess it.

Dwight.

Everybody in the water go quiet, like startled a Blackface could talk.

What'd he say? Talia asks.

I think he called Dwight. Did he call you, Dwight? says Kimmie an I wonder Those girls suddenly go deaf? I don't even look at her, my eyes fixed on the figure starin at me from the bank.

Dwight.

You better answer him.

Talia clearly wa'n't talkin to Carl but here come his two cents: Why? No one invited him. Al Jolson. Everybody turn sharp to Carl but he seem to take no notice, laughin at his joke, divin under.

Get rid of him.

This time I decide to answer Talia, my eyes like stone. It's a public crick. He can be here if he wants.

Well I wonder if somethin's wrong with him.

Me too, says Kimmie.

Like maybe he's a little bit retarded, continue Talia.

He's *not* retarded. My voice quiet, my underwater hans tight, fists.

Whaddya gonna do, act like he's not there?

I try to act like *Richard* ain't there, but course he gotta go on: Pretend it's not your name he's callin?

Dwight!

I breathe deep before I swim toward shore, stayin far enough away I still gotta tread.

What.

You said Sundays off you an me.

I went to your house every Sunday, you were always too tired!

I said, Come back nex Sunday.

I *did*!

Not today.

Every other Sunday! Geez, Roof, maybe I got tireda always No. An don't look like you were off today.

They needed extra men to blast the new hole, me an Daddy went in, three more hours.

Stare at him. He stare at me. A fish plop but the crick behine me where all the human beins is ain't stirrin.

Come outa the water.

No!

Roof say nothin but gimme the steel eyes.

It's hot!

So make me yell crost the crick?

We're not yellin. An then I glance over my shoulder. Three. No tellin where Carl swum off to. I turn back to the shore. Come ere, I say, an swim to edge a the dock.

Roof breathin heavy, from where I'm treadin I can hear it, deep an fearful. Then he take a cautious step by step, inchin down the pier toward me. He stop well short a the front, a safe distance a the better part of a foot between him an the edge.

I looked everywhere for ya. Messengill's an D'Angelo's, the railroad tracks. Then I remembered. You goin to the crick one day. With him.

I said that lass summer! How'dju remember it now?

Roof starin.

Look, I'll come by an play later.

When?

I don't know! You need a bath anyway. Take a bath an by that time I'll be aroun.

Roof start coughin. The coughs are small. Then the coughs are big. Then the coughs are bigger, bigger, like an orchestra from Music Appreciation barrelin toward a huge cough crescendo.

You're startin to cough like your dad.

AAAAAAAAAAAAAAAAH!

A screamin banshee come sprintin, poundin crost the deck behine Roof. Roof swerve aroun, his face alight with the terror, losin his balance an fallin backward *splash!* Gone.

Everybody freeze. Cep the smilin blond boy banshee on the dock, who speak: Teach him to swim.

Seem like a hour but prolly not three seconds fore my wits come back, I'm bout to dive under searchin for him when he crash through, screamin for help. Wavin frantic, then back under, pop to the surface, fall under. I swim fast, reach him, *Grab on to me, Roof!* But his whole bein is panic, snatchin at me but slippin off. Richard an the girls now swum to the scene. Finally Roof manage to get close enough to the dock so the banshee standin atop can reach down an grab him under the arms.

Gotcha, says the rescuer an laughs.

Roof's head hinge back to look right up into Carl's face.

NO!

Roof throw hisself outa his deliverer's clutch, apparently choosin death over bein saved by Carl. The thrust send him flyin outa all our reach, and he paddlin wild, Drownin! Drownin! Drownin!

Swimmin.

Hey, says Richard.

Roof. Roof! *You're swimmin!* I yell it, catchin my breath. I yell it!

Yay! cheer the girls.

Toldja, says Carl.

Roof do the doggie paddle, Roof backstroke. Roof floatin face up on calm waters, Roof smilin, look at peace. Then freestyle to the dock.

Uh-oh, says Carl an jumps in before he gets jumped in. Roof pull hisself up on the pier, standin, lookin down at his audience in the water. Grinnin.

Yay, Roof! Kimmie an Talia whistlin. Me an Richard smilin. Carl smilin but his smile seem a little too much, or a little too little.

Niggers, says Roof. Dirty dumb niggers, all the goddamn lotta you.

Everybody still. The waters still the birds still.

How could I be friends with *niggers*?

What the *hell*? Richard all gapin.

Niggers? say Carl. Well guess what *you* look like right now. Everyone turn to Carl, confusion. The dip in the crick cleaned some a the black off Roof's face, but not all. Thunder.

Make no mistake, Talia says. There's only one nigger here who'd call *you* a friend.

Why you gotta *be* like that, Roof? asks Kimmie.

Filthy Bartons, says Talia. That trash your friend, Dwight?

Nobody *colored* pushed you in, Roof, says Kimmie.

Roof's eyes on me: No. 'Twas Dwight's friend pushed me in.

Damn right, says Carl.

Trash Bartons, says Talia.

I pushed you, and I *saved* you. You can swim now, you got me to thank.

Dwight's best friend, says Roof. You all got badminton planned for today?

You need to go home an clean yourself up, I say.

This is the thanks we get for saving his life! If I hadn't been here, you'd *still* not know how to swim, you'd be *dead*! If I hadn't been here—

If your mama'd only *hop! hop! hopped*! better, says Roof, you *would*n'ta been here.

The sound that come outa Carl ain't nothin like anybody here ever before heard on earth, puttin us all to silence. Carl look at me, then back at Roof whose murder eyes still stuck on Carl. Then Roof turn aroun, walkin away.

You stinking piece of shit! Moron, you po white trash *nothin*! Then Carl dive under.

I toldja never to repeat that! I'm yellin but all I see's his back, him movin away, not fast, not slow. *You hear me, Roof?*

Carl up from the water, rock in his hand. Hurls it but it go wild, missin Roof by yards. Stupid piece of trash shit!

CONSIDER U.S. NO LONGER FRIENDS, ROOF!

Roof jus keep walkin: Like we ever was, Dwight.

Piece of coal mining trash! Goddamn shame to the white race!

Like we ever was, Dwight, an Roof disappear into the woods.

Carl fly out the water, vanish where Roof jus did.

White boy fight! Talia gigglin.

He ain't gonna catch him, Richard says.

Way he tore outa this water? Yeah, Talia repeat, he gonna catch him.

He ain't gonna catch him cuz he don't *wan*na catch him.

Why Roof gotta be like that, Kimmie ponderin aloud.

Ain'tchu gonna go after him? Richard askin me. Ain't he your friend? Yeah, ain't he your *friend*?

Shut up, Talia.

Talia glare at Kimmie. Don't tell *me* to shut up.

He ain't gonna catch him cuz it's a fight he won't win, an he damn sure know it. Then Richard dive under.

Talia holdin her arms like suddenly she cold. Somebody better go, make sure they're not killin each other. Then she scream, Richard come under her, pull her up on his shoulders, throw her off backward.

It sure is quiet out there, says Kimmie not to anyone in particular but I'm the only one leff to hear it. I sigh an slow move to the shallow. Step onto the bank, then stop cuz here come Carl walkin outa the woods.

I couldn't catch him. Carl starin at me. Everyone in the water quiet now, starin at Carl. Flock a geese screech overhead.

I'm going home, says Carl, and turn into the woods. I quick grab my clothes an his, jog to catch up.

Carl walk fast. I know he hear me comin up behine but he persist with the speed, don't turn aroun. Then I hear: I shoulda killed him.

I'm scamperin to keep up.

I shoulda picked up another rock, cracked open his skull. Then Carl pick up a rock, throw it hard into the trees. A twig snaps, falls.

He sure ain't no friend a mine no more.

Carl swing aroun so quick I near barrel into him, his eyes burnin me red hot. I owe him my attention but not long can I hold it. Look away, but I owe him explainin I catch my breath catch my breath.

He was talkin bad about you. Most an gen—*Usually.* Usually we don't say anything about you, but this one day. An I was jus tryin to say, you know, you got your problems too, your mother, you. He thought you was jus some spoiled rich boy, I was jus sayin other people's got their problems too, I was tryin to—

Dwight the peacemaker. Any more a *your* diplomacy, guess we'd be entering the *third* great war.

Why some chuckle escape outa me I can't say. Carl sure weren't makin no humor an I sure ain't feelin no joy. The look he gimme now. Not hate. Worst. I don't know the word for what he's lookin at's so nothin it ain't even worth the energy to hate. Wunst Eliot threw a dictionary at my head. *Sycophant.*

Carl pick up another rock, hurl it, yellin. Smelly piece of miner trash! Pick up another, this one big, yellin. Dead meat!

An there's Parker.

Carl starin at the cat. His hand tightenin roun the rock I feel sweat cole sweat pop out my forehead. Rumble a thunder.

We better go, I say. Your mother'll be fixin lunch for you, wonderin where you are.

Carl kneel. Here, kitty kitty.

Parker suspicious. Parker eyein Carl.

Here, kitty kitty kitty. Here, tabby.

That cat bites, remember? You better leave that cat alone. An I liff my leg high, gonna stomp gonna send Parker runnin but Carl's faster, Carl grab my leg midair near topple me over.

Hey!

Parker flinch. Parker crouch into himself.

Oh don't be scared, kitty kitty. Carl movin careful toward Parker. Nobody's gonna hurt you.

Parker flinch again. Now Carl gettin closer, Parker hiss an take off. Carl hurl the rock at Parker's head. Funny Carl miss Roof by a mile but this time bull's eye. The stone bang Parker's skull, bounce off.

Parker stop, tryin to trudge on in his path but dizzy. Carl movin in closer, close. My mornin toast on its way back up, sour my throat, *Carl.*

Parker hiss harsh an swipe a claw at Carl, who jump back nicka time.

You bitch, says Carl, then picks up the rock an give Parker another whump, close range. Blood.

Carl!

Oh she can take it. Hey kitty.

It's a he. Air soppin humid but my mouth dry.

Carl teasin Parker with the rock, like it's some ball a yarn. Parker swats. Can you get it? Parker swats. Can you get it? Parker pants.

Carl, come on.

Can you get it?

You hurt him enough, Carl, come *on*. Parker swats an slashes Carl's han.

Oh boy, you're in for it now. An Carl straddle Parker, usin inside a his shoes to gentle push Parker side to side, Parker havin trouble keepin balance. Hey kitty. Carl pick up the rock an smack Parker a bit, right side a his head. Hey kitty. Carl smack Parker a bit, leff side. Hey kitty. Parker bleedin, staggerin. Now Carl stand up straight, studyin Parker. I figure he finally got tired a the game. My breath come back, I start to speak, no. Keep my big dumb mouth closed, Carl done stopped on his own, leave it.

An sudden with all his might Carl whip his arm back forceful, the rock high in the air, ready for the big crush.

Carl!

PARKER!

We turn toward the scream. He stans tremblin. Numb.

Eliot. My throat tight.

Parker!

Eliot. Whatta ya doin here?

Eliot pantin, starin at Parker. Then his wild eyes turn to me.

Oh I wasn't really gonna hit the damn cat. Eliot an I snap back to Carl. He laughs. I was gonna throw *by* the cat, scare him, see?

An before Eliot or I can move, Carl slam the rock on Parker's head. The stone bounce off. There Parker's head on the groun, half of it flat an somethin oozin. Brain.

PARKER!

Eliot run to the cat.

Oops.

Parker! Eliot cradlin him. My body froze but the world warm, world blurry an world clear, clear. My mouth open but no words, mute.

God, I really meant to miss it. Chucklin. I really am a bad shot.

Parker! Eliot bawlin, me starin at Carl through my eyes blurry ha-ah ha-ah ha-ah ha-ah

Jesus. No wonder I never made pitcher in the summer camp games.

I feel no legs but make my body move, my eyes on Eliot only Eliot, I'm close, I reach out to touch him gentle. Eliot flinch like Parker, Eliot flinch hard from me.

That was one mean tabby. Carl swing himself up to sit, low branch of a tree. Shows his han. Look at that scratch.

Eliot. I try again, reach out touch my brother but Eliot scream an swing wild, slap my arm away. An now he stare at me, his eyes terrible his eyes confused, like he don't know who I am, like maybe he never did.

AAAAAAH! Me an Eliot turn to Carl, what now? But nothin hurt him, he laughin. Discovered in the distance number three, Uncle Sam decked out in his regular red white n blue, hung. Carl whoopin so hard he fall back, hung from that branch by his knees an upside-down he still can't stop the giggling, face red, red, mad rush a blood.

Parker. I turn back to Eliot, my baby brother holdin his cat. *PARKER!* Eliot runnin through the woods, Eliot carryin Parker's corpse clutchin Parker to his heart.

Eliot. I wipe my face an run, follow, not too close. *Eliot, Eliot.* An feel like those the only two words I'll ever know resta my life.

1959–60
PRAYER RIDGE

I

Decay. Knot. Split. I write the defecks a the logs on my chart. Wipe my wet
forehead with my wet arm, glance over at B.J., him all concentration, movin
logs along the carriage to the big ole head saw. Lunch break called, I go set
with the fellas though I don't talk much, them discussin the photographs a
the earth appeared on the TV lass night, some of em claim it's all fake, ain't
nobody in no outer space, them blurry pictures coulda been anything. I
don't say how I marveled, all along thought we was the entire universe, then
August 1959 roll aroun here's the picture prove otherwise: historical. My
brother by hisself in the corner readin like usual. *A Farewell to Arms*. Even a
five-minute break he pull a book out. Well why not, cep for me nobody sure
know how to han-talk with him. People workin with him jus mimes what
they need. My hans: How is it? He smile, right fingertips tap his chin then
bring backa right han down to leff palm: Good. Always I ask bout his books
though never do I pick up one. Lost interest after I dropped out, now all I
read's the paper.

When I was nineteen an still got some energy, read in the ads bout some
crash sign language course in Selma, three long days. Me an B.J. trades our
work schedule an goes. What we learned! Still, can't help here an there
throwin in our ole made-up words.

Fifteen an barely a year workin when Ed Kessler says Boy, gimme a stick
a that damn Wrigley's cuz often I had a wad in my mouth, and I go I ain't
got no more, jus like that, I ain't got no more all natural pop out. Hadn't
talked that way since before I started school, like I got educated and lost
ain't, replaced it with grammar, but not twelve months sawin logs an ain't
come flyin back, simultaneous the better words slowly driftin away. When
I'm mad I say mad. Or angry: that's it. Useta have a whole slew a vocabulary
for mad. An glad. Sad. All his readin, I know B.J.'s dictionary been steadily
increasin whilst seem like I'm goin backwards.

Whistle blow an we back at it. I wave, catch my brother's eye. Comin for
supper Saturday?

Yes.

Even though it's the routine tradition him over every Saturday, I don't
ask he won't come, like not to presume. I gaze at him, checkin the sharpness

a the teeth before startin again. When I was a kid I'd hear these radio shows, the villain tyin up the woman, then puttin her on the carriage for the head saw to saw her in half. That wa'n't the way Pa went. Two months after my eighth-grade graduation, saw jus swallow his arm. Life insurance he mercifully had take care a the burial, an September I fine myself in the mill steada the high school. Still, I don't worry bout B.J., careful in his work. I done the head saw myself here an again, an oddly I find a certain peace, the magic, spinnin logs into lumber. Wonder if Pa felt that before it all turn to blood.

Saturday watchin Erma pull the oven door down, peekin at the roase chicken. Couple months ago, sweatin an swingin at the VFW, home in bed after an she go This is the night, I feel it. I ride her slow, like that how ya make a baby. Minutes later the alcohol have her dreamin, she ain't no regular drinker but wunst in a blue moon. I stare at the ceilin. Plantin seeds a babies ain't never proved a challenge, she got a speck a one stuck up in her now. Keepin it in incubation, well. This be try number five.

Met three years ago, bar over in Cuttery. Tole Ma it was a dance, dance sounded nicer n bar. Erma a cute little short thing, on the slim side but not too skinny, dark hair, bob, an to this day her style ain't changed much. Still livin with her mama an daddy, her mama originally from Texas. After three dates brung her home engaged, we both thought she was with-child. I felt love for her fast, so happy we got a excuse to tie the knot, an while I near cried when it all come to a red mass in the toilet, I wa'n't a bit regretful she wearin that ring. When we firs tole my mother bout the engagement, she pleased as punch since she figure a daughter-in-law mean more grankids, though Benja already amply supplied her that department. Then we hear B.J. pullin up in his truck, gettin in from work. When Pa passed on he inherited his ole pickup but that died years ago an B.J. finally replaced it with somethin used in good shape. We give him the news an he smile like he spose ta, then kiss Erma on the cheek, then go up to wash up for dinner. Firs time she seen him.

He s'tall, Erma go.

Yeah, took after my pa. I's the one got stuck at five-eight. What I don't mention is Pa stopped at six foot, B.J. kep goin on to six-six, what I think but not say is I'm not entirely sure *was* our pa give B.J. that height.

Erma likes the Saturday night suppers with B.J., give her a chance to play hostess, lay out the embroidered napkins, the weddin china gravy boat her aunt give us. At the table she do the talkin, I do the hand-interpretin, B.J. do the polite listenin, readin her lips but mostly my hand. Doin it years now, sometime I lazy-man it with jus the one hand, eatin with the other, don't even look up from my plate. Now Erma talkin bout her mother an sisters, bout the wonder a the earth pictures, bout how look like nex week Hawaii make statehood, how strange it is takin territories not land-connected an makin em states an how those people didn't exactly look American an how forty-eight stars made a pretty flag, but since they went on an brought in Alaska this year may as well take Hawaii, make it an even fifty. My leff han flyin conveyin it all while the right feedin me mash potatas while my head plunge to the near future, the day she gonna abruptly stop the chatter, when the house go to mournin again after the baby turn to blood in the toilet again like all the rest, then my mine roam back to that day when I firs brought her home. What's that? she said, lookin at somethin framed.

What's *that*? Read it, whatta ya *think* it is? I don't say that but guess she see it in my eyes. Purse her lips. An that's how I come to find out Erma is one hunnert percent illiterate. Cuz

CERTIFICATE OF ACHIEVEMENT

This is to certify that

Randall Jason Evans

has been selected for the
honor of valedictorian for the
class of 1942
of Prayer Ridge School

is pretty damn self-explanatory.

Certificate of achievement.

Achieve what?

Upstairs is a wall picture, me a newborn. You interested? She nod eager an we climb the steps. She got shame for never catchin on to readin which is lucky cuz it keep her from ever askin bout that damn certificate again.

I use to thinka Hawaii like China, like some foreign country but now guess I better start thinkin of it like Tennessee, just another state. Whatchu smilin bout, Randall?

She snap me back to the present.

Nothin. This roase chicken sure is delicious, hon. An she grin wide cuz she see I'm interpretin, B.J. gettin what I'm sayin an he nod, agreein.

But what I was *really* smilin about. I remembered! Maybe I ain't such a hopeless case, ole senile man at thirty-one can't even recall another word for mad, sad, cuz all the sudden middle a this here dinner the vocabulary jus come floodin back! Mad: Enraged! Resentful! Bitter! Sad: Melancholy! Misery! Despair!

2

Standin near the reference table touchin that big ole globe he like, fingers grazin Russia. *Anna Karenina* tucked in his arm, guess he jus checked her out. Figured he be here, Wednesdays like regular. I get close enough he look up, smile. Then see my face ain't returnin it. Benja, I sign.

Hey! You didn't say you was bringin B.J. too, both my brothers! Come in! Hey yaw, come say hi to your uncles. Oh they was in my hair all day. Sid-down, I'll fix the coffee. This place look like a cyclone, all the damn toys *Stop pullin her plait!* Look at that broke fire truck. Christmas ain't a week gone an already they done tore it all up. *Destructive*, that's what yaw are! Listen Randall, sorry bout the tears over the phone, didn't mean to be ruinin your mornin off. An B.J., ain't Wednesday your lie-bary day? Oh you already got your book *God*, Randall! Look at your hands flyin: somethin else! Don't know if I ever toldja how jealous I feel sometimes, way you kep up with the signin. B.J., remember Palm Sunday, you had to come late to supper cuz you volunteered to pick the weeds on the lie-bary grouns, so you wa'n't here yet but Randall signin everthing automatic like you's in the room! Like he doin now! All habit, we had the biggest laugh over that *Give it back to her!* Yaw stayin for dinner? *Lunch*, now all the kids calls it *lunch*. Chicken salad. Oh you all do *not* have to pick up that damn tree. I don't even remember seein it fall, Aaron an me get to screamin, nex thing the tinsel flyin every-where! Had to sweep up pieces from them glassy balls fore the kids come through. Well thank you, you didn't have to do that, always take the tree down New Year's anyway. Nineteen sixty. You thinka that? Two days be a whole new decade. The space age. Well listen. You don't got ta worry, I took my medicine I'm fine now. Boy, look at your fingers move! Sorry B.J., when I got married I got busy, stopped practicin. Busy makin damn kids, five, *five*! I ever get pregnant again think I'll shoot myself. No, Aaron. No, I'll shoot us both! *There!* I *told*ja do it again yer gettin it! An shut up that damn cryin fore I give ya somethin to cry about! If ya can't stay for dinner, at least some Oreos with your coffee. Look. Yaw gotta wipe them looks off your faces, whatchu thinkin. I do that again? Over *him*? He can stay out all night he wants. Sometimes I think What a fool, jus cuz he's a good war pen pal I think that make a good husband, I *should*a married that *firs* bastard, one got his legs cut *off*, *he* wouldn'ta been goin nowhere. Sorry, I oughn'ta laugh! But anyway, yaw ain't got to be all concerned about me. See? I ain't touched my bandages, I can tell my wrists is healin. An Aaron ain't touched me neither. Not since he seen I am serious with a razor. Sorry, that ain't funny! Butcha know, maybe it ain't such a terrible thing, lass week. I ain't gonna do it again! Don't worry! But what I'm sayin is maybe it scared him, make him think twice before ballin up his fists so fast. Ain't *that* a blip? He out trackin pussy an I call him on it, then *I'm* the one kissin knuckles! I wanna go to the pictures! Yaw wanna go to the pictures? I wanna see The Hanging Tree! I wanna see Gary Cooper, yaw wanna come? You can do the signs for B.J.! So nice we went lass year, that was the firs time I went to the pictures in I don't know when! Break another crayon, see whatchu get. An you're the oldest Leslie Jo, you *know* better. I like goin to the pictures with my brothers but wouldn't ya think my husband take me out *sometime*? The Streetcar Name Desire! remember that one? I sure like Marlon Brando. Cep that ole man behind us, hard a hearin, his wife whisperin everthing to him, drive me nuts! See, with B.J. you jus sign, yaw don't disturb nobody *Bed*! *All* a yaw! Right now, goddammit! What was the name a that actress played Stella? Stella! Him callin. Stella! Stella! I *said* bed! No matter how bad he treat her she always remember Marlon got his good side too.

3

Sundays at two everybody walkin the south side. Me an Marietta an Henry Lee walk the north.

Ah! early spring's my favorite. March has such a nice crispness to it, like the last bit of sparkling dew before the dawn.

Ooolg, says Henry Lee in his wheelchair.

Had to run some errands yesterday, happened to drive by the school at recess. All those white children running around, screaming and laughing. Well, they staved it off another season. Integration. It won't last forever.

Ooolg.

Five years now. Do you realize that? Five years since integration went nationwide *with all deliberate speed,* said the Supreme Court, well. The South certainly has its way of interpreting that.

A little girl on the south side starin at Henry Lee till her ma smack her, drag her by fast. We hit a bump in the sidewalk.

Sorry, Henry Lee.

September come, I bet the federals crack down. The Negro children brought in, English together with the white kids, phys ed together with the white kids.

A good thing?

Yes. Yes, Randall, I believe it is a good thing. Remember Sally's son Roger? What a bright boy! Why couldn't he sit next to Henry Lee and you in class, take advantage of all the white school had to offer? Once I asked Sally what she thought about things. Separate but equal. Her answer surprised me. She said she'd be just fine with it if separate *was* equal, but it never is. I never forgot that!

Ooolg.

We reach the corner an turn aroun. Our walks with Henry Lee never cross the street. From the east corner to the west corner, from the west corner to the east.

So what do you think? Desegregation.

I shrug. I don't see this town changin.

But it will. Nineteen sixty now, Randall, late in the day! Eventually we'll be asked to adhere to the law.

Then I'll adhere to the law. Sorry, Henry Lee.

Randall, all these years on this walk, you hit that bump every time! But she smilin, glad wunst a week have someone else push his wheelchair, somebody else to talk to.

Hey Frankenstein! Some teenage boys on the south side, laughin.

All the choices in the world, what makes a fifteen-year-old boy drop out and join the army? One little growth spurt enough for him to claim eighteen and for those bastards at the draft board to pretend they believe it. A fifteen-year-old does not imagine that he'll come home with no legs, half a face, half a brain, the induction officers did not mention that when he signed the dotted line. A boy enlisting, the farthest his foresight may go is to think he'll either die there or come home fine, never considering what's worse is in between.

Woman walkin toward us with a baby carriage. She don't see us, stooped over, coverin up the baby. Or cooin to the baby.

He should be married now. He should be married and me a grandmother. Oh I'm sorry, Randall!

It's okay.

This last one didn't take either?

It's okay. Not everybody meant to be parents.

That's true, but if you want to be. I mean there are so many abandoned children in the orphanages—

The young mother look up see us, cuttin off Marietta's thought. Then the young mother cross the street.

You go ahead! Damn you all, *stay* on the other side! He's a war hero! You were fine when he was there fighting for your freedom, a war hero!

Mother with the baby walkin head up like she ain't even heard Marietta yellin, like we on that TV show, what's it called? Some fourth dimension, us unheard unseen by other humans. Cep teenage boys.

Marietta stoop in fronta Henry Lee. Well, my son. Have you had your exercise for the day?

He say somethin to her, move his hans everywhere.

You sure? she ask. It hit me: *Twilight Zone.* Name a that show. Then I speak: He need somethin?

She gazin at him, stands, shakes her head. Alright, let's go home. Which is two houses away. At the bottom a the porch steps I help her lift him up. How she do this when I ain't aroun?

Thank you, Randall.

I nod.

Visiting every Sunday. You're a good friend to Henry Lee. You always were.

He was a friend to me.

She nods.

He was just telling me, reiterating. She pause fore she go on. He would like you to have his train set. Could you come in and get his train set?

I look at her. I look at him.

I know, I don't understand myself. He enjoys it, looking at it. I turn it on and. Yesterday he told me. He said you'll take care of it, he said. He's been giving things away! One by one, like he knows, he—

Wisht I had a clean hanky to offer her but I already blown my nose on mine.

Henry Lee gonna be aroun a long time, Marietta.

It's hard. Hard for a mother. My only child.

Henry Lee gonna be aroun a long time.

In the basement me an him like the ole days, he tole his mother leave us alone. I don't like deprivin him of his train, but packin it up I ain't seen him so lively, not since he's a kid, puttin every piece in its special box, he already wrote on the boxes. FREIGHT CARS. PASSENGER CARS. TRACK. AUTOMOBILES. PEOPLE. SIGNS/LIGHTS. HOUSES. BUILDINGS. His writin squiggly but readable. He fill a box an put it in my arms, then push the box into me liketa emphasize I'm to keep it. Henry Lee an I separate ways that lass year, him in high school ninth an me at the sawmill after the sawmill taken Pa. But summer before tenth Henry Lee signs with Uncle Sam, he ain't gone but ten weeks fore that grenade come flyin, itty thing he coulda held in his han lay out resta his life. I see how ginger Henry Lee be with them boxcars now an it spur on a memory a him always sayin he gonna hop the trains an my knee take to shakin.

Carryin it all require three trips back an forth his house to mine. Lass roun there Sally swayin thoughtful on the porch swing, on the floor beside her a big burlap bag fulla the lass boxes a train waitin for me. I ain't seen Sally in I don't know when. She only part-time now, an I don't usually go inside a Henry Lee's an she don't usually come out. Gray. Glasses. Few pounds thicker.

How you, Sally?

Fine. How you, Randall?

Fine.

I pick up the boxes, ready to go.

He turn out to be a nice man, didn't he?

Henry Lee?

Uh-huh.

Yes he did.

The swing creak soft.

Make me wonder if it all a bad side a the brain. Like there's a section reserved for meanness, prejudice. All us got it, but some of us use it more n others, Henry Lee made *good* use a his once. She sigh. He was a child. But maybe that parta his brain's the part that explosive shot off. Lotta other people roun here could use that kinda surgery.

I don't believe Sally really takes stock in the theory she's puttin forth. Still, the picture she holdin of it in her mind give her some faraway sweet sad smile.

4

When the lass time you come to a meetin?

Buppie with a cigar, some new fool thing he started recently. Sittin near the grill, Lily's yard. Few years back she started her own tradition: all the family at her house, Confederate Memorial Day.

I dunno, I tell him. Long days. Sip my beer.

We all got long days, we all tired. That on't stop rest of us.

I pay my dues.

Yeah you pay your dues.

Dusk. Over by the big oak I glimpse Benja's Aaron sittin alone, in the doghouse like regular. Lily at the picnic table with Deb Ellen, them two sisters havin an after-dinner smoke an the latter say somethin funny an they's both laughin. Even though she matronly rounder in Lily's smile I get a flash from when I was a kid, crush on my older cousin. Their mama come sit with em, Aunt Pearlie with that sad smile she pretty much been wearin since the war. Her oldest Jack they was all worried about, he come back unscathed but here Artie Ray, younger son signed up seventeen, killed in the Pacific three days before Hiroshima.

You know what's been goin on in this country. Integratin the schools everywhere else, how long till you think it come here?

I shake my head. Ain't no one gonna let that happen but no sense me tryin to tell that to Buppie once his mine's made up. Hard head.

Remember Little Rock? How they tried to stop it? An now the little niggers sittin right nex to white.

Confederate Memorial Day work out nice, April 26th fall on a Tuesday. By lucky coincidence this week I'm given Monday off an the whole mill closed today, two free in a row feel like some island vacation. Erma come out the house now, join the women at the picnic table.

You listenin, Randall?

When *is* the damn meetin?

Toldja. Sunday.

Yaw wanna slice a lemon meringue? My mother suddenly there, smilin. Hopeful.

That your homemade, ain't it, Aunt Bobbie?

Sure is.

That soun like a winner, I think I will.

Randall?

No thanks.

Lemon meringue! Your favorite.

No thanks.

She stan there a few seconds. Know she lookin at me but I ain't lookin at her.

Then she say, Yaw went to the cemetery today, Buppie?

Sure. You know Ursula's daddy past away November.

Yes, I sure was sorry to hear boutcher father-in-law. Randall an Erma come over this mornin. We cut roses off our bush, then us an B.J. gone up, lain em on Ben's grave. An your granmother. Didn't we, Randall?

Yep.

Can't believe how long since Uncle Ben gone.

You know, I got into an argument with Annabelle Maizy from church, sayin Decoration Day's only about them that served an died, like I'm some kinda blasphemer honorin my poor mother.

Way I was brung up not jus the soldiers. Ya honor *all* your dead loved ones.

That's what I told her! Oh Buppie the roses jus bloomed today! Didn't they, Randall? Prayin, prayin they be ripe for Decoration Day. An I looked out this mornin an there they was! Miracle!

I know she lookin at me, waitin for me to look back, smile at her miracle. I don't. She walks away.

Thurgood Marshall, *he's* the bastard. Remember him?

I shake my head.

You *ought*a remember him, he's that nigger lawyer from New York, one done it in the Supreme Court. Schools.

Somebody colored on the Supreme Court?

No! Well not yet, who knows the way things're goin. He made the case *to* the Supreme Court.

Whatchu think the buyout mean.

The who?

I give him my eyes.

Oh. Buppie sigh. Guess I don't like to think about it. When some other company take over a mill, it don't usually mean cuz they wanna *expand* the employee roster.

I sip my beer, stare at my beer.

You been there a long time, Randall. Since you's a kid, me almost as long. Gonna be lass hired, firs fired, I think our positions is secure.

I ponder on that. I nod. I ponder on that.

But tell ya what. Come a day you need a job, plenty a businessmen in the Klan. An hirin time come, guess who they look to firs?

You wanna beer, Aaron?

No thanks, Randall.

Why you wanna call him over? Buppie tryin to whisper an bite my head off same time.

Lookin awful lonely over there all by his lonesome.

Like you care. Only reason you reach out to him is change the subject.

He a member too, ain't he.

Yeah, he could learn you a thing or two about commitment.

I take a swig.

Him an Benja on the outs again? Buppie still keepin his voice low.

When ain't they?

Here ya go, Buppie! Oh I didn't even ask if you wanted some ice cream with your slice.

You see this belly I'm growin, Aunt Bobbie? I think pie alone'll do me fine. Don't it look creamy.

You want some ice cream, Randall?

No thanks.

She jus standin there again. I look out in the direction a the park, swig a beer. Be able to see the fireworks from here, though they be tiny little pop stead of a big boom. Don't know why for but the honorable town council decided fireworks Memorial Day *an* Fourth this year. I take another swig. She walk back to the house.

Cut her a break.

I beg your pardon?

What happened? You an your mother use to be lovin.

I gently advise you to mine your own goddamn business.

It only happened once.

I look up an now here's Aaron.

It only happened once, he repeat, eyes on me.

Once what?

The skirt chasin. But your sister won't forget it. I was a dickaroun in the army, them nurses, WACs, but since comin out, jus that one girl that Julia. Benja don't belee me.

Lotta late nights.

Runnin from the screamin! Kids screamin, *her* screamin, I keep my pants up. Jus head for the bars, *you* seen me in the bars, ever notice I pick up some woman? *No.* Jus gettin out the house, away.

How bout that black eye she had?

Only happened once.

Aaron.

We all turn aroun hearin that voice. Benja an her stressed face. Come ere. Walkin off, soff talkin, I drain the lass bit a my Bud an my han already grabbin the bottle opener for the next.

I wanna suggest somethin. Buppie, not knowin when to let go of a subject. I'm gonna suggest somethin an might be you won't like it. Maybe logical why you ain't so worried bout the innegration a schools, seein as you an Erma don't seem to be contributin to the population a the school system any.

Buppie on his back so fass I don't even remember flippin him over outa that chair. Sorry! he say, palms up, surrender, Sorry!

Benja an Aaron run over. What happened! You okay? Aaron stoopin, in Buppie's face.

Whadju *do*, Randall? Benja say, an I storm off, away from em all. Jus fore I open the screen door to Lily's kitchen I turn aroun. Benja an Aaron's back to me, talkin to Buppie, him still on the groun, like me knockin him eight inches to the grass paralyzed him or somethin, an then there go Aaron's han gentle on her waist, an just a nudge she lean into him.

I slam the goddamn screen door. How long till that han aroun her waist ball into a fist smackin her jaw again? Yeah, black eye happen only once. An her broke tooth only once. Her broke ankle, arm. What make me go soff an offer the bastard a beer anyway? Him sittin all alone? Alone's where he oughta be!

Randall honey, you alright?

I storm past her, carryin aroun her goddamn lemon meringue. Maybe you oughta ask your nephew, he's the one flat on his back, I say without turnin to her an down the basement steps.

Big commotion sudden come to a stop, hearin my feet on them stairs. Must be twenty little boys, all some kinda who knows what kin to me, all wrasslin an laughin till my presence make em freeze.

Go ahead, I say, I ain't here. Swig a beer. They approach with caution, but forty-five seconds later all of em back in full swing. Distant *pop*. It's startin, they say, It's startin, stampedin me to fly upstairs out to the yard. Whoever planned it space em out maybe three a minute, hopin to stretch the light show to a good half-hour.

In the quiet I see framed on a shelf one a Lily's, high school football quarterback, the town star lass fall an too young to know those three months a glory prolly be the best a his entire life. On the shelf above: schoolbooks. *Organic Chemistry. Pop* go a firework. I open it, flip right to a chart take up two pages acrost: Periodic Table of the Elements. It ring a bell, I remember once I had some kinda curiosity about it. Riflin through I glimpse density an matter an atomic theory an balancin chemical equations an suddenly I wanna take it home, read it cover to cover! But it gotta be one a Lily's kids'. Put it back. Muss be somethin similar at the library. B.J. get to the library regular, I'ma start to too, *pop*.

Throw my empty bottle in the garbage, head on up the steps. Now Erma sittin where I'd been, Buppie still there, finally pulled hisself back up on the chair. No hard feelins, Buppie say, I overstepped, overstepped. *Pop*. Blue stars an green.

I go over by where the vehicles parked. Benja an Aaron somewheres near in the dark, laughin an kissin. I light a cigarette, sit on my truck's runnin board. B.J. lookin out at the works from inside, upstairs winda. Light in the bedroom he stand in make it easy to see him, but in the night imagine I'm invisible as Benja an Aaron. This solitude I like, no one see me, but boun not to last. Here come Erma.

I got an idea.

I take a puff.

I was jus talkin to Lily an Deb Ellen, an Deb Ellen said lass week she run into her ole friend Sandy Whiner in the market by the produce, Sandy Whiner who she went to school with an played ball with, now also married with children.

What I think but don't utter to Erma is contrary to her family tradition a quittin after sixt, Deb Ellen went to eighth where her an Sandy Whiner was the star girl athletes them lass two years an where her an Sandy got real tight, maybe *too* tight people said.

Well Sandy tells Deb Ellen they're startin the ladies' leagues, sofball. They don't start till middle a June, after school's out since most a the players are mothers. Aw Deb Ellen you *gotta* pitch, Sandy tells her. An Deb Ellen: How? an point to her overflowin shoppin cart, referrin to all her babies. Only once a week, only Wednesdays. The men's leagues take up all the fields over the weekends. An who gonna watch em? Deb Ellen asks.

Us! That's what I jus told her at the picnic table. Once a week, few times over the summer. We don't mind havin a little practice in our future parentin. Well Deb Ellen look at me not sure, say I oughta check in with you. She also say her an Calvin happy to pay: ten dollars a night. I say, No! But she insist.

I look at Erma's pleadin eyes. All eager, advertisin to the whole damn clan WE ARE CHILDLESS an her desperation not to be.

How Deb Ellen end up with that Calvin I'll never know. His own business, sellin swimmin pools to the rich, income ain't nothin they never worried about. Their eighth anniversary few months back somehow we end up babysittin their litter, Deb Ellen lookin all uncomfortable in her blue dress, seem like she only feel like herself in pants, an Calvin all in love, grinnin ear to ear. Their oldest seven an five behine that one. Enda the evenin look like some tornado gone through our livin room, little Deb Ellens tearin up everywhere.

On the other han ten bucks a week supplemental. An the mill buyout, whatever that mean.

Sure.

Aw, thanks honey! She gimme a big hug an kiss. I'll tell her! A louder bang an we both turn. Big purple an blue one.

He's right you know.

I turn back to her.

Buppie. Bout the school innergration. We need the Klan strong, solid if we gonna prevent it. Buppie said he also joined the White Citizens Council, every ammunition we got. You considered that? The White Citizens Council?

What else he say? Offer any specific theories about why he thinks I ain't been so committed as I oughta?

Everbody's tired, Randall, all the mill men got long hours.

I take a long puff, smoke flow out my nose.

Hey, B.J. lookin at the fireworks! I thought he was a-scared a the fireworks.

I shrug. He still don't like to go to the park. He feel the vibrations there, feel the explosions set the world movin.

How come he so spooked?

A dud make a harsh bang even this far from the park an me an Erma flinch. B.J. stare, don't stir.

He was little, some kids. He thought they was bein friendly. Put firecrackers on his shoulders. Lit em, burned him.

Erma turn to me, starin wild a minute fore she speak, eyes all shiny. I *hate* kids! No, *parents*! *They* trained em. Nut don't fall far!

A cricket right on the groun in fronta us. Thirty-two I turned week an a half ago an still can't help but smile: good luck. So I near most fall off the runnin board when Erma stomp it, smash it dead.

Why God give all the fertility to them prolly couldn't raise a puppy proper, let alone a child!

My mother comes to the winda, puts her arm aroun B.J., kisses him, then look right at us, her mouth wide open in some fake surprise while it obvious she come jus for the opportunity for me to see her. So guess I ain't so invisible. Why she always after me anyway? She points in Erma's an my direction for B.J., who squints, tryin to make us out, then start wavin big, like we all some long-loss friends. Erma wave back smilin, wipin her tears.

See yer ma, Randall? An B.J.? Your brother sure loves his family!

Big bang. Some a them thousands a cousins got home works, a red-orange sizzler right in the yard, an B.J. jump, back away from the winda, I know he wanna go home. But steel hisself to stay. In the ole days she be givin him a little comfort hug round about now, but grown man, guess he old for that. An somethin else. Occurs to me for the firs time he ain't her favorite no more. What I hoped for my whole life I got an till now didn't see it, I moved into my mother's favored position jus by no longer bein interested in it.

In spite a the periodic too-close booms, B.J. stan there, all mesmerized gazin, little smile on his face. My guess is that's the advantage a deaf. Our ma right nex to him but he got the choice. He can be with her but he also got the grand option a jus goin inta hisself, alone. Erase us all.

5

Thirteen hours straight at the mill, I sure make no complaints. Two a the young guys recently laid off. Feel bad but jus prayin them's all the adjustments needs to be made with the buyout. Get home all I wanna do is hibernate like the bear, starvin an too tired to eat. Which is good cuz I notice no sign a supper.

In the guestroom I stare at it.

Oh Randall! Honey I forgot to cook, I'm sorry. I jus got all excited.

I stare at it. Crib.

I *know* I'm jumpin the gun but. Well, waitin for you to get home, workin so late, I couldn't wait no longer. I wanted to see the crib in here! The doctor said. Oh I *know* I'm jumpin the gun but this time I jus feel it, I *know* this baby gonna pull through. Sixt try's a charm!

She kiss me an I kiss her, she smile an I smile. Many a time in the past I think to take a ax to that goddamn crib.

Course I'd asked B.J. to Saturday night supper so it's TV dinners, which he accept all gracious like that Salisbury steak's a T-bone. All the while she reiteratin Buppie's appeal, impressin upon the special importance of attendin the meetin tomorra night with a little one on the way. The part bout the little one she mouth, move her lips but no sound, which mean I ain't sposed to sign that part to B.J. but since she exaggerate her lips enough for me to read then surely he can read em hisself. An Sunday, she go on, You'll have all day to rest up before the gatherin. I don't insert *Rest up?* Ain't I gotta mow the lawn, yank the weeds?

I ain't got the energy for arguin so while she puttin dirty dishes in the sink I ask B.J. he wanna come.

Pa did it?

Yeah, remember? His robe she threw in with the colors, turned pink.

He grin.

Sunday afternoon I'm clippin the hedges, she comes up. Your mother called. Since you're goin by to pick up B.J. for the meetin anyway she figure she celebrate his birthday a day early, you show up nine instead a ten: she got the cake. I keep workin, don't answer. I know my mother made this plan so if I don't show up early, look like I slighted *him.* Dammit! Clipped a blamed big hole in the hedge.

Benja's there with her brood, runnin aroun like somethin wild an native. An like it ain't raucous enough, B.J. hammerin, mendin Ma's knickknack shelf, here's how he celebrate his birthday. Somethin that seem to come natural to him not long after he gained language: fix-it man.

Where that bruise on your jaw come from? I ask my sister.

Fell. Minutes later she head to the bathroom, return with more cake makeup like that big blacknblue don't shine right through.

She wanna get the kids home an in bed so we get the cake done. Afterward Ma insist on a Polaroid a the whole gang. Then B.J. say he wanna take one with Ma in it. But Ma: No, you're the birthday boy. Thirty-seven-year-ole boy, I think. He insist, an for his shot he put the kids sittin in front an us standin behind: Ma in the middle, Benja on her one side, me on her other. I ain't been this close to Ma in years an I don't appreciate it. Ma put her arm around us. Benja put her arm aroun Ma. My arms hang loose. After the flash I say, Let's go, an I head for the door an lass second I turn to see B.J.'s arm aroun Ma, her with the teary eyes.

Turns out it ain't just a regular ole meetin. It's a rally, cross-burner which always draw a crowd, newcomers as well as the slackers in the general membership. Me an B.J. close, sweatin from the flames. An from the six-pack I got us for an appetizer. The guy railin on an on about job competition an Northern agitators an a course school innegration, I'm signin it all fass to B.J., You gettin all this?

He smile, sign back: Nigger Kyke Nigger Kyke.

More brew at the gatherin so we come back sloshed an stumblin, an I know better n go home to Erma stinkin a liquor. She so happy I went to the meetin, tomarra jus tell her me an my Klux fellas was plannin till the wee hours. I go in with B.J., tiptoe upstairs. My brother had every right turn our ole room inta *his* room but never did. I lay on my twin jus like comin up, he on his. But he don't turn out the light, meanin he wanna talk. My eyelids heavy, comin down

BANG! with the pilla.

I jump awake, stare at him. He got the mischievous grin, I sign, You gonna regret that, son. Grab my own pilla.

You never had to go to the mill.

I stop. He ain't grinnin no more.

After Pa died. Now B.J.'s hans flyin. She never said quit school and go to the mill, *I* went to the mill. *I* make enough to take care of the family, *you*'re the one decided you had to quit school and work, I didn't ask you to. She didn't ask you to.

Where *this* come from? Usually B.J. don't overdrink, now I see what happen when he do: his hans get way too damn chatty. An even with that bitta bloodshot, his eyes look pretty sober to me.

They weren't payin you right! *That's* why I went. They were payin you deaf wages! Still do!

I made enough.

For the whole damn family? You think that then you ain't got no math sense.

Blaming her because you dropped out. Nobody but you.

Who said I was blamin her? I don't ever remember discussin this subject with you! Maybe her an I jus don't got nothin in common, maybe people jus grows apart.

He stare.

Well she never stopped me. Did she! She was the mother, she coulda stopped me goin to the mill.

She was mourning, she didn't know what to do.

She was the mother, she shoulda stopped me!

Nobody but you.

Bolt up outa that bed, run down the steps, slam open the damn door. Light click on, I see it from her winda, see she jus woke turned it on, hell with em all. An even in my rage I know I'll do somethin tomarra to make up. Drive by, I won't turn off the engine but she'll come out, Ma come out all hopeful an I'll say I'm goin to the market, you need anything? An she'll smile wide, Aw, I'm all set but thank you for thinkin a me honey! We both know she got B.J. to run to the store for her, the offer jus symbolic an then her an I okay a while. I park a block away an walk so the truck don't wake up Erma, catch me stumblin.

Sleepin with a frown. The daylight she happy hopeful, but nighttime I know the toilets filled with blood rip through her dreamin.

Tiptoe to the nursery, that what she be callin it how long. Three weeks? Two months? All them fertilizins ain't never swoll her belly out a smidge.

Move a chair to the crib. Lean forward, lay my tired head on the side bar. Some people find it hard to believe I got a memory so early, but I recall bein a toddler standin in my own crib, Ma's big face in mine, holdin this stuffed bunny. Her cheeks puckered out, ticklin me, kissin me, an I'm squealin happy, Hey Randall, Ma loves you, Ma loves you.

Spring day. I'm out in the yard an hear, Daddy look at me! My little toddler girl up a tree, twirlin aroun, dancin on a branch. I'll catch ya, sugarplum! In my dream tryin to comfort her, thinkin she's scared but my daughter jus keep laughin an dancin on that branch, happy like the sun.

6

Here come Deb Ellen in her sofball jersey, white letters on orange, carryin that baby still not a year yet, the other five fallin in line behind. Late June, me an Erma's third weekly shift: zookeepers to the beasts.

Mommy can I have some milk? Mommy I have to go potty. Mommy you kiss my booboo? But like she ain't hearin none of em, her eyes in the meer, make sure her uniform got all the wrinkles ironed out, checkin her teeth for stuck food. Deb Ellen got a thickness, big girl, but don't seem like middle age. She always was athletic so her grown-up stockiness feel right for her. Mommy can I put on your baseball glove? Thank you for keepin an eye on em thrown over her shoulder as she sail out. Mommy Mommy cryin at the door. On the table a ten-spot. We don't ask but Deb Ellen feel better about it: pay upfront.

Yaw want Aunt Erma bake ya some chocolate chip cookies? Holdin the infant, smilin like they's all the angel a angels. Randall, why on't you show em Henry Lee's train?

In the tradition a Henry Lee I got it set up in the basement an some Sundays after walkin Henry Lee I might come home an work with it a hour or two.

What kinda car is this? says A.R., oldest boy, name after his uncle Artie Ray that passed.

LaSalle.

What's a LaSalle?

Manufactured by GM, 1927 to '40. Built by Cadillac. You hearda Cadillac? Well this here's his offspring.

Except for the occasional question, they're quiet, miracle! watchin the trip past the school, the market, roun the mountain, by the lake. Then Erma, Cookies! They all fly up the steps. Cep the firsborn, girl with the long dark hair. Seven an I never see her speak a word besides Stop it or Behave to the rest, seem like she never have play-fun all her own. But the train she can't keep her eyes offa.

How you doin in school, Lou Mary?

She jump a little, like forgot I was there. Guess no one seem to speak to her much. Outa all a Deb Ellen's litter, she the only wheel ain't squeaky.

Fine.

Whatchu think you like to be when you grow up?

She bite her lip. Teacher.

Teacher? That's a good thing. You gotta go to college for that. You plan on goin to college?

Nod her head. Train goin through the mountain tunnel. Sometime I imagine I'm ridin on top, through the blackness, but there's always the hope up ahead, peek a light. Now approachin the crossin, safety stick comin down, bell ringin, always remine me a Henry Lee's penchant for very tragic accidents.

You went to college?

That question catch me off guard. Usually Lou Mary ain't one to speak less she spoke to.

I wanted to go to college. Be a lawyer. You know what a lawyer is?

In court?

Uh-huh.

How come you ain't one?

You like to work the controls?

She nods, eyein me like she ain't sure I really mean it. I wave her over an she come runnin. Laughin, ain't it a delight to see it comin outa that solemn girl!

Lou Mary. You better come on up here fore no cookies left.

My little cousin highly reluctant to leave the train but follow after Erma. I turn it off an come on up, the brats all peaceful roun the table, crunchin, glasses a milk. Cep I don't see that Marky, worrisome cuz lass week he come up missin in action, later I fine my garden hose cut in two.

I go upstairs lookin for the little devil, half scared what I might see. An hear a soun give my belly a ache. There he be in the guestroom, thrustin the walls with the toilet plunger, rings appearin all over the wallpaper. I'ma smack you to kingdom come, boy. He try to fly past me, but on the way I snatch the plunger out his hands, whomp him on his hide. He keep runnin, down the stairs, not even a tear. Ain't even four years old, only Deb Ellen could make em that bad!

You know what that boy doin upstairs?

All innocent, hidin behine Erma, peekin out at me.

Whatever it is, I'm sure you whooped him for it.

Damn right. An I ain't finished. I make a move an he fly out the back door.

When's Deb Ellen gonna grow up, take care a her own?

Lease she ain't screamin at em all the time, like your sister.

Ya gotta *notice* em to scream at em, Deb Ellen pop one out every five minutes an forget about em. An where's Calvin? Prolly enjoyin some peace an quiet, ear glued to the radio, Cardinals game.

She ignore me, all wide-eyed baby-talkin. This argument we have every Wednesday.

Wait till you see that guestroom.

Now her all teary, dammit. My slip: spose ta say nursery. But her hurt feelins can't lass long aroun here, what with one screamin an the other slappin an the firs one bawlin an Erma called upon for arbitrations. Where Marky go? she ask.

How'm *I* sposed to know? I think. Cep I know she weren't askin no question, what it was was *Please* go look for Marky.

How the hell he climb up the tree that high? I sure hope this boy go for sports cuz otherwise all that energy he headed for firs-class lawbreaker. Come on down here, Marky. I ain't mad atcha no more. Come on down to this branch, I'll ketcha from there.

But that boy come flyin down from way up where he be, oh my Lord! I step back fass, I got him! I got him!

You okay, Randall? You okay? Erma in my face. All them kids, why I'm lookin up at em? At the sky?

Now in the car, how I get here? Erma drivin, Erma don't know how to drive! He awake, Aunt Erma, one a them monsters say. Erma turn to me: Randall? I see that Lou Mary lookin concerned, I hope she *do* go to college she *do* become a teacher. I hope she stick it out in school

Cousin Erma, he fallin to sleep again!

You've had yourself a concussion, Randall. I'm gonna stitch you up. And then, Erma, you keep the coffee brewin. Don't let this rascal go to sleep tonight.

Randall. This is Dr. Mattingly.

Mattingly, Mattingly. Somethin in his eyes. Hospital so clean white gimme a headache.

Can you hear me, Randall? It's me, Erma.

Where the kids?

Calvin come an got em. Once the doctor say okay for Marky to go.

What about Deb Ellen?

Said they won six–four. Three a the innins she pitched three up, three down. An there's only seven innins in softball.

I'm gonna stitch you up now. Keep talkin, Erma. This'll sting a little, Randall.

Somethin familiar. Dimple.

Marky fell an you caught him an you saved his life, but you fell back an banged your head on the groun. He seemed fine an the doctor said he's fine. You saved his little life.

Ouch!

That's one stitch, Randall. There's gonna be six.

We know each other?

Dr. Mattingly look at me. You don't remember? Eighth grade?

I stare.

Earl Mattingly? Practically I whisper it.

He turn to Erma, See there? Can't be brain damage he remember that.

Lookin at me again, then he throw back his head, hollerin the laughter. Close your mouth, Randall! I know what you're thinkin. What turned that bumblehead into a doctor? When I entered the ninth, dumb football player, they all figured at best I'd be on the business track.

Sssss.

Sorry, Randall, I know that stings. Hey, Betty, why on't you bring some more cotton in here? Earl Mattingly squintin while he work.

Well here's what happened. That freshman year I found myself sittin in your place. Quarterback, away game in Montgomery, somebody sacked me and I saw stars. My concussion was worse than yours, I was told how lucky, the right doctor in emergency, how close I come to permanent mental ramifications. Anyway, I quit the team which I tell you made a lotta people sore, studied night and day and by God by graduation I was the class valedictorian! So now we got that in common!

Aaaaaaah.

Sorry, one last stitch. College, worked my way through the summers, graduated at twenty, then med school, residency. And now here I am back home, M.D. Earl Mattingly cut the thread. Done.

3:30 a.m. me an Erma in the livin room drinkin drinkin. For variety, sometime I say milk, sometime sugar, sometime sugar an milk, sometime cream. Mean I pee a lot, an she even folla me to the bathroom, make me talk the whole time, make sure I ain't dozin. Finally wore out my taste for dairy, this hour jus take it black.

What was it Dr. Mattingly said yaw had in common? Soun like. Victory?

For a second I'm back in eighth grade in our caps an gowns, principal call my name an I take the valedictory podium but jus fore I start, Earl Mattingly stand, announce to the whole world I cheated, copied offa his standards test, he tell that lie then *he* take the podium, make the speech. I go back to my seat an watch him. It's better, I think. His speech is better n mine.

Randall! Snappin her fingers at me. Wake up!

I focus on her. The clock tick tick tick.

Valedictorian, I say.

What's that mean?

As it turns out, nothin.

You know what? I'm gonna give you some grouns a coffee an you gonna chew em up, raw. That oughta keep ya a while.

When you got word to Deb Ellen, her game over?

Still had a innin an a half to go. Calvin tole me the number for the field phone booth, everybody use it for calls.

An what you tell her. I'm hurt? Her son maybe hurt?

Sure. We didn't know about Marky then, yeah I alert her as to the situation, takin both yaw to the emergency. Calvin on his way.

An she play the game out? Jus posepone the matter a her kid in the hospital till the game through?

Erma hesitate.

She was tore up, tryin to decide. The game was tied then, she's the star player, she'da left they'd surely lost. I got her top a the sixt, you know there's only seven innins in softball. An she call back checkin before bottom a the sixt, before top a the seventh, before bottom a the seventh.

So she never left. Played the game out to the end.

Erma purse her lips.

Knew it! An I laugh so hard one a the stitches near pop out.

7

My breathin breathin heart thump thump. In come Mr. Holliman.

Oh hello there, Randall. Well I ain't gonna beat aroun the bush with ya. Demand's down. Tryin not to have the whole mill shut. We gotta let some men go.

I try to speak. Nothin.

It ain't personal. Your work's fine, we had to go random. Well some lazy bums got their asses fired, they went firs. An the new guys. But wa'n't enough of em. We had to go to the capable workers, we had to go random. Sorry to ruin your weekend.

He look at me like he want me say somethin. I wanna but.

Things were boomin a while. But guess no business stay profitable forever. Thankin the Lord we was good long as we was, sure supported a lotta Lefferd County for a long spell.

Mr. Holliman. Mr. Holliman, I'm sorry about lass week. I'm sorry about missin Thursday, the doctor, he said with the concussion nex day, he advised—

Randall, you ain't called in sick a day in fifteen years, you think I'm s'heartless to fire someone cuz they missed one Thursday in fifteen years? This ain't a firin no way. A layoff, nothin to do with work quality. Your work's fine, I give ya a good recommendation. Jus economics, supply n demand. Nothin nobody can control.

My father.

I know your father, I know you got legacy. Know who else's father worked here? Everbody's!

My father died.

Oh. Oh yeah, accident. Mr. Holliman look down. He sure was a good man.

He keep lookin down. I wonder is he cryin, or prayin, or jus bein respectful. I don't know what Mr. Holliman talkin about, my father was a good man, Mr. Holliman was in fourth grade when my father died. Maybe *his* father told him bout mine? Mr. Holliman lookin down at his feet, an right where his feet is is a patch a mud somebody tracked in. After Mr. Holliman spend a respectable amount a time respectin my father, he take a tissue from his desk an wipe up the dirt.

Why the buyout people buy out if demand's down?

The buyout people bought out sayin they know how to run things more efficiently.

We lookin at each other, don't know who gonna speak nex.

B.J.?

B.J.'s stayin. You don't got to worry boutcher mother.

Phone.

Hello? Oh hi Charlie!

Mr. Holliman smilin, sittin on the edge a his desk, turnt away. The phone call go on, him turnt away whole time, so finally I turn to go.

Sarah gotcher lass check, Randall. Now he lookin at me, his han over the receiver. You can leave anytime you want, we already covered your pay for the day.

Buppie unloadin logs from the truck. They pay B.J. peanuts, he says, that's how come they kep B.J.

The head saw screamin, B.J. shootin planks through. His face showin the moisture but never do I see him wipe his brow.

What about you?

I'm the random luck a the draw. An maybe they worry, half my family works here, maybe they thinkin fire one of us we all quit. But listen, Randall. You wanna job, I can get you a job.

B.J. look up at me, signs, They pay me peanuts. That's why they keep me.

I look over at Mr. Holliman's office. Kirby Wright who I went to school with an whose pa lost two fingers from a mill saw come walkin out slow, somebody shut the door behind him. Kirby starin in space like he in shock, starin at the pink paper in his hand.

I take no charity, I work my whole day an end of it I see Mr. Holliman comin outa his office. He give a start, sprised to see me there waitin for him.

Eighteen years. You said fifteen. Eighteen years, I been workin here since I's fourteen years ole. Then I walk out, wipin all the perspiration an wonderin whether the swelterin dog days ever end.

8

Why you got that damn ham sanwich? Buppie keep his eyes on the road while he ask it, not even the speck of a glance my way even though ain't another car for miles.

I ain't had supper. An you said they ain't servin supper, only cocktails.

I bet you didn't even bring your toothbrush. Meetin potential employers smellin like ham an mustard.

I look in the rearview. Wipe the mustard, corner a my mouth. Dressin up my Sunday suit an they ain't even feedin us.

We'll stay a few minutes, politeness, do our business an leave. It's a fund-raiser an I don't think you exactly there to write out no checks.

Cocktails. All I see's them big weeds. Chuckle.

That's *cat*tails.

I *know* that.

Look air. Some gum in that glove compartment. An spit it out fore we walk through the door. An spit it out in this here ashtray, not on his front lawn!

Mansion. Bay windas, figures millin aroun inside, who they are you can't even tell behine the curtains. *Ding dong.*

Buppie! Come in. And Randall! I'd forgotten he was bringin you.

Hi. I don't say his name in the moment cuz I'm a little unsure. Dr. Mattingly or Earl?

May I get you gentlemen a drink?

Whatever you're havin, says Buppie.

Whatever you're havin Earl, I say. I ain't got to call nobody who ain't at present examinin me doctor.

What Earl's havin an thus me an Buppie is scotch. I have a swallow then take in my surroundins. Bout twenty men in the room, they have their drinkin huddles. I was a mite confused when Buppie tried to explain this affair to me, but now I see it. Meetin a the minds: the high court a the Klan an high society. How Buppie got me into this gatherin a professionals I don't know but I don't question. He ushers me over so we're standin nex to Ike Martin a Martin's Shoes. Ralph Goody the lawyer says he'll give money to the Klan but he feels more comfortable claimin membership to the White Citizens Council. Earl Mattingly says he'll contribute but won't take out official membership in neither. Ike Martin says I give no money to no group I'd be ashamed to proclaim active membership in, an ya might note I've given to the Klan *an* to the Council.

Mr. Martin this here's my cousin Randall. I mentioned him to ya.

Ike Martin gimme the long look. Whatchu know about shoes, Randall?

My mouth open but nothin come out.

He's in the Klan. An his daddy, Ben Evans. Was.

Oh yes, I remember Ben. Tragic. Tragic.

From this angle I catch a glimpse a the kitchen, spyin a colored maid lookin over the snacks. Hors d'oeuvres. No one else see her, an she never make her appearance out here in the party.

Sellin shoes is a knack, either ya got it or ya don't. Think ya got it?

I glance at Buppie, his eyes hard on me, tellin me I better answer right, true or lie.

I think I got it.

Comin downstairs there's Dr. Mitchum, full robe regalia, everything but the hood. Not sure why he's dressed to the T's an no one else but no one else seem bothered. Big grin, he always bright up a room, maybe that's what makes him a good pediatrician. Still recollect his teasin when I was six, makin my visit for a diptheria vaccination almost pleasant: *Here it comes, Randall, it gonna tickle! And then a big cherry sucker! Or grape?*

I have an employee leavin to start her family in a couple weeks. Tell ya what, you come in Monday, you can overlap with her for your trainin. Course you're paid for the trainin. That be fine?

That be *very* fine. Thank you, sir!

Trial basis. Like I said, sellin shoes is a knack. You be on probation a month.

I understand.

Monday 10 a.m. An by that I mean 9:45. Monday's the firs. August already, don't the time fly?

The maid in the kitchen done set down, chewin on a olive on a toothpick. By accident I meet her eye, an I expect now she'll feel caught, jump up an hurry on back to work. But she jus turn away an go right on chewin, like not carin if the grass ever grow.

9

You are on trial for four weeks an while you are on trial you will get minimum wage. Minimum wage is one dollar. If you make it past the trial you will get minimum plus a nickel plus commission. Commission starts after you have sold more shoes than minimum. In other words, if I work ya forty hours a week that's forty dollars for your minimum, an if in that week you only sell shoes add up to a thirty-dollar commission, all you get is your basic forty dollars. However, you sell enough shoes add up to a sixty-dollar commission, well! You just traded your forty-dollar paycheck for a sixty. Understand? After your four weeks a trainin you should definitely be makin more than minimum. If not, you an I will have to have a talk.

He speakin to me in the back storeroom. I'm a sweater an I can feel it already! Erma sewed pads into my shirt armpits so they won't be soppin.

Sellin shoes is a professional job. You come to work clean, wear a tie an a smile, you're halfway to your commission right there.

Ting-a-ling.

Don't worry, Brenda Jean an Diane's out on the floor. Can't be a customer yet anyway, keep the door closed till ten.

Hi Mr. Martin.

Hi Imogene. This is Randall, startin today.

Hi Randall.

You show him aroun?

Sure. She go someplace to put her pocketbook down. She clearly expectin.

You shopped at Martin's Shoes before? he ask.

Yes, I lie. Martin's far outa my price range, an growin up we never seen the adjoinin room neither, Martin's Children's, for the rich kids. Our loafers came from Discount Denny's.

After your trial, as an employee you may buy Martin's Shoes at a substantial reduction, cost plus ten percent. An I expect you will. What kinda business our salespeople not even wearin our shoes?

On a shelf behind him's a gold trophy cup: WORLD'S BEST DAD.

Randall. We are brothers in a vital organization and that got you your trial. I just need to reiterate it did *not* get you a permanent position, *that* you'll have to earn.

Home I flip through the dictionary: Di.

Whatchu doin? She bastin the roast.

There's a word. I knew this word.

Meatloaf be done five minutes. An boiled potatas. You want applesauce?

At the table she pourin the ice tea.

Well. How was your firs day?

A dichotomy. Sellin shoes is a dichotomy. You know why?

Shake her head, cut her groun beef. I know damn well she don't know dichotomy an illiterate can't look it up like me, but she hopin if she pay attention she catch up.

You go in shirt n tie, they tell ya professional. Then all day you kneelin before customers! Take off their shoes, touch their feet. Pretend it don't smell, ack like you see no corns.

Don't fill up eatin biscuits fore the resta your food.

Dress like a lawyer, kneel like a slave.

I felt somethin! Oh Randall, I jus felt somethin new. The baby. The baby moved. Feel it here. No here!

I don't feel nothin.

Here, Randall! Here!

I don't feel nothin.

I think it's a girl. I know it's a girl! I was thinkin Ruby, she was my favorite aunt. Ain't Ruby a pretty name for a girl?

In bed starin at the ceilin. I *did* feel somethin. All them prior pregnancies, can't remember anything ever movin in there. But think I tell her that? Always the joke on her. Now ya feel it, now ya don't.

10

> Henry Lee Taylor was a war hero. Highly decorated. He joined up when he was only fifteen, so patriotic, willing to die for his country. He came back crippled

Walk out to the kitchen, Erma an B.J.
Would you say Henry Lee was crippled?
Huh? she ask.
What happened to Henry Lee. Would you call that crippled?
You gonna write that?
Is that what he was?
I don't think that's the word you oughta use. Maybe wounded.
I consider it. Then I say, I don't think wounded works for what I'm sayin.
Well I don't think you oughta say crippled.
Well I don't think wounded quite captures he had half his face blowed off.
Randall, watch!
She scratch on a paper.
Look! My firs word! I mean I already wrote it once, this is the second time for practice.
Her paper say ERMA.
B.J. teachin me to read!
Back in the livin room, starin at the paper.

> Henry Lee Taylor was a war hero. Highly decorated. He joined up when he was only fifteen, so patriotic, willing to die for his country, ~~He came back crippled~~ and he paid the ultimate price. If it wasn't for ~~people~~ soldiers like him, we would not a won the war. He was brave to have ~~gone~~ served so young.

It seems kinda dry.
What?
Maybe I should write somethin about *us*. Me an him.
Like what? Then she turn to B.J. What's that word?
B.J. pronounce it bess he can, motions like coverin up himself.

Cover? Oh, cover*ed*!

I think I gotta find somethin more personal.

What kinda personal?

I don't know. Like we useta sneak out on the school fire escape at lunch an smoke.

I don't think people wanna hear that. You gotta find the good, Randall. What's that word?

B.J. holds up ten fingers, which Erma counts. Then B.J. holds up two fingers.

Twelve? Oh, *twelve*!

Well it's dry. It's borin.

Well I don't know what to tell ya. It ain't like it's sposed ta be a USO comedy hour.

Slow, slow, she sound it out, book on her lap.

> *In an old house in Paris*
> *that was covered with vines*
> *lived twelve little girls in two straight lines.*

Paris, France? I *always* wanted to go to Paris, France! Let's go there, Randall! Tenth anniversary. Never too early to start plannin somethin that big!

He was brave to have ~~gone~~ served so young. We were the same age but I never went, I never got the chance because legally we were too young. But Henry Lee was very curratious.

I could ask B.J. how to spell it but guess I done interrupted em enough. I get the dictionary. Courageous. In the kitchen I hear her slow workin out the readin a somethin he wrote for her.

Erma loves her mother and father.
Erma loves her sisters, Lizzie Jo, Amanda, and Toodie.
B.J. loves his mother and his sister Benja and his brother Randall.
A family should be together always.

Outside the winda a chirpin. Eastern bluebird. Plenty here the winter escapin the Yankee cold, but there's also loyal ones stays, spy em in July, August, all year roun. An the neighbor's spider lily finally come to bloom after a couple a rains, butterfly flittin over it, Henry Lee sure liked them spider lilies. Summer's the months Henry Lee seem to favor. Me an his ma walkin him up an down that sidewalk an while resta the population draggin in the sultry, him all aglow, laughin, hearin the bluebirds, reach out try n touch the butterflies, Ooolg he say an I remember once a butterfly alight right on his knees, all three of us don't speak, this miracle we a part of, delicate, we don't wanna make no move don't wanna make it break, make it break—

Randall! Randall, honey whatchu cryin for? Aw come on, honey. I know he was your friend.

I gotta call her! I gotta call Marietta, I can't write no eulogy, I ain't no writer! Way he liked August, why'd them spider lilies have to wait till *now*? They bloomed just a few days ago he coulda seen em, why they have to wait till *now*?

B.J. hans me my pad, which is to say jot down what I jus said. I look at him. I ain't sure. Then I write.

He signs. What else?

I think about it. His trains, I say it an sign it. The Ole Smoke Escape. I sign it don't say it so Erma can't hear.

Hours pass, Erma gone to cook supper an my brother pulled up the hassock, sittin on it close to me, my han runnin nonstop the pages, I ain't suffered writer's cramp like this since the eighth grade.

11

There weren't no severance from the mill. So between my lass day July the 22nd an delayed action on my initial shoe store check, my firs pay in three weeks be tomarra, Monday August fifteenth. My trousers gettin looser but in the scarcity I keep a eye, make sure Erma don't try sneakin me a bit more, if anybody get extra it's her, with child. Whatever that mean. Well I ain't complainin. Ain't we blest, another job foun s'fast? *Knock knock.*

Aaron! Whatchu doin here? Everthing okay? Benja? Me an Randall seen her in church this mornin.

We fine. An whilst you all was gettin religious, I was gettin lucky on the river. More n we can eat. Yaw take some a this carp off our hans?

Feast! Pickin my teeth, Erma with the dishes, You think they really had extra, Randall? Or Benja jus send him over, knowin things been tight aroun here.

Tight no more, tomarra finally gettin that check! I ain't have another day off till nex Sunday, why'nt we celebrate now? We got some merriment comin to us. Ice cream?

Lickin my chocolate cone, her a vanilla purist, strollin quiet downtown in the hot n humid. All the stores closed cep Kelley's Sweet Freeze.

Shoeshine, suh?

Ole Bruce. Lookin up at a white man in a suit. He sure wouldn't be addressin me, all he do is look at my shoes, know a colored shine a luxury beyond my means. The white man sit, put his feet up. Bruce in the sun but position his chair so the customer in the shade, Bruce know good business.

Ever time I come here that ole man workin, says Erma smilin. Bet he been sittin on that corner fifty years.

You got a vanilla mustache. She giggle an wipe it.

There she is. Handin out suckers to her brood. Then look up, smilin.

Randall Evans.

Hello, Margaret Laherty. Mrs. Woodhouse.

All around her's Alexander Woodhouse an them four little Woodhouses an Margaret's belly lookin damn close to turnin four into five.

You ever met my wife Erma?

I did, church lass Christmas. Good to see ya again.

Good to see you. But sorry, I don't recall. You a member of our church?

Margaret snorts. Lucky I ever set foot outside my house with this army. I think you know my husband Alex?

How're yaw? His smile bright white. Dentures. Some war accident, Korea. An he return, become a dentist.

We ain't regulars. Jus Christmas an Easter goers, as the holier-n-thou peg us. Erma purse her lips. Margaret look embarrassed, Not yaw! Her hair still long, still that pretty auburn. Few strands a gray but healthy. Shiny.

That one sure is your spittin image. Tryin to save Margaret, lookin all red-faced over nothin. Not that Erma ain't been known to accuse a congregant or two a bein a Christmas an Easter goer which she practically rank up there with killin an covetin thy neighbor's wife.

That's my oldest, Caroline. Say hi to Mr. Randall an Miss Erma.

Hi.

I heard things got tough over there at the mill. Hope you got spared the ax.

Matter a fact, I did not. But another source a gainful employ pop right up. Workin at the shoe store. Salesman.

An Margaret Laherty glance at ole Bruce.

Hey! Ma, he took my grape! He took my grape outa my pocket!

You weren't eatin it.

I was savin it! Ma, he finished his cherry, now he took my grape!

Give it to your sister.

The boy shake his head.

Give it your sister!

The boy shake his head, stick the sucker in his mouth. The girl scream.

Bam! Margaret slap the backa that boy's head, pop that grape lollipop right outa his mouth an Margaret catch it expert like some trick they been practicin. The boy bawlin while Margaret give it to the girl, who promply stick it in her mouth.

Nex time I buy em you don't get any. Margaret wipe sweat from her brow, move her hair outa her face. The boy hollerin louder.

I hope yaw think long an hard fore you decide to start a family. Nice seein ya again, Randall. Let's *go!*

With Margaret's crew gone the day's quiet again. Ole Bruce had two consecutive customers, now stand in the shade, fannin hisself. My cone ancient history but Erma a slow-eater, still a bit left. Then she throw it away, lost appetite, an I know what's comin.

Women like her don't know how lucky they are.

Wipin moisture from her cheek, she ain't decided yet whether she's perspirin mad or cryin.

She don't even got the patience. Way she whomped that boy!

Whatchu think I do? My job?

She stop. Huh?

Jus wonderin. I been at the store two weeks now. What would you call my occupation?

Shoes! Whatchu talkin about?

Like that? I look toward Ole Bruce. Where Margaret looked.

What?

I'm askin—

You comparin your job to nigger work?

I'm askin do you see a difference.

Yes I see a difference. You *sell* shoes, look like he *sell shoes?* You work *in*side, you're a professional, shirt n tie. An you ain't a nigger!

She storm ahead toward home. In the distance I hear another a Margaret's gang hollerin, or maybe it's the same one, an I stan there, feelin this odd sensation. Satisfaction. *Lucky* about my sorry propagatin status, childless maybe not such a bad state a bein. An a little guilty about thinkin it but maybe not guilty as I should be feelin. Couple drops, I look up. The hot n humid just about to come to a fass climax. Ole Bruce quick to pick up his gear. His own shop, I think. Own boss.

I start to run but still caught in the downpour, prolly good Erma rushed on ahead mad cuz she musta made it home dry. Soaked, no need to bother hurryin anymore so I mosey. An the thought a those fine gentlemen in their crisp newly shined shoes now sloshin through the mud have me whistlin all the way to my front door.

12

School starts 9 a.m. Wednesday, but we got people comin early as seven.

I nod. This sure is some good potata salad, Benja. Jus like Ma's.

Thank you. We don't want any funny stuff goin on, them tryin to sneak em roun the back, we got all doors covered.

Where *is* Aunt Bobbie anyway? says Deb Ellen.

Ole folks' home, she fixed food for em. Give her somethin to do now an again, she be by later. An they ain't beatin us there neither. Principal assured us, teachers arrive eight but no kids in till eight thirty earliest. You don't gotta be to work till ten.

Nine forty-five.

It'll all be over by nine, plenty a time for you to get over to Martin's.

That'd be somethin. Erma chimin in. That'd be somethin for the baby, wouldn't it? Know her daddy protected her school for her even before she's born?

Cracka the bat. I turn. There's Labor Day our side a the park, Labor Day their side. In the middle the kids play together, ten-year-olds, twelve. Colored with white, all they care about's enough for baseball teams. Deb Ellen watchin the game. My mind ain't on school nor baseball, bein distracted by Mr. Martin takin me aside Saturday. Been a month, Randall. Toldja we'd be havin us a talk your commissions don't raise above minimum. Now sometimes there's the late bloomers, takes a little longer to get the knack. But consider this your firs warnin.

What's the score? I ask Deb Ellen, tryin to change the subject in my head.

Fifteen–three. But don't worry. That age, it ain't over till it's over, nex innin underdog might score twenty.

We need a solid wall a people at the high school, Randall, we need to show we mean business.

Your kids is still in the elementary, Benja.

Thinkin bout the future! Wait till they get over to the secondary to take care a things, too late!

Whew! I jus felt the baby kick. You wanna feel it, Benja?

Whoever don't show up can't complain later when some nigger's asked their girl to the senior prom.

Clamorin from inside a Benja's house, B.J. fixin the kitchen sink.

Why you ain't keepin a watch on the primary? *Your* kids?

Cuz the parents a the little ones is smart. They ain't tryin to invade, jus keepin their kids right where they are, colored school.

Hard times prolly made a good salesman out of a man or two but I'm the other breed. I nodded to Mr. Martin, which to reassure I'd try harder, but the truth I don't say is me an Erma's grateful for every penny, lass thing we need is someone tryin to give us the hard sell on luxury shoes so why would I do that to somebody else? On the other han such a philosophy apparently never entered the heads a my co-workers, Brenda Jean an Diane practically tackle me racin to the floor when they hear incomin customers through the entrance *ting-a-ling*.

Randall, you got Sundays off, store closed, right? I got a roofin job, repairin the holes, tarrin. Be my partner? They pay fifty, that be twenty-five apiece. Day's work.

I stare at Deb Ellen. Yes!

We mean business. What kinda colored parent gonna send their kids into all that? Danger. Separate but equal's been workin fine.

Ain't that a blessin! We really could use that money, Deb Ellen. Give Randall somethin to do too, all he do Sundays now is down in the basement with Henry Lee's train. Watchin TV with me useta be his favorite pastime but think he got sicka baby this baby that. Ah, new fathers!

We mean business. Those niggers try innegratin our schools, someone's gettin hurt.

B.J. come out for a little break, deviled egg. He see Benja all intense, he sign to me, What? I sign back, Tell ya later.

Lucky you got today off. People's tryin to change the blue laws. Wanna make stores open Sundays, stores open Labor Day.

I doubt that, Deb Ellen. How that make any sense? Make people labor on Labor Day. Then I pick up a big dill pickle. Crunch.

We're thinkin a namin her Ruby. You think that's a pretty name?

It sure is. Benja settin out the ketchup an mustard, not even botherin to look at Erma.

Cracka the bat, gran slam homer for the trailin team. Hey hey hey! says Deb Ellen.

Two a mine's your godkids, Randall.

That's right, sweetie, we gotta do right by Benja's kids, our godkids. An Ruby.

Honey.

We look up. Aaron all sheepish. Benja glarin at him. Cautiously he approach.

Honey. Honey, I'm sorry—

Quick Benja untwiss the jar an hurl mustard all over his shirt. Erma gasps, everybody go quiet. Aaron look down at the mess, up at Benja, down at the mess, up at Benja. Then turn, walk away.

That oughta earn me a broke wrist, she says. Worth it.

Hello hello! My mother. Looky what I brought!

Peach cobbler. Holdin it out for everbody to see but I note her special quick glance to me. What I wisht she brought was a spare mustard as I am not much of a fan a burger with ketchup.

13

It's six in the mornin.

I know.

How come you all dressed? Nobody gettin there till seven.

Thought I stroll by early.

What for?

I dunno. Since I got laid off from the mill don't get much of a chance to greet the dawn no more. Birds. Go back to sleep, I'll see ya after work tonight.

You wamme make you a egg?

Go back to sleep.

There is the birds an I stroll the ten minutes to the high school. I was here, inside, once. Visitation Day, the eighth grade. Preparin myself for a four-year educational career, an then who knows. College? Law school? Everthing seem a possibility, them days.

The school windas clear an sparklin, clean blackboards, ready for start a the year. I loved the firs day! Peek in. Inches below me I spy a texbook lyin top of a low bookshelf. *History of Western Civilization*. An now I remember that commitment I made to myself in April, that cookout at Lily's, start goin to the library. Forgettin about it till now pretty much clarify how empty that damn oath was.

I don't wanna get no hopes up but I count the days an this time two weeks longer than Erma ever held a baby before. I don't wanna jump to no conclusions but glance at her belly coulda sworn I spotted a bitty hump. Here's where he'd go to high school. Or she. She wanted to play basketball I'd be all for it. Him singin in the choir? My kids, I give em the freedom. Some days B.J. come over, their uncle take em out for cartoon movies.

Firs spark a sun peepin over that hill, now the rays spread everywhere. I gotta smile, why the sunrise always give that promise?

Yellin in the distance. Five men in a pickup. No, two men, three high school boys. So guess it's startin.

Don't know em but I greet em. One's drinkin, share the bottle with his son. It ain't yet 7 a.m.! They offer me but I say No, I gotta go to work. You can't drink an work? What *are* you, a surgeon? Yeah, I'm a neurosurgeon. Everbody laughs. Others driftin in, an the quiet an the birds give way to the day an this mutterin hullabaloo. This is not gonna happen an We gotta come together protect the children an Who they think they are? I see Benja in a group a other women. Smile ear to ear soon she spy me. Randall! I didn't think you'd really come! This is my brother Randall.

By 7:45 quite a crowd. A truckload suddenly pulls in in their checkered shirts. These ones riled up, mad, but in some way happy excited, chance to make a stand. Teachers startin to go in. They all disappeared into the buildin by eight, an by 8:15 the front schoolyard's jam-packed. Loud. I see a teacher lookin out from a second-floor odd wing winda an another from a firs-floor even.

At 8:30 sharp the light green station wagon pulls up, an they step out. Five of em, lookin clean an pressed an polite carryin book satchels. In the mornin chatter I heard they are seventeen, seventeen, sixteen, fifteen, fourteen. The fourteen is a girl, lookin even tinier than I was then an I was a runt. The one boy looks to be fifteen. They are black but the terror in their eyes make em seem all ghost white.

An here it comes.

Don't you goddamn step any closer!

Who the hell you think you are?

Nigger bitch, don't you even think about settin foot in this school!

Nigger nigger nigger nigger nigger!

The colored children are bein led by a grown-up colored woman an man in their thirties. The tiniest girl suddenly turn tail, run back to the car bawlin.

That's right, little Nigress, you better *turn aroun!*

The adult woman runs back for the girl. Then the five of em approach again slow, huddled together. The screamin so loud hard for me to make out individual words.

Then one voice so shrill it rise above the rest. *I don't care if it goddamn Brown or Black or High Yella versus the Board a Education, no niggers goin to school with* my *kids!*

I turn to see that screamer is Margaret Laherty, who I didn't notice before. I wonder if this is good for that baby still swimmin aroun in her big ole belly.

The face a that black seventeen girl, tears streamin down but she don't stop she keep movin slow slow, my cheeks hot. The face a the white men an women, the grannies all hate, dark eyes an spit, I ain't never experienced a lynchin but these gotta be those faces, sure glad they leff their baseball bats at home. An somehow seem scarier n weapons. Hate like this don't need a gun.

Look like all the colored adults an kids got separated, the white parents yankin em apart, screamin in their faces the kids cryin Lemme go! the little fourteen-year-old tears Please! Please!

I'm starin between this girl an that boy an their colored man an colored woman, what kinda adults take these kids to their executions? An jus then out by all the parked cars I notice B.J. Leanin gainst his truck. What's *he* doin here? He ain't in the bulk a the crowd, standin jus outside of it, his face registerin somethin I ain't sure of.

A cry. The fifteen-year-old boy been tripped, his satchel flies. He reaches for it but somebody kick it away. He crawl for it an another one kick it again, all laughter. That boy crawlin wild, knees a his new pants torn, crawlin, bawlin—

STOP!

Everyone turn to me. Everything stop, everyone confused eyes on me so yes I guess I actually did say it out loud. With maybe the exception a my valedictory I ain't never had attention like this an it kinda funny the way they all with the open mouths an I don't know why, this chuckle escape me.

Randall!

Benja's eyes furious. Explain! her eyes say.

Jus let em get back to their car. They wanna go, jus let em go.

But everbody still, nobody move.

Yaw wanna go, right?

The grownups nod slow an tired, the kids nod fass an eager.

They wanna go, let em go.

The white folks back off. The coloreds start to move toward the station wagon. As they get closer a cheer suddenly erup from the crowd, like it jus hit em: the coloreds retreatin.

Tingle in my stomach, watchin their black selves movin away. Peace. Peace! *I* done it. *I* brought about a nonviolent solution for all, everbody listened to *me!*

Make it to their vehicle. Everbody get in, kids in the back, the man at the wheel, woman front passenger. She the lass one, stand with the door open. Then turn around an say to alla us,

We'll be back tomorrow.

Roar from the crowd! an this n *not* happy. Fly to that car! The woman jump in, slam the door but before Mister can start the engine white men block the front, sittin on the hood, cover the entire windshield with their bodies, that car goin nowhere. The colored girls wailin again that dumb bitch! That goddamn dumb black bitch *why?* Couldn't she a held her goddamn smartass tongue till they pulled away? Why'd she have to say *any*thing? If you're stupid enough to come back tomorra, why ya gotta announce it? Well, *I* won't be here! *That* dumb, go ahead. Come back tomorra get yourselfs killed, an those poor colored kids with ya, *I* won't be here to save ya!

An someone with a hammer crash the windshield, the colored man an woman leap to the seat behind, the kids in the far back leap ahead, all seven huddled screamin in the middle seat a that station wagon an what's nex happen so fass I'm starin right at em an miss it. So fass the white men on the car misses it, this other white man. This other white come up to the coloreds nobody notice, just another white man joinin in the fun but nex thing we know the whole goddamn colored car is emptied an like lightnin the bed a the white man's truck fulla the whole entire colored gang an he's drivin away, the white man's drivin away, B.J.'s drivin the coloreds away! Takin em all gone, outa our reach! The white men still on the colored car all gapin, open mouth. By the time they register it a mad scramble to go after em, but there's mass confusion with all the boxed-in vehicles an by the time somebody finally fine their own car, key in the ignition B.J. an company's long gone.

RANDALL!

Benja about to burst a vessel in her head.

Go after him!

An do what?

You see what B.J. jus did?

I come on foot, Benja! You wamme to run after that truck on foot?

She get close enough only the two of us hear. This reflects on our family. They're all lookin at our family.

Shut up! an I storm away.

Go on over to Ma's, it's nine-twelve, still got a little time till work.

Oh Randall! I'm so glad you're here, you wamme make you a egg?

No I gotta go to work. Why ain't B.J. at the mill?

This week he traded with somebody, he's doin second shift. I don't know why, he never has to—

You tell B.J. drop by my work, you tell him I gotta talk to him.

Alright. But now stay for jus one cuppa coffee, it's all ready—

Tell him what I said! an I'm out the door.

Diane an Brenda Jean better stay outa my way, all I gotta say. An Mr. Martin, god*dam*mit! Why didn't that fool jus get in the car an go? That black bitch fool. An B.J. What the *hell'd* he think he was doin? I'm sweaty, a little dirty for sales work, god*dam*mit!

I walk in the store *ting-a-ling* an there they all stan starin at me.

Then applaudin.

We heard all about it, Randall. You was a hero!

You *tried* to tell those niggers. Help those niggers. Well. What can ya do?

They ain't comin back. From what I heard they was damn sure outnumbered. I think it's awful, grown woman like that leadin them little children—

I'm all for separate but equal. But they jus ain't never satisfied.

While the ladies chatterin Mr. Martin jus gazin at me. Smilin. Then I note he carryin a bakery sack.

Went to Orloff's for buttermilk pie. Little celebration.

It's slow so we lounge in the back, chewin.

You really think they comin back tomorra? Brenda Jean wanna know. She like my mother's age, goes to our church. Been workin Martin's Shoes twenty-seven years, Diane eleven.

Be crazy if they did. Lick my fingers, the mad melted all outa me.

Well they crazy to wanna innegrate in the firs place, says Diane. I think that damn nigress jus had to get the lass word in, that's it. All hot air.

An once they get in, then they want everything, says Brenda Jean. It's *football,* tackle *football,* who wanna have to touch a nigger? An is that fair to the visitin team? Where's Mr. Martin?

He went to the bank, says Diane. Why you think they doin all this anyway? Thinkin they white. They ain't white!

Ting-a-ling. Brenda Jean an Diane race to the floor, eager for the customer. Then Diane peep her face back in, the curtain dividin the floor from storeroom.

Randall?

I'm confused, but go out to see.

There stan B.J. Both the women dead quiet which tell me they heard all about that too. I move toward him. The ladies mill aroun, pretendin they oh so busy.

What the hell you do? I sign.

He jus stare at me.

I *said* What you *do?*

You saw.

It was nunna your business!

He stares.

You think niggers should go to a white school?

I don't like mobs. I wasn't going to watch them get killed.

You think niggers should go to a white school? My arms wild, the ladies glance my direction.

I don't like mobs. I wasn't going—

This reflects on our family! They're all lookin at our family!

There's a board loose in the porch floor, Ma asked me to fix it. I'm going now—

No! You defend *them, I* couldn't go to that school but you let *niggers?*

I couldn't go to that school.

You're *deaf,* B.J.! How the hell you gonna go to school? You're *deaf* playin dumb, hard head, I could *kill you!*

B.J. turns to walk out the door. In my head ain't I callin on the Lord, Oh my God oh my God I can't believe, can't believe.

Grab him. Tight by the waist, Don't you walk away from me! Yellin now even if he can't hear it, *Don't you walk away from me!*

But like no effort B.J. throw me off. We ain't never fought like this. I was his little brother, he was my little brother. Now B.J. tall like a tree, never occurred to me before he got the physical strength come with it. He stare at me, then turn to walk on down the street.

I storm out onto the sidewalk, almost follow him. Then I turn aroun, go back inside, nobody on the floor. Back to the storeroom, Diane an Brenda Jean starin.

Mr. Martin back from the bank, sittin at his desk, looks up.

Mr. Martin I'm sorry to disturb you but I gotta make a phone call I gotta make a very important personal phone call—

An quicker n I expect he shove his chair away an walk out, not mad but jus to gimme what I need. Yesterday I was his rotten seller on probation but like defendin segregation I'm owed new respect, for the day.

Hello?

I went after him. I had to go to work but I told Ma send him to the store an he come an I talked to him. Stubborn! He won't budge won't admit he's wrong. But I talked to him.

Okay.

A toddler cryin in the backgroun which she ignore.

Anything else? she finally say.

You okay?

Yeah, soundin like she shruggin. I wait. Yeah! Whatta ya mean?

Jus wanted to make sure you okay. Jus checkin.

You mean checkin if I'm okay so I don't kill myself over my brother actin like a fool in public?

Jus checkin.

Listen. If you all actin the idiots were enough to push me over the edge I'da been dead an buried long ago. I got *plenty* good reasons to blow my brains out, that little drama this mornin don't even make the top two hundred. *Click.*

Randall, there's a customer here insist *you* the one she wanna buy her shoes from. Diane grinnin. That emphasis on *you* she meanin friendly, givin me the pep talk, but we both know a customer requestin me's in the category a *Well guess there's a first time for everything* since thus far I been proven bout the lousiest shoe salesman the world ever known. I follow her out to the floor.

Miz Letterbeck stan there, big ole smile. Oh Randall I heard about the school this mornin. Good for you! We need more young men like you.

What kinda shoes was you lookin for?

You tell me!

Miz Letterbeck is one a them customers most notorious for tryin on a dozen an takin none, especially irritatin given she got money, her husband own the plastics factory. She got the commonest shoe size, 6, so we always got hordes in stock for her. I go to the back an randomly grab a sensible shoe, a high heel, an a sneaker. Come back, slip off her loafers, exposin her seventy-year-ole bunions.

Afraid this all we got in your size today, Miz Letterbeck, I lie, as she stare startled at the selections an I pull my shoehorn outa my pocket. Twenty minutes later she's leavin with her shoppin bag, carryin all three.

14

On the roof Deb Ellen an me both in suspenders, her spread eagle like some man hammerin aroun a hole.

I see somethin?

She look at me, then down at her stomach, slightly protrudin.

Fuck, she say. Then sigh. Guess I hoped it go away. Back to hammerin, chucklin, Guess I tried to *help* it go away! Sprintin the high school race-track, hard-jumpin every step top to bottom. But miscarry don't seem to be in my belly's vocabulary.

I look up an she don't an I see her face red cuz she jus remember who she spoke that word to. Too embarrassed to say Sorry which I sure am sicka hearin anyhow, an to make certain she don't say it I speak next.

I sure preciate this work. All I been gettin at the shoe store's minimum.

Uh-huh. Well that's retail.

Sometimes you make more, commission. But if people ain't buyin. Well times're hard.

When ain't they? Look at these holes! Can't believe the whole house didn't roll out to sea with the firs rain. Toss me more nails?

Times ain't never hard for Calvin an Deb Ellen is what I'm thinkin. I know they don't even need this damn roofin job except she get bored house-wifin an Calvin indulge her. But I ain't complainin, half the pay's mine.

Hey we got leftover deer meat from Calvin an his brother's huntin. Wannit? Almost run it over to yaw yesterday fresh, but then I remember B.J. comes by Saturdays an he don't like venison, do he.

I keep hammerin.

Yaw *still* sore?

Hey, we never uninvited him, he jus didn't show up.

Amount to the same thing. You tole me you don't invite him special every time he won't come.

Why I always gotta do that anyway? Always put *me* in the place a expectation, why don't *he* take some responsibility?

Well the time to suddenly *stop* invitin him an wait for him to take the initiative is *not* after yaw jus had a great big fight, cuz it pretty clear the message he got is he ain't welcome.

I hear ya, Deb Ellen, now drop it.

Poundin, half the nails she get in with jus one slam.

You think I was wrong? You think B.J. shoulda done what he did?

You know somethin? I don't get the goddamn big deal. The colored kids learnin beside ours, so what? They play with each other all day excep school anyhow.

I can't believe you said that! You're a mother!

Well I said it. Deb Ellen dip her roller in the tar tray.

Whatta you care? You never liked school no way. *I* dropped out cuz I had to, support the family, but you. An never wanted no kids didja? Jus pop em easy like a gumball machine an after they out in the world you could give a damn!

She look up, her eyes narrowin.

Be that as it may, I don't see what all the goddamn hysteria's for.

The *hysteria* happened *nex* day. Wa'n't *that* fair, a few concerned parents versus the goddamn National Guard! This ain't Little Rock, Prayer Ridge ain't no city! How the hell the blamed government even hear tell of it? Oh guess they make us an example. Glad I wa'n't there for *that,* but I seen my friends from the day before! All in the national newspapers, what the hell you hummin for?

Nothin. *Hum-te-dum.* (An smilin!) *That* was somethin. One damn day *not* borin in this frickin hicksville.

Tell ya what. Benja said all the parents thinkin on private school, put together some new kinda private school affordable for *everbody,* close the damn public school system.

That didn't go over too well in Little Rock.

You got a answer for everthing, dontcha? I'm jus tryin to be a responsible white man! Responsible father. I say father on purpose, wonder she gonna snort at it.

But she jus say We about ready to lay the tar. Take a cigarette break first. That's five, not ten.

We take our five sittin on the roof edge, legs danglin. Deb Ellen blow smoke, then say How you an Erma doin these days?

Fine. Wipe my brow, the sun bearin down hard. Regular. Her all up in arms. I ain't been to church in a couple weeks, I ain't been to Klan meetins, when I'm gonna commit to somethin. Like my one day off I got all the leisure energy to—

I sigh. Open my lighter flame. Close it. Open the flame, close it.

Don't mean to bring up a tender point, but if things don't work out with you all again, you can have this n.

I stare at her.

Your new *baby?*

I don't care if ya legally take it. We'll all keep the lie, it never gotta know it was adopted. Or you can tell it the truth, raise it an it call me mom an you uncle. I don't care. Jus too many mouths at our house.

Think maybe firs you oughta talk to Calvin about this?

Deb Ellen blow smoke. Makin love lass summer. Well it always backa our minds but neither of us ever sayin. So Calvin finally brung it up. Here's a plan, in case, he said. An I go, Wow. Why didn't *I* thinka that?

A few seconds fore I can speak. Middle a innercourse, Deb Ellen an Calvin discussin me an Erma's reproduction desert.

That was potential, I say. Now the baby somethin real Calvin might feel different.

She shrug. I'll ask him.

I take a puff, starin at the roof nex door. Which could use some major patchin itself.

Even if he says yes, I dunno how Erma'll feel.

I'll check in with Calvin an letcha know if the offer still stans. This ain't to jinx yaw, maybe things'll go alright this time. Still yours might wanna sister or brother. Or cousin in the house.

Can't be no more jinxin than her tellin every damn body she know. One a my damn co-worker ladies run into her in the supermarket, Erma runnin off her mouth like—

I sigh hard.

Maybe she figure may as well be happy while it lasts. Deb Ellen put out her cigarette, stand up. We get movin now, half-hour lunch at one, oughta finish by six.

I stand up. Deb Ellen go to pour tar in the trays.

What if Calvin say yes but Erma say no. What chaw gonna do?

Deb Ellen shrugs. Guess I jus have to get a extra husband for supplemental income. Or Calvin bring home another wife. An now Deb Ellen all dreamy like. Yeah, that's better, she do the housework, take care a the kids an I get a outside job, full-time. Three of us, guess we need to get a king-size bed. Deb Ellen ponder this, rollin her roller in the tar, her eyes all glinty an a smile. I'll be in the middle.

15

It's slow. Eventually Mr. Martin says he got business to attend to, he be back three-ish. He's a mainly easygoin boss but no matter how easygoin the boss it's easiest goin when the boss ain't aroun. Me an Brenda Jean an Diane relaxin with our packed lunches in the back. Today I ended up in Mr. Martin's chair, which he don't mind when he's not here. Well I never actually asked him if he mind but I seen Brenda Jean sit in it before. Then again she been here twenty-seven years an always jump up when he walk in, an he say No, don't get up, Brenda Jean, but she do an he never argue a second time.

I think it's a silly burden, says Brenda Jean, expectin the girl's parents to cover all the costs.

Silly? returns Diane. It's a blessed right. There's a reason they call it *holy* matrimony.

I think it's holy crap.

Well then all I can say is good thing you an Leonard didn't have no kids.

Me an Leonard's pretty happy bout that ourselves.

Oh Brenda Jean!

My sister an brother-in-law tearin their hair out makin sure my princess niece get the best dress an best flowers an best dinner, well! Only one more week an it all be over. Nex Saturday's the ceremony, Halloween weekend. Hah! After that—

Ting-a-ling.

Oh!

Brenda Jean fly out the stockroom, onto the floor.

You see that? So anxious to snap up the customer before you or I get to em, she interrupt her own thought.

I chuckle, workin on my lunchmeat an mustard.

You shouldn't let her do that. You got a baby on the way, Randall, you need the money. You need to start makin more commission money, it's not fair you always the lowest an her grabbin all the buyers from the both a us.

Desk phone rings.

Martin's Shoes.

Randall! Glad you answered, honey. I'm in the paint store lookin over colors for the baby's room. Course I won't do pink or baby blue, but I was thinkin a neutral mint green. Whatta ya thinka mint green?

A bottle opener tied to a string hangin from the wall. I pull out my Orange Crush, flip off the top, take a swig.

Honey?

Mint green sounds fine.

I thought so too. Okay. I love you. I'll see you tonight. *Click.*

You on till six this evenin, Randall? Closin? You make sure you step up that last hour, when the Friday after work rush happen. Don't let Brenda Jean take all the customers! You need to step up!

Ting-a-ling. Diane fly out to the floor. But a second later she back, peekin her head in.

There I go, not even check with you. You want this n, Randall?

I liff my Crush.

Still eatin.

Sure?

Sure.

She disappear. *Ring.*

Martin's Shoes.

You think I'm some nut! I'm gettin mint green cuz mint green can be for anybody, if we gotta change it from a nursery back to a guestroom, mint green for the *guest*room. *That's* why I wanted mint green! *That's* why! *Click.*

Brenda Jean come back a-mutterin. She wanted them damn Espadrilles an not even interested in a thing else, why can't people be more flexible?

I drain my Crush, throw out my lunch wrappins, head to the bathroom. Wash my hands an stare at my face in the meer. If ya get close up, the eensiest little lines. If ya take your fingers through, spot a gray now an again. *Ting-a-ling.* Diane surely got that customer but I better make a show a goin out there anyway.

Walkin through the stockroom toward the floor I see Mr. Martin at his desk, the ting-a-ling was him come back early.

Hi again, Mr. Martin.

Hi Randall. Where ya goin?

Seein if there's any customers.

Brenda Jean an Diane got it covered. Looky here.

Mr. Martin open a file cabinet behind him. Today his wingtips are black an glistenin. Mr. Martin shine his shoes hisself or do a shoeshine boy service him daily? He pull out a graph chart.

Can you read this, Randall?

I think so.

What it tell me. About you.

I swallow.

Seem to say I remain slowest horse in the commissions race.

By several laps.

He starin at me. I look at him. I look down. Practically need sunglasses to look at his shoes.

I already give ya one warnin a while back, but cut cha some slack after your day at the school. I was honored to have you in my employ. *Am* honored. Still. Business is business.

I look at him. Behind him some new picture, him an his wife an kids on a quiet beach. Tanned an smilin.

So this warnin is your second an final.

I let out a breath, hope he don't notice. What he mean to put the fear a God in me actually come as relief, one more day I don't got to go home to Erma with the bad news, watch her face contort up like she the longest-sufferin since Jesus.

Mr. Martin put his chart away, then turn to me, suddenly all bright.

So! Monday. You heard?

I stare at him. I shake my head.

The voter registration. Tuesday's last day, so coloreds thinkin they're sneaky, plannin to show up at the courthouse en masse the 24th. Monday.

Now seated, he peelin a red apple. Mr. Martin's slim, I ain't never seen him have nothin for lunch cept an apple.

All that ruckus at the school. Vital, but some citizens don't realize the bigger issue's the vote, which can impact schools an everything else. Unfortunately I think the school thing kinda wore a lotta people out but we gotta hold strong.

Diane grinnin, rushin past us. Mother with five kids! Hope we ain't outa the saddles.

You count heads, you find more black in this town than white. You know that? Those shacks on the outskirts. An droppin babies every five minutes, fifty-five–forty-five, they outnumber us. Fifty-five–forty-five.

I almost nod my head. Then I almost shake my head. Mr. Martin halfway down that apple peelin one long peel, he ain't lifted the knife.

They vote, they gonna tip the election! You know what could happen that Kennedy gets elected? Integrate everything! And Nixon i'n't much better. Schools jus the start. Water fountains! Toilets! Churches! An they gonna push for it, all of em, even the nice ones. My maid Tory been in the family forty years, raised me. Tory, you want the vote? Yes suh, Mr. Martin. You know that nigger convicted a rape from Avery Junction? Electric chair? When that verdict come down, Tory, whatchu thinka that? That jury wa'n't his peers, Mr. Martin. What! You think colored shoulda been on that jury? He raped that girl! It was *alleged*, Mr. Martin, how she even know that word. *Alleged*. Niggers can't hardly read but they sure know them three syllables, spent enough time facin the judge. Lemme tell you, put black on the jury, oh wonder what *that* outcome be. They all stick together, not guilty! All a black on a jury need's to see's a black at the defendant's table, not guilty!

Brenda Jean flyin through. She was a pill but her husband's a dream! Two pair a Red Wing boots he wants! Two! *That way when the one wears out I have the other.* Gigglin.

The registration board at the courthouse'll tell em no an they'll go home. Simple. We just need some people like you there to make *sure* everything go smooth, but I really don't foresee no trouble. Okay?

My head quiverin, like I jus fell in a vat a confusion.

Sir?

You ain't been to no Klan meetins recently but I excuse it. Know you got to take care a your wife, expectin, I know you had your troubles there in the past. Still, I'm sure you continue to support our cause. You can have Monday off. Spend it at the courthouse.

Brenda Jean's nearabouts fifty an practically skippin, carryin two big boxes out on the floor.

The whole day, sir. That's a healthy chunk outa my paycheck, tell ya the truth.

Mr. Martin's face get twitchy. He don't like what I said, but don't quite know what to do with it neither. He feast on it quarter of a minute.

Awright. I'll give ya minimum for the day.

Thank you, sir! It's just the baby comin an all.

My brown wingtipped are the cheapest in the store, not fine like Mr. Martin's. But a good expert shine spiff em up, bring em back to near jus-new, then maybe the customers see I'm a truthworthy representative.

Useta be I coulda got some a my investment back from the deposit on my empty Orange Crush bottle, but these days that offer's been rescinded, bottles been reclassified as garbage. I start to throw it out, then remember one a Benja's asked to save em for a art project.

Bruce already got a customer so I wait my turn. While he's whooshin the shine rag he glance up at me. A fass look I interpret as he seen me aroun many times but never expected a shine be in my budget. Still, he finish his current customer who pay up, then turn to me like I'm a regular ole deservin gentleman. I sit in the chair. Throne! Like I got my subject kneelin before me. I work hard makin myself not grin, this polish jus everyday casual.

Ole Bruce is a professional, fast an thorough. I *do* see a reflection! I'm thinkin soon's I walk away outa sight I'ma take em off, walk in my socks so's I don't scoff em before work tomarra. I know Mr. Martin'll glimpse that shine an be pleased, if there's one thing Mr. Martin notices is everbody's shoes. While I'm searchin my pocket for the dime I see the shadow a the nex customer cast over us.

I get a shine?

Ole Bruce turn aroun, lookin up. A finely dressed colored man. I don't know nothin about fashion but his suit is least as nice as Mr. Martin's best. I have learned a little about shoes, an his we'da sure placed on the expensive shelf. Now Ole Bruce practically scream.

When dju get in? Boy, my sister don't tell me nothin!

They're laughin an chatterin, forgot me sittin here on the throne. Then the fancy dresser finally see me, somethin registerin in him. An I note somethin familiar too. I stand.

I'm sorry, suh, but this my nephew I ain't seen in a couple years. Now that he's a bigshot Chicago lawyer.

Bigshot, the lawyer mutters, all modest.

This is Mr. Roger Thomas, Esquire.

I step back, near drop my Orange Crush bottle.

We know each other. Well, from kids. Hello, Randall.

It's my sister Sally's birthday. I shoulda guessed. Ya come home for your mama's birthday, didn't ya.

Hi Roger.

Good! he come back with even though I ain't asked how is he. Doin *real* good. How're *you*, Randall?

My breathin breathin

Just a visit? You ain't here on no official business?

Roger lets out a big laugh.

If you're worried I'm an *outside agitator* you can put your mind at ease. Family affairs, that's all the interest I have in Prayer Ridge.

You brought the kids? Where's Herman an Georgie?

At Mom's. So's Carrie. You know we're expecting again.

Already? Boy, yaw been busy! You hopin it's a girl this time?

Here's your dime.

Thank you, say ole Bruce, hardly lookin at me, all distracted with Roger. I notice he didn't say Thank you *sir*.

When we were in high school, Randall lent me some of his books. Keep up with the white kids.

He *did?* Ain't that nice.

You were in high school, I was younger.

Good to see ya, Randall. An like that moment a few weeks ago with Margaret Laherty, I detect a quick glance from Roger, he givin me the once-over an know he don't even need to get the details on how my life turnt out, it all too clear.

My bladder suddenly callin which is unfortunate cuz three doors away already I hear the screamin an cryin from inside my house. An her mother's voice, tryin to calm her down. Can't see now how I'm gonna relieve myself with the toilet apparently fulla my baby, so I head for the woods.

When I'm finished I zip my pants an pick up the bottle. I keep readin it over an over, touchin it, the letters raised in the glass: NO DEPOSIT NO RETURN. The wind musta taken a turn cuz deep as I am in the woods, for just a second my ears glimpse Erma's wailin an I crash that Crush bottle gainst an ole elm. I stare at my bloody hand an too late see the red drops stainin my newly shined wingtips.

16

Lyin in bed starin at the ceilin 1 a.m. I get up an strike the match, put it to the curtains. Take a few seconds but it catch, then flash the whole bedroom, dresser, chest, bed. The closed door hot, flames cracklin, kissin it. Then the blaze splits, some of it take the guestroom, bathroom, some creep on down the steps. There it firs consume that rottin front door, then take its good ole time in the livin room, ease on through to the dinin, the kitchen: explode.

From the outside the whole place is lit. Occasionally I hear sirens in the distance but no fire truck ever shows up. I was in the house, but now I mus be outside cuz I'm seein it all, there go my toolshed, there the big ole oak Marky fell outa, the hedges *whoosh*. Sometimes the conflagration continue down the street, sometimes the whole neighborhood combust.

Lyin in bed starin at the ceilin 2 a.m. Tired a pyromania fantasizin in the insomnia, sleepin alone I have trouble with, an Erma in the guestroom, third night in the guestroom since the blood in the toilet. Four an a half months I stayed my side a the bed, she afraid *anything* close to her rattle that fetus, but now it all gone she on't seem any more interested than she was before in the tender touch. Nothin but sobs that firs evenin with her mother, sobs the second day. This mornin she skip church, come out to see me sippin coffee which'll be the whole a my Sunday breakfast an seven words she say: I know it ain't your fault, but. Who said it *was?* That all she utter in days, both us right in the same house. Every so often I peek through the keyhole, make sure she ain't dead. Guess she eat while I'm at work *if* she eat. Today my day off, damn if she didn't stay in that room all day, waited till I gone to bed to come out. Held her pee all day! Went to get my hedge clippers outa the toolshed yesterday an there they be—two cans a mint green paint. Imagine they stay there, unopened till eternity.

Earlier I tried stretchin out the whole bed, may as well take advantage a the sorry situation. But what if she come back all the sudden? Her place gotta be ready for her, I keep to my half, her side crisp clean fresh. *Ring.* Who the hell callin blacka the night mornin?

Randall, this is Sugar Schaeffer, Benja's neighbor. He's killin her!

At her place in a flash but by then he's gone, nothin but a house a screamin kids an her bloody an barely there. I call the ambulance. Sugar take the kids over to her house while I ride beside her on the gurney.

No surgery. Knocked her out but besides that guess she ain't bad as she looks. I sit in a chair by the wall gazin at my sister, the other bed for the moment empty. Nurses an doctors in an out, checkin her bags an tubes. Starin at her an suddenly it all burst into flames, the hospital bed, curtain, Benja

Randall.

My eyes pop awake.

It's after eight.

I squint at her. She say that like years ago, like we at home late for school.

Don't chu gotta be gettin to the voter registration before it open at nine? I wipe the sleep slobbers.

What? My sister had holy crap kicked outa her lass night an now speakin clear as a bell, I'm the one with the slurry words.

You tole Mr. Martin you hit the voter registration.

My sleep-deprived eyes try to focus. How the hell she know about that? I ain't doin it now.

Why not?

Why *not*? She stare at me. *Why not?*

If you mean cuza this. If there weren't the voter registration you'd have to leave me anyway, you got a wife in mournin at home. An you *got*ta get to the voter registration, it's the nex thing comin. They got the schools, they can't have this.

I thought you said you an the other parents gonna make up some kinda private school.

That's provin harder n we figured. She sighs. Believe me, the rich *are* gettin their kids into the private.

She look at the IV stuck in her arm, sigh again.

I ain't gonna try to kill myself no more.

She say it like it some casual but determined decision, like I ain't gonna break my diet no more.

If he want me dead so bad, me stayin alive, that'll serve him right.

Well good mornin! How ya feelin. Nurse all cheerful.

My back hurts. My ribs hurt. My mouth hurts.

I bet. Here, you take these little pills.

Then the nurse pull that cord. Venetian blinds go up, daylight blindin.

They'll be bringin your breakfast in soon. She gone.

Randall—

I ain't budgin. What if your bastard helpmate happen by?

That's what the cop's for.

Cop?

She frown an tip her head toward the door. Sure enough, the man in blue standin guard.

I still ain't leavin my sister practically kilt to go to some damn demonstration or whatever you call it.

You *wan*na get fired?

Who said anything about gettin fired?

Benja roll her eyes, turn to the winda.

Who said anything—

You know Brenda Jean an me on the communion committee. They had communion yesterday mornin, so Saturday while we cuttin up the bread, pourin the little grape juice glasses, Brenda Jean an I talked.

Benja stop there like the rest self-explanatory.

So?

So? Her eyes narrowin, the imprint a his fists all over em.

Dr. Weiss, please come to emergency, requests the public-address system. Dr. Weiss.

Brenda Jean don't know nothin. Any firin goin on, or *not,* that between Mr. Martin an me.

Brenda Jean said you ain't no salesman! She didn't mean it mean, she likes ya, tryin to help, but anybody know people ain't salesmen ain't gonna last in no shoe sales!

I stare at her. How my sister in a hospital bruises head to toe manage to make *me* look the pathetic?

Mr. Martin likes ya too. You're young, you got spirit. That's what he says to Brenda Jean. He was inspired by the thing at the school.

You know what? If one more person bring up the goddamn thing at the school, like it the only accomplishment I ever accomplished my whole damn life.

Dr. Weiss, please come to emergency *immediately.* Dr. Weiss.

Well you gotta be makin a paycheck, that's all.

No kiddin.

It bears sayin since I don't think you particularly like sellin shoes, I think you might *wan*na get fired.

I ain't arguin with you about this, Benja. I ain't gettin into no fights while you look like somebody threw you in a wood chipper.

We ain't carryin ya, Randall!

What did you—

We got our own things! Aaron an me can't support nobody else.

Who asked you to? What, cuz you give us the damn fish? I'da known that I'd thrown the damn fish back in Aaron's face!

Good, cuz we been savin. Hopin to repeat our honeymoon. Savannah.

I bout fall off my chair laughin.

Too bad they ain't brung out my breakfast tray so I could throw it atcha!

I'm practically rollin on the floor then in fly Ma. All she got to see is Benja's face to bust out bawlin.

Aw little girl, what he do to you?

Ma, it ain't that bad. An now *she* cryin. Stop cryin, Ma. Stop.

Why i'n't you call? Turnin on me. I'm phonin over to Benja's, wonderin why nobody answerin, then I get scared, call over to Sugar Schaeffer's.

Now there's B.J. standin in the doorway, musta drove Ma here. I know he see me but don't look my direction. We ain't talked since that day at my store but this ain't about mad now. He jus can't take his eyes off Benja, his chest risin fallin risin fallin. Then he turn an gone.

I get up, go to the cop.

You found him yet?

Who?

The husband. Her husband.

I wa'n't lookin for him.

Ain't he at large?

She ain't pressed no charges.

You seen what he done to her.

That's why he come by I ain't lettin him in. Not till he cool off.

Till he *cool off*?

Look. I don't like domestic. I feel like some Peepin Tom, intrudin between a man an woman, their business. But till he calm down, my job's to keep em apart.

So you ain't arrestin him?

For *what?*

I take a walk down the hallway keep movin keep movin or I'm a god-damn punch this cop's lights out. Come back to the room.

Where's B.J.?

I shrug.

I thought you went after B.J.

I was talkin to the damn public servant at the door.

You gotta find B.J. You gotta find him! I don't want no trouble!

You seen your face? Little late for that.

Randall! If I was close enough, Ma'd prolly hit me.

Find him! Find him! Like some nutty women's chorus.

Okay! I think he jus went to the bathroom!

You gotta find him! Why Benja pourin all these tears now Ma's in the room? An they ain't fake. Ma got that effect.

I'll *find* him!

Take me a breath.

I'll find him. Don't worry, I'll find him.

What, she think B.J.'s out searchin for Aaron, beat him up? Big as he is, B.J. never won arm wrasslin with me comin up, pretend like he lose for fear a hurtin me. Which is to say, he ain't the aggressive type. Where B.J. went is to the bathroom to cry after he seen Benja. Or throw up, an meanwhile them women whipped up in some wild frenzy, God! What a family!

He ain't in nunna the bathrooms. I go back to the room. Her breakfast tray in fronta her but she ain't touched it, look up when I walk in, worry face. An tired, the pills gettin to her but she fightin it.

He was in the bathroom. But he tole me he had to go to work.

Ma an her jus stare, mouths half open.

An I gotta go to that voter registration. I locate a tiny spot on my sister's cheek ain't bruised an gentle kiss it. I'll be back this evenin.

Walk past the dumb cop to the stairs, fly down em, out the door. Half runnin, fury sure is an accelerator, I'd ever had this kinda fury in school I'da been the track star. All roads leadin to Benja's, don't ask me why I'm headed there. Her idiot husband surely ain't nowhere in sight, always vanish after his little episodes, the bar or some friend's.

When I get to her place, all quiet. Eerie, I'm s'use to the commotion a all them kids. I step through the yard, through the kitchen door.

Thud! backa my head, the room spinnin an I'm lookin up from the floor. Aaron poundin my face.

You an your fuckin brother! Kill you *both,* this is *my* property! *My* house!

I think I'm about to go out, then Aaron suddenly pulled up, away, suspended in air like God come down yanked him offa me. A struggle, but I manage second try to lean up on my elbows, adjuss my eyes.

Aaron white as a sheet. Close to his face is B.J. B.J. behine Aaron an towerin over Aaron, B.J.'s right arm aroun Aaron's torso tight, his leff hand on Aaron's jaw, one twist an all over for Aaron. B.J.'s right fingers move.

He wants to know if you want your neck broke.

Uh-uh, *uh*-uh, *uh*-uh bess Aaron can say, his jaw in that position. B.J.'s fingers move. I reach into Aaron's hip pocket, pull out his wallet. Aaron's eyes try to follow.

He tole me get your wallet. You *always* walk aroun this much cash, boy? Pay day pay day.

That's right, Pay day Friday out at the see-ment mixers.

The tears rollin slow down Aaron's cheeks. B.J.'s fingers move.

He says he checked your car, you got plenty enough gas to get to your mother's. You go there an cool the hell off. The money'll stay here with Benja. An ever touch my sister again, I'll kill you.

Aaron look at me. My face red warm.

I mean *he'll* kill you.

B.J. releases Aaron an Aaron falls to the floor. His neck an arms is all shades a purple. He stares at us both, specially at B.J. Then stumbles out the door.

I sign: Where did you come from?

I was here before, I knew he was hiding. I knew he saw me so *I* hid. Till he showed his face.

B.J. goes to the sink, washin his face an hans with the bar soap. I stare at my brother, my *big* brother. Aaron was scared a *him,* not me. Aaron look at B.J. he see somethin. What's the word? *Formidable.* But Aaron come outa hidin for me, Aaron look at me, see nothin.

Just as I'm thinkin I ain't heard no car engine start up, I turn to the door an here come Aaron approachin fass with his pistol aimed straight at B.J.'s back.

B.J.!

But course my brother ain't heard me, wipin his face with the towel.

Aaron, no!

B.J. sense somethin an swerve aroun, facin Aaron, who got the revolver close range, close to B.J.'s heart.

You dummy, says Aaron. You goddamn deaf an dummy.

Aaron. Aaron, you don't wanna—

When you checked my car for gas, it mighta benefitted you to check the glove compartment cuz guess what I had stored there.

AARON—

Click.

Aaron jump like me, like he didn't quite mean to pull the trigger, jus him all hot n crazy he slipped. But now his face confused: why come nothin happened?

Click.

Click.

Aaron lookin all mystified, peerin down the barrel, shake the gun like it's a flashlight gone weak, need a jiggle.

An all calm B.J. slip his hand in his front pocket, pull em out. Bullets.

Aaron's mouth fall wide open. An defyin any logic he turn the aim back on B.J., tryin again. *Click. Click. Click.*

Then he turn toward the door, like embarrassed.

In a second B.J. got him, slap Aaron's right palm down on the kitchen table, then slam that pistol hard into it *slam slam slam*, Aaron screamin. When B.J. through Aaron raise up that bloody thing use to be a hand, starin at it. Then Aaron turn, walk out the door, through the yard. My brother an me follow but stay on the porch. A neighborhood crowd all gathered by now, I see no Sugar nor kids so thank God she musta took em somewheres. Aaron get in his car, start it up. His leff hand on the steerin wheel, he pull out, slow an gentle, on down the road.

B.J. turn back into the house lookin tired.

You think it's all over? Bastard's gonna *kill* you.

B.J. see my signin, then look down to count the cash in the wallet like I ain't said nothin. Guess ain't enough leff after Aaron been to the bars all weekend, B.J. pull out his own wallet, add some dollars to it. I slap his arm.

Hey!

He look up.

What happens when he takes all this out on Benja?

Somethin breaks. Now somethin crushin on B.J., lookin like a loss little boy, like he made a terrible mistake. *Yeah,* maybe you shoulda thought a that, I say an sign, but his face down, an I know he seein in his head Benja an her broke bones in the hospital. Or the morgue. I fly outa there. I gotta get home an clean up God I jus hope Erma's still in her damn mood, still in her damn room cuz seein her pitiful face is just about the lass thing I need right now.

Dammit! Why's he always gotta undercut me? *I* wanted to kick Aaron's ass! But a course B.J. get there first, B.J. the one put the fear a God in Aaron. An everbody *said* I was the hero at the school, but then B.J. got to come, ruin it all. An no shame! Always thinkin he's in the right, no matter nobody else feel that way.

Soon's I'm in my door there she stand. Mr. Martin called all hoppin mad! You ain't at the voter registration! He give you the day off an you didn't even show up! Then he. What *happened* to you? You got blood all over your. Randall. Where ya goin? *Randall! Where ya goin?*

My head bout to explode, countin the church bells. Ten. Ten o'clock, how the hell he know I *ain't* showed? Courthouse opened just a hour ago, an he jus got to work hisself, wait. Unless he went over there before work to check. God*dam*mit he got up early, went over there before work to check up on me!

Bout two hundred niggers in line. Hot as hell already, no shade for em, an they look like they been here a while. Dressed like Sunday, like they bein job-interviewed for some goddamn executive position. Some of em wearin a *coat,* sweatin. Standin with em's what looks like a few professionals, nigger North lawyers stirrin up mess no doubt. In the white faction which is all men, there ain't nearly the crowd as there was for the school, an things don't seem so tense. I didn't know better I'd say the colored *an* the white lookin kinda bored.

Except my entrance on the scene seem to shake things up a bit. The white men look at me funny. So does one or two a the niggers. Then I remember I never got to wash myself, blood an all.

Well they can jus stare cuz I ain't explainin a goddamn thing. How long everbody been here?

Some a *them* been here since seven, he tell me, lookin at the coloreds.

Any of em get in?

Couple. But you better believe they got turned aroun empty-handed, ain't none of em gettin registered.

Pretty early to be in the bars, mutters somebody to his friend, but really talkin to me.

I go right up in his face. Twiced my size but don't he take a step back. You smell any alcohol on me? I ain't been to no goddamn bar.

Some ole auntie come outa the courthouse then, face scrunched up, lookin ready to spit nails. A chubby man giggles.

Guess she flunked the test, says Fatty.

What test? I ask.

The test ya gotta pass to register.

Rack my brain. I don't recall takin no test when I registered to vote. *What* test?

Well, it varies, says he, this crooked smile. Then cuz he can't hold it no longer: How many pine needles on a Christmas tree? An he whoop an holler. Some a the others join him, though too hot an too early to laugh too hard. There's blacks also hears the joke. They frown but don't look our direction.

Randall Evans.

I turn aroun. Man about my age. Over six feet, near tall as B.J. Dark hair, mustache. A beer-sipper an it barely past ten but he don't appear drunk. Grinnin huge.

You don't remember me?

Oh look, says Fatty. That ole auntie tryin to protest to the cop. This oughta be good!

Francis Veter.

I stare at Francis Veter. I ain't got a clue.

I seen you at that cross-burner lass summer, he says only half confidential. *Surprised* to see ya. Figured you gone on to college.

Another nigger musta got in cuz the entire line take one step forward while my brow furrows, tryin to work out who the hell standin before me.

Well you was the firs debate team!

I almost trip backwards. *Debate* team? Who the hell recall *that?*

Still remember your rebuttal. Hawaii. I didn't know what the hell you was sayin! but I sure knowed we shoulda beat St. Mary's.

My mouth open all bafflement, an him all starry-eyed like we talkin bout the days I quarterbacked the football championship.

An then the valedictorian. Can't *believe* you didn't go on, higher education. Course if ya had prolly you'da moved away. Wouldn'ta been here to do what you done at the school. I was there.

Oh, you was the one at the school, says somebody. Another nods some kinda polite acknowledgment, but it all ole news now.

You still don't remember me! No wonder. We sure ain't never shared no classes. Well I was two years ahead but even if we *was* same age I scarcely cracked a book, barely made it through the sixt. Then dropped out.

My head dizzy. My father died, I quit school an went to work—same ole story. That's all people thinks a me, who the hell else outside my family recall valedictorian? An spite of it all I'm brought back: lookin out, seein Benja an Ma in the graduation audience smilin all pride. An Pa. An B.J.

That speech you give, with everyone smack in the pain a war? Brought a tear. We all felt it.

B.J. who reads every book he can get his hans on never set foot near a school till my graduation. An there in the audience grinnin, like my valedictory's the happiest day a my brother's life.

I seen you before all that but you didn't know. Well how couldja? I was in my robe. Francis Veter grins, an speaks softer. We was Klan kids together, remember? I spied you at a midnight meetin once.

I gotta go, I say to Francis Veter. I gotta check in at my workplace.

Oh, okay. Hey, listen, Randall, we should talk about things. Nex steps, ya know? He glances hard at the coloreds in line, then back to me. You in the phone book?

I'm walkin, my back to him but my head nods. Glance up my way out, I see some ole uncle exitin the courthouse, rantin an a-ravin. The cops make a move toward him.

Oh he musta got question number two! I hear Fatty sayin. Where does a hula-hoop begin an end?

Ting-a-ling. There's Brenda Jean an Diane both with lady customers, an all four look up at me, mouths wide. Shit, I keep forgettin I ain't cleaned myself up!

Mr. Martin come flyin from the back. Out.

Mr. Martin, I can explain this mornin—

OUT!

I go back out on the sidewalk, wait for Mr. Martin to come talk. But I hear clickety-click, turn aroun to see he's locked the door! With customers in there!

I storm roun the block. Who the hell he think he *is?* I been workin there near three months, I deserve a hearin. I deserve a hearin!

Go home. There she is, bawlin. He said you don't even need to come back! He jus called, said he'd mail your lass paycheck to ya!

Oh I'm goin back, says I not stoppin head right for the bathroom shut the door.

Whadju say?

I turn on the sink, start scrubbin.

Whadju say?

I get all nekked for a deep cleanin. When I'm washed off, I open the cabinet door meer so it faces the toilet. Look at my face. Stand on the toilet I see my torso my privates. Partial view a my hairy legs. Not bad.

By the time I get back to the store it been unlocked an I go right in *ting-a-ling.* No one in the adult half, Diane arrangin a display in Martin's Children's. With the door ring her an Brenda Jean both race to adult shoes. Stop real short when they see who it is.

Oh hi Randall. Diane all nervous.

Where's Mr. Martin?

Jus then he come out. You need to go on home, Randall. I already called your wife about the arrangements.

Arrangements? He think I'm *dead?*

Mr. Martin, I deserve a hearin.

I don't think you do.

My sister's in the hospital! Her husband. Somethin happened, I had to take her to emergency.

I'm sorry to hear that but—

An then I *did* go to the voter registration! After no sleep all night I went, an there ain't nothin goin on! Bunch a niggers standin in line for hours jus to get rejected! There ain't gonna be no trouble, Mr. Martin. I figured I'd be doin more good at work here than jus standin there. Since you promised to pay me for the day's trouble anyway.

Well whether you there or here seem like you still expect me to pay you to *not* sell shoes.

Like I can *feel* my pupils dilatin.

Go on home, Randall. Until today you been a very pleasant young man, I'll give you a good recommendation for your nex job. Long as it's not sales.

I look at him an Brenda Jean an Diane all starin, goddamn pity in them women's eyes. I turn toward the door.

I hear they're hirin out at the chicken farms, he says to my back. Slaughterin the hens. They train ya, you don't need any skills—

I'm throwin the display shoes at em, the high heels an slippers an espadrilles, rain rubbers an boots. All of em duckin runnin screamin, I clear all the shoes off the shelves fass, shoes everywhere, then I pull the damn shelves down too! The store a mess in seconds, like a hurricane an the lass thing I do is take off my own goddamn Martin's wingtips an hurl em at the store owner himself.

Stormin down the street in my stockin feet I don't know nor care where to go nex. Then I hear the distant siren an know that's one decision I won't have to worry about makin.

Nappin. When I wake dark out, there sets some kinda gruel, cold now. I eat it, lick the tin plate shiny till I see myself. Lookin a damn mess again. Guess I was a teeny bit resistant to the arrestin officers an got a teeny bit banged up for it. In the reflection I glimpse somethin dark an familiar in the cell nex door.

That ole uncle twas throwin a fit at the voter registration. He stare straight ahead, his face all rage, like I was feelin. But the nap suck most a my fury out.

Now a young colored in a suit let in by the guard, who clearly jus been woke up from his own siesta. The attorney an the ole uncle speaks in low voices, an I catch enough syllables from the younger to definitely reckonize Yankee. Then he walkin away, right past my cell.

Hey!

He keep walkin.

Hey! I ain't got no lawyer!

He keep walkin. The guard snickers.

Whatchu in for, uncle? Nothin, he gimme nothin. An I know that ole man ain't deaf way he was whisperin with the nigger in the suit, why the hell everyone ignorin me?

Now the lawyer returns with the sheriff.

Let him out.

The guard starin at the sheriff.

Let him *out?*

His bail was jus posted, open the cell.

He was resistin arrest!

I turn to the ole one. Now I see. The black eye, bloody chest. That arm look broke.

That's for the judge to decide, now unlock the goddamn door, Jesse.

Jesse does an the ole codger is thus released. The nigger attorney lettin him lean on him.

This is not the way we usually do things here, Jesse says.

An for the firs time the lawyer say somethin, mutterin: I bet some of it is. His eyes on his client's bruises.

What did you say? Jesse's eyes narrowin.

Hey! I ain't seen *my* lawyer! I ain't made no damn phone call!

Yes you did, says the sheriff. You jus don't remember.

I stare at him, an for a second I wonder if I *did* make a phone call an forgot. As they's all filin out, I notice the lawyer glance in my direction, finally givin me two cents. Lookin down: my stockin feet. Disappearin down the hall.

I ain't no indigent! That damn sheriff tryin to make like I am, I ain't drunk! You know what kinda day I had? My sister beat to bits by her bastard husband an the cops do *nothin, I* had to find her on the floor lookin like put through the shredder! *I'm* the one taken her to the hospital *the cops do nothin,* then I get *fired* for my trouble! I threw those goddamn shoes at Martin's head, I'd do it *again!* Come back here! You listened to *him, I* got a story to tell! *I* got a story to tell!

Ten minutes pass. Twenty. An finally the sobs breakin through, sad sobs but I take my forehead, bang it gainst the see-ment wall, turn em into mad sobs. By the time I see blood on the bricks, no tears left.

I'm back at Benja's, repeat a this mornin, Aaron comin at B.J.'s back with the pistol. B.J. turn aroun, show the bullets in his hand. Aaron shoots. *Bang!* One bullet left in the cylinder, right to B.J.'s heart. B.J. look surprised, starin down at the hole in his chest. Then fall down, gone.

Benja an Ma cryin, walkin by the casket. I come up to it, my brother peaceful laid out.

Hey B.J., I say. Open your eyes.

He don't move.

B.J., it's a dream, you in my dream you ain't really dead. Talk.

He don't stir. Then I get it.

Oh!

Course he ain't answerin, he can't hear me! So I reach for his han, put it aroun *my* han so he can feel me finger-tell it. But his han's ice cold, stone hard. I try movin his fingers, workin all my strength. Then his pinkie snap off an fall to the bottom a the coffin, *clink*.

Wake up, Randall.

My eyes flash open. There stan the guard, that Jesse. A little light shinin in from out where the sheriff's desk is.

I got a present for ya.

I don't react a jot.

That Yankee nigger lawyer? You know, he a good man. He apparently got a tenderness in his heart for po white trash. Went back to whatever nigger's house he hidin in an come back here. He come back for ya, Randall.

From behine his back Jesse pull out two wingtips which he promply throw through the bars at me. They ain't the finest quality but they ain't bad. Just a little worn through, still in good shape.

This is what he said: I brought these in case some Negro needed em, but then. An he tips his head toward your cell, turns aroun an leaves. See, Randall? He foun you more pitiful than the worstest-off niggers.

Now the phone ringin at the sheriff's desk. An I hear every blamed word.

This is Sheriff Tucker.

Ma'am, ma'am, now calm down.

Who again? Mrs. Evans? Mrs. Randall Evans? You his wife? Yes, he's here. Yes, his bail's set at—

Ma'am, you gotta stop cryin now, I can't understand ya. You gotta calm down now, ma'am, you gotta calm down!

17

Near midnight by the time he's released. He ties the colored lawyer's shoes together, flings them over his right shoulder. She and he walk home in silence, her gait brisk and a few feet ahead of him. She goes into the house, proceeds directly to the guestroom and shuts the door. He heads for the basement.

He gathers every freight car and passenger car, every automobile and tree, the school bus, fire station, stop sign, traffic light. He collects the park bench and baby stroller, the pedestrians and the little terrier, every bit of track, all thrown into a couple of old burlap potato bags. He carries it all up the steps through the house, through the kitchen, out to the yard. He goes to the toolshed, grabs his gas can and, because there is just a sliver of the moon, a flashlight.

He drives to the junkyard, steps out of his truck. He is alone. He brings the bag to a clearing and empties it.

He sets up the town—the school and the police station, the streets and the park, the drugstore and the butcher and the automobiles and the mother shopping for groceries and the shoe store. He lays the track and arranges the train on it. He walks back to his truck, siphons gas into the can, carries the can back to Train Town and holds it high over the miniature metropolis: a gentle spring shower.

"It was all a very tragic accident."

He tosses the match and the town blazes. He throws one of the colored lawyer's shoes into the flames, then the other. He remembers a Sunday school verse: *And they burnt all their cities wherein they dwelt, and all their goodly castles, with fire.* He stays throughout the incineration of the homes and the businesses and the people and the train. The inferno is reflected in his baby blue irises, and though forty-five minutes later there's nothing left but gray cinders and ash, the fire in Randall's eyes continues to flash and burn.

1959–60
INDIANAPOLIS, ET AL.

There are six floors and the rickety elevator stops at the fifth with a worrisome jolt. The bus driver steps out. He did not know what to expect and yet imagined the law offices to be something a trifle more elegant than this shabbiness. Fingerprinted walls, threadbare carpet. The carelessness signals to him instability, yet he knows the establishment has been in operation a good twenty years. The receptionist is a slim, medium-dark woman wearing a brown blouse and deeper brown skirt, her shoulder-length straightened hair equally sensible. She checks her appointment book, makes a call, and the middle of three closed doors is opened. The attorney who now stands before him is a slender, handsome, dark man of about five-eight, no older than mid-twenties. He wears a suit, presents a professional air. His smile is close-lipped, and he holds out his hand. "Hello. I'm Eliot Campbell."

The table in the conference room is old and marred, but clean and polished. Eliot offers the potential client coffee, and they sit.

"What can I do for you, sir?"

J.C. Kane, paper-bag brown, middle-aged, and carrying forty pounds too much, twirls his bus driver's cap between his fingers. Such a personal issue. How can he discuss it with a stranger? He is not here because of a battle with a landlord nor because he has been embezzling money from his company nor because he is contesting his millionaire uncle's will, though he supposes on some level they are all private matters. Anyone coming to a lawyer is exposing himself, opening up his most vulnerable wounds for the world's judgment.

"Sir?"

"I was workin a twelve-hour shift. There was the usual. Woman tryin to claim her ten-year-old son was five, free fare. Drunk refuse to get off enda the night. So I come home, not a lot to ask, dinner on the table. She ain't cooked nothin! Not a damn kidney bean, she sleep! I know she big, expectin, but this behavior was goin on before. Also, since she been withchild the house seem to go to pot. Like a steam locomotive run through it, sink full a dirty dishes, stuff flung all over the livin room. This our firsborn, she can't handle things now how it be our fourth? Also, we live right here in Center Township like everybody else, lately she been talkin bout wantin to move when the baby come, better neighborhood, now what realtor gonna sell a house to a Negro north a Thirty-eighth Street? Dreamin! Also, she on the phone with her mother *all the time.* Lucky it a local call, long-distance woulda bankrupted me. Also, she has not been lately interested in anything marital. An I hear for some women this condition can continue for months after the baby come out, well what *else* I'm sposed to do? Also,"

"'What else'?"

The attorney's tone is dry, noncommittal. J.C. has been pouring it out to him, all his frustrations of the last months, and in the lawyer's face he can read nothing but detachment. The bus driver looks down at his cap again.

"Well, I can't. I need."

He sighs, then notices the clean ashtray in the center of the table.

"Can I smoke?"

Moving only his index finger the lawyer pushes the object a few inches closer to J.C., who pulls out his Kents, lights up, and sits back, as if acting more relaxed will make him so.

"What about we jus ain't happy together no more?"

"That's not grounds for divorce."

"It oughta be!"

Eliot says nothing. J.C. puffs, the cigarette faintly trembling between his fingers.

"I *told*ja she ain't doin her wifely duty."

"If that was not the situation before she became pregnant, it's not grounds for divorce."

"The house a mess!"

"That's not grounds for divorce."

"She ain't gettin no younger!"

"That's not grounds for divorce."

J.C. Kane slams his cap against his knee, stands, turns away to face the door, hands on his hips. Eliot glances at the clock, then speaks.

"When you said What else were you supposed to do."

J.C. Kane does not turn around.

"I'm a man, ain't I?" His chest rises and falls, deep silent breaths. "She. This girl. I'd seen her before, work up on The Avenue. Barmaid. She jus."

Eliot allows for J.C. to go on. When he doesn't: "That *is* grounds for divorce."

J.C. swings around, his face now bright, hopeful. "Yeah?"

"Your wife's grounds. If you've been unfaithful."

"Well. That's okay!" J.C. smiles. "What's the difference?"

"The settlement. She'll likely get it all, the house, car. And alimony."

J.C.'s smile fades. He stares at the younger man, whose expression of dis-engagement has remained unaltered throughout their interview. The bus driver roughly stamps out his unfinished cigarette and puts on his cap. "*That* I coulda got without speakin to no attorney." He yanks open the door, then turns back around. "All them years a law school. For *that?*"

"Definitely *not.*"

J.C. Kane stares at the lawyer, confused. Then leaves, noting the extraor-dinary period of time since Eliot Campbell has batted an eyelash.

2

Eliot is startled by the ring.

"I was so surprised when the mail come! seein the shape of it. Another book! I don't know any other mothers, their sons regularly sendin em poetry."

He smiles. "You're welcome, Mom."

He hears Beauregard Greene's pencil sharpener again, his neighbor to the right seeming to employ the device twenty times a day. The walls are thin, the three tiny rooms, wherein sit the three lawyers, having once been one large office, now partitioned. As the rookie, twenty-five-year-old Eliot has been placed in the middle between fifty-something Beau and forty-something William Mitchell. The modest rest of Winston Douglas and Associates is comprised of the conference room/library, the reception area, the larger office of Winston Douglas himself, and the bathroom.

"You should see the size a the turkey! An I know how you like pineapple upside down, I made that an punkin pie both."

Eliot gently moves his finger along a scratch on his desk.

"Don't tell me."

"I tried. Really! But I think it's too late. I was waiting to see if I could've gotten off early but, Wednesday afternoon, you know how the traffic'll be."

Silence.

"I'll be home in a month for Christmas." Nothing. "You know I come when I can. I just saw you in August."

"Yes, when you knew Dwight an his friend were takin their fishin trip, he wouldn't be here."

"I'll be home for Christmas."

"Good, I'll tell Daddy an we'll all be expectin you. An Christmas is Friday this year so you'll be able to stay the whole weekend."

After he puts the receiver back into its cradle, he stares at his closed door, his coat and wraps hanging from it. Dwight and his friend.

He walks out to reception, glancing at the gold nameplate: ANDREA MEYERS. She stops typing to look up at him.

"Andi. Can I talk to you a second?"

She doesn't reply, as if her staring at him is answer enough.

"I wish. In the future, could you please buzz me to let me know who's on the phone before putting it through?"

Her eyes remain fixed on him, though he perceives a flicker.

"It was your mother."

"I know but—"

"Sorry. Usually I do buzz you but I had three people on hold and it got a little hectic, sorry, I thought you wouldn't mind speaking to your mother."

Is she *reprimanding* him? "Andi. I know you're busy. Just, I'd appreciate—"

"I'm sorry. Honestly. My fault. It won't happen again," and she turns back to the typewriter to resume her previous task. He feels clumsy as he often does after conversations with her. In addition to her receptionist duties she serves as secretary to the four lawyers, so he never has been certain if her abruptness is because she never much cared for him or because she's just very busy. Noting the way she expertly ignores him while he remains awkwardly standing at her desk, he presumes a little of both.

As he starts to turn back into his office, the elevator gate is pushed open.

"Miss?"

A middle-aged white man dressed in his Sunday best, hat in hand.

"Yes?"

"I'm wondering if I could see somebody. I have this problem. Could I talk to somebody?"

Andi and Eliot stare at him.

"Sir." Andi is delicate. "You realize this is a Negro law firm?"

"You turn white away? I'n't that discrimination?"

"We have had a handful of white clients. I just wanted to be sure you knew—"

"Don't I get it from the white *an* the black. I'm colored!" He sits on the couch. "That's my curse."

Eliot puts his hands into his pockets, speaking in a steady tone. "How exactly is being colored a curse?"

"No! Lookin white! I *want* to live among other colored people, but all those places." He shakes his head. "So I find a very nice house with a very nice yard for my three kids plus one on the way an a very nice flower garden for my wife, an it's affordable! More affordable than the ghetto." He sighs. "But all the neighbors. They favor me. Which is to say they do not look like my brown-skinned wife, they do not look like my light brown kids. I said yes, I signed on the dotted line. These nice places I have been shown before when my family is not with me. I have said yes before but it never went so far as me being shown the dotted line because I would always mention, in case it wa'n't clear, that I'm colored, and suddenly there would be some other family who'd got there first but that fact had slipped the realtor's mind till now. So this time as an experiment I neglect to mention I'm not white. I am never asked and I do not volunteer the information." He chuckles. "You shoulda seen the surprised eyes of our new neighbors on moving day! Oh that first week there were the dirty looks, 'Nigger nigger' screamed at my kids comin home from school. But I thought, Sticks and stones." He sighs. "Eight days after my family crossed the threshold, the first *real* stone come crashin through the livin room, Sunday evenin while we watchin *Ed Sullivan* narrowly missin my nine-year-old daughter. We barricaded ourselves behind the couch. Called the police but they did not arrive until sixty-five minutes later, just five minutes after the bombardment suddenly subsided. Interestingly. The police acknowledged the extensive damage to our home. The television a pile a scrap, our furniture. However, it was obvious from the looks the officers gave us that little would be done in the manner of investigation. For the present we are all crowded in with my wife's sister's family. The realtor, who out n out claimed I had deceived him by not tellin him I was colored, says that he can nonetheless set aside his feelings for the sake of business, the realtor is eager to sell. Well I don't like him, an I can't set aside *my* feelings." Here the white black man pauses.

"What is it you wish us to do, sir?" asks Andi.

"Put em in jail!"

"That would be the job of the district attorney."

The man lets out an exasperated breath.

Eliot speaks. "Perhaps you'd be interested in filing a civil lawsuit?"

"Yeah! Sue em all! The cops an the neighbors an the goddamn realtor!" He holds out his hand. "I'm Roscoe Foster."

Forty-five minutes later Eliot sits at his desk, his office door open. He looks over a divorce case related to a husband's gambling obsession. He hears Winston Douglas's door opening. The quality of Winston's polite farewell to Mr. Foster clarifies for Eliot that the case has been accepted, and as soon as Mr. Foster has closed the elevator, Eliot flies to his boss's door.

"May I speak with you, sir?"

Winston Douglas's office may be large compared to his associates' but there is no indication of executive luxury. His sofa a bit frayed, the file cabinets somewhat dented. Eliot sits forward on the couch to make his case.

"Sir, when you hired me eight months ago, I felt honored. I knew that your firm had taken on job discrimination suits and housing discrimination suits, that you had defended Negroes in claims of police brutality and black men falsely accused of rape when colored service institutions shied away from such cases. I was thrilled to start a new life in Indianapolis, I felt *privileged* to have been invited to be a part of such a vigorous, vital organization, and I am eager to start contributing to your esteemed mission. Once I heard Charles Hamilton Houston speak. He said that the Negro students he taught at Howard Law School were to become more than lawyers, they were to become *social engineers* as his protégé Thurgood Marshall has already proven, and every civil rights case we accept is on that path. Right, sir?"

Eliot had always found his boss to be fair and understanding. Winston Douglas, born in Indianapolis, a self-named "lifelong Hoosier," a man who remembers well the heyday of "The Avenue" of J. C. Kane's barmaid, Indiana Avenue, the historic Negro cultural hub. This respected attorney wanted his birthplace to be more than revived to its former glory but to be *better,* Eliot is certain Winston had not brought him here just so he could spend his career divvying up the spoils of wrecked marriages. Now the elder gazes at his recruit.

"Eliot. This establishment could never survive on civil rights cases alone, most of which we do pro bono or nearly so. We are supported by the income of divorce cases, of accident claims. You are still our junior member, you are young and earnest and are learning quickly. When you're ready, you certainly will be assigned race discrimination cases, there is unfortunately no shortage of that work. But for now, I'm giving the Foster case to Beau. I *do* have a new assignment I'd like you to look at. A woman almost had a knock-down drag-out with her sister at their mother's funeral. Contesting the will."

Eliot is back in his office, slamming the pages of *The Probate Law and Practice (of the State of Indiana)*. Usually he works till at least seven but today when the clock strikes five he's out the door. It's still later than everyone else who left early, three, for the holiday weekend, with the apparent exception of Beau Greene, as Eliot still hears the irritating grinding of his pencil sharpener through the wall. The usual six-minute wait for the ancient elevator is interminable.

"Hold that for me!" when the bell finally sounds. Beau comes running.

Riding the lift down, the older attorney asks, "My wife'll kill me if I forget to pick up the cranberry sauce for tomorrow. You have big plans?"

Eliot shakes his head, not turning to Beau. Then a momentary fear erupts, that Beau, in the spirit of the holiday, might actually ask Eliot over for dinner with his family. Eliot quickly mutters, "Wanna catch up on some work."

"So Winston's giving you all the crap cases."

Eliot's face flushes warm, keeping his hard eyes trained on the elevator door. It had not occurred to him that his colleagues may have perceived his impatient ambition, and he remembers now the thin walls, wonders how much of his pathetic appeal to Winston was not the closed-door conference he'd assumed. Beau laughs loud and hearty.

"You can't become the Negro Clarence Darrow overnight. Patience, boy. Patience!"

Like a piñata. It is suspended, the vague semblance of a man, a Giacometti. The elbows lifted, fists tight like Popeye flexing his biceps, but only a nub where the right hand was. Both feet gone, nothing below the right knee. The entire body burnt black, hanged. A loincloth, mockery, as if anything beneath it would appear remotely human. And the white men staring into the camera, sneering, smug, a good twenty in the photograph and presumably many more beyond its frame, their little boys with them. Pride, as if a white multitude kidnapping, torturing, and murdering one Negro were some astounding feat of courage. Scrawled on the flip side of the postcard:

> This is the
> Barbecue we
> had last night
> My picture is to
> the left with a
> cross over it your
> son Joe.

The Giacometti man is a boy. Seventeen-year-old Jesse Washington. He was mentally retarded and a laborer on the farm of Lucy Fryer, a white woman who was murdered in May 1916. Washington confessed to the crime, though the validity of such an admission by a Negro youth with the mind of a child to a bloodthirsty white horde intent on finding him culpable would be dubious at best. The Waco, Texas, jury deliberated four minutes, and despite the guilty verdict that would have meant the harshest state punishment, the mob assumed authority. The boy was beaten, castrated, his ears amputated. Then set on fire. Wailing, he tried to escape and had his fingers slashed off. To prolong the torment he was repeatedly lowered and raised into the fire, out of the fire, into the fire, his agonizing death displayed on the public square for the entertainment of fifteen thousand white men, women, and children.

Douglas Winston and Associates is defending Otis Hill, a farmer from Harnsgrove, Indiana, who shot a man to death. Mr. Hill claims it was self-defense. Seymour Tillman is Mr. Hill's white neighbor, another farmer. According to Mr. Hill, Tillman envied the Negro's successful crop and became infuriated by Hill's refusal to sell his land to him. Tillman had allegedly threatened Hill's family, and when Tillman came with three other armed white men to "talk" one midnight, bullets were exchanged. Mr. Hill's family was miraculously unharmed but Tillman was wounded and his acquaintance Augustus Peabody lay dead. Mr. Hill, in jail, claims he feared he and his family would have been lynched if they hadn't defended themselves. Winston Douglas is taking on the case himself, and has asked Eliot to spend the morning at the public library, collecting photos and taking notes on lynchings as a way to bring this reality home to the jury.

Another picture, dated 1911, is of a newly built bridge over the Canadian River in Oklahoma. About fifty white people span its length, mostly men but also women and children, all facing the photographer who is apparently on a boat in the water. Hanging from the bridge, spaced perhaps twenty feet apart, are two Negro bodies: fourteen-year-old L. W. Nelson, who had been accused (and obviously convicted without trial) of shooting and killing a deputy whose posse came to search their cabin for stolen meat, and his petite mother Laura. The boy's pants have been ripped off, dangling from his ankles. His mother in her long print dress seems intact. The lynchers deliberately chose a Negro settlement as the execution site: an example. Eliot stares at the small woman, remembering that Memorial Day when he and Dwight were children and Uncle Sam came to them in the night to speak about the lynching of his mother Tiny back in Humble. "Lookin like she asleep, so peaceful," Uncle Sam had said.

Eliot reads about another fourteen-year-old boy whose hands were slowly burned off in a stove, the whites demanding that he accuse his father of derailing a train. In agony the overwhelmed child finally gave in, telling his torturers what they wanted to hear whether or not it was true, at which point the white men promptly riddled the boy's father with bullets.

In 1918, Mary Turner, eight months' pregnant, spoke openly in her town of Valdosta, Georgia, about her determination to have justice served regarding the lynching of her husband. For such an insolent challenge to white authority, she was abducted by a mob who tied her ankles together and hung her upside down from a tree. They poured gasoline on her clothes to burn them from her body and, while she was still alive, cut her child from her abdomen. The baby fell to the ground and gave a cry before being crushed by the heel of one of the crowd, immediately inciting the bunch to fire, hundreds of bullets honeycombing the body of the suspended woman.

The North and West, albeit with less frequency than the South, are also well represented in the pictures. The 1920 hangings of nineteen-year-old Elias Clayton, nineteen-year-old Elmer Jackson, and twenty-year-old Isaac McGhie, three Negro circus workers in Duluth, Minnesota, accused of raping a nineteen-year-old white girl. The morning of the allegations, the young woman was examined by a local white physician who found no evidence of assault or rape. Nevertheless that evening the city jail, where the Negroes were being held, was surrounded by a frenzied mob of thousands.

And here in Indiana, the infamous photo of eighteen-year-old Thomas Shipp and nineteen-year-old Abram Smith, both hanged for the shooting death of a white man in 1930. Unique to this lynching is the fact that evidence implies the young men actually may have been guilty of some of their charges (robbing and killing a white man during an attempted robbery but *not* raping his girlfriend). The picture became notorious because of the smiles and smirks at the camera, the festive picnic atmosphere of the onlookers numbering in the thousands. (Many who have viewed the image are surprised to know of the locale, having assumed a Dixie setting.) The two young men had been so brutalized, with everyone in the mob trying to get in a blow, that at least one was quite dead before ever seeing the rope. A third victim, sixteen-year-old James Cameron—guilty only of association as he was traveling with the older boys but who, frightened, ran away before any crime occurred—was also viciously beaten and had a noose placed around his neck when, astonishingly, a single woman's cry for mercy silenced the horde, allowing for the boy's deliverance from death. (No one but Cameron seems to remember the voice; only that, inexplicably, at the last possible moment the rabble had a change of heart.) The boy had recognized many of his would-be killers, including his white schoolmates.

The 1899 lynching of Sam Hose in Newnan, Georgia, was promoted so widely as to bring in two thousand spectators, some by chartered train. Hose had asked his planter employer Alfred Cranford for a pay advance, which some claimed were actually wages Cranford already owed Hose and had not remitted. The white man refused, and the next day Cranford, peeved that Hose would have the audacity to even ask for such a thing, drew his pistol as Hose was chopping wood. In self-defense, Hose struck Cranford with his ax, killing him. This was Sam Hose's story, and was confirmed by Cranford's widow. But apparently no one cared to ask her until after the fact, the press having promulgated an altogether different narrative, including Hose's rape of Mrs. Cranford while her dying husband looked on. Hose's ears, fingers, and genitals were severed, his face skinned. He was still alive crying to God as the flames gradually consumed him, the crowd delighted by the slow process of his body's disfigurement, his eyes bulging out of their sockets. Pieces of his corpse were sold at exorbitant rates as souvenirs.

After two hours, Eliot has had enough. He checks out his items, putting them into his briefcase and shutting it, relieved to no longer look at the pictures and yet being acutely aware of their weight in his attaché. Outside in the crisp air there are lights and wreaths, the distant sound of carol recordings. He crosses the street and into a patch of frozen grass crunching beneath his soles, then along the east sidewalk of the American Legion Mall, on his way back to the office.

Because the pictures are all decades old, he isn't sure how useful they will be to the case, whether or not the jurors would regard them as relevant. Lynchings are certainly not all a thing of the distant past, but thank God are exponentially less commonplace than at the top of the century when incidents were reported literally every other day. (And who knows how many went unreported?) They also are no longer so universally celebrated in white America, and thus photos of more recent episodes are scarce, other than after-the-fact journalists' shots meant to document the horrors of the phenomenon. Horror was clearly *not* the intention of the photographers behind the specimens he had viewed this morning, but rather a sinister comradeship with the smiling, sadistic bunch.

"You look like you've seen a ghost."

He looks up. Andi the receptionist on a bench with her packed lunch facing the Scottish Rite Cathedral across the mall. It's in the forties, too chilly to be eating outside, but it doesn't occur to him to question her about it. He sits, allowing a good two feet of space between them.

"I was doing lynching research. For the Hill case."

"Hm." Whatever vague hint of a civil smile that might have been on her face now vanishes. They are silent for several moments, gazing absently at the holiday shoppers toting their packages.

"It happened to someone I knew," she murmurs. "His father." The grassy area of the mall dips several feet from its sidewalk borders, like a casserole dish. A pigeon alights just below them on the slushy green, and Andi hurls a bread-crumb from her sandwich yards beyond it, causing a flock to descend. "I grew up in Des Moines, but this was a couple hours away, out in the boondocks. My cousins. He was a neighbor kid, I'd see him every summer when my siblings and I visited. I kind of remember some altercation with a white man: hunting dispute, or border dispute—whose land ended where. So one night they came. Beat him, tied him to a railroad track, burned him to cinders. I was eleven. My parents debated letting us go the summer after, but I begged till they gave in, and I guess it would have looked funny to my aunt if all of us just stopped coming. Everything seemed normal except. That kid. Quieter than he used to be, and everybody quieter around him. Still, he played with us, he played hard. And white kids played with us, and one day some white boys we regularly played with came over, I could tell by their faces something was up, and they put a little black square in that boy's hand and said, 'That's a piece a your dad.' And that boy. Stared at it, like his eyes went blank. And then he was on his knees, he fell to his knees, his eyes still blank, and those white boys laughed and walked away. All of us fell silent, and then all the sudden he snapped out of it. Like he had passed out just halfway, to his knees. He looked up at us, and then he looked up at the sun, and he said, 'Who turned the lights out?' And then he looked at us again and at the sun again and then he got up and walked home. He never came out to play after that, and a week later his family moved. Omaha, we heard." A group of carolers who'd gathered near the North and Meridian corner, half a football field away, all white except one colored woman, begin "God Rest Ye Merry, Gentlemen." "Maybe it was a piece of his father and maybe it wasn't. It looked like it could have just been a chip of tree bark to me."

Eliot wants to kill the carolers. He wants to take a shotgun and *bang!* Reload, *bang!* He likes the snap of the barrel, the smooth feel of the stock. No, wait. With a machine gun he could quickly wipe out the entire choir before he is inevitably shot down himself. He would try to miss the Negro woman. On the other hand, what the hell is she doing with all those white people anyway?

Andi takes off her gloves, as if her hands had suddenly become hot. "Well, that was back in. I guess, '29 or so."

Eliot frowns. The math doesn't seem to add up. Andi laughs.

"I'm older than I look."

He is taken aback and trying not to show it. That would make her nearer his mother's age than his own. Has he been treating her with proper elder respect?

"*Well!* The good ole days. Now I worry a hell of a lot more about *legal* lynchings. Remember all the sensation about Willie McGee? Well, no. You were just a kid then."

"I know about Willie McGee." Does she think he lives under a rock?

"Okay then. Have you heard of Sherman Street?" He reluctantly shakes his head. "No one has. Negro prisoner in the same jail as McGee, labor organizer, and all so conveniently he's suddenly charged with raping a thirteen-year-old white girl. Rushed to the chair in about three seconds flat." She is quiet a moment, then laughs harshly. "Nineteen fifty-nine and they can't even enact the anti-lynching bill! Refuse to offer us even the *pretense* of humanity." She hurls several crumbs quite far, causing an excited rush of birds wondering which way to turn.

Eliot glares at his target, the unsuspecting chorus which has now attracted a small audience. No, not this arbitrary slaughter: he must be accurate. He would bring his shooting spree to Newnan, Georgia. And since it would essentially be suicide, he would pin a note to his shirt: "Remember Sam Hose." Some of his victims would remember, and some of his victims would be descendents of Sam Hose's murderers, and if he's lucky some of his elderly victims *would* be Sam Hose's murderers which, as far as he's concerned, would be anyone who witnessed Sam Hose's murder: *Black's Law Dictionary* be damned.

Andi turns to Eliot with a half-smile. "Thanks for ruining my appetite. Would you like the other half? Chicken salad."

"Those pictures." The steam from Eliot's mouth puffing larger. "I wanted to kill em. I wanted to be there, I wanted to riddle *their* bodies with bullets, I wanted to give *them* a slow torturous death." He feels childish, a temper tantrum, and doesn't care. He imagines her contempt, waits for her to laugh at his infantile fantasies. He shrugs as if she already has. Her prerogative.

But she surprises him. "When they build that time machine, let me know. I'll be riding with you."

The choir seems to have put some rehearsal effort into "We Three Kings," with solos assigned for certain verses. All the wise men are white, which, according to the tradition handed down in American Christendom, is technically miscasting. Still, the Balthazar tenor is pretty good.

> *Myrrh is mine, its bitter perfume*
> *Breathes a life of gathering gloom.*
> *Sorrowing, sighing, bleeding, dying,*
> *Sealed in the stone-cold tomb.*

4

Barely 10 a.m. and already the young mother is in the kitchen fussing over dinner. The two little girls in their pajamas sit and chatter at the table, holding dolls and eating Christmas cookies. A man walks in to say something to his wife and one of the little girls impulsively jumps up to hug her daddy. Her sister, not to be left out, runs to the man and he stoops down for a three-way embrace.

Eliot stands on his family's back porch in his trench coat, hands in pockets, leaning against a pillar, gazing right into his parents' new neighbors' home. Everything is altered—there is no more Miss Onnie—yet he racks his brain for something very specific that's amiss. She had lived to a ripe old ninety-one. When she passed on three years ago, his mother had called to tell him. She had not seen her neighbor for a few days, and with trepidation went to knock on Miss Onnie's door, careful not to step on the thousand cats roaming the yard and porch. As Claris raised her knuckles to rap on the screen, an odor from inside overwhelmed and horrified her. The police arrived, finding the corpse mostly whole, though a bit of her face and hands had been eaten away by felines ravenous since their mistress's demise. At the time Eliot was a law student on a meager budget and couldn't get away from his classes for the funeral, but had asked his mother to send a very large arrangement of roses, promising to pay her back with his first paycheck after finishing school, which, over her objections, he did. She and his father had gone to the service which she had described as intimate but sincere. And suddenly Eliot realizes what's missing. The aroma forever linked with the memory of his childhood friend: cat smell.

Now the young mother glances up, startled to see her family has an audience. Eliot takes his hand out of his pocket and waves with his closed-mouth smile. And as if this gesture excuses his voyeurism, the whole clan returns the wave and smile. Perhaps people are more tolerant over the holidays. Still, to continue his watch at this point would seem awkward, so he turns and goes back into his parents' kitchen.

His mother is prepping the turkey for the oven. Without looking up she remarks, "You need to be buttonin up your coat you gonna stand out there that long." Apparently she had been observing him observing them.

"How long they been living there?"

"More than a year. You didn't see em when you were here in August?"

"Uh-uh."

"Maybe they were off visitin their relatives. Nice family. You wanna go in the icebox an get me some butter?" He hands her the stick, then walks into the living room. Aunt Beck speaking to his father.

"It's gotta be the same people."

"It's not the same people. For one thing, that one lass month, those Clutters, that was Kansas. This recent one Florida."

"Whole family tied up, throats slashed. And this Florida one, little teeny babies murdered. Six days before Christmas. Monsters!"

"Monsters," her brother agrees, shaking his head.

"So how that not be the same killers? Different states, you sayin the murderers don't know how to drive?"

"There's this thing. The crime happens, then some copycat gets the idea an does the same crime."

"Now who gonna copycat killin a whole family?"

"It's a thing. It happens."

"That such a thing? Mr. Attorney-at-Law?"

"I've heard of it."

"Aw, you jus stickin up for your ole daddy."

After the war, with the new prosperity in the country, several manufacturing industries popped up in Humble, most of them hiring Negroes, and the traditional discriminatory practices in the established factories were also eased. So when Lon's defense job ended in Baltimore, he was able to get on at Humble Glass. His sons were in the eleventh and sixth grades by then, and for the first time he worked at home, seeing them every day, even if shift work meant that it was only briefly at breakfast when he was just coming off.

"So how's the law business goin, nephew?"

"Fine."

"Fine, fine. Don't matter if they five or twenty-five, that's all you get out of em."

He thinks but does not say, You know marriage counselors, the ones trying to keep a husband and wife together? My job is pretty much the opposite.

Claris walks in. "Anybody want some coffee?"

"Hear, hear!" says her sister-in-law.

After nine hours' driving, Eliot had quietly slipped into the dark house with the porch light left on at three this morning. His parents and aunt were briskly moving around by seven and he had risen to wish everyone a merry Christmas, but suddenly the sleeplessness is weighing heavy on him and he ascends the stairs for a nap.

He lies supine on his old twin, not bothering to get under the blankets. Dwight said he'd arrive today around eleven, and would probably stay till ten or eleven tonight before driving home. He had moved to Lewis, West Virginia, about forty miles away, and had been working as a postman there these last seven years. Dwight had elected to be neither too close nor too far from their parents.

When Eliot was still very little, he had decided he was ready for his brother and himself to have separate rooms. Despite Dwight's earlier yearnings for the guestroom, it was Eliot who had moved into it. So for many years it had been transformed into a boy's room, boys' sheets and boys' curtains. Two years after Eliot had gone to college and their mother had finally somewhat come to terms with her empty nest, the space had been converted back into a guestroom. Their childhood room however was untouched, forever a shrine to young boys. As men, in the rare instances that their paths had crossed at their parents' and Dwight had stayed too late to make the same-day drive back, Eliot had taken the guestroom as if it were still his, and Dwight slept on the same twin his parents bought from Ryan's Used Furniture when he was thirteen and Eliot seven. Sleeping arrangements for tonight were unclear, however, since with relatives coming, it would be a houseful.

Eliot wakes and turns to the clock. Twelve twenty-five. Two hours: he'd hoped to have slept only half that long. He sighs, then hears Dwight's laughter from downstairs.

In the kitchen he stands, telling some elaborate story about being chased by chickens while delivering mail. Lon, Claris, and Beck sit at the table in hysterics. Dwight is big, a good six feet and well filled out. His laughter is easy and hearty, which has endeared him to much of the extended family. On the other hand, slight Eliot, who had stopped growing at five eight and a half, had seemed to become more aloof as his years of education went on, until finally he echoed his social distance from the family with a geographic remove to the Midwest.

Despite his captive audience, Dwight spies his brother as soon as he walks into the room, has clearly been waiting for this moment since his own arrival. A year since they've seen each other.

"Brother!"

Dwight grabs Eliot and gives him a warm bear hug. Eliot is considerably more reserved. As is often the case with siblings, he and Dwight have grown up to be very different people, except Dwight doesn't seem to have noticed. Still, what the younger brother does *not* want is any kind of scene in front of the family, and he thus returns the embrace, albeit in a markedly shallower fashion.

"*Finally*," says Claris, scuttling into the living room. All morning she had been holding off giving her sons their presents until they were both here to open them together. She returns now with the two wrapped mysteries. They are men's pajamas, such as neither Dwight nor Eliot would ever wear. The style is identical, Dwight's blue plaid, Eliot's green plaid. With their age difference, Claris could never dress them alike as children, so it is as if now in their adulthood she is making up for lost time.

"Thank you, Mom." They each smile and kiss her cheek, and she basks in the glory of having picked out just the right thing.

Within a half-hour, Claris's sister Peg-Peg shows up with her gang, setting the house in a state of confusion. Peg-Peg's daughter Liddie, now twenty-four and a bit round with motherhood, carries her newborn. Her four-year-old twin girls happily run throughout the house. In the afternoon Lon, Aunt Peg-Peg's husband Rick, their son Mitch, and Eliot sit in the TV room while Dwight stays in the kitchen entertaining the women with anecdotes. Uncle Rick sighs.

"It worry me." He looks at Mitch. "He's draftable now. Eighteen."

Mitch laughs. "Them two American advisors ambushed in Indochina lass summer, now he's convinced there's gonna be a war. *American* war. It ain't Korea, Pop."

"Never know where them things lead."

"It ain't Korea, Pop."

Eliot goes to the bathroom. When he comes out he is surprised to see his mother sitting alone in his parents' bedroom, on the edge of the bed, away from her cooking tasks and the extended family hullabaloo. In her hands she holds *Annie Allen,* the book of Gwendolyn Brooks poems Eliot had sent her at Thanksgiving. Having stolen a moment of peace to glance at a passage, she puts the book on her lap to consider what she has just absorbed, taking off her glasses and caressing them, nodding as she is wont to do whenever stirred by her reading. Eliot gazes at her, his mother always seeking truth and therefore finding it. He quietly walks past and down the stairs.

At dinner, the topic of war comes up again, and Claris is not interested in having the holiday meal ruined by a heated discussion, so she says, "I have a joke." She tells the story of a man named Big John. When she finishes, laughing at the outrageous humor of it all, she is confused to see everyone staring at her blank. Then she realizes she screwed up the punch line. Family common knowledge: Claris can't get a joke right. But everyone is always tolerant, either forever hopeful that this time she might surprise them or just enjoying the fun of how badly she gets it wrong. Eliot smiles.

"Feels like it might snow today," remarks Aunt Peg-Peg. "You been gettin a lotta snow out there in Indianapolis?"

"You can *have* the city," says Aunt Beck, before Eliot can answer.

"You practically *got*ta live in the city you wanna professional job," says Lon.

"You sayin there's no lawyers in Humble? That's funny cuz I remember us goin to one when Mama died."

"How's Lewis treatin ya?" Uncle Rick asks Dwight.

"I like it. But the winters. Whoo!"

"Yeah, yaw *way* up in the mountains. Mus be snowin by Labor Day."

"Practically."

"Dwight, you ever do your drawins anymore?" asks Aunt Peg-Peg.

"Aw, naw. Well not so much."

"I like to draw!" says one of the little girls.

"I like to fingerpaint!" says the other.

"Better stay away from that." Aunt Beck lowering her eyes at the child. "Give ya cancer."

"Beck!"

"Didn't Amy die of it?" Aunt Beck challenges her brother. "Our baby sister, paintin missiles for the damn war effort turn her skin orange, nex thing she gone."

"Wa'n't nex thing. Fourteen years. We don't know for sure was the missile paintin done it."

"That's how it works! Chronic. Makes it harder to prove."

"That's true, Dad," says Dwight.

"Radium! In the paint they used on the missiles so they glow in the dark in the cockpit."

"I thought that was World War I," says Aunt Peg-Peg. "I thought that was them paintin the soldier watches and lickin the paintbrushes."

"This time they was breathin in the gas, don't tell *me* she didn't die of it." Aunt Beck's eyes hard slits on her brother for the latter phrase.

"Okay, you got all your facts, Beck, don't mean you have to tell the baby about it. She's finger paintin, it ain't the same chemicals like in those missile paints."

"How *you* know?"

"Lotta secrets from them days," inserts Uncle Rick. "Read this story bout a soldier just after the war, put into atomic bomb testin. The military brass wearin all this protected clothin, the rank an file sent out in shorts an sneakers. No one never told em they were bein exposed to radiation nor what exposure to radiation meant. Today both this soldier's legs amputated, his one hand five times bigger n the other. Five times! Jus waitin to die." The little girls stare at their hands.

"Damn shame," says Lon.

"Well," Dwight says, his eyes on the frightened twins, "I use to love finger paintin myself. What's your favorite color?"

"Blue!" says one.

"Purple!" says the other.

"You really shoulda gone into that, Dwight," says Aunt Peg-Peg. "You was so good at drawin! Like in the paper, the funnies."

"Hard to get those jobs," he replies. "Newspapers." He shrugs. "Anyhow my comics weren't so funny."

"Now how in the hell funnies not be funny?" Aunt Beck twirling around her mashed sweet potatoes with marshmallows.

"I like the funnies!"

"You *do?*" Claris asks the twin. "Which ones?"

The little girl stares agape at her great-aunt.

"They're still too little to read em theirself," says Liddie, "so I read to em. Dagwood an Snuffy Smith an Snoopy."

"Snoopy!" the girls cheer.

"I don't know how in the hell you can tell em apart," Aunt Beck remarks. "Freda an Fido?"

"Fiona and Felicia!" the girls yell.

"Well that don't help me with which is which, so guess I jus have to call each one a yaw Fiona-an-Felicia." The children turn to their mother, confused. Liddie smiles and winks at her daughters.

"I hear you like campin, Dwight," says Uncle Rick.

"I *have* come to like it. An there in Lewis the woods come right to your backyard. Me an my friends, we jus pack up an go."

"We use to enjoy fishin. Remember, Peg-Peg?" Uncle Rick asks his wife.

"Mm hm. I like fishin, an hikin. I stop short a overnight though. Bears I don't like."

"We live in Bear, West Virginia!" Mitch reminds his mother. "Why you think they call it that?"

"Bears don't usually come into town."

"An whatta ya mean 'stop short a overnight.' Bears are in the woods in the daytime too."

"Yeah but in the daytime I can see em comin!"

"Stop with all that salt, Lon." Lon grunts. "Claris, I hope you keepin tabs on my brother."

"He's been much better with it lately, Beck."

"Much better. Use to serve him a pork chop an he practically turn it white with the sprinklin, man ack like he ain't got high blood pressure."

"You don't do the drawins at *all* no more?" Aunt Peg-Peg back to less volatile subjects. "You were so good!"

Dwight chews on a piece of gristle. "I do them. Occasionally." He doesn't look at Peg-Peg. There is a pause, all waiting for him to continue. He doesn't.

"I like Dennis too!" says Fiona or Felicia.

"Dennis the Menace." Liddie smiling at her child.

"They call em undergroun comics," says Dwight. "Jus mean I do it for fun, kinda for my friends, an their friends. Jus to keep my hand in it."

"I didn't know you did that," says Claris.

"See? Our kids never tell us anything," says Lon.

"I'd like to see those undergroun comics sometime," says Claris.

"Sure," says Dwight, his eyes on the hunk of turkey he slips into his mouth.

"This is what *I* wanna know," says Aunt Beck. "How come Peg-Peg's settin here with three grankids an you an Claris all empty-handed."

"Aw, Beck!"

"It's a legitimate question."

"Beck," says Claris, "Dwight's very busy with the post office. He's had his girlfriends there, they just ain't none of em worked out yet. An Eliot's busy with his law firm. An he's only twenty-five, plenty a time."

Beck turns to Liddie. "How many kids you got, Twenty-four?"

"Sister, *you're* not married!"

"Exackly. You want your sons to turn into bitter ole me?"

"You seem to be doin fine for yourself," her brother tells her.

"Eliot's a lawyer, Aunt Beck! That is somethin we are *all* proud of!" Dwight's big smile big personality to the rescue. "Finished college in *three years,* then straight to law school."

"Three years, spendin his summers at school when he coulda been home." Claris referencing an old quarrel.

"He's gonna be the nex Thurgood Marshall, count on it!" Dwight goes on. "An you don't got to worry about me. I have my girlfriends, one of em'll work out one a these days."

"Well I jus think—"

"An I got *friends!* I feel like a wife is easy to come by, every one a them women let me know they're ready when I'm ready, I'm jus waitin for the right one to come along. *Friends,* though. I think they a much rarer commodity."

Most of the oldest generation nod vague, a somewhat confused assent.

"What's the difference anyway?" says Mitch. "I got a new girlfriend every week. I ain't plannin on settlin down anytime soon."

"Unless one a them gal's papas come after you with a shotgun, you don't watch it," says his father.

"Eliot!" says Dwight. "I like that Ford Falcon you drivin. Them new compact cars, real good gas mileage, right?"

"Those things are fine for the single person, but once you boys start your families gonna have to trade it in," Uncle Rick says.

"Oh they got more room than you think," says Liddie. "I got a girlfriend drives one, three kids an a baby."

"I wanna take a ride! An I want you to see my truck. You ain't never seen the inside a my Dodge."

"Yes I did." It is the first time Eliot has spoken. "Last Christmas. Remember, you and Dad went someplace, and Mom had that big box of your old stuff and asked me to take it out to your truck."

"Oh, I don't know if I knew that. The truck was new then! Well, new used. We need to drive in it sometime, I need some one-on-one time with my brother! You should come out to Lewis, see my place."

"And while I was taking the stuff out to your truck, I found one of your underground comics that you draw for your friends lying open on the seat."

The Campbells are dark-complexioned, but insofar as it's possible for Dwight to go chalk white, it is happening now. Eliot holds Dwight's horrified gape for only a moment: too quickly for the other adults to quite register but long enough for the brothers to understand each other. Having made his point, Eliot reaches for a biscuit and begins buttering it. "You know what, Aunt Beck? I *have* been thinking about marriage. But kids? Uh-uh."

"What are you talkin about? Lon, what is your son talkin about? This generation!"

"Aw, he's pullin your leg, sister." The dinner repartee continues with Eliot typically and Dwight notably not participating.

After the meal, the little girls are racing wildly through the house, Liddie yelling in a futile effort to get them to settle down. Finally Eliot, ready for a breather himself, offers to take the children for a walk. Their mother bundles them up, then Eliot takes each twin by the hand. They chatter like chipmunks but he is patient, answering their questions when asked. Around the block and coming up Colored Street. On one decorated house, lights blink accompanied by a bell rendition of "The First Noel." Several houses later a party is going on. Through the window he sees people dancing, drinking, happy. The festive music from here,

> *Stagger Lee shot Billy*
> *Oh he shot that poor boy so bad*
> *Till the bullet came through Billy and it broke the*
> *   bartender's glass*

Twenty minutes after the start of their stroll, Eliot and the girls are nearing the Campbell home, the children worn out, quieter. Walking by Miss Onnie's, the new neighbor girls are playing in their yard.

"Hi!" They come running. "You all live nex door?"

"My mother and father do."

"What's your name?"

"Eliot. And this is Fiona and Felicia." He doesn't even try to identify which is which.

"I'm Alicia!"

"I'm Alexa!"

"I'm seven!"

"I'm eight!"

By the time Eliot opens his door with the twins, they are falling asleep standing up, and Claris is laying out their bedroll.

"Where's Dwight?" Eliot asks his mother.

"Went on home."

"It's not even seven yet."

"Said he didn't feel well. I thought somethin. Way he got all quiet at dinner."

In the living room, Uncle Rick chastises Mitch, "You went with her *an* her sister? You playin with fire, boy!"

"There's punkin pie out there," Claris tells her younger son. "An pineapple upside-down."

"No thanks."

"No to *pineapple upside-down?*"

"My stomach feels a little funny."

Claris shakes her head. "I hope you an Dwight ain't comin down with the same thing."

Eliot walks out to the back porch.

"Eliot!"

It's the neighbor children, still outside.

"Come see our dolls!"

He almost steps off the porch to oblige the request. Then it occurs to him that the children's parents may wonder what the hell this grown man is doing, spying on them this morning and now entering their yard to talk to their little girls.

"I can see from here."

"This is Kitten!" says Alexa.

"This is Cathy," says Alicia, markedly less enthusiastic. Kitten is a white blond doll, and Cathy, identical, is Negro. When Eliot was a kid, the only kind of black doll he'd ever seen was Mammy. But perhaps the pendulum has swung *too* far in the other direction, the Negro doll's lips and nose as Anglo-Saxon as her white counterpart, her dark hair curly but not nappy.

"Looks like you girls had a nice Christmas."

"Yes! Yes! Yes!" says Alexa, jumping around happily while alternately swinging and clutching her white doll. Alicia eyes her sister bitterly.

"Alexa's oldest so she got the good one." This segues to a bit of a tug-of-war over white Kitten, interrupted when their mother comes to the door, snapping at her daughters to stop fighting and come inside to go to bed. They rush in crying, and even with the door closed their sobs can still be heard a little, as Cathy the black doll lies alone out on the cold ground till morning.

5

It had started early in the week with about thirty, those who could not afford a television. As the days passed more came, many who did own a set but who felt a compulsion to be among others, a good two hundred Negroes now in the February evening cold, the northwest quadrant of Monument Circle, their eyes fixed on the televisions in the display window. The irony that they are standing outside a Woolworth's in Indiana to watch history being made at a Woolworth's in North Carolina is not lost on any of them.

On Monday, Ezell A. Blair Jr., Franklin Eugene McCain, Joseph Alfred McNeil, and David Leinhail Richmond, students from North Carolina A&T, walked into the Greensboro Woolworth's and sat at the lunch counter. Seating had been reserved for whites while Negroes were expected to eat standing. The four young men were not welcome and they were not served, but they were not evicted and they did not move. The manager hoped the spectacle would be an isolated incident. On the contrary, the number of Negroes making the quiet protest had increased throughout the week. Today, Saturday the 6th, three hundred were sitting in, including young women and some A&T football players, the latter to provide an extra bulwark of resistance should anyone even consider forcing the expulsion of the group.

They had come upon the assembly independently. Andi had needed to run some domestic errand at the five-and-dime after work, Eliot and Will had had business in the nearby Marion County Courthouse, all distracted by what appeared to be a spontaneous gathering of Negroes in front of the department store just in time for the evening news. They had only noticed each other at the end of the broadcast. Every day since they had come together. They'd made no plan for the weekend, so Eliot is pleasantly surprised to glimpse both of his colleagues among the multitude. When the Greensboro story is over, the crowd disperses, most in a silent awe as if uttered words might break the spell. Eliot walks over to Andi and Will. They smile, then quietly walk to the corner where they separate to find their cars.

Eliot drives up Meridian. A few middle-class Negroes had belatedly colonized the Grandview Settlement to the north in Washington Township, but the vast majority of blacks remained south of Thirty-eighth Street in Center Township, and here in the Higher Twenties Eliot makes a left. He wears his glasses, which he only needs for driving. His childhood cross-eyed condition was corrected with prescription lenses, but as an adult it had developed into farsightedness in one eye and nearsightedness in the other. He spies the building, pulls over to the corner, and waits. Ten minutes later he glimpses movement in his rearview mirror, seeing her car turning the corner. She parks, gets out, locks the door, and strolls, smiling, absently swinging her keys. He thinks she should not be so careless with her keys while walking down a dark deserted street. She glances up, then passes her building, moving directly toward Eliot's car. He rolls down the window, and Andi speaks.

"Hope you remembered your toothbrush this time."

□ □

Wellman's *The Art of Cross-Examination. The Principles of Judicial Proof, or the Process of Proof as given by Logic, Psychology, and General Experience and Illustrated in Judicial Trials,* Clarence Darrow's *Attorney for the Damned.* Oliver Wendell Holmes's *The Path of the Law* and *The Common Law. The Proem to the Ideal Commonwealth of Plato: An Introduction to the Language and Method of the "Socratic" Dialogues.*

"You like garlic?"

Eliot looks up from Andi's bookcases. She stands over the stove, sautéing ground beef, her five-five frame seeming slightly taller in the slenderizing black shirt and slacks. Her apartment is small but functional, similar to his: kitchen, living room, bedroom with bath attached. They had not planned on meeting today but, since it happened, they made love earlier in the evening than usual, before dinner, and are now famished. It would depend on her mood, how much studying she had to do, whether he would be invited to breakfast as well. He's already longing for the hash browns that had become their morning tradition. He had never heard of the dish before, something she'd picked up spending a college summer in Boston, and while he is still partial to his mother's fried potatoes and onions, he'd developed a certain taste for this more stark treatment of the spud.

It had begun on a Friday in mid-January. A storm had started in the afternoon, sleet turning to snow, and everyone with any sense departed around 4:30 before driving would get worse. That left Eliot alone, Eliot who had just a bit more work, who promised to leave within the half-hour. Rushing to finish his task, he was surprised when ten minutes after the mass exodus he heard the elevator. Andi had just discovered she'd locked her car keys inside her vehicle. He heard her trying a couple of mechanics. Then sighing, apparently no one answering given the blizzard. City buses would be running intermittently if at all, so she called a taxi company. He heard her exclaiming into the receiver, her incredulity that she would be put at the end of a two-hour queue in which case, depending on the storm developments, a cab *might* come. While she was dialing another car service, Eliot interrupted her, saying he would drop her off at her home. It had been on his mind all along to offer, but he had worried she might take offense. And she did seem a bit taken aback, embarrassed, but at this point of desperation mostly eternally grateful. By the time he got to her place, the ten-minute drive taking nearly an hour, he could not argue with her insistence that he stay the night. Her living room couch turned out into a bed, and she made it up for him, putting cases on both pillows in case he preferred two. She fried chicken, the sole item left in her freezer, and had the ingredients for salad. She served them with wine, and afterward they sat on the couch-bed and stared out at the storm and talked for hours, about work, about the state of the country, Black America. Around two in the morning they were both bushed, and she had gone into her bedroom, closing the door. An hour and a half later, he'd awakened in the dark, and was startled to see her there, her back to the window, leaning on the radiator and staring at him. Caught, she began nervously chattering about how uncomfortably warm it was in her bedroom, how the radiator handle was permanently stuck on full blast, how she often came out into the living room to cool down, Was he cold?, she could get him extra blankets, and finally he had gently cut in, "Hey Andi," lifting his blankets to reveal the side of the couch-bed closest to her, that part of the sheet and the pillowcase still crisp clean, and she had slipped in under the covers and that had been the first time.

Eliot has picked up the Plato, glancing through it. "Pretty light reading."

She smiles without looking up from her cooking. "I'm forty-two, I don't have time to waste. I wanna know right off the bat if I'm gonna follow through with this law school business, no cake courses. Wanna come out here and slice up the bread?"

They are sitting at the kitchen table twisting forks around spaghetti and meatballs when he asks her why. She chews several moments, considering, before replying.

"I guess law school had always been in the back of my head. Just got delayed. English undergrad."

"Where?"

"University of Iowa. Tough for my parents, we were very poor."

"Seven brothers and sisters."

"Probably a mercy I was the only one inclined toward higher education. My parents were determined, and I worked my way through. I was about to graduate and already applying to law schools when Zay came along."

"Zay?"

"My husband."

He is agape. She laughs. "Yes, I used to be married. Xavier Meyers. I'd known him, philosophy, some of our courses overlapped. Also wanted to go to law school, eventually, and wanted me to stay home and make babies. Okay, I guess at the time I wasn't so passionate about all those extra years of study as I thought I was. We had a wedding, he got a job with the city cleaning buses, I cleaned house for a white family. And then came a war." She takes a bite of bread and shrugs, apparently having decided to end the story there.

"Then?" Eliot is aware that until now their post-coital discussions had usually gone back in history no further than the recent goings-on at the office.

"Then he enlisted. I got a defense job, Rosie the Riveter. We were both twenty-four." She smiles. "I bet your mama and daddy hadn't even thought about you back then."

"I was around." He doesn't say he was seven. She always finds a way to maneuver in their age difference lest either of them ever forget it for a second, a pattern he finds irritating and unfair.

"So he enlisted, '42. Sent to Europe. Still there '44, then his letters stopped coming. When it was all over, I found out he'd been taken prisoner. Highly unusual because colored men were mostly banned from the front lines. Then the Battle of the Bulge. So many Allied casualties from Hitler's last-ditch effort, they *had* to bring in the Negro troops. They held him—I'm not sure how long. As I understand it, the SS mostly killed colored POWs and pretty nastily, so I assume he escaped. He never talked about it after he came home." She absently dabs her mouth with her linen napkin, red roses on a soft gray background. "Or, something of him did. Skeleton. And not just the starvation, they took a whole lot more than his flesh." She sighs. "Do you want seconds?"

"What else did they take?"

She is quiet a few moments, staring at the two burning centerpiece candles, her sole effort to elevate the meal above the humdrum.

"Like some zombie movie. Body snatchers, I'd married this very nice man who sailed overseas and what returned." Her eyes find Eliot. "Wrinkle in his shirt. An overcooked roast, his *fury*. I don't remember how many times I ran home to Des Moines, busted lip, arm in a cast. My mother said don't go back. If my father were still alive he'd've killed him. But my favorite aunt, the youngest one, teenager when I was a kid, Aunt Geri always with the laughter and good advice said stay. Aunt Geri said, Your vows were till death. So I went back. It almost *was* till death one night, his fingers around my throat. I'm watching the veins in his neck, his face quivering hate all hate. He ripped off my underwear, opened his fly, he." She takes a breath. "On top of me. Crushing me, *tearing* me. I hit him with a lamp. I don't know where that lamp came from. Blood! Everywhere, head wounds bleed like rivers and I ran. Out in the street, I don't know if my wearing a dress was a curse as it made it easy for him in the first place, or a blessing as it made it easy for me to cover myself again when it was over. Trying to bring air back into my lungs and as soon as I did: screaming. The police came and he cried. Zay looked at me and he cried, not at my bruises. My terror, he saw how terrified I was of him, saw what he had become. It broke him." She gently touches hot drips rolling down the side of the wax sticks.

"Then you left him."

"Yep." She wipes her fingers on her napkin, pushes her hair back from her face.

"He could've killed you." She doesn't reply. "You should have left him long before."

"Yes. I could have walked into your office and you would have given me that detached glazed-eyed look: another trivial divorce case."

He is thrown. "Andi."

"And then with your perfectly dry voice you would have informed me that a man can't rape his wife."

"I don't think your situation compares to a husband who wants a divorce from his pregnant wife to allow him more freedom to slip around with young girls!"

Andi nods, her thoughts distant. "You're right, it doesn't." She stands, goes to the refrigerator. "Strawberries and cream for dessert?"

At the table he slices the berries. He tries remembering the clients for each of his divorce cases, specifically how sensitive an attorney he had been for them, or how not.

"The rape. I got pregnant."

He puts the knife down.

"You have a child?"

She is momentarily confused. "Oh. *No. No!* I don't have a child. I ended it. With Aunt Geri's help. She knew a woman. I had a dishwashing job in a diner then, cost me a paycheck." She picks up the knife and hands it back to him. He resumes his task, his slicing more agitated. "I can't describe the pain. An operation without anesthesia. Without a real doctor. I bled for two days, I was afraid it wouldn't stop. Then all the sudden, it did."

He stops slicing, holding the knife perfectly still. "It sounds like you need to stop taking advice from Aunt Geri."

Andi's eyes narrow. "It was not bad advice." She sighs and mutters, "Not the abortion part anyway. It's not her fault that—" She sighs again. "It hasn't been easy. You have no idea what it's like to be a woman in law school, the condescension by some of those damn professors." Shaking her head. "My previous job? Before Winston Douglas? I don't think getting pinched on the ass should be an accepted inconvenience of the profession, I don't think male divorce lawyers preying on female clients is just par for the course. Winston is one of the precious few firms that forbids such behavior. I'm lucky to be here now, but unless one of you moves on, I'll likely be looking elsewhere after I pass the bar so I think, Am I *insane,* going into this? Then I think, That's why I'm going into this. Those lynching photos. What's going on in Greensboro. A thousand Negro whys, yes, and a few female whys too." She takes a berry slice from his bowl and chews. "It came up in the women's bathroom. I was suspicious, what motivated this white law student to go to the Negro law student as if she assumed I'd know all about it. And then I thought, Whatever her reasons, we, women, need to strategize, to work *together* toward legalization: safe, hospital abortion. It was all hush-hush, cautiously investigating the viewpoints of other co-eds. Most of whom had no interest, the women in law wanting to assimilate as best they could into the world of male law, same for the budding physicians, though the nursing students were more open. Four of us now, two white, two Negro. We meet Thursday evenings after my class."

She can't read him, for all she knows he may be sickened and furious to imagine decriminalizing abortion. She stares unblinking, to make clear she has no intention of backing off her stance.

"Where's Zay now?"

"He hanged himself two years after the divorce."

He drops the knife. She laughs.

"I promise you that's the end of the saga. Okay you've sliced enough berries, I can take it from here."

Eliot pushes the fruit around his bowl, watching the half 'n' half turn pink.

"Why?"

He looks up at her, then understands that now it is his turn. He shrugs. "I'm sure you know." She waits. "We should be able to live where we want, our kids going to the neighborhood school. We should be able to stroll the streets without being stopped and harassed by the police, whether in Mississippi or Massachusetts. We have a right to a fair trial, we have a right to goddamn *be* without some Southern cracker or Western cracker or Northern cracker setting us on fire cuz it's Burn a Nigger Day."

Andi spoons red berry and cream through her lips, and something in the movement of it, something in the candlelight bouncing off her face and hair and eyes. Eliot believes it's the most beautiful image he has ever seen. "That's pretty generic."

"*What?*"

"I think you'll concede my reply to that question was a bit more personal."

He looks down into his dish, takes a bite. His previous bite tasted better.

"I don't think of myself as an especially open person, but you. We've been together several times now, and I don't even know where you're from."

"Maryland, I told you. Humble, Maryland."

"I'm the secretary at work, Eliot, that much I knew from your job application."

"I don't know, hick factory town. Mostly white people."

"Did you have brothers and sisters?"

"I thought the question was why I became a lawyer. We are all in law because of a lifetime witnessing injustice. Now you ask me to pinpoint it all to one moment of my life?"

"No, I'm asking for *a* moment. One you wouldn't happen to tell any damn stranger you ran into at a political rally."

A memory flashes before Eliot's eyes, his seven-year-old hands wildly waving away the parasitic flies before his mother closes and seals the shoebox which is Parker's coffin. They buried the cat in the backyard. Eliot had read from the Bible, some verses about Noah and the ark that had nothing at all to do with the present situation but that had been his Sunday school lesson that morning. Then he and his mother had sung "Jesus Loves Me, This I Know," and she had planted seeds for violets over the grave. Dwight had not been invited to the funeral. At one moment Eliot had glanced up and seen his brother's face staring down at them from the boys' bedroom window.

"High school senior year I was going with Jeanine, girl I'd known since before first grade. I came over to pick her up for the prom, and she and her mother are in the living room with this man, hat in hand, and soon as I walk into the room I can tell he's a stranger to them. He stands and they sit looking up at him, starkly serious on a night I planned on being all about dancing and laughing and kissing. Jeanine waves me to come in, and I sit, holding the corsage I bought for her in my lap. I don't recall where the man was from, or where he was headed, but he was passing through Humble and remembered the name of the town from Ramonlee, Jeanine's uncle, and was overcome by this urge to look up Ramonlee's family. They had been soldiers together, Ramonlee a teenager when he was drafted and teenager when he came home in a box. Not from France and not from the Philippines, the boy never got further than Pennsylvania, the army always remaining frustratingly vague on the matter. The man standing in Jeanine's living room said that everything was Jim Crow on the base, that there were German prisoners of war who could move about freely but the Negro soldiers were confined to the Negro quarters which naturally were the swamps. There were several movie theaters for white soldiers but none for colored. When they finally set up something makeshift in the Negro section it was small, and a soldier would have to stand in line outside at least the entire two hours of the previous screening in order to make it in for the next. The PX was white-only, and a fed-up black soldier at long last went in to buy a beer, and for his uppityness had the shit kicked out of him, but that wasn't enough. Within minutes, jeeps of white soldiers came rushing into the colored section, firearms cocked and ready. They shot everything in sight, and before the spree was over several Negroes lay dead. This man standing in Jeanine's living room and Ramonlee were both wounded, Ramonlee badly, and transported to the infirmary. On the way the Red Cross worker assured the ambulance driver that quote, Niggers don't bleed that fast, unquote. There is some dispute over whether Ramonlee was treated as quickly as he should have been, at any rate in the end both his legs were amputated, but not quite properly and he bled to death." From his chair at the table Eliot had been staring, though not seeing, out the window. Only now does it register that it has started to snow. "It got late. Jeanine and I never made it to the prom."

"It'll happen soon." He is startled by her voice, by the present. "Your first civil rights case."

"How do you know?"

She smiles. "Given your workload, I think by now all the colored couples in Indianapolis have divorced. Nothing else left for you to do."

She jumps into the bath and he tucks the corners of the blankets. They have agreed making love is most satisfying on clean sheets, or at least on a made bed. In the corner of the room is his briefcase, always with him. He opens it and takes out of the inside top pocket the page his boss had handed him during his first days on the job, something until now he had forgotten about.

Useful Tips When Confronted by Southern Hospitality

by Winston Douglas, Esq.

1. When in Rome. From your hotel window, gaze out. Observe. Take note of the physical cues passed between Negro and white.

2. Be polite to whites, but avoid looking them in the eye. If you are male, <u>especially</u> avoid making eye contact with WHITE WOMEN.

3. If there is a white man, or white men, approaching on the sidewalk, and someone has to step off the curb to allow room for passage, make sure that someone is you. To be safe you will <u>always</u> want to step off rather than risk coming anywhere close to a white woman; to be saf<u>est</u> you will always want to step off rather than risk coming anywhere close to a white anything.

4. (a) Make sure you have absolutely ascertained that a restaurant is a Negro establishment before entering. (b) Avoid at all costs the patronage of bars or saloons or roadhouses, even if they are Negro establishments. Alcohol impedes alertness, and one thing you do not want impeded as a Northerner in Dixie is alertness.

5. Never ever ever drive at night.

6. If you find yourself driving at night, get out of town as fast as your (g)as can carry you. If they catch you, you will be arrested for speeding regardless of whether you were going 15 or 50, so don't let them catch you.

7. Get used to saying "Yes, ma'am" and "Yes, sir" to white people. It is not always necessary, but it may be, so it is a good idea to practice it until it automatically slips off your tongue. Think Pavlov.

8. Get used to hearing the word "nigger" casually thrown around by whites. Get used to not impulsively clenching your fists when you hear the word "nigger" casually thrown around as there will be many more white fists to clench and white fists to clutch objects that can do considerably more bodily harm than clenched fists.

9. If you are female, do not ever find yourself alone with a white man, or white men. This can lead to rape. If you are male, do not ever find yourself alone with a white woman, or white women. This can lead to lynching.

10. Before you leave home, make a will and have it

notarized. Having properly considered in detail and
legalized your posthumous arrangements generally
makes one much more likely to adhere to Rules 1
through 9.

A dog starts barking, wild and vicious. Andi's apartment is on the fourth
of six floors, practically a skyscraper compared with most Indianapolis resi-
dences. Just below on the third, a German shepherd—Eliot takes her word
for the breed since he's never seen the animal—sits behind a door, flying
into a maniacal tirade every time they walk past. He turns on the radio to
drown out the sound. A ballad.

The snow is falling harder, three inches already. She will be aware of
slippery roads: if she is going to send him home it will be now or not till
after breakfast. They have never been on a real date, all their rendezvous
occurring here at Andi's. His reasoning for the clandestine nature of their
relationship has been the fear of running into someone from the office, how
such awkwardness might be detrimental to their work environment. Does
he know for certain that's *her* reasoning? Despite the physical intimacy,
he has always detected a certain distance from her. Is it because he has not
opened up to her about his past? And if so, didn't that change a bit this evening when he spoke of Ramonlee? Or maybe her reticence is something else
altogether. The worry that has unsettled him: Does she take him seriously?
Take *them* seriously? Is he a man to her, or a boy? What if he suggested they
take a weekend away? If they pooled their resources surely they could find
a hotel within their means in Gary. And there they would be in no danger
of encountering Winston or Beau Greene or Will Mitchell. Would she be
willing to go with him then? Be with him?

"Andi." It's out of his mouth before he thinks, and at that moment the
bathroom door flings open. She is naked and grinning. His mouth opens in
awe, and she falls into him, turning off the lamp as she does and they make
love again as Brook Benton assures them both that it's just a matter of time.

6

The white entrance guard leans back in his chair, legs stretched, feet crossed and propped on his desk. His blue eyes glance up over his newspaper. "Thought you were waitin for that gal." Though he's relaxed, he is not exactly rude. A Negro boy of about twelve sweeps the floor, empties the wastebasket. Behind the guard stand two flags, one representing the state of Georgia, the other the United States of America.

"She's five minutes late. I don't want to lose any more time with my clients." The impatient young attorney seems a bit perturbed with the tardy party. Beads of sweat appear on his brow, not used to heat like this in mid-April.

The guard unlocks the gate, leading him down the hall. They come to a closed door on the left, another guard leaning against the wall next to it, absently smoking.

"Donnie Ray." The entrance guard points his thumb in the visitor's direction. "There's the lawyer."

The guard throws his butt to the floor, stamps it out, and unlocks the door. The room is small, cramped, and uncomfortably warm with no windows or fan. A rectangular wooden table and chairs. They are adult chairs, yet the four grownups stand while only the two little Negro boys are seated, their legs dangling. They work in coloring books. When the lawyer walks in, all eyes turn to him. The older child sits on the opposite side of the table facing the door, which the guard now closes as he exits. The younger's back is to the door so he has to turn around to see the visitor. He is the first person in the room to speak. "Are you Mr. Campbell?"

"Yes," says Eliot, who takes off his hat and holds it in his hands, "I am."

The boy scrambles out of his chair to stand and shake his attorney's hand with the formality of the gentry. "How do you do."

The adults are Claudette and Ronald Price, the parents of seven-year-old Jordan, and Howard and Minnie Williams, the parents of nine-year-old Max. They introduce themselves to Eliot.

"Where's Didi?" Mrs. Price asks. Eliot is confused. "Miss Wilcox."

"She must've gotten held up."

Jordan's mother seems stricken, as if this is yet another bad omen.

"This a fire truck, Mr. Campbell," says Jordan. "Fire truck, I color it red." He makes a siren sound, moving his picture through the air.

"Can I wear your hat?" Max asks, and Eliot gives it to him. Max puts it on and it falls over his eyes. He giggles, then pushes it back on his head so he can see before resuming his coloring.

"This a Dalmatian," says Jordan. "The page is white but white crayon make Dalmatian whiter. This is the *fire* man. Max make him pink but I jus leave him be, like the page white but not white like the Dalmatian. I traced it, see? I traced it, look like the real picture, see?"

"I see. What did *you* color, Max?" Eliot takes a chair, sitting on an end of the table between the boys.

"Train." Max had done a very studied rendering of an engineer standing outside a passenger car, kindly talking to a porter. Both men are pink.

"That's very nice, Max. But you know, you could have made those men brown." Both boys stop coloring to look up and gape at Eliot.

"My father was a porter. Like him. And colored men can be engineers and firemen too."

The children look down at their pictures, then back up at Eliot, blinking. Eliot asks gently, "You boys wanna tell me what happened?"

Max sighs, tired of the question. But Jordan jumps in, seeming to delight in this reversal of Children should be seen and not heard: whenever he tells *this* story, he has all the adults' undivided attention. "We was playin with Ginny Dodgson an Leecy Pike, an Ginny Dodgson's daddy's a *fire* man an he the *mail* man too, an I don't know what Leecy's daddy do, an Ginny go 'How old is you?' an I say 'Seven,' an she say 'I'm seven too!' an Max go 'I'm nine' an Leecy say 'I'm eight' an Ginny say 'You wanna play dolls?' an I say 'Dolls is for girls!' an she say 'You wanna play Hide n Go Seek' an I say 'Okay, 5, 10, 15, 20, 25, 30' an we fine her an Leecy in Miss Dellarose's bushes an Ginny go 'You wanna touch my hair?' an I say 'Okay,' her hair straight an yella, an Leecy go 'You wanna touch *my* hair?' it red, an I say 'Okay,' an Ginny go 'I seen Beeber and Sissy Gompers kissin,' Beeber Ginny's big brother, an Ginny go 'You wanna kiss me?' an she stick her lips out an I go 'Okay' an I kiss her right on the lips peck! an she laugh an Leecy go to Max an Leecy say 'I know how to kiss' an Max say 'Okay' an Leecy go to Max peck! an we find a frog we pick up that frog but it slip away! hop hop an we go home for supper an knock on the door an Mama get the door, then she go 'Jordan! Ron!' an me an Daddy come runnin to the door, her voice soun like we oughta come runnin to the door! an a po-lice standin there! An po-lice man say, 'You kiss a white girl, boy?' Po-lice man look mad! Po-lice man say Ginny tell her daddy we was kissin, po-lice man say, 'You know that's a white girl! You know that's a white girl!' an po-lice man got a gun in his pocket he keep tappin it, an then they put the hancups on me click! an they put me in the paddy wagon an Mama cryin an me cryin an then they drive, an then they park, they park a long time, an then come Max in the hancups cryin, they put him in the paddy wagon with me, his mama cryin, an in the jail they punch us in the tummy, they punch in the legs an the back a long time bang! bang! bang! my tummy hurt, an every day we say 'Can we see our mama?' an they say 'Shoulda thoughta that when you go rapin little white girls' an then our mama an daddy come an then the judge say 'The reformatory' so they send us here, the reformatory, an they make us pick the strawberries in the sun, hot! an they make us talk to the psychaw-jegist an the psychaw-jegist say 'You oughta be cashtrated' an the psychaw-jegist say 'You know what cashtrated mean?' and we say 'No' an the psychaw-jegist tell us!"

Jordan's eyes are filled, his demeanor completely changed, as if at the beginning of his narrative, his enthusiasm in having a new adult as a captive audience had caused him to temporarily forget his story's terrifying end. Eliot turns to the other child and speaks softly. "Now you tell me, Max."

"Like he say." Max had continued to color throughout Jordan's testimony and doesn't look up from his task now.

Eliot talks to the parents quietly a few minutes. They are interrupted by a quick knock followed by the guard poking his head in. "Two minutes." He shuts the door.

Mrs. Price wipes her eyes. "Come give Mama a kiss goodbye."

"No!" Jordan runs to his mother, throwing his arms around her legs. "I wanna go home!"

She reaches down, embracing him. "That's why we goin to talk with Mr. Campbell now, baby, that's what we tryin to figure out."

"You be a good boy, alright?" Mrs. Williams instructs, and she and her husband walk over to kiss Max, who never looks up, never stops coloring.

"May I have my hat back, Max?"

Max stands, takes it off and hands it to Eliot. Then he stares up at his lawyer.

"Can I ask you a question?"

"Of course." Eliot stoops next to the child, and Max cups his hand around his own mouth and Eliot's ear.

"When my mama kiss me, that don't count as 'rape.' Do it? It only 'rape' when I kiss back. Right?"

Though he had confirmations by three locals that the establishment was colored, Eliot is nevertheless relieved to see a Negro family enter the place just before he does. It's 10:30 on a Thursday morning, the restaurant half full. The family, a couple with two small children and a girl of about fourteen (Eliot wonders why the kids aren't in school), are seating themselves. Peppered about are three single men sitting separately, two middle-aged women chatting, a table of high school kids, and isolated away in a corner is a pretty fair-skinned teenager. Eliot is startled when the girl waves him over.

"Deirdre Wilcox?"

"Didi. And you would be Mr. Campbell." She smiles, standing to shake his hand, a Southern drawl spiced with Northern education. Her hair is naturally wavy, light brown and falling below her shoulders, her eyes medium brown with golden sparkles. She takes in his baffled look and laughs. "You thought I was eighteen, right?"

"Seventeen was my guess."

"Well you don't look much older, but if my investigation is correct, you and I are the same age. Twenty-five?"

She apologizes again for missing the meeting with the boys. She had been with the case the last two weeks, and had promised she would be there yesterday afternoon to make the introductions. When she spoke to Eliot on the phone last night, she told him about running into unexpected traffic problems. She'd found a pay phone and tried to get the message to him through the correctional facility staff but, Well, you know how that goes. She accepts full responsibility: her seamless drive last week had left her cocky, when she should have known to have allowed more leeway for her travel from Chicago just as he had from Indianapolis. She had spent her early childhood here in Red Bank, a small Georgia municipality in the rolling hills of the middle of the state with near equal Negro and white residents, and had known extended family of the boys, so when an old friend called to tell her about the situation, she rushed here the next day to provide any assistance she could. Unfortunately she was twenty-four hours too late: the children had been given their disposition orders the preceding morning. They would be confined to the state colored reformatory until they were twenty-one.

"I went to the parents who were completely distraught, having tried several local lawyers to appeal, all of whom turned them down. There is one Negro attorney in the county who advised them free of charge as best he could, but in addition to his regular overextended load, he was now involved in a few local high-profile race cases—defending the young people arrested for trespassing after they peacefully tried to integrate the public library, defending the Negro who asked his white boss for back pay and is suddenly, mysteriously accused of company theft—well, the poor man just had his hands full." Of the other lawyers in the area, some didn't want to be involved with a case so controversial, others claimed to be in the business of trying to keep adults out of the penitentiary and would not deign to lower themselves to juvenile law, the most dire consequences of which being a stint in reform school, "as if it were a trip to the circus," Didi remarks, shaking her head. The local NAACP was sympathetic, but the legal defense team of the national organization refused to get entangled in what it termed a "sex case." So she had plunged into researching private firms. Two were in Chicago, and a schoolmate from Indianapolis had suggested Winston Douglas. Before making the call, she had investigated the institution scrupulously (but quickly—there *is* the deadline to file for appeal), and when the case was accepted pro bono and the junior attorney recommended, she had scrupulously investigated *him*. She carried no delusions about taking on the job herself given her lack of experience, and is well aware that the prejudices to which a judge and jury may be inclined against her race and gender would only be compounded by her youthful appearance. What she needs to do is to start heavy drinking and smoking so as to age herself, and she laughs heartily.

Eliot could have likewise undertaken a more thorough background check on her but the effort seemed somewhat redundant, given that over the phone she freely gave away all manner of information about herself without prompting. She is not yet tied to a firm. She stayed in the city after graduating from the University of Chicago Law School a year ago, waitressing to pay the rent while studying for the Illinois bar which she passed in the summer. But despite her impressive academic record, she has become painfully aware that gender discrimination in Negro law firms is yet one more hurdle to clear, and consequently maintains her full-time position in the diner. Eliot thinks of the time taken off from her job to travel South, the long-distance phone calls, the hotel fees, and wonders how she has managed to cover her legal expenses thus far.

"Cuz I'm rich!" She laughs. "Really! My father's a tailor, he owns three shops in Atlanta. We moved there when I was nine. He's semi-retired now but still raking in the dough. My mother gave private piano lessons, not because we needed the money, but because what else would a Southern bourgeois colored woman do?" Then why does she need to waitress? "I'm not being carried! I support myself. But I am not in denial about my safety net. If I get in trouble, they'll wire cash. Worst case scenario I can always go home. I am well aware at the end of the day when we collect our tips, for me it's a matter of personal pride. For the other girls it means survival, and a slow week the lack thereof."

The waitress comes, and Eliot is assisted in his order by Didi. As she gives hers, he notices a girl from the teenage table standing at the jukebox, contemplating. The waitress walks away as the room is suddenly filled with the initial chords of Ray Charles's "What'd I Say." A responsive gasp of delight from the younger patrons.

"When Mrs. Williams went to visit Max last week, she signed in with a friend who she explained had driven her. The friend turned out to be a reporter who sneaked in a camera. When the pictures hit the international press, well, you know the rest. Mrs. Williams looked at me worried, knowing the outcry had agitated the governor, Had she done the right thing? 'Yes!' I assured her, 'and we have only begun to fight. From here on out the boys *will* be properly represented.'"

Eliot nods, gazing at his utensils atop the red-checkered tablecloth. He wonders exactly how "properly" represented these innocent children will be by a twenty-something lawyer whose only previous experience has been divorces and accident claims.

"You're going to have a team." Didi picks up her briefcase, pulls out a file, and hands it to him. "Two local whites. Diana Rubin and I met in an oral argument seminar. Both of us from this hick town but going to segregated schools, we didn't know each other till Chicago. She's smart, graduated top five percent. She suggested a local white man, and a local white man is always useful in the South. Steven Netherton. You'll meet them both this afternoon."

She sighs. "Juvenile justice. It rang some distant law school bell, but the system is *so* preposterous I didn't really grasp it until this crash course in firsthand experience. When young offenders' law came about in the eighteenth century, the idea was that the state would act as *parens patriae,* a stand-in parent, that no longer would a small child be imprisoned with grown men, hardened criminals. All well and good, but the trade-off was the state took away the youngster's due process. No right to counsel, well. If Max and Jordan's families had had the financial means and a reasonable amount of time *maybe,* but the boys were held incommunicado the first six days, not even their mothers could see them, let alone an attorney. You knew that."

"My boss told me."

"And on the seventh day, the parents were called in just long enough for Judge Sawyer to sentence away the boys' childhood. 'Disposition orders' in the delicate parlance of the juvenile court, as if the confinement of a human being for well over a decade were not a sentence but rather a father telling his child to go to his room until he has grown a beard. So a: no attorney, b: the case is based on unsworn hearsay testimony, *that* I had to drag out of the probation officer who, believe it or not, is considered the child's advocate, which brings me to c: There's no written record of the proceedings! Perfectly legal for a juvenile hearing, apparently we're lucky to have been apprised of any charges as they could just as well have claimed 'The judge deems the boys delinquent,' oh *there's* specificity, try and appeal *that!* And this is the treatment the *white* youth face. Multiply that by the fact that these are Negro boys, the victims so-called, white girls. The hysteria! Crime of the Century, my *God.* They burned crosses in the yards of the boys' families every night until the judge's decision."

She takes a sip of water, then sets her glass down with a hint of force. "So. Let us talk strategy. Fortunately you will be appealing to a different court and a panel of three new judges in Atlanta. One place you might start: The parents had *no idea* what was going on with their little boys after the arrests, every day they came to the police station begging to see their sons and were refused. These circumstances obviously precluded the opportunity for them to secure an attorney. Another thing. While most local people couldn't give a fig about international opinion, the brouhaha does seem to have unnerved the governor, there's always the possibility of a pardon. Meanwhile, Diana and I consulted a former professor in Chicago. On his advice she's quietly speaking to some highly regarded local citizens in the hopes that they can approach the judge for leniency. Further, and here's where you can use the vagueness of the system to your advantage, in a year you can come back to Judge Sawyer to tell him how well the boys have been doing at the reformatory and to ask him for a modification in his disposition orders. I would hope—"

"A *year?*"

"Unfortunately our professor felt it would not be appropriate to approach the judge any sooner. At that time you can stress that the past twelve months have successfully rehabilitated the boys, while any longer could reverse that rehabilitation, as few would argue reformatories, conceived in good faith, have declined into vocational institutions for training criminals. Of course with any luck you will appear before the appellate court before that. And we will naturally hold out hope that all will go well there, yet we need to be realistic about—"

"Are you working for the prosecution?"

Didi looks at him, momentarily dumbfounded. Then sits back, her eyes narrowing. "No. I am *not* working for the prosecution. I *am*—"

"But you're suggesting two children who played an innocent game stay locked up a year till we come crawling back to the judge pleading his mercy, his 'modification' of the disposition orders. *What* modification? Get them out at eighteen instead of twenty-one?"

"Mr. Campbell. I certainly would hope the modification would mean *immediate* release, I'd like—" She sighs, shakes her head. "While those poor little boys were being held incommunicado, being beaten by police everywhere but their faces knowing the children's clothing would conceal the bruising elsewhere, while all this was happening on the inside, on the out there were nuts around here screaming, 'Rape! Try em like adults! Set an example!' The courts seriously bandied about the possibility a while, and do you know what the penalty is in the South for a black man convicted of raping a white woman?" Eliot stares at her, his silence severe. "It is an appeal, Mr. Campbell. There is no room for challenging the law's morality or lack thereof, an appeal as you know is about examining procedure or *interpretation* of the law, so it would be in the boys' best interests for you to grasp, not to condone but to *grasp,* the mind-set that resulted in those children's confinement. Otherwise I'm afraid you will find yourself skipping from landmine to landmine in Dixie."

"I don't need to take a course in the peculiar practices of the Deep South, in the twenty-four hours I've been here I've already worn my shoes out stepping off the damn sidewalk for whites."

"Good. Because like it or not, as far as that judge is concerned the boys *are* guilty. And the appellate judges you'll be facing will be just as Georgia as Sawyer. Max and Jordan *did* kiss those little white girls, which the state, in accurately representing its white constituency I would submit, has deemed the toddler equivalent of rape, and feels exceptionally charitable in its grudging reduction of the charges to seduction, assault, and lewdness."

"Those kids can't even spell that, let alone know what it means."

"According to the Code of Georgia, seduction—"

"*I* know what it means! I was musing on the insanity to apply it to a second grader."

"No argument here."

"Even at the outstretches of anyone's imagination, that seven- and nine-year-olds would understand what seduction is, it was instigated by the girl."

"That's according to Jordan and Max. According to the probation officer who spoke to Ginny's father who spoke to Ginny and that's as close to an affidavit as you're going to get, Jordan started it. At any rate, the officer claims while in custody the boys confessed that they did all the kissing, not the girls."

"Oh you mean in between getting slugged by a couple of two-hundred-pound cops?"

"I presume before the beatings. Those big white policemen would have made those helpless little Negro boys aware in no uncertain terms that things would go easiest on them if they confessed. And after easily securing those confessions, *then* they would have pummeled them. But try proving any of that to the judges."

"Confession or no it was clearly consensual, no evidence of force."

"Seduction needn't involve force. And consensual? I wouldn't advise it. Negro males and white females, you're nudging the miscegenation laws right there."

"Again I would like to ask, are you representing those little boys or the state."

"And *I* would like to ask how *you* plan to approach the appeal."

"*I* never said anything about appeal."

She frowns. "Well we can't motion for acquittal. Sawyer will say there was no trial and therefore no conviction to acquit, he merely *disposed* the children as is consistent with the juvenile court. Are you suggesting a new trial? Again we cannot motion for a *new* trial when technically there was no *first*—"

"Habeas."

Didi stares at him, stunned. Then abruptly breaks into laughter. Then abruptly stops laughing. "You can't be serious," she says because she sees that he is.

"This whole thing is ludricous, I'm getting it thrown out and having those little boys released pronto."

"A *habeas corpus*."

He stares at her. She chuckles. "You've rather flabbergasted me, Mr. Campbell. I did not come prepared to consider such a radical plan of action. Especially as a court would never consider granting a writ, the *Great Writ* no less, until all other avenues have been exhausted. You think they would overlook the fact that you've completely circumvented the appeals process?"

"You just elaborated at length upon the fact that there are no court records, and sans court records an appeal, an investigation into whether procedures were administered properly, is impossible, so it would appear the extraordinary remedy of *habeas* is applicable here."

She leans forward, elbow on table, chin in fist. "A *habeas* begins at the same court level as the original hearing."

"I'm aware of that."

"And are you also aware that in this small town, in this small *county* there is no separate juvenile judge? Sawyer was pulled from the two men representing the Superior Court. That means when you file your *habeas* there's a fifty-fifty chance it will go right back to him."

Now it's Eliot who is taken aback. He considers this latest information before countering. "With a *habeas* I can introduce new evidence, something I could *not* do with an appeal. *Habeas* I can start from scratch, maybe Sawyer'd see reason since this time there would actually be a defense lawyer in the picture to present reasoning for him to see."

"And all the while we're waiting to see if the *habeas* is granted, the clock is running out on our chance to file for appeal and guarantee new judges."

"A writ's heard quicker. If it's granted, the boys won't be lingering in the kiddie state pen a year or three waiting for an appeal."

"And if you're granted the writ and the judge still doesn't buy it."

"Then I appeal the *habeas*. To the state appellate. And if that doesn't work to the state supreme court, and if that doesn't work to the *U.S.* Supreme Court did I say something funny? You think this case is funny?"

"Oh no, I don't think the *case* is funny, Mr. Campbell, if I was smiling in any dubious fashion I wasn't making fun of the *case,* I was making fun of *you.*"

"I did not drive six hundred miles through the damn Bible Belt just to try and appeal phantom proceedings, to play kangaroo court!"

"That's the point, Mr. Campbell, you *did* come down here, you *aren't* from here." She falls back against her chair. "Kangaroo court!" She laughs again. Eliot's silent breathing is slow and heavy. "Well maybe it's fortunate you weren't around for the original hearing. Flaunting all your Northern values might have had half the white citizenry ready to commission the design of a tot-size electric chair."

"Don't give me that naïve Yankee crap! I grew up below the Mason-Dixon, damn Jim Crow town."

"Sweetie, South Carolinians call North Carolinians 'Yankee' so you haven't exactly pulled out your Dixie credentials with Maryland."

He is caught unawares. "You *did* do your research on me." She smiles. He sighs, sits back. "Seven and nine years old, no attorney representation and their so-called confession holds up."

"The Fifth doesn't apply to children. Nor the Fourteenth, nor any of the rest." She caresses her flowered linen napkin between her thumb and pointer. "When I said they had no visitors their six days in jail, that was a slight exaggeration. Apparently on the third night two local Ku Kluxers in full regalia entered their cell, terrorizing them. Just a prank, good ole boy fun."

"When I go back to Sawyer on hands and knees as you have counseled, perhaps I can use that little anecdote to clarify that the boys have been *most* 'rehabilitated.'"

"*I grew up here, Mr. Campbell!* A child of Red Bank, a Georgia girl till college. If you believe I am thrilled about any of what I have suggested to you, you are sorely mistaken about me, about Southern Negroes. There are certain mores that are untouchable, chief among those being the preservation of white womanhood, and white womanhood starts when a white woman is born. Those innocent little boys walked into a lion's den they knew nothing about. It's done and cannot be undone, that's the tragedy. I don't want to exacerbate it by leaving their fate from here on out in the hands of self-righteous adults who prioritize some utopian ideal over Southern reality." His hard eyes turn to the floor. "I've noticed your penchant for the first-person singular. Do you plan then to go it alone, without a team?"

"*No.*" His face warm. "Of course I. I said 'I' but I meant—"

"Glad to hear it, because you'd be delusional, pardon me, *certifiably insane* if you thought a Northern Negro attorney could come down here and fly solo on this one." She rests her elbow on the table, the side of her face gently leaning into the L of her index finger and thumb. "It will be your case, your *team's*, not mine. So petition for the *habeas* if you wish, if you can get your partners on board. As I say, there's a good chance you'll be in the initial round facing Sawyer on that one, and when he refuses you can go to the state supreme court, and when they refuse you can go to the U.S. Supreme Court, with the boys all the while languishing behind bars. I will be right there, cheerfully hitting the law library for any research you need, cheerleading you and Diana and Steven Netherton all the way, wishing Godspeed for your success. But should you fail. It will be quite late in the day *then*, Mr. Campbell, to beg Judge Sawyer for mercy."

The fourteen-year-old in the family suddenly belts out "Say you will!" in accompaniment with Jackie Wilson's tenor plea. She is promptly smacked on the arm by her mother.

"Eliot," he says, an assent to drop the formalities.

Didi smiles. "Eliot." She opens her briefcase fully so that he can see inside. Two small chocolate bunnies. "Technically they're contraband, but I trust you can keep a secret. I'm going to slip them to the boys when I see them today." Eliot stares at her, then looks at the children across the restaurant, and then at the counter, for the first time noticing a plate of colored eggs in a nest. "Oh my God, you're such a Northern heathen! You didn't realize Sunday's Easter? Why do you think the kids are out of school? It's Maundy Thursday!"

The waitress brings the food and sets it in front of them, then walks away. Eliot inspects his grits, the recommendation of his breakfast companion, not quite sure if they are what he had had in mind. Didi nearly falls off her chair laughing. "Welcome to Down Home, my friend. Oh, and if you ever again ask a waitress if they make hash browns in that damn Northern accent, I'll have to slap you. Yankee mess!" as she sloshes her biscuits around in her gravy.

8

"You must be Mr. Campbell."

Eliot steps back, confused by the gray-haired white man, no taller than himself, who has opened the door.

"I'm Sol Rubin, Diana's father."

"Mr. Campbell!" Ten feet behind Sol, at the foot of the stairs, a young woman smiles. Pretty, petite, black hair and eyes.

"You broke one of the sacred laws of the South," Diana says when the two are alone in the "drawing room." "A Negro coming through a white person's front door."

"Oh," Eliot says, looking back vaguely in the direction of his entrance, trying to remember whether this was a part of Winston's top ten Dixieland *dos* and *don'ts*. Diana laughs.

"If I didn't want you to break that law, I would have warned you. It's nothing dangerous in broad daylight, given that everyone on the street could see I was expecting you. And I guarantee you they were looking, peeking behind their blinds. Always suspicious of their Hebrew neighbors."

"You grew up in this house?"

"I did."

"Your neighbors have always known you."

"Yes, my entire twenty-six years. My father was born and raised in this town, you might have thought by now he would have graduated to their *neighbor* rather than their *Jewish neighbor*. He went to Philadelphia for school, met my Philly native mother during his residency. Doctor, nurse. He persuaded her to move here with him. *He* should have been a lawyer."

"Do you plan on staying?"

"Heavens no! I'm getting married in July, moving to Sacramento. Are you married, Mr. Campbell?"

"No." He suddenly realizes he had forgotten to put the penny in the pocket of his pants this morning. Andi had found it on the ground as they strolled to her apartment the evening before he traveled South, Lincoln's shiny profile. "Heads. Good luck," she had said before she gave it to him.

"I *do* plan on continuing law, my fiancé and I are both preparing for the

California bar. I certainly didn't study all these years just to spend my days arguing the virtues of Comet versus Ajax!"

A Negro maid of about forty appears with a tray: coffee, petits fours. A childhood image flashes through Eliot's mind—his mother ironing in Miss Idie's house.

"Thank you, Bertie." Bertie must have noted Eliot's glance but leaves without ever meeting his eyes.

"Thus far I've only passed Illinois so we will both have to motion for a *pro hac vice* to practice here."

"And you worked for a firm in Chicago?" Eliot asks carefully, taking a sip.

"Oh I'm afraid I've had some trouble this past year securing work, firms can be damned prejudiced against women. *So.* This case is my first!" Something in Eliot's pupils deflates Diana's broad grin. "You're disappointed, Mr. Campbell."

"No."

"Were you under the impression I had more experience?"

"Well. Miss Wilcox—"

"Didi's a scream! She was a year behind me but we became fast friends. I spent a week with her and her family one summer, lovely people."

"There was little time between my late breakfast with Miss Wilcox and now for me to peruse the paperwork she handed me. Still in my glance I was impressed by your academic accomplishments. And I did note one professional appointment. An internship?" He takes another sip, noting how his presumed legal partner's physical energy seems more akin to sixteen than twenty-six.

"Are you going to fire me, Mr. Campbell?" She is half smiling but he detects the vaguest worry, *pout*, beneath her words.

"Miss Rubin. After I graduated and passed the bar—"

"Both in record time!"

"My first appointment as an attorney, as you probably know from my CV, was to assist a former professor in his efforts toward mandating equal pay for colored and white janitors in Baltimore. *Just* an assistant, research and paperwork, no real responsibility. His office could scarcely afford me part-time, well, to *pay* me part-time regardless of my workload, and I was happy to oblige. But it was understood I was looking for a full-time salaried position. I worked there five months before being offered the job in Indianapolis last March. A firm I have greatly admired for its political rights record, but. As a young lawyer, my thirteen months there have been entirely devoted to divorce settlements, probate disputes, accident claims. Until now. I have been familiarizing myself with Georgia law but I." He sets his cup down. "To be perfectly honest, I'm a bit concerned that the cumulative experience of yours and mine will add up to a rather big zero for little Jordan and Max."

"*No,* Mr. Campbell, I don't believe that at all! We are both smart, and driven. And we have Mr. Netherton! Did you have a chance to look at his résumé?"

"Briefly."

"Well then you know! Steven Netherton is a very capable attorney. And a white male Protestant who *grew up here, exceedingly* useful!" A grandfather clock indicates half past the hour. "Mr. Campbell. I hope you don't think I'm some silly naïve girl. I'm very much aware of the gravity of the situation, I would not suggest we go through with this if I did not think we were ready. And besides. I worry what alternatives, if any, the boys would have if we pulled out."

"Perhaps they'd get a more experienced team."

"And perhaps they wouldn't. The parents certainly have received their share of rejections." She picks up her cup and saucer, sitting back in her chair. "I presume you are not here because there's a lull in your civil work and you need something to fill the time. I would guess this is more in line with what you had in mind when you went to law school, but of course it doesn't quite sink in until you are *in* it, the reality of criminal law, the stakes that could not be higher: a person's life in your hands. Of course the juvenile court is technically civil, but what's the difference if we're talking about a client being deprived of his liberty for the next fourteen years? So we accept this responsibility, are aware of that responsibility our every waking working moment. Otherwise we just get out of the whole thing and stick to accident claims." She sips. "If we're going to do it, then we must commit. We have to decide, given all the circumstances, the best possible outcome for the boys, then work toward that goal confidently. *Optimistically.*" Her eyes peek over her cup at him.

He holds her gaze a moment before speaking. "The goal I would be working toward." He pauses to prepare himself for her inevitable shock. "*Habeas.*"

"*Habeas corpus*, yes! Just before you came Didi rang to tell me. Now that *is* optimism!"

"And?"

She puts her cup down and leans forward. "We should be candid, Mr. Campbell?"

"Please."

"I was a bit terrified." A soft giggle. "Didi and I didn't get to talk long, she just relayed to me the basics. And we hung up, and I pictured some arrogant bully whisking in here, demanding to run things, gunning for his own Supreme Court glory. That is not the impression you have made on me, Mr. Campbell. I don't know you at all, but I'm a pretty good judge of character. I think we could work well together. I am willing, *eager* to go on this journey with you."

Some neighborhood children beyond the screened window. "One potato two potato three potato four."

"I'm glad to hear it," Eliot says, and while his tone is controlled, she senses an incredible relief.

"Now. With regard to my judge of character. Some people—" She takes a bite of cake, her brow furrowed in concentration. "Some people may not be especially. *Genial.* But they possess other necessary qualities, enough so as to encourage a compromise. Mr. Netherton." Taking another nibble. "Mr. Netherton and I talked very briefly over the phone, he said he'd rather discuss things face to face. In just three years since law school, his CV has become impressively packed. He has taken on a lot of clients other attorneys refused, this won't be his first race case! So we are *very* fortunate to have Mr. Netherton! The attorney." She absently crumbles the remaining cake in her fingers. "Regarding Mr. Netherton, the *man.* There *are* one or two, oh Mr. Campbell, your coffee is getting cold!"

"There are one or two."

"It seems that occasionally. *Occasionally* Mr. Netherton has been known to drink a bit much. I do *not* believe this has affected his professionalism, I've only met the man once myself, but I have heard from very trustworthy sources that he has never missed a court date! Still I thought you should be alerted as it's something you and I may notice while we are all working together."

Eliot takes a sip, sets the cup back on its saucer, and places the saucer on the table. "What else?"

"Well." She drains her cup, then refills. She takes the prong, picks up a sugar cube, and plops it in. Another cube. Another. Another. "Not to be redundant but, yes, it is very auspicious that we have working with us not only a white Protestant man but a *local* white Protestant man." She stirs the sugar rapidly, the cup clinking. "So you must understand, Mr. Netherton *is* a man of the South. Which means—"

"Another gentleman for you."

Diana stares at Bertie in the doorway, then looks at the clock. *"Already?"*

Laughing and talking as Mr. Rubin and the guest approach.

"Hello!"

Diana and Eliot stand to greet the newcomer, a white man with premature hair thinning and twinkling, mischievous blue eyes.

"Mr. Netherton! You're early!"

"I hope that is not a problem."

"I should think your promptness would be a perfect start to a fine working relationship," her father asserts, smiling broadly. "Diana, I *thought* I recognized the name. We have a cousin in common! You attorneys are distant relations."

"By marriage only, Mr. Rubin. A fourth cousin on my side and, I believe, a third on yours."

"Well!" says Diana. And after another moment, "Well!" Her smile outrageously huge.

"And this," Sol continues, "is Eliot Campbell." The younger men shake.

"I am told your alma mater is Lincoln University, Mr. Campbell."

"It is."

"Appears to have some reputation. A colored university with graduates arguing cases before the Supreme Court. And shaking up our South!"

"Mr. Marshall is a fine lawyer!" Diana chimes in.

"Oh I wager Mr. Marshall will one day *sit* on the Supreme Court, if there ever will be such a time and place for a Negro. Do you agree, Mr. Campbell?"

"I wouldn't be surprised."

"And I do believe it was his work that integrated your own law school, was it not? The University of Maryland?"

Eliot nods. *"Murray versus Pearson."*

"Mr. Netherton, please forgive me, I have not even shaken your hand yet."

"Well you seemed rather caught off guard by my punctuality, Miss Rubin. I hope you two weren't speaking ill of me when I walked in."

"Of course not!"

"Bertie, maybe you can refresh the coffeepot. And Mr. Netherton, may I offer you anything stronger?"

"Thank you, Mr. Rubin, but I would very much be obliged for just a tall glass of ice water. This kind of heat in April does not bode well for the coming season." Bertie takes the pot and exits.

"Mr. Campbell also declined my offer," remarks Sol. "A roomful of tee-totaling attorneys."

Steven Netherton chuckles, his smile intimating some private joke. "I have been called a lot of things, Mr. Rubin, but 'teetotaling'? *That* is a first."

"I am so sorry about my rudeness before, Mr. Netherton," Diana apologizes when the attorneys are alone. "I was just confused, not expecting you until two."

"Think nothing of it. I am pleased to make your acquaintance, Miss Rubin. Or shall I say 'Cousin Diana.'"

"We have met before, Mr. Netherton, though you may not recall. The Larsons' Christmas party."

"Oh. Parties! When the cocktails are complimentary, who remembers *any*thing later. Now! If we all agree to carry through with this diabolical plan, we shall be spending a *lot* of time together in the coming weeks so I suggest we hereby dispense with the formalities. May I call you 'Eliot'?"

"Please."

"And I'm Diana!"

"And I'm Steven. Plain old Steven, an old man of nearly thirty who did *not* get my law degree at twenty-five and make the bar on my first try like my esteemed colleagues in this room."

"Eliot passed at twenty-three!"

"Nearly twenty-four. My birthday's late."

"And *you*, Steven, are being modest. You have already built a reputable career, the courage to take on so many cases other lawyers wouldn't touch."

"Yes, Diana was just expounding on our good fortune that you are considering being part of our team."

"Eliot and I have our passion and drive, and you bring your experience. I imagine we will have much to learn from you."

Steven, who had been glancing between the two of them with a detached amusement, now laughs heartily. "Well! I don't remember playing instructor to anyone since I taught my younger brother how to mix wine and beer without bringing it back up." He snaps open his briefcase, taking out a file. Bertie enters, setting the ice water in front of him and replacing the coffeepot. "Then let this unstoppable legal team get right down to the business of freeing those fast little pickaninnies!"

"More petits fours?" asks Bertie, holding up the near empty dish. Diana stares at her agape, then turns to Eliot, who replies.

"No thank you."

The maid turns to the white man.

"Oh none for me. Trying to keep the weight down!" as he pats his faintly round tummy. Bertie leaves. Steven peruses a newspaper clipping. "Now. Between what Diana told me over the phone and according to the *Red Bank Sentinel,* our local bulletin of record, the incident occurred on Thursday the 31st of March, two weeks ago today, and the boys were given their disposition orders on—" He has looked up and is surprised to see the others staring at him. "Yes?"

"Steven!" Diana laughs. Now Steven stares. "'*Pickaninnies*'?"

Steven appears confused, then turns to Eliot. "Well what do *you* call them?"

"Eliot." Diana takes a breath. "Steven Netherton is a man of the South. As such, there are certain words. They may seem insensitive to you, but down here. They are often regarded, by *some,* as neutral—"

"I would ask that you *not* speak for me, Diana."

"Steven, you must see from Eliot's point of view—"

"I am a lawyer. I believe after practicing law in the state of Georgia for three years I have at least earned the right to defend myself in a drawing room conversation."

"Look," says Eliot.

"What's wrong with 'pickaninny'? Pickaninnies are cute little darkies."

"*Steven—*"

"Oh can it, Diana, I did not just emerge from a cave. I *know* the preferred term is 'colored.' No, *knee-grow.* The nicest word I grew up saying was 'Nigra,' which will be the same with the appellate judges we are to face in the capital, and *believe me* the good people of Atlanta will not be so welcoming given the entire state of Georgia has been indicted by the international press, the constituency demanding those uppity little boys *stay* locked up at *least* until adulthood. And they *are* the constituency, Georgia appellate judges *are* elected, and if they want to get *re*-elected they very well may find it expedient to appease the cracker masses. If I'm going to be a part of this, I will not be made to feel uncomfortable every time I open my mouth in a private colloquy with the two of you. I *could* train myself to say what's proper in Mr. Campbell's presence, but quite frankly we don't have time for that and, more to the point, those little boys don't have time for that. If either of you are disturbed by my manner of expression, please speak now and I will gladly leave. Go find yourself a Northern white liberal attorney, yes, we'll see how far *that* gets you. With the sensationalism of this case, we will undoubtedly be called upon to make statements to the press. The men and women who'll stand outside the courtroom waiting for those accounts, or who will read about them in the paper the next day. I know all those white folks, if not personally then let's say we are all of a kindred spirit, and I can guarantee you they will *not* be impressed if I start putting on airs, speaking in all the Yankee-sanctioned vernacular, and neither will our panel of judges who are merely a J.D. removed from the horde. And perhaps I should reiterate here, Cousin Diana, that you and I are kin *only* through marriage. Make no mistake: my lineage is one hundred percent Protestant. And the men of the appellate court we need to persuade and I are of like blood and like minds and you may as well know now that, for the most part, I agree with them. Our common grievances regarding all the changes suddenly being thrust upon our states. I am *very* conflicted on the subject of school integration, and I am categorically opposed to miscegenation. But to send children *this* small to the youth penal colony. Well it's absurd. Esteemed fellow members of our potential legal team, I would submit that I, if any of us, would have the trust of those judges, enough that they may actually also come round to seeing the absurdity of it all. But! Whether or not those judges see my name on the briefs. Up to you." And with one long, luxurious swallow Steven downs the ice water, then sets the glass on the table. Diana looks to Eliot. Her hand clutches her knee, white knuckles.

Eliot gazes at Steven's empty glass, then looks up at him. "I want to petition for a *habeas*."

Steven stares at Eliot, stunned. Then throws his head back, guffawing. "Did I say Mr. Marshall would be the first Negro to sit on our Supreme Court? I do believe I am in the presence of one who will give him a run for his money!"

"I say this because—"

"Oh you needn't explain, Mr. Campbell. *Eliot.* I follow your line of thinking to the letter and I am all for it. The Great Writ! Why not?" He laughs again, incredulous and merry.

"Then?" They turn to Diana, who continues: "We are a team?"

Eliot studies Steven, considering it all one last time. Then nods. Steven's eyes remain fixed on Eliot. "It appears to have thus been decided, Cousin Diana."

Diana jumps up, clapping her hands. "Now," Steven begins, flipping through the pages in the file as Bertie appears behind him in the entry, "the way the judge will see it is niggers gotta know from the start the way to be around white women, which if at all possible is *not* to be around white women. A lesson well learned, but who would expect children so young to understand the proper societal rules yet?"

"More ice water?" Bertie asks.

Steven smiles. "I think I have sufficiently quenched my thirst in that department, thank you. However, I believe I *will* have that coffee after all. And perhaps you might squirt a bit of gin into it?"

9

Eliot gazes at Andi's small law library. He has a vague memory of seeing her running around this morning, pulling out her hair curlers and putting on a girdle (something he never understood in shapely women, let alone one as slim as Andi). After he heard the door close he had given his mother a quick call, catching her before church, and then gotten back under the covers for a couple of hours. When his eyes opened again at 10:38, he already felt tardy about starting his workday and dragged his ass off the mattress. It would be well into the afternoon before Andi returned. The trips he's made South over the past month coupled with her studies have considerably abbreviated their hours together.

He had expected resistance to the *habeas* that would prompt his legal team to appeal to a higher court, so he was rather stunned when the initial motion was granted a little more than a week ago. It's still not entirely clear when the hearing will take place, but he and his partners are hopeful a date will be set in the coming days. Ironically, after his argument to Didi that the accelerated *habeas* process would result in the children's earlier release, he (and his associates, he presumes) is apprehensive about an imminently approaching deadline that might catch them unprepared.

Didi had been right about Diana Rubin. Smart and creative, never shying away from hard work while making it clear to her male partners she would undertake no more of the tedious tasks than they: she was nobody's secretary. Steven Netherton was another matter. As would be expected with a lush, his punctuality when they were introduced at Diana's turned out to be an anomaly. He and Eliot nearly came to blows after a meeting with the children's parents when Steven had arrived tipsy and insisted on sipping a rum and Coke throughout the conference. On the other hand, his work was solid, and he spoke so well to the press in his typical faintly inebriated state that Eliot had declined from suggesting he ever face them sober.

He sits on the couch and snaps open his briefcase. The pages he had photocopied from *The Code of Georgia of 1933,* the most recent volume, pertain to adult crime, but since Max's and Jordan's alleged transgressions have actually been named, the legal team will make use of the Superior Court designations. Regarding "assault," his time in Red Bank has already clarified that there certainly is something to Didi's assertion that locals equate seven-year-old interracial kissing with rape.

CHAPTER 26-14. ASSAULT AND BATTERY.

26-1401. (95 P. C.) DEFINITION OF ASSAULT.—An assault is an attempt to commit a violent injury on the person of another.

26-1404. (98 P. C.) ASSAULT WITH INTENT TO RAPE.—An assault with intent to commit a rape shall be punished by imprisonment at hard labor in the penitentiary for not less than one year nor more than 20 years.

CHAPTER 26-61. LEWDNESS; LEWD HOUSES; DISORDERLY HOUSES; OPIUM JOINTS; AND KEEPING OPEN TIPPLING HOUSES ON THE SABBATH.

26-6101. (381 P. C.) LEWDNESS AND PUBLIC INDECENCY.—Any person who shall be guilty of open lewdness or any notorious act of public indecency tending to debauch the morals shall be guilty of a misdemeanor.

CHAPTER 26-60. SEDUCTION.

26-6001. (378 P. C.) DEFINITION AND PUNISHMENT.—Any person who shall, by persuasion and promises of marriage or other false and fraudulent means, seduce a virtuous unmarried female and induce her to yield to his lustful embraces and allow him to have carnal knowledge of her, shall be punished by imprisonment and labor in the penitentiary for not less than two nor more than 20 years.

He sighs. Even in the warped Dixie viewpoint, how could such child's play be defined as "carnal knowledge"? The charges brought against the little boys are a boldface fiction, and Eliot and his team will now have to contribute to that farce, active participants in the Sisyphean task of proving red is red to men determined to believe it is green.

He's briefly startled by the envelope he had absently tossed into his attaché yesterday, and now opens it. A wedding announcement. He had not been in touch with the bride and groom since their college days, both from rich families, which he deduces provided for them to invite everyone and his brother to their nuptials. He has no intention of paying for a bus to Detroit plus hotel fare to celebrate the marriage of two people he no longer knows, and as for a gift, he wonders if anything within his paltry means could be regarded by the couple as other than well-meaning kitsch. He'd send a card. By rumor, Eliot has heard tell of just about everyone with whom he went to school tying the knot. He's twenty-five, high time to be starting a family himself, yet he doesn't feel ready. Perhaps Andi's right when she condescends to him about his age.

Well who *would* he marry? The four months he had been with her had pretty much set a record in stamina after his handful of fleeting relationships in college and law school. But would she feel embarrassed to call someone so much younger "husband"? When he had brought up the weekend away in Gary, she appeared to have liked the idea, but every time he tried to nail her on a date she seemed to put him off.

Is he ashamed of *her?* In truth, he doesn't know. He would like children someday. He knows little about female biology but is aware she still undergoes a regular menstrual cycle and that would seem to be enough. He tries to imagine bringing her home to meet his family, but finds it impossible to separate his own emotions from the fact that she would likely feel so awkward as to infect everyone with her discomfort.

He realizes he is ravenous. There's little in the fridge and he has a craving, so he grabs his jacket and heads out the door. On the landing below he jumps wildly, jolted by the sudden ferocious barking from the other side of the closed door. The notorious third-floor German shepherd. Eliot can almost *hear* the saliva running from the canine's deranged jowls. Its owner had bizarrely built an eyehole at the dog's level, something Eliot cannot fathom since the dumb mutt must hear and smell all anyway. "German police dogs," he remembers Aunt Beck would call them, and down South he recently had had a brief confrontation with one that clarified for him precisely how justified was the nomenclature. He gallops down the remaining flights, out into the sunshine.

When Eliot was eight and Dwight fourteen, their father brought home a six-week-old collie mix. Eliot made his disinterest decidedly apparent. Dwight on the other hand was instantly enraptured, and he who had been intended to be "the boys' dog," or more generally "the family dog," quickly became "Dwight's dog." The duo would gleefully wrestle all over the living room floor, and some of these playtimes Eliot would glare, on the tip of his tongue *I sure wish I could have Parker to do that with* or *I sincerely hope what happened to Parker never happens to Rex* and Dwight, as if he could read his younger brother's mind, would at once cease the roughhousing and sheepishly race the dog out the back door, his eyes never meeting Eliot's. Dwight had taken Rex with him to Lewis, and when the animal died two years ago, his companion was so distraught their mother made a special trip, for the second time in her life comforting a son grieving the loss of a pet.

At the market he buys eggs, Swiss cheese, peppers, onions. He considers picking up a box of dried pasta and the makings of a good sauce, yet knows the likelihood of her letting him stay for dinner on Sunday, a crucial studying day, is slim to none. He pays for the omelet ingredients.

Eliot leisurely strolls back to the apartment in the spring warmth. He had ordered a dozen roses for his mother which arrived yesterday. When she returns from church, Dwight will undoubtedly be there to hand her his own bouquet in person. She doesn't especially like going out to restaurants so he would bring dinner to warm up, and Dwight is not a bad cook.

Eliot squints into the sun. It isn't just about Parker, his differences with his brother. Why was it that growing up Dwight only seemed to strike up friendships with white boys? And the white-boy thing continued into adulthood, secrets Eliot had gleaned with absolutely no interest in knowing the details of.

"Just catch the key!"

A man's head sticks out of a top-floor window of Andi's building. At the entrance stands a young white woman with short brown hair, staring up at him.

"But what if I miss it?" Her face all worry.

Now the man notices Eliot. "Hey! You mind lettin my girlfriend in?" Eliot has seen him before. Obese, blondish, mid-thirties. The girl looks twenty tops.

"Sure." Eliot puts his key into the door. She walks in.

"Thanks."

Eliot nods.

"I'm not his girlfriend. I don't know why he said that." She glances up the stairs. "I just came to look at the apartment. I called the landlord from the phone booth, said he's on his way over but if I wanted the guy could let me in till he gets here." She leans in, whispering. "I think he's getting evicted."

Eliot looks up, as if he could see the sixth floor from the first.

"You like living here?"

"I don't. Live here. My girlfriend does." And he inadvertently shudders, having rarely uttered "my girfriend" before and never with respect to Andi.

"Oh."

"Her apartment's nice."

"Yeah?"

"I guess they're all alike. The neighborhood's nice."

"Oh. Okay. Thanks." And she starts to run up the stairs.

"Hey!"

She turns back around.

"You okay?"

She smiles. "Thanks. Yeah, I'm not fool enough to go in there alone with my 'boyfriend.' But the landlord said there's a nice view from the corridor window up there." Nice view of the empty lot across the street, Eliot thinks, but she is up the stairs before he can say anything else. He waits, listening to be certain she doesn't knock on the nut's door after all. The outside door opens, and he recognizes the brawny sandy-haired Scottish immigrant landlord. The man remembers Eliot and greets him before heading up, and when Eliot hears a murmuring of the Scot's and the young woman's voices, he lets go of his concern for the girl and ascends the steps himself. He wonders whether the rumor regarding the sixth-floor tenant's eviction may be true, though it would seem odd given his compliance in opening his home to a potential replacement. Eliot had seen him once or twice racing out the building as he and Andi were coming in. She seemed to find him a civil if not especially friendly neighbor.

AARGH GARR RARR RARR

Eliot had completely forgotten about the fleabag. He jumps backwards, grabbing the banister to prevent serious injury, but the carton of eggs falls out of the bag. He snatches up the mess and, blinded by fury and humiliation, runs up the last flight to the apartment, slamming the door behind him.

There's one slice of bread left: the heel. He sautés an open-faced cheese sandwich with the vegetables. Seated on the couch with his plate, he eats his breakfast while skimming through Andi's *Indianapolis Recorder*, the Negro paper. Afterward he takes out his briefcase to catch up on some divorce cases. As he opens the first file, it hits him. When that white girl, that stranger, had walked past, when the landlord walked past, the Terrorist of the Third Floor hadn't uttered a sound. What the hell?

Two hours later, a key jiggles in the lock. Eliot, sitting on the floor, his back against the couch and papers spread all over the coffee table, looks up to see her. Aqua skirt suit and matching gloves and pillbox hat. She carries a paper bag of groceries, a loaf of bread sticking from the top.

"How was it?"

Andi kicks off her shoes. "Good music. I was touched by the sermon. I should go more often."

"Than once a year."

"If they kept track, they probably wouldn't know what to make of me. They expect the tourists who only show their faces Easter Sunday, but I'm the oddball who makes her annual appearance on Mother's Day."

The prospect of him accompanying her was never raised. Despite the fact that he hadn't criticized her decision to attend services, it seemed she'd intuitively sussed out his lack of interest. He didn't know if he could be properly called atheist or even agnostic, given that he just didn't think much about the existence of a Supreme Being nor lack thereof. When he was eighteen "under God" was added to the Pledge of Allegiance and P.L. 84-140 enacted, demanding "In God We Trust" be printed on all U.S. currency, but by then law school had long been in his sights, all *his* trust placed in the U.S. Constitution wherein the word "God" never appears.

She smiles, leaning over to him, and they kiss. "You had breakfast?" Walking into the kitchen.

"Yeah."

"Then I guess this'll be lunch." She glances at the clock. "Jesus! Damn Methodist Negroes hold you all day."

"The Baptists I grew up with weren't any better."

"We can eat in a half-hour, then I kick you out." She starts taking the groceries, including a dozen eggs, out of the bag.

"If I'm going, I'd rather you fed my libido than my belly."

"Hmm."

"Seriously. I can always pick up something on the street to satisfy my stomach."

"Your libido too."

He smiles.

After sex, she lies on her back and tells him about her tenth-grade basketball try-outs back in Iowa, one of the few school systems in the nation supporting girls in the sport, even to the tune of a celebrated high school state tournament. She and another colored girl had made the most free throws as well as garnered the most points in active play, yet neither was chosen for the team. Hoping to prevent a scene, she had said nothing to her mother but the other girl, Gail, told *her* mother, who called Andi's mother, and the next afternoon both Negro mothers were sitting with their daughters in the locker room office opposite the phys ed teacher slash coach. The stocky woman with short auburn hair asserted that while points are a quantitative assessment of a player's performance, other considerations were also factored in: attitude, being a team player. The mothers were well aware that these abstractions were a pile of crap, but the principal defended the coach. The mothers' tempers seethed for a year until the girls were juniors and their mothers and about one hundred other Negro parents, some who had only sons, showed up for girls' basketball tryouts. The principal was summoned, as if this sudden interest by adults in their children was tantamount to some hostile revolutionary coup. He entered the gym, his face a stunning shade of crimson, and ultimately strong-armed the coach into putting both Negro girls on the team. But the victory was bittersweet. Despite their stalwart athleticism, the coach screamed at Andi and Gail constantly, often forcing them to do extra laps, sometimes benching them for entire games even when such a decision sabotaged the victory. The frustrated white girls fluctuated in targeting their anger, at the coach one day, at their Negro teammates the next. The pressure to perform and to perform extraordinarily under such high-stress circumstances finally defeated Andi, and she refused to try out her senior year, she and her mother having a screaming match over the pronouncement. The principal threatened to fire the coach if her antics led to another losing season, and Gail wound up traveling with the team to win the state tournament. Andi did not even attend the games as a fan, had looked at the team's picture in the local paper without comment, each beaming player holding a trophy, Gail grinning third from the right.

It was not until graduation, when the shocker of the ceremony was a black girl's citation as most valuable girl athlete—Gail, of course, the one who had *not* quit—that Andi could feel her hands shaking, and when the seemingly endless closing exercises finally reached their conclusion, and while all the other students were tossing their caps into the air, she had sprinted to the bathroom and sat in the corner alone, bawling for a half-hour straight.

While there must have been a few, Andi can't recall offhand a single other significant disagreement with her mother. It has only been since she died two years ago that Andi had begun these annual church visitations as a small tribute to the woman who had given her life and nurtured it, and who had never missed a Sunday service throughout the year.

It was a gift. These sensitive insights into her history Andi does not freely impart, and Eliot is unspeakably grateful to be the recipient of such a bestowal, the astonishing privilege of intimacy. Those states where schools were integrated at the time of his own upbringing (in the case of Andi's Iowa, since 1868 after a Negro man took his struggle to enroll his daughter in the white public school, the *only* school, to the Iowa Supreme Court)—it all felt like a foreign country to him. In Indianapolis, the fluctuations seemed schizoid. Once elementary schools were segregated but high schools integrated; then in 1922 Crispus Attucks High was built to segregate secondary Negro students (coinciding chronologically with a number of Klan members influential in local politics); then the 1949 desegregation on paper, which changed little in fact (in part because the discrimination practices keeping Negro teachers out of white schools meant that the Attucks faculty was phenomenal—master's degrees, doctorates, attorneys—so why would a parent want their child to be transferred to the less impressive white institutions?); then in 1955 Attucks became the first Indianapolis basketball team to take the state championship, and by then its persistent crushing of other city schools led many whites to *complain* that Negroes were segregating themselves—that it wasn't fair that black students (meaning talented athletes) were abandoning the schools in their own neighborhoods to attend Attucks—while other whites still had, and have, their hand in redistricting toward the continuance of racial separation. This twentieth-century history of his adopted city, coupled with the stories Andi has shared over these months regarding her own integrated educational experience, has only made him feel exceedingly fortunate to have graduated from his own all-Negro school. A few weeks ago, she'd mentioned being harshly admonished by a teacher for suggesting that George Washington Carver ranked with Edison, Whitney, and Bell.

Her generosity is especially notable in the presence of one so stingy in a like regard. Though he has never exactly lied on the matter, Eliot is certain she assumes he is an only child since none of the few family stories he has shared have included Dwight, which took some doing on his part.

"Did you call your mother?"

He nods. "I'll pay you back the long-distance. Just let me know—"

"Don't worry about it. So who's cooking today? Her or your dad?"

He smiles. "When I was little and my father was off from the porters one Mother's Day, he tried to cook and I tried to help him. They were the toughest pork chops we ever had in our lives."

They laugh, then Eliot's stomach growls.

"Uh-oh! Sounds like libido was the wrong choice." She tugs on his ear, then gets out of bed and goes to the dresser, humming as she slips on her pants. He doesn't quite understand where the sound came from. He's not really hungry since breakfast wasn't more than three hours ago. But lunch would be an excuse to stay.

"Aren't you cooking anyway?"

"Not for you."

"Isn't it just as easy to cook for two as for one?"

She gives him a crooked smile. "My mama used to say, 'Nothin beats a fail but a try.'" She shrugs. "Probably just make a peanut butter sandwich. I've gotta study."

"I like peanut butter. What's the song?"

She stops humming, thinks. Then laughs.

"'Sometimes I Feel Like a Motherless Child.' Swear it was subconscious, I wasn't begging for sympathy."

"Sounds pretty."

"Thanks. You're still evicted, buster." She walks out of the room, resuming her humming. Buster.

Eliot, dressed, walks into the living room and sits on the couch, putting on his socks. Andi stands in the kitchen holding a carrot in her mouth as she spreads peanut butter across a slice.

"I can make you a sandwich to take with you."

He snorts. "To go."

"What?"

"Nothing."

He stands and walks to the kitchen doorway. "So what about Gary?"

She looks at him, talking around the carrot as if it were a cigar. "What about it?"

He stares.

"*How?* With you going South every other week."

He nods as if this explains everything, goes back to the couch and rapidly starts putting on a shoe.

"What's wrong?"

"Nothing."

"Eliot."

"Maybe I just hate walking by that damn dog downstairs."

She laughs gently, carefully. "I guess I've gotten used to it. Hardly even notice it anymore." She bites the carrot.

"You know it's a racist dog."

She stops chewing. "What?"

"That mongrel. It only barks at colored people."

"No it doesn't."

"Have you ever seen it around white people?"

"Of course."

"When?"

She frowns. "Well I can't think of a *specific* instance, but—"

"*I* saw your landlord walk by that thing today. Not a peep."

"So? I'm sure Kyle's been in the apartment now and then, the dog knows him. I've only walked past the door."

"Did you know the big guy upstairs is moving out?"

"Pete? No. *Really?*"

"And this girl comes to look at the apartment today, says she thinks he's getting evicted. Stranger, never been here before, this white girl walks right by the third floor. Nothin."

Andi agape.

"Do you even *know* the owner of that monster?"

"*Yes.* I see him at the mail sometimes. *And* the crazy dog. The two of them moved here from Boston, the guy was born there. He apologized, soon after he adopted the dog five years ago he got the job here, moved here, it always goes nuts with strangers he said, he apologized—"

Eliot stares at Andi, then begins throwing his papers back into his briefcase. She looks up toward her ceiling.

"Pete's been here forever. Before me."

Eliot, stooping at the coffee table, looks up at her.

"That's all you have to say?"

"*What?*"

"I *said* your neighbor has a racist dog."

"I *heard* you, Eliot, I don't care about the damn dog! I just hope Pete isn't getting evicted."

"You don't even like him!"

"Doesn't mean I wanna see him tossed out into the street! He just. He never appears to have a job."

"Well he seemed just fine today showing his apartment to young girls, I wouldn't worry too much about Pete. What do you mean, you don't care if your neighbor trained a dog to attack Negroes?"

"I didn't say that!"

"You said—"

"He's my neighbor! I'm *not* gonna just make a big presumption like that, turn this building into a race riot on a maybe!"

His pupils fixed on her.

"You have no proof!" She had not meant to screech.

"No." Snapping shut the briefcase. "Some white woman, some stranger off the street it lets walk by, fine. You, some *Negress* it's known most of its life, ready to tear you limb from limb. All circumstantial."

The term infuriates her, as he knew it would, but she takes a breath, bites hard on the vegetable, chews slowly. "Alright, you've proven your case. You have successfully made me feel completely depressed about my own home."

Their eyes like knives.

"You might understand my hesitation in jumping to conclusions based on *your* assessment, since you think *all* white people are out to get us. The *enemy*."

The dog starts going wild. Eliot races out Andi's door, flying down the stairs. He returns smirking in triumph. "Huh, I didn't know the couple across the hall from Rin Tin Tin were also colored."

She sits, her back to him, taking a harsh bite of her sandwich.

"I can't believe you're defending him."

She swerves harshly around. *"I'm not defending him! I said you're right. Okay? You're right!"*

He allows a moment to pass, then speaks quietly. "I don't believe all white people are the enemy."

Now she smirks.

"I don't believe Diana Rubin is the enemy."

A momentary fear flashing in her eyes. It had not been his intention to put it there. Her constant reminders of their age difference. Buster. Her deflection of Gary. He had never known for certain she would care enough to be jealous.

"I'm considering dropping the case."

She nearly falls off her chair.

"Of course I'll find a replacement first, I'm not just gonna." His breaths coming deep. "Well she's barely out of school! Competent, she's *very* competent but. And *him!* Cracker and a *lush,* I just think. The little boys, I just think—"

"You were granted the *habeas* only a week ago and now you're going to drop everything?"

"Yes, now, before it's too late. I just need to—"

"All you've talked about is wanting a civil rights case."

"*Yes!* but not. I think maybe I needed a *little* more practice before being thrown into something like. They're babies! *We're* babies, none of us is *thirty* yet! I wouldn't want us. If *I* was the client, I wouldn't want—"

"So you're just gonna walk out on those little boys."

"Are you *listening?* I'm trying *not* to! I'm trying to think of *them,* not myself. If it was about my damn ego, *sure* I'd keep it. The publicity? Nice little entry on my CV!"

"Who're you gonna replace yourself with."

He looks away. "Whoever takes it, I'll." He swallows. "I'll brief them, we've put a lot of work in, I'll make sure they—"

"*Who,* Eliot?"

"I don't know! *Winston!* He has the experience."

"Oh after begging him all these months for something besides divorce, something *important*—"

"You act like I don't take the divorce work seriously! I take the divorce work seriously!"

"I'm not talking about the divorce work, Eliot, I'm talking about Winston entrusting you with a very delicate case, Winston having the faith that you *are* ready and now you're gonna tell him, 'No thanks, do it yourself.'"

"Beau could! Or Will!"

"You know they're overbooked."

"Why *would* Winston give me a case like this? Why would he make those little boys my training, my *learning* experience?"

"Every case is different, you know that. Every case is a learning experience."

"Oh which of your esteemed professors are you quoting now."

"Think about why he gave this to you, Eliot. It's a *juvenile* case, civil law, he wants you to cut your teeth on a court case, an *important* court case, but one where the consequences are less dire than in a Superior Court."

"Please tell those little boys set to spend the next decade and a half in the reformatory with embittered *big* boys and vicious guards that this case is less dire."

"Well if you can't handle this, what do you think the likelihood is of Winston assigning you to a jury trial anytime soon."

"I know. I *know*, I can't think about that. I've gotta. I've just gotta think about those little boys, I need to—"

"Would you rather Winston gave you a capital case? You wouldn't be the first lawyer fresh out of school holding a man's life in his hands before some cracker judge and jury."

His eyes narrow. "Wait till it happens to you."

"If you think I'm saying it's easy, you misunderstand me." Lost appetite, she stands and throws out the remaining sandwich, then leans against the sink to face him. "What I'm saying is unfortunately you can only gain experience *through* experience."

"I feel like an impostor, Andi! Every time I talk to their parents, every time I talk to the *boys*—"

"Eliot, it's okay to be scared."

"No. It's okay for Max's mother and Jordan's mother to be scared, for those children to be scared, because in the end it's all gonna boil down to the formidable team of a boozer bigot, a college girl, and a divorce lawyer with barely nineteen months' experience terrified out of his mind."

His heart thumping. He'd made a terrible mistake. Law school. On better days he imagines the future, when this is all behind him. But in those fantasies he doesn't dare look back on the outcome for Jordan and Max. "Optimism," he remembers Diana saying.

"Okay, Eliot. But then really be honest with yourself. Are you afraid for the children? Or are you afraid for your own failure?"

"It's the same thing, Andi!"

"Not quite."

He swings open the outside door, slamming it behind himself. Races down the steps, deliberately stomping on the third floor. To his surprise, there is no response. He goes right up to the door, stooping to stick his pupil into the eyehole. A blur.

How could she ask such a question? And how *could* he separate his feelings about his own limitations from how these would play out in Max's and Jordan's fate? On the drive back from Georgia two days ago, he had stopped outside Memphis to fill his tank. Then a police car pulled into the station. An officer and a German shepherd got out, and the pooch seemed to take no notice of the white service attendant, nor the white family in the station wagon, but had gone wild at the sight of Eliot. He had stood frozen. He'd heard rumors of such things, dogs trained to attack Negroes, but he had never seen it before, and given the recent changes that were threatening the Great White Dixie Way, he wondered just how these animals might be utilized in the very near future. After a month of stepping off sidewalks for white women and trying to avoid looking whites in the eye and holding his bladder long past comfort level till he found a colored bathroom, his own Jim Crow upbringing multiplied exponentially, after all that it took a confrontation at a service station with a white supremacist canine to finally bring home to him Deep South reality, and how two small children became tangled in its enigmatic web.

As he hits the second-floor landing, the outside door now visible below, he stops short. Just inside by the entrance stands a middle-aged white man Eliot has never seen before, sporting a healthy gray head of hair and beard. His mailbox door is open, and he peruses the envelopes in his left hand. In his right he holds a leash connected to a German shepherd. Eliot takes in the tableau a second before the dog looks up to see him and goes insane, its spine-tingling gnarl all too familiar, teeth gnashing, a desperate frenzied attempt to snap the cord and fly to Eliot's jugular. But it is almost as if Eliot had seen this coming, and he regards this part of the picture with a strange calm. It is rather the next moment that causes his legs to buckle, falling to sit on the steps, his hands trembling. The eyes of the beast's master—the Boston Yankee glowering up at Eliot, a violent loathing of the stranger before him, the black trespasser—which eclipses any malevolence on the part of his dog by light-years.

10

Diana sits on a braided throw rug covering a section of the mercifully cool cement floor. Behind her is the coffee table and couch, a living area situated in the middle of the Rubin basement, dubbed the "rec room" by virtue of the ping-pong table off to the side. This space, two floors separating it from the bedrooms so as not to disturb her sleeping parents, the curtains drawn against nosy neighbors, had become the de facto office of Max and Jordan's legal team.

She wears a long white shirt and black stretch pants, her legs spread in a V and between them the index cards she meticulously arranges and a large pink mug of coffee. She jots notes on a new card regarding a recent incident involving little Ginny Dodgson, one of the two alleged victims. Last Wednesday, the first day of the new school year, one of Ginny's classmates sat too close to her and she screamed rape. She appeared to be angry rather than frightened, the event having everything to do with an ongoing feud from the previous year between herself and the culprit, a boy who considered Ginny bossy and, to take her down a peg, occasionally pulled her pigtails. Apparently he had decided to let her know on Day One that this year would be no different than the last, and the frustration of it, undoubtedly coupled with the scrutiny she had been under since the spring, caused her fuse to be short. The teacher was at a loss, called upon not only to quell the confrontation but then to face twenty-three second graders all wanting to know the definition of rape. Ginny the expert jumped in to explain that kissing was rape, which resulted in her nemesis making it clear that he *in no way* raped her, that he raped no one but his mother. As the teacher desperately worked on damage control, the dismissal bell rang. The next day, the boy's parents walked into the classroom wanting to know what the hell went on the day before and what their son was being accused of. Diana had relayed the anecdote to her partners, and they had all held their stomachs, the ache of laughter, a welcome release after their long hot mostly humorless summer. The episode had not been raised among them since, but it had come back to her at this very late hour, wondering how these misunderstandings by *all* the children might be capitalized upon tomorrow: The Hearing. She looks up at Eliot.

He sits at the desk in a low lit corner beyond the couch, writing on a legal pad. His coffee mug is navy. She observes his concentration, the dark circles under his eyes. There was a moment way back in May when she had begun to worry, this vague panic in his irises, a distance. He had never said anything to the effect, but after leading them down this *habeas* path, she was terribly afraid he might just quit. Whatever she was reading in him, it all had abruptly vanished, and she had forgotten about it until now.

Their fears that they would suddenly be assigned a fast-approaching hearing date had proven absurdly groundless: with officials of the court vacating sultry Georgia for more pleasant summer climes, the scheduling of the date had been repeatedly postponed. Given the controversial nature of the case and the publicity it had generated, the defense team suspected the delays were also related to some closed-door meetings between the governor and the court, and thus the hearing to address an incident that had occurred on March 31st, was disposed by Judge Sawyer on April 6th, and granted a *habeas* on April 29th was at last set for 9 a.m. Wednesday, September 14th—ten hours from now. The attorneys had relaxed into their routine and seen the children regularly, each visit ending either with the boys crying to come home or, even more heartbreaking, fighting their tears in an effort to be brave. What exactly was happening to two innocent children in the unprotected company of bigger boys, and in the unprotected company of reformatory guards, the lawyers shuddered to think, but the staggering guilt would newly energize the legal trio in its pursuits. Over the oppressive summer, their output of hundreds of pages would seem to render them, if anything, *overly* ready. They narrowed their thoughts to a thirty-seven-page brief which was now in the hands of Judge Farn. It had been decided, to the relief of the defenders, that the *other* county Superior Court adjudicator would preside over the case, and thus the little boys' fate would not once again be in the hands of Sawyer. It would be Farn's first juvenile case, and the defense team held out hope that this bode well, intimating a more open mind.

One evening in the grocery store, purchasing TV dinners and snacks in anticipation of a long night, Diana had tapped Steven next to her in line, and had winked at Eliot near the door. (The latter had given them the money for his frozen meat and potatoes since his presence in the queue would only hold things up, as every single white customer would be served before he could pay for his own provisions.) Diana's subtle signals had called attention to the fact that Judge Farn was two places ahead in line. He seemed formidably stern, a fiftyish white-haired slim man, setting his collards and lima beans on the conveyor belt. At that moment he looked up. Recognizing Steven, he broke into a guarded smile. "Afternoon, Colonel."

"Afternoon, Judge." The polite acknowledgment had been the extent of the conversation. Steven and Diana later explained to Eliot the tradition in the local legal world of Georgian lawyers being referred to as "colonel," something rumored to have started during the War Between the States, or by some other historical state militia, when lawyers were conscripted as colonels.

Beyond the predictable commendations for the children (well liked in school and in church, never before in trouble with the law) and their parents (reputable hard-working Negroes), the brief went radically further in challenging the juvenile justice system with its presumption of paternalism as a substitute for due process: the lack of a court record (citing *Griffin v. Illinois,* 351 US 12 [1956]); the children being subject to self-incrimination (citing the Fifth Amendment); the parents being informed of the hearing only the day before, allowing them no time to secure a lawyer (general right to counsel in *Uveges v. Pennsylvania,* 335 US 437 [1948], and the incompetence of children to waive their right to counsel in *Williams v. Huff,* 142 F.2d 91 [1944]); the case wholly resting upon unsworn hearsay testimony as the juvenile alleged victim would never be subject to cross-examination (the Sixth Amendment); the confessions by the children having been coerced by psychological means (*Watts v. Indiana,* 338 US 49 [1949]) and very likely physical means (*Brown v. Mississippi,* 297 US 278 [1936]); the conflict of interest given that the probation officer was simultaneously charged with making the case against the children while serving as the boys' only legal advocate (the tenets of our entire American adversarial system of justice, stipulating two opposing sides in order to, presumably, arrive at the truth).

The document concluded with an emphasis on the boys' extreme youth, too immature to begin to understand the infractions they had been accused of, and contrasted a return to their well-respected parents with the ominous ramifications of a prolonged stint in the reformatory. The oral presentation tomorrow would reflect all these particulars, while the lawyers had made a decision to avoid mention of the crosses locals had burned in the children's families' yards, of the Klan visitation to the boys. After much discussion, they had agreed to conduct their argument as if Max and Jordan were white children, tabooing anything racial that might incite the judge or his constituency.

Eliot had sought Winston's advice on the brief, Diana and Didi had stayed in close contact with their law school professor. They were assured by those with decades of experience that they had done the work and their case was strong, that now it depended on 1) driving it all home in the oral argument and 2) the judge. And yet in their hours together this last day, Eliot, Diana, and Steven had all experienced the nagging sense of a missing piece, the link that would reach a Georgia adjudicator, to have him reconsider the conventional wisdom. Steven had made the suggestion, since their discourse had begun to go around in circles, that they break for a couple of hours to clear their heads and rendezvous back at "headquarters," as Steven referred to Diana's basement, at nine. Following the brief recess, Eliot had gently rapped on Diana's door at 8:55. They waited fifteen minutes for Steven before going downstairs, assuming their senior partner would show up sooner or later.

He and Diana had bounced around ideas for two hours, and for the last forty-five minutes had ceased the jabber to work independently. Now from their subterranean lair, they hear the drawing room grandfather clock striking twelve tolls. The official marking of *the day of* has not caused Eliot to break in his writing.

"Just in case," she begins. There is no response from across the room. "Just in case, we should be prepared to go this alone. The two of us."

"What do you think I'm doing." He still doesn't look up from his task, remarkably successful at keeping the testiness out of his tone if not out of his words.

"He'll come. I believe he—Well, midnight, you know that's still quite early for Steven."

"You or me?" He is looking at her now.

She turns away. "I don't know, Eliot. Men around here call elderly colored men 'boys' and forty-year-old women 'girls,' so I honestly can't say which of us stands a better chance." She moves a card from one column to another. "Maybe you. If Farn walks in the courtroom with suspicion in his heart, at least he wouldn't see you as a traitor to the South."

"No, he'd just think all niggers stick together." He stares at his pad a few moments. "We'll split it."

"But who will go second?"

Eliot's pencil tapping the desk.

"I think it should be you. The lasting impression. I honestly worry he'll see me as some little girl."

"Maybe, but—"

"Eliot, we could just as soon toss a coin. Instead I'm going to make an executive decision. You'll conclude. Okay?"

He considers, then nods. She turns back to her cards. "In the future, I want children. I was thinking. I can speak from the viewpoint of a potential mother."

"That's good. And maybe a compelling reason you should go last."

"We'll see." Eliot turns back to his notes.

"I couldn't believe." She bites her lip. "Do you think we were too hard on him yesterday?"

"Are you *kidding?* He was plastered in court!"

"We were just turning in the brief, we weren't really '*in* court.' And I don't think the clerk knew, no one could tell but you and me. Steven *does* know how to hold his liquor."

He gives her a look.

"He *does!*"

"I could smell the alcohol from five feet away, Diana, and he was right up in that clerk's face muttering some damn Steven joke the guy clearly did not find funny."

"Well! It happened, it was over and done with. What good did it do for us to chew him out all the way to the reformatory?"

Silence.

"I *know!* I just— He's *not here!* We *need* him! He seemed fine today but how can anyone guess what's going through the mind of Steven Netherton. Perhaps he was acting civil just to fool us." She sighs. "I don't even want to think about the expressions on Claudette and Minnie's faces if we walk in without him tomorrow. They'll look at us, then they'll look at their little boys, *God!* He *never* comes to court drunk! He has his failings but they never affect his work, that's what I was told. I never would have suggested him if—" She picks up a card and moves it to another column. Picks it up and moves it to another. Picks it up and moves it to another, snatches it and rips it in two. "Dammit!"

"It's not your fault." His voice is soft. She turns, gazing at him.

"It's a whole new world, isn't it? Just this summer, how many African countries won their independence? And Woolworth's! I wish I could have been in Greensboro when they served their first Negro. And have you read *To Kill a Mockingbird*?"

"Not yet."

"You must! I went out and got it as soon as it hit the bookstores, I'll loan you my copy. Everything is changing!"

"Too quickly, your neighbors would say."

"But we don't want to be *completely* left behind."

He looks at his notes, momentarily considering before quietly replying. "You know that's not the direction we decided to go in."

"I know, I know." She sighs again. "Everyone around here would happily lag into the twenty-first century, *Segregation Forever*. No colored child sitting next to a white in kindergarten, no colored man buried next to a white in the graveyard." Eliot goes back to writing. "To celebrate V-E Day we had an all-school party. The pictures from the death camps hadn't come out yet, but the rumors. While the sixth graders all sat at our desks with our pieces of cake, Clay Hummer to my right just stared at me. 'What did the krauts have for dessert?'" Eliot is looking at her. "I knew not to engage him, I looked away, but he answered anyway. 'Cherries Jew-bilee, fresh out of the oven.'"

"What made you think of that?"

She swallows. "The picture in the *Sentinel,* those picketers outside the courthouse, the fury in their faces. *They're* not afraid to raise the race issue. The judge's constituency. They think of me as an outsider nearly as much as you." She turns to him. "His mind is already made up. It has been, from the beginning. Right?"

"Optimism, Diana."

She nods. "Optimism, optimism."

"Your parents were born here. You said."

"They had siblings in Warsaw. Cousins. Most of them starved to death in the ghettos before anyone ever thought up the word 'extermination.' Well. Anyone since Andrew Jackson." She opens a new package of index cards. "When my father was twenty he was threatened to be lynched. Did I tell you?"

"No."

"Writing all these letters to the local paper in support of the Scottsboro boys. They *were* boys! The youngest just twelve, did you know?"

Eliot nods.

"And tried like adults. No gynecological evidence of rape, then one of the two so-called victims recanting, admitting she made the whole thing up. It was as if the more truth my father reported, the angrier his towns-folk got. He sent money to the International Labor Defense. I'm not sure what they found more revolting, him supporting Negroes or him providing funds for their Communist legal team, but one day he received a package in the mail with no return address. A noose." She gazes at a mosquito dancing around the ceiling light. "Eliot. I never thought until now. If the judge might remember my father from those days, hold it against us."

"I think with all the screaming protests we would have heard about it if it were in the forefront of the collective memory." He goes back to his writing.

"Oh! Didi came across some letter to the editor Farn wrote back in 1940 in favor of *Chambers against Florida*. If that's true, if he *did* support the decision to reverse those *adult* Negroes' convictions because of coerced confessions, well. There's a little encouragement. Have you seen Didi lately?"

"Mm hm." The affirmative, not interrupting his work.

"She'll be there tomorrow of course, but she really should be facing the judge with us, she was the team before there *was* a team. I wanted her to stay here with me, but I guess she preferred taking a room in the colored hotel, being closer to the parents. I know she's been *such* a comfort to them, someone with knowledge of the law keeping them constantly abreast." Diana picks up a pad and makes a few notes. "You're *both* so good with the boys. They always look so happy when you arrive, Jordan just runs when he sees you and Didi coming! Even Max, reticent as he can be, I see the hope in his eyes when you two walk in. They even get along with old Steven." She chuckles sadly. Eliot looks up at her. "They sure never run to me. I guess they're terrified now to come close to *any*thing white and female."

"We have to get through this, Diana."

She turns to him. "If he doesn't come I'll call him, even if it's goddamn three a.m. I'll tell him to be at the courthouse by seven so we can brief him on what we've talked about tonight. If he doesn't show, or shows too late. Or shows up *drunk*. Well obviously we'll have to send him home."

"Really?"

She nods warily. "Steven can be very persuasive but he also has to be alert, tomorrow the judge can and will cut off and challenge his precious soliloquy at any time. Tipsy he can manage that dance, but if he walks in loaded." She shakes her head. "Maybe we can use it to our advantage. Having to dismiss an—*incapacitated* member of the team just before we make our oral argument could prove very useful in getting us an appeal. Perhaps it's all part of Steven's brilliant plan that he just failed to mention to us." She looks at her partner. "But seriously? I believe he *will* show. Tonight."

"Since neither of us has ever worked with him before this case, I guess the answer to that mystery only time will tell."

"And when he *does* come walking down those steps and into this room. There will be relief, but maybe also a bit of disappointment. All the eloquent words we're scribbling now that no one will ever hear."

Eliot sits back in his chair. "I know."

"Because no matter what you and I write, it will matter a thousand times more coming out of the mouth of a local white man."

"I *know*."

"What *are* your eloquent words, Eliot?"

"Give me another half-hour."

"Can I have a hint?"

He looks at her.

"Alright, alright!" He goes back to his pad. "It's just. Like you said. They don't like things to move too quickly down here. I *know!* you're the one who keeps reminding *me*, no race. I only. It's late, we're exhausted. Who knows what crazy ideas might be popping into our heads."

"Diana, I have been coming *down here* for five months, you and I and Mr. Jack Daniel's have been practically glued together the last eight days. I hope by now you know me enough to trust I'm not here to make any speeches about the lunacy of Southern customs and institutions, I'm here to do the best I can to save those little boys, *whatever it takes*."

The outside door above them opens: footsteps through the house. Then slowly, carefully calculating each step, he makes his descent. When he has reached flat ground in one piece, his face easily betraying his relief, he squints through his bloodshot eyes to properly focus on his partners' images. Grins.

"So! Ya'all waited up for me."

Eliot turns back to his work, finishing off at the bottom of one page and slamming onto the top of the next. The room quickly filling with the smell of alcohol and tobacco.

"Very thoughtful of you to leave the front door open."

"After the *last* time you came pounding completely tight in the a.m., waking up my family and half the neighborhood."

The elder attorney laughs. "I never understood 'tight' as a synonym for 'drunk.' Because right now I can't imagine feeling any more loose and mellow." He takes a seat on the couch. "Well, team! Are we ready?"

"Steven. Eliot and I were not even certain you'd be showing up. We were deciding what to do in case you—"

"Oh I'll be there. I'm all prepared." He pulls out of his hip pocket several folded sheets of paper, balls them up and basketball-shoots them toward the desk. The wad impressively lands on Eliot's writing hand, rebounding onto the page he's composing.

"Did I mention what a shock I had the other day? That picture in the *Sentinel*—well I've never been caught at such a bad angle. There I was between a coon and a Jewess, and I declare I appeared to have the largest nose!"

"Have you thought of this case as nothing but a joke, Steven? From the start?"

"Oh Diana, are you about to take me to task again? Because those lectures are really beginning to bore me. And what kind of hostess are you? You haven't even offered me a drink."

"I'd *like* to offer you a punch in the nose."

"So would Invisible Man over there, but right now he'd rather play the Noble Savage." He sits back smiling. "Well, my esteemed Hebrew colleague, aren't you even curious as to what I've written regarding our adorable little black predators and their second-grade sluts?"

"Every word. I'll read it when Eliot's done. Meanwhile I *will* offer you a *cup of coffee*. Would you like that?"

"I've never seen you in pants so snug, Diana. What a pleasant change from your usual schoolmarm look! Wear them tomorrow. If we have nothing else in our favor, the outlined curve of your little round bottom might be somewhat inspiring for the judge."

Diana opens her mouth, reconsiders, closes it. She gathers her mug and Eliot's before ascending the stairs, muttering something unintelligible.

"Have you read it? *Invisible Man.* By one of your people. Extraordinary. Or perhaps *Native Son*?"

"Yes." Eliot does not look up from Steven's wrinkled papers, moving on to the next sheet. Water is heard running in the kitchen overhead.

"Which?"

"Both."

"Well! Then you can understand why a white man might feel a little bit nervous. I mean it's one thing with the wild masses, but these notions of violence coming from the darkie intelligentsia. Oh what did that gentleman from the so-called Harlem Renaissance call it? The Niggerati!" and Steven throws his head back laughing.

"It's good." Eliot has finished reading and is looking at his partner. "Different than we planned but. It might sway him." He gently touches the text Steven had penned. "They're the words of a white man, Diana and I couldn't step in. Are you going to be there to say them?"

Steven turns to him. "I am no Cyrano de Berge—de Berge—" He giggles. "I'm afraid I am one drink past the limit of French pronunciation! What I mean to say: If I create the words, they are for *me* to utter."

Diana descends the steps, carrying a tray holding three mugs of coffee and a pitcher of ice water. She sets the tray on the table in front of the couch where Steven sits, takes Eliot's mug to his desk, puts hers on the floor near her cards, then picks up the pitcher and flings its full contents into Steven's face. He stands sputtering, his mouth and eyes flung open.

"Sober yet? Colonel?"

In that moment he recovers his composure, turning forty-five degrees so as to easily look from Diana on his right to Eliot on his far left and, in fact, suddenly does appear to be sober.

"Your honor.

"Between the brief you have before you and the oral arguments we have presented, we have quite comprehensively examined our concerns vis-à-vis our current system of juvenile justice, which in the *parens patriae* mode has abandoned children's constitutional rights in favor of a benevolent, paternal role to be played by the court. We have weighed the consequences of this state of affairs, challenging the presumption that the reformatory is a place where wayward youth may be rehabilitated, given that evidence has universally demonstrated reform school is merely a juvenile penal institution, complete with all the unspeakable perils and alarming recidivist rates.

"In maintaining this legal path, however, we have tiptoed around the elephant in the room: the sensationalism engendered by this case. We have been speaking of Maxwell Williams and of Jordan Price, as is appropriate, yet we all know the issue is bigger than these two boys, *far* bigger. The incident has caused great embarrassment for Red Bank, and though I know, Judge Farn, you would never let such factors as the picketers outside influence the judgment of this court, I do feel we would be remiss not to directly address the basic facts—that two little black boys kissed two little white girls—so that you may make a most informed decision on what is best to be done about it.

"To try to put it all into perspective, let us briefly again go back to that notorious date, Thursday the 31st of March, or perhaps more accurately for most of us, the next morning, April Fool's Day, when we opened our papers and were shocked. And confused. How to deal with such a transgression when the children are so very young. We, a community of white folks and colored folks who have gotten along well for generations, but of course the international media was not interested in that. No, it took one dispute that has divided us to bring in all this worldwide attention, and I would wager we would not *be* so divided were it not for the egging on of the busybody outsider press.

"I don't believe those incensed citizens are out there on the steps because of this isolated event. No, this episode which sent a chill down their spines was the latest in a string of setbacks: the bus trouble in Montgomery, these recent disturbances in Greensboro. And most frightening for all of us: the forced desegregation of our schools. What happened with Max Williams, Jordan Price, Ginny Dodgson, and Leecy Pike confirmed all our worst fears about where school integration might lead.

"But was the incident with these children *really* an abomination? Or a blessing in disguise? Something happened, yes, something undeniably unfortunate happened, this kissing game had ramifications unforeseen by any of its players as they engaged in it, but oh have little Max and little Jordan been thoroughly upbraided for it since. You may have heard something of the surprise visit to the children in custody from our local Klan, and I am certain I needn't tell you that little black children in Georgia may not know what kissing is but they definitely know what the Klan is. Yes, Max and Jordan may not have understood that what happened with those little white girls was wrong when they did it, but they surely do now! Anyone who has looked into their terrified little eyes will know they will never ever make that mistake again. And as far as an example being made, the boys have already provided it: Negro mothers and fathers have learned it is *never* too early to tell your little boys that they are forbidden to *ever* kiss, or anything *else,* a little white girl. Problem solved.

"But what about retribution? Isn't society owed justice in the matter? The outraged cries of our neighbors are an assertion to the world that we have had enough, that we will not allow this manipulation of the South from the outside to go one step further. But I as a Southern man would like to show the meddlers, whether they be from Europe or New York, that we are not the vicious barbarians they claim us to be, brutes out to destroy innocent children. We are decent law-abiders who defend our customs, and who handle the breach of those customs in a just and dignified manner befitting Southern gentility. We are not here as reactionaries to the judgment of intruder fools, we are not stubborn crackers but reasonable men. And whether the world likes it or not, we *can* solve our own problems.

"Because I must say I worry. If these little boys, on top of everything else they've been through, are asked to spend their entire childhood in a dubious environment away from the loving guidance of family, I *do* fear a different lesson will be learned by them, and by all our colored folks: Go to the outside for justice.

"So let me return to the salient question: *Have* the boys learned their lesson? *Are* they reformed? It would be hard for you to fathom as their testimony today may have seemed tentative in the intimidating atmosphere of this courtroom, but if you were ever to talk to them one-on-one you would find that little Jordan is the chatterbox. It was very clear to me from the beginning how sorry he was, he said as much over and over, but then there was nine-year-old Max. The quiet one. Frankly I often just didn't quite know what he was thinking. The addendum we submitted this morning to the brief. It is testimony from our visit with the boys on Monday, our last time to speak with them before this hearing. I decided to take Max aside. He sighed, I would wager because he assumed he would be interrogated for the thousandth time regarding what happened that awful day when he and Jordan played with Ginny Dodgson and Leecy Pike. Instead I simply asked him if he was ashamed of what he had done. He stared at me. Again I asked, 'Are you ashamed?' and again he did not reply. I asked a third time, and a fourth, now beginning to become exasperated. 'I am not playing a game with you, Max, you must answer the question! Are you ashamed? Are you ashamed? Are you ashamed?' and finally little Max spoke, very quietly: 'What *ashame* mean, Mr. Netherton?' 'Well, Max, shame is an awful sad feeling that you did something terribly wrong, and you're very sorry and you won't ever do it again, but not just because you got into trouble. It's because you know you were bad, and it hurts to know you were bad, it hurts so much that you can't ever ever erase that you were bad, the best you can do is just try and be better.' And little Max stared at me, and slowly the shine came to his eyes, and as he tried hard not to cry he said, 'I didn't know that word before, Mr. Netherton. I kept looking for that word but I couldn't find it, I kept looking for that word, that word's in my heart.' I believe, your honor, *that* is about as rehabilitated as rehabilitated gets. I'd hate to see Max and Jordan spending the rest of their tender years in the reformatory, two small boys raised away from their parents, in the company of robbers and rapists and a murderer or two, these innocent children growing into their manhood and becoming increasingly bitter with what life has dealt them for a mistake they made before they were old enough to begin to comprehend it. I would hate to see that shame, which would have stayed with them and guided them on the right path, well I'd just hate to see that shame knocked right out of their hearts."

At which point Steven drops to sit on the couch. "And that, lady and gentleman of the rec room, is that." He picks up his cup and saucer, sips. "Mmm. Now *this* is good coffee, Diana, you will make your future husband proud. If only it had just a shot of" and Steven is dead asleep, sitting up.

His partners stare at him, looking incredibly balanced and poised holding his cup, The Thinker at tea. Gradually Diana finds her voice. "We were trying to avoid it but." She turns to Eliot, dazed. "It might work." She turns back to Steven, hypnotized. Then snaps out of it. "That might do it! We'll have to drag his dumb ass off that couch early, you'll dress him, I'll coffee him up but." She beams in the direction of her conscious colleague. "We might win. Eliot! We might win!" She throws blank index cards into the air and laughs. "Oh my God, playing fire with cracker fire! You said, 'Whatever it takes,' well!" She shakes her head at the irony. Then realizes in the dimness she has not been able to see clearly across the room to the desk. "Eliot?"

"Yes. Optimism," she hears quietly from the corner, and it is because she knows it is *not* sarcasm, that Eliot *does* believe now they stand half a chance for the boys' release and his tone is nevertheless so devastatingly hollow and wretched that she will never be able to bring herself to utter the word again.

II

"Oh I made every mistake in the book first year out. *Rape* cases?" He whistles. "I remember this one. College girl trying to press charges against her professor. Her *white* professor, I gotta hand it to her, she had *cojones*! Clearly forced himself on her but this was some tenured guy, published about a hundred books, Reconstruction and Scottsboro and a crack at fiction, his own slave narrative, you get the idea. And the girl *loves* his class, obviously infatuated with the guy, now how the hell'm I supposed to prove it wasn't consensual? That Professor Progressive is really a skunk? It didn't help that the girl lived with a man, of the *Caucasian* persuasion no less, so in the first place she plainly wasn't a virgin, and in the second I don't care if we *are* 'up North,' those sorts of choices don't exactly sit well with the general populace. *So* I enter into the *voir dire*. First error: I'm so thrilled to get a Negro on the jury, *any* Negro, I don't stop to investigate where my only rep of the race is coming from. What do you think he thought of a promiscuous colored girl and her white boyfriend? That she's willing to give it away to any Anglo-Saxon dick, that's what! Another beginner's misstep: selecting some sculptor beatnik. You'd think given who I was trying to prosecute I should have known better than to make any assumptions about white liberals or perceived liberals. Guy turned out to be the biggest cracker of all!"

Eliot, at his desk, wonders if Beau Greene plans to stand in his doorway the rest of the day, lest the junior attorney misconstrue the reasons for his legal team's losing the children's case as related to anything other than his own rookie *naïveté*. A redundant exercise: on the long drive back after Wednesday's decision, Eliot had fluctuated between blaming himself for what he had or hadn't said in court and blaming himself for failing to quit early on and finding a more experienced replacement. And of course his haughty, uncompromising drive toward the *habeas,* refusing to even entertain the notion of an appeal. Steven's oral arguments were at least as effective as they had been in Diana's basement, and with what appeared to be minimal deliberation on the part of the judge over his lunch hour, it had all gone exactly as Didi Wilcox had predicted. And now seeming worse than before. How long would it take for an appeal? Had they gone that route in the first place, they could have already been through it, with a panel of comparably impartial judges in Atlanta having no connection whatsoever to Red Bank. And her suggestion to come to the judge after a year to ask for a modification of the disposition orders. Had the clock started over on that? Five and a half months the boys had already moldered behind those walls, and Eliot feels a little ill now, remembering the look of eager expectation on their faces in the courtroom, with their families near and the attorneys they had come to trust. Though it had been explained to them numerous times that the hearing *might* result in their release, their innocent child's hope interpreted *might* as *will*, and thus the boys were not merely disappointed but stunned to find out at the end of the day they would be returning to the reformatory. And Eliot was suddenly aware of how much he had also accepted that the children would be eating supper with their families that very evening, feeling stupidly jolted back to the miserable reality of what he as attorney, while not presuming, certainly should have been emotionally as well as strategically prepared for: Judge Farn's concurrence with Sawyer's decision that Max and Jordan stay put until twenty-one, near Eliot's age now.

Immediately after the 2:30 announcement, the legal team set aside its personal devastation to offer the parents assurances regarding appeal, and Eliot was on the road by three. He had gotten back to Indianapolis Thursday evening and lain on his bed, staring at the ceiling. Around nine his phone began ringing and he ignored it, as he did when it rang again at 9:30, and at 10, finally lifting the receiver off its hook.

Andi had stared at him when he walked in this morning. It was presumed he would have had post-mortem discussions with his legal team after the hearing Wednesday, then driven Thursday and Friday, not getting back to Indianapolis till this evening after work, and thus not back to the office until Monday. His former girlfriend, or whatever she had been, offered her quiet, heartfelt sympathies, which he graciously and gratefully accepted. They had had little to say to one another in recent months, having not met outside of work since the Mother's Day episode. Their relationship, never officially named, had been equally ambiguous in its breakup, although both parties seemed to have come to recognize that it was over. He wondered, in the way she had trouble looking at him when she had told him how sorry she was this morning, if she felt that he may hold it against her, her insistence that he stay with the case when he had wished to replace himself with someone more seasoned. But if there were blame there, he laid it on no one but himself. After her commiseration, she had told him Winston wanted to see him. Eliot had sighed.

In his boss's office he reported the details of the hearing, and then conveyed the preliminary thoughts he and his colleagues had bandied about regarding appeal. Winston offered quite copious praise of his young recruit for his work on the case before handing him the file on a local police brutality incident that had materialized while he was down South. This afternoon he would meet the man in the hospital. As Eliot returned to his desk, Will Mitchell had stopped him to express his condolences and to assure him that in his absence Winston could not stop talking about how impressed he was with the junior member of his staff. While gratified by all the support from his colleagues, Eliot was still haunted by flashbacks of the children's proceeding, and it was only when he opened the file and was flabbergasted by the graphic photos of his pulverized client-to-be that he was catapulted, for the moment anyway, out of Red Bank, Georgia, and into the present.

He had just put the paperwork back into its folder and pulled out an ongoing accident claim when Beau had come to his doorway to offer his own brand of solace.

"Well of course the prof walked. Though I believe things were shaken up at that school a bit, don't think any Negro co-eds found themselves alone with Professor Broadminded again. As for that poor gal—"

"Beau? Thanks, but I really need to get back to this fender bender."

"Oh. Oh sure." Beau turns around to the reception desk. "Andi. Coffee?" And as if he is suddenly so busy that he cannot wait even the minute for her to pour and bring the cup, Beau enters his office and shuts the door, meaning she will have to knock. As soon as she is seated at her desk again, her phone rings.

"Winston Douglas." At that moment Eliot happens to glance up, and sees she is staring at him. "For you."

From the look on her face, he knows who it is.

"Thanks, Andi." He gets up to close his door just before the ring.

"Hey."

"Hey. Am I speaking to the crazy attorney who rushed right out after speaking to the clients' parents *without saying goodbye* lest he dare miss a day at the home office?"

He smiles. "Sorry. How are you?"

"How are *you?*"

"I've been better." He rolls his pencil between his pointer and thumb. "Well I think 'I told you so' is in order." He laughs and is caught unawares by the subtle cry that escapes.

"It could have been a lot worse."

He takes his thumbnail and scratches at the writing on the pencil.

"You were right. With the *habeas* there's finally a record of procedure. *Now* we can properly appeal."

"And how many years do you think that will take."

"Maybe not as long as you think. The outside pressure has not died down, it's still a cause célèbre. We're lucky there."

A memory flashes before him of a day when the four attorneys came to the reformatory, and walking the corridor toward the visitors' space they passed a room where two teenage colored boys were painting the walls under the suspicious eye of a seated guard. Returning from the meeting and chatting, the lawyers were abruptly rendered silent as they inadvertently glanced into the room again, one of the boys having taken off his uniform shirt in the heat which exposed numerous lashes on his lower back and apparently continuing down to his buttocks.

"I kept trying to call last night but you didn't pick up."

He swallows and hopes she cannot hear. "Where are you now?"

"Chicago. Remember? I flew back. The only way to go, honey."

He grins. "Your high-powered position."

"Yes, civil rights law is certainly the jet set. And listen. The next time you're in my town I'm taking you out to Lutz's for chocolate éclairs."

"Maybe we should hold off celebrating until we see if we get the appeal."

"What about celebrating my job?"

He sets his pencil down. "You're right. But then that would be *my* treat."

"You're right."

"I could have taken you out while we were down South but that would have compromised the agreement."

"It would have. And if you'd've escorted me into some backwoods hogs 'n' dogs place in Red Bank, Georgia, and called that 'celebrating,' you would have been looking for another lawyer to slip into cheap hotels with."

The agreement was that no one in Red Bank, including Didi's old friend

Diana (Didi had felt a bit guilty about that), would know that Didi and Eliot had been sleeping together. There had been faint signs suggesting such a destiny in the instances when they found themselves alone, the smiles, glances, but nothing had been consummated, or even a word suggesting such until Independence Day. They had an appointment with the court clerk scheduled for the 5th, so Eliot had gotten in his car on the 3rd and arrived the afternoon of the 4th. He had met with Diana, Steven, and Didi for dinner, and afterward he and Didi had returned to the modest colored hotel. Eliot's room was on the second floor, Didi's on the third and top. As they were about to enter the lobby they heard the first bang, and realized everyone in the building was on the roof watching the fireworks. They went up, enjoying them together, and when the show was over they both walked down the steps to the third floor. Eliot never made it back to the second until morning. At the time it had been eight weeks since the blowup with Andi, and while this start with Didi had left him with some vague feelings of guilt, there was no regret. Rather he had felt a bit relieved, as if this finally marked some sort of closure that he and Andi had not been able to find themselves.

Naturally there was suspicion. Diana would look at them sideways. Steven made up a song: "Young Coon Lawyers in Love," and after he had crooned it enough to commit it to collective memory, he would simply hum it whenever Didi joined their threesome. But she was expert at deflecting, and occasionally in the astonishing feat of shutting Steven up. "Oh yes of *course*, me and Eliot. Well I thought about making it me and *you*, Steven, but then I noticed how your hands and feet are disproportionately small compared to the rest of you and I thought that does not bode well."

And Andi. With her it had gone beyond suspicion. Didi called often, and Eliot's laughter on the phone, Andi had apparently deduced, indicated a place much deeper than colleague repartee.

A month ago Didi had interviewed with a Negro firm having a mission not unlike that of Winston Douglas, though considerably larger given its Chi-town locale. Two weeks later her future supervisor called her in Red Bank to offer the position, and given that her commitment to the children's case had been in part what had impressed her associates-to-be, they were more than tolerant in allowing her to see the work through. Her first day would be Monday.

"Ready for it?"

"I think so. Though I imagine I *will* miss my old life as a cop."

Eliot guffaws, then covers his mouth. He doesn't want Andi to hear. Well why *shouldn't* she hear? By sparing her feelings, if she does in fact have any left for him, he only confuses the fact that things are over, so he lets the laugh out, then gags himself again: Beau might complain. As loud as his own pompous ass could be, the older attorney could get surly about other noise around the office.

Since things started, Eliot had spent two weekends in Chicago. He had been surprised and somewhat disappointed to find out Didi's apartment was no bigger than Andi's, or his own, then was ashamed. Was he with Didi just because she was a rich girl? Well, in a manner of speaking, yes. She was smart, she was educated, she was using law as a serious conduit for civil rights. And she was *fun*. She could do all that vital work without being uptight, a trait he and Andi were both sorely lacking. He remembers this particular quality from the privileged students in college and law school. The *ease* of the wealthy.

And of course there was the other matter, the fuse that had lit all the drama that last awful afternoon: Andi's umpteenth rejection of his offer of a weekend together in Gary. He could only interpret her reticence to fully be with him, her younger lover, as a lack of seriousness in them as a couple.

On the third Saturday in August, as they both lay on her bed naked, Didi told Eliot to go through her closet and bureau and come up with an outfit for her. She promised that whatever he'd pick out, she'd wear. He had been granted the power, then, to dress her in the silliest or the most provocative fashion, but rather than enjoy the fun of it, he was seized by a paralyzing terror that he might make a mortal miscalculation. If he chose wrong, would she secretly resent him for it? He cowered and put together an ensemble he had already seen her wear. "You have impeccable taste." Next she picked up the underthings he had singled out and burst out laughing. "What?" he had cried. "What!" How could he have gone wrong *there*? Underwear is underwear! But she put on everything and refused to tell him what she had found so amusing. At a deli lunch, the guilt of cheating overcame him, and he confessed to having dressed her (except for the underclothes) as he had already seen her dress herself. His shame over the matter only enhanced her merriment. He asked again about the underwear error, but began to see the more he pressed the issue, the more she delighted in his exasperation, so finally he gave up.

The permission to search through her drawers, and the drawers *in* her drawers, had not made Eliot feel closer to Didi. It was very possible he was the first person she had ever asked to dress her, and it was equally possible he was the hundredth. Sharing was not satisfying, not a gift, as it had been with Andi, because Didi seemed to have no problem expounding upon intimacies with strangers, or at any rate what others would regard as intimacies. She knew little about Eliot, and he was certain she would have been open to hearing him if he had wished to talk, but since he didn't volunteer the information she didn't pry. It was all part of Didi's composure, her smiling effortlessness which meant their relationship was not *fraught*.

They were strolling along Lake Michigan that afternoon, sometimes hand in hand, none of the clandestine measures that he and Andi had taken in Indianapolis, or that he and Didi had taken in Red Bank for that matter, and this public display of affection soothed for the moment his nagging curiosity about what Didi did in her spare time when he was not around, and with whom. A seagull alighted in front of them as Eliot had asked Didi if she had considered going into law enforcement.

She frowned. "A *lady cop*? No! Why?"

From her reaction he was tentative about continuing, but there was no turning back now. "When I went through your closet, I saw those handcuffs." She had had to double over holding her stomach, the ache of her laughter.

Now he hears the phone ringing in the office next to him, followed by Beau's voice loud through the wall: "*Monday?* Now it's *Monday?*"

"I better go," Eliot says, realizing he'd been on the line a good seven minutes.

"Alright, but first I have a little story for you. A priest, a rabbi, and a cracker judge are all sent to meet St. Peter."

He is grinning in anticipation when there's a knock.

"Come in."

"Sorry to bother you. Beau needs some documents in triplicate right away and I'm out of carbon paper. Do you have any?" Andi is businesslike, unsmiling.

Her kindness this morning about the children's case had not only been a comfort to him but also a relief to see something close to tenderness in her eyes. Their relationship had deteriorated to this chilly remoteness, more Andi's doing than his, especially after he had begun feeling pretty gratified by his new Windy City distraction and just wished for bygones to be bygones back home.

And right now he has no time for dramatics, his mouth watering for Didi's punch line. He indicates the file cabinet. "Go ahead and check." As she does, he grins into the receiver. "Okay, give it to me." Eliot is fussily organized, and alphabetically a file is marked CARBON PAPER. Andi turns to him again. "I'm sorry."

He looks at her.

"There's only two sheets left."

He waves dismissively, implying for her to take them both and leave, his mind focused on following the details of the gag. Suddenly he explodes in laughter. "No, I *had*n't heard it. Our jokes are *clean* in Indianapolis!" Andi leaves, quietly shutting the door behind her.

Late morning, Eliot walks to the conference room and finds Andi using her fifteen-minute break to read a chapter in one of her law books. She doesn't look up. He notices how tired she seems, dark circles. Returning with the cup of coffee he poured, he overhears Beau in Winston's office, bellowing about some judge who put them off for months and now suddenly has set the hearing for just after the weekend.

Eliot works through lunch. He had inadvertently left his door cracked, and hears Will go out to ask Andi something. The conversation begins professionally, but then Will must have said something funny because Andi starts laughing. It continues, the murmur of their voices and her giggling and it begins to irritate Eliot, distracting him from his work. The two have developed a rather flirty relationship as of late, or perhaps it was always there but has come to flower since she and Eliot stopped seeing each other. Andi and this married man, father of five. None of Eliot's business but what *is* his business is the fact that he can't concentrate because of their frivolousness. He could just close the door but he likes Will and doesn't want to antagonize him, nor does he want Andi to mistake the gesture as some act of jealousy on his part, so he waits out their talk which goes on a good twelve minutes. When Will finally returns to his office, Eliot allows about three more minutes, buffer time to prove he is not responding to them, before quietly closing his door.

He leaves for the hospital at one, and at 1:25, five minutes early, he stands outside the room. He tells the white police officer that he is the patient's attorney and is permitted entrance.

The man lying on the bed is motionless but awake. He breathes heavily and even. He is covered in a sheet, his right arm on top of it, everything bandaged from his biceps to his fingertips. A handcuff is locked around the bars at the foot of the bed, the shackle attached to something under the sheet, presumably the patient's ankle. The only visible flesh, his neck and face, is completely black and blue, and there's an awkward shape to his head as if the side of it had been flattened. His nose and lower lip are split open, his left eye swollen completely shut, the blood vessels in his right eye bright and appearing to be on the point of bursting. But something is working behind that eye because the man has managed to fix it on Eliot.

On a chair next to the client sits a thin woman in her late forties, a care-worn face. She stands. "You Mr. Campbell?"

"Yes."

"Sam. This the lawyer." She turns to Eliot. "I'm Petronia Daughtery, and this is my son Samuel Daughtery."

"How do you do, Mrs. Daughtery." According to the file this would be the proper address, though there was no clarification of a *Mr.* Daughtery excepting her son. Eliot shakes her hand. "How do you do, Mr. Daughtery."

Samuel Daughtery closes his right eye, holding it for about three seconds.

"He jus acknowledgin you. Usually that means yes. He blink twice fast for no."

"I'm sorry this happened to you, Mr. Daughtery."

Sam Daughtery stares at his attorney.

"May I have a few moments alone with your son?"

"He jus blinked twice."

Eliot had missed it, having turned to the mother.

"Would you prefer if your mother stayed?"

Sam Daughtery holds his right eye closed.

"Alright. Please sit down, Mrs. Daughtery." Eliot sees another chair on the other side of the room and walks over to pick it up for himself. He tries to think what his first question will be since the intended "What happened?" is obviously not going to work.

"Mr. Daughtery. Do you understand the charges that have been brought against you? Possession of a concealed weapon? Racketeering? Resisting arrest, I am not yet asking whether you committed any of these crimes, only, do you understand the charges?"

Sam Daughtery holds his right eye closed.

"As your attorney I am here to help you as best I can. I can only do that if you are honest with me. Anything I don't know that comes out later can only hurt us. Do you understand?"

Sam Daughtery holds his right eye closed.

"At the time of your arrest, were you in possession of a gun?"

Sam Daughtery blinks twice.

"At the time of your arrest, were you in possession of betting slips pertaining to the numbers racket?"

Sam Daughtery blinks twice.

"At the time of your arrest, did you resist the officers in any way?"

Sam Daughtery looks at his mother.

"I think he needs you to be more specific."

"Did you hit the officers?"

Sam Daughtery blinks twice.

"Kick the officers?"

Sam Daughtery blinks twice.

"Strike the officers in any way?"

Sam Daughtery blinks twice.

"So you did not resist the officers."

Sam Daughtery looks at his mother.

"People who was nearby tole me he said, 'I know my rights! I get to talk to a lawyer!'" She raises her volume when she quotes her son, her eyes burning into the officer standing at the door. The officer faces away. If he hears her, he makes no indication of it.

"Is that what you said, Mr. Daughtery?"

Sam Daughtery holds his right eye closed.

"Didn't he have a right to say that?"

"Yes, he had a right to say that. And did they reply?"

Sam Daughtery holds his right eye closed.

"I imagine they said a lot of things, Mr. Daughtery, and we can talk about that in a few days when you have healed a bit. But for now, with a simple yes or no, can you tell me what was their reply when you asked for a lawyer? When you demanded they recognize your rights?"

There is a movement, something slowly sliding under the sheet. With great effort and apparent considerable pain he pulls it out, his left arm, and lifts it, tight and strong, in reply to Eliot's inquiry, the answer the police officers gave him when he asked about his rights: a fist.

It's three by the time Eliot gets back to Winston Douglas. Andi is not at her desk. Then Eliot hears Beau's voice booming from his office, formulating a letter so Andi must be trapped in there taking dictation. Eliot shuts his office door, jotting notes regarding the information he had garnered at the hospital. Around 3:45 he jumps when Beau's door slams open. "Andi! Get in here *now!*"

Eliot had never heard such a belligerent tone from Beau. He hears Andi enter his neighbor's office, then Beau spewing a hysterical tirade wherein such phrases as "dumb secretary" and "dumb office girl" are tossed about liberally. From bits and pieces, Eliot gathers that some simple but crucial error was made and, by virtue of the carbon paper, Andi had triplicated her mistake exponentially. The rant is terrible but brief, or cut short when Andi runs crying out of Beau's office. Eliot had never seen her cry, and he flies out of his own office. Will is already standing there, staring stunned at Beau's open door, and Winston is in the room trying to calm Beau down. Eliot dashes to the bathroom and knocks. "Andi. Andi, are you alright?"

A silence, Andi instantly cutting off her sobs, seeming to have been caught by surprise and thus further humiliated to know that everyone has heard the incident though they would have had to have been in a coma to have missed it. Her voice is small. "Yes." When she emerges several minutes later, she is startled to see Eliot still standing there. Her eyes are red, swollen. "I have to go to the office supply store and buy more carbon paper, we're out."

"I can do it. Do you want me to do it?"

From Beau's office they hear Winston. "No, Beau, I am *not* firing her!"

She is instantly sobbing again. "He kept me here all night! He knew Tuesday and Thursday evenings I had class but he said he had his deadline today, I missed my exam! I flunked my exam! And now the Opal case is moved up to Monday—" She bawls fully a moment, then abruptly suppresses it. "I gotta get to the office supply store before it closes," and she quickly walks out.

Eliot keeps his door open the remainder of the day, his eye on Andi retyping Beau's documents. It's already five and her pile is huge. She has taken no notice of Eliot's attention as she is anxiously focused on not making another blunder. The elevator sounds, and Andi and Eliot look up.

She wears a dazzling red dress, sleeveless and provocatively cut at the neckline, snugly fit to clarify every curve from shoulder to hem, the latter barely concealing the knees. Gold hoops dangling around her wrists, a white hat accessorized with a red sash, red gloves, and four-inch shining red heels. But most striking as she steps toward the entrance to Winston Douglas is something in her eyes, in her closed-mouth smile: confidence. This is what causes Andi, and Eliot in his office, to inadvertently stand.

"May I—" The receptionist does not get the question out. She has never before seen Didi, but now she looks at the visitor staring at Eliot, and at Eliot staring at the visitor, and Andi needs to ask nothing. The two women are standing next to each other, Andi wearing an outfit as drab gray as her mood, and in an instant Eliot finally sees Andi's age, and knows now what Andi had understood all along, why she never really wanted to go to Gary with him, to take that step: the universes that divide them. She sits, resuming her typing, the rat-tat seeming to underscore her despondency.

"What are you—" He too gets stuck mid-question.

"What am I doing here? I don't know. I told that stupid travel agent 'Chicago' and look. She sends me to Indianapolis," all the while striding toward his office as if she had been here a thousand times before. They shut the door and when, after a long period of quiet, a burst of their laughter causes Andi to mistype, she calmly tears out the sheet and replaces it, resigned to be sitting here another long night. When she calls to order her dinner for the third time this week, the man already knows chicken chow mein before she says it.

12

She points her index finger at him. "Tell me what you're thinking."

Lying on her side, torso propped up by elbow, cheek leaning against fist. Their naked bodies covered by the flowery hotel spread. She teases him about his wandering mind. Just a game to her, keep him on his toes.

Plenty of injustice in their American world. That's why she became a lawyer, that's why she had volunteered her time, her *self,* for the little boys. But less consequential concerns that drive those who can afford it to analysis and those who can't to Jesus—she is immune to such trivialities, tossing it all off with a laugh. He has never before met someone who had her priorities so straight, and he tells her this now, *that* was what he had been thinking.

He's surprised to see her smile fade. She rolls over onto her back. "Hmm."

When she'd called this morning, she was dialing him from this hotel room. She'd hoped he would be with her here last night, but of course he never picked up his home phone. So she devised the strategy to show up end-of-day at his office, spending the afternoon exploring Indianapolis. He waits for her to say how boring it all was, but then Didi can make any place an adventure if she sets her mind to it. As an art and architecture enthusiast, she made visits to the Tudor-Gothic Scottish Rite Cathedral, the neoclassical Soldiers & Sailors Monument, the art deco state library, and, since she was in the capital, of course the Parthenon-inspired statehouse. She was charmed to walk the various bridges crossing the canal, and finally made certain to hit Walker Theatre on The Avenue. Afterward, she quickly found the little boutique to purchase the red dress just in time to hop into a cab to the east side, step into his firm promptly at five, and drag him away in case he had any intention of working late to catch up on all those damn divorce cases. In his car to the hotel they were giddy with anticipation, but when she put her key into the door and they entered, glimpsing the charming décor and the beckoning queen-size bed, they'd stopped short. Something was wrong, something vital forgotten. And then without speaking it they knew, and for two hours they sat at the table discussing Max and Jordan's case, what they'd done right and their missteps, not wallowing in guilt but rather evaluating the process as objectively as they could. And when at last the topic felt exhausted for the present, their brains picked over and worn out, *then* they had sex. And then they had sex again.

"Whatever you see, or think you see. I wasn't born into it. Yes, I went to a nice North Carolina Negro college, and I was in the esteemed sorority with all the other light-skinned rich girls. Not exactly maverick thinking on my part. And we felt superior to the dark poor girls and all that, and the boys made us feel superior the way they were always up under us, and some of the dark poor girls made us feel superior with their envy. But of course we knew deep down it was all a ruse." Her eyes on the ceiling fan, her mind far away. "This girl. Renaissance Art, junior year. I'd wondered if her parents were Africans, that's how coal black she was. *Stunning.* Even with our twisted ideas of American beauty, no one could dispute that girl was anything but gorgeous. Transfer student from California, she didn't know anything about me. Turned out she was brilliant as well as beautiful, an international studies major with a four-oh average who took an upper-class overview of Leonardo and Michelangelo and the van Eycks for the hell of it. And once she happened to catch my eye, and I tried to smile, I was embarrassed because I realized I had been staring, I mean she was so striking. And she returned my smile with this look, this. *Contempt.* With one glance she pegged me, a frivolous girl desperate to fit in, and desperate to be thought of as anything but that." Didi makes herself dizzy, her eyes fixed on one blade circling the fan.

He is aware she has given him a gift, perhaps the first ever. *This* story she would not tell just anyone.

"Were you pre-law?"

She laughs. "Those days I wasn't thinking about anything but my MRS degree. Art history." Her eyes lower, toward the framed flowers still life above the desk. "And then Emmett Till. I'd just graduated." She sits up, arms outside the covers hugging her legs. "Those pictures. He was a *kid*, and that. *Thing.* That mutilated, disfigured *thing* that was left after those goddamn bastards were through with him, and suddenly at twenty-two I'm infused with purpose. And my rich daddy pulled some strings and a week later I'm sitting in a Chicago classroom jotting notes on the Magna Carta." She turns to Eliot, his eyes fixed on her. She smiles. "So what's with you and your secretary?"

He stiffens. "What?"

"'*What?*' '*Who?*' The woman who practically fell off her chair when I walked in today. Not that I didn't have my suspicions before. When a receptionist puts you on hold all she says is 'Just a moment,' but I sure have noticed how the tone of 'Just a moment's changed since you and I started screwing."

"I *doubt*—"

"Don't get me wrong, she's always professional. Can't say I knew for sure until this afternoon, the way she looked at me, the way she looked at you. For a prude, you sure seem to have trouble keeping your pants up."

"Yes! You're right, okay? Something happened between us, it's over."

"Not for her."

"Things take time. She's having a rough go of it now." He sighs. "There's this jackass at work—"

"There always is."

"And she's going to school. *Law* school, *and* working full-time. I try to be sympathetic."

Didi gazes at him. "What's her name?"

"Andi." He picks up the room service menu from his night table. "Wanna order in?"

"So what's she interested in? I'd think after her insider look at public interest law she'd be sprinting to a corporation."

He studies the offerings, relieved to see several reasonably priced entrees. "Pretty much going for the same stuff as us." He shrugs. "Says she'd like to work toward legalizing abortion."

"Good for her."

Eliot looks up.

"This old sharecropper woman where I grew up." Didi absently scratches an insect bite on her arm. "Her whole life in mourning after her sharecropper daughter died trying to prevent her eighth child because she and her sharecropper husband and her seven sharecropper kids were already starving." She shakes her head. "Should have been done in a hospital. Safe."

He is quiet.

"What?"

He swallows. "Just for the record. If it happened, you wouldn't be alone. I don't run away from my responsibilities."

"What are you talking about?" The hairs around her face gently blowing with the whipping fan.

"If you became pregnant. I'd marry you."

She stares at him, her mouth agape, then roars in laughter, falling onto her back. "Well! *There's* a comfort."

"What?"

"Eliot! A kid wouldn't change *your* life."

"Of *course*—"

"And which of us is gonna be staying home to raise it while the other continues practicing law? *I* have work to do *too,* you know!" A fly buzzes near her face and she harshly swats it away.

He speaks quietly. "There's that birth control pill."

"Honey, we're just gonna have to keep making do with my diaphragm cuz I don't touch *nothin* the first year the FDA approves it, let somebody else be the guinea pig." She stretches. "Your boss seems like a nice guy. Letting her go home early."

"Who?"

"Andi."

"Oh. Yeah, Beau would have made her work all night, *again.* Winston loves him, or at least feels loyal to him. Beau's been there since the beginning. So he gets mostly free rein, but once in a while he goes too far, has to be pulled back. Never saw him so crazy like today though."

"It must be more than loyalty if Winston's kept him on."

"Yeah, I'm sure he's great at his job, luckily I've never had the pleasure to be assigned to work closely with him." Eliot goes back to the menu. "I don't want to spend the rest of the evening talking about Beau Greene. You want steak or chicken?"

"What did Winston say about the outcome of the case?"

He looks at her, then gazes out the window. "That our arguments were sound. That we'd done our job and it all came down to the judge. But then all I gave him were the legal facts. Not the important stuff."

"What's the important stuff?"

A streetlamp weak, flickering. "The boys. They have no concept. We took Claudette out for a late lunch the afternoon I got there, eight days before the hearing. She said when Sawyer had given the disposition orders, her son clearly heard the judge's words, that they would be sent away until twenty-one, and yet three days later Jordan asked the guards, 'Is it almost time for me to see my mama?'" His eyes lower. "I didn't tell Winston when

Farn announced his decision there had been that momentary silence of disbelief. And then as the guards started dragging Jordan and Max away, the mothers began wailing and the fathers began moaning and Jordan started bawling, screaming for his mother, only now fully comprehending that he was going right back to the reformatory, and Max. The guard leading Max toward the door and he turns around to tell his mother, 'Don't give my fire truck away.' Max, who may be a grown man before he's released, and at the exit he turns again: 'Don't give my scooter away.'"

His steak is well done, hers medium rare. They eat at the table, she in her robe, he in his underwear. Then she calls the front desk, and he's surprised when minutes later a small watermelon is delivered.

"I bought it earlier, asked them to chill it." She eagerly slices the fruit. "Growing up, it was my favorite. And when I came to school in the North, it was the first thing I disowned. Afraid it made me look bumpkin. Pickaninny. Recently I've reclaimed it. Looks like a sweet one." She glances up to find him staring at her, and points her finger. "Tell me what you're thinking."

He looks down. "I can't."

"You must."

His voice cracks. "I was thinking how lucky I am to have found you."

"Yes, you're the luckiest man on earth. Now here's the thing. Am I on the train back to Chicago in the morning or am I staying at your place tomorrow night? Because my budget can withstand two hotel nights, but that's the limit."

"Oh." He looks around, their fleeting lap of luxury. "*I'll* pay."

"You'll pay starting tomorrow night. *Or* we go to your apartment. Unless you're hiding a wife there."

He smiles. "I need to clean it."

"Oh you're such a neat freak! Alright, you get your butt home in the morning to dust your knickknack shelves while I do some more shopping. We'll meet for lunch, then a museum. Your condolence party officially ends tonight, tomorrow begins my gainful-employment celebration so *you'll* be taking *me* to a nice restaurant for dinner, then back to your place. A plan?"

"A plan."

"Okay. Now. Inspired by the watermelon, let's talk about the South."

The main reason she had wanted to get together, besides gratifying their carnality, was to make sure he doesn't give up on the balmy states. It could be discouraging, a case involving innocent children and *still* the forces of evil triumph, but it is only if we continue to fight the good fight that those forces will eventually subside, wither, and die. It will be a long struggle, progress would be slow, but there would be progress. There are school systems six years post-*Brown* that still refuse to integrate, there are poll taxes and fraudulent tests designed to deny Negroes the vote. Much to be done, and they could use every good lawyer out there and she assures him from her observations over the last months that he is a *superb* lawyer, and this embarrasses him. Of course there's also plenty to do above the Cotton Belt, God does she know that. But the atrocities occurring in the Northeast and Midwest ghettos still pale in comparison to the savage collective White Power of Georgia and Alabama and Louisiana and Mississippi.

"Okay, there's my pitch." He looks down, his eyes fixed on the watermelon rind. "What?"

"Did you know Clarence Darrow once bribed a juror?"

She stares. *"Really?"*

"Evidence points that way."

"When?"

"Nineteen twelve. Labor disputes. Two white brothers blew up the *L.A. Times* building. If they were found guilty and it was pretty clear they would be, the AFL feared it would bring down unions in the whole country."

"The McNamara Brothers, I've read of it. People died. Right?"

"Twenty-one. A hundred injured."

She takes this in. Then looks at him. "And Darrow *bribed* a juror?"

"Appears so."

She shakes her head. "God." She considers it again. *"God!"*

"Okay. What if it was a colored man accused of raping a white woman, South Carolina. No physical evidence, no credible circumstantial evidence, every damn person in the courtroom knows he didn't commit the crime, that likely a crime was not committed at all, and still this poor farmer, this father of five sent to the chair. That is if he's lucky enough to make it there before the mob gets him. Same old story, right? But what if an opportunity arose. Slip a few bucks to a juror. What's the ethical choice? Stick to the book and let an innocent man die? Or fudge a little, and possibly save an innocent life. Is respect for the law more important than justice?"

She considers his question, looking for the answer on the table, the walls. "Would you? Tamper?"

He runs his finger through a puddle of water in the rind. Sighs silently.

"Guess I could never bring myself to do it. Some faith ingrained in me, the American court system was designed for justice and, eventually, justice will prevail. Guess that'd be the last words I told my strapped-in trembling innocent client before they flipped the switch."

They put the room service tray outside the door and slide under the sheets. He caresses her most private areas which she has generously shared with him, kissing her from there up through her belly, her breasts, her throat, where her sweat-beaded smiling face awaits him. When it's over they lie on their backs, his arm around her. She looks at him, the picture of tranquillity, his eyelids falling in a distant sleepy fashion, and now he is the one fixated on the turning ceiling fan. She points her finger. "Tell me what you're thinking."

What he is thinking is why in the hell Will found it necessary to take Andi out for an after-work drink tonight. Yes, she had had a hard day, but here was Will, a married man, and Andi in a very vulnerable emotional place. Winston had negotiated, telling stressed Andi to go home and rest, then return at her leisure over the weekend for a few hours to finish up the work. Eliot and Didi were only a few steps behind, but in the elevator Andi and Will only seemed to see each other, appearing like a very attractive couple, she looking easily a decade less than her early forties and he all of his forty-six, her Chinese delivery tucked under her arm for later, and through eyes still moist she looked up at him with her sad smile. He pulled the gate over and, as the door was falling closed, Will had gently, tenderly, touched her upper arm.

Eliot turns to Didi, delicately stroking her breast. "I was thinking I'd better run to Woolworth's in the morning for a new toilet scrubber, my old one's worn out." She slaps his arm and rolls on top of him, both of them laughing, she more easily than he.

13

Eliot flips over the page of his day calendar: Tuesday, October 4th. He has not been to the office during regular hours since Sam Daughtery's trial began Monday a week ago, stopping by only in the evenings after court. In that time he would occasionally find a late-working Beau or Will or Winston. Andi never. But he's here early now, Winston having left a memo yesterday to let him know there would be an all-office meeting at 9 a.m. The boss had promised to keep things brief, plenty of time for Eliot to get to court by eleven, the start time of today's proceedings.

As he scratches notes, he gradually becomes aware of how frequently he has glanced at his telephone. It has remained equally silent when he has been here in the evenings, as has his home number. And Didi knows what his schedule is like these days, at what times she can reach him.

Saturday of their weekend together had even surpassed the high standards set Friday in the hotel. As planned they had met for lunch—she carrying a shopping bag from her morning tasks—but right after she took him to a shoe store. He said his six-month-old wingtips were fine, but she replied they weren't buying, that the game was to select their "dream" shoes no matter how expensive and to walk around the store in them. He said he found window shopping dull and expressed his concern that this would waste the clerk's time, she called him a worrywart and then they were in the store. As the merchandise was segregated by gender they divided, and twenty minutes later she walked up to him wearing four-inch heels, leopard or faux leopard. He told her in his opinion they were exceedingly ugly, that he hoped they *were* faux because killing an animal for the sake of high fashion disgusted him, and at any rate they hardly appeared comfortable given she had hobbled just the thirty steps from the women's side of the store to the men's. She smiled through his little diatribe, then said she agreed on every count but they were the most expensive ladies' shoes in the place and therefore her dream selection. She was not surprised to see he had gone the dull conventional route, wingtips again and moderately priced at that, with all those posh styles staring him in the face. He countered that this was the pair he liked best in terms of fashion, comfort, and, yes, cost, because his dream shoes were those that suited both his aesthetics *and* his wallet. In fact, he'd decided he would purchase them to be ready for when his current pair wore out. Nope, she declared, putting them back into the box, it was a window-shopping game, no buying allowed, prompting the white balding clerk to glare at her as they walked out. They spent the next couple of hours at the Art Association of Indianapolis gazing at paintings mostly by Europeans, sometimes seriously discussing, sometimes whisper-giggling. They went to a diner for a leisurely coffee before she announced she would go off alone to change for dinner. After the evening meal they went back to his place where she surprised him, presenting him with the wingtips. Luckily the same clerk was still there, as she would have felt a little bad giving the commission to someone else. "He snarled when I first walked in, but as he rang up the sale he was beaming. 'Please, come back again!'"

On Sunday they arrived sleepy-eyed at the depot, twenty minutes early for her nine a.m. departure, the only Indy-to-Chicago daily. Her train was delayed, allowing their farewell kissing to drag out a half-hour more. They planned for him to drive to her town the following weekend, though he would've returned crack of dawn Sunday to prepare for the Daughtery trial starting Monday.

But now, sixteen days later, he tries to suppress the needling worry that, since her night at his place, whatever communication had occurred between them had been initiated by him. When he'd brought up the planned Chicago visit she'd sighed and apologized, they would have to postpone as her first week with the firm was outrageously busy and she would probably have to work Saturday. Being in the middle of court the following weekend, the one just past, he couldn't leave town, and activity at her office was again much too hectic for her to consider coming out to him. She sounded tired. If what she said was all true, her caseload and his combined could certainly be a damper on their future time together. But the more nagging concern was what if it wasn't all true. If after such an intense intimate weekend, she was now backing off. He reasons that a new job, her first real job, and a new relationship simultaneously *do* amount to a lot of emotional information for one person to sift through, so while he still calls periodically it is not as often as he'd like, giving her space, and warily he hopes for the best.

Today Sam Daughtery's mother, and likely Sam Daughtery himself, will take the stand. In the couple of weeks before his first jury trial began, Eliot had second-chaired a civil trial under Will in the magnificent Marion

County Courthouse which, Eliot lamented, would soon be demolished to make way for the nondescript modern rectangular City-County Building being erected just behind it. In court with Will, Eliot had participated in a minimal way but was mainly there to learn, and during lunch hours had spent time observing other trials. Still on his first day in court in defense of Mr. Daughtery, Eliot had nervously hesitated to raise objections, and now would legally never be able to bring up those particular points, even in the case of an appeal. To make up for his initial reticence, on the second day he had objected to practically every sentence the prosecutor uttered, only to be nine times out of ten overruled by the judge and thus, he feared, pegged by the jury as a lunatic. He took a deep breath and, by Day Three, had begun to force his mind-set into a certain self-assurance or at least, for the sake of the jury, the outer appearance thereof.

By 8:45 everyone has arrived. Life at Winston Douglas had been mercifully less volatile. Beau, evidently warned by Winston and, Eliot would like to think, shamed by his own outburst, has been cordial to Andi, piling on less work and even thanking her when she brings him his coffee.

Eliot heads to the conference room himself for brew, on the way noticing Will and Andi chattering and laughing at reception. Having not glimpsed her the last week and a half, Eliot is ludicrously surprised and relieved to see she looks exactly the same. After drinks that terrible Friday, she and Will had made a pact to share an end-of-week liquid refreshment every Friday, three thus far. Eliot overhears Will asking her if they can reschedule this week's outing for this evening—family obligations presenting a conflict for the end of the week—and when Eliot comes out of the conference room he is startled when Will asks him if he would like to join them. He surmises Will had assumed he'd heard them planning and thought it would be rude not to include him. Eliot looks at Andi, who is not looking at him, her smiling face fixed on Will. This could mean she does not want him to come as he would be crashing in on their fun, or that she *does* want him to come because she has hope that a spark may still exist between them and thus is afraid to look at him, or that she does *not* want him to come for fear that a spark may still exist between them. Eliot politely declines the offer, explaining he is back in the office every evening after court catching up until seven or eight. "Next time," Will says, and Eliot nods, certain the next time will not come unless Eliot invites himself, which he won't. Now

Andi does turn to smile at him, a different smile from the one she shone at Will, and Eliot believes he detects in her eyes something like gratitude for his begging off. He goes to his office, closing the door for just a minute to settle his breath before the meeting. Finally he admits to himself that he is envious of Andi and Will's friendship. That he wishes to have both Didi as a lover and Andi as a friend, but that's fickleness and unfair. You can't have everything, and at the moment he seems to have nothing.

The meeting takes place in Winston's office. He announces that as of yesterday they had been assigned to help monitor the activities regarding Negro voter registration in a small Southern town. There were a couple of local NAACP officials, but they had asked for legal assistance as the anticipated large turnout would likely result in arrests and possible police violence. The mass gathering has been whispered to happen the penultimate registration day, Monday the 24th, twenty days hence. Winston details the traveling schedule before speaking a bit about the Southern Christian Leadership Conference and its recent offshoot the Student Nonviolent Coordinating Committee. Eliot eagerly waits for an opening to express his interest, but before he has a chance to do so Winston tells them that he has already decided who would be going down South in three weeks: Beau and Eliot. Beau seems to accept this news with perfect composure. By contrast, it is only with gargantuan effort that Eliot's eyes don't pop out of his head, and there appears to be similar strain in the faces of Andi and Will: *Beau and Eliot in close contact for six days?* The meeting ends, and Eliot stands to spend the last half-hour before he has to leave for court in his office, a little work and a little brooding. But after dismissing the others, Winston asks him to stay a few minutes.

"Did I ever tell you I knew Ida B. Wells?" Eliot, concerned that his voice may betray his irritation over the meeting, shakes his head. "Wonderful lady. Spunk! Once during Reconstruction she was traveling on a train. Bought her ticket and sat in the seat she had paid for, but the conductor walked by, telling her since she was colored she had to go back to the smoking car. She refused, which resulted in a little altercation, which resulted in her biting the conductor's hand! Another time. Women's suffrage parade in Washington, she was asked not to march with the others in the Chicago contingent, the *white* ladies, for fear it would offend the Southern onlookers in our nation's capital. The Negro women were slated to bring up the rear. So there stood Miss Wells on the sidelines with the spectators, and weren't they all surprised when the Chicago squad marched by and she jumped right in with em! Nothin they could do."

"Hmm." Eliot hears his boss's laughter while seeing himself in a car next to Beau, the latter driving the automobile as well as the conversation, no doubt a lecture related to the elder's vast experience and the younger's analogous deficiency.

"Of course Miss Wells, *Mrs. Wells-Barnett,* was most known for her tireless efforts toward the criminalization of lynching. I was fresh out of law school when she came to town to speak, The Avenue, the way it *was,*" and Winston gets that look of lament he always does when referring to Indiana Avenue, the once bustling cultural and business center of the black community with Madame C. J. Walker's Theatre at its nucleus, now declined to urban blight. "I was in awe, and I introduced myself. Over the next few months I stayed in touch, came to know her a bit, or, more importantly, she came to know *me,* enough that when a certain lynching transpired in Montana, two teenage boys tied to a railroad track and burnt to a crisp, I received a letter from her.

"Oh I was eager! Hot-footed out there to meet my man, Mr. Freddy McDonnell. Negro attorney, quarter-century my senior. A local colored family put us up, and in the kitchen we were left alone after supper, at which point he reiterated the particulars. The murdered boys had worked for a logging company, and one had allegedly smart-mouthed their despotic white supervisor who in turn allegedly broke the boy's jaw, then had the teen arrested as well as another of his workhorses, innocent bystander, the boss claiming both colored youths assaulted *him.* The young men were subsequently seized from their jail cells and the mob match lit. We were there for a potential civil lawsuit, a claim from the victims' families that their sons' civil rights had been violated by their murders, though we had little faith it would lead to anything. In truth, we were all yearning for something more substantial in the way of justice: someone going to prison. After the shoddy, indifferent work of the police, it was left to Freddy to undertake a thorough examination—to serve as detective as well as legal representative—grounded in the hope that he would be able to identify viable suspects, then pressure the police to arrest and the district attorney to prosecute. Given that lynching itself was not illegal, the culprits might be tried for the crime of kidnapping.

"That encompassed the first forty-five minutes of our introductory meeting. The subsequent hours were filled with Freddy's long-winded tales about his esteemed law career, his chutzpah: a *thousand* times more obstacles for Negro barristers in his day compared with the easy walk for *my* generation. Then, apropos of nothing, he began to recount the various sexual exploits of his lifetime, the sheer number of which would have been arithmetically impossible. This was a grandfather married to the same woman for decades, mind you.

"In the morning we went to question the local frightened Negroes who not surprisingly had little to contribute, and in the afternoon we spoke with the police captain and lieutenant. The authorities barely went through the motions of replying to our questions, and then. *Then* swaggering Freddy suddenly transformed. His shoulders drooping, *yes suh, no suh,* nodding like a dog. I was aghast! And said something that caused the white men's eyes to narrow onto me. Fortunately Freddy caught this before it escalated and put me outside fuming, pacing. Then Miss Hannah Casey, an elderly washerwoman, walks up to me. 'Looky what I found in Mr. Aubrey's basement,' and there it was: photograph of four white men grinning in front of the just-slaughtered Negroes. At that moment Freddy comes out of the police station, seeming tired. I held up the picture. He looked at it, looked at me, snatched the photograph, muttering, 'Stay out here,' and ran back inside. For a moment I was stupefied. Then ready to spit nails, I stormed in! And stopped short. There's Freddy all humble. And there's the captain and lieutenant looking at the photo. *Really* looking at the photo. Then they looked up at me, and this distaste crossed their faces, and Freddy mortified to see me standing there. As if a moment before they were seriously entertaining the possibility of acting upon the evidence, but my presence brought them back to their senses, now ready to discard the absurd idea, prosecuting lynchers. 'Sorry,' I stammered. 'Sorry,' and I backed out the door. Twenty minutes later Freddy walked out with the two officers, him in meek tow. The cops disappeared, and after an hour they returned—with two of the white brutes in handcuffs! They were convicted on kidnapping charges: two years for the ringleader, fourteen months for his sidekick. Outrageously lenient, and yet a victory, *miracle* it happened at all."

Winston takes out his pipe and lights it. Eliot glances at the clock. He needs to leave for court in four minutes.

"I kept Miss Wells apprised of the details, and later, when it was all over, I cautiously relayed to her the difficulties I had had with my partner. 'Yes,' she said, 'Freddy can be a jackass. But I thought the two of you would make a good combination.' She *knew* there was value in our amalgamated talents, and that we could rise above our petty differences. In the end I came to respect Freddy McDonnell, have regretted we never had occasion to work together since." He puffs. "Do you understand?"

"Yes sir, I understand."

"Good." He indicates for Eliot to rise to his feet, then pats him on the back. "I hear things have been going acceptably in court this week. Think you'll rest soon?"

Eliot isn't sure what "acceptably" means so sticks to the question. "At this rate probably Thursday or Friday."

"Well then. You and Beau will have all next week to start strategizing. I know you'll take good care of each other down in ole Dixie."

Eliot rushes back to his office to grab his briefcase. Standing in wait for the decrepit elevator, he remembers Didi's smile as she told him she wished she'd written her will before getting on "The Lift of Terror." He glimpses Will coming out of the conference room with coffee and stopping by Andi's desk. "Got one for ya. A priest, a rabbi, and a cracker judge are all sent to meet St. Peter." Will's voice then lowers to an animated whisper. The cage finally arrives and Eliot steps in, closing the gate, and just before the corridor outside Winston Douglas and Associates disappears from his view, he hears Andi's raucous laughter, and Will joining in.

14

"As this is the last chance I have to speak with you before you're excused to deliberate, first and foremost I want to express my sincere gratitude to each and every one of you for your time and attention over the last nine days.

"On the surface your task appears to be simple. Given the evidence, you are asked to decide if you believe Mr. Daughtery is or is not guilty of the crimes with which he has been charged, which are resisting arrest, possession of a concealed weapon, and racketeering. If you decide that he is guilty of one or two or all three of these, you are bound to have reached that conclusion beyond a reasonable doubt.

"And if you find Mr. Daughtery not guilty of any or all charges. What makes this determination so complicated is that you would in essence be implying your uncertainty regarding the honesty of the police. There is no concrete proof that any crime took place. All the evidence is circumstantial based upon the testimony of the officers: their word against Mr. Daughtery's.

"With respect to the charge of resisting arrest. That Mr. Daughtery suffered critical injuries on the day of his apprehension by Officers Crawley, Pfeiffer, Sheradon, and Wooley is not in question. The policemen claim that Mr. Daughtery's resistance to his arrest was to such a threatening degree that they were obliged to restrain him with extraordinary force. There *is,* as we all know, disagreement over whether that force continued after Mr. Daughtery was handcuffed and in custody at the stationhouse, but I'll get to that in a moment. For now we have Mr. Daughtery, whom *each* of the four officers has described in his testimony as, quote, 'big and menacing,' unquote. He has not seemed so big in this courtroom but, in fairness, a man in a wheelchair *does* appear small. He is able to stand for intervals of a few seconds, at which point his height can be determined to be five feet eleven, though I did have to curve the tape measure since his body seems to be in a fixed stooping position *and before Mr. Ingram puts forth the objection that he has just stood to raise* I will remind you that Mr. Daughtery's physical condition should not affect your judgment regarding his guilt or innocence, that if the four officers inadvertently caused injury, permanent or otherwise in the necessary course of their duties, then the damage to Mr. Daughtery's person would be considered an unfortunate but inescapable consequence of the policemen's engagement.

"Where I become confused is in the officers' claim that all four of them, and they are certainly not small men themselves, but *all* of them were required to exercise *such* force to restrain Mr. Daughtery, that the defendant physically overwhelmed them. By contrast, Mr. Daughtery has stated that his *only* resistance to the police were his verbal assertions that he wanted a lawyer, that he has rights, and words alone do *not* warrant physical restraint, let alone the fact that Mr. Daughtery was completely within his rights to utter those words. Of the nine civilian eyewitnesses to the arrest who have testified before you, not one saw Mr. Daughtery assault any of the policemen in any way, but, as you'll recall, the officers have stated that all of those witnesses are either lying or, as Officer Pfeiffer put it, 'blind.'

"With regard to the officers' assertion that the defendant was not harmed in custody, that he was not beaten after he was handcuffed and defenseless, that all his injuries were sustained at the time of his apprehension. Mr. Daughtery was arrested at 4:35 p.m. on Monday, September 12th. The medical report established the time of his admission to Emergency as 11:32 that night. If Mr. Daughtery's injuries all occurred at the time of arrest, I find it strange that Mr. Daughtery was not taken to the hospital until seven hours after his arrest, given that his injuries were hardly minor. Let me read for you again the physician's report, a head-to-toe examination.

> *Head trauma with fracture of the left temporal bone. Medial blowout infraorbital fracture (left), with moderate displacement and disrupted soft tissues of the eye. Hemorrhage within the orbit. Three upper left teeth dislocated. Displaced fracture of the left mid clavicle. Left ribs # 6, 7, and 8 fractured in mid axillary line. Fracture right distal radius, fractures of the right hand (navicular, metacarpals #2–5). Spleen is ruptured and surrounded by large hematoma. Pelvic fracture, bladder laceration, ecchymoses of penis and scrotum, with scrotal edema. Extensive lower extremity hematomas.*

"But even outnumbered four to one as Mr. Daughtery was, he would still pose a legitimate threat were he armed, and here we may move on to the second charge: possession of a concealed weapon. The officers allege, after confiscating the defendant's merchandise, that later, back at the station, they discovered Mr. Daughtery had cut through the pages of several books, turning each tome into a storage area. Most of these makeshift chests were used to hold policy betting slips, and one was obviously cut in the vague shape of the thirty-eight caliber pistol the police claim Mr. Daughtery illegally possessed. So, in putting all this supposedly found evidence together, the weapon and the betting papers, the officers came to the conclusion that Mr. Daughtery's sidewalk bookshop was actually a front for a numbers racket. There is no dispute as to the existence of the weapon and the betting slips in Mr. Daughtery's books. The question is when and how did they get there.

"The gun and its clever concealment, as well as the numbers slips, paint Mr. Daughtery as a shrewd and dangerous criminal. But since the weapon was not discovered until later at the precinct, Mr. Daughtery's weapon so inaccessible he could not get to it when he needed it most, he suddenly does not appear so shrewd nor so dangerous. But perhaps the defendant was smart enough to know that even if he were to get off a shot, there would be three officers left standing to fire back. This would explain his failure to reach for the gun. It would also conveniently deflect suspicion away from the very real possibility that the officers planted the gun and racketeering evidence into Mr. Daughtery's confiscated possessions while the defendant was in police custody. At any rate, whether the weapon was Mr. Daughtery's or whether it was put there by police, at the time of arrest Mr. Daughtery was unarmed and therefore would not appear to be such an ominous menace to the four officers attempting to subdue him.

"The third and final charge: racketeering. In specific, Mr. Daughtery's alleged involvement in the policy racket, and not as a mere runner. No, we are asked to conclude that the defendant's book table was in reality a policy *bank*—headquarters for the neighborhood numbers game, and Mr. Daughtery the boss. Never mind that Mr. Daughtery has no history of violent crime, that the *only* violation on his record is a misdemeanor four years ago regarding his lack of a permit to sell his books, for which he paid the fine and now holds a proper license. Never mind the numerous character witnesses who spoke highly of Mr. Daughtery as an honest street merchant, let us examine this portrait of Mr. Daughtery as the local crime czar. Officer

Crawley in particular has portrayed the defendant as a self-serving wolf concerned for himself only. He didn't mention the defendant's mother, with whom Mr. Daughtery lives and provides for. After she testified quite emotionally on behalf of her only child who, as she stated, since his young teens has always worked hard to support the two of them, never asking anyone for a handout, suddenly Mrs. Daughtery *did* exist in the eyes of the prosecution, but as a woman indulging in the criminally ascertained wealth of her gangster son. I would like to point out that while Mrs. Daughtery has always come to court dressed respectfully in her Sunday best, her humble attire is hardly the fruit of some extravagant shopping spree.

"Mr. Daughtery claims that he had been harassed on several occasions by the police. That during the last such incident before the events of September 12th, the defendant had asserted to Officers Crawley and Sheradon 'I know my rights!' He has told us that he was afraid, and that he was praying this reminder that he was legally owed basic human dignities would stop the intimidation. Sadly, it appears Mr. Daughtery was naïve. It was only when the two officers returned the next day with the reinforcements of Officers Pfeiffer and Wooley that Mr. Daughtery realized he may have made a fatal error, that to have mentioned his rights may *not* have endeared him to the officers and *yet*. Yet, he knew he was an innocent man in America, and as the wall of brutal authoritative power descended upon him with fists and batons and pistols at the ready, he proclaimed it again. 'I know my rights! I know my rights!' This is what you heard when Mr. Daughtery testified yesterday. His speech was slow, and strained, and slurred, but those were his words.

"The defendant's instinctive fear of the officers. I imagine it makes little sense to most of you, who probably think of the police as the protectors of citizens. I would like to tell you that Negroes on the whole do *not* think of law enforcement that way. We generally consider the police an entity to dread and to avoid, and we have ample reason. I don't mean to say *all* policemen harass Negroes on no other basis than that they *are* Negro, but unfortunately there have been enough such incidents to have warranted our general feeling of mistrust and foreboding. You may recall during the *voir dire* when the question was posed, 'Have you ever had any tussles with the police?' that every single colored man save one raised his hand, and that sole Negro male for whatever reasons was excused by Mr. Ingram. From that illustration we can come to one of two conclusions: either ninety percent of the Negro race *is* criminal, or ninety percent of the Negro race is *presumed* criminal. Thus I stand before you, ten white men, a white woman, and a Negro woman, and though I don't by and large consider you a jury of Mr. Daughtery's peers, I trust that you will all judge him fairly.

"My final point. In their testimony, Officers Crawley and Sheradon characterized Mr. Daughtery as a mobster who neither knows nor cares about his 'front' merchandise. This depiction would contradict those witnesses who spoke of Mr. Daughtery's loquacious discourses regarding his books. It would also contradict something you were all a witness to yesterday. You will recall as I was questioning Mr. Daughtery, my client suddenly became agitated. Despite the trauma he has undergone, I didn't imagine at this late date he would be rendered into such an emotional state that the court would have to take an early lunch to allow my client to pull himself together. Here was my error. When I had informed Mr. Daughtery long ago about the evidence the police claimed to have found, that it had been stuffed into several of his books, I failed to mention *which* books. Mr. Daughtery sold titles mostly of Negro interest, with a few popular paperbacks thrown in. In this courtroom, I picked up the damaged volumes as I questioned him. James Michener's 1,056-page *Hawaii* harbored the gun. *The Lord of the Flies* contained some of the policy forms. As I held the defaced copy of W. E. B. Du Bois's *The Souls of Black Folk,* I noticed a flicker of distress in Mr. Daughtery but, foolishly, I ignored it and continued with my examination. By the time I got to the mutilated copy of *Invisible Man,* Mr. Daughtery was howling. I was bewildered as to how I had aggrieved my client. He was well aware his books had been damaged, why this eruption of emotion *now?* When he could finally articulate, barely, you'll remember he asked in his broken speech, 'Why'd they do that? Why'd they do that?' And just before the recess he completed the thought: 'Why'd they do that to Ellison?'

"Because Mr. Daughtery is a man who cares deeply about literature. After court was adjourned yesterday, I went to a bookstore and purchased a copy of *Invisible Man,* the one you see on my table. I'd just like to share a little from the beginning.

> *I am an invisible man. No, I am not a spook like those who haunted Edgar Allan Poe; nor am I one of your Holly-*

wood-movie ectoplasms. I am a man of substance, of flesh and bone, fiber and liquids—and I might even be said to possess a mind. I am invisible, understand, simply because people refuse to see me. Like the bodiless heads you see sometimes in circus sideshows, it is as though I have been surrounded by mirrors of hard, distorting glass. When they approach me they see only my surroundings, themselves, or figments of their imagination—indeed, everything and anything except me.

I'll stop there, as I just wanted to give you a taste of the book that so affected Mr. Daughtery, an extraordinary novel that requires a contemplative and committed reader. Someone with more investment in his merchandise than merely as a façade for illegal operations. That line again,

I am invisible, understand, simply because people refuse to see me.

When the police officers began harassing Mr. Daughtery, did they see a well-read man who conceived of his own honest business to provide for himself and his mother? Or did they just see another Negro from the ghetto, someone of such low stature as not even deserving the rights of other Americans. And might it have infuriated them that such a person had the audacity to inform them that he *did* deserve those rights?

"Mr. Daughtery. I bought *Invisible Man* for you. Please accept my gift.

"I cannot help but to think of how, until September 12th of this year, against all odds, Mr. Daughtery was able to scratch out a living by his simple, entrepreneurial endeavor. One that provided for his family as well as for the social and artistic enrichment of the community. It never made him a wealthy man, but his humble contribution to the literacy of his people rendered him vital to our collective humanity. And what more could any of us ask of life?"

As Eliot concludes a brief cry erupts from his client. Everyone in the room turns to the defendant, Eliot especially unnerved by the outburst. Sam Daughtery, who initially seemed wildly confused when his attorney had handed him the book, gaping between Eliot and the paperback, now clutches his new, whole, unblemished copy of *Invisible Man*, holding it tight against his chest, nodding, nodding, a single tear rolling down his cheek.

15

Andi pours the champagne.

"So Winston Douglas and Associates finally *wins* a case!" She laughs.

"Hey, *I've* won a time or two." But Will is grinning. They stand around Andi's desk.

"I was shaking."

"From what I hear," Will tells Eliot, "no one could tell."

"I was shaking! But I just kept my hands in my pockets. About ten minutes in, guess I calmed down. Good thing I didn't plan to pick up *Invisible Man* till late in the argument, any earlier it might have trembled out of my fingers and hit a juror in the face!" Eliot giggles. Giddy as if he were six years old again, all he can do not to cry out: I love Andi! I love Will! I love champagne! Hahahaha!

The summation had happened yesterday, Thursday, the deliberation lasting two and a half hours, and Eliot is still incredulous. Not guilty. Not guilty. Not guilty. The verdict on each of the three charges pronounced separately by the foreman, a white construction worker. Sam Daughtery's mother had run over to embrace her son long and firm, and in his weakened physical condition, Sam's attempts to return her hold were poignant in their awkwardness.

Eliot is glad Beau's a little late this morning as he might be a bit of a wet blanket, though he wonders when Winston will get in. But too embarrassed to ask, a kid wanting to know when Daddy will get home to show him his straight A's. Serendipitously, Andi answers the unspoken question. "Mr. Douglas called first thing. He sounded thrilled. He had meetings but'll be back after lunch." Her smile is radiant. Andi and Eliot, friends again, at least for today.

"So what do you think?" asks Will. "Sue the city?"

Eliot grins and doesn't reply. The district attorney's office had made it clear it would not indict the police officers so that avenue was unavailable, but after this verdict. It would be an audacious long shot but this is what he'd dreamed about after that tort law course. The damages in a civil suit would not only be a godsend to Sam Daughtery, whose medical bills continue to drain his and his mother's meager resources, but, in arriving at a pecuniary amount far beyond a paltry slap on the wrist, the city might actually be jolted into learning a lesson or two: to start keeping better tabs on its police officers, to start training those officers to respect their Negro citizens as well as their white.

The elevator sounds. Beau pulls open the gate and steps out.

"What's all this?"

"Eliot's victory party," Will replies. "Have a glass?"

"Oh yes, many congrats, Eliot," smiles Beau. "Shame Mr. Daughtery's in that wheelchair or he could be here dancing too." He strolls into his office as the others stare silently after him. So socially oblivious, it's very possible Beau hadn't intended to spoil the party, yet Eliot and Will now find themselves quietly retreating to their own lairs.

But behind his closed door, Eliot can't wipe off the smile. Half an hour later, a probate case open, he gazes at the telephone, thinking of how he would like to share this happiness with her. But he doesn't want Didi's same tired, distant voice to dampen his mood. He pulls out two other files, accident claims, to provide himself with a vaguely pressured feeling of being backed up in his work, and his concentration partially returns.

His first tête-à-tête with Beau regarding the voter registration case happens at 10:30 as scheduled, in Beau's office, naturally. As with refraining to contact Didi, Eliot decides he is not going to let Beau's condescension get a rise out of him. As the meeting progresses, he becomes pleased to learn that Beau has good ideas, and is stunned to see that yesterday's triumph in court—Eliot's first opportunity to present closing statements—must have impressed Beau, who seems almost humble and very much interested in Eliot's thoughts, all of which the senior attorney takes seriously. Encouraged that they are starting off on the right foot, Eliot allows himself a rare luxury, leaving the office for his full lunch hour rather than munching at his desk while working.

He eats his packed sandwich on a park bench, gazing at two pigeons in conversation. He *will* call Didi when he gets back to the office. Her excuses for disregarding him as of late may be all true, perhaps she is just very busy at work. If so, he's sure she'd gladly take two minutes away to enjoy this day with him, to be happy for Sam Daughtery. And if something else is going on. Well. It's time he knew for certain. If she wants it all to be over, at least his present euphoria would provide some bit of emotional cushion from the blow of romantic heartbreak.

When he returns, Andi, seated at her desk, is staring at him. "Your brother phoned. He said you need to call home *immediately*." In that instant, Eliot sees in her face the sense of full betrayal, the artifice of their so-called relationship wherein even the most basic information, her assumption that he was an only child, had been a lie.

But he has no time to worry about that now. Dwight has *never* called him.

He emerges from his office twenty minutes later. The look on his face and his reddened eyes are enough for the hurt in Andi's eyes to change instantly to alarm.

"My mother died."

Her mouth opens. "Oh. Eliot." His breath is quickening. "What happened?"

"I don't know. She was alive today. Dwight said she was alive today, he called her today. And then she died." His fedora trembles in his hand. "I think I have to go home."

"Yes."

"I have to go home now."

"Yes, I'll tell Mr. Douglas."

He goes back to his office, retrieves his briefcase, and walks out to the elevator. He wears his hat but no other outerwear. Andi hurries to his office to snatch his trench coat, then runs it out to him. He stares wildly at a blank corner of the corridor. She notices he has pushed the Up button. She hands him his coat and pushes Down.

"You're driving right from here to Maryland?"

"I have to go to my apartment and pick up some things, my black suit. Oh! I should give you my number there."

"We have it. Your paperwork—" She stops herself. When he was hired, for life insurance purposes he had listed his mother as next of kin.

"Okay." The elevator arrives. Eliot starts to open the gate but Andi gently blocks him. He is confused. The lift continues going up.

"Don't worry about anything, Eliot. I'll tell Mr. Douglas you've gone, it'll be fine."

"Okay." Then a panic. *"My briefcase!"*

"You have it."

"Oh. Okay." The elevator arrives. A Negro businessman stands in it.

Eliot steps in. As Andi pulls the gate closed Eliot suddenly snatches it, his eyes crazed. *"Will you tell Winston I've gone?"*

"Yes, I'll tell him."

"Okay. See you Monday," the words automatic, as if this were any other Friday.

He makes several wrong turns, increasing the nine-hour drive time. He pulls over and begins convulsively bawling twenty minutes straight, and when it's over he is glad to have gotten it out of his system before he has to deal with the family dynamics.

He arrives half past midnight. The house is full of relations, and he is polite but avoids their comforting touches for fear of unleashing a sob or two that might still be left in him. Everyone knew there was heart disease on his mother's side, but the family concern had always been his father's high blood pressure. Claris's sudden death at fifty-four was astonishing, absurd. She had been sitting at the kitchen table going over the bills, and had apparently simply slumped over. Lon happened to have had the day off from the glass factory, but was at the hardware store buying items to repair a leak in the roof. By the time he returned she was already cold. Dwight tells his brother that Didi had called, looking at Eliot curiously, and that she had said Eliot could call her back as late as he wished. Eliot says nothing. How did she know?

Over the next three-quarters of an hour the house clears, as if they had all been waiting for Eliot to arrive before they could leave. Only Aunt Beck remains, and Dwight pulls out the couch-bed and makes it up for her. He had given his own house keys to Aunt Peg-Peg so that she and her brood could stay at his place in Lewis, much closer than their home in Bear, while he sleeps here in the boys' old bedroom. Dwight tells Eliot he doesn't know if any other family will come into town and need the guestroom but, for tonight, Eliot is welcome to sleep there. Eliot brings his suitcase to the middle bedroom. It is past 1:30, the rest of the house dark, when he makes the call.

"Hello?"

"I woke you?"

"Of course not." A pause. "I called the office to say hi, and Andi told me. She gave me your family's number. She thought you might need someone to talk to." Another pause, Didi waiting for a response. "It was thoughtful of her."

"Hmm." His eyes are fixed on the afghan his mother crocheted for the guest bed while he was away at college, to help her sift through the reality that both her boys were grown and gone. He gently taps a tassel to watch it sway. Vaguely he has a sense of significance, Didi finally calling after a silence of so long.

"I'm so sorry, Eliot."

"Thank you." The tassel, a soft pendulum.

"Listen. Do you need me to come?"

There is a universe of difference between Do you want me to come? which is I am there for you, and Do you need me to come? which is I will if I have to. Eliot understands the distinction and is surprised that he is relieved to hear it. To know that she would come but would rather not. Because, he realizes, while he truly appreciates the offer, he also would rather she not.

"No, I'm fine."

"Sure?"

"Uh-huh."

"Do you want to talk?"

"No. I mean I'm tired. It was a long drive."

"Of course." On the lower wall behind the dresser, an expertly rendered sketch of Little Orphan Annie and Daddy Warbucks, now faded. You would have to be sitting in this precise spot and looking from this precise angle to notice it. Eliot remembers coming home from school when he was still very small and finding it: a surprise gift from Dwight. He didn't thank him. At some point, Claris had apparently moved the bureau to cover her firstborn's wistful vandalism for the sake of guests, but Eliot sees that she never painted over it. "When is the funeral?"

"Monday morning."

"What church?"

"No, a funeral parlor. My brother and I have to go pick out the casket in the morning."

"Uh-huh. What's the name and address of the funeral parlor?"

"Waverly's. I forget? I forget—"

"That's okay, I'll find out the street." A brief lonely cry from his father in the next room. Eliot had thought he was asleep.

"Alright. Well I'm going to call to check on you again tomorrow. If you want to talk that's fine, and if you don't want to talk that's fine too. Okay?"

"Okay."

A silence. "Okay. Well I'll call tomorrow. Maybe early in the afternoon, after you get back from the funeral parlor."

"Okay."

"You get some sleep."

"Okay."

"Okay. Okay. Good night, Eliot."

"Good night, Didi."

He has not eaten since lunch, and after all the admonitions from his aunts to put something into his stomach, and with a refrigerator already stuffed with food from just the first day of bereavement visitors, he goes downstairs to see if he can tempt his appetite. He opens the fridge and stares for several minutes before giving up.

Back in the guestroom he dials a number.

"Hello?" Her voice sleepy.

"Sorry! I woke you. What time is it?"

"Eliot! Don't worry about it. How are you?"

He swallows. "I'm fine. Andi?"

And Eliot tells her about his earliest memory, still a toddler, his mother giving him a bath in the kitchen sink. Her smile. And about being wrapped in a blanket on her lap, with his brother on the floor with the Sunday funnies, and her uttering "lynching," the first time he'd ever heard the word. About sitting on the front porch sliding chair with his mother and brother, his mother saying that the heavy raindrops smashing against the pavement were people dancing in the streets. And then he speaks about Miss Onnie and her cats, and feeding the birds with her, and Parker. Miss Onnie saving Parker, and Ramonlee's puppy, and Eliot trying to teach Parker tricks. About Colored Street and Mixed Street, about being cross-eyed and getting his first pair of glasses, and earning the Perfect Attendance certificate. About his father the porter and A. Philip Randolph's visit and his father's Baltimore defense job and the coal mountain in the basement and his disappointment at the canceling of the March on Washington. About the Bartons and the little baby girl Barton who drowned and Roof Barton becoming a kid miner. About being in trouble with Miss McAfee for coloring the white schoolbook children brown. About Jeanine almost getting hit by the car driven in the snow by the white man, and the new used twin beds, and the long ride on the school bus to visit Helen and Ellen Brown and their big family. About that Memorial Day at Aunt Beck's, and the Dream Man, Uncle Sam and his lynched mother Tiny. About Jeanine's rabbit in the box. About his father getting the glass factory job and the time he brought home two prisms from work, one for each of his sons to hang in their windows and watch the rainbows dance around their rooms. About Dwight. His big brother, always chasing after Dwight. Tarzan movies with Dwight, Dwight teaching him to make snow angels. Dwight the artist, Dwight's cartoons, Dwight's chalk lynch drawings. Dwight always letting Carl run over him, and Dwight was *better* than Carl. Dwight's dog Rex, and Parker's tragic end. Eliot talks about being chosen class valedictorian, and his high school moments of shame: the time he refused to dance with a heavy girl at the Valentine's Day hop, the days he watched an outcast boy being bullied and did nothing in his defense. His high school sweetheart Jeanine over junior and senior years, wholly innocent and his longest relationship, as each of the four girls from college never stuck around, or he didn't, longer than a month. His undergrad sick drunk night that permanently terminated his taste for hard liquor, his antisocial law school days. And Miss Onnie's passing. And Christmas, walking Liddie's twins and meeting the little girls next door and that black doll. And Dwight's job with the postal service. And Dwight's underground comic, and Dwight and his friends. When Eliot is finished, he yawns. He looks at the clock: almost four.

"I've kept you up!"

"It's okay. I was already awake after the phone rang."

"I've done all the talking!"

"It was a nice change of pace."

"The long-distance! I'll have to pay my dad back, in the morning I'll tell him—"

"Eliot, it's really the least of your worries," and with that a cry spontaneously escapes him, then expires just as quickly.

"Andi. Can you come here?"

There is a silence, and instantly he feels ridiculous. They are not together anymore, and what? Does he expect her to miss work Monday? So everyone will know about their former relationship? Though he imagines they'd figured it out by now anyway, given all the weird energy between them. She wouldn't go to Gary with him when they were together, and now with it all over he presumes she would be willing to become sucked into the middle of it all, his *life?* And what must she think, him asking her to drop everything and come to Maryland after he's been with Didi all this time?

"Andi, I'm sorry, that just popped out. But I really appreciate your listening." Still no answer. "Andi?"

He hears the receiver jiggle. "Okay, go ahead."

"What?"

"Oh sorry, Eliot, I had to put the phone down. With all the books and notepads strewn around here, you wouldn't think it would have taken me that long to find a pen and paper. Alright, give me the driving directions."

16

"These are some of the samples we have in right now." Stan Waverly the funeral director, a short, stocky fifty-something white man with white hair and much pink in his smooth, fair complexion, sits at his desk, holding up a three-ring binder. A picture album, except these pages are neatly filled with photographs of caskets. Dwight and Eliot, sitting next to each other opposite Stan, stare at the images, both brothers looking like they've been through the war, confusion and exhaustion, but Stan is used to that appearance in his clients. Despite Eliot's phone call into the wee hours, the time seemed to have dragged until this 10 a.m. meeting, having woken every half-hour from vivid dreams. Several vases of artificial flowers adorn the room, one placed on a tall chest made of cherry wood, as is Stan's tidy desk, both pieces unmarred. A cup on the desk is filled with pens (WAVERLY FUNERAL HOME with the address and phone number), a standing American flag is situated in a corner, and on the wall is a framed diploma authorizing Stan as a Mortuary Technician. Undertaker. Until now, Eliot had not thought about how literal the word is: he takes them under.

To spare their father, Dwight and Eliot have taken on as many tasks as possible: choosing the coffin; writing the tribute to their mother, assigned by Dwight to Eliot the lawyer before he arrived; the organization of the cars for the funeral procession and other logistics (Dwight); arranging the pallbearers (Dwight again). Eliot had remarked that the elder seemed to have unfairly burdened himself with the bulk of the work, but Dwight assured him he had not taken on more than he could handle, and Eliot left it at that.

"Most people choose steel. Very sturdy and economical. It may seem cold, but it comes in a variety of colors. White, pink, tan. And of course silver, gold. I assume an open casket for the viewing, closed for the funeral?"

The brothers stare at him blank.

"That's the general custom. See here, the upper half of the casket is open so that visitors can see her face. The bottom half is always closed so you needn't bring shoes."

Again the brothers gape in utter confusion.

"You will have to pick out an outfit for her to wear of course."

Eliot and Dwight look at each other.

"I can do that," says Dwight. "Or. I can pick out something, and then I'll check with you." Eliot nods.

"Alright, so you'll notice the design on the inside upper half. This one with the praying hands is very popular, as is this. With the roses, 'Mother'?" Dwight looks to the lower part of the page. "Now *that* we call 'Going Home,' very simple, very tasteful." Stan Waverly allows a few moments of silence while the brothers stare at pictures, turn pages. "These," he begins again quietly, "are in the range I imagine you're looking at. But I should also—" He turns several leaves to the wooden models. Eliot notices that the prices have now doubled. "These oak and mahogany pieces are quite elegant. I'm especially partial to the ebony." Four times as much as the steel. "I've already reserved one for myself." Stan softly chuckles.

The brothers stare for a few moments. "My mother's life insurance benefit for the whole funeral is a thousand dollars," Eliot says finally.

"Certainly," says Stan, and moves to turn back to the budget section.

"Wa-wait! Let's jus look at a few a these," says Dwight, his hand holding the page with the ebony model. Eliot's face slowly turns to his brother. Dwight doesn't notice.

"Well the ebony is certainly very striking." Stan smiles broadly, then glances at Eliot and tempers his expression. "Now, some families prefer the cherry, more affordable than the ebony. A little color. Softens things." The cherry is half the cost of the ebony but still twice as much as the steel.

Dwight leans forward, turning the sheets, studying, frowning. At last he sits back in his chair. "Well! I say we go with the ebony." As if injected by a boost of some stimulant, he suddenly seems brighter, smiling at Eliot. "Whadda ya think?"

Eliot stares at Dwight as if his brother is from Mars. "What do I think? I think the ebony's two thousand dollars and we only have one thousand for the entire funeral."

Dwight ponders this, as if Eliot were sincerely posing a question. Lightbulb: "I can pay for it."

"What?"

The elder laughs. "I been workin with the postal service a long time, little brother. I put some away, savings. It can be paid in installments?" He is looking at Stan now.

"I'm sure we can work something out."

"What do you need installments for. I thought you had savings."

"Well I don't have *all* of it!" Dwight laughs. "But I can cover half up front. And the rest." Dwight leaves the sentence dangling, the idea having already been completed by the discussion of partial payments. He seems delighted to have resolved this issue so quickly.

Eliot stares at Dwight, then turns to Stan, whose face is frozen noncommittally. After a moment, the latter speaks. "You know, I have some other business I need to attend to. Why don't I leave you two alone to talk." He walks out, closing the door behind him.

Eliot turns back to Dwight, his eyes narrowing. Dwight, befuddled by the heat he is gathering from his brother, does a doubletake.

"What!"

"I'm not letting that bloodsucker prey on our grief. The five-hundred-dollar casket is fine."

"'Fine'? *'Fine'?* That's good enough for your mother? We only have one chance to do this, Eliot!" And Dwight bursts into tears. Eliot glares.

"It's *my* money! What's the difference if that's what I wanna do with it?"

"The difference is she's *our* mother, not *your* mother, and I say no."

"Eliot! I been workin longer than you. I know you don't make much your kinda law, I know in the city rent's high. I don't mind doin this. I *wanna* do this!"

"You wanna be a fool for that parasite."

"It's not about him! It's about Mom!"

"Oh you think Mom wants this? Letting some white man bamboozle her grown sons she thought she'd raised with some sense?"

"It ain't about black n white, Eliot! *every*thing to you's about—" Dwight takes a breath. "And if it was, you think if we were white he'd be sellin us the cheap junk? If you'll recall, that's what he started us with. *Maybe* I'd like to show him niggers can afford the ebony good as the whites."

"Yeah I'm sure that's just what he's hoping. Nothing he loves better than when the spooks are trying to keep up with the goddamn white Joneses, he loves *that* all the way to the bank."

"Who cares what he thinks! Who cares if he gets rich? It's not about him!"

"I know, it's about Mom, who as you know would be rolling in her grave if she knew after she took out that life insurance policy to cover all her expenses, we were sitting here contemplating going into debt on a damn two-thousand-dollar coffin."

"*My* money! I said I'd pay for it! And whadda *you* know about Mom anyway? How many times the last few years you seen her? *I* seen her every Sunday, called her every day! Every day! I called her yesterday mornin and she was *fine!*" and Dwight is wailing again. Eliot is violently silent. Finally Dwight wipes his face. "Don't worry, I'm not gonna tell anyone. People'll jus think we both paid for it," and it is with every fiber of his being that keeps Eliot's fists clutching his chair and away from his brother's face.

Forty minutes later they stand outside, having settled on the more moderately priced cherry, Dwight committing to making up the fiscal deficit. Parked in front of the parlor is an old red pickup truck. The street is one-way, and the truck parked on the left so that the driver's side is next to the sidewalk. Behind the wheel sits a slim blond man, late twenties or early thirties. He looks straight ahead. Not at the funeral home, despite the fact that there are many parking spaces and there would be no reason for him to park where he is unless he had business with the establishment. Not at the brothers, despite the fact that they are the only people on the street and only a few yards away from him. He wears a flannel shirt with both sleeves torn off leaving his arms bare, a tattoo of some kind on his left near the shoulder. Poster boy for trash, Eliot thinks, though he allows that at least the guy looks clean. Dwight glimpses the truck, then looks away.

"Eliot, listen, you go on ahead home. I got some things I gotta do, I'll be there in a while."

Eliot's hands are in his pockets. "Who's that?"

"What? Oh, him! That's Keith, he's a friend."

"Friend."

"I gotta go, Eliot. I got some stuff to do, I'll come by the house later," and Dwight runs to get into the passenger side of the pickup. The moment he closes the door he breaks down sobbing again. The driver steals a glance at Eliot before pulling off.

At home he is grateful that the constant flow of relatives and friends paying respects seems to be a comfort to his father, and that his assignment to write his mother's tribute means he is excused to shut his door against all visitors. He needs to finish before tomorrow evening, in time for Dwight to look it over and provide any input. They would also need to decide who would read the piece, someone close to their mother but not so close as to break down emotionally before finishing. Uncle Rick?

At 4:35 a soft rap at his door. His cousin Liddie, noticeably rounder since Christmas.

"Hey Eliot."

"Hey Liddie."

"You got company."

He comes to the top of the steps, and when he sees her he dashes down. He takes both her hands, their faces beaming, eyes shining.

"I didn't expect you till tonight!"

"Well. When we got off the phone I knew daybreak was coming in a couple hours, thought I may as well pack up and hit the road. I must've put as many gallons of coffee in me as gas in the tank. Speaking of which. The bathroom?"

After Andi freshens up, he brings her to the guestroom. With the door closed, he reads aloud the first draft of the tribute for her feedback. He manages an impressive emotional detachment, simply presenting the words, so is surprised to look up at its conclusion and see her wiping tears. "I wish I could have met her."

Then she says, "Eliot. Can I have a drink of water or something?"

"Oh. Oh, yeah. Are you hungry?" Only now does he remember that he hasn't eaten since lunch back in Indianapolis yesterday.

On the way, he gives her a glimpse of his parents' bedroom, then they walk downstairs. In the living room, he introduces her to his father, who is surrounded by people. Despite his grief, Lon seems pleased to meet her, the first time since Eliot was in high school that the elder has ever been introduced to anyone from his younger son's life. She offers her condolences, and Lon takes her hand, smiling through glassy eyes.

Eliot leads her through the crowded TV room to the kitchen. He pulls a huge meat-and-cheese platter out of the refrigerator. They make sandwiches and talk. Aunt Beck and Claris's oldest sister Carol chat quietly nearby.

"How long yaw known each other?" Aunt Carol finally ventures.

"We work together," Eliot says flatly. He already knows where this line of questioning is going, and has decided it's not.

"Well," Aunt Beck taking her turn, "I bet *you* been workin there a lot longer n he has. Right? Andi?"

Andi starts to answer but Eliot stands. "I'm gonna show her the neighborhood before it gets dark." He grasps her hand and they are both out the back door, leaving half-eaten sandwiches.

The temperature is in the low fifties and sunny, fortunate since Eliot had not bothered to grab their coats. He shows her Miss Onnie's house and Carl's and Roof's, Colored Street, and Jake's Hill where the kids used to, and he imagines still do, fly down on their sleds in the winter. The space where D'Angelo's Market once stood, now an empty lot. He takes her by his old school, and Miss Idie's, the white lady his mother had worked for when he was growing up, and the railroad station where they used to meet his father when he was a porter. They stand on the bridge gazing at the crick, its banks recently fortified by cement levies to prevent the periodic floods he remembers from childhood.

"You know they were asking about my age." Andi's smile is wry but sad.

"They need to mind their own business."

"From what you said on the phone last night. Your Aunt Beck sounds like quite a character. Once you get to know her."

"She is. And she needs to mind her own business."

When they return, Dwight is waiting for them at the back door, holding an outfit of their mother's. He is in a panic. "I been lookin all over for you! I have to give the funeral director Mom's clothes."

"Dwight, this is Andi. Andi, this is my brother Dwight."

"Hello."

"Hi, nice to meet you. Eliot, he said he'd only wait till 6:30!" The clock on the wall reads 6:07. In his right hand Dwight holds a hanger, and draped over it a burgundy skirt-suit their mother often wore to church, complete with her faux pearl necklace. In his left hand Dwight holds a pair of her good brown loafers.

"He said no shoes."

"I don't like the idea of her barefoot!"

Eliot takes a breath. "It's fine," and Dwight flies out the door.

Dinnertime, and there is a lull in the crowd, the house quiet. Eliot notices that Andi's eyes are now heavy from driving all night. He tells her to go up and take a nap on the guest bed and she nods gratefully, dragging herself up the stairs. He walks into the living room to study the photos on the wall, pictures he's seen a thousand times but never *really* looked at. Shots of him and Dwight from babies on up. His father in his porter uniform, his father with another man at his defense job. Eliot at the lectern giving his high school valedictory speech, Eliot and his parents and brother when he received his law degree. Dwight at fourteen with Rex the dog, Dwight in his postman's uniform in front of his house in Lewis with elderly Rex. It occurs to Eliot that because mothers are often the ones taking the pictures, they are the most absent from them. He does find one image of her alone, Lon having caught her in action throwing icicles on the Christmas tree.

Eliot walks up the stairs and eases open the door of the guestroom. Andi had always had the habit of disappearing under the blankets, her head eventually popping out while she dreamed. Turtle. He waits for this to happen but before it does, he hears a faint restless cry from his parents' bedroom. His *father's* bedroom. Eliot gently taps on the door, and when there's no answer he discreetly peeks in. Lon lying fully clothed on the made bed, eyes closed and breathing evenly. He wears a suit to receive visitors over these three days. Eliot starts to gingerly close the door and leave.

"I'm awake."

His father's eyes are now open. Eliot steps inside, shutting the door and leaning against it.

"You okay, Dad?"

"Mm hm." Lon stares at the ceiling. A rumble of thunder. Usually such an incident would be answered by his commentary on the weather, but this evening he doesn't seem to notice. Gradually he lowers his eyes to Eliot. "That Andi seems nice."

"She is." Did he introduce her to his father? Eliot can't remember.

Lon looks at the ceiling again. "Dwight's tryin to figure out the music. 'Nearer My God to Thee.' Guess that's pretty standard. And 'Just a Closer Walk with Thee.' That sound good?"

"Yeah, that's great, Dad."

"Oh. While you boys were lookin over the caskets, the grave marker people called. I jus told em 'Claris Louise Campbell, 1906–1960, Loving Wife and Mother.' That okay?"

"That's fine."

Lon's chest rises high and falls, a soundless sigh.

"Think I might go ahead an take my vacation this week. Ernie down there can inventory the jars an bottles for a few days."

"You want me to call them?"

"No, I know what to say to em." Eliot follows his father's gaze at the ceiling. He wonders if they are staring at the same crack, or if Lon is seeing any cracks at all.

"'Sweet Bye and Bye.' She liked that one."

"Oh yes! Thank you, son."

He watches his father, who continues to look at the ceiling. A sudden downpour, the sound filling the room. Eliot slides his back down the door so that he is stooping, staring at nothing for twenty minutes, thirty minutes. When he stands again Lon's eyes are closed. Eliot steps out, quietly shutting the door behind him.

The guestroom door is open, the bed remade. Eliot walks downstairs. He finds her sitting out on the porch in the sliding chair, gazing at the pouring rain.

"Hey," he says.

"Hey." She smiles, nap-refreshed. She wears her coat, unbuttoned.

He sits beside her and stares at the evening cloudburst. Eventually he cautiously reaches for her hand, holding it, and she squeezes back, neither of them ever taking their eyes off the shower.

"Look, Eliot," she says. "All the people dancing in the street."

When the rain stops, they walk back inside. It's nearly eight and Andi is famished after their interrupted lunch, but when she sees Eliot has lost his appetite again she keeps her meal lean. They sit at the kitchen table, and a new worry nags him as he watches her chew her boiled egg and dry toast. When he invited her, he never considered sleeping arrangements. What he would really like is for Andi to sleep with him in the guestroom, but he has no idea if by asking her to share his bed he would offend her, or if by *not* asking he would hurt her. Another complication: though all he really wants is for them to hold each other this night, he believes the implication of more with a woman who is not his wife would be disrespectful to his father. He supposes the logical solution would be to give her the guestroom and go back to his old twin, sharing the room with Dwight.

"What's the matter?"

He is startled to see her looking at him.

"Oh! Nothing."

She takes a drink of water.

"So am I sleeping on the guest bed? Or the couch? Or I can check into a hotel if you're full up with family."

He remembers she didn't know he had slept in the guestroom last night, that she obviously expects to sleep without him, and he is relieved that the decision has been made with no injured feelings.

"The guestroom. Aunt Beck's the only one staying here, and she sleeps on the couch."

"I can trade with her if she'd rather."

"Thanks. We always ask her and she always says no. She likes the couch. Pulls out to a bed."

"Can I see your old room?" She means his and Dwight's, and he realizes he has shown her every space in the house save that one. They climb the stairs. He points out that his was the twin next to the inside wall, Dwight's against the outside wall and back window. Andi asks, Is this your pogo stick? Who carved that face with the tongue into the dresser? This photo of the toddler boy smiling with your mother, you or Dwight? Eliot answers all her questions, even as sleep is overtaking him and he lies on his bed. Then Andi is gone and Claris walks in wearing her burgundy suit. She seems distracted, going through drawers, looking for something.

"Mom!" Eliot sits up. "I thought you died!" He's so happy to see her!

"Oh that was a mistake," she says absently, never turning to him, finding a small box on top of the bureau and scrutinizing its every corner.

He is abruptly awake. Looks at the clock: quarter to midnight. The lights in the room still bright on. Dwight sits on his bed, going through notes. His face is strained, calculating logistics, probably figuring out the funeral procession car assignments.

"Andi's in the guestroom." Eliot's voice startles Dwight. The older brother frowns, as if trying to understand some deeper meaning in the information just conveyed to him, then nods and returns to his task. Eliot sits up and takes off his shoes, letting them drop to the floor. He is too exhausted to do anything else in the way of undressing, so he lies back down and finishes his thought. "So I'm sleeping here tonight. And tomorrow night. If it's alright with you."

"It's alright with me if it's alright with you."

"It's alright with me," says Eliot, and turns to face the wall.

"I might be gone in the mornin," Dwight says. "I'll leave a number. Where I can be reached."

No answer.

"You hear?"

"I hear."

Dwight writes a few more notes, then looks up at his brother's back. "It's Keith's number." He allows a few moments for this to sink in. "I'm going to see Keith. Remember Keith? From the pickup truck? He lives out at the trailer park, I'll be with *him*."

Eliot is so still Dwight wonders if he is already back asleep. Dwight continues regardless, his eyes stinging and determined, the pen in his hand trembling. "I'll be with *Keith,* at the *trailer park*. I'll leave a number, if you need me, I'll be at *Keith's*." Silence. "*Okay?*"

"Gotcha," replies Eliot, and no more words pass between the brothers that night.

□ □

It's close to nine when Andi wakes Sunday morning, ravenous. She knocks on the door of the brothers' room.

"Come in."

Both beds are made. Eliot sits on his, editing the tribute. He glances up just long enough to identify Andi, then, his mind far away, looks back down at his page. Dwight is gone.

"Shall we have some breakfast?"

"You go ahead." He doesn't look up. "I'll be down in a little while."

Andi's impulse is to insist that he eat, to tell him he needs his strength, but she's conflicted, not certain if her own growling stomach is her real priority. She could go on downstairs and grab a bite as he suggests but she hears voices, extended family and friends already and of course Aunt Beck, and all she needs is for those biddies to see Eliot's *mature* girlfriend, or whatever they think her relationship to him is, stuffing her face while poor Eliot is left alone to struggle with the memories of his mother.

"Alrighty then, maybe I'll go for a walk."

"Okay." Eliot rises, and Andi is hopeful that he will come along, that they will go downstairs together and she can convince him to eat even a little food with her, but he retrieves a thesaurus off a nearby shelf and sits back down to his work.

"Okay. I'll be back." She descends the steps, hearing the crowd talking around the smorgasbord in the kitchen, and walks out the front door. She remembers passing a corner market in her stroll with Eliot yesterday. ("That wasn't here when I was coming up.") She finds the place, buys three six-packs of orange-colored cheese crackers with peanut butter, takes them out to the small parking lot, and greedily gobbles them all.

There are two viewings, 2 to 4 and 7 to 9. Stan the funeral director had suggested the immediate family be there by one to "have time alone with her." Andi comes with them, Dwight driving his father's car (rather than his own two-seater truck), but without being asked by them for privacy, she stays in the lobby while the three men, all wearing black suits, walk into the large parlor. She looks around at the red furniture, too comfortable, too formal, at the guest book ready for signatures. She glances out the window, the sky heavy gray. It had been drizzling on and off all day. At one point she walks over to glance in at the family. Lon stands next to the casket looking down at his wife, Dwight sits far to the right in the front pew looking down at the floor, Eliot stands far to the left, hands in pockets, staring at his mother. All three seeming lost, and utterly alone.

A few people come right at two, and the place is crowded from 2:30 on. Both brothers are gracious and stoic. After a while Eliot wanders around, gazing at the plentiful flower arrangements, reading the cards, most with a printed note, "In Sympathy," followed by a handwritten name. A generous autumn bouquet is signed

Winston Douglas and Associates
Winston, Andi, Will, Beau

Eliot smiles, knowing that Andi would have been the one to put in the order and thus the sequence of names her decision. A smaller arrangement is signed "Affectionately, Andi." And another, a dozen long-stem roses, simply "Didi (Wilcox)."

Andi tries to be with Eliot when he wishes, to leave him alone when he would desire that. His cues are not so clear, and finally she whispers: "Would you rather I sit down? Or do you prefer I stand with you?"

"Uh-huh," he replies, smiling at his mother's cousin Delores, just in from Ohio.

Eliot goes to the bathroom, and when he returns he stops short. He is looking at their backs: Dwight standing at the casket with Keith beside him. Keith wears a respectful black suit. Dwight is talking quietly, evidently telling Keith about their mother. Eliot looks around to see if others are also stunned, but either no one else seems to take note or they are all pretending well. After a few minutes, Dwight walks Keith to the door. Keith pats Dwight's arm, the same way their cousin Monroe had done to Eliot when they first saw each other yesterday, and Keith leaves.

Lon sits quietly in the front middle pew, as close as possible to Claris, letting people come to him. At five minutes to four, almost all visitors now gone, he breaks into uncontrollable sobs. Dwight runs to kneel before his father and talk to him softly. Eliot stares at them, the nearest he has come to weeping himself since arriving home.

Outside the building, a handful of family members waits. Dwight emerges through the door, now using a clipboard for his notes, making him appear like a children's football coach. He announces that the prayer service will commence at "the house" at five, immediately followed by a meeting of the pallbearers. Monroe is driving Aunt Beck and Lon home, and just before the new widower gets into the passenger side he turns to Eliot, Dwight, and Andi, the only ones remaining on the sidewalk. "Would you like to ride with us, Andi?"

It is a gesture of kindness, revealing that Lon has noted the petty gossip regarding Eliot's guest and he isn't having it. Andi looks at Eliot, unsure. Eliot smiles. "Go ahead."

After they pull off, Eliot turns to Dwight, the latter's eyes still on the clipboard. "Prayer service?"

"We told you about it last night when you got in, guess you were too tired. Reverend Fairbanks." Dwight sighs. "It'll be in the living room, he said it shouldn't take longer n twenty minutes."

Eliot has had experience with what Reverend Fairbanks calls a "short" service. He nods. "Bunch of baloney, I'm not going."

Dwight snaps. "Can't you do it for *Dad?*"

Eliot stares at his brother, then swerves away to walk the two miles home alone. He cannot believe Dwight *of all people* still buys into that conservative hypocritical bunk. He hears his brother starting the car behind him and doesn't turn around.

People are already gathered in the living room when Eliot gets home.

Andi stands next to Lon. She exchanges glances with Eliot as he enters, and it is clear in her face that it is clear in *his* face that he had just had another confrontation with Dwight. He goes up the stairs, shutting himself inside his room until Andi taps on the brothers' door. "Eliot. The pastor's here."

There are seventeen in the living room, standing in a circle. "Let us hold hands," the reverend begins, the last thing Eliot wants to do. Luckily Andi is to his right, and one of Liddie's little girls to his left. The minister has bowed his head in prayer, and everyone but Eliot follows suit. He is at first surprised that Andi goes along with it, then remembers: *Oh* yes, Mother's Day—the annual holy supplicant. The preacher reads from Isaiah and Ecclesiastes, the assembly chorusing intermittent "Amen"s, and the session concludes with a quiet 23rd Psalm, surprisingly over as promised just twenty minutes after it had begun. The pastor shakes Lon's hand firmly and embraces him, gives Dwight the same treatment, and finally Eliot. "Okay, can the pallbearers please come into the kitchen?" calls Coach Dwight.

With the exception of the summoned, no one has left the room, most thanking the pastor. As a pallbearer Eliot is grateful for the out, but before he can leave Andi asks if he has eaten anything today. This time she really is concerned more about his nourishment than her own hollow stomach. He smiles. "You and I'll get something after the pallbearers' thing." He walks out to the kitchen to find the other five bearers: Dwight, Monroe, Uncle Rick, his mother's brother Uncle Mookie—and Keith. Dwight is already in mid-lecture. "So Eliot and I'll be holdin up the front—"

"What's *he* doing here?"

Dwight stops talking. All in the room stare at Eliot.

"I *said*, what's that white boy doing here?"

Keith whispers to Dwight, "I'll come back later."

But the whisper is not quite low enough. "Oh no you *won't!* We got seven hundred relatives can bear *this* pall, you are *not* needed here."

"Eliot! you don't jus get to decide—"

"How's he rate?" The younger's eyes boring into his brother. By now the chatter in the living room has also fallen to silence. "I mean, all the relations to choose from, how the hell's *he* go up, top of the list?"

"Eliot." One of the uncles, but Eliot does not take his eyes off Dwight.

"I *said*, how's he rate?"

Now both uncles jump in. "Eliot, you got to calm down."

"We know you're feelin it hard, son, your mother—"

"I'm not talking about that!" Nearly screeching. Are they blind? They don't see what's going on here? "I asked a simple question. Can anybody answer a simple goddamn question?"

"Eliot!"

He swings around at the sound of his father's voice. Standing in the doorway and Andi with him, horror in their faces. Eliot stares at them, then turns back around to see the pallbearers all gaping at him. And he flies out the kitchen door.

Beginning to drizzle again. "Eliot!" Andi's voice behind him. He walks faster, doesn't turn around. *"Eliot!"* He sprints in his suit and dress shoes, eventually removing them to run in his socks. He doesn't know how far he runs but it's long past the point of exhaustion. The rain pours.

He must have gone a good fifteen miles because as darkness falls he finds himself on the outskirts of town. He had slowed to a fast walk, but never stopped moving. A lonely highway, houses now appearing only occasionally. The rain letting up. He tries to identify where he is, then realizes he is on Old Mill Road. He remembers the Andersons lived out this way. Richard the firstborn, around Dwight's age, who Eliot had heard painted something inside the old Messengill house leading to it being torn down. But now everything seems different, the dirt road paved, trees cleared. And he comes upon the trailer park.

▫ ▫

In the guestroom is a small framed photograph of five-year-old Dwight sitting cross-legged on the floor, giving a bottle to his infant brother in his lap, their mother's arms visible around the child and baby. Andi holds it, smiling. Little Dwight grins down at Eliot, a wondrous awe.

Dwight had asked if Andi wouldn't mind staying home while they were at the second viewing and answering the phone in case any out-of-town relatives called needing driving directions. "Sure," she had said, grateful to be of use, grateful to have an excuse not to go back to the funeral home without Eliot. She knew Dwight was kindly offering her this out, and she also suspected that he wanted someone to be in the house with his brother when Eliot came home, that in reality all visiting relatives were already in town, a notion confirmed when Dwight continued: "I know you came on short notice so if you need to make any calls, go ahead," which would obviously tie up the line. She graciously thanked him.

Andi pulls a textbook out of her suitcase and sits on the bed, her back against the headboard, preparing for an extended study session when the phone rings.

"Hello?"

"Hello, may I speak with Eliot?"

Andi flinches, recognizing the voice instantly, feeling catapulted back into the role of Eliot's receptionist. "He's not here right now. Can I give him a message?"

A momentary silence. *"Andi?"*

"Hi, Didi." They have never before addressed each other by first names, and it is at once strange and as if they have done it a thousand times.

"Oh." A pause. "Oh."

"Didi, listen. He asked me to come. We're friends, that's all. He asked me to come. As a friend."

"Uh-huh."

"Please, believe me."

"I believe you."

Another silence. Then a sigh. "I've tried to call the last two days but either someone picked up and said he wasn't there, or there was no answer. I guess I should've left a message, but I didn't want to bother anyone."

"Well. I could—"

"I can't leave a message with *you!* Like he doesn't have enough worries, all he needs is to hear I called and you answered!" Didi laughs heartily, but a cry cracks through.

"Why don't you call in the morning? Eight our time, seven yours. You can catch him briefly before the funeral."

"Oh. Oh, that's a *great* idea. Thank you, Andi."

"You're welcome."

Andi waits for Didi to say goodbye, but she doesn't.

"Well."

"Andi. Andi. Can I ask you something?"

Andi tenses. "Sure."

"Three weeks ago. That Friday I came to your office. Eliot and I had a very nice weekend but then." Trying to catch her breath. "I am *so regular!* I should've gotten it two days later. Then three passed. Four." She begins exhaling. "We weren't fools! My diaphragm. It's always worked before." A little cry. "I didn't know what to do, I waited to make sure, then I was sure and I didn't know what to—" She sighs. "I finally decided to tell him, to call and tell him and then you said his mother." She swallows. "I made an appointment. I made an appointment but I'm *scared!* I'm so," a violent trembling in her voice. "Eliot said. Eliot said you were interested in abortion law, I wonder. Maybe. Maybe you know women who know what to expect? What it's like, what I'm gonna—" She is suddenly bawling. "Sorry, Andi, I just needed to talk to someone!"

"Oh, Didi. Sh. Sh." Didi sobs for several minutes. When the spasms subside, Andi begins to speak quietly. "A few women from school. One of them has drawn up this checklist. To make sure it's safe as possible. I'm certain she'd be happy to talk with you. Would you like me to put you two in touch?"

"Yes." Didi hiccoughs. "Oh yes, Andi. Thank you!"

"Okay." Several moments pass before Andi speaks again. "Would it be helpful to talk to other women who have gone through it?"

"*Yes!* That would mean so much to me, Andi!"

"Alright." Andi gets down to sit on the floor, making herself comfortable. "Listen. When I was young, I was married to a very, very sweet husband. Then the war came."

◻ ◻

Eliot had heard the trailer park was out in this direction but had forgotten until now. He hesitates, then walks onto the grounds.

A couple of homes have lights on and no curtains, putting their business out in the street, which embarrasses Eliot. But the vast majority are discreet enough to have drawn their blinds. He strolls around, confused, hoping he is not spotted and pegged as a prowler. Do colored people live out here? Are they allowed to? He turns a corner and some children are running and playing just before they're called in for the night. He turns another corner and sees a woman taking laundry down from a line. Sheets and towels and baby clothes. She seems exhausted, a sleepless young mother, and though

Eliot knows it's madness, he has an overpowering desire to tell her to go back inside and rest, he'll finish the job and bring the basket to her door when he's done.

"Eliot."

He swerves around. Keith, taking out the garbage, stares at him. Eliot stares back.

Keith looks around. "Where's your car?" Though Eliot had stopped running twenty minutes ago, he is panting again.

"You *walked* out here?"

Eliot wants to reply but the words are locked, the knowledge of speech. Keith sets the rubbish bag into a metal can and replaces the lid. "Come on. You're soaked, you need to dry off." He walks over to a nearby trailer and opens the door, stepping in. Eliot has followed him with his eyes, but he cannot move. "Come on."

Eliot regains the use of his legs and follows Keith inside.

"I'll get you a towel." Keith disappears. The first thing that surprises Eliot is that in a trailer there's enough space to disappear into. The second thing is to find that, besides the bare necessity of furniture pieces, what has filled Keith's trailer is paintings. They are everywhere, on the walls and one on an easel, in process. This is Keith's home, and it is also his studio.

He returns with the towel, handing it to Eliot. Then, following his guest's line of sight, he snorts, embarrassed. "I'm not good. Not like your brother. I think. I think a little more red might help this one."

Keith is right. He doesn't have Dwight's visionary eye. But he clearly has passion and perseverance and humility, and aren't they the seeds of all greatness? Until this moment, Eliot had only seen Keith and Dwight as two groping bodies having but one thing in common: that they both happened to be homosexual. A frivolous lifestyle with an irresponsible, juvenile interest in only the present carnal instant. He had had that sort of nothingness himself with at least one of his four girls in college, one-night stand, but he always knew eventually he would want more: love, marriage. It had never crossed his mind that a homosexual, that his brother, might want the same. But in the paintings he now glimpses something between Dwight and Keith that had not occurred to him. Something kindred. Tender. Sacred.

Keith hands Eliot a full glass of water. "You're missin the second viewing," he says.

Eliot, who wasn't aware he was thirsty, downs the entire glass in one gulp. Keith refills it and brings it back to Eliot, who swigs it again.

"Listen, lemme drive you." Eliot cannot take his eyes off the paintings. "They'll close the casket before you all get there in the mornin. Tonight's the last time you can see her."

Eliot looks down. "I'm sorry." His panting again. "I'm sorry, Keith, I shouldn't have said. I don't know why I—"

"Eliot, you just lost your mother."

Eliot's right leg spontaneously begins shaking, fast and furious. They both stare at it, Eliot baffled. He expects it will stop momentarily, but instead it quakes increasingly harsher, now his foot stomping a rapid rhythm. Finally Eliot reaches down with his hands, seizes his knee to hold it in place. It stops.

"Whoa," he says, an embarrassed chuckle, "*that* was weird."

Keith grabs his truck keys, opens his door, and stands out on his step, waiting. "Come on."

Eliot looks at Keith, then down at his own drenched clothes. "I don't think they'll let me in looking like this."

"Don't worry," Keith says. "Your mama's seen you before."

By the time Keith and Eliot pull up in front of the funeral home it's 9:30. All the mourners' cars are gone. The place is dark, except for a light in Mr. Waverly's office. Keith gets out of the truck, followed by Eliot. The driver raps on the metal knocker. When no response comes, he bangs the knocker hard.

The door opens. Stan Waverly works hard to suppress his irritation. "Yes."

"Listen, I'm sorry but there were some family circumstances, and Mr. Campbell was not able to come to the evening viewing of his mother. He'd like just a few minutes alone with her now."

"I'm sorry, the viewing ended at nine." He turns to Eliot. "I'm very sorry, Mr. Campbell, but it's impossible at this point. I was just about to close the casket, and—"

"He won't be longer than ten minutes."

"Again, I'm very sorry, but—"

"How much did he pay you?"

The large room, the front half of which had neatly contained the rows of white wooden folding chairs for the viewings, is now full to capacity in preparation for the big turnout expected tomorrow. Eliot is impressed that Mr. Waverly managed to put it together so soon after the last guests left at nine. Alone in the silence the room seems cavernous, and Eliot approaches the casket. His mother's face appears frozen in a frown, as if he and Dwight were still kids and she had just found a window blind on the floor, accidentally torn from its roller, and was trying to figure out which of her knucklehead offspring was the culprit. Eliot's eyes shine. "Hi Mom."

Keith drops Eliot off at home close to ten. Eliot knows he should say something to his father but Lon is already asleep, whatever sleep means these days. He should say something to Andi but as he passes her room, he sees she is on the phone, her back to the door. "Well, in the end it'll be nothing compared to the pain when you get this long-distance bill." And then she laughs, the kind of laughter that is some sort of release after an endlessly long period of mirthlessness. Eliot is suddenly more exhausted than he has ever been in his life, not able to hold his eyes open, and decides he'll have to postpone any apologies until the morning.

Dwight sits on his bed, wearing his pajamas. They are the blue plaid that match Eliot's green, the Christmas gifts from their mother. Usually Eliot sleeps in an undershirt and boxers, and had worn the pj's only once previously, Christmas night for his mother's sake, but he felt compelled to pack them for this trip, and he notices the set Dwight wears appears to be equally mint condition. Dwight frowns, staring down at his clipboard. At this point everything should be in place for a smooth go tomorrow, the car passengers assigned, the pallbearers ready, the tribute written. There's no logical reason to still be poring over the lists except, as it finally dawns on Eliot, his brother's obsession with order is the only thing keeping Dwight from falling apart.

"Hey," Eliot says.

Dwight looks up with such a piercing hatred that Eliot nearly trips backward. The younger brother is momentarily confused, then remembers Dwight has no idea that Eliot has already apologized to Keith, which surely would have at least mitigated the glower. Eliot undresses, hanging up his suit to dry. In the morning he'll have to wash that bit of mud off the leg bottoms and give the whole thing some sort of quick ironing. He gets into his pajamas.

"I was supposed to get to read the tribute, but you weren't here to show it to me so guess I'll jus have to wait an be surprised tomorra."

Eliot pulls the pages out of a drawer and hands them to Dwight.

"I may wanna add a few things."

"Whatever you want." Eliot gets under the blankets and turns away from his brother to face the wall.

As Dwight reads what Eliot has written, he softens. "Oh yeah." After a moment he laughs out loud. Then, wonder: "I *forgot* about that." There are sniffs and tears and Dwight finally finishes, wiping his face and looking at his brother's back. "It's beautiful, Eliot."

Eliot is silent. Dwight looks down at the pages in his hand. "Beautiful. Jus. There's jus one thing. It might be dumb but, I was thinkin. What do you think we added somethin, I don't know, ordinary. Like, remember when Mom would be readin, like the way you hooked her onto Gwendolyn Brooks? And somethin would impress her, or make her sad, and she'd take off her glasses and sigh, an start touchin em, rubbin the frames—"

It is so powerful it comes out like a scream, Eliot's sudden wailing, sobbing, the torture as if he were being stabbed over and over not catching his breath, his pillow soaked in seconds and the flood won't stop, Dwight rushing over to lie next to his brother, behind his little brother who shakes so violently the headboard harshly and rapidly bangs the wall, and Andi and Lon rush in but leave quietly, neither of the brothers seeing them, Andi and Lon running into Aunt Beck on the stairs, the entire house lit up with Eliot's torrential grief, it won't stop, for two hours it won't subside and Dwight holding him, and Eliot letting Dwight hold him, and Dwight not letting go.

17

"'Sweatin like a nigger in court,' sure you heard that comin up. Big joke till you confronted with it literally. Cracker judges, I'd consider it a resounding success to get a life sentence. Least it's not the chair. Not a lynching, victory you actually *made* it to trial. And God don't let the charge be raping a white woman, when everyone knows damn well the experts on interracial rape are white *men*, thinking colored women are theirs for the taking. One time this ole judge look like he falling to *sleep* during the proceedings, a man's *life* on the line and—" Beau stops himself, seeming shaken. He looks at Eliot, who wears his glasses for driving. "I'm talking too much. You rather I be quiet, you just concentrate on the road?"

Eliot, a vague smile on his face, shakes his head in the breeze whipping through the windows, rolled down even in late October to provide some relief from the Cotton Belt humidity. Beau had been much more considerate where Eliot was concerned since his mother's death fifteen days ago. It is late afternoon Saturday, and Eliot has been driving since they departed Indianapolis yesterday morning, waving off Beau's offers to take the wheel. On Friday, as planned, they had gone as far as Memphis, then started early this morning to make their Deep South destination before sunset. Just inside the border they had briefly stopped by the home of a local man, who hid Eliot's Falcon out back and loaned them his 1954 Plymouth turquoise two-door station wagon. Thus for their two-night stay, Eliot and Beau have in-state license plates.

"You're just being nice. You want the radio?"

"No, I wanna hear what happened with the judge who fell asleep in court." What Beau doesn't realize is his windbagging has become a comfort to Eliot. A sense of normalcy, of life before.

"Oh you *were* listening!" Beau chuckles self-deprecatingly. He finishes the tale, the trial outcome dismally predictable, then switches on the dial. "Let's see where we are." Mostly static, two stations playing country music. Then, "Hey!"

"What!"

"What did that sign say?"

"Nathan, Alabama, Population something. We're still fifteen miles away."

Beau sits back. "Huh."

"What?"

"That's where my sister lives. I had no idea it was so close."

"You wanna stop in and say hi?"

Beau shakes his head. "Haven't seen her in twenty years. She and I get to talking we'll be there hours, and you and I will *not* be driving ole Dixie after dark." He stares out at the high weeds lining the road. "But maybe I'll call her tomorrow." Beau falls into a pleasant world of far-off memories, for the first time in the entire drive saying nothing for so long that when an announcer begins a mellow monologue Eliot turns up the volume, to get a feel for the local landscape and to fill the silence.

They pull onto the grounds twenty-five minutes later, half an hour before dusk. A tiny poverty-stricken Negro village at the edge of town, the houses resembling little more than shacks, but this particular shack happens to have a telephone and thus was the one the locals felt would be most useful for the Northern visitors. The hosts come out to greet their guests. Martha Coats is brown, about five feet tall and stout, her darker husband Jeremiah a sturdy six-five.

"An this is our granbaby Leona," Martha says. Whether Leona, who looks about ten, is the offspring of their daughter or son, and where that daughter or son is now, neither Eliot nor Beau inquire. The one-story home contains two bedrooms of equal small size, and the lawyers are loaned what is apparently the child's room, a single bed and several blankets on the floor.

"You can roll it up in the day if you need walkin room," she suggests to Eliot. "I'm assumin Beau bein the elder will have the bed."

But Beau looks at Eliot nervously. "You want the bed, Eliot?" This sensitive generous thing is all new to him, and he seems flustered every time he speaks a kindness as if he may have done it wrong.

Eliot sets his suitcase next to the unfurled bedroll. "My brother and I used to camp in the backyard. Least now I won't get eaten by the mosquitoes."

"You still might," says Martha.

There are pigs' feet and greens for dinner, and they sit and get acquainted for a couple of hours. Before retiring Beau asks the Coatses if he might use their phone to call his sister in Nathan tomorrow morning before she leaves for church. The couple is delighted to hear he has people so close.

"You wanna call her now?" asks Jeremiah.

"I imagine she still goes to bed with the chickens. Last time I phoned after nine she laid me out so bad by the time she finally got around to 'How are you?' my whole long-distance allotment had been exhausted. I had to tell her, 'I'll let you know that next call.'"

The crickets are loud, and Beau's snoring louder. With a small flashlight, Eliot reads a while, then stares at the ceiling. In a variation of a recurring dream, it is Eliot's twenty-seventh birthday, a year from now, and he is home in Humble with cake and ice cream and Dad and Dwight. "We have a surprise for you," Lon says, and in walks Claris. Eliot is in an ecstatic awe, and everyone laughs. "We *knew* we could fool you!" his mother says.

Early the next morning Beau phones his sister. By his tone, it's clear she's thrilled to hear from him. After a few minutes he says, "Rosie. Guess where I am?" The whole house hears her screaming response.

"Come on, make yourself useful," Martha says to Eliot, and he follows her outside to the chicken coop to help collect eggs. "You won't be seein me an Jeremiah in the voter registration line tomarra. We're already registered."

"Really?"

"Bout five of us they let on the rolls. Make it look like they ain't prejudiced. Don't ask me how we made it to the fortunate few, probly jus drew our names from a hat." She counts eggs to herself. "Where your people from?"

"Maryland."

"Whereabouts?"

"Humble."

She frowns. "I don't know that one." She blows on an egg. "Well I bet your mama must be proud a *you*. Lawyer."

Eliot doesn't pause in his egg collecting. "She was."

"Aw, she not with us no more?" Eliot shakes his head. "When she pass?"

"Two weeks ago."

Martha nearly drops her basket. "She *jus* passed?" Eliot nods. "Aw. Bless your heart." Martha collects more eggs. "Bless your heart," she says again softly to herself.

When they get back in the house, Beau announces that Rosie will visit later that morning. She wants to prepare a meal for Beau, and since he can't get out there, she told him to ask Martha not to cook. She would be bringing enough for everyone, dinner *and* supper.

"Would you rather take the car and drive to her?" Eliot asks.

"Nope. Never know what might come up, we need the car."

At 8 a.m., the three representatives from the local NAACP arrive. They are dressed casually, as if they are farmer neighbors, and perhaps they are. Warren, who gives the impression of the leader as he does most of the talking, appears to be in his mid- or late forties. Joe Archie seems mid-thirties, and Les around Eliot's age. They thank Beau and Eliot again for being here as there are no local Negro lawyers. Then they all discuss the strategy for Monday, tomorrow, over breakfast. Warren mentions a recent hysteria sparked by the integration of the high school, so they should be prepared for troublemakers.

"I hate to say it," says Martha, "but we ain't lettin Leona go to the white school, not till things calm down anyway."

"Wait for that, she might be graduated," Warren says.

"Then that's the way it's gonna be. Sure, I'd like her to have the nice new books. But mostly I like havin her in one piece."

Beau remarks, "Indianapolis schools been legally integrated since '49, but don't they do every kind of gerrymandering, trying to keep the old separate ways."

Joe Archie grins. "Yaw Up-South, huh?"

"Sure," Beau says. "And make no mistake: Up-South go all the way to Boston, at least."

Rosie's car pulls in around 10:30, a half-hour after the NAACP men have left. She is light-skinned with brown freckles. Like Martha, she is short and rotund and in her fifties, as if these were traits of all local women. Beau walks out to greet her, and she has barely stopped the car before she runs to him. Her eyes dance, and Eliot sees that she adores her brother.

And Beau seems a completely different person around Rosie: soft, affectionate. Leaving the talking to her, which she does a lot of. Amusing the table with anecdotes of Beau as a boy, of their family and childhood neighbors, of the crazy colored and white folks out in Nathan. The Coatses reluctantly leave for their 11 a.m. church service around 11:45. ("Never starts earlier n noon," Martha had remarked.) Rosie feels a little guilty for skipping church herself, but "I know the Lord'll forgive me missin this once. My brother's in town!"

Eliot decides it would be nice to leave the siblings alone to catch up, so he tells them he brought some work with him and should go into the bedroom now to look at it.

"Just a minute first," says Rosie. She puts her hand on Eliot's. "My brother told me about you losin your mama recently, an I jus wanna say I sure am sorry."

"Thank you." At moments Rosie reminds him of his mother. But these days a lot of things remind him of his mother.

"We all gotta go through it. Beau was only ten when he lost his."

"Yes, Lord," Beau says softly, far away.

Rosie registers the confusion on Eliot's face. "Oh, you didn't know. I'm Beau's *foster* sister. We grew up together in Arkansas, an my husband Roy too. Beau was the only one his family, Miss Nancy an Mr. Melvin tried an tried but another baby never come. Beau's mama, dark as she was, still the prettiest woman in town. One day walkin down the street, these four white men start to touchin her. Broad daylight! His daddy, *big man,* find em standin outside the white saloon that night, he say real quiet, 'Don't you never touch my wife again.' An them four men jus stare at him, shakin in their shoes, terrified to say a word. This we know for true cuz a neighbor a ours happen to be walkin by then. People was sayin, 'Melvin, get outa town! Them white men gonna come after you!' Well he don't budge, an three days go by, four, five, he figure they done forgot all about it. Then the seventh night, everybody asleep, they come outa nowhere, hootin an a-hollerin." She turns to Beau. "Took her, didn't they, Beau-Beau. Takin turns with her till she died."

Beau nods, his sad eyes staring at something on the table no one else sees.

"Right in front a her ten-year-old son."

"What happened to his father?" Eliot has fallen into Rosie's pattern of referring to Beau in the third person. Beau too seems to be reliving the tale from a distance, an outside observer, albeit not a neutral one.

"They held him to watch everything they did to his wife fore they ready for him. I don't even wanna get into what kinda mutilations before they burned him alive, an *conscious,* make sure he still got life in him before they tie him to the railroad track. His screams wakin everybody within a mile, wake me an my family. An not jus the terror. The grief, shock: what they done to poor Miss Nancy. A full hour till the locomotive come cut him in two, his wailin fill the air, seem like it burstin with all the horrors a the world. Never forget the sound till the day I die."

Eliot stares at Beau. How could he have gone through all that and never spoken of it? How could Eliot have never *sensed* something of it in him? "You saw it?"

"I saw it," Beau says quietly. "They meant me to see it. It was a show for *me*."

"So my mama an daddy took him in. An we been brother an sister ever since."

Another quiet. Then Beau says, "Now tell me how that rascal Roy's makin out."

When Eliot feels he can leave without being rude, he excuses himself. In the bedroom he pulls out his work and stares at it for the next two hours, never comprehending a word.

At supper Beau is quiet. Martha asks why Rosie's husband didn't come.

"He's a veteran." Beau buttering a biscuit. "Army, had his legs blown off. He moves around on a little cart in the house, but hurts him to ride in the car."

Jesus Christ! thinks Eliot, what next? *Well Rosie, Roy and I were just having ourselves a little vacation in Hiroshima back in August of '45, when all the sudden*

Beau sighs. "Sure wish I could've shook hands with ole Roy though. Rosie and I figured it out. Lass time we seen each other was our mama's funeral, '38. Twenty-four years."

Martha marvels on the wild coincidence of their proximity. "Yeah, they moved here soon after they got married, can't remember why now." Beau gazes out the window. "Until yesterday Nathan, Alabama, wasn't anything to me but an address on the envelope."

At bedtime Beau goes to the outhouse as his roommate unrolls his bed. Eliot looks up, sensing another presence. Leona, looking sad.

"Hello."

"My granmama said I gotta be nice to you cuz you jus lost your mama."

Eliot smiles. "You have a very nice granmama."

"Wamme tell you a joke to make you feel better?"

"Yes."

"What's the biggest pencil in the world?" and without giving Eliot a second: "PENNSYLVANIA!" She doubles over in laughter, running out of the room, overcome by her own cleverness.

In the morning Beau and Eliot are at the courthouse at 7:30 as are the three NAACP men, and about forty Negroes are already lined up though the building won't open until nine. The government employees start rolling in around 8:45, conspicuously ignoring the two hundred colored men and women in single file. An assemblage of casually dressed white men stands near the queue, clearly *not* here in solidarity with the Negroes. Beyond them a squad of police officers with a van at the ready.

The temperature is already nearing eighty, and Eliot has noticed that the line, as monitored by a white official, is directly in the sun, and needn't be, given that a clump of trees is nearby. Most of the hopeful registrants seem to be in their best attire, including coats if outerwear spruces up their appearance. Eliot remembers the shoes. At Didi's suggestion he would bring items for the poor on his trips South—used clothing, toiletries, school supplies—and the gesture was always deeply appreciated. It had occurred to him, since he now had the new wingtips she had bought for him, to give away his old, still in good condition. (He'd considered donating the new pair but worried it would be ungracious to dispense with a gift.) The moment he met giant Jeremiah he saw there was no point in offering his size 8s to him. As he looks at the queue now, he notices a few who appear to be in need, but it may be insulting to pick someone out of the crowd because his shoes look shoddy, or for that matter to approach one man and not his neighbor in line who may be of equal want.

The white protestors are in the shade. Eliot recalls Warren's caution about the school integration madness. By contrast the whites here seem bored, as if this is a special chore they are required to finish before getting back to their real work.

By eleven, only three people have been let into the building, and none of these allowed to register. Eliot had been warned about this and tries to keep his temper in check, standing in the oppressive sun. Periodically he or Beau gently inform the people of their rights, and are sometimes asked questions. Eliot becomes concerned about the frail elderly, some beginning to breathe unevenly, and he expresses this to Beau. Beau whispers to Warren, who nods, and Eliot isn't sure if he is considering some sort of action or if he assumed Eliot, through Beau, was simply commenting on the state of affairs.

The fourth rejectee, a tall thin old man, exits the courthouse furious. A couple of police officers walk over. The senior citizen is waving his arms wildly. One of the officers grabs at his arm, and the elder swings. The cops handcuff him, take him to the police van, lock him in and pull away. An old woman, apparently the man's wife, runs as best she can after them, yelling and crying. Eliot, urgently wanting to intervene, looks at Beau, who is looking at Warren, who says, "One a you come with me?"

Eliot now notices that Beau in his middle age seems to be waning in the heat himself. And while Warren had asked for either of them, his eyes were on Beau, presuming him to have the greater experience.

"You wanna go, Beau?" Eliot asks.

"Okay." Beau is relieved, and he follows Warren to the jailhouse, apparently walking distance despite the cops' fanfare with the van.

There is absolutely no movement in the queue now, and at precisely one o'clock many employees pour out carrying lunch bags. Some NAACP volunteers, mostly women, arrive with sandwiches and water for those in line, but the police won't let them near, claiming they are obstructing the people's right to register to vote. Les has had about enough and goes to talk to the cops, who laugh in his face. At two o'clock, the employees return from lunch. At 2:05, a buzzer is heard, and the entire building empties, "Fire! Fire!" some say, laughing. At 2:10, the fire department shows up and runs straight through the queue, pushing people out of the way, causing tension among some of the standers who begin to argue about who was in front of whom. The firemen are in the building for some time, doing nothing that anyone can see, many of the Negroes surmising they are drinking Coca-Colas to kill time. At 3:10, precisely one hour after their grand entrance, they emerge, the captain announcing that the problem is electrical wiring and that the building will have to be closed the rest of the day, Come back tomorrow. This should legitimately have brought about a collective moan if not a riot, but the people, having by now anticipated this, sigh and quietly disperse. Eliot feels himself hyperventilating from a heat inside him having nothing to do with the sun, but he takes a breath and follows Les and Joe Archie to the jail.

When they walk in, the deputy briefly glances up from his newspaper with distaste. Beau and Warren sit nearby, both looking frustrated and Beau in particular worn out. The wife of the arrested man sits a few feet away, lost in her own thoughts.

"That's Delaware," Warren says, out of the officer's earshot. "Said the sheriff has other business to attend to, which I reckon is a leisurely supper, and that he'll be back at six. The earliest we can see Mr. Yancey."

Eliot looks at Beau. Beau, exhausted, stares at the floor. Eliot walks over to speak quietly to his colleague. "Why don't I drive you to Rosie's? I can get there and back by 4:30, 4:45, plenty of leeway."

Beau stares. *"What?"*

"I can counsel Mr. Yancey, Beau. Only one arrest, we got lucky. I'll leave you off at your sister's. You can see Roy, then I'll come pick you up in the morning on my way out of town."

"What are you talking about? Go off and socialize when I came here to do a job?"

"You did your job. You stood with the people, advised them. If we hadn't been out there, some kind of deterrent, I imagine there would have been a lot more arrests, and worse." Beau is anxiously unsure. "You don't look good, Beau, I think you got a little sunstroke. You could use the rest."

Eliot notices the NAACP men looking in their direction. He indicates for them to come over. Warren does, as Joe Archie checks on Mrs. Yancey.

"I'm concerned about Beau. He seems pretty fatigued after being out in the sun all day. He has relatives nearby, and since there was only one arrest that I can offer counsel to, I thought I'd drive him to his family and he can rest for the evening. I'll be back before six."

"I didn't ask him to! He just suggested, he—" Beau takes a breath. "I will be happy to stay here and do my job."

Warren glances over at Les, who seems to be in a bit of a tussle with the deputy.

"You *do* look a little peaked. Whatever you two decide, I'm okay with." He walks over to Les and the officer. Beau and Eliot stare at them, and after a few minutes Warren turns around to wave them on.

"Come on," says Eliot. "Let's go so I can get back."

"No, I haven't decided yet! This doesn't feel right." Beau's hat oscillating in his hands.

"Excuse me." Mrs. Yancey suddenly standing near. "Can somebody fine me the colored bathroom?"

Beau and Eliot are baffled. Mercifully there had been an outdoor facility next to the courthouse for colored use, but here in the jail, the cells undoubtedly filled with Negro inmates frequently, the only lavatory visible is marked **WHITE ONLY**. Joe Archie is looking in their direction, and walks over.

"She needs a bathroom," says Eliot.

"Oh. Oh yes, ma'am, we'll find it," and Joe Archie walks the feeble woman outside. Eliot is aware that this man who has lived here all his life is clearly not certain there *is* such a thing as a colored restroom in the vicinity.

"Well?" Eliot asks.

Beau struggles a few moments. Finally, "No! I came here to do a job, not to have a family reunion!"

Eliot stares at Beau, then moves away from him. He gazes out a window, hands in pockets, thinking of the recent reunion in Maryland of his own family, something getting smaller.

"I didn't mean that." Eliot turns around. A softness now in Beau's face, and Eliot realizes the elder has surmised his thoughts. "I mean. Yes. Thank you."

When Eliot drops Beau off at Rosie's, she is jumping up and down, and runs to hug her brother. Eliot steps out of the car but stands leaning against it, not wanting to intrude. He stares at the house, by no means indicative of wealth but certainly a few degrees above the Coatses' level of hardship. Rosie scampers over to embrace Eliot as well, then leads him by the hand into the house.

"I know you can only stay a minute but I wanted to introduce you to Roy."

Roy on his cart is in the kitchen mending a pair of dungarees. From the top of his head to the floor he stands about three and a half feet. "Roy, this is Eliot."

If Eliot's face reveals the shock and pathos he feels, no one seems to notice. "Nice to meet you there, Eliot," and Roy shakes his hand.

Beau enters. "Whoa," says the visitor, "looks like you lost a little hair there, partner."

"Well now I see your big fat belly I guess you ate it." They both laugh heartily, then Beau goes down on one knee, like some fairy-tale marriage proposal, something Eliot never would have guessed he could do so effortlessly, especially after the day in the sun. And now Eliot sees that just being with his family seems to have put Beau back in optimal health. The brothers-in-law embrace so tightly and for so long that Eliot becomes embarrassed and looks away.

"Here's your supper." Rosie comes to Eliot. "It's a roast chicken sandwich an boiled egg. I didn't have time to peel the egg but I figure you can handle that."

"Oh! You didn't have to."

She gazes at her husband and brother. "Well you didn't have to neither. But cha did."

When Eliot gets back to the center of town, it's 4:55. He walks to the park, a rectangle bordered by the jail, courthouse, and other public buildings. He makes certain to identify the Negro area before sitting on a bench to dine.

It's the first time he has been alone with his thoughts in a few days, and there has been plenty to process. After the funeral and a couple of respectful hours at the wake, he had gotten on the road, Andi (who had called in "sick" to work that Monday morning) following in her azure Beetle. Barely another hour had passed before he was suddenly aware that he was famished, and they pulled over to a small diner. They both ordered huge plates of spaghetti with garlic bread, and though neither of them said as much, they each came to recognize this as the first time they had been *out* to eat, what might be called a *date*. Eliot had wolfed down the pasta and still felt hungry, surprising himself by ordering a second full plate and finishing that one off too.

"How much have you eaten since Friday?" Andi had asked, and only then did he realize how empty his stomach must have been. "You made me hungry too," she added, and told him about the cheese crackers episode, and for the first time in days they both laughed, and heartily. He then revealed, cautiously, that he wanted to be with her, and she answered, cautiously, that he had been through a lot recently, that she wasn't saying no but if they even considered this it would have to be taken slowly. In answer to a question he was afraid to articulate, she had admitted to her reluctance in the past, why Gary never happened, her fear that their age difference would eventually leave someone brokenhearted and she guessed she didn't want that someone to be her. But on her drive to Humble, she finally reasoned that age is only one of a thousand reasons relationships don't work, or do. Then she sipped her cherry cola. "Have you spoken with Didi lately?"

He had nodded, saying nothing more. Didi had called that morning before the funeral. He was very happy to hear from her, but it occurred to him that he was touched in the same way he would have been had an old friend called—not a lover, and certainly not a girlfriend. He knew he would have to have a more difficult conversation with her soon, but decided to postpone it until he felt a little stronger. He promised himself it would happen before anything started with Andi again.

Two days later, Wednesday evening, Didi had called him at home to tell him she had had an abortion the day before. She had been torn between laying this on him now and keeping something so important from him. He could hear the physical weakness in her voice and was upset that she had gone through it alone, but she said a friend had given her some contacts, and one woman, a registered nurse who had already been through such an ordeal herself, not only went with Didi for the procedure but stayed overnight at Didi's place to make sure there were no complications, all at enormous risk to the woman's career. "I'm sure she and I will be friends for life."

Eliot was quiet. "Please at least let me pay for it."

"Eliot, it's not your fault. You didn't know. And, believe me, I'm lucky compared to all the women making appointments with back-alley butchers. I'm rich, remember?" He was silent. "Alright. If it'll make you feel better, send me a check." She paused. "I suppose you thought I hadn't been calling because I'd lost interest." He could hear a smile in her drained voice.

"You suppose right."

"Not yet, though you have definitely been on probation ever since the day you picked out those ridiculous underthings for me to wear." He had laughed softly, and pondered what to say next. Before he could work it out, she continued. "This all kind of knocked me for a loop though." He heard her swallow. "I'm thinking maybe we should back off a while. At least a year, till I see how this birth control pill thing is panning out." A joke, and not.

She had made it all so easy for him, his moving on, and he felt a little sick with guilt. And then she had said, "Once when I called Maryland trying to get you, Andi answered."

He caught his breath. "We didn't. We didn't—"

"I know you didn't. But you will."

He sighed quietly. "Didi—"

"Listen, sweetie, if you were going temporarily out of commission, I can guarantee I wouldn't be a nun waiting for *you*. So what's good for the goose."

"I don't know about Andi and me." He was about to say more, he felt he owed her some sort of honest explanation, but she had laughed then, suddenly the old mysterious carefree Didi laugh that she knew drove him nuts by her refusal to ever define its subtext. He shook his head, a wistful smile, wiping a tear.

"I'm going to call tomorrow. And I'm going to keep calling. To see how you are."

"Oh good, because I was seriously considering becoming a lesbian and avoiding all this drama. You'll be the first to know."

"You'll make a lot of women very happy."

He was quiet all Thursday, sequestering himself in his office. At five he walked out to Andi's desk, noticing her putting her things together to leave. She looked up.

"I talked to Didi."

She had stared, her eyes shining.

"Can we. Can we talk tonight?"

"I have my class."

"Oh! I forgot."

She continued softly. "Let's talk tomorrow."

Friday was busy, and he couldn't find a moment alone at Andi's desk until mid-afternoon.

"You and Will going for a drink tonight?"

She had looked at him, an odd smile. "Uh-uh."

"I thought you always did on Fridays."

"We had been. But, I don't know. Neither of us brought it up today. I'm kind of looking forward to going home and washing my hair, getting to bed early."

"How about dinner first?"

Her eyes still on him. "I'm kind of tired, Eliot." He nodded, a bit embarrassed, and turned to head back to his office. "How about tomorrow night?"

He turned around smiling, hopeful.

"Slow," she had reminded him.

"Definitely."

And they had taken it slow. They picked up a pizza and went back to

Andi's just to talk. And they kept things slow all through dinner, and all through the long evening chat, and all through their ice cream dessert, and all through sex that night and all day Sunday, periodically hearing the crazy neighbor dog which now caused him to laugh.

As promised, Eliot had called Didi a few consecutive evenings, and on Monday morning, six days after the procedure, he rang and there was no answer. His heart beating, he tried her at work and was relieved and elated when she answered, sounding like her old self. She told him her colleagues were glad her rough bout with "the flu" was finally over, then began enthusiastically elaborating on a case she had just been assigned. For a moment he worried that her giddiness indicated she had forgotten that they were no longer together, as the decision was made in her fragile fog of the previous week. Then he wondered if she were forcing a deliberate smiling face to prove how she had already emotionally moved on. No, she seemed genuinely jubilant. And then it hit him: how life-threatening her out-of-hospital surgery was, and how grateful she was just to be alive. And he loved her. No longer carnal desire, but rather his admiration for her unceasing courage and drive and unparalleled strength, and he fiercely hoped that he would always have the honor of calling Didi Wilcox his friend.

He'd forgotten it was his birthday until his father called later that morning. Because it was his mother who'd always made this call, it was all Eliot could do to be gracious during the two-minute conversation, and instantly after hanging up he had placed his palm tight on his mouth to gag the sobs. At 4:30, his colleagues surprised him with cake in the conference room. At five, Andi had to rush off to study for an imminent and crucial exam. As things were just starting with them again, he certainly wouldn't have expected her to take him out for his birthday, and at any rate he was hardly in the mood to celebrate this first motherless one. But when he returned to his office he found on his desk a small box, as if to hold a ring, and a note: "Happy 26th." A shiny new penny. Andi's gift of luck for his next Dixie venture, just as when she had found the heads-up cent and given it to him for his travels to Georgia. When he turned the coin over, he saw that both sides were heads.

Eliot holds the egg, happy that Rosie didn't peel it because it is this tactile activity he loves most about the food. He watches a pickup baseball game, colored children and white. He marvels. By pubescence the lines would start being drawn, but at this age, even in the Deep South they could put aside their differences so as to collect enough players for a team. So when exactly does it begin? The point of no return, when race defines *every*thing?

He remembers his undergraduate days, a few mixed mixers with other local colleges wherein he had had his share of run-ins with a certain faction of the White Left and its patronizing arrogance. Befriending Negroes on *their* terms. They might say schools should be integrated, but would they send their children to the former colored school, to have them taught by black educators? The answer to that had left many Negro teachers supporting segregation for fear of losing their jobs, their dire predictions ultimately proving wretchedly accurate. And if a liberal socialized with you, did they consider you another distinct human being or merely a symbol of their broadmindedness?

But what about the whites who truly struggle for equality, who risked their own lives coming South to fight with their black brothers and sisters? And the progressives who lived in the South. Diana and her father come to mind, daring committed souls Eliot had come to trust, to be deeply fond of.

What about Keith? And like an avalanche the reality comes crashing down: What had really irked Eliot was not his brother's sexual relationship so much as the fact that Keith was white. Not that Eliot would have been exactly thrilled had Dwight appointed his male colored lover as a pallbearer but, in seeing a sixth black man complete the assemblage, Eliot certainly would not have made that ugly scene that shames him now. And after all that, it was Keith's graciousness that had allowed him to see his mother for the last time. Evil is epidemic in White America—and Eliot thinks bitterly about the fate of little Max and Jordan—but it is not universal.

The image comes back to him now of Beau and Roy's embrace: more like brothers than brothers-in-law, and Eliot wonders if he and Dwight could ever be that close. After Eliot's emotional release the night before their mother's funeral, the brothers had remained stoic at the service, comforting their father when necessary but otherwise left to their own private ache. Yet there were words that needed to be spoken between him and Dwight. Well. They had both promised to come home and be with their father on Thanksgiving and Christmas too. There would be time then to start the conversation.

The courthouse clock strikes 5:45, and as Eliot strolls back to the jail he hears a crack. A Negro boy has hit the ball to the farthest outfield, and now runs as if victory in this game will win him the world.

Eliot crosses the threshold to see Warren, Joe Archie, and Les quietly talking. Warren smiles. "This your first time down South, son?"

"No," and Eliot tells them about Max and Jordan. The local men are jolted by the case, and impressed by Eliot's part in it. He asks where Mrs. Yancey is.

"I talked her into staying home until we came for her," says Joe Archie. "Close to a bathroom she can use."

The sheriff walks in from the outside, not looking in the direction of the Negroes and continuing to ignore them after he takes the deputy's place and begins paperwork. Warren, flanked by the others, goes to the desk. "Sheriff Tucker, I would like to—"

"Bail's set at one hundred dollars." Tucker doesn't look up.

Warren seems confused. "Sir?"

"You heard me, an one a you can go back. *One.*" He holds up his right index finger for emphasis before returning to his work.

Warren takes the colored men aside. "I don't have that kind of cash on me right now but I can get it. If you could talk to Mr. Yancey," Warren is looking at Eliot, "let him know it's on the way."

Tucker unlocks a door. "Double shift tonight, Jesse," he utters to the guard, which sounds less like a friendly reminder than something between a reprimand and a warning, given that the watchman clearly just snapped to after a little shut-eye.

There are only two prisoners, a young white man with reddish-blond hair looking a bloody dirty mess who gapes at Eliot as they pass, and in the cell next to him Mr. Yancey. Eliot looks in at his client. A black eye, blood on his shirt. His arm hangs lazily, in a way that suggests it's broken. Eliot is astounded, and then angry at himself for being so: as if they wouldn't do such a thing to a frail old man. He turns to the guard, glaring. The guard smiles a little, shrugs. "Resistin arrest." Glancing at the white man, Eliot thinks, Seems like a lot of that's going around. He makes himself focus on his client, speaking quietly, informing him that he is his attorney, assuring him that help would arrive momentarily in the form of bail, that he would be out soon and taken to the hospital. The old man nods. "Can you please tell my wife I'm alright?"

"I don't want to leave here until you are released, sir, but when the other men come back, I promise one of us will let her know." Eventually Eliot hears Warren's voice from the front desk area, and he starts to walk out.

"Hey!"

The white inmate. He sounds agitated, indignant, the tone Eliot associates with a preamble to a spat of racial epithets, and because Eliot cannot afford to lose his temper now, he keeps walking.

"*Hey! I* ain't got no lawyer!"

The guard snickers. He unlocks the door, and Eliot walks through to find Warren posting bail. The sheriff accompanies Eliot back to Mr. Yancey, ordering the guard to release the prisoner.

"Let him *out?*"

"His bail was jus posted, open the cell."

"He was resistin arrest!"

"That's for the judge to decide, now unlock the goddamn door, Jesse."

In a huff, Jesse does as he has been commanded and, with difficulty, Mr. Yancey steps out, aided by Eliot.

"This is not the way we usually do things here," says Jesse.

And Eliot, staring at Mr. Yancey's injuries, no longer able to fully restrain himself, mutters, "I bet some of it is."

"*What did you say?*" Jesse snaps.

"Hey, I ain't seen *my* lawyer!" chimes in the white prisoner. "I ain't made no damn phone call!"

"Yes you did," the sheriff says. "You jus don't remember," and the inmate seems utterly confused. Eliot sees now that he has no shoes, his socks torn and filthy.

"I ain't no indigent! That damn sheriff tryin to make like I am, I ain't drunk! You know what kinda day I had? My sister beat to bits by her bastard husband an the cops do *nothin,* I had to find her on the floor lookin like put through the shredder! *I'm* the one taken her to the hospital *the cops do nothin,* then I get *fired* for my trouble! I threw those goddamn shoes at Martin's head, I'd do it *again!* Come back here! You listened to *him,* I got a story to tell! *I* got a story to tell!"

The next morning Eliot wakes early, before his hosts, before dawn, and walks outside to gaze at the twinkling remaining stars. In a few hours he would be leaving, heading back north to home. The whistle of a lonely train in the distance, and then the birds chirping, something he hasn't heard since sunrises in Humble. As day breaks, he gets into the borrowed local Plymouth station wagon.

When he walks in, the jailhouse guard is talking to the sheriff. Eliot is surprised to see them both still here, then remembers the latter's remark yesterday evening about a double shift. They turn to Eliot, confused and vaguely alarmed. He sets the shoebox on the desk, opening it so they can see its contents.

"I brought these in case some Negro needed them, but *then*—" and at that moment Eliot spies in the wastebasket a lady's handkerchief, a delicate light fabric and intricate handmade needlepoint design, apparently something Mrs. Yancey dropped and the officers scrapped, and he remembers his mother making things like that once, she had wanted doilies to adorn the couch end tables in the living room and couldn't afford the store-bought laces, and suddenly the events of the past nineteen days—the agony of losing his mother and the drama of the funeral arrangements and the complications of romance and the bittersweetness of Mr. Daughtery's trial and the horror of out-of-hospital abortion and the vexation of another bout with Deep Southern hospitality—all seem to well up in Eliot at once. He tilts his head toward the cells, then turns and leaves quickly.

As he packs up the car at the Coatses', the couple stands with him to bid their adieus before heading off to work. Martha is a laundress, Jeremiah a janitor at the bus station. He shakes Eliot's hand, and asks when he'll be back this way again. Eliot says he isn't sure.

"Well you know you can always stay with us," says Martha, giving him a few sandwiches to share with Beau on the road.

Truthfully, Eliot imagines he won't be returning. He had asked the NAACP men if he should stay for today, the last day of voter registration, to try again. They said they would be there, but they imagined most of the Negroes would not be able to spare another day off work, presuming a repeat fiasco. And yet the activists did not seem defeated, preparing to continue their drive, if not for this election, then the next. In a couple of weeks it will be President Kennedy or President Nixon with or without the Southern black vote. (Of course with both pledging their support of civil rights, many segregationists are still holding out for independent President Harry F. Byrd and running mate Strom Thurmond.) Winston Douglas and

Associates would certainly continue to support and defend the struggle in the Deep South, but they would not be back to Prayer Ridge, Alabama, for a while, if ever.

Leona, dressed for school, dashes out of the house to offer Eliot a farewell riddle. "What kinda coffee they serve on the *Titanic*?"

"I don't know."

"Maxwell House!" She runs back in, giggling her head off.

"I'ma pray for you an your daddy an your brother," says Martha. "You know your mama's always lookin down on you," and she gives Eliot a warm hug and a kiss. Eliot gets in the car. He puts on his glasses and turns on the ignition, then Leona comes racing out in a panic. "I mean SANKA! SANKA!"

As he pulls off Eliot starts laughing and finds he can't stop. He is reminded of how his mother could never get a joke right, and for the first time since her death he is able to enjoy her memory without the simultaneous undertow of pain. He is still chortling fifteen miles up the road as he pulls into Rosie's yard and sees Beau waving at the window, and Eliot wonders if he'll laugh the whole way to Indianapolis.

1970s

I

Shit, piss, puke, blood. If you can modify your perceptions so that bodily excretions are no longer repulsive but rather merely parts of a riddle to solve, then you have prepped yourself for significant remuneration: a free apartment.

Mrs. Garcia opens her door. A rotund woman in her sixties, she speaks quickly, then suddenly puts her hand over her mouth embarrassed, as if it were an insult to me that she has uttered words when I cannot hear them, or perhaps it's just that she feels foolish. I smile politely, and she points me in the direction, too ashamed to accompany me on my first glimpse of the foulness in her backed-up toilet. Her mortification, common among my clients, is beneficial for me as I enjoy working alone, being left with my thoughts. I start with my plunger (though I presume this ultimately will be a job for the snake), and as I work I marvel on today's milestone: the tenth anniversary of my arrival, this rural Alabama boy's entry into New York City.

When I left Prayer Ridge on a Tuesday afternoon, I wanted to get as far away as possible, geographically and otherwise, and Manhattan seemed to be the place. The bus pulled into the Port Authority depot at 2:30 Thursday morning, November 24th, 1960, and I found a corner and there I set my suitcase, the container of all my worldly possessions, laying it flat and laying my torso on top of it, and I slept. I woke a few hours later, washed in the public restroom and, carrying my valise, started walking south down Eighth Avenue looking for work. I was stunned to see so many institutions closed in the city I had thought of as always awake, and then I remembered that it was Thanksgiving. In the 30s I strolled toward Seventh Avenue and Macy's, captivated by the parade balloons. From there I had a clear view of the towering Empire State Building, conclusively bringing home to me where I was.

When the show was over, I ambled through the hordes, and on the window of a diner in the 20s spotted a sign: DISHWASHER WANTED. Being handicapped has its advantages. Employers believe that I'm lucky to get any job and therefore feel they are in their rights to pay me less than other workers, and underpaid work comes easily. I began immediately, breaking at seven for my Thanksgiving dinner, a toasted fried egg sandwich with pickle. The restaurant was open twenty-four hours but I was let go at eleven, and the cook pointed me to a nearby flophouse where I made my home the next several weeks.

One mid-afternoon while the waitress was on break, a customer walked in and I was asked to serve him. I touched my ear to indicate my deafness, handed the man a menu, and asked him to indicate what he wanted. Thereafter the man began coming regularly, weekdays at 3:10, and every day I served him. On a January Friday, two months after my arrival into the city, he handed me a note.

Window washing: <u>More $!</u>

I didn't even know this man's name and yet he offered me this kindness. Of course I know it now, Sheldon Wise, because we worked together for two years, high in the sky. His boss was at first reluctant to hire a deaf man but finally could think of no good reason why my disability would be a hindrance and, again, he realized he could compensate off the books below the standard rate, which was still exponentially more than I earned dishwashing. The raise allowed me to move out of the flophouse and into a basement apartment in Hell's Kitchen. One room and no windows, but I had my own private half-bath: sink and toilet. The work was good, perfect solitude fifty storeys above Fifth or Lex, seldom noticed by the office dwellers any more than had I been some decorative plant. This invisibility I much preferred over my conspicuous presence in the diner, where I was periodically subject to a sudden hostile jab in the back from a customer frustrated by my insolence to have ignored his party after he called me three times.

One day I was going through my mail, which had never been anything but the electric bill or advertisements, and discovered a hand-delivered note.

Dear Mr. Evans,
 I don't know if you knew the night super is moving to Arizona. I need somebody in case somebody calls in the evenings or middle of the night or Sundays. (I take care of Saturdays.) It's really

just for emergencies and you wouldn't have to do much. That time when the Murphy's toilet overflowed and you got up there and fixed it before I could get there I was impressed. I could train you. Since you don't have a license (I guess) YOU WON'T GET PAID but you'll get a FREE APARTMENT. (Including utilities.) Also 2 weeks vacation. You can keep your old apt. or you can move into Jerry's old apt., which is bigger. Leave a note under my door, yes or no.

Lloyd Fischer,
Super.

Not only is the living room of Apartment 3B easily twice as large as the entire space of my subterranean studio, but the bedroom and small kitchen are separate, and three rooms is an enormous upgrade. And a full bathroom with tub, *and* two large windows! Not much sunlight on the third of a six-floor walk-up, but if I'm awake early enough on bright mornings, for fifteen minutes the room is bathed in nature's warmth.

At some point the window-washing became slow, and I was asked to start coming in only for the afternoons. The Metropolitan Museum is admission by donation so, at fifty cents a pop, I began spending my mornings gazing at masterpieces. I am perpetually enraptured by Mr. Miró, and for a period of time *Le Carnaval d'Arlequin* was on loan to the institution. On a Friday in January of '63, as I soaked in its magnificence for the fourth consecutive day, I happened to glance at the security guard, a slight dark woman I had seen often, and who was now strangely smiling at me. And then she signed: Would you like a job?

I'm a private person. I am in no way ashamed of my deafness, but the fact that she had deduced it left me feeling exposed. A *job?*

Before I could respond she continued. You come here often, seem to appreciate the work. There are deaf groups who visit. You could lead the tour. Mary's been doing it but she's about to go away to graduate school.

I looked at her, then at the roomful of treasures, my thoughts racing: I have never studied art. I have never been to school. I'm ignorant.

During my first year in the city, I had taken the subway to visit a museum in Queens. In the borough streets, perplexing to even seasoned Manhattanites, I became lost, and by chance happened upon a group of deaf people.

I asked for directions and they politely gave them, arguing about the best route. With the exception of a brief course years ago in Selma, until this point I had never signed with anyone but my hearing brother, and I found myself confused, not knowing which signer to look at, not understanding many of the signs nor the syntax, and I could see them frowning at my own manual information. Finally a woman asked if I were deaf or hearing. Though I don't believe she intended to insult me, but rather to be more helpful by this clarification, I was nevertheless humiliated. I didn't sign with another person until two months later when I came across an advertisement for adult education instruction in the sign language. I followed up my first class with more advanced courses, finally eliminating the thick hearing accent in my language, so that now I signed deaf rather than deaf-taught-by-his-self-taught-hearing-kid-brother, or so I was assured. (Years later I came to realize that the hearing also use the term "accent" with regard to variation in spoken language.) Still, the mortification of the Queens episode stayed with me, and I've since mostly avoided conversations with the deaf.

This, however, was more explanation than the museum guard needed so I kept it simple: I have never studied art.

You're in here studying the work quite often, I'm going to make a guess you know enough. They need someone fast and available. It's too late in the season now to recruit some college art student intern, which would be in line with the pay scale. Also free admission to the museum.

I hesitate.

You'll meet Mary. She'll help you, she won't hire you unless she feels you can handle it. Are you interested?

I nod.

Be at the main entrance Wednesday at eleven for the tour. I'll tell her to expect you. What's your name?

Benjamin Evans.

I'll tell Mary to expect you, Benjamin Evans. If there's any confusion, just mention Perpétue sent you.

And then in reply to my unvoiced question: It's Haitian.

And then in reply to my other unvoiced question: My sister's deaf.

Why don't *you* want the job?

She laughed. Museum tour guiding doesn't pay enough for me.

I spent the next five days in anxiety, deciding whether I should go, but before I'd made a final decision, it was Wednesday. I bathed and dressed in my only suit, arriving at 10:40. I noticed a group of sign-speakers beginning to form, and at quarter till a young Oriental woman appeared. Over the next hour Mary Kim gave an overview—European paintings, Greek and Roman sculpture, ancient pieces from sub-Saharan Africa, China— followed by a Q&A. The tour was over at noon, and Mary told everyone they were free to continue exploring the museum on their own. Because the guide had in no way acknowledged me, I began to wonder if Perpétue may have forgotten to tell her, or if Mary was less inclined to hire someone with no art education. I was just turning away to leave when I was tapped on the shoulder.

Benjamin?

Yes. I wondered how she picked me out of the assemblage. Then she laughed: You *are* tall.

We began retracing our steps, her asking me to lead the tour. I was worried now that she would find me out to be an impostor, a home-schooled deafie, but to my great relief we chatted easily, and I felt at that moment, whether I was hired or not, I had *passed:* crossed over into the conversational deaf community. In celebrating this grand accomplishment secretly, I was not even aware at how impressed Mary was that I'd retained so much of her earlier lecture.

What draws you to that Rembrandt? She had noticed me glancing at a painting she hadn't mentioned on the tour.

The chiaroscuro.

Chiaroscuro! And I remembered she had talked about light and dark but had not evoked the technical term in her whirlwind lecture. I felt embarrassed, as if I had been showing off.

I think I'm recalling something from an art book I read. I looked down a moment. I don't have any formal art education.

If you did, you would have gotten an A-plus.

I was quite nervous at first, but the more I conversed with other deaf, the more agile I became in the language, and as for the content of my lectures, my tour groups seemed universally pleased. I learned that it's customary for the educated deaf to ask where one was from, and when I would answer "Alabama," they assumed that I was referring to the Alabama Institute for

Deaf and Blind. They also seemed to take for granted that I had studied at Gallaudet College. I couldn't lie, nor did I want them to feel they were being cheated in having a layperson for a guide, so to avoid awkwardness I did my best to keep the discussion on the art.

During one of these sessions a woman walked up to me. She was a hearing person, smiling. This was not unusual, as there are museum patrons who seem oddly moved by an open display of deaf art enthusiasts, some of these patrons walking up to congratulate me on my charitable work, only to become flustered and embarrassed to realize the tour guide is also deaf.

But this woman was not confused, and handed me a note.

> My daughter goes to a private school in Greenwich Village. In addition to Spanish, French, and German, they would like to offer a class in the sign language. They are looking to hire a part-time teacher. Are you available Tuesday and Thursday afternoons?

I smile and write a reply, admitting that I hold no academic degrees.

> I'm somewhat embarrassed to say that may be an asset. I have a sense that the budget could not withstand the going rate for someone properly qualified.

I love my students! Younger children in the noon group, the teens at one. I use flash cards and mimeographs, but mostly hands-on handspeak, insofar as possible keeping vocalizations out of the classroom. Many people would regard my decision to quit my comparably lucrative window-washing job in order to teach a few classes as foolish. But my free rent allows me the luxury of part-time work (I still spend Saturdays dishwashing as a pecuniary supplement), and I am stunned and honored to be a fine arts museum guide and a language teacher. I, who never had any formal education!

Among the many features of my adopted city that were not available in Prayer Ridge: foreign films. I'm not a snob about Hollywood releases. On the contrary, I see the marquees and long to be in the cinematic know of my fellow citizens: *Midnight Cowboy* and *Easy Rider* and *Hello, Dolly!* and *They Shoot Horses, Don't They?* But a movie sans subtitles is utterly frustrating. Lip reading is not so easy a task as the hearing seem to presume. For the hard of hearing it is sometimes a useful auxiliary tool, but the most expert deaf lip-reader gleans thirty percent of the language at best, and with films there is the additional matter of voiceovers and off-camera dialogue. So I satisfy myself with either American films of a bygone era (I'm a huge Charlie Chaplin and Buster Keaton fan) or screenings from abroad: *Battle of Algiers, Persona, The Bicycle Thief.*

And once I happened upon a retrospective of the Moving Picture Committee of the National Association of the Deaf. At the advent of motion pictures, these silent shorts were shot completely in the sign language, no translations into English, *by* the deaf and *for* the deaf. I sat in an audience who fluttered their hands in applause. The pieces varied widely—the serious and the humorous. Significant was the advocacy for manual communication, threatened by the then-current movement for oralism: forcing the deaf to renounce hand-speaking and talk, something that could never be perfected without hearing and thus would always leave the deaf at a disadvantage. Especially striking was the 1913 "Preservation of the Sign Language" by George Veditz, a former NAD president and multilingual deaf man who was also an award-winning horticulturalist and newspaper editor, who launched a campaign against the Civil Service forcing Teddy Roosevelt to allow for the hiring of deaf in government jobs, and who once played the world chess champion. (It was a draw.)

Monday mornings, with most museums closed, I sit in the reading room of the main public library, the entrance guarded by the noble stone lions. If Abigail the librarian is on shift, she always smiles and often holds out a book she thinks may be of interest to me. One afternoon in 1967, my seventh year in New York and fifth as a night super, she handed me a slim hardback—*Helen Keller: Her Socialist Years.*

Some years ago I met a gentleman who was introduced to me as Mr. McKelway, editor of the Brooklyn Eagle. *It was after a meeting that we had in New York in behalf of the blind. At that time the compliments he paid me were so generous that I blush to remember them. But now that I have come out for socialism he reminds me and the public that I am blind and deaf and especially liable to error. I must have shrunk in intel-*

ligence during the years since I met him. . . . The Eagle *and I are at war. I hate the system which it represents, apologizes for and upholds. When it fights back, let it fight fair. Let it attack my ideas and oppose the aims and arguments of Socialism. . . . I can read. I can read all the socialist books I have time for in English, German and French. If the editor of the Brooklyn* Eagle *should read some of them, he might be a wiser man and make a better newspaper. If I ever contribute to the Socialist movement the book that I sometimes dream of, I know what I shall name it:* Industrial Blindness and Social Deafness. *(1912)*

It seems to me that they are blind indeed who do not see that there must be something very wrong when the workers—the men and women who produce the wealth of the nation—are ill paid, ill fed, ill clothed, ill housed. Deaf indeed are they who do not hear the desperation in the voice of the people crying out against cruel poverty and social injustice. (1913)

This is not a time of gentleness, of timid beginnings that steal into life with soft apologies and dainty grace. It is a time for loud voiced, open speech and fearless thinking; a time of striving and conscious manhood, a time of all that is robust and vehement and bold; a time radiant with new ideals, new hopes of true democracy.

I love it, for it thrills me and gives me a feeling that I shall face great and terrible things. I am a child of my generation, and I rejoice that I live in such a splendidly disturbing time. (1913)

I closed the book. *This changes everything.*

I began taking classes: boilers, heating, ventilation. Twelve weeks later I stood outside Lloyd Fischer's door holding a note and some paperwork, and I knocked.

> Dear Lloyd,
>   I am submitting to you documentation certifying that I
> have passed all requirements for licensed employment

as a building superintendent. Thus, if I continue to be employed as a night/weekend/emergency super, I must be paid and receive applicable benefits. If you feel you cannot comply, I hope you will understand that I will have to speak with a union representative about the arrangement under which I have been laboring here. I have enjoyed our friendship, and hope that none of the aforementioned engenders ill feelings.

Sincerely,

Benjamin Evans

For a while it did engender ill feelings—I have wondered if Lloyd had been getting some sort of kickback by virtue of my "voluntary" labor (and, regarding my outdoor work which I was about to end, I have also pondered about the sleight-of-hand involved in my hire as a window cleaner without mentioning the union)—but Lloyd nonetheless went to the building management and I was officially hired, becoming a Local 32B member. Naturally he began to give me extra duties in light of my substantial wage increase up from zero, which I have not minded at all. I like earning my paycheck.

Oh what a rich life I have lived in New York! I am overwhelmingly grateful, aware of the domino effect that has brought me to this juncture, ten years since my arrival. Through the dishwashing job I met my friend Sheldon Wise who arranged the window cleaning, which afforded me my move out of the flophouse and into Hell's Kitchen, leading to my meeting my friend Lloyd Fischer who offered me the night superintendent job, which provided free rent and the time to go to the library and explore museums, where I met my security guard friend Perpétue leading me to my friend and mentor Mary Kim and the Met job, which led me to Penny Appleton who arranged the teaching job (her daughter being one of my students), and my library visits leading to meeting my friend Abigail who gave me Helen Keller's book inspiring me to demand my just treatment as a New York City superintendent, I am a lucky man! And if it seems odd that I call all these people my "friends," I would counter that anyone who has offered me the opportunities each one of them has is a friend to me.

The snake has finally jiggled something free. I pull out an eight-inch long rubber alligator, definitely making my top twenty list of strangest things I have ever found that have impeded plumbing. I clean up my area, then wash off the reptile before bringing it out to show my client. Her face red, Mrs. Garcia cries *"Nieta! Nieta!"*—explaining that her granddaughter must have flushed it. I smile politely, hoping my neighbor will admonish the child not to play in the toilet in the future, then I have her sign the services-rendered form before I run downstairs to take my shower. It's 7:15 and I don't want to be late for my own anniversary banquet!

I walk into my favorite restaurant at 8:05, only five minutes late. The friendly waitresses are happy to see me. To be polite, the hostess always asks how many are in my party, even though the answer is always the same. I hold up one finger.

It's a celebration, so I order the sushi *and* the teriyaki, then red bean ice cream. I savor the sweet scoops as I look around. A young Oriental couple. Two white middle-aged women. A Negro family, mother, father, two children. Three Hispanic teenagers giggling. Though I appear to be the only one in the restaurant who is alone, I'm not. I have brought my friends *Franny and Zooey*. I look down and turn the page.

When I get home, I read a bit before retiring promptly at ten. I'm a chronic insomniac, something that began my last few agonizing weeks in Prayer Ridge, and the 10 p.m. curfew allows me a few hours' shut-eye before the inevitable waking at two. At that point I am a wide-eyed zombie for at least three hours, and I have never been able to sleep past seven. But for tonight I have a plan. This afternoon I visited the brand-new Mid-Manhattan branch of the public library, stood before the woman behind the information desk and handed her a note: **Cookbook?** This will be my secret weapon against insomnia!

At the restaurant are Abigail the librarian, Lloyd the super, Perpétue the security guard, Mary the museum guide, Penny the private school parent, Joy the principal at the private school, Mrs. Garcia from upstairs, even Sheldon the window washer whom I haven't seen in years—all my friends! At first they are smiling, chatting, but now they seem uncomfortable. I can read their lips: Where's Benjamin? And I realize I'm not there! Now I leave my building, I'm coming! But no. I'm lost! The restaurant is only two blocks north but I'm in Times Square, then Grand Central Station, then the Chrysler Building—I can't find my way! Now I stand in Central Park, a circle of seven hippies seated cross-legged in the grass. They gaze at me with benevolent wise looks, knowing something I don't.

My eyes flash open at 1:55 and I pick up my defense. But as I carefully study each term in the glossary from *aerate* to *zest,* and as I identify the calorie counts for various casseroles and stews, and as I incorporate my arithmetic skills—if a cup and a half of flour is needed for four dozen cookies, how much for three dozen?—awaiting sleep to overcome me in the mundanity, I am suddenly seized by a profound melancholy and when I feel my eyes burning I throw off the blankets and run to the kitchen breathing, breathing.

As I gradually calm I become aware that I'm staring at my hundreds of books. I had nearly forgotten my decision to donate a few boxfuls to the public library, and now it occurs to me my own library could use some organizing. Knowing the hour is late, I am gentle in emptying the bookcases covering my walls so as not to disturb my neighbors, and in an hour my floor is covered in tomes. I'm alphabetizing, classifying—merge biography with history? separate fiction from poetry?—while setting aside dozens of volumes for my public library contribution. I'm barely halfway through when daylight seeps through the blinds, and I remember I'm out of milk and should go to the corner grocery now to beat the morning pedestrian rush on the sidewalk.

I never heard the voices of my family nor of my neighbors nor of the other men at the sawmill, yet when I read Faulkner I have an impression of things familiar, of coming home. I'm not in the least interested in ever returning to Dixie, but there's a certain comfort in this identification, a fellow Southerner who can so richly convey, for better or for worse, the intricate peculiarities of our very distinctive region.

I turn the page. It's the 5th of December and the uptown E is packed, some headed to Saturday night social events, some suburban holiday shoppers. Squeezed in the horde are four deaf students, their hands moving rapidly. The colored girl says Kennedy started the escalation, and the colored boy says the first U.S. casualty was way back in '56, Eisenhower, and the Oriental girl says when they began defoliating the jungle that was the real beginning, and the colored boy says *What?* and the Oriental girl says My brother was there, it comes in big cans with an orange stripe, "Orange," and the white boy says it started with the origins of the Cold War, and the Oriental girl says who *cares* where it started, three hundred thousand American troops there *now*, killing and dying and killing.

At Times Square there's always the mass exodus of passengers replaced by a mass influx, the colored girl the only remainder of the students. Her flawless smooth skin is dark brown. She wears a miniskirt and tights and sports a large Afro. Moments after the doors have closed and the train pulled off I glimpse her stricken face, and I recognize her distress: she had wanted the uptown local train, the AA or CC, and just realized she's on the E to Queens. The girl is not aware that I have been observing all this because I've learned to absorb the goings-on around me without appearing to have lifted my eyes from my book. She moves through the throng to the map and seems to make a plan. At 50th, the next stop, she exits the train, as do I. My building is three blocks away. I walk up the steps and notice there's some sort of police action that has temporarily halted the uptown AA and CC. I feel someone tap my back.

She stands before me with that panicked look again. She is five-five or -six, a good foot shorter than I, and stares up into my face as her lips move, apparently sound is being uttered from them as she gestures with exaggeration. She assumes I can hear. Her distorted sound might only confuse a hearing person but, fortunately, her strained pronunication allows me to easily read her lips. "Cross over?" She would like to know if at this station she can move from the uptown to the downtown side without exiting and thus avoid paying an extra fare. I smile sympathetically as I shake my head. She looks as if she's going to cry. I don't know what else to do so I turn away. She grabs my arm, a bit frantic. She has pulled out a small notepad and writes furiously.

> *I am deaf. Earlier I gave all my money to a hungry person, I don't have 30¢ for a token. May I please borrow?*

I have many friends. Abigail the librarian and Lloyd the super and Joy the school principal and Perpétue the museum guard and none of them knows anything about me, no one has ever asked me a personal question and this has made for me a very culturally rich and safe life. I keep my chats with Perpétue brief, and holding conversations with hearing people who are not sign-speakers is exhausting for both parties so I've been able to maintain respectful boundaries with all of my good friends. To begin a conversation with a stranger in the sign language is to risk complications. I could give this young woman the thirty cents, then have her walk up out of the station to cross the street then back down into the station on the other side to take the E or the AA or the CC one stop downtown back to the Times Square station to then walk up and over from the downtown side to the up to wait for the northbound AA or CC.

But there's an easier way.

I sign: Do you need the CC uptown?

She stares at me, startled that I am hand-speaking. Yes! I'm going to 94th and Amsterdam.

You can walk to Columbus Circle and catch it there. I'll give you the thirty cents.

Thank you! Thank you so much!

And as I am reaching into my pocket for the quarter and nickel, her hands begin moving rapidly. She lives in Greenwich Village and never comes uptown but a friend of hers from college has just moved to the city and is having a housewarming party. It started at seven but then you know how parties go, you get there when you get there. She couldn't come until now because of her Friday afternoon class with the people she was on the train with.

Yes, I thought you were students. We have come out of the subway and are walking up Eighth Avenue, the night clear, in the forties.

Continuing education students, I think you mean. I'm thirty-three. It was a fiction writing class. Have you ever written stories?

No.

I haven't done it since Gallaudet. I'm really glad I went there. I liked D.C. After high school I debated whether to go to a regular college or deaf, but I guess I've always been around deaf people so I felt more comfortable there. My parents and most of my siblings are deaf.

Really?

Her fist nods briskly. I've never been to a housewarming before. I wasn't sure what to bring so I brought wine. Do you think I should have brought something for the apartment? But I haven't *seen* the apartment. So I just brought wine and I'll ask Marielle when I get there if she needs anything for the apartment. That's her name, Marielle. Well, actually, it was Mary Lou until she took the name Marielle in *classe de français* and kept it. The young woman smiles, rolling her eyes. Oh I love these decorations! I know it's all commercial but I just can't help it, I get in the spirit. I'm going home to South Carolina for the holidays. I have six brothers and sisters and they're all deaf except for my sister Ramona. She's the third oldest, I'm right behind her. We'll go to church Christmas Eve and she'll sing in the choir. She wanted to sing in her high school chorus in tenth grade but she was afraid it would insult our family and when my mother found out she was livid. So junior and senior year there she was, her whole deaf family in the front row watching her lips move. Were you born in New York?

I have held onto every word and still it takes me a moment to realize she has paused for a reply.

No. Alabama.

A fellow Southerner! I thought for sure you were native Gotham, you sign so fast! How long have you lived here?

It seems strange for her to remark on my velocity, given that her own hands have been flying a mile a minute.

Ten years.

Oh you're a real New Yorker then! When I graduated from Gallaudet, I stayed in D.C. a while. Another English major I knew got me a job proofreading at her law firm. Then three years ago I was talking about coming to New York and I wrote to my old sophomore roommate who was already here. Well Toni tells me she's about to move to Seattle to get married and her fiancé is allergic to cats so would I like to sublet her place and take care of her cat? *Would* I! The young woman stops a moment. You must think I'm some dingbat, walking around with no money. When I carry it I have a bad habit of spending it, on coffee, a candy bar, junk I don't need and then I'm broke. Thank God I don't smoke anymore. I smoked my freshman year, then my aunt died of diabetes, I quit cold turkey. I know diabetes isn't lung cancer, but every day they seem to discover some new disease smoking causes, I'm not taking any chances. Now I can't even stand to be around cigarette smoke though I know they'll be smoking at the party, they always do. Do you smoke?

No.

So after spending way too much on crap I started leaving my apartment with no more than a dollar. But then right outside the building where my class was I saw this destitute man, skin and bones. I'd already bought my token to get to the party so I gave him the rest. I figured after I got to the party I could borrow thirty cents from somebody for the token home. So it would have been all okay if I hadn't made that mistake just now and got on the E when I should have been on the CC. She shakes her head. That poor man had no shoes. In December! It made me feel grateful to have a job. Even if I hate it. Temped the first two years here, now I'm a secretary in an ad agency. I was told it's the way you break in. Except I'm not sure anymore I *want* to break in. What do you do?

She's a college graduate and I'm a janitor who never went to the first grade. I want to say I'm a teacher but I'd feel like a liar. At any rate it's part-time, and I teach sign. Nothing impressive for her.

I'm a building superintendent.

She stares at me, wide-eyed. *Free rent?*

I smile.

Fantastic! You know, I'm thinking very seriously about a career change. I have a friend who works at the Bronx Zoo who thinks she can get me something. That'd be great, outdoor work. And I love animals! How old are you?

Now I truly consider lying. But I believe she has told me the truth about her age, it's only fair. Only fair. My sigh is private.

Forty-seven.

Really? I would have thought a lot younger. Mid- or late thirties.

My face warm, crimson.

I never come uptown. I'm missing out on a lot, you know? You ever been to the Cloisters? Top of Manhattan?

Yes.

I've always wanted to go! She breathes in the air. What a beautiful night! What's your name?

We are caught at the corner of 61st by a red light. I indicate for us to cross Broadway, and she follows. When we are on the sidewalk, I reply.

Benjamin.

Benjamin. And what's your sign name?

As directed by my sign instructors I had created a concise moniker, an embellished *B*. But the name I grew up with, the name I have never mentioned to anyone in New York, is compact enough. I swallow before I form the two letters.

Hello, B.J. I'm April May June.

I stare at her. She smiles.

It started with me being born in April. And my parents the Junes had a sense of humor. What's *that?*

Lincoln Center.

Lincoln Center? Wait. We passed Columbus Circle.

I thought I would walk you up to 94th. You can use your thirty cents to get home after your party.

She stares at me, and I know I have made a terrible, presumptuous mistake. Some strange man offering to walk her all that way, and up Broadway through notorious Needle Park in the 70s no less! What am I thinking?

Or I can just give you the other thirty cents if you want to get on the subway now. I keep my eyes low, fixed on her hands. I say, You'll need the other thirty to get home later.

I was going to borrow it from somebody at the party.

I nod.

You got out of the train at 50th. You don't mind walking so far out of your way?

And now I glance up and see she's smiling. I tell her, I like to walk.

She takes her little notepad out and scribbles something, tears off the sheet.

My address. You can write to me sometime. Now she turns to Lincoln Center, across from where we are standing.

I swore I would never come here. They removed San Juan Hill to make way for this. It sounds Puerto Rican but it was black, a poor black neighborhood decimated. Did you know?

I shake my head.

Come on.

I follow her, and after navigating the heavily trafficked crisscrossing of Broadway and Columbus, we arrive at Revson Fountain, the centerpiece of Lincoln Center which currently houses the symphony, opera, and a theater, and has future plans for the ballet. Her hands are motionless now as we gaze at the gurgling flow. She smiles, the lights of the cascade dancing in her eyes. Finally she looks up at me, studies my face a moment before her hands gently speak. My sign name. And with a flourish she gives me her flowing, fused *A M J*.

The water suddenly shoots high into the air. April May June and I laugh, surprised, standing next to each other, mesmerized and washed by the crystal spray bedewing the crisp, clear night.

My last day of classes before Christmas break I receive a message from Joy. I wonder if students realize that teachers also live in mortal fear of being called to the principal's office. I have all my basic needs met from my super-intendent career so losing the school position would not mean financial ruin. But I *enjoy* teaching.

When I walk in, she smiles and hands me a note.

Dear Benjamin,

We are all so pleased to have you as our sign language instructor.

I had been wanting to speak with you about your first-term reports. I am concerned that giving every <u>single</u> student an <u>A</u> does not conform to the rigor we have established at this institution. Your pupils all adore you, but I also want them to respect you as a teacher demanding that they strive for their best. You certainly don't want students to register for the sign language class simply because it has come to be known as a "cake course."

Joy Ross

I read the note carefully, then scribble my reply. I imagine Joy is stealing glances at her watch so as I write I don't look up, as it would only embarrass both of us.

Dear Joy,

Though some of my students have picked up the sign language more quickly than others, I believe every one of them is enthusiastic and putting in his/her very best effort. I would not have given an <u>A</u> otherwise. If this makes signing a "cake course" and therefore attracts <u>every</u> student to it, to more extensively bridge the communication gap between the deaf and the hearing, then I am all for it.

Benjamin Evans

As Joy reads the note, I see her laugh out loud. Then she turns the paper over.

> Touché.
> Happy Holidays, Benjamin! See you back here on the 4th.

Two nights later, after a dinner of canned pea soup and saltines, I take my customary annual Christmas Eve stroll sixty blocks uptown and stand in front of St. John the Divine. I sip my deli hot chocolate and join a couple dozen other night wanderers waiting in anticipation on the steps of the Episcopalian Gothic Revival cathedral. The midnight bells. I know when they begin by the smiles on the faces of the others, the Merry Christmas embraces. I keep to the side, smiling myself, observing. When the doors open, I move quickly before the midnight service crowd comes pouring out.

Trekking home I pass a lit window at 92nd and Amsterdam. Apparently the tradition of this Hispanic family is to open gifts just after midnight. The children are in heaven, wildly tearing off the wrappings. The mother seems just as enchanted, the father sitting in his chair smoking, trying to smile but looking exhausted. I watch them for a quarter-hour before the chill forces me back on my way. The next evening I embark on my other holiday ritual, Christmas dinner at my favorite Japanese restaurant, but for some reason this year the establishment is packed, a line out the door. I sigh and pick up egg rolls at the corner takeout to eat at home alone.

As Hell's Kitchen is adjacent to Times Square, every New Year's Eve I plan on getting all that needs done early so I needn't leave my apartment past three. Darkness falls and I stare out my window, wondering if April May June might be among the swarms.

I never wrote her. When I came home that night, I taped her address to the free dog-photo calendar from my bank. I told myself I would dispose of the timetable on the day of its expiration, January 1, 1971, thus setting myself a fast-approaching deadline. But I nervously put things off and now, nearly a month since the evening I walked through Columbus Circle with a companion whose hands spoke to me with such vibrancy, I feel I've missed my chance.

At 11:30, I am inexplicably inspired to rush down into the multitudes. There was some attempt by the police to have barricaded out all latecomers, but this plan seems to have been overruled and I am shoved into the mob. People drunk and happy. I see screaming and broad laughter, I see horns blowing, it seems noisiness is an important part of the celebration. And then their lips: Ten. Nine. Eight. No one in my vicinity can see the lowering ball and still people are jubilant and in one moment they all cheer and embrace, and someone embraces me, and someone kisses me, and someone pours me a plastic glass of champagne which gets knocked out of my hand in the big crush but it's alright, I have not been embraced nor kissed nor touched other than anonymous accidental brushes on the sidewalk in over ten years, I am trembling and relieved they are all too inebriated to be aware of my tears.

It takes me half an hour for the five-minute stroll home. I walk into my apartment and pull out pen and paper.

> Dear Ma,
> This is your long-lost firstborn Benjamin. It is New Year's Day in New York City, where I have been living the last ten years. I have a nice job and a nice apartment. I miss you, and think of you often, especially on holidays.
> Ma, I know you were so upset and hurt when I left. I never ever meant to hurt you. You were always everything to me.
> I hope you and Benja and everyone are well—very healthy and very happy.
> Please write back to me when you can, Ma.
> > Love always,
> > Your son
> > B.J.

I couldn't have tasted more than a few drops of the spilled champagne and yet I feel drunk and merry, dreaming she will write back, that we will begin to correspond regularly, and I will invite her to visit me in New York, I'll pay her way and take her to the Statue of Liberty and the Empire State Building, to the theater (I live in the Broadway district and have never seen a show!), to Macy's and Gimbels and when she comes again in the spring we'll have a picnic in Central Park.

This optimism directly contradicts my apprehensions in recent years that my mother may have passed on. She would be sixty-nine now, a senior citizen, but then many people live to that age and beyond, and she had been a healthy fifty-nine when I saw her last. Had she wanted to contact me she couldn't since she had no idea where to reach me.

The second letter is suddenly easy after bolstering myself for the first.

> Dear April May June,
> Remember me – the man who walked you to your friend Marielle's party on the Upper West Side and showed you the Lincoln Center fountain? It is New Year's Day, and I hope you have a wonderful 1971. And if you ever have time for a cup of tea, please let me know.
> B.J.
> (Benjamin Evans, Jr.)

It's going on two, and I walk to the mailbox now because by postponing it until tomorrow I'd undoubtedly change my mind.

A cold January of periodic snow and sleet passes slowly. On the 27th, my Met tour group informs me they're interested strictly in nineteenth-century Impressionism. I smile as always and internally sigh: the request is a common one, and I am notably less taken with that particular movement coupled with that particular time period, so I cheat in a few van Goghs and Matisses, which garner no complaints since they are famous names.

On an early February Thursday I plod through slush, my feet soaked by the time I get to school. More than half my students are home with the flu, and the ones in attendance are irritable, embittered by the endless winter. I'm hardly in top form myself, my regular insomnia rearing its head with a vengeance the last week. By the time I leave for the day I have a pounding headache.

On the subway home I notice a card next to me. On one side are sketches depicting the manual alphabet, on the other side an appeal. I look up to see the deaf beggar laying cards next to the other passengers of the sparsely filled car. Many working deaf consider ABC peddlers a disgrace and would have given him hard looks and no money. He goes back to collect the cards, leaving them as a gift for those who offer him coins. I give him back his card along with a dollar. He signs Thank you and when I return You're welcome, he grins.

My migraine is worse on Friday despite the heaps of aspirin I've swallowed. In the afternoon I sit in the library reading *The Wretched of the Earth*. At 4:15 I leave, as my superintendent shift will start at five. While checking out the book, I realize I left my coat around my chair on the second floor. I go back up to retrieve it but it's gone. I had absently worn only a cotton shirt, no sweater, and now walk the twenty blocks home, the icy air penetrating my bones.

I stop by the drugstore to purchase a sleeping aid. I look over the various brands and decide to buy three large bottles, mixing and matching. The cashier eyes me suspiciously, and I present a warm smile to assure her how happy I am.

I'm shivering everywhere by the time I get to my building at 4:45. The entrance door has been left slightly ajar, meaning the lock is frozen again. I walk in, and am immediately greeted by a thick curtain of water falling hard from the lobby ceiling. I run through the wet cold wall and up to 2F, banging on the locked door but getting no response. I sprint upstairs to my apartment for the passkey, dropping the over-the-counter barbiturates in my living room, then race back down to 2F. The tub is overflowing, the apartment a flooded mess. I turn off the spigot. I notice folded clean towels in a laundry basket and I instinctually grab them, trying to sop up the liquid from the carpet, obviously damaged beyond repair. Minutes later, a fist slams into my back, the force of the punch pushing me forward, and I swing around to see the tenants, Mr. and Mrs. Wolinski, screaming at me. They are in their coats and dressed nicely, apparently returning from some afternoon formal event. The wife snatches her towels from my hands, the husband keeps pointing at the carpet and the ceiling, and it dawns on me they have astonishingly deduced that the whole mess originated in the apartment above. After much effort I manage to bring the couple to their bathroom, the source of the disaster blatant now, yet they seem determined to place the blame elsewhere. Finally I leave, the heat of their incessant screeching rage against my back.

I knock on Lloyd's door, who will likely be in trouble with the management if they find out he left before five. I leave a note, then go to my apartment, flop down supine on my bed.

Why would I think my mother would reply after all these years? Her last words to me, her last tearful screams enunciating every syllable to be sure I understood: *You betrayed your brother! You betrayed your family!* Six weeks today since I sent off those letters, a fool to open up all those old wounds again. And April May June. I remember she had planned to spend Christmas with her family but *no* job would tolerate holiday time-off to continue into February, she would have returned weeks ago and received my note. Well, the lack of response from her is less surprising. She may very well have a boyfriend, I don't know anything about her. And given my tardiness in writing her, all she knows about me is that I apparently have some emotional complications, and who would want to start any kind of relationship knowing that?

I take down my plastic green pitcher. Generally I have bad luck with sleeping aids, my insomnia so powerful as even to defy narcotics. Success may require a hundred pills so this is the plan. The plan is to pour the contents of all three bottles into the pitcher and to swill it, one gulp. To drink too slowly might mean I'd fall asleep before I have taken enough to not wake and the goal is to *not wake*. I stir, the water turning chalk white.

I scratch a brief note, bequeathing my only treasure, my books, to the public library. Had I any other valuables there'd be no one to will them to anyway. A nagging sense of responsibility drives me to investigate the wreckage in the lobby, to make sure the ceiling isn't about to all come bursting down. I walk down the stairs. It will withstand the night. I would go ahead and repair it now, leaving no unfinished business, but I can't make an official decision on a public space without Lloyd's say-so.

I glance at the mailboxes. In all the excitement I had forgotten to check my mail, as if it would be anything other than an advertising circular.

I stare, my heart thumping. A personal letter. I take it out.

The exact same letter I'd sent to my mother six weeks ago, but now with a special stamp by the post office: DECEASED. RETURN TO SENDER.

4

I have no idea how long ago my mother died but for me it just happened and I weep, my body violently convulsing with the torrent but I'm silent: a deaf person learns early on the awkward and unfriendly looks his utterances can attract and thus perfects the art of soundless emotion.

Would it have been so painful to have mailed an occasional postcard, just to have kept her apprised of my whereabouts? Even if she refused to respond immediately, she may have thought differently later. Why couldn't I have been loving son enough? Man enough? If she never answered, at least I would have been at some peace knowing I'd tried. For all she knew I could have been dead. And might this stress have contributed to her own passing?

At 1 a.m. I glimpse a note being slid under my door.

> Benjamin,
> Want to get started in lobby by 7 – come down soon
> as you get up.
> Lloyd

I'm ordinarily off Saturdays, but this task is definitely classified under the emergency on-call feature that's part of my job description. I don't sleep and at 6:30 start to force myself calm, at seven leaving my apartment. Lloyd is not in the lobby so I knock on his door, and when there's no reply I knock harder. He wakes, and by 7:15 we begin the formidable chore. An all-day job and, against union rules, I work through lunch as I fear a break could catapult me into another sobbing episode from which I may not easily recover.

Seven in the evening, the work completed, I lie on my bed. I should write to Benja. I need to know the cemetery, where to send flowers. And when did she pass on. And was she at all happy those last years? And are *you* alright, sister? And your children? My Lord, the oldest must have graduated by now and suddenly it comes flooding back, the last time I'd seen her, barely healed from the pounding her husband had given her and when I'd seen *him* last I'd just removed the bullets from his pistol. What happened after he bought more and reloaded?

I fall into an anxious sleep, waking at 4:30. I throw on a couple sweaters and walk hours in the predawn darkness. I wind up at St. John the Divine as the doors are opening for the day, and I enter, sit in a pew, not knowing what to pray for but I missed my mother's funeral so this is the place I believe I should be now. Twenty minutes later my solitude is broken by an influx of congregants, and I remember it's Sunday and early morning services will start soon. In the neighborhood I discover a thrift shop and stop in to buy a used coat. Walking home the seventy blocks I begin to feel dizzy, and by the time I step into my building I have fever and chills. I go into the bathroom to splash my face and am taken aback to see Ma staring at me from the mirror, how much I have come to resemble her with age. I have occasionally pondered that I have not inherited even one of my poor father's physical features. I shake my head. What's the difference? He fed me and clothed me, and the rest was the business of him and my mother.

I realize I haven't eaten since lunch yesterday and check to see if there's any canned soup in the kitchen, where I find the pitcher of dissolved pills right where I'd left it. I'd forgotten. And if I hadn't, how selfish to have killed myself rather than to have given my mother her proper mourning. Only now does it occur to me: How would my young students have taken my self-inflicted demise? I'll have to remember for the future that no matter how alone you are, you cannot escape affecting others. If I ever make this decision again, I'll be considerate enough to plan it during a summer break. I pour the concoction down the sink.

I turn in early, and when I wake in the morning I'm still a bit light-headed but strong enough to hold a pen.

Feb. 8, 1971

Dear Benja,

I imagine you're surprised getting a letter from your long lost brother. As you could see from the return address, I now live in New York City and have been here the last ten years.

Benja, I'm writing because I just found out that Ma died. I'd like to send flowers to the cemetery. Can you tell me where please?

Also, I would like to know how you and your family are doing. I'm so sorry we lost touch all these years.

Whatever happened, I never meant to hurt you or Ma.
Please write me back.
I hope you are all healthy and happy.

> Love,
> Your brother
> B.J.

Tuesday morning I feel somewhat better, and I walk down to see how the lobby ceiling is holding up. It's fine, but I'm reminded about the broken entrance door lock, something I'd mentioned to Lloyd Saturday and which he should have repaired yesterday. I walk up to his apartment. He shrugs and says he needs special parts and has sent away for them. I'm not sure he's telling the truth. An hour later I commence the fifty-block walk to my classes and when they are through I walk the fifty blocks home, not certain why since the news of my mother's passing I keep choosing my feet over the subway. I step through the unlocked outside door and open my mailbox, pulling out the drugstore circular. I'm surprised to see a personal letter behind it, no name, only the return address. I recognize it instantly.

February 6, 1971

Dear B.J.,

I QUIT MY JOB!!!!!!!! I don't remember if I told you the night we went to the fountain—I hated being a secretary! So I'm going on "sabbatical"—haha. Meaning I have a little money in the bank which will last a little time. Meanwhile I ran into my friend Carmen at a party. She's going to grad school (MBA—yuk) and has all January off—winter break—and was going to spend it in her family's cabin in the woods of Maine, quiet time to relax, did I want to join her? I'd be welcome to use the time to write. Um—YES. So after Christmas week in South Carolina I took the train straight to Maine do not pass go do not collect $200. I was writing like gangbusters when Carmen had to go back on the 30th, but she said if I wanted to stay on I was welcome to, long as I didn't mind being alone. It was a little creepy but I stuck it out. I wrote four short stories there! (Jesus it was cold though . . .)

I got back yesterday and lo and behold, among the junk mail and the tons of Christmas cards, there's a letter direct from Hell's Kitchen. (Um, you're a rather slow correspondent . . .) So listen. A bunch of Gallaudet alums are going to have this party here in the Village next Sat., Feb. 13th. If you come by my place at 8, you can tag along. But be prompt: April May June waits for no one.

P.S. You know "June" is my last name, right? Because you addressed me "April May June" in your letter. People call me "April," my family calls me "April May." Maybe I'll let you be the first to give me the whole shebang. I think I like it.

Terrified of train delays, I am waiting for the IRT at seven and standing in front of April May June's townhouse at 7:25. I was afraid to walk and build up a sweat even bigger than my nervousness already has. She may not be pleased to have me here this early, so I stroll around Greenwich Village checking my watch every two minutes.

Her letter arrived on the 10th, giving me only three days' preparation. Though the only reply it had called for was my showing up tonight or not, I was so worried she may get the wrong idea that I wrote back immediately.

> April May June,
> I'll be there!
> —B.J.

After mailing it, I fretted that its delivery may be somehow delayed. I considered sending a second note,

> In case my other message got lost in the mail, I just wanted you to know I'll be there on the 13th!

but feared if she got both messages she may think I'm a lunatic.

And while receiving her letter was the single happiest event of my New York life, I was racked with trepidation regarding this party. My only comparable experiences were childhood birthday celebrations with my family. I had requested tea, a one-on-one with her, not a roomful of people. But of course after my long silence she couldn't be sure she could trust me. If she invites me to accompany her to a party and admonishes me to be punctual or she'll leave, then if I don't show she wouldn't feel stood up, or not *very* stood up, having arranged that me or no me she has social plans for Saturday night.

At 7:55 I stand outside April May June's four-storey building and try not to panic as I wonder how I will summon her. It's a quiet street, no one going into her building to whom I could pass a note to slip under her door. Not knowing what else to do, I push the buzzer. To my surprise, lights flash on the top floor. She comes to the window and waves, then signs something but it's too dark to see. A few moments later she opens the outside door, smiling. She looks very pretty in her miniskirt, and seems to have spent time on her cosmetics. I wonder if I have dressed properly, the secondhand pinstripe suit I purchased for the occasion, not knowing who to consult on these matters. She takes the flowers I have brought, and invites me up.

Her studio apartment is neat, clean, a bit cluttered. Used furniture, hanging beads. She signs Goodwill was her decorator. I realize since coming to New York I have never been in another person's home, unless it was because I was asked to fix the toilet or radiator. I tell her it's a very nice place. She smiles and signs, Rent-controlled. A long-haired gray cat appears.

That's Mr. Peoples.

She asks me to sit while she goes to the bathroom to apply her lipstick. When she returns, she sees I have unbuttoned my suit jacket in her warm flat, though not taken it off.

My, you're formal.

I look to the floor, embarrassed that I have apparently made the wrong fashion choice, assuming this will embarrass her. I feel her coming closer to the couch and I look up.

What's wrong.

I hesitate.

I've never been to a party.

Never?

I shake my head.

Are you looking forward to this?

I'm looking forward to spending time with you.

She sits on the green soft chair, taking me in.

Would you rather not go?

They're your friends. You'll have a good time.

Would you rather not go?

I sign No, then I sign Yes.

Have you had dinner yet?

I shake my head, hopeful.

That party will go on till the wee hours. What if we eat now, then I can go on and you can come with me, or not. Up to you.

I nod, so grateful!

Diner okay?

We have burgers and fries and I worry her food will get cold as her hands chatter on, but I take in all she's saying, it's only with enormous effort that I don't constantly smile. She tells me she was able to secure another proofreading job, children's textbooks. She speaks about growing up with deaf parents and mostly deaf siblings. I wonder to myself what it must have felt like, to have been raised in a family and not felt so alone, within it and outside of it at once. I tell her I'd never heard of genetic deafness until she described her heritage, that I have since been researching it. She speaks of the phenomenon, not an especially rare one, then mentions a Georgia clan, two parents and twelve kids, all deaf. We knew them from the Atlanta deaf club, she says, which was the closest black deaf club to us. I have no idea what she's talking about but, afraid she'll think of me as a complete bumpkin to all things deaf, I try to conceal my mystification.

You don't know about deaf clubs?

Feeling my blush, I shake my head.

Cultural centers. Play performances and sports teams, card playing. Job recommendations. Sprang up during the forties, when people congregated to cities hiring deaf for the factory jobs the hearing men left when they were sent off to Europe or the Pacific. So the clubs were mostly blue-collar.

She dips a fry in her ketchup. And segregated. The sports league was very organized among the white clubs, national basketball championships. They would actively recruit black deaf players, offering them money or jobs, but refused to let them into the white clubs. And I'm not talking about the South. It happened in Detroit. It happened in New York! Then she sits back, a wry smile. Are you confused by my signs?

I tell her I don't understand her question.

Well! Plenty of white deaf have told me they're surprised when they *do* understand. That I'm the first black deaf person whose signs they can make out. Her eyes roll. They guess I went to Gallaudet, assume that's where I learned to sign white. But my family could always sign both ways. For a while I had to translate for another black student who was as baffled by the white signs as they were by his. She shrugs. They call white signs "standard," but during the oralist movement, the white schools tried to force their students to speak while most black schools kept signing, black sign language was never interrupted so wouldn't that make it the purer language? Then April May June touches her thumb to her chin with her fingers outstretched, a fan comb pointing up. The sign for *mother*—except she begins wiggling her fingers.

The black sign for *mother*, she informs me. Do you know the black sign for *color*?

I shake my head, presuming it's not the gesture I recognize, wiggling fingers touching the chin. April May June lightly strokes her cheek with her index finger, and I see that in the Negro sign language *color* and *race* must be the same.

Of course, she continues, black signs vary state to state, county to county. She sips her root beer and asks about my interests, and I hesitate before mentioning my love of books, and the museum job, and the teaching, wondering if she will find me a great bore. She thinks the museum tours sound like fun (I only guide two groups a month) and the teaching job sounds rewarding (I'm only part-time).

Stop putting yourself down! Now, would you like banana cream pie? It's their specialty.

The waitress comes with the bill and I'm now seized by a new anxiety: Will she think I'm a chauvinist if I pay the entire check or a cheapskate if I suggest Dutch treat? I timorously take it, leaving a generous tip.

She smiles. Thank you. Next meal's on me.

At eleven we are strolling back to her apartment because she needs to pick up a book she promised to lend to someone at the party. As we cross Seventh Avenue, she remarks that when she entered Gallaudet in '55 it had only been four years since they'd started admitting Negroes. (Her term, as it has consistently been all evening, is *black*, but after my Alabama upbringing where even in my deaf isolation I was aware that *black* was considered a cruel insult,

I'm still working to wrap myself around the new word.) My deaf university, she goes on, was established in 1864, a mandate of Abe Lincoln, but it took almost a hundred years for the Emancipation Proclamation to come to Gallaudet! She laughs, then goes on a light rant about the segregation of deaf schools reflecting that of the general public school system, separate and very unequal facilities, even in cases where the black and white children were on the same campus, and she details her own experiences at the South Carolina School for the Deaf and Blind and then asks, What was it like at Alabama?

I had promised myself I would be honest with her about this, though somehow I am still caught off guard when the moment is thrust upon me. My hands utter the words that have been on my mind all evening: I have never been to school.

She stares at me. I swallow.

I have never had any formal education. My brother. When I was a teenager, my younger brother taught me some signs, he taught me how to read. We took a short course on signs once, and I took more courses after I came to New York. Then my hands stop because there's nothing more to say.

But you teach. You lead art tours.

I'm self-taught.

She nods, not looking at me, absorbing the information.

I sigh. Well. It's getting late.

No it's not.

I think—

Why do you want to leave all the sudden? You don't want to be friends with me because you find my formal education pretentious?

No!

She smiles. Good.

When we are just a block from her building, she turns to me: Tell me about your girlfriends.

I catch my breath. Naturally she notes my reluctance, and I hope she will take mercy on me and begin a new topic. I'm most comfortable when she's the one talking, which is usually, but she patiently waits for my response.

There's not much to tell.

There's *always* something to tell. I'll tell you about my boyfriends.

I look at her.

Nobody right now, she clarifies.

I look down. I stop walking. She stops walking.

I've never had a girlfriend.

She stares at me. Have you never been intimate with anyone?

I shake my head.

Her hands move gently. I was a late starter too.

Not *this* late.

She smiles again, and we continue walking to her place. Since you teach right here in the Village, you should stop by my place sometime after class.

When?

Surprise me.

Never.

She looks up.

You're inviting me to drop by uninvited, and that sounds like an invitation for trouble.

If I get sick of you, I'll just pretend I'm not home.

I'm not coming uninvited.

Then come Tuesday after your class. You're invited.

The paperback she came to pick up is on a small bookcase in her living room. It turns out she is also an avid reader, and we sit and begin to talk about Richard Wright and Hemingway, Salinger and Fanon, then civil rights and women's rights, Idi Amin and Vietnam and then she begins to kiss me and touch me and I'm awkward but I accept what she's offering and I watch as she effortlessly pulls out her couch into a made bed and she leads me to it and takes off my jacket and takes off her cardigan and unbuttons my shirt and caresses my chest and unbuttons her blouse and removes it and begins lowering my pants zipper, *Stop!*

She stops. I'm panting panting.

I'm afraid.

She gazes at me, her smile surprised but tender.

That's alright.

We lie on her bed, eventually undress down to our underwear, and we hold each other, and we sleep. She never makes it to the party. In the morning, which neither of us remembers is Valentine's Day, she offers to make breakfast: Raisin Bran or Froot Loops?

By my definition, that night was the first time we made love, though we had not technically engaged in intercourse. That didn't happen until Tuesday after class.

5

April May June is partial to the tapestries, but I'm captivated by the intricate ivory pieces on the subterranean level, breathtakingly detailed carvings of complicated, bustling scenes, an entire three-dimensional world inside a locket!

She took the IRT from the Village, the last car of the train as we'd agreed, and I joined her at Columbus Circle where we continued uptown to the top of Manhattan Island. A quiet Tuesday at the Cloisters—the Medieval Art arm of the Metropolitan Museum, the structure resembling a castle. Perhaps because of its decentralized location, visitors are comparably sparse in striking contrast to the rest of the sardine city, the spaciousness luxurious and accentuating the hollowness of the edifice, its mystery. April May June's proofreading schedule is irregular—afternoons/evenings. Today she happens to have off, and my students are on spring break, my superintendent shift not till five—so we're fortunate to have this time, avoiding the gallery's somewhat more bustling weekend hours. April May June and I walk together and articulate our wonder. Sometimes we separate to have our own individual experiences, and from this I learn that we comfortably enjoy each other's company as well as our independence.

Afterward we stroll through the adjacent gardens. Little is in bloom so early in the season. The air is cool but we're fine in our spring jackets.

Yesterday was the Ides of March. She smiles as she tells me this, but I notice a vague despondency behind her expression, something I've sensed since we met today.

Is anything wrong?

No.

I perceive an ellipsis behind the sign. She sits on a bench. I sit next to her.

When I checked the mail on my way out to work yesterday, there was a rejection letter for my story. Her left foot is on the ground while her right foot faintly swings. I didn't open it till I got to work. I guess I didn't want to know. Or maybe I wanted to hold out hope it was good news long as I could. She kicks a stone. I should be used to it by now. Rejections are the only kind of mail I get.

I know that's not true. In the month we've been together she has received at least three letters from her sister Ramona and two from her mother. But I also know not to point that out just now.

I would like to read your stories sometime.

She looks at me, then back at the patch of tiny wildflowers before us. The wind gently blows them. Something lavender.

They're not very good. Obviously.

I would like to read them.

They're not even fiction really. When I was taking that writing class, when we met? I told the teacher they were all true stories, I said I call them fiction but they're really autobiography. He had this knowing smile, he said, Yes, thinly veiled. After that I didn't come back to class. April May June pulls up her legs, sits with them crossed on top of the bench. I wouldn't be the first person to use personal anecdotes in fiction. I just wish I had more imagination. Especially since my thinly veiled autobiography apparently isn't very well written anyway.

April May June. My fingers rapidly spelling her full name, the appellation she has reserved for me alone, but before I can go on, her hands move again.

I half feel like an assimilator anyway, English isn't my first language, sign language is my first language, why'm I writing? I should tell stories in sign. She sighs. Two months ago I *did* get an encouraging rejection for the first time. They wouldn't publish the story but they liked a lot of it, please send more.

Did you send more?

I sent another the same day. I haven't heard anything yet. She plays with an ant in the dirt, repeatedly blocking its path with the toe of her sneaker. The letter I got yesterday said We've narrowed it down to seventeen hundred thousand submissions and yours didn't make the cut. It did *not* say We'd like to read more of your work.

I'm deciding whether I should ask for the third time to read her stories when her face changes, brightens.

Alright, enough feeling sorry for myself today. Let's catch the bus. I know a great burrito joint down on the Upper West Side.

◰ ◳

April Fool's Day I stand perplexed in the gift shop of the new Studio Museum in Harlem. There's the book of photographs by Gordon Parks, and the book of paintings by Jacob Lawrence. April May June loves both artists. Would it be too extravagant, too forward in our relationship, to buy her both large volumes?

I need to get this shopping task behind me because tomorrow Ramona is coming, and April May June seems to have made many plans for all three of us so I'm not sure how much free time I'll have over the next few days. I'm terrified! We've only been together six and a half weeks. Isn't that early to be meeting family? I mentioned this to her a few days ago, trying to come off as joking but praying she would have mercy and suggest I wait until her sister's next visit. She replied with a smile that if I hadn't taken so long to write to her in the first place then we would have been together longer and I wouldn't be in this predicament now. She says that she's told Ramona all about me. I hope that's true because I couldn't bear the look of shock and disapproval on her sister's face were she to be confronted with unpleasant surprises. That I'm forty-seven. That I'm a janitor. That I'm white.

Late Friday afternoon I wait with April May June at Port Authority. I realize I've not been here, the arrival gates, since I first disembarked the bus from Alabama over a decade ago. I've never left the city. To go where?

Ramona comes flying into April May June's arms, the sisters embracing tight and joyously as if they haven't seen each other in twenty years. Same nose, mouth. Ramona a couple inches taller than her sister's five-five. She also sports an Afro, not quite as large as April May June's. A pink blouse and black slacks, differing from her sister's perpetual miniskirts. Ramona has playful eyes and now trains them on me, and signs: So this is B.J. We shake, and she shares her sign name with me: her first two right fingers crossed in an *R,* horizontally touching her cheek and twisting, similar to the sign for "candy." When she smiles, I see why the sign was placed where it is: her dazzling dimples. Then she takes April May June's hand and subtly signs something to her I am not privy to. The sisters exchange smiles and I assume I've just successfully cleared some hurdle. We take the IRT to the Village. Ramona is starving and we find an Italian place. The sisters' hands are flying at lightning speed. I gaze at them, only half paying attention to their stories. There was certainly love in my own family, but never such an obvious manifestation of it.

After dinner I offer to carry Ramona's suitcase back to April May June's apartment but she waves off my offer, having traveled light for her week in New York, and then I leave them alone to catch up. April May June protests my early departure, but not too passionately, understandably wanting intimate time with her sister.

On Saturday while they're at the Museum of Modern Art, I do some cleaning of my apartment, not knowing if the Junes may surprise me with a visit. I meet them for an Italian dinner before we stroll to a theater on West 48th to see my very first Broadway show, a nineteenth-century play called *Hedda Gabler*. Ramona has splurged on the twelve-dollar orchestra seats and refuses to let me reimburse her. She sits between April May June and me, and our eyes flutter from the stage action down to Ramona's interpreting hands in her lap. A shocking story!

We go out for dessert, and April May June chats a bit regarding her curiosity about the recently established National Theatre of the Deaf. Directed and choreographed by hearers, the rapid movements, according to accounts she has read, are visually arresting but confusing for the deaf as there is no time allowed to properly understand the signs. The hearing, on the other hand, can use sound to keep abreast of the story. Ramona crinkles her nose to indicate she's listening but she's fading, having not slept well last night. You have no idea, she tells us, how loud this city is. Those damn sirens! Tomorrow I won't see the Junes as I will be on-call as the Sunday super.

Monday at eight, April May June pointedly reminds me. It will be her birthday, April 5th, my first party and this one I had better not miss.

Thank God I didn't come early, she remarks to her sister now.

You mean thank God you were a day late. You *were* supposed to be born on the 4th. It isn't until I leave them and notice a flyer for a prayer service in commemoration of the third anniversary of Martin Luther King's April 4th assassination that I realize what they were talking about.

On Monday when I arrive at her Village townhouse, I'm the only guest. April May June admits that she knew I'd show up right on time before anyone else, having no concept of fashionably late, and Ramona, apprised of my punctuality habit, had discreetly waited until 7:50 to slip out and buy decorative flowers.

I miss you, April May June says, and for a while we kiss. Then I give her the presents, both art books, which she loves, and the card that I agonized over. I tell her she can wait until later to read it, and by this I mean *Please* wait until later to read it and she knows this and opens it anyway.

April 5, 1971

Dear April May June,
    Happy Birthday! To the reason the last two months have been the happiest of my life.
                                                    —B.J.

She stares at the words, and I can tell something doesn't sit well with her, but she forces a smile and says Thank you. This is exactly why I wanted her to open it later! It would put her on the spot for me to ask what's wrong. *Happiest.* Was that going overboard? Does she think I'm exaggerating? I'm not! Or does she believe me and that's what's making her uncomfortable? Or does she wonder, if I'm so happy then why didn't I sign the card with love? But isn't it too early for that? I don't know the rules!

Ramona, who's gone so long I think she must have planted and cultivated those chrysanthemums, finally returns to find April May June and me awkward and relieved by the interruption. At quarter to nine a few guests arrive, and by ten the place is packed by people of various races, most in their late twenties or thirties, the apartment smoke-filled which April May June apparently tolerates for the sake of the occasion. Most of the crowd are deaf but there are a handful of hearers talking in a corner. Many of the invited make a point of greeting me, and their smiles imply whatever April May June told them about me must have been good. I'm grateful for their sociability because otherwise my impulse would be to take my champagne glass and sit alone in a corner, my shyness possibly mistaken for snobbery. April May June has guests flocking her all evening, in addition to the deaf the good hostess taking time to speak verbally with her hearing friends while periodically sending glancing smiles in my direction.

She has insisted on all thirty-four candles, claiming if she blows out any less she won't get her wish. We sign the birthday song while the hearers sing, and afterward, eating my chocolate cake, I realize how sleepy I am. Ten forty-five, and I'm ordinarily in bed by ten, so here's the next dilemma: If I'm April May June's "steady," is it improper for me to leave earlier than everyone else? As if in answer to my prayer I feel someone coming from behind, slipping her arm in mine.

Tired?

I smile, so grateful for this touch.

Go home, go to bed. Would you like to come to the movies with us tomorrow?

Yes.

An American movie! With familiar New York scenes! Ramona sits between us again, interpreting. The film is called *Shaft,* and though I'm not partial to the action genre, it's thrilling to enjoy a contemporary film from my own country, even this somewhat outlandish representation. The sisters appreciate the racial truths, find the drama intermittently silly, and love it beginning to end.

After the movie we sit in a diner, Ramona and I saying our goodbyes. Tomorrow morning she and April May June will take the train upstate to see an aunt, and Thursday, Ramona's last full day before catching the bus early Friday morning, the girls plan to visit a few tourist sites. April May June has clarified to me in no uncertain terms that it is no longer proper to refer to grown women as "girls," and I agree with her, but I must admit, in observing them, this is the word that keeps popping into my mind: the way they smile and hold secrets like teenagers. In the booth they are side by side across the table from me.

And I wanna get a picture of the skyline, Ramona tells her sister, who is detailing their upcoming sightseeing agenda on a napkin.

You came right as it's changing, April May June remarks. Construction's just finishing on the second of the two World Trade Center towers, supposed to be done in the summer. They surpassed the Empire State Building. World's tallest.

Ramona turns to me now. I'm so happy we met, B.J. The warmth in her eyes tells me she's sincere.

I hope you come back again soon, Ramona.

The Brooklyn Promenade's probably the best view of Manhattan, right? April May June asks me. How do we get there again?

As I jot directions on another napkin, Ramona unexpectedly turns around and speaks to the table behind us, four young white men, probably college students. They smile and respond. When she turns back to us, she says there's a song on the restaurant speaker, *Thank You (For Letting Me Be Myself Again)* but the singer cleverly titled it as he pronounces it, and she takes my pencil and flips over the napkin: *Thank You (Falettinme Be Mice Elf Agin)*. She had overheard the young men referring to the recording artist as James Brown when it is Sly and the Family Stone, and she'd felt the need to correct them. She rolls her eyes and says with a smile to her sister: White boys.

Because Ramona means the last remark as a joke, April May June smiles back at her, then at me so I won't feel left out. But her smile is confused because neither she nor I wholly get jokes about music, about slang pronunciation. The moment had clearly been more about flirtation than anything else, Ramona being just as pretty as her sister, which is to say *very* pretty, and this teasing exchange was coordinated through their common knowledge of the aural art. I wonder if it's a relief to Ramona, after a week speaking with her hands, to chance upon this occasion to communicate verbally, and I'm momentarily envious of her ability to smoothly segue between our world and theirs.

□ □

Friday night after Ramona's departure, I stop by April May June's as she and I had planned. We make love, and everything seems alright, but it still nags me, whatever it was that bothered her on her birthday.

What?

I swallow. Did you. Were you upset by my card?

She looks at the ceiling.

Was I too forward? Not forward enough?

Yes. Yes.

I frown. She smiles and pulls the blanket up over her shoulders.

I don't know how I felt. Just because I've had lovers and you haven't doesn't mean I have all the answers. I can be confused too.

I'm not confused.

She looks at me, smiles again, and doesn't respond.

I fixed the door.

The outside door? To your building?

Lloyd was never going to do it. I finally bought the parts and did it myself. And billed him.

For your labor as well as the parts, I hope.

Better. I told him I would not charge him for the labor, but he'll owe me a favor.

Like what?

When the time comes, he'll be the first to know.

I sit up, my lower body still covered, knees bent.

I thought about rigging my place like yours. Your door light. But it's complicated.

She nods. I was fortunate to get this place when I did: deaf-ready. Toni my friend, the former tenant? Took her four years of cajoling to get her landlord to comply. I'm paying rent like all the other tenants, she told him, I need to know when I have guests too.

You're the only guest who would need to get in *my* door. So I thought.

I take a breath, then reach over to my pants on the chair and pull out of the pocket two shiny new keys. I eye her carefully, searching for any more signs of "confusion."

She stares at them. And, after a moment, gently takes them.

This is good, she remarks. I was just about to inaugurate my career as a stalker.

□ □

I hope I was not being miserly in choosing the double. April May June's is, and we fit quite nicely. King-size would crowd my bedroom, and even the queen seemed greedy. Well it's certainly a comfort-level step up from my previous single.

But I'm irritated. It's twenty past five, and when the store manager wrote on the note that my new bed would arrive sometime between ten and six, I didn't really think it would take all day. With no light fixture summons connected to my apartment I've had to wait here, sitting on the steps facing my building entrance for over seven hours, leaving my post only twice to race to the bathroom.

The door cracks open. I can never stay angry about anything when I see her smile. Warm this late April day, and over her pale blue blouse and denim miniskirt she wears only a light yellow sweater.

So what's the big surprise? She kisses me.

I'm still waiting for it.

She notices I'm reading *Crazy Horse,* Mari Sandoz's biography, and she becomes excited, telling me she loved the book, then extolling the virtues of the American Indian Movement. I nod and intermittently respond while wondering what to do should the bed men not show. If there was a problem they obviously couldn't call, nor can I call them now. In my mind I make various complicated plans, feeling a headache coming on, when at 5:40 a truck pulls up. With her first glimpse of what the two Trinidadian men are carrying into my building, April May June's broad grin and sparkling eyes make the long wait since this morning more than worthwhile.

I've bought new linens, and we tuck the sheets and spread the blankets together. Before we replace the pillows, she takes off her shoes and sits on the bed, clutching her knees, back against the headboard.

Perfect.

I take off my shoes and sit where the other pillow will be, and though we don't know it yet, we have just established that she will always sleep to my left. Her thoughts have gone far away.

What?

My father's had a lot of trouble with his vision lately. He finally went to the doctor. She caresses her necklace, something African, leather. Sugar. His sister died of it, I told you. He's not obese but. Too many seconds, he never could say no to cherry pie. She sighs. Your parents still living?

She's starting a conversation we've never had. Since her family is a frequent topic, my lack of likewise contribution has been conspicuous, but she has not addressed the subject directly until now. In reply to her question, I shake my head.

When did they die?

My father. Almost thirty years ago.

Your mother?

I don't know.

She stares.

I've not been in touch with them since I moved to New York. I only recently found out she passed.

Why have you been out of touch?

I swallow.

I did something.

I massage the fingers of my right hand with my left.

I betrayed my brother.

I sigh. I go to the bathroom, wash my face, my underarms. When I return she has not budged, her eyes still fixed on me.

You don't want to talk about it?

I don't want to talk about it.

A housefly enters through my cracked window, doing a figure 8 between us before disappearing into the other rooms.

Do you have a picture?

Of my mother?

I go to my desk and pull out the drawer, reaching in the back where I keep the old billfold. I can't remember the last time I looked at the photos. I show her the only image I have of Ma, standing in front of our house.

She has a nice smile. April May June gently strokes the plastic slipcover.

And she begins flipping to the few other pictures. I suppress an impulse to snatch the thing back.

Your sister?

Her senior picture.

Your father and brother?

Yes. His eighth-grade graduation picnic, not long before my father died.

The brother who taught you to sign. To read.

I say nothing. She ignores my grave face and continues, getting to the last portrait. Who's that?

Incredibly, as I'd handed the wallet to her I'd forgotten about it. A newspaper clipping photo of the young Negro man.

I gently take the billfold back, walk over to my desk and shut it in the drawer, then turn to her.

There's a new egg roll place on the corner.

Walking back from the eatery, we lament the immediate succession of dictator Papa Doc by son Baby Doc in Haiti, applaud the Supreme Court decision endorsing school busing, consider the gas chamber sentencing of the Manson family, but beneath it all we're both giddy in our eagerness to initiate my latest furniture addition. I stop to go through the motions of checking my mail and thus sweetening the anticipation, and am surprised to find a letter.

What is it?

Nothing. I slip it into my inside jacket pocket, and though she clearly wants to press the subject she doesn't.

There's something reinvigorating in our relationship, still quite young anyway, in making love on a new bed. I wait until she's in a sound sleep before I slip out from under the sheets, closing the bedroom door behind me. I turn on the kitchen light and sit at the table.

April 19, 1971

Dear B.J.,

Sorry it took me awhile to write you. I had to get over the shock of getting a letter from you first. After ten years, we didn't even know if you were still alive, and if you were, well, I guess I assumed you'd just forgotten all about us.

We lost Ma seven years ago. It was colorectal cancer. I guess you don't know but the symptoms started six months after that thing with you and Randall. Over the next couple of years she would have little improvements and we would be hopeful, but they'd eventually always be followed by some kind of relapse, one step forward two steps back. Funny even when we knew they'd sent her home to die how you're never prepared, when she really left us it still hit like a bombshell.

Randall has been gone about as long as you have. After everything, he was made to feel like some kind of pariah in his own hometown. He went to Texas, and moved around the state before settling, but has stayed in touch, a Christmas card at least. It was hard to be at Ma's funeral when two of her three offspring didn't show up. Randall did send flowers. You asked me where to send them but you should know she's buried right next to Pa out off of Swamp Road.

B.J., I was so angry with you for such a long time. I blamed you for everything bad that ever happened to our family after what you did. But four years ago I got sick

myself and that gave me a new outlook on everything.
It was very hard so soon after Ma, and because there are
certain body parts you think you need or you're not
really a woman anymore. But I'm doing okay without
them, and it has put the sickness in remission. I also lost
all my hair but it has grown back.

Yes, Leslie Jo and Todd graduated. Leslie Jo has two
little girls. I didn't much like the boy she married at first
but he did right by her, giving the baby a name.

I'm reading this letter and wondering if it comes off
madder than I feel. I guess I did get upset when I got your
letter, out the blue you suddenly wanting to act like the
caring son. And I guess I had a lot of stuff stored up that
I had to get out of my system. But you get close to death,
you really do see things differently. I would like us to act
like a proper brother and sister again, but forgive me if I
need a little time to get used to it.

Here is a picture of the whole gang we took last
Thanksgiving. Leslie Jo named her oldest Estelle Roberta
(Roberta after Ma, of course) and the other Caroline. It's
still hard to believe I'm a grandmother! And you're a
great-uncle.

Your sister,

Benja

□ □

On an unseasonably warm Saturday near the end of May, April May June
and I go to a demonstration in Harlem in response to the shooting death by
police of a ten-year-old boy, a case of mistaken identity. Afterward we grab a
bite at a nearby cafeteria-style restaurant on East 125th. I'm delighted with the
Southern cooking, the chicken and collards, vegetables generously spiced with
ham, when I look up to see she is picking at her macaroni and cheese, sullen.

What?

I need to move to Harlem. What am I doing in the Village? How many
black people are in Greenwich Village? I only moved there because that

rent-controlled place fell into my lap. She twirls the pasta around. I waited too long to come to New York. I missed Malcolm. You ever read his auto-biography?

Of course.

He *worshiped* Elijah Muhammad. Yeah, some Messenger of God, Muhammad in his fat mansion, well guess how he got so famous? The flock was about three sheep before Malcolm! And the FBI and NYPD all infil-trating, no protection for Malcolm's family, and the press dismissing his assassination like some black gangland war, the Powers That Be were fine when they could call him a hatemonger, but after he went to Mecca, after he started preaching brotherhood for all. *That's* when he became dangerous.

I watch her. I'm not sure whether she wants me to agree. Then her hands are moving furiously. He was a kid! Ten years old, they just kill us! Cops shoot, one black looks just like the other.

We have had similar conversations regarding police killings of deaf men, mistaken identity complicated by the officers rapidly jumping to wrong conclusions when the alleged perpetrator fails to respond to the cops' verbal orders, but April May June is making clear that the "us" to which she now refers does not include me. I don't believe such brutal misconduct is the practice of every police officer, but it's true for *too* many of them. I know, however, this is not the time to make that distinction. Her anger is unwieldy, she needs to place it somewhere and right now I'm very conve-nient.

She smashes her macaroni with her fork. It's like we never left the South.

No it's not.

What's the difference? That boy's just as dead.

I pick up my cornbread, tear off a piece to chew. Now *I* am angry. *What's the difference?*

The difference is there weren't police out at the demonstration today with vicious dogs attacking us, white people spitting on us. The difference is you drink from the same water fountain as I, sit in the movies with me, go to the same bathroom as white women and this is not something very recently imposed upon the white population which they bitterly and vio-lently resent. The difference is you and I go to museums together, walk in the park in public, sometimes holding hands, and while we may get the occasional dirty look we are not playing Russian roulette with five bullets in the cylinder, we are not about to be lynched and by that I mean a slow, brutal, torturous death.

That boy's just as dead.

Yes, he's just as dead. Then I stop moving my hands, wishing we hadn't paid already so I could ask for the check now and signal our departure, the end of this "date," as I can't bring myself to just stand up and walk out. Our first argument. She's from Dixie, she knows exactly what I'm talking about and yet she's determined to be stubborn.

You've never been back South since you left?

No.

When will you go?

Never.

Because of everything you just said?

Yes.

She salts her food liberally and unnecessarily, then moves her hands, still looking at her plate. Is that why you're with me? And now she looks up. Because I'm black?

My eyes narrow. I will be forty-eight in a week. I waited my entire life to be close to someone in the way I'm close to you and now you *dare* ask me that?

Three young men are suddenly at our table snarling. They all talk at once so reading their lips is even more confusing than usual, but from scattered words and the looks of disgust I get the gist: What's a pretty black girl like you doing with that old white man? It is only now that I realize I'm the only white person in the restaurant. I turn away, wondering if April May June in her present mood will be inclined to agree with them.

She begins to sign to them. Not only is the idea ridiculous, the chances of them knowing the sign language slim to none, but her hands form complete nonsense: father, run, say, D, hate, ball, M, Y.

"Hey," they're obviously saying through their laughter, "we don't know any sign language," at which point she gives them the middle finger. They are taken aback, a huge laugh but it's now a bit nervous, confused, embarrassed, and they leave.

She turns to me with a smirk, finally picking up her fork to eat and with her left hand she speaks: The universal sign.

Sunday, June 6th, I'm home on-call all day, but Lloyd has kindly given me the evening off so that April May June may take me out to celebrate. She enters my apartment at seven as planned.

Ready? She smiles but her cheer seems forced.

Are you alright?

I'm fine. She kisses me. Happy Birthday.

She takes me to a new restaurant in my neighborhood, brightly lit the way we like it so as to read each other's signs, and to that end as soon as we sit we move the centerpiece to the side. I've never had French food before, presuming it to be beyond my budget (and usually lit atmospherically darker), but the prices here are reasonable, the salmon melt-in-your-mouth. My companion is trying to be happy for me but I see her mind is elsewhere. I know there's no sense prodding her, she'll never tell me what's wrong until she's ready.

During dessert she hands me a book she constructed herself, colored paper and yarn, her own calligraphy: poems by Loy E. Golladay. She's told me about the writer's style, often applying sign-language syntax to his English verse, the pieces frequently droll, always surprising. Deaf authors being discriminated against in the mainstream, he has not yet been published in book form so she has anthologized the work herself. I am, as a hearer would put it, speechless.

I need to use the bathroom. There's only one toilet, which I prefer as multi-stall situations can be embarrassing to the deaf. (It took several red-faced episodes for me to determine that the odd, and sometimes glaring, looks I received from other men was related to my aiming for the pool of water in the urinal bottom rather than quietly against the urinal wall.) The door is closed so I wait. I don't like trying the knob which may disturb an occupant. If no one comes out in a few minutes, I'll assume it's empty.

A white man, about six feet tall so several inches shorter than I, stands behind me. Less patient, after about five seconds he gives me a look before walking ahead, knocking harsh and brief, turning the knob and, scowling in my direction, stepping into the empty lavatory. As he starts to close the door I'm stunned to see April May June suddenly appear to hold it open against his strength and say, as I read her lips, He's deaf, you moron.

The man is startled and vaguely frightened. But he quickly recovers, then laughs, and to himself, though we can clearly see it, he mocks her enunciation as he turns away and starts to close the door again. April May June smacks the back of his head, hard. Instinctively he rears around, pulling back his fist, and I quickly insert myself between her and the bastard. He stomps away, leaving the commode free.

I turn, my eyes hard on her.

I had to come and find you. They were clearing away our dishes and I needed to know if you wanted to take some of that fondue home.

Are you *insane*?

Fuck him. And she swerves around and exits. I follow her, the toilet remaining unused.

We head back, her gait rushed, her hands uncharacteristically still.

When do you plan on telling me what's wrong.

I hate hearies! Skipping ahead of you! Making fun of my speech!

Rude people. Then I think better of it, the image of that monster rearing his fist back at her. *Ugly* people. You mean you hate ugly people.

I know what I mean!

I think, Do you hate Ramona? but know better than to be reasonable right now. We get to my building and she flies in, running up the stairs ahead of me.

I walk up the two flights. When I get to my apartment, I use the toilet before heading back to my bedroom. She is sitting on my bed and already seems to have done a bit of crying, something I've never seen from her, and force-stopped it. Next to her is the current *New Yorker,* open to a short story.

Read it.

I take the magazine and sit in my desk chair rather than on the bed, to give her space. "72 Hours" by John B. Caulfield. As I read, I periodically sneak glances at my guest who had eventually lain down on her back, staring at the lighting fixture on the ceiling.

When I'm finished, I toss the weekly on the bed near her. She sits up.

So?

The writing's fine but the plot's not to my tastes.

Notice anything familiar?

I frown. The tale of a junkie in withdrawal who murders a man, and no one I know fits that description. Before I can reply she answers for me.

John Caulfield was at my birthday party! I met him at some temp job, and we were having all these conversations because we're both writers. He was that white guy with the reddish hair, a hearer. *No,* nothing happened, we were just friends, I asked him to my birthday last year too and that's when he must have written that, how about that part with the silent party? Being at a party with all these deaf people, and how can they call it a party with no music? I guess he *used* my party for his damn research, jackass! She opens the magazine and rips it in half, longwise from the mid right page to mid left, which is impressive, then flings it. Don't tell me I don't hate hearies, how about your wonderful hearing boss, the one whose deaf assistant gives free labor in exchange for *favors*. How many *favors* has he granted? I bet he doesn't even have a plan for you if there was a fire. You couldn't hear the fire alarm! My lights are attached to the fire alarm, what about you? Your skin-flint boss would just run out and forget you!

One of your stories was just rejected?

And she cries and cries and I go and hold her. When her sobs subside, she shows me the letter which she has crumpled into her handbag, addressed "Dear Fiction Submitter." Then she reaches into the bag again, pulling out three well-used composition books.

Wanna see them?

I sit beside her and read. Many stories: she's quite prolific. After a while she tries to put *The New Yorker* back together and read other articles. Eventually she falls asleep. I wake her gently.

The billy goat tale made me want to weep.

She tentatively smiles. Really?

I tell her what I liked, which was plenty, and what I didn't like, which was rare. Which stories had great beginnings but endings that left me unfulfilled, which stories had ingenious endings but seemed slow to start. I'm initially hesitant to say anything less than upbeat, not only because of her sensitivity but because of my own insecurities as I am no writer, but she encourages all the criticism, excited at long last to be discussing her work, thrilled for my praise and intrigued when I am less satisfied, which she seems to eagerly incorporate into her plans for revisions.

Two hours into the discussion she sighs. The problem is they're all auto-biographical. And sometimes life is boring.

Then you can embellish. It's fiction. Which leads her to ask more questions in this vein, and I smile answering, between the poetry book and the stories her two "homemade" gifts of literature have made my forty-eighth the happiest birthday I've ever had.

At 2 a.m. she decides she'll make us omelets. I see her searching through my neatly stacked pots and pans for a fryer, the whole assemblage tumbling out. I imagine it has caused quite a racket, which I hope hasn't awakened the neighbors.

She takes the round alarm clock she's brought in her bag and sets it for 7:30, then puts it under her pillow where she'll feel the vibrations of the ring. She needs to be at work by nine. The worst thing about being deaf, she remarks, is that you can't just pick up the telephone and call in sick. It's close to five and she has lain down on top of the bedspread, still asking me questions but her voice is fading, when her eyes fly open in a panic: We forgot to have sex! and the next moment she's gone for what's left of the night.

I come to a groggy arousal at 8:35. Since I've been with April May June, my chronic insomnia seems to have all but vanished, but I'm still hard pressed to ever sleep in. She has not stirred. I gingerly remove the clock from under her pillow. In her middle-of-the-night fog she had set the time but forgot to turn the alarm on. I gently rise and go into the kitchen. Put on the teapot, then open my pots and pans door to see what damage she has done to my order. As soon as I pull the knob the cookware flies out again, covering the floor. I glance at her under the blanket I had laid on her before turning out the light a few hours ago. The crashing vessels have not caused her to bat an eyelash, her deafness apparently as total as mine. I consider what she said about the fire alarm. I know the system—any fire in any apartment, including mine, would set off the alarm for the entire building—and while I've always been aware this would do me little good, I'd just accepted the risk. But it's no longer only me. In case of emergency two lives would be at stake.

At nine I knock on Lloyd's door. He answers with bed hair and stubble. Technically his workday also begins now, but as long as he gets his job done the tenants don't complain about his taking liberties with the schedule.

Lloyd, I need you to do me a <u>FAVOR</u>. April June needs you to call in sick to work for her.

He chuckles at the note, the import of *favor* clear. He is lazy about notes, but has learned to enunciate clearly toward my lip-reading efforts.

"Well, Mr. Evans, I can't just say she's calling in sick. What should I say she has. Flu?"

I shrug, nod, and show him the number in her address book which I'd retrieved from her bag. He makes the call while I watch him from the doorway.

"Anything else?" I know from his expression this is sarcasm, and yet I jot another memo.

> As a matter of fact, I have been wondering about the fire
> safety plan. As you know, I cannot hear the alarm.

There is the trace of a smile on Lloyd's face as he motions for me to step inside. On the back of his door is a paper on which he has neatly written SUPER'S PROCEDURES IN CASE OF FIRE. A list of eight steps in order of priority. Number 1: *Wake Benjamin.*

▯ ▯

Deaf who grew up in a deaf family or deaf schools tend to be more physically demonstrative than hearing people, something I first observed at April May June's birthday party. She and I are private people, or perhaps more accurately I'm a private person and April May June has taken my cue, or perhaps more accurately April May June and I would just as soon not have an afternoon stroll ruined by a stranger's scowl at an interracial couple holding hands—but even our minimal show of public affection is reduced to nil once we cross the Mason-Dixon. Just our sitting together on the bus has garnered enough glares, though we are cut some slack as deaf people: not knowing any better.

Over the summer she had made monthly trips to South Carolina to be close to her rapidly declining father. On Wednesday, September 8th, Ramona called the textbook publishing house. April May June was summoned by the receptionist, a woman she barely knew, who jotted down Ramona's news that their father had passed on. When she came to me an hour later, her eyes so full of profound shock and grief, I betrayed my vow

▫ 555 ▫

to myself and, without her asking first, told her if she wished for me to accompany her South for the funeral, I would.

The Junes live in an eight-room house, the largest dwelling on their street, an all-black (here they still say "colored") lower-middle-class neighborhood. The immediate family is very warm to me, the extended family polite, if guarded. It's obvious that of all her siblings April May June is closest to Ramona, and we spend a lot of time in her room, formerly the one she shared with April May June. Ramona had been living an hour away, but moved back home to help her mother care for her father the last several months. April May June will sleep in this room with her sister, and I'll be on a couch in the basement. Ramona has a small television, the only one in the house. On the news is a report of a mass riot at Attica, a New York state prison near Buffalo which, as near as we can piece it together, seems to be related to inhumane conditions at the penitentiary. Momentarily we are removed from our immediate tragedy as we stare at the disaster unfolding.

Dinner around the big table is a mishmash of bereavement food left by friends and extended family. Only the immediate family, spouses and children, and I are here now, and there's bittersweet laughter, everyone having an anecdote about the recently passed patriarch. And other family lore: firstborn Cecil ribbing April May June for her annoying childhood habit of facing one of her siblings while shutting her eyes in the midst of a squabble, thus closing off the other's manual arguments. In time the conversation quiets to a more serious tone, and April May June and her three brothers and three sisters begin their gentle persuasion of their mother to have the funeral conducted in the sign language. It would seem an obvious choice given the deceased's closest relatives would miss half the service were it in spoken English, yet it takes some convincing since many hearing relatives will be in attendance and Mrs. June is naturally accommodating. In the end she concedes, and the next day a multi-page bulletin is printed, translating for those who don't communicate in sign.

The funeral takes place the subsequent morning, Saturday, and everyone has been forewarned, but it's as if the hearing did not imagine the minister really would be deaf, that the *entire* service would be silent, and many are miffed as this reality gradually sinks in. I'm the only white person present. There's one white in the family, married to a cousin in Philadelphia, but while the cousin is here he had cautioned his wife, for both their sakes, to stay home.

As we walk up the hill for the interment, a woman passes a note to April May June. I had noticed her in the church. She didn't seem perturbed by the quiet but rather had closed her eyes, seeming to have gone to a meditative place. April May June reads the message, smiles at the woman and nods. A minute later she subtly slips the paper to me, telling me the woman is her father's sister.

> April May,
>   I have thoroughly enjoyed this service. The quiet and the sign language made me feel like Johnny Lee was right there in the room, still with us.
>   Do you mind as the casket is lowered, can we sing "Will the Circle Be Unbroken"?
>
> Love ya'll,
> Aunt Ruth

At the coffin's descending, a glassy-eyed April May June smiles at her aunt. The elder begins the song, and the hearing, surprised and happy through their tears to finally take part, join in.

April May June wishes to stay an extra day to see what needs to be done, so we plan to take the bus back Monday. Sunday I wake earlier than everyone else and walk just outside the front door, gazing around at the early morning stillness, my first moments alone with the Cotton Belt in over a decade. A police car appears, slowly patrolling the neighborhood. The two white officers seem flabbergasted to find a white man here. I wait for their expressions to metamorphose into some judgment, suspicion and disgust, but it's worse: they smirk, leering, as if I'm here for easy sex, and we three white men are all in on the joke. I stare at the vehicle as it vanishes around the corner, my body hot in its fury, and I turn back into the house to cool down.

There are few bright spots over the long weekend, but Sunday night Ramona invites us into her room. She directs me to sit in front of her two-foot-tall left stereo speaker, April May June in front of the right, having us each place our hands on our respective sound box. She flips on the turntable. We are delighted by the vibrations seeping through our fingers, our bodies. Ramona begins to dance and sing: *I want to thank you falettinme be mice elf agin.*

In the fall my classes fill to twenty capacity with waiting lists. I'm pleased the sign language is so popular but I also need to work harder to ensure every student is getting the necessary individual attention. As autumn passes, April May June makes her holiday travel plans, wishing I could join her in South Carolina, but I couldn't possibly ask Lloyd for more time off after the days he allowed me for the funeral in September. She'll take a predawn bus Christmas Eve, and the evening before we have dinner in my neighborhood, then head back to my apartment, walking distance to the bus depot. I present to her *Custer Died for Your Sins,* a book she'd heard about and had been eager to read, and a kente cloth scarf I'd purchased from an outdoor table in Harlem. She gives me *Nobody Knows My Name,* a book of essays by James Baldwin, the author whose novel had mesmerized me on my original long bus ride out of Prayer Ridge to New York, then she goes into my closet—how did she hide something there without my knowing?—returning with a surprisingly large box. A beautiful new winter coat. She has clearly splurged and I'm thinking I'll save it for special occasions, which she apparently intuits because she snatches my consignment shop frock, *that raggedy old thing* as she puts it, exits my apartment, and dumps it in the shoot for the building incinerator. After sex and very little sleep, I in my new coat walk her, her suitcase, and her big bag of gifts to Port Authority. When the coach pulls up we kiss goodbye, with the promise that I'll come see her the evening of her return, Sunday the 2nd.

Lloyd has finally broken down and purchased paint for the lobby, assigning the task to me. Having confined myself inside on New Year's Eve to avoid the Times Square madness, I decide to use the hours constructively and pull out the stepladder. I'm about halfway through the job, 6:30 in the evening, when I remember the deaf tourists from the subway today, Italian flags sewn on their duffel bags. I was fascinated by their foreign manual language, and now I make wild spontaneous plans to learn Italian sign and then to travel with April May June to Venice in the spring. The entrance door cracks open, but it's a struggle for whoever is trying to get in, being jammed among the throngs. After some effort the mission is accomplished and April May June emerges, wild-eyed and clutching a bottle of champagne, slamming the door behind her as if she had just made a narrow escape with her life. I stare at her, unbelieving, and she is startled to see me looking down from the ceiling, roller in hand. I nearly fall over the ladder in my rush to embrace her, this surprise gift of her return two days early to be with me on New Year's Eve. She's not at all disappointed by the meager canned tomato soup and crackers I have to offer for dinner, just so long as she doesn't have to go out and face that mob again. We eat staring out at the crowd, and my eyes fill as I remember being in this same place a year ago, wondering if the stranger in the miniskirt I'd met in the 50th Street station might be among the multitude, overcome with the gratitude that I drummed up the courage to write her that night. When we see the lips of the revelers moving with the final ten-second countdown, we face each other and raise our glasses, our counting fingers moving in unison with the millions.

A cold, wet January kicks off 1972. On Tuesday, February 8th, I organize a game of Gossip with the teenage class. Confidentially I give the first person of each of the two teams a message in sign syntax: "gray goat sleep where, big tree, under." By the time the sentence moves down the line, my assertion that "the gray goat sleeps under the big tree" has been distorted by one squad as "two red rabbits eat a house," and by the other (with obviously some deliberate embellishing along the way) as "President Nixon is a toad."

After class I stroll by April May June's as usual. I wonder if she remembers that our anniversary is fast approaching—one year since the night I first came to her apartment for the party we never went to. I'm surprised she's not at home and has not left a note, so I leave one. When I come again after Thursday's class and again there's no answer, nor a reply to my previous message, I begin to feel uneasy. I leave another note.

AMJ,
    Our anniversary is on the 13th! (Sunday!) I want to take you out, wherever you want.
    I'll come around 7.
B.J.

The next afternoon I'm leaving my building to pick up a few groceries when I see a note taped to my mailbox.

I haven't been feeling well lately, B.J. Can't do Sunday. We'll get together later on.
AMJ

In her "illness" she managed to travel over fifty blocks to my building to leave a message, and made no effort to see me? I get on the train to the Village and push the button connected to her flashing lights for a half-hour, no intention of leaving, until she comes to the entrance door, glaring.

I told you I don't feel well.

Then I should come up and make you some soup.

She rolls her eyes, turns, and I follow her up to her apartment.

Are you angry with me?

No, but she doesn't look at me. I've got hot water on. You want tea?

Thank you.

She returns momentarily with two cups. I'm sitting on the couch, and she sits in the right-angle soft chair. I put my cup down without sipping and lean forward.

Are you pregnant?

Her cheeks are instantly covered in flowing tears but she tries to suppress it. It's okay, it's early, thank God I spotted and went to the doctor, it's really early, it's just a pinpoint of a pinpoint, I know a place where I can get it done.

Is it safe?

I don't know. I don't know!

Is it what you want to do?

She wipes her eyes. I don't want to have it just to give it up for adoption. Little black kids don't get adopted so easy. And if they get adopted by whites, raised white, they don't even know who they are. And what if he's deaf? Could spend the rest of his life in an orphanage! She sighs. Your tea's getting cold.

You don't want to keep it?

She looks down, she doesn't say anything. What she is thinking, I think, is how hard it would be to raise a child on her own, all by herself. But she doesn't say anything. I take my hand and gently raise her chin so that she can see my signs.

I would like to get married.

She studies my face a long time. Then shakes her head. Shotgun wedding! she signs, a weak laugh.

I say nothing and she looks at me again.

B.J. We've barely known each other a year.

But I see the trace of a cautious, hopeful smile.

Mr. Peoples appears, picks up his front paw, and taps her, sign language for Lunchtime!

◻ ◻

In Gimbels I can't help fingering the infant wear, though April May June, even with a belly swollen eight and a half months, is superstitious and forbids me to make any such purchases until after the baby is born.

But I do research without telling her. Since April May June's deafness is genetic, I want to know where a deaf child is taught. As it turns out there are several institutions right in the city, including Public School 47 on East 23rd. I would be able to see my child every day just like the parents of hearing children! Where I grew up, there was but one choice in the entire state—the Alabama Institute for Deaf and Blind up in Talladega—and I imagine my mother just couldn't bear to send me so far away.

I walk out into the fall chill that has suddenly hit this late October Thursday. Passing by a deli, I stop and consider. April May June seemed fine today, but after what happened last night, bringing home a tub of strawberry ice cream, her favorite, may not be a bad idea toward the maintenance of her present tolerable mood.

The evening began pleasantly enough. We were expecting our first guests as a couple. In fact, other than April May June in the days we were dating, they would be *my* first guests of my nearly twelve years in New York City. Ida Jo, a childhood school friend of April May June's, was traveling through town with Ted, her husband of two years, a professor at Gallaudet, whom April May June had never met. She invited them for dinner, and we managed to make room at our small table.

The prospect of, for the first time, having an outside eye inspecting our home, what we have made, caused me to step back a moment and give it the once-over: not bad. And we could share our news about the imminent, and *emi*nent, upgrade to an even more spacious flat.

In August, Lloyd informed me of his plans to retire at the end of the year. He wasn't liking the changes, the building going co-operative which, despite its commune-sounding appellation, actually led to a certain exclusiveness, and he was already sensing a more critical eye directed at himself. Anyway he'll be sixty-seven in a year: it's time. Would I like the job? I could have his apartment: two-bedroom. In the transition he's also allowed me more day hours, and the swollen paycheck is a godsend for my burgeoning family. I've already ordered the tools to rig up our future home so that the building buzzer and, more vitally, the fire alarm will be linked to the lighting.

The new position will mean leaving my Met job and the teaching, the latter of which I'll especially miss. Joy also laments my forthcoming departure, and has been embarrassingly flattering in her scramble to find a way to keep me. Since school starts early, how about having each of my two classes once a week rather than twice, 7:30 to 8:15, before my building management duties start at nine? Half my current hours but three-quarters my current pay? I was tempted to say yes on the spot, but I do need to think about taking too much time away from my wife and baby. How fortunate to be a super, a stay-at-home dad! The principal has asked that I give her an answer by Thanksgiving, and April May June and I persist in weighing the pros and cons.

As for now, we continue to share this one-bedroom. She moved in last April. It broke her heart to give up her Village sublet but she felt greedy holding on to two apartments, one rent-controlled and the other free, so she passed her studio on to a recent Gallaudet graduate, new to the city. Mr. Peoples would have moved uptown with her but during her pregnancy she developed an allergy to his long hair. As it turned out, the new tenant's elderly cat had died just weeks before so she was thrilled to have the company, and April May June gave her old companion a teary farewell embrace.

Yesterday she scrubbed and polished our place, assigning me cleaning tasks whenever I happened to take a break from my janitor duties. Her final touch was to set out our small wedding album. The March ceremony was very modest, at the courthouse downtown. It was rainy and cold, and April May June and I entered the building in our wedding clothes, her simple ivory dress cut just above the knee and my navy suit, both of us soaked and shivering and laughing. The court clerk and officiant, a pleasant, smiling woman who had come to New York as a child with her Puerto Rican family, didn't know the sign language, but an interpreter was found. The fifth person in the room, the legal witness and sole guest, was a beaming Ramona who had arrived with good wishes from the family and armed with her camera, embracing her role as self-appointed wedding photographer.

And so, with many good tidings to share, and my wife's eagerness to meet her old chum's husband, it was with great anticipation that we opened the door last evening. April May June and Ida Jo had not seen each other in over a decade, and the huge joy in their reunion was multiplied by the fact that my wife had kept her secret—thus her obvious pregnancy came as a shock and a delight to her old friend. Kisses, warm embraces.

And then things began to take an unfortunate turn. It became quickly apparent that Ted, Ida Jo's husband, was engaging in Signed Exact English and that Ida Jo was following suit. Very recently this rejection of sign language syntax in favor of signing with precise English grammar—inserting articles, inventing words for pronouns rather than simply pointing at *her*—had become a volatile topic. An assimilation to hearers, and elitism: rejecting the traditional manual communication still embraced by the working class. We had heard of deaf people engaging in SEE with hearers not proficient in sign, but to be in a room of *all* deaf and have an educated couple speaking in this clumsy, pretentious fashion was rather unsettling. As host I could maintain my composure but I knew hell was bound to break loose as April May June is not one to temper her opinions nor temper her temper. I agree with her in principle but these *were* our guests, and I was irritated to suddenly be cast in the role of peacemaker when my wife knew very well I would have much preferred spending the evening in the library while she entertained her old pal. The couple argued that this compromise—speaking manually in the way we deaf are comfortable while using grammar in the way the hearing feel at ease—could facilitate a new universal vocabulary. My wife retorted that sign language is its *own* language, it's *not* English, and then the sarcasm: Oh wouldn't it be great if America could get the whole *world* to speak English! And worse: So what's next for the two of you—the Alexander Graham Bell Association? Bell, the son and husband of deaf women (his invention of the telephone arose out of his wish to develop devices to help the deaf hear), was a crusader for oralism and, in his zeal to force the deaf to speak, campaigned to abolish the sign language, even advocating for the closing of deaf schools and to outlaw deaf couples marrying. For my wife to insinuate that her dear old friend and spouse would support such an organization was the ultimate low blow, and as I stood there awkwardly offering the apple sour cream pie, our first guests hastily grabbed their coats.

In the quiet hour after their departure, I suggested to April May June that she write Ida Jo to patch things up. She categorically refused. I cautiously reminded her that our language is undergoing its own identity introspection, no longer to be referred to generically as "the sign language" but as "American Sign Language" or "ASL" and *Yes, I agree with you* but perhaps we need to be tolerant of others' ways of engaging with the manual tongue during these changing times. That's when I got *the look*. It wouldn't matter to me if it weren't for my concern that my wife may come to regret tossing away a lifelong friendship based on one philosophical disagreement. Well, perhaps she'll soften after the baby is born. Thus far today she has been sweet as pie, uttering not a word about last night as if it never happened, which is a bit ominous. I am no fool: should any remnant of that mood return, I am armed with a gallon of strawberry, and chocolate syrup for good measure.

I open my building entrance door. A fluke: someone's key had broken in the lock so once again the door sets ajar until I fix it. I picked up a few other groceries along with the ice cream and hold the shopping bag in my left arm as I pull out my mailbox key when I turn and see him, sitting on the steps next to a duffel bag. Twelve years older, a touch of gray, but I know him instantly as he does me. I'm frozen except for the key I feel trembling in my hand. He smiles and, as always, speaks as he signs.

"Hello, brother."

6

Randall's fries are drenched in ketchup. He still prefers mustard for his burger.

"Aintchu eatin?"

I shake my head. The glass of water the waitress put in front of me remains untouched.

"Surprise! Bet you thought you never have to see me again this life. Hey, miss, I run outa ketchup, you bring some more?"

It's quarter to five so the dinner rush hasn't hit yet, the place half empty.

"Well I can't believe how funny you're actin, visit from your long-loss brother. Whatcha think, I come lookin for a kidney?"

What *do* you want?

"I ain't seen you in twelve years! I gotta have a reason? Hey, we close to Times Square, ain't we?"

In his manual speak, I'm reminded of some of the signs he and I made up when we didn't know the proper gesture. In any case someone who speaks and signs simultaneously compromises either the spoken language or the sign language so it's fortunate, given my brother's very familiar mouth formations, that I am able to lip-read enough to fill in the gaps.

"New York City! Can't believe my brother from Prayer Ridge find hisself here!" He takes a big bite of burger. "You know, I was tryin to watch the calories, but how can ya have burger an fries without a Coke? Miss?"

Randall wears a flannel shirt and blue jeans. For all I know they may be the same flannel shirt and blue jeans from Prayer Ridge. I notice the shirt is buttoned to the top, concealing his neck.

"You ain't changed a bit, brother, lookin all slim. I got just a little bitta paunch. Well, Monique feeds me well." He sticks some fries into his mouth. There are utensils but he ignores them, licking his fingers and wiping them on the napkin. He smiles, sly. "Guess you don't know bout my new wife Monique."

You should have let me know before you came.

"I understand you're feelin that way but here's the thing. Me an Monique got our vacation from the factory. Calculators, handheld things with big brains an teeny parts. We always take our week off together visitin relations a hers, she got enough all over Texas. But ain't been able to get it outa my head, what Benja wrote year an a half ago: she heard from you an here's your address. Wanted to come lass summer but Monique: 'Over my dead body, after what he done to you?' Respected her wishes at the time, but sooner or later I knew I was gonna see you. Started brushin up on the signs, took a course out at the community college, she thought I was bowlin Thursdays. Useta be fast with my fingers, remember? But ain't had call to use it in more n a decade, outa practice. So here we are, firs day a vacation, her packin for a visit to her cousin Stella Mae in Fort Worth an suddenly I know I ain't goin, I know I'ma be on a bus to New York. All impulse, see? Now by the time I'da written you an you'da written back, the vacation'd be over. Why'd they bring that little thing a coleslaw? I didn't order it."

You should have planned. You should have written early enough to let me know.

"All hindsight now. Anyway what would your answer a been?"

So you just show up? Force me to take you in?

"You know what? This whole conversation feels a little upside down, you with the judgment since *you* backstabbed *me!* But guess you don't see it that way. Hey miss, that apple pie in the glass good? Okay, couldja fetch me a slice à la mode?"

I lean forward. I'm married.

"*Married?* Why didn't ya say! When was the weddin? Shoulda let me know!"

No wedding. We went down to the courthouse.

"Well. I wanna meet her!"

We're expecting our first child very soon, and I don't want to upset her.

"Congratulations! An what the hell you think I'ma do, take her out drinkin an smokin? When's she due?"

I hesitate. It all feels so personal.

Thirteen days.

"Ah! Now that is a bless'ed event. Thank you, miss. Look, she brung a spare spoon, you gotta help me with this mountain." Randall takes a heaping serving. "Mmm. Pie's dry, but the ice cream helps."

She's black.

His second spoonful freezes midair, his mouth open. Then he lets out a huge laugh. "Shoulda knowed it! My brother, the great liberal. Lemme guess," and for the first time Randall signs without speaking: *Some hooker you got pregnant, only my brother would feel obligated to marry the whore.*

I stand.

"I'm jokin! Swear I won't say nothin to her like that." I'm unmoved. "Come on, B.J., you gotta admit this news is a little shockin to your brother from Prayer Ridge, Alabama."

You're not meeting her.

"So where'm I gonna sleep. The street? That bus depot, Port of Authority? I saw what kinda place that is right off, you put your brother out with the derelecks?"

You can take the bus back now.

"No I cannot because there's only one bus a day: 11:30 in the a.m."

I'll give you the money for a hotel.

"I ride twenty-eight hours cross-country to get here firs time I see my brother in twelve years an you send me off to a hotel. Ma muss be rollin in her grave."

I take a deep breath, and sit.

You can sleep on our couch. You'll leave in the morning.

"I appreciate the accommodation. Here's your hat what's your hurry ain't exactly the family hospitality you was brought up with, but guess you done got New York'd." I wait. "*Yes,* I will be on that damn bus in the mornin."

I watch him dip crust into the soupy vanilla. My hands move carefully. *Please don't say anything to hurt my wife.*

"Lord, whaddya think I am?" He pushes his plate away, the dessert half-eaten. "Miss! Coffee please?" He lights a cigarette. "So what's her name?"

I sigh. *April.*

"Nice name." He blows smoke. "Let me tell ya a story, how once I had a wife named Erma an now I got a wife named Monique."

Outside my door I turn to him.

Could you please wait out here a second? So I can prepare her?

"Prepare her for *what?* This is a reunion, B.J.! Oughta be a family celebration, bygones be bygones." When I don't reply, he shakes his head. "Do whatcha gotta do. Feel like some stranger off the street treat me more brotherly."

Before I enter I calm myself so she won't be worried. April May June is pouring herself a glass of milk. In the heat of the summer, she'd cut her big

Afro so that it's now no longer than two inches. She looks up at my smile, and is instantly alarmed: What's wrong?

I brief her on our guest, and I can see she's conflicted between her knowledge of my sibling feud, the details of which I've never revealed, and her excitement at finally meeting someone from my family. If I allow another minute I'm worried Randall may start pounding and disturbing the neighbors if he isn't already. I open the door.

He enters smiling. April May June smiles, timid, holding out her hand to shake, which he takes but also gives her a gentle peck on the cheek. He and I have not touched since he arrived. "Hello, sister-in-law."

As I prepare dinner, he seems to enjoy having another person to converse with in sign, and she follows, trying not to frown in her bafflement when he tosses in our homespun signals. I still don't have an appetite but I sit to eat a little with my wife. Randall, full from the diner, takes just a few mannerly bites, filling the meal with his questions for April May June. Where's her people from? When did she move to New York? *Why* did she move to New York? What sort of work does she do? Does she hope it will be a girl or a boy? I clutch my fork and wait for the other shoe to drop, but he conducts himself as a proper gentleman. "Superintendent? My brother never tole me that! That mean yaw get free rent?"

When dinner's over, we retire to the living room. I'd never owned a television before, but April May June had purchased one for herself the summer before last and brought it with her when she moved in. Without our requesting it, Randall begins interpreting the news. Henry Kissinger has just proclaimed "peace is at hand." April May June and I say nothing, though we're both weighing our mistrust of Kissinger against the hope that he wouldn't make such a pronouncement if he imagined he would soon lose face over it. Around eight, she says she's tired and is going to bed. I follow her to see if she needs anything, then come back out to the living room.

"Well? Ain'tcha gonna show me New York?"

Crossing my fingers that no emergencies arise as I skip out on my evening super duties, we walk Times Square, the New York Public Library, Grand Central, the United Nations, back to Radio City, Rockefeller Center, St. Patrick's Cathedral, up Fifth Avenue, over to Carnegie Hall, lower Central Park, Lincoln Center. I give him a ride on the subway uptown. Stroll around Harlem, then Riverside Church, Columbia University, St. John the

Divine. The train again, to the bottom of the island. Battery Park to look out at the Statue of Liberty and up at the Twin Towers, then north to Chinatown, Little Italy, Soho, Lower East Side, Greenwich Village, up to the Flatiron. I sign little other than to identify the sites. After the Empire State Building I tell him, That's about it. Except for the two underground rides we've been walking, four hours walking, and even as a seasoned New York pedestrian my legs are giving out. But Randall never complains. We stand on the southeast corner of 47th and Broadway, Times Square, five minutes to home, and he asks me to stop, he'd like to take it all in. We gaze at the flashing neons.

"You never asked about me."

I don't respond.

"It hurts that you don't even care."

I sigh.

"I like her. Your wife." I look at him. "Surprise surprise, maybe I ain't exactly the same man I was twelve years ago. But you jus—" He kicks his toe against the pavement. "You ain't told her nothin."

No.

"Good, cuz it's not fair, her gettin jus your side." The colossal flickering Coke sign reflected on his cheek.

"I know you're in 3B now. I know starta the new year you'll be in 4F. That right? Case I wanted to write ya?"

I stare at my Prayer Ridge brother, now surreally framed by the glitz and rush and multitudes of Manhattan. If you wrote to me at my building, I'd get the letter. Either apartment number.

He jumps, and I realize a police siren had unexpectedly gone off just a few feet from us. "If I write you, will you write me back?"

I consider the question, and give him an honest answer.

I don't know.

I'm surprised to see him smile. "Well. I thought you'd jus outright refuse, so guess that means you're warmin up to me."

It's nearly one by the time B.J. and Randall get back to the elder's apartment. B.J. is exhausted and ready for bed, but Randall notices the deck of cards on the shelf.

"Brother, I may not see you for another dozen years. Or ever. Can'tcha just gimme these lass few hours?"

They sit on the couch, cards on the coffee table. The game goes slowly, owing to B.J.'s sleepiness and Randall's interest in chattering. Through a fog B.J. watches his brother's lips moving rapidly, knowing he wouldn't wake April May June but hoping he's not loud enough to disturb the neighbors.

"You ain't even asked me if I got any kids."

Do you have any kids?

"Matter a fact I do. This time aroun I seem to get a wife with all the parts in workin order. A son. Randall Jr. Randy."

B.J. nods, concentrating on keeping his eyes open.

"You ain't even asked how old!"

How old?

"Ten. He's a regular athlete. Baseball. Soccer. An jus gettin to the age for basketball, we put a hoop out back. He was in the kids' football leagues too, he was *good,* but less a football fan. It jus come natural to some kids, that ability. Don't even need to like a game to excel at it. Look."

He takes his wallet from his hip pocket and tosses it on the table, open to a picture of the boy in baseball uniform. B.J. can't help but smile.

Like you spit him out.

Randall grins. "Everybody says that. Monique, they tell her, looks like all you did was carry him them nine months cuz everything he got he got from his pappy." Randall picks the photo back up, gazing at it. "Good thing, otherwise I might wonder. All that natural talent with a ball, but one thing he got no time for is school. Now where he get that from? Remember me his age? Couldn't catch a high fly to save my life, but the books, there I was the star." He chuckles, shrugs. "Long time ago." He turns to another picture, sets it on the table. Randy with his soccer team.

Looks like a fine boy.

With his fingertip, Randall flips to the next photo. The whole family:

Ma, Pa, B.J., Benja and himself in front of the tree, that last Christmas before their father died. B.J.'s smile fades. Randall laughs ironically, shaking his head and putting the billfold back into his pocket.

"I don't know, brother, erasin your entire history. Listen, I think I wanna cuppa coffee. No, don't get up, I see everything. Now as I recall you're a *tea-totaler*. Okay, there it is."

B.J. makes the mistake of winning the first rummy game because Randall tells him it's only fair that he give his brother a chance to redeem himself. As they continue Randall talks about his son, his work, life in Texas. B.J. fading, but Randall seems more energized as the night progresses. When the second game is finally over, Randall the victor this time, he announces a tiebreaker is now in order.

"Randall!"

Randall stops, his eyes shining. "I ain't heard my name from you in—" He swallows. "Your pronunciation's got a lot better."

B.J. doesn't see how. He never speaks anymore, has no interest in oral communication. Randall starts to gather the cards, then, "Oh!" He runs to his duffel and pulls out a piece of paper.

"Almost forgot. Benja sent me one a the bulletins from Ma's funeral. Copied it for ya. It ain't as pretty paper as the original, but."

B.J. stares at the page, a small photograph of his mother smiling at the top. His breath is shallow, quick.

Randall shuffles. "Benja's youngest girl, that Tessa wrote a poem to her grammaw. Printed in there." Randall deals.

Day breaks, and at 7:30, full up on coffee, Randall decides he'd like one of those hot chocolates with whipped cream advertised in the window of yesterday's diner. He'll be back in a few minutes.

He takes the drink to go and strolls over to Broadway for a last look at Times Square, more subdued in the early morning. He'd come looking for some reconciliation. The worrying possibility that B.J. would be unforgiving had haunted him much of the trip, but as he neared the Northeast he calmed himself, hoping for the best. And still B.J. had stubbornly clung to history, shutting his brother out. Randall takes a swig of the brew and singes his tongue.

The apartment door was left unlocked for him. On the table is a note, B.J.'s sleepy scrawl.

> Randall, Lying down a second. Reach your hand in
> bedroom door & wave & April will wake me I'll come out.

The bedroom door is slightly ajar. Randall pushes. It slowly opens wide.

April May June sits up, knees bent, the latest issue of *Ms.* magazine propped against her thighs, turning pages with her left hand. On the bed to her left are other periodicals: *Silent News, The Deaf American, Essence.* To her right B.J. lies dead asleep, fully clothed, his mouth open, one leg on the bed and one off, as if he were climbing up to her, his right hand on her round stomach. With her own right hand she absently strokes his hair, but as she sees the door creep open, her hand freezes. She had been expecting Randall to merely stick his hand in, to "knock," and she is stock still, her eyes alone moving, up from the magazine to fix on her brother-in-law.

"Boy, he gimme the tour lass night! There sure is a lot to Manhat*tan!*" Randall laughs, signing and speaking. "Well. Looks like you both made a nice life here for yourselves. An I guess I can't complain neither. Good wife, good son. *Great* son! Life ain't all a bowl a cherries but it sure could be worst. But listen. Didn't you never wonder what happen between my brother an me?" He crosses his arms, leaning his back against the door. A vague smile appears on his face, staring at nothing. "Once upon a time there was Erma an Randall. They met at a dance, 'twas love at firs glance." He giggles. "Might not a been marriage on second glance if it weren't for real fast Erma tellin Randall he done plant one in her, but it was awright, him feelin pretty ready for man an wife, for You an me an baby makes three. Cep the only three they ever got was a blob a blood in the toilet but that's okay, nex time. But nex time he fertilize her, scrambled eggs again. An nex time. Nex time. Nex time so guess it Me an you, jus be us two.

"Well Randall, he took it in stride. Or maybe he didn't but weren't no room for Randall to express any kinda heartbreak what with Erma's connniptions fillin their whole damn world." His eyes somewhere above April May June, where the wall meets the ceiling. "Randall, go to the meetin!' 'Randall, come with me to church!' 'Randall, I know it ain't your fault, *but.*'" Randall bouncing his shoulders against the door, tiny rapid motions. "Then ridin with his sister in the ambulance, stayin overnight in the hospital with her lookin like the grave after her lovin hubby's fists done turn her face inta groun meat, but ain't *she* still orderin: 'Go to the voters!' Same thing like his boss told him, shoe store owner what give him gainful *employ* so he *do* go an yet an still nex thing he knowed he's fired. Fired! So whaddya think happen nex? *I'll* tell ya what, Randall takes all them goddamn shoes off the goddamn walls a the goddamn store an pitch em at his goddamn boss! Which subsequently give him a bloody face to match his sister's an make him a overnight guest a the Lefferd County Po-lice Department, he don't even get no lawyer then his sweet wife come to take him home. So she can let him have it herself!" He guffaws. "Oh the *tears,* the *tears!*" He lets his mirth ride, gradually subsiding to a smile. "Erma'd just had the sixt incubation gone awry before postin bail on her jailbird till-death-do-us-partner. For her nerves the doctor give her these high-power prescription tranquilizers." He had lowered his eyes but now looks up at April May June. "Grind up them pills an pour water over em, easier for her to swallow. I know the proper dosage. I know what's overdosage. I got A's in everything, English, history, math, science, *science.* I know there's chemicals can speed a heart up I know there's chemicals can slow a heart down. I know these is the latter, if Erma's heart go patpatpatpat, a pill over the dosage slow it down to pat, pat, pat, pat, pill over that dosage pat. Pat. Pat. Pat. A pill over that, pill over that, pill over that:

Pat. Pat.   Pat.   Pat.   Pat.   Pat."

Now a very long silence, Randall's and April May June's eyes locked. Then he turns to his sleeping brother, his voice nearly a whisper. "'I have very strong reason to believe.'" He turns back to her. "That's what he told em. The *po-lice,* 'I have very strong reason to believe,' how he know?" Randall's eyes shine. "How he do that to me! His own brother! Then everyone in town wanna." He glares, his signs becoming huge. "How I stay in Prayer Ridge after that? *Huh?* My own hometown I'm banished from cuza my own brother!" Randall takes the crook of his arm, roughly wipes his eyes with his shirt. *"I never woulda done that to him!* Own flesh an blood! my own—"

He slams his hand against the wall behind him, his breathing heavy and quick. He stares at B.J., wipes his eyes again. Then turns to April May June and gives a start, as if he had forgotten she was there.

Her face tight, eyes registering horror. Her hands tremble as she speaks: Erma died?

He stares at her, confused, terrified. "I didn't say that! I didn't—" He tries to calm himself, and eventually his breath softens. He looks down as he signs.

"Hard growin up. Him five years older, the oldest, yet *he's* Ma's baby. Took me decades to lose all interest in bein her favorite, so naturally that's when I become it. So here he's the one stayed with her, took care a her, an the only thing she ever took him for was for granted. Then me an Benja get married, an Benja all them kids, we had *lives*, what did *B.J.* have? So I guess I get it. The bitterness. Guess he finally find a way to pay me back."

Randall gazes at his sleeping brother, B.J.'s chest rising and falling deeply. "Those days when I firs come to Texas. The *vengeance*. Come up with a pistol behind him, *bang*. Watch his flesh explode, pieces a B.J. brain flyin Alabama to New Orleans. But then he'd never know. Even the one half-second before death when he mighta heard the sound, known what's comin, well course he *wouldn't*a heard it. So I had to think up somethin else." He chuckles. "It got pretty elaborate. There were a couple a bricks comin loose outside Ma's house, I'd tell him we gotta fix em. We walk outside together, me behind him. An I'd wait. Him stoopin, his back turned away from me *wham!* Break that brick over his head but jus to stun him. He be weak but he be aware, lyin on his back, he see me liff that brick high, he know what he done unto his brother he havin done unto himself, *wham! wham! wham!* Flatten his face, nothin leff but blood, bone. Brain spillin the grass."

His smile is far away. Then fades. He shrugs. "Just a fantasy, had to get it outa my system. All that." He runs his fingers through his hair, suddenly tired. "Ugly. Ugly time. I don't bear hard feelins no more. Life's short. I only got one brother." Glances up at her. "He forgets. That goes for him too." He pulls from his pocket a napkin from the diner and tosses it onto the bed, his mailing address written on it, then walks out to the living room and picks up his duffel bag. At the door of the apartment, he stops. He has a direct view into the bedroom, at his sister-in-law who hasn't moved, her eyes full with terror. "Why you lookin at me like that? *April?* Ain't nunna us perfect! What, you think when you meet St. Peter *your* slate be spotless? Yeah, doubt it. An *him.*" His eyes rest on B.J. one last time. Randall's blue irises are full again, wet and stinging but hard. He speaks quietly as he signs to April May June without ever removing his eyes from his sleeping brother. "Sometime you might wanna ask your hubby bout his ole days in the Klan," and with that Randall walks out of the apartment, shutting the door behind him.

Twenty minutes later B.J. abruptly wakes, confused. He looks at April May June, then out through the bedroom door.

She signs, He's gone.

B.J. sits up next to his wife, resting his elbow on his knee, his forehead in his hand. His expression is something between profound worry and relief. After a few moments he looks at her.

What? He gently takes her hand.

She searches his eyes.

He's a. Murderer?

He drops her hand, staring at her, his eyes wild, then turns away. She touches his hand, and with great effort he turns back to her. He begins hyperventilating, his fear transforming into fury, and something she doesn't understand.

He said. He brought it up, murder. She swallows. But then he said he didn't do it. So did he—

Yes.

She is violently shaking everywhere, and he puts his arms around her, gently caressing her, and she's gradually calmed but also knows his comfort will not go so far as to speak any more on the subject. In that rare moment when it was briefly on the table, in B.J.'s *Yes,* she had glimpsed something in his eyes she'd never seen before. She remembers Randall's word: bitterness.

In the afternoon, B.J. goes downstairs to repair the building entrance door. April May June tidies the living room. She wipes the coffee table, then opens the drawer. Inside is the photocopied funeral bulletin. She reads the citation of descendants with its mention of her husband, not being able to tear her eyes from the final word.

Roberta ("Bobbie") Evans is survived by three children and seven grandchildren: her daughter Benja Sprigg, husband Aaron and their children Leslie Jo, Todd, Eliza May, Tessa, Kip and Beattie of Prayer Ridge; son Randall Evans and wife Monique and their son Randall ("Randy") Jr., various parts of Texas; and son Benjamin ("B.J.") Evans Jr. (unknown).

8

On the corner television eight feet off the floor, the returns are starting to come in, but for those in the hospital waiting room, the election results seem distant and insignificant. B.J. is standing, not looking at the set. He had wanted to be with April May June every step of the way, but there were complications, he was confused and frustrated that they weren't being explained to him properly, none of the hospital personnel knew the sign language, and around seven he was handed a note: *Cesarean,* which he knew was major surgery with general anesthesia. Near midnight he's tapped on the shoulder, and he swerves around wildly in his anxiety to face the Jamaican nurse. She knows her manual letters: G – I – R – L. And just as he is about to inquire as to his wife, the smiling RN hands him the note: *Mother and daughter are fine.*

He's eager to see his child but there's some delay, and after all the fierce and fluctuating emotions of the last several hours he is unexpectedly fatigued, dropping into a chair, instantly asleep. He snaps awake an hour later, and the nurse, passing by and noticing he's sitting up, indicates for him to follow her. She goes inside the nursery, picks up an infant, and brings her to her father waiting on the other side of the glass. B.J. nervously holds his daughter, barely bigger than his hand. Black hair and plenty of it, rosy cheeks, her coloring halfway between her mother's and his own.

The next morning April May June is beginning to come more clearly out of her post-op daze.

Iona. It came to me when I woke, I just made it up. Do you like it?

B.J. smiles. *I–O–N–A,* he feels it in his fingers, over and over, the beauty of it. He wonders when he and April May June will give her a sign name and what it will be.

How'd McGovern do?

It takes him a moment to remember the election was yesterday and not months ago. He and April May June had had high hopes for fellow New Yorker Shirley Chisholm, and when the first black female American presidential candidate didn't receive the Democratic nomination, the comparably less inspiring McGovern had secured their votes against Nixon. B.J. shakes his head. Oh well, the new mother sighs. I admit it wasn't my biggest prayer the last twenty-four.

April May June sleeps much of the day while B.J. runs around the city, an industrious consumer: body suits, bibs, bassinet, blankets, bottles so he can feed his breast-fed baby too. When he returns to the hospital in the evening April May June is nursing. B.J. touches the tiny fingers. Iona. November 7th, 1972.

Watch, April May June says. She picks up a rattle, a gift from the hospital, holds it four inches above Iona's head, above the infant's ears, and gives the toy a shake.

The baby flinches.

□ □

The April rains and sunshine bring
The birds and bees and flow'rs and spring.

Iona's parents arrived an hour early to guarantee front-row seats, but had they been further back in the packed auditorium they still would have found it easy to read their daughter's lips, having rehearsed the lines with her dozens of times. For the school spring pageant, Iona was one of twelve kindergarteners chosen to recite a verse related to a month of the year, and she begged the teacher to be assigned April, her mother's name. (Had it already been taken, she would have settled for May or June.)

B.J. and April May June stroll home, arms around each other's waist in the warmth of mid-May, Iona two feet in front and walking backward, talking excitedly with her hands, apprising her parents of all the program's backstage gossip. Her eyes are very large and very dark, her deep brown hair wavy, dimples deep as her Aunt Ramona's. A happy child, rarely sullen, and those periodic foul moods dissipating only minutes after their debut. When the school year finishes in June, her father has promised to paint her room, and the color she has chosen is purple. B.J. hopes that choice can be clarified as something soft akin to a lavender rather than in the black-light arena.

They'd adored their daughter from the start, but April May June had appeared somewhat apprehensive and, B.J. suspected, remotely disappointed, to have had a hearing child, a baby born handicapped by a lack of deafness. For him it hadn't mattered, deaf or hearing, so long as his daughter was healthy. But April May June had grown up in a deaf family, gone to deaf schools. Her natural impulse to raise her child as her own mother had raised her would not be wholly applicable here, but more unsettling: the wonderful deaf public school they'd visited, where the class sizes were small and the teachers spoke to the prospective parents in sign, would now have to be abandoned for the overcrowded, chaotic, and perhaps dangerous mainstream public school. Though private school was well beyond their means, as Iona matured it became apparent she was an extraordinarily bright child, reading before kindergarten (owing to the influence of her well-read parents), and could conceivably earn a scholarship. But was that what they wanted? One of the major contributors to the breakdown of the public school system, they believed, was the proclivity of parents with the privileged advantage of supplemental time and energy (generally coinciding with supplemental income), those parents who *could* demand better public schools opting instead to send their children to private institutions. So Iona's parents ambivalently enrolled her in the neighborhood public school with hitherto good results: their five-year-old already reading third-grade books. B.J. and April May June were gratified when the new president, upon relocating to Washington, chose to register his own young daughter in a D.C. public school. (The irony of any elected public servant eschewing free taxpayer-supported education for their own children in favor of elite private schools is not lost on B.J. and April May June.) Thus far B.J. very much likes President Carter. He never thought he would vote for a Southerner.

Iona's godmother and favorite aunt Ramona visits frequently, and when her niece was three, Ramona had complained to her sister and brother-in-law that, while Iona's hands were a chatterbox, it would be like pulling teeth to get her to speak, a skill that would certainly come in handy in her mainstream school. And while she had been very happy at home, on the playground Ramona had bloodied the nose of more than one hearing boy who mocked her for speaking like a deaf kid. She had no regrets there, but saw no reason Iona need waste her childhood in comparable brawls. Iona's parents thus began taking her to a jungle gym in Central Park to interact with other children there, who by odds were hearing and garrulous. The plan nearly backfired when Iona began teaching her playmates ASL, but in the end the peer pressure sometimes to sign and other times to speak resulted in all the kids enjoying a rich bilingualism.

Iona plops herself in front of the television as soon as the family walks in their door after the pageant. Ordinarily the rule is homework first, but Fridays she has a reprieve. And April May June has her own homework. After a five-year maternity hiatus, B.J. has convinced her to go back to writing her stories. A revision of the billy goat piece that had so moved him was published in the *North American Review,* the couple receiving the happy news when Iona was two months old, but since then, despite her husband's gentle cajoling, there had been no sign of April May June putting pen to paper. Then last October, six weeks since Iona's entrance into the public school system, B.J. had come home one afternoon after checking on the building boiler in preparation for the coming winter. The apartment was empty, and he went into their bedroom to undress for a bath. On his desk lay a newish composition book, a note attached: *Read at your leisure.* He sat down to read immediately, her first story in five years! They had had a lively feedback session after she brought Iona home from school, and without discussing the matter, it became their routine for her to leave her notebook out for him whenever she'd finished a new story. In the last year she has written three and started a fourth. No luck with her submissions yet but she's not discouraged.

Four months ago B.J. received a letter from Leslie Jo, Benja's oldest, saying her mother had passed on. His niece wrote that she unfortunately did not have B.J.'s address at the time of the December funeral, five weeks prior, but had found it later as she was going through her mother's things. B.J. and his sister had kept up a sporadic correspondence after that first letter back in '71, seven years ago. And her tone did soften over time, the siblings coming in the ballpark, he felt, to being as they once were. But she had never mentioned a recurrence of the cancer. His eyes moist, he wrote back to Leslie Jo, telling her how sorry he was and asking if there was anything he could do. She responded the moment she'd received his correspondence, updating him for twenty pages. Details of the illness, her own feelings that her mother's hard life was a contributing factor to the disease. While at the time of her death at fifty-two Aaron had not beaten Benja in more than a decade, Leslie Jo had never forgiven her father, and had even spearheaded a family boycott at Christmas, only the baby Beattie showing up with his wife and toddler, leaving the patriarch devastated. Leslie Jo's remorseless comment: "He *oughta* cry." In the letter she also mentioned fond childhood memories of Uncle B.J., her favorite uncle, a fact that took him by surprise and he wiped his eyes.

In the days following Randall's long-ago visit, B.J. decided it was at last time to talk with his wife about the circumstances that led to his estrangement from his brother. He couldn't burden her while she was still pregnant but promised himself he would sit down with her soon after the baby was born, and when Iona was three months old he had gazed long at April May June one evening in their living room, and when she looked up his hands began to move and they did not stop, he knew they could not stop or he would never get out the whole truth, his childhood, his young manhood, his mother and father and sister and brother, the library and the Klan robe turned pink, long hot days at the sawmill and the cross-burner he and his brother attended, Sunday dinners with his brother and sister-in-law and the awful school desegregation day and the awful day he saw his sister's face beaten to a pulp and his confrontation with his brother-in-law *and*. He had taken a breath to prepare himself to tell the worst, and in that pause her hands finally began to cautiously move, to convey the terror she had been carrying, so profound she couldn't broach the subject: the specifics of her private conference with Randall. B.J. was stunned, as her understanding of the events that culminated in his alienation from his brother differed radically from the facts. And then he was telling her, *the* episode that led him to betray his brother and flee Prayer Ridge, Alabama, and the South forever. And afterward B.J. and April May June had cried all night. Over the years Randall has never written, despite his intimation to his brother during his one and only visit that he would.

Every summer April May June and Iona spend at least a week in South Carolina, Iona always excited to see her doting grandmother and aunts and uncles, to play with her cousins and there seemed to always be a new one. Someday she would ask her father about his family. He didn't know how he would answer but he'd cross that bridge when he came to it. He goes to the kitchen now for a little boost—he imagines he's getting old, fatigued often, and these days coffee has proven a stronger stimulant than his formerly preferred tea—and from his standpoint he has a perfect view of April May June writing in her notebook, of Iona laughing at the Cookie Monster. He and his family have been very happy in this Hell's Kitchen two-bedroom, and after B.J.'s participation in Local 32B's seventeen-day strike a year ago, he was gratified to be bringing home higher wages and an extended health-care package. He marvels on the changes of time. Once he had a family—parents, a sister, a brother, all obliterated in a crushing denouement. And now he has another family. He wonders if Iona would ever abandon him as he had done his mother. He shudders at the thought. Then again in two months he'll turn fifty-four, and by the time she would be at an age to even consider such a thing he'd be an old man, perhaps so irrelevant to her life there would be no dramatic departure but rather a natural and gradual falling away from each other, though she would be the one to initiate that gentle separation as he would certainly cling to his child with every fiber of his being. Well, such was life. He would be utterly grateful for what he had had while he had had it.

B.J. takes out the unopened can of coffee grounds. Now April May June and Iona are bickering, their hands rapidly fluttering, assuredly the same dispute they always have related to Iona's one-hour television limit. He watches amused, paying more attention to the drama in the living room than to his own task and thus accidentally cuts his right index finger with the can opener, drawing a few drops of blood. He washes the tiny wound and interrupts the living room debate by summoning his daughter, who loves to play physician. She puts the antiseptic on the Band-Aid and smooths the compress over her father's injury. After dinner B.J. is surprised to see the bleeding has persisted, and Dr. Iona replaces the bandage. After she's in bed, April May June frowns to see the blood has soaked through again, and this time she wraps her husband's entire finger in gauze.

When B.J. wakes the next morning the dressing is saturated bright red, surrounded by a circle of blood on the sheet, the circumference of a 45 rpm record.

9

Randall's face is close to his work. One by one he picks up the thirty-eight minuscule keys with the tweezers, snaps them into their positions, sets the microchip in place, and attaches the keyboard membrane to the sensors. He's suffered migraines lately and it's been suggested he get prescription glasses, but the company won't pay for them so the best he can do is grab whatever's at the Salvation Army. Monique's job is to ensure each assembler has each of the thirty-eight keys for each calculator. When they first started working here she had asked him, "What's the checkmark? What's 'cos'? What's 'tan'? What's the two eyes and the nose?" Regarding the last he had to look to see what she meant. "That's percent," he'd replied. "The checkmark's square root. The rest I don't know, it's trigonometry an I never got that far."

Now he smiles at his wife, lost in her concentration, wearing the glasses with the pale blue frames that she has owned for years, putting them on upon awakening and rarely taking them off before turning the light off at night. He marvels how they have pulled through all the trials and tribulations of life. After a lot of moving around in Texas, they'd settled here in Shelbourne eleven years ago. Good jobs for the both of them, a lovely new home. And yesterday they received another letter from Randy, sounding excited about some new plane he was flying.

Nineteen seventy-eight had been rough. The boy had never taken much of an interest in football, but his natural prowess in spite of his detachment, not to mention the special affection girls have for football stars, had enticed him to play on the school team, second-string quarterback. He was a junior and had recently hooked up with a blond sophomore cheerleader, a rich girl who chatted incessantly about the virtues of her father's calling, the marriages he'd saved via post-mastectomy reconstruction, the second chances in life he'd given to burn victims who had lost half their faces. Outside of Bridgette's reports, Randall and Monique had only known of Dr. Taggert by his reputation for flawlessly turning B cups into D's, Bridgette's mother being a dazzling example of the surgeon's handiwork.

The crisis was launched when, during the last football game of the autumn of '77, Randy had stepped back in preparation for a long pass and was surprised by a sack, and his leg going crack. The break meant he would be on crutches all of basketball season and, unlike his apathy toward football, Randy's greatest joy in life (that didn't directly involve his penis) was basketball, his NBA dreams encapsulated by his bedroom adorned not with posters of Queen nor Blondie (though he played them both incessantly) but of Bob McAdoo and Kareem Abdul-Jabbar. (He was only five-ten but knew boys still could grow into their early twenties, and while he was painfully aware of his father's deficit in that area, he was encouraged whenever he met tall men on his mother's side.) His forced immobility engendered a sullenness, a marked change from his ordinary easygoing demeanor. Arguments with his parents became increasingly ferocious, and he began spending more time at the Taggert estate.

The problem was that Bridgette's sole sibling, the brother she despised who lived in the basement, seemed to have been doing little since his graduation the prior spring other than spending the bottomless pit of his familial endowment on drugs and, unbeknownst to Randall and Monique, Randy had gradually grown less enchanted with Bridgette than with Brian's glorious subterranean pharmacy. There began to be calls to the Evans household from the principal on the subject of truancy, and the screaming between Monique and Randy became unbearable. Randall would slip off to their own basement turning on the radio or TV, but always following Randy's inevitable door-slam exit came Monique's race downstairs to transfer her frenzy onto her husband. Hostilities reached a new peak when Monique found a plastic baggie filled with white powder that she was fairly certain was not baking soda, decidedly upgrading the concept of Randy's substance abuse from the abstract and alleged to the achingly concrete.

In May their landlady of the previous eight years informed Randall that she had heard too many complaints from neighbors about the hysterics, and that they would have to be out by June 1st, adding a threat to call the police on their "addict" son if she were given any grief on the matter. So coupled with everything else was the stress of finding a new home quickly (which they mercifully did) and moving.

By early summer of '78, the family dynamics had reached an absolute nadir, and after the lying and the stealing and the onetime threat to his mother while brandishing a butcher knife, in one horrific blowout it all came to an unforeseen head with Randy's uncontrollable sobs and desperate cries for help. His parents checked him into rehab at an expense that would put them into debt for years, and he came out in early August clean and with two announcements: he had been studying for the fast-approaching GED exam and, related to this, he would like to skip his senior year and join the air force. He had just turned seventeen in mid-July, the earliest he could enlist, but as he was still a minor he needed their signed permission. It was not the future they had dreamed of for their son, Randall's long-held fantasies about collegiate athletic scholarships fading before his eyes, but after the trauma of the last year he and Monique gave in with few objections. Randy passed the test and, after some ardent intervention by his drug counselors coupled with the fact that the infraction had occurred before Randy had reached his majority, the air force had suspiciously accepted the former junkie on a trial basis. It had all worked out beautifully. Randy's letters always sounded upbeat and enthusiastic, and when he recently came home on a short leave in his spiffy uniform, he seemed calm and content and quite the gentleman, doting on his mother till she was brought to tears. And as the months of merciful tranquillity passed, Randall and Monique came to make peace with each other and, occasionally, love.

At the end of the workday, Randall and Monique walk together to their car. It's the middle of June and an oven outside. Still Randall buttons up his shirt to the top so as to conceal an old injury—a shallow cut on his neck. The diagonal wound had once begun by his ear, with only the section below his chin, a shadow of the former scar, still refusing to vanish. Ten minutes later they pull into the garage of their home, a duplex connected to a three-unit building. As Monique prepares dinner, Randall gazes at Randy's eight by ten framed photo on the wall, head and shoulders in his air force uniform, brilliant smile. A strange trick of nature that the boy looks a mirror image of Randall at that age *and* is universally considered handsome, something his father had never been mistaken for.

With the stew cooking, Monique rests with Randall in the living room a moment. On the TV screen, Lucy and Ethel are singing onstage while tearing each other's dresses apart.

"What's on tonight?"

"*The Waltons* or *Mork & Mindy* and *Benson*." Randall doesn't even bother to pick up the *TV Guide*. The phone rings and Monique goes to the kitchen to answer it. The murmur of a conversation.

"That was Elizabeth. She said she been holdin onto our mail long enough, we don't go over an get it tonight, she's throwin it out."

"Let her throw it out."

"Hon." He groans and gets up to drive over there. It took the post office months to forward their mail properly since their move a year ago. Elizabeth had called before on this issue, Randall gathering she had only held onto the mail this long out of guilt for kicking them out so abruptly after they had been good tenants for the better part of a decade, and he enjoyed the idea of her bruised conscience. But Monique was damn anxious to get those outdated letters from her family. When he rings Elizabeth's doorbell she tries to be friendly but stiffens at his chilliness, and as she hands him the plastic bag he notes with satisfaction that her eyes seem glassy and hurt as he turns his back on her forever.

He eats his dinner on a standing tray watching TV while Monique goes through the envelopes in the kitchen. Finally she comes to join him with her own plate. "Letter for you, from New York."

Randall freezes, staring at her, though she has already become distracted by Dick Van Dyke tripping over his ottoman, dipping her buttered bread into her chili. He puts down his fork, sets his tray aside and walks out into the kitchen. Not a regular envelope, but some sort of express mail thing that required a signature. Did that witch sign and then not even bother to tell them he had an urgent letter?

July 17th, 1978

Dear Randall,

I know you must be surprised to hear from us. I hate to write with bad news but your brother is very, very sick. He has acute myeloid leukemia and desperately needs a bone marrow transplant. I know that is a lot to ask, and I wouldn't if there was any other way. Neither I nor my relatives are genetically compatible. I wrote to someone in your family in Alabama but have not heard back. The doctor has been grim about his chances of survival unless a donor comes forward very soon.

I know you and B.J. have had your differences but I remember what you told me, that you only have one brother. I'm begging you now to save your only brother's life. He recently slipped into septic shock, which is like a coma, and was rushed to intensive care. He does not know I have written you.

So, for the sake of your brother, I have taken it upon myself to beg you to consider. I will happily pay for your travel. You are sincerely welcome to stay with us, or I will pay for a hotel. And Randall, if you and Monique are in need of money, I will pay you more, no questions asked. I hope you will accept this as an offer of gratitude, and are not in any way offended. <u>I AM DESPERATE!</u>

If you feel you can make this sacrifice for your brother, for which we would all be eternally grateful, please call the Cripshanks at 212-388-4125. My friend Marielle is deaf but her husband Jonas is hearing and will answer.

I hope you, Monique and Randy are all in good health, and I long to hear from you soon.

Your sister-in-law,
April

P.S. I have enclosed a kindergarten school picture of your niece. Her name is Iona.

Randall walks into the living room. He turns off the television, and Monique stares at him. He reads the letter aloud.

After a few moments of silence, she speaks. "Sorry, hon."

Randall's eyes stay fixed on the paper. "Maybe—"

"She said 'very soon.' That was a year ago."

He doesn't say anything more. After she goes to bed he dials Marielle Cripshank. *The number you have called is no longer in service.*

June 20, 1979

Dear April,

I did not get your letter until now. We moved and the mail service was not forwarding.

I was very upset by your letter. I pray my brother is still among us. If he is not, please let me know, and I will pray he is at peace. But if he has held on, my bone marrow is his. Here's my number: 325-252-6736. My wife and I just squeeze by with the bills. I don't have money for the airplane, and I would need the hotel only if you would prefer I stayed there. Besides that, I don't need another penny.

April, I said some terrible things to you in New York. I was so ashamed I cried half the bus trip back to Texas. I guess it hurt my feelings, me wanting to know my brother again and he seemed to just want me gone. But I never should have come there, sprung myself on ya'll than expect open arms. And those things I said from Prayer Ridge was for your husband to tell you not me. I been owing you an apology for a long time and I hope you except it now.

I meant it when I said it. I only got one brother.

Randall

P.S. Randy is in the air force and doing real well.

Over the next several days Randall is clandestine—when Monique is grocery shopping, busy in the kitchen with dinner, at the mall. He goes to the library to look up leukemia and checks out the colossal white pages for Manhattan. There are a few Cripshanks, but no Marielle nor Jonas nor M nor J. He slowly moves to *E*, his heart racing, and counts five hundred nineteen Manhattan Evanses. Maybe their daughter can hear, and if so might they have a telephone? But apparently not or April would have written that number on the letter. Then he starts at the beginning of the book—hundreds of infinitesimal entries to a page—and on Sunday while Monique is at the farmers' market he finds it: 247 W 53. The name connected with the address is A GARCIA.

"Yes, I remember Mr. Evans." An elderly lady, and Randall detects an accent. "Very kind man. Quiet. Well, the deafness," and it's with this positive identification that Randall's heart begins to beat rapidly. "I remember he got sick and his family moved out. I didn't realize it was that serious." A silence. "Tell you what. Let me go to his old apartment. Maybe the new tenants know something."

"Oh thank you!" He's so happy for this little offer of assistance he nearly hangs up before she asks for his number.

Tuesday after work, he is writing a check for the electric when the phone rings.

"Randall." He looks up. Usually she addresses him as hon. "Somebody callin boutcher brother."

Randall runs to the kitchen.

"Hello?"

"Hello. I'm calling about Benjamin Evans." A man.

"Thank you! Should I hang up an call you back on my long-distance?"

"No, no. It's fine."

"Oh thank you. Jus one second please, I'm here in the kitchen where my wife's makin dinner but I wanna take you to the bedroom, quieter in there." He puts his hand over the receiver and looks at Monique, who is staring at him. "I'm goin in the bedroom. You hang up, hon? Promise I'll explain soon's I get off." She makes no sign of a reply, but when he runs into the bedroom and picks up the receiver, "Hello?" he hears a click and the kitchen noise vanishes.

"Yes. You're the brother of the deceased?"

Randall catches his breath. Everything in the room disappears, some other dimension.

"Hello?"

His voice quiet: "Yes."

"I didn't know him. We just bought this place six months ago." The man clears his throat often and sniffs occasionally, as if suffering from allergies. "When we bought it, no one told us the previous tenant had died. The super, right?"

"Yes."

"Yeah, we were told the super died. Just nobody told us before we moved in we were living in the super's quarters. 4F, right?"

"Yes."

"Sorry to tell ya. You didn't know your brother passed on, huh."

Randall feels something wet in his palm. Blood. He realizes he is still holding the pen he was using to write the check, and has stabbed himself. He stares at the thick red feeling no pain, a stream slowly rolling down his wrist, his arm.

"I'm sorry. Condolences," in a tone that also sounds like "Goodbye." Randall speaks quickly.

"You don't? You don't know where his family moved to?"

"No, I think there was a little lag time between when. You know. And the time we moved in."

Monique waits in the kitchen, dinner ready but not served, her arms crossed.

She's furious to find out Randall would make such a decision, to offer his bone marrow, without consulting her. She says she would leave him if he ever did such a crazy thing, but thank God that won't happen because B.J. is long gone. She is instantly remorseful of her outburst, and the one-sided argument is over. They are silent in bed that night until she says, "He'da never done it for you."

"You don't know that."

"He was ready to let you sleep in the street when you come visit him in New York. His own brother. He wanted nothin to do with ya, so what's that tell you bout if the tables was turned."

"You don't know that," and Randall wipes his cheek, rolling over to face the wall.

A week later Monique sees the letter first, the same one he had written to his sister-in-law, now stamped RETURN TO SENDER, ADDRESS UNKNOWN. She leaves it for Randall and he finds it and they never discuss it.

She spends Saturday morning at the mall and when she comes home she stops, staring at the framed pictures on the wall and on the mantel above the faux fireplace. Something has been altered. All the photographs are of her numerous relatives with the exception of the one taken on the occasion of Randall's sister's nuptials: Benja in her gown smiling with Aaron, her groom and soon-to-be batterer. To the left is their mother, a bittersweet smile which Monique had always attributed to her sadness that her husband was missing this, Randall's father snatched away from them so tragically only two years before. To the couple's right is tall B.J. at twenty, and next to him Randall, a diminutive fifteen. And now she discovers what is out of kilter. This family gallery, this parade of happy white folks, and now stuck in the lower-right corner of Benja's wedding, as if she were part of the family, is a school photo of a small brown child. Monique sighs. The resemblance is uncanny, the girl unmistakably B.J.'s. And when she peers closer, she is startled to note a touch of Randy in his first cousin.

10

In the summer of 1980, Randall and Monique received the news that their son Randy had expired in a crash during a routine air force training exercise. Randall, who had vigilantly prayed the country would stay at peace, was astonished and bewildered to envision his son's death in a practice drill, though in his frenetic mourning-engendered research he was to discover that fully 1,556 active soldiers had lost their lives by "accident" in 1980 alone (and an additional 174 by homicide and 231 "Self Inflicted") while precisely zero had died by "Hostile Action." The grieving father bitterly demanded of the heavens what he had ever done to deserve a life of nothing but misery, but as he quickly realized the answer was too painfully obvious, he rephrased the question so as to insert Monique's name in the subject line. At any rate, he didn't believe it was fair for the sins of the father to be visited upon the son. (In a bizarre coincidence the Taggert boy, also rehabilitated from illegal substances, had gone the rich-boy route of college—his family relieved that he now partook of nothing but booze—only to be found dead that fall after a dorm keg party: alcohol poisoning.)

The months following Randy's death saw Monique's paralyzing grief give way to a new horror: Randall's bereavement over the loss of his son had blossomed into a renewed search for his brother—an energetic awareness that, unlike the conclusiveness of Randy's charred remains, he had never gotten concrete confirmation on the issue of B.J.'s demise. On his two monthly Saturdays off he would drive to Austin and spend hours in the new central library, the *New York Times* microfiche, checking every day since his brother's alleged passing for his name—not just the obituaries but, optimistically, the front page, local page, sports, arts, as if his brother may have committed some act of heroism or depravity so remarkable as to have made the Gotham press. In addition he would approach anyone at work, stranger or not, if he heard they were going to New York and ask if they wouldn't mind stopping by 247 West 53rd Street to inquire if anyone there might know anything about Benjamin Evans. (Monique never found out about the private investigators he'd phoned, the one avenue Randall quickly discovered was universes out of his financial reach.)

After months of reasoning and pleading, Monique was through. She demanded a separation of sorts, banishing him to the basement since two apartments were not in their budget. Because she didn't want to cross paths in the kitchen but also didn't like cooking for one, the arrangement was that she would have her own dinner at six and leave his plate on the table for him to have promptly at seven. When he emerged the kitchen would invariably be spotless, the cookware washed and Monique nowhere to be found, though he could usually hear the television faintly from their bedroom upstairs. Work mornings she would already be in the backseat of the car when he was ready to depart and, like a cabbie and passenger, he would drive his wife and himself to work, not a syllable passing between them. At first all this was obviously awkward, but as the months dragged on to a year, then two, they settled into a strange meditative comfort in their isolation. Occasionally they might briefly catch each other's eye at the factory, but an unknowing observer would peg them strangers.

Somewhere in the silence Randall had discovered word-find puzzles. He stands holding the lightbulbs he'd just picked up (Monique had left a note telling him they were needed) and staring at the Walmart magazine rack. He sees he has already gone through all the issues up to the present, May 1983, so on the drive home he decides to stop by that new little periodical place. He'd not been there before but, as it's a specialty shop, he imagines there may be more to choose from.

The store is quiet, and Randall appears to be the only person in it other than the bearded heavyset man perusing an *Esquire* behind the counter, but the space is a maze of tall shelves so it's possible there may be another customer hidden somewhere. As he walks through the aisles searching for PUZZLES AND GAMES he passes FITNESS, GUNS AND SPORT, CELEBRITY and after turning a corner: LITERARY JOURNALS. Some impulse from his long past, of lustfully devouring books and having a report card to show for it, draws him here. *The Antioch Review*, *Granta*, *The Paris Review*. He's never heard of any of them. On the cover of one of the journals under the subtitle FICTION BY he skims several names, and his perusing freezes at "April May June Evans."

April Evans may be a common name, but when he ate dinner at their table in New York didn't she say she was a writer? And some joke about her whole name, that it *was* three months? Randall opens to the table of contents. The story is called "The Purple Room."

Paulina, who is black and deaf, exits a New York subway train and finds herself lost. She hands a note asking for directions to a very tall gentle-looking white man, Orville. He hesitates, then signs back, thus blowing his cover as another deaf person. Paulina is delighted, as she had known somewhere in her heart there was a reason that, of all the people in the station, she had singled out *this* particular man for help. Later she invites him to a party but instead they spend hours at a diner, and that burnt burger and greasy fries will remain the best meal she has ever eaten in her life. She finds out that night that he has never been physically intimate with another person, and she deduces, and is later proven more correct than she even imagines, that he is a terribly lonely man. No family, no friends. She has had several lovers in her life, all black. She's from the Deep South (as is he) and had never before had any interest in being with a white man—yet from the moment she'd met *this* white man . . .

Their days and nights are blissful, and yet there are times when she glimpses him, when he's at his bedroom desk alone and doesn't realize she's awake, or even when he's sleeping, and a terrible affliction crosses his face. Some torment from his past he cannot escape.

They are recently married and Paulina very pregnant when Orville comes home with news: Surprise! His long-lost brother has shown up.

"You buyin?"

The man from behind the counter.

"You been here half an hour, you can't jus—" Randall, sitting on the floor cross-legged, looks up and the man trips back. "Oh! Sorry, you okay? You need somethin?" Randall is confused, then realizes what he is feeling must be registering on his face. He looks down at the journal, turning to the front cover. $5.50. He pulls out his billfold, hands the cashier a ten.

"I can get the change on the way out." His voice is quiet.

"Yes sir." The man nods and walks away.

Something in Orville's wild eyes as he tells his wife that his brother is about to walk through the door, coupled with Orville's silence on the matter of his family, frightens Paulina. And yet her heart pounds with a certain eagerness: her first in-law! A window to Orville's past! And at dinner Edmund is courteous, even warm. Soon afterward Paulina retires for the evening, leaving the brothers to themselves. She lies awake a while, something bothering her, haunting her, despite Edmund's cordiality, perhaps *because of* Edmund's cordiality, which doesn't seem to correlate with Orville's secrecy. Then she's in a room surrounded by monsters, men in men's clothes with grotesque faces. At one point in the dream she recognizes the gait and gestures of one of the monsters as those of Edmund's, and she's afraid, but the dream doesn't truly kick in to a nightmare until she is suddenly aware that Orville is among the monsters, his presence is palpable, and she's not distressed that he's a monster per se but rather that she can't discern *which* monster, she doesn't know who he is, going from one beast to the other in a panic, trying to pull off their masks except they aren't masks so they won't come off.

The next morning Paulina sits up in bed reading a magazine. He stumbles in, having pulled an all-nighter with his brother, seeming to be sleepwalking, and he tells her he would like to nap just five minutes, that Edmund had stepped out a moment, and Orville places his hand on Paulina's stomach and is about to ask a question about the baby, his hand signing the question, but before he can complete his thought he has conked out.

Something intrusive and inexplicably sinister when his brother slowly pushes their bedroom door wide, and proceeds to have a private chat with Paulina. Edmund has a confession to make.

Randall claps the journal closed, trying to steady his breathing. The pages are now damaged, sweat and tears, so he feels it's only right he has made the purchase. He slowly opens it again.

Edmund tells Paulina that when he was in high school he got into a fight with another boy over a girl. The girl finally chose the rival, and although Orville warned his younger brother to let it go, Edmund could not. He hunted down his enemy and stabbed him to death. Reform school till twenty-one.

A cry escapes Randall. He holds the periodical tight against his chest, eyes closed. He's certain everything he has read up until now has been fact, and he whispers to his sister-in-law his relief for this single departure from the truth: "Thank you."

> *The dog days of summer had descended upon them when Paulina accompanied Orville to the clinic. She had told him, It's nothing, It's nothing, her hands still inadvertently speaking the words over and over even after he had been taken in*

for examination and she was sitting in the waiting room. She looked around at the others. Many of them would receive bad news, and she selfishly prayed to be among the few winners in this game. She was returning from the bathroom when she saw the doctor standing there, staring at her. His face. He turned, expecting her to follow, but her legs were frozen, her body stuck. She had not yet heard anything devastating, she would stay here fastened to this moment, in this moment safe.

Sitting with Orville in the ambulance transporting him to the hospital, her hands were aflutter. That Dr. Alvarez has said the patient survival rate had improved in recent years, that Orville had been otherwise healthy, didn't smoke, rarely drank. Orville nodded without responding. When the nurses asked Paulina to step outside the room as he underwent a procedure, he asked her to go home, to open his lower desk drawer and find the superintendent's contract he had signed and to bring Felix, her old lawyer friend from Gallaudet, to see him. As the two men discussed his pension, how it would go to her, and Orville was being advised on the drafting of his will, she was burning with fury. She would not jump to the worst-case scenario. They only needed to find a donor.

The problem was family would make the best match, not to mention would be most likely to volunteer, and his parents and sister were all dead. And his brother. When they had exhausted every possibility for a bone marrow donor Orville still refused her pleas to contact Edmund. In desperation she finally stooped very low, suggesting that his feud with his brother had taken precedence over his love for his daughter, that in clinging stubbornly to the grievances of his past he was apparently more than willing to allow his daughter to grow up fatherless.

Even after all the moments she had ascertained that unnamed misery in Orville's eyes, she had never seen anything like the anguish she had provoked now, and it broke something inside her. And at that moment Jade came running in, followed by Paulina's babysitter friend Nina who stepped out to leave the family alone. If Paulina could never bring herself to believe Or-

ville would leave her, then she certainly couldn't suggest such a thing to their child, but Jade's father had become weaker with each visit, the tubes in his arms, coming out of his nose, and suddenly the five-year-old seemed to understand everything. She burst into tears, holding her mother, her back to her father. And then he asked her what shade of purple she would like her room to be. This was a subject that had been dropped since his illness had consumed the family, and the child turned to him, showing new interest. She asked him what purple he liked. And he told her a story that he had never before shared with Paulina, of being a youth in Alabama, and his jealousy when his only brother had suddenly found a new friend and, Orville had felt, abandoned him. There were days when Orville would go alone to a field of heal-alls. The violet wildflowers could grow two feet high and he would sit, only his head above them, and he would be calmed, finally fully comprehending the plant's namesake.

The babysitter came for Jade. When they were alone Orville gazed at his wife, a tenderness in his eyes. She was certain he was reconsidering contacting his brother. But then he fell asleep. She vowed to ask him again as soon as he woke, but in his slumber he acquired an infection which put him into septic shock, and he was rushed to intensive care.

So without his permission she wrote to his brother. For the rest of her days she would have to live knowing her last desperate words to her husband had been so deeply hurtful, and that with her next deed, in going directly against his expressed refusal regarding Edmund, she had betrayed him. She never heard back. They had not been in touch since Edmund's visit, and for all she knew he may have moved and never received her request.

In intensive care Paulina put her unconscious husband's hand into hers and her fingers spoke to him. Jade asked for a haircut. We argued, and she won. Actually it looks quite cute. She said she can't wait for Daddy to see. Oh when you come home you'll be surprised. We have completely rearranged the living room furniture! Then Jade decided she wanted to hide plastic Easter eggs—in August! She hid the whole dozen but there was one I couldn't find, and she couldn't remember where she hid it. We turned the apartment upside down and finally I told her it was alright, but she began to bawl. And bawl, and bawl, and bawl, I could not get her to stop.

Her husband's breathing was quite shallow now. She sat back in her chair gazing at him. She dozed. In her dream he held their daughter on his knee and opened her favorite book, the child seeing it through his signs and hearing it through her own voice, the story she loved to hear but that he never could.

In an old house in Paris
that was covered with vines
lived twelve little girls in two straight lines.

She had not been asleep more than two minutes. When she awoke, momentarily she forgot everything and decided this summer the three of them would go to the South Carolina beach she used to enjoy with her parents and siblings when she was growing up. Why had she never thought of that before? And then she realized Orville was gone.

Eighteen years in New York, and he had never made strong bonds outside of his wife and daughter. Who would present the eulogy?

By happenstance on the corner of 43rd and Ninth she ran into Clifford Manz, a former student of Orville's from his sign-language teaching, who expressed his sincere sorrow. Learning sign had led him to find his wife, a deaf woman. If there is anything he can do. Paulina replied instantly: Can you deliver the eulogy? You only need read it and interpret it for the deaf. The young man was naturally taken aback, but he hesitated only a moment: It would be an honor.

The day Orville had told Jade about sitting in the patch of heal-alls, which was the last time he had seen his daughter, his last conscious hour, Paulina had taken Jade to the paint store to buy the violet she had requested. Two days after Orville had passed, the evening before the funeral, Paulina was in their bedroom making final edits to the eulogy, glancing at Jade who was asleep in her mother's bed as she had been the last six weeks since her father's admittance to the hospital. Paulina walked to the kitchen to get a glass of water and happened to pass by the can of violet paint, which she had forgotten about. It was only then that she began to cry for the first time and she didn't stop bawling until dawn.

Although Orville tended not to become close to people, he had touched a great many and they came in droves to pay their final respects. Clifford Manz stood when he was introduced to read the eulogy. He looked down at the paragraphs Paulina had written, and he spoke them with his hands, never uttering a word.

Randall stares at the cover of the journal, his eyes fixated on the word: FICTION. Wishing to garner from it some remnant of hope but, at last, he knows. After three long years of searching, five since B.J.'s passing, someone, perhaps their mother, had intervened, bringing Randall this gift of closure, that he may finally begin the process of mourning his brother. And, as a sob suddenly escapes, he realizes he can also now truly grieve his son. He would tell Monique, and she would be relieved, and he would move back upstairs and they would go back to being a family again. Minus one.

It occurs to him that B.J. must have died within eight months of Benja. Randall had gone to his sister's funeral, arriving just in time for the final viewing Tuesday night, staying for the service Wednesday morning, and then he was gone. It had been his first time back to Prayer Ridge since he'd left seventeen years before. Monique did not accompany him. There with his relatives he'd felt like he was sitting in a room full of strangers. He'd leaned over and kissed his sister in the casket goodbye. And now the clarity of B.J.'s passing. There was no one else left in the world who could understand the joy and the pain of growing up with the Evanses of Prayer Ridge, circa 1940.

He starts to walk out of the shop when the cashier reminds him of his change. Randall waits as the man opens the register.

"May I have a bag please?" Randall is not sure why, but suddenly he feels the need to wrap the journal in something. Protection.

The man is pulling out the sack when the phone rings. "Yeah, the latest *Rolling Stone* should be in," absently glancing in the direction of MUSIC. When he hangs up, holding the change and magazine in its bag, he realizes his customer is gone.

1983

I

Dear Uncle Dwight,

How are you?! I can't believe how long it's been!

All's well here. I just completed my finals and am looking forward to graduation next week. (Thank you again for the check!) I did well overall, 3.6 average. I know that I fluctuated for quite some time, but in the end I settled on Poli-Sci with a minor in Black Studies, a pre-law schedule. Yes, I'm following in the footsteps of my "esteemed" parents!

But I would like to live life, to learn a little about the world and myself before heading back to academia. An old dormmate of mine has been in Togo a year with the Peace Corps and has invited me to come over and visit him. Say no more—I bought a one-way ticket! (That took care of the credit card I had just been bestowed . . .) My plan is to work and save money over the summer (and learn French!), then to fly to Lomé, stay a few weeks or months with my friend to be of use in any way I can, and then do a little traveling around the continent.

Regarding the summer job. Sadly with the recession many full-time positions have dried up. (Did you know it's been predicted by the end of the year more banks will fail than during the Depression?! Thank you, President Reagan . . .) So I feel very fortunate, having applied for internships with law firms all over the country, to have been offered three! The one that speaks to me most is Morrison & Foerster in San Francisco.

Corporate law? you may ask. Eliot's son???
Haha! Well, I can't see myself spending the rest
of my days there, but MoFo will certainly look
impressive on my résumé when it comes time to
apply for law school.

 This is a long way to say—Uncle Dwight, might
I stay with you for the summer? I know that's <u>a</u>
<u>lot</u> to ask! But I promise I'm neat! My internship
starts June 1st so I'm flying into San Fran May
31st (TWA, arriving at SFO 2:08 PM) and the job
ends August 30th so I would depart September 1st.
(Flying to Africa that evening!) If this seems <u>huge</u>,
then perhaps I could stay just one month? June?
That would give me time to find another place for
the rest of the summer, a youth hostel if nowhere
else, and a first paycheck or two to offer for it.

 I hope I haven't put you on the spot. I had to
ask. As The Judge always says, "Nothing beats
a fail but a try!" ☺ And if it's not possible, <u>I</u>
<u>completely understand</u>. Where there's a will there's
a way, and I'm sure I can drum up somewhere to
crash.

 But please at least consider my request, Uncle.
Because the truth is I chose the San Francisco job
so I would have an excuse to spend some time with
my father's brother. It has been way too long!

 I hope you are well, Uncle Dwight—healthy and
happy and thriving.

> *Love,*
> *Your Nephew,*
> *Rett*

Dwight sits at his drafting table, absently caressing Carver on his lap, the early morning sun flooding through the east-facing picture window. He reads the neat four-page letter for the twentieth time since its arrival three days ago. Not a scratch mark, meaning Rett is either very self-assured in getting it right the first time or very meticulous in having written a first draft prior to what was sent. Dwight doesn't remember his nephew writing to him since high school, and he hasn't seen him since the boy was in the second grade. The last time he remembers even talking with him on the phone was when Rett had first started college, the fall of '79. Soon after Dwight lost control of his life again.

He looks at the balled-up papers in front of him.

> Dear Rett,
> I'm sorry but at this time

> Dear Rett,
> I am so happy to hear from you! What a treat.
> Well before I elaborate on how proud I am of you, I know you really need an answer to your question. Unfortunately at this time

> Dear Rett,
> I have enclosed a little sketch I made of you playing your guitar, inspired by that picture you sent me years ago. What were you then—tenth grade? Do you still play?
> It <u>has</u> been way too long! And I do so hope to catch up with you soon. Unfortunately at this time

He looks out the window, the bay in the distance, then stands, Carver hopping to the floor, and turns around to gaze at the loft-like space called his living room, the dining area on the other end and beyond that the kitchen, with doors along the north walls leading to the two bedrooms and bath—his bright, spacious, quiet apartment. Keith's apartment. Dwight walks over to Keith's two paintings on the south wall, each two and a half feet wide by four. One a self-portrait, the other titled *Dwight, 1960,* both somewhere between post-modernism and abstraction. Dwight didn't think it was ego that made him feel the piece representing himself was Keith's greatest artistic triumph. By no means was it the only time he had rendered Dwight on canvas, neither could Dwight say the composition brought him any joy, but Keith, for the only time Dwight could remember, had clearly worked without the burden of self-conscious adherence to some convention or to some approved *un*convention, had instead simply followed his instincts and depicted with astonishing precision the rage and torment Dwight was undergoing at the time. Because he so recognized himself in the work, upon its completion a year after the date in the title Dwight had snarled to its artist that it belonged in the garbage. Given the unrestrained shouting match that ensued, he assumed Keith had followed his instructions to the letter, and for good measure had also tossed any other likenesses of Dwight Campbell he had been fool enough to waste his time on. So Dwight had wept when he found the piece in Keith's collection posthumously. He'd hung it as a reminder of what he was and never hoped to be again, and as a tribute to his closest friend.

Dwight sits at the drawing board again. After a few moments he carefully reaches for his pen.

> Dear Rett,
> YES! YES! YES!!!!!!!!
> (And stay the whole summer.)
>
> > Love,
> > Uncle Dwight

He studies the note one last time, bites his lower lip, and seals the envelope.

He dishes out a wet canned breakfast and pours fresh water for tan Carver and her black brother Banneker, cleans the litter box, and by quarter to seven leaves his apartment to walk the three blocks to the school. He is fifty-four and slim, wearing one of his three identical gray jumpsuit uniforms. On the way he passes the mailbox. He pulls down the trap, and sees a little woman hanging inside. It's Tiny, Uncle Sam's mother, the one the whites lynched. She's freshly dead, the noose around her neck, head tilted lazily to the side. Then she comes back to life, lifting her face to look at Dwight. "Sure you wanna do this?" He drops the letter in and shuts the door with her still hanging, then heads off to work.

He's always the first to arrive, last to leave. After he climbs to the third and top floor where his small office/broom closet is tucked away and sets down his jacket and shoulder bag, he rolls out his cleaning cart and takes the freight elevator down to the first floor. He vacuums the administrative offices, emptying the wastebaskets. Then he moves on to the bathrooms: filling the soap dispensers, replenishing the toilet paper, and on the second floor where the older girls are he empties the sanitary napkin receptacles. He finishes around eight, then goes outside to gather any after-school playground litter—a pink sweater and plastic ball for Lost and Found. He notices a screw loose on the swing set and tightens it. Between 8:15 and 8:30 the teachers materialize, most of them waving and smiling at Dwight in greeting. A few don't wave. A few are suspicious of the custodian, knowing his history, but most of the faculty consider themselves progressive, all about granting second chances.

As time moves closer to nine the children begin arriving, many of them waving with innocent exuberance, "Hi, Mr. Campbell!" Dwight smiles and waves back.

After the late bell he works alone again, oddly feeling the guilt-giddiness of a kid who's supposed to be in school but is not, some Pavlovian ingrained response. On his way back inside a little white girl comes running out to find him, trying to suppress her pride at being chosen for the important mission of conveying a directive to the janitor. "Mr. Campbell, Heather Addlewood threw up in Mrs. Eisentrout's class!"

"Okay, I'm comin." The child runs back in, wishing to beat Dwight so she would be able to make the crucial announcement of his impending arrival before his appearance rendered her proclamation moot. Dwight had been hoping puke patrol would be over by the end of February. He prays this isn't the start of some school-wide epidemic.

He enters Mrs. Eisentrout's classroom armed with cleaners and disinfectant, the students mysteriously missing. He has no trouble locating the soiled area, the stench greeting him instantly, the third-row desk overflowing with the gunk. The teacher is writing on the board today's schedule for her fifth grade.

"Thank goodness they had music first thing and I could send them all to the auditorium. Little hard to keep their minds on long division when the room reeks of upchuck." She shakes her head. "The nurse called her mother. Why do they send their kids to school sick?"

Dwight shakes his head in sympathy and in something like solidarity, except as he is alone in wiping up the revolting muck he has no real sense that he and Mrs. Eisentrout are in this together. He's finishing the task when he notices something carved into the adjacent desk. It will be his job to take a scraper and rub it out. He'll bring that tool with him when he does such chores after dismissal, but for now he shows the graffito (the word's singular form he'd learned when once given a citation for such an infraction) to Mrs. Eisentrout.

MIKE ZIEGLER IS A FAG!

The teacher sighs. "I'll talk to him."

At 10:30 Dwight goes back to his office, taking from his bag his reading glasses and a paperback, *Song of Solomon*. He sits at his well-worn wooden table, an ancient high school student desk. When this job was offered to him last summer, he was informed of the irregular hours. Some work needs to be performed before the start of the school day, other tasks post-dismissal, so the schedule was Monday through Friday 7 to 10 and noon to 5. When he asked for a slight adjustment, 7 to 10:30 and 12:30 to 5 so he could finish his hour-long 11 a.m. meeting, the principal was kindly accommodating. The Presbyterian Church is just a five-minute walk away so at 10:50 he closes his book and gets up to leave, always making sure he's a little early to allow for any unexpected delays because at eleven the room is locked and not unlocked until the meeting is over.

There are nineteen in the circle, various genders and races and sexual orientations. The space is already filled with cigarette smoke. They sit quietly, the attention of the room moving around to the left, all who wish to take a turn speaking, all who speak respecting the three-minute limit. When the person to his right begins to utter quietly, Dwight's heart starts pounding, hearing little in anticipation of his own turn.

"My name is Dwight, and I'm an addict. Some of you regulars know it would take too long for me to list all the drugs, let's just say I did em all, OD'd twice on speed, three times smack, every day I'm grateful, every day aware a the miracle I'm still here." He is momentarily silent. "I haven't dropped acid in three or four years. But I just had a flashback. My great-aunt was lynched, that's not the drugs, that's the truth. Well she just talked to me through the mailbox." He laughs softly. "I think this is related to the fact that my nephew is comin to stay with me for the summer. He just graduated from college, wants to go to law school like his daddy, my brother. Over the years I'd receive the occasional correspondence from him, hardly ever did I reply but he never gave up on his uncle, never—" He swallows. "He's got it all together. I haven't seen him since he was a little boy, haven't heard his voice in years. But that letter. You just feel it. *Confidence.*" He takes a breath. "I'm scared. I haven't been around family in a while. Been clean two years, I don't wanna go back and oh God I don't wanna go back in fronta—" Wiping an eye. "When he asked could he come I thought *no, no, no.* And then. He's all grown up. I say no now, might never get another chance." Looking at the floor, he smiles. "I think my sponsor and I will remain in very close contact till September."

He's back at his office by 12:05. He spends the last twenty-five minutes of his break reading while partaking of his habitual packed lunch: egg salad sandwich with an orange for dessert. On days when he volunteers to clean up after the meeting, he gets back with just five minutes to devour his meal. He doesn't mind these service tasks, even emptying the ashtrays despite the fact that he is in the minority as a nonsmoker. Nicotine was certainly among his numerous vices for many years, but he'd made a pact with himself when he finally decided once and for all to give up chemical addictions that it would be *all* chemicals.

He sweeps the floor and stage of the auditorium, then mops before rolling out the several dollies on which are folded hundreds of metal chairs, the smaller ones for the little children to be placed in front. Not easy to make neat lines with seats of such assorted sizes but Dwight takes pride in the orderliness of his aisles and rows.

At 1:45 the students start flowing in. Dwight stands at the back and is as mesmerized as the small children by the Chinese acrobats. (The fifth graders are the oldest, and are divided between those gladly giving into the experience and those trying to maintain a cool distance.) In addition to their astounding gymnastics, the performers present mind-boggling tricks with props, such as the woman who tosses saucer, cup, saucer, cup, saucer, cup on top of her head, pitching them without seeing, each new dish landing perfectly balanced on top of the others until there are ten sets. With every new demonstration Dwight holds his breath, worried for the tumblers and jugglers, their humiliation should a blunder occur. And one does, an exhibition with stacked chairs, someone slipping off, but the man merely catches himself and without missing a beat remounts, and the stunt is resumed to its breathtaking finish. Dwight smiles. Mistakes needn't be catastrophes.

One of the second graders sitting at a middle aisle seat is a spellbound black child, and in his expression of eager delight a memory is sparked in Dwight, of coming to Indianapolis for a visit and taking Rett to the circus. The boy was seven, and Dwight never would have guessed it would be the last time he would see him until this coming summer. A decade later the uncle would become disgusted after learning of the abusive treatment of circus animals, but at the time it had seemed that nothing in years had made him so happy as seeing the enchantment on his nephew's face while he stared at the dancing elephants. Afterward they went to an ice cream parlor, and as they sat at the table Dwight taught Rett to draw a three-dimensional box starting with two overlapping rectangles. The child laughed, jubilant, making boxes over and over, squealing every time he had successfully rendered one, and Dwight had laughed, kissing and embracing Eliot's son until finally Rett had to squirm away in order to create his eighth box.

When the assembly is over, Dwight applauds enthusiastically, the curtain call concomitant with the dismissal bell, and the custodian slips out quickly, hearing (after he has made his own escape) teachers yelling at the children for order amid the mad rush for the exit. In his office, he takes the marble composition book out of his bag. He has had memory lapses lately and when a moment comes back to him, such as the Rett circus story, something he hasn't thought about in years, he writes it down so that he will have preserved the recollection before it vanishes forever. By the time he's through logging his entry the building has fallen silent, and he walks down to the auditorium to fold and bus the chairs. Afterward he begins his regular Friday afternoon erasing and washing of the classroom chalkboards and is surprised to find Mrs. Eisentrout hasn't bolted for the weekend like the rest of the faculty but is still at her desk, grading papers.

"I took Kevin Winters aside and told him what you found. He was cantankerous as ever, but after I had a few choice words with him I did get some kind of grudging apology."

Dwight had forgotten about the offensive defacement. He walks to the desk.

MIKE ZIEGLER IS A FAG!
AND SO'S MR. CAMPBELL

Dwight proceeds to rub the words into oblivion.

2

Saturday morning Dwight sits at his drafting table making the finishing touches. He had mentioned in one of his meetings his history with underground comics, and Mervin, an addict who had successfully turned his life around, had taken an interest. The black businessman had commissioned Dwight to imagine some sort of poster that could be displayed around the city and that targeted "us." Recently the virus, the ghastly existence of which no one could any longer deny, had finally been given a proper name: Acquired Immune Deficiency Syndrome. (The first draft of the appellation from months before, Gay-Related Immune Deficiency, had been pitifully inaccurate regarding the wide range of victims, ultimately proving more effective at raising the level of homophobia than of consciousness.)

The significance of prophylactics in prevention of the disease has been a major breakthrough discovery as, even a year ago, Dwight and many he knew were making wild hysterical stabs at the epidemic's cause. (The club sex-enhancement drug "poppers"?) Dwight's concept is a cartoon of Shaft and Superfly getting into bed together, a one-night stand. Shaft wants to use a condom but Superfly doesn't. Referencing the theme songs of each, Shaft says, "The problem with *you* is the only game you know is do or die!" and, halfway through the comic, Superfly turns to the reader to say, "Wow—he *is* a complicated man!"

At 10:45 Dwight slips the prototype into his portfolio and walks over to the church. He is gratified by his commissioner's enthusiastic response to the model, Mervin rattling off all the places he plans to post the placards.

An hour and a half later, Dwight sits at the bus stop in the late spring sun. Saturday mornings he reads or sketches in his apartment, on nicer days a park, and after his 11 a.m. meeting he partakes in a quick lunch at his favorite taquería, then walks or rides the bus to a museum or gallery. He invariably tops off his outing with an early dinner in Chinatown before going home to retire for the evening. Routine, routine.

On the bus he stares out at the cars. He misses driving. The second to last time he was behind a wheel was in September of '75, when his Nova swerved and rammed into a guardrail. It was his final DUI, license revoked. He had never been entirely certain if this sentence was for life but, given the recently established harsher penalties for drunk driving, had been reluctant to go to the DMV for verification on the point.

His last time driving was in May of '79. He had just been soothed by a hit after nearly twenty-four hours of a violent withdrawal, and took out the envelope he'd been carrying in his pocket since the end of April. Something had prevented Dwight from severing all ties with family. This, and perhaps some holdover from being a mailman, had resulted in him always maintaining a post office box, the rental of which being the *only* bill he paid faithfully each month, even if it meant skipping illegal substances for a day and undergoing the terrible sickness.

The card, liberally smudged from Dwight's repeated fingering, announced Rett's high school graduation in two weeks. In his medicated state, Dwight focused on the pretentious archaic font his nephew's high school administrators had chosen, the eff-looking esses, when he heard something on the television and raised his eyes. A public interest story about a boy who had had a difficult beginning that he had overcome, an exemplary law student who would speak at the UCLA closing exercises the following day. Dwight had stared at the screen long after the two-minute segment was over. He switched the box off and walked the two miles to Keith's, pushing the buzzer. The proprietor was home. Dwight climbed to the third and top floor, saw that the apartment door had been set ajar, and walked in to find Keith on the couch facing the door, glaring at his visitor.

"I jus need a shower. An my suit."

Keith didn't blink. Dwight collected a towel and washcloth from the linen closet and went into the bathroom to cleanse himself, something he hadn't thought to do in some time. When he emerged three-quarters of an hour later, the towel wrapped around his waist and legs, he walked to the small closet that had become the storage unit for Dwight's stuff. Now Keith was turned away, staring at the television though it wasn't turned on. A new TV, Dwight noticed, as the previous one had disappeared along with various other of Keith's belongings, pawned by Dwight for drugs. Hanging in the closet was Dwight's only suit, the one he reserved for funerals, and some decent shoes. He left a few minutes later without uttering another word, Keith still turned away from him.

It was around one in the morning when he walked to the quiet, residential neighborhood. He selected the car, a Chrysler Newport, hot-wired it, and drove it to the PCH going south. He kept a bit of narcotic in his system to maintain equilibrium, prevent the nausea, but, as best he could, this day he wanted to be sober. The blue Pacific to his right seemed to wink its approval.

He entered the Los Angeles city limits and took the 405 to Downtown. A mile from campus he finally found street parking, then walked to the university grounds where he discovered thousands in various lines. After he located the ceremony for which he had come, he strategically waited until he spied a large black family and fell in with them in the swiftly moving queue, preparing to slip in on their ticket. As it turned out, the law school commencement was open, requiring no prior reservation.

The seating was outside, the announcements of special awards and honorary degrees seeming to drag on for hours. At long last Maxwell Williams was introduced. Though Dwight had a relatively decent view of the handsome young man, he was grateful to have caught a better glimpse of him on television the night before. Even with the sound system reverb, he did not miss a word of the address.

In February of 1960, four black students from North Carolina Agricultural & Technical College began to sit in at the Greensboro Woolworth's lunch counter. It was by no means the first such civil rights action in the South, but it set off a year-long epidemic of similar demonstrations from Richmond to Nashville to Houston. In April 1960, students from Shaw University in Raleigh held a conference that soon gave birth to the Student Nonviolent Coordinating Committee.

And on March 31st of that year, seven-year-old Jordan Price and nine-year-old me played a kissing game with a couple of little white girls that exploded into a local cataclysm and an international clamor. The state of Georgia in all its wisdom had planned to incarcerate us until adulthood. In those pre-Gault days when youth were afforded no due process, coupled with Bible Belt racism, we were helplessly at the mercy of a judge's whim, and we may well have served out that verdict if it weren't for the public outrage and the miraculous entrance into our lives of attorneys of extraordinary courage and forti-

tude. Their choice to petition for a habeas corpus *was bold, and when their initial attempt failed they immediately filed for appeal, and three months later Jordan and I were released. Thus I stand here today, a graduate of one of the finest law schools in the country, and without a doubt I owe not only my youth and freedom but my life's ambition to my family and to those four lawyers, grown-ups to me then, but now I fully comprehend how young and fierce they were. All of them still in their twenties, three younger than I am now. They were: Deirdre Wilcox, Diana Rubin, Steven Netherton, and Eliot Campbell.*

He then elaborated, praising each of them individually in the order he had introduced them, and with Max's first sentence about Eliot, Dwight was already wiping his eyes.

When Max's speech, which drew a standing ovation, was over, Dwight wished to slip out but, not being close to an aisle, it was impossible. As he glanced about restlessly, he snatched a profile two rows ahead. He held his gaze, hoping telepathically to force her to turn to him, he was almost certain it was she but he hadn't yet gotten a clear look. When tassels were being moved to the left twenty minutes later, he watched her stand and it was unmistakable. She was rushing in the direction of the podium, no doubt to catch Max before he disappeared into the throng, and in a panic he called her name. She kept moving, and then he was rudely jumping chairs, pushing through parents Excuse me, Excuse me, *"Didi!"*

And now she heard, and turned around, staring at him, stunned. Then slowly breaking into a smile, her eyes glistening.

"Dwight." He had caught up with her, and she reached out to hold his hands firm and warm, no other words coming to her but to repeat it. "Dwight."

She led him down to the front, to Max and his parents who were surprised and thrilled to see her as they had long ago lost contact. There were warm hugs, and when she introduced Dwight, the family was very touched as if he were Eliot's proxy, embracing their former attorney's brother as well. The Williamses had restaurant reservations and invited Didi and Dwight to join them, but they both declined, saying they needed to get on the road.

When the family had gone their way, he turned to her to initiate their adieu. "Well."

"Oh not yet for you, mister, we have a little catching up to do. Take you to lunch?"

It was a quiet place, and they ordered salads. Didi would be forty-five now, looking gorgeous as ever. She chatted on, the same ease and delight Dwight had remembered from that weekend long ago, Rett's chistening as an infant, she and Dwight among the godparents, and another time when they were both in Indianapolis for the boy's fifth birthday. She had been living in San Diego seven years now and loved the weather if not the political conservatism. She had Nellie, a black German shepherd she cherished, a pool, and her walls were adorned with the work of local artists.

"Would love to buy something from you. Have a drawing of yours in my home."

"Be happy to make that happen, but it would be a *gift,* no buyin."

When the salads, which were quite large, were brought to them, Didi had dug into a chunk of chicken, chewing, her thoughts drifting back to the events of the day.

"Funny to think now about the conditions we worked under, defending those little boys back in '60. All the progressive Supreme Court mandates that came down later that decade, and I mean in *addition* to the civil rights laws. *In re Gault* established constitutional rights for juveniles, we would still have been dealing with race, but had *Gault* been in place we wouldn't have felt *so* mice against mountains. Then *Gideon*—did you know before '63 there was no federal directive for a public defender? The poor accused of felonies sent away to the state pen *years* because if they couldn't afford a lawyer, they just had to stand up and defend themselves in court: a layperson against a district attorney! And before *Miranda* '66, the police were under no obligation to inform an arrested individual of his rights, oh my *God!* how did we *do* it?" She shook her head. "But I suppose if we *hadn't* been doing it *then, then* would still be *now.*"

"You know what become a the other little boy? The little chatty one?"

"Jordan?" She sighed. "The latest was five to ten for robbing a convenience store. Both those boys spent the rest of their growing up targeted as pariahs by the local whites. And between the bigger boys and the guards, who knows what happened to them those months they were in the reformatory. Jordan became the criminal they all made him. The miracle is Max didn't." They were both quiet a few moments.

Dwight noticed no wedding band around Didi's finger. She began telling amusing anecdotes about her life since moving to the West Coast, and at one point she mentioned a Glenn twice in the course of three minutes.

"Is this Glenn someone special?"

"Yes. He can hold an erection for thirty minutes straight." She had squealed with delight, seeing the embarrassment on Dwight's face. "Oh Dwight, I have no interest in marriage or children! I just like having a good time." She smiled. "Thirty minutes straight. That would be a good line for Tease. Next installment."

Dwight's face went blank. "You don't know I'm a novelist? I've written a whole series! Black lawyers, mysteries. Ludwig and Tease, attorney partners and lovers."

"Well. Congratulations!"

"Thank you. Not that I have any delusions that I've created great literature. It's crap. But it's page-turning crap, and it's fun." She fed herself an olive with her fingers. "I guess something snapped one day, and I finally got too tired and frustrated with the reality of the legal system. So I decided to write it as it *should* be. And if I attract readers who generally do all their book shopping from the supermarket checkout line, then maybe I'm not just preaching to the choir, maybe my life's served some kind of purpose."

At a far table, a black girl in cap and gown chatted energetically with her proud family. Between his elbowing with all the parents at the graduation and this restaurant lunch, Dwight had been feeling like an impostor all day. Being among folks who had normal functioning lives. His own existence generally fluctuated between part-time and full-time junkie, peppered with sporadic vows to go straight which lasted from a few days to (in one particularly inspired period) six months. Even the year and a half he spent in prison—burglary to support his habit—he barely remembers a day of sobriety. He routinely slept with men who would provide him with a temporary roof. He was doing just that at the time, the apartment where he'd seen the news broadcast that had brought him to L.A. was leased by his latest, a Vietnamese immigrant. (He'll never know for certain whether it was some inadvertent narcotized memory confusion or petty passive-aggressiveness that caused him to shower his filthy self at Keith's rather than at "home.") These were times of semi-temperance. At worst, Dwight's home was the street. But today had made him long for the luxury of ordinariness and, once again, he made mad promises to himself as he smiled at Didi over the flower vase centerpiece.

"And you?"

"Me?"

"What sort of purpose is *your* life serving these days? Remember you're in competition with a fluff paperback writer so I hope it's something equally lofty."

He had looked into his plate, a smile thinly concealing his shame. "I guess I'm not doin much at the moment."

"Anybody special?"

He did not recall an occasion ever to have discussed his sexuality with Didi in the past, but if she would have a problem with it, he may as well find out. "What you said about Glenn? Thirty minutes? Nunna my men been *that* special," and Didi had cracked up. Then she sipped her wine.

"I heard you were having some troubles."

Dwight, still staring at his plate, sighed irritably.

"I'm not going to get into your business. But I hope the struggles are a thing of the past." She had then gazed at him meaningfully. "Like *all* the bad times."

He had looked at her quickly, then away, and nodded.

"Hey. You hear about Andi's good news?"

"I got an announcement for Rett's graduation and there was a letter. He mentioned somethin. Gonna be a judge?"

"Not just *any* judge. She was appointed to the federal court, Southern District of Indiana. *Very* prestigious!" Didi had then sat back in her chair, taking in what Dwight had said. "Eliot's son graduating *high school?*"

"Coupla weeks."

A wistful smile and a shine returning to her eyes, her thoughts far away. "Time flies."

As she perused the dessert menu, Dwight felt it coming: sweat, tremors, fear that he might retch.

"Say, Didi, I think I gotta get on the road. What do I owe you?"

"If you recall I offered to take *you* to lunch. The only repayment. I'd better see that artwork in the mail."

"You got it. And I'll definitely be lookin for Ludwig and Tease." Dwight had stood, then Didi.

"I'm gonna stay a little while longer. The brother at the bar has been giving me the eye, and without you sitting here cramping my style I'd like to see where that goes." She hugged him, kissed him on the cheek. "It was great to see you again, Dwight."

"You haven't changed a bit, Didi."

"I'm gonna opt to take that as a compliment."

Usually it would be easy to ward off the monster near a college campus, the dorms full of provisions, but with graduation, classes were on hiatus until the summer sessions began. In the neighborhood, however, Dwight was able to make contact with a few fellow travelers, the score calming him for the drive back up the coast. At 3 a.m. he pulled into the neighborhood where he'd snagged his lift the night before, parking three blocks away. The following weekend he had strolled the scene of the crime in broad daylight and noticed the car in its original place, so San Francisco's Finest had apparently proved worthy in returning the auto to its owner, if not in ever resolving the mystery of its borrower.

Dwight exits the bus and walks the two blocks to the gallery. The show is a collection of racist mainstream cartoons, screening everything from Betty Boop's visiting a reservation to teach ignorant Indians how to make *real* music (jazz, ironically) to Sunflower the Centaur, a Buckwheat-like character of Disney's *Fantasia*. Among the print comics are the World War II anti-Japanese images Dwight remembers from his childhood. He had reconciled with Dr. Seuss over the years, appreciating that the man had regrets for those days and wrote *Horton Hears a Who* in support of a more internationalist point of view, the book dedicated to a Japanese friend of the author's. "The Sneetches" blatantly condemned prejudice, and the story concludes in a beautiful redemptive spirit, but for Dwight there were aspects of the violent Jim Crow era of his young adulthood that he will never forgive, a tight ball of bitterness formed and expanded in his soul. To that end, he finds the sentiment of the whole ugly generation more epitomized in the Seuss story wherein the north-bound Zax and the southbound Zax obstinately refuse to step aside to let the other pass, and therefore neither goes anywhere. Though the creatures were meant to represent opposing opinions, to Dwight the bigger issue is both of them united in their clinging to set ways, perfectly analogous to the Southern stubborn, and often lethal, defiance of even federally mandated change. And change happens, the entire world built around the bullheaded Zaxes, who still in the end remain unmoved.

3

Dwight waits at the TWA gate. He finds it odd that the internship would start right on June 1st, a Wednesday, but who knows the bureaucracy involved in these programs. To make up for taking the afternoon off, he'd worked an extra hour every day last week. After dinner yesterday he held Rett's senior picture, the one enclosed with the boy's high school graduation announcement and which Dwight had miraculously managed to keep all these years, now framed and prominently displayed on the coffee table. Eliot all over, Dwight had thought when he looked at it the first time, so he didn't imagine he would have trouble picking his nephew out of the deplaning crowd.

It has crossed his mind that Rett might not be on the flight. What if Dwight's reply had gotten lost in the mail so Rett made other plans? Or if something unforeseen had come up at the last minute? Did Rett even have Dwight's phone number? After all his anxieties regarding his nephew's visit, he realizes only now that for it all to *not* happen would be a bit devastating.

And out of the blue flashes a memory of being thirteen and sitting on his bed. He hadn't been outside in days since the brutal death of Parker the Cat, and Eliot had not said a word to him. His mother had told Dwight she wanted to talk to him, and it was her gentleness, the tenderness in her eyes, that had terrified him. She sat down softly next to him.

"You been wantin your own room, right?"

He'd stared at her. Eliot had vigilantly lobbied against this.

"Your brother said he's ready now. Eliot's gonna move out, into the guestroom, so you get to have the ole room all to yourself."

And Dwight had bawled harder and longer than he had ever remembered, his mother holding his violently shaking body. Where Eliot was during all this—outside and aware or not that his directive was being handled at this very moment, or in the house and unmoved by his brother's sorrow, his overwhelming guilt and regret—Dwight would never know.

Agonizing as the recollection is, it's still a part of him, he can't just let it go. He sighs and takes out the composition book from his bag. He's just finishing when the arrival of the flight from Dallas is announced, and he stands. For those who had originated in Indianapolis, he had calculated a ten-hour travel time including layover, thus the many fatigued expressions now emerging through the gate. Dwight nearly drops his coffee when he sees him, the high school photo having not prepared the uncle. The spitting image of Eliot, only Rett is about three inches taller. Slim, and dressed neatly in what appears to be a new, crisp outfit: jeans and a green and white horizontal striped shirt. He dons dark-framed eyeglasses. Earphones hang from his neck, the wire falling into the duffel bag he carries, where presumably is the attached Walkman. In the other hand he holds a guitar case. He walks up to Dwight with a tired smile.

"Hi, Uncle Dwight."

After all the time and distance, it doesn't occur to either of them to embrace. Dwight is still marveling on Eliot's genetic photocopy when Rett says, in reference to the instrument, "I hope you don't mind. I'd like to practice sometimes in the evenings after work."

Dwight smiles. "I don't mind at all."

The uncle splurges on a taxi, and after they're dropped off, Dwight gazes at his home, seeing it for the first time as Rett might. A lovely old three-storey mansion, now converted into three single-floor apartments, Dwight's at the top. "The bus stop's just a block away. See it? If you gimme the address of your workplace, I can call, get the Muni directions."

"Oh thanks, but I can call myself. I'm usually better hearing directions firsthand."

They climb the two flights, and Dwight unlocks the door. Rett takes it in: the large living space, the comfortable couch with matching chair and loveseat. "Wow. This place is great, Uncle Dwight." And Dwight believes Rett is earnest but has noticed nary an exclamation point in the boy's unwasted words—polite but solemn. Rett gazes out the picture window at the spectacular view.

"Well I kind of inherited it. It was my friend's place. I'll show you your room."

He does, and Rett sets down his things. Then Dwight brings him back out to the living room and hands him a set of apartment keys and a piece of paper.

"The phone number here, till you memorize it. Make yourself at home. Eat anything out the fridge. There's the big stereo out here, the smaller one in your room, you're welcome to either. Headphones so you won't disturb me if I'm workin and vice versa. And you can call home to Indianapolis anytime, don't worry about the cost."

"Thank you."

"You need to call your mother, let her know you arrived?"

"Yeah. In a little while."

"Tired? Wanna nap?"

"I'm okay."

"Want some juice? Water?"

"Water please."

Dwight nods, gazing at his nephew. "Guess you're legal now. At restaurants you can order your wine or beer, but nothin like that in my home please. No alcohol, no drugs. And marijuana is a drug. And cigarettes, if you don't mind keep all that outside. Okay?"

"I don't do that stuff, Uncle Dwight. No drugs, and I don't want lung cancer. And I hardly ever drink. I won't do it at home."

"I appreciate it."

Dwight goes to the kitchen.

"We have these."

The uncle looks into the living room. Rett is referring to the seven books in the Ludwig and Tease series, displayed on a bookshelf. Dwight smiles. "Page-turners. You read em?"

"Only the first. Guess I'm not much into law stories. Get that enough at home."

"I bet." Dwight brings in water for Rett, cranberry juice for himself. "But you still interested in law yourself?"

"Oh sure. But reading about it in fiction too. Guess it makes my life too redundant."

Dwight chuckles. Rett studies Keith's two paintings on the wall for some time, then walks to the drawing board. "This architect table's great."

"Mm hm. Also was my friend's."

"Keith's?"

Dwight is startled. "Yes. Keith."

"I heard about him. I'm sorry."

"Thank you." Rett moves to some framed photographs on a mantel. He picks up the one of Eliot graduating from law school, flanked by his beaming parents and brother.

"You all have a copy of that, don't you?"

"Uh-huh." Rett sets it back. "You don't have any of when you and my father were little?"

Dwight shakes his head. "We didn't take millions a pictures back then like people do today." He hesitates. "I think. I useta keep a storage unit, but. When I missed some monthly payments, guess they got throwed out with the resta the stuff." He had sobbed a year later when he'd remembered, during a sober moment, about the photos in the compartment. Before he can slip into a minor melancholy, Carver enters, walking up to Rett.

"That's Carver greetin ya. The black one's Banneker. He'll show his face eventually. Aloof." Then a sudden worry: "You're not allergic, are ya?"

"Oh no." Rett stoops down and strokes the feline. "Hi, Carver."

"I was more a dog person growin up. But then I found em, two abandoned babies. The other two in the litter lyin beside em dead." He picks up his shoulder bag. "You like Chinese?"

They walk around Chinatown, and Rett seems to come alive a bit in the bustle of the neighborhood.

"This your first time in San Francisco, right?"

"Uh-huh."

"Well we'll have to ride the cable car back."

Rett smiles.

"We got the whole summer for sightseein. Maybe I'll show you around a little Saturday? Golden Gate Bridge? Japanese Tea Garden? Or Lombard Street?"

"It all sounds great."

He takes Rett to his favorite restaurant for dinner. As Dwight chews on his kung pao chicken he studies his nephew, who looks around as he eats, speaking only when spoken to. Something doesn't jibe with the confident young man who had written that letter, taking the daring plunge of asking a long-lost relative if he could crash at his place the entire summer. But then Dwight remembers his reply, the exclamation points *ad nauseum* that intimated an enthusiasm that was certainly an exaggeration if not a boldface lie.

"So what's this internship all about?"

"Oh I don't know. Probably a lot of xeroxing, gofer stuff. Whatever's too tedious for the *real* personnel." He pushes his beef around his rice and onions.

"You know I'm a school janitor."

"You wrote that in the letter when you sent my graduation check. Thank you again for that."

"My hours are 7 a.m. to 10:30, 12:30 to 5."

"You come home for lunch."

"No." Dwight takes a sip of water, considering before he speaks. "I have meetings. Narcotics Anonymous." His eyes glued on his nephew.

"That's great, uncle."

Dwight gazes at Rett a few moments before nodding. "They're at eleven every day except Sunday, Sunday the meeting's at four. So we wouldn't be able to do our Saturday outing until after I finish at noon."

"That's fine."

"Weekdays I'm up by 5:30, out by 6:45. I don't know what your schedule is but I'll try not to wake you."

"I should be getting up around the time you leave anyway." He smiles. "Thank you for saying yes, Uncle Dwight. I'm really happy I'm here."

Dwight gazes at Eliot's grown son. "I'm really proud of you, nephew."

"I'm really proud of *you,* uncle."

They take the California line cable car west and then walk the several blocks home. Dwight is putting the doggie bags into the fridge when he hears Rett exclaiming from the living room, "You have a VCR!" The younger runs to his bedroom and returns with a videotape.

"Looks like you have a VCR too."

Rett chuckles. "Hardly. The Judge thinks they're a waste of money. Some guy at school made em, sold em."

Dwight is amused by his nephew's moniker for his eminent mother. Rett sticks the tape into the machine. The uncle has not stayed current with music, but he likes the sound of this band that keeps making references to *The Funk.*

"Song's old," says Rett. "'Seventy-six. But look at Bootsy with that bass!" And Rett air-guitars.

Look at *all* of them, thinks Dwight. The song is called "Stretchin' Out," and what strikes Dwight, besides the highly skilled musicians and the near obscene relationship one of the guitarists seems to have with his instrument, is how *happy* everyone is. He has seen many bands play, the members having a good time, but this differs from the utter jubilation he witnesses on the screen now. And Rett seems happy, finally a truly unbridled smile. Andi's smile, Dwight realizes, her chromosomes apparently having not gone completely to waste. Nephew and uncle bounce to the beat, playing the tape five times before Rett says he probably should get to bed. It's eleven, and that he has made it this far after his long traveling day coupled with the time difference is a testament to the astounding energy of youth.

Rett asks Dwight if he has any milk, remarking that he usually drinks a glass before bed. "All I have out there's juice. Cranberry, pineapple. That do ya?"

"I'll just have water then, thanks."

"Okay. I'll pick up milk tomorrow and remember to stay stocked. Come ere."

Dwight shows his nephew the water dispenser on the fridge door. Rett stares.

"I can't believe you still have this."

Dwight is spare about his refrigerator adornments. On the freezer one item: a plaque with the Serenity Prayer, a gift from his N.A. sponsor on the first anniversary of his being clean. But what Rett refers to is the article taped to the lower door: a crayon drawing. When he was about six, Rett had sent it to his uncle. Two figures, an adult holding the hand of a child, supertitled in a little boy's scrawl: "Uncle Dwight" and "Everett."

Dwight is moved himself, remembering the argument. Keith threatening to throw out Dwight's things and Dwight countering with a suggestion that Keith throw it *all* the fuck out for all he cared. But Keith did not throw it all out. Dwight had found the drawing later, gingerly preserved by his friend, wrapped in cellophane and placed in its own box. Now he touches the curving lower right corner of the yellowing paper, where his nephew had placed his tiny signature just as he had seen his uncle do in his own work. With his fingers Dwight irons it out, but as soon as he lets go, it stubbornly rolls up again.

4

The adjustment to his quiet, isolated existence as evoked by the sudden presence of an extended-stay houseguest is not initially so monumental a transformation as Dwight had feared. For the remainder of the work-week he resumes his regular morning routine of rising early to meditate on the day that awaits him, eating his bran cereal, showering, doing a little sketching, and feeding the cats before leaving for work. When he returns at 5:30, Rett is winding down after his own workday by playing his guitar or watching MTV. Dwight cooks simple meals, and when over dinner he asks how things are at the law firm, Rett invariably shrugs. "Yesterday I got to xerox for the white lawyer, today I got to xerox for the black lawyer. Never a dull moment."

On Friday, Dwight comes home to overhear his nephew in his room talking on the phone to Indianapolis. The last time Dwight had dialed that number, eons ago, it had become yet another lecture about his using. With these episodes, Dwight's indignation was consistent, regardless of whether he was telling the truth or lying. Well it had been two years now, his longest clean stretch by far and the first time he had admitted to being an addict—not just saying the words (he'd gone the Twelve Step route in the past with little success) but finally accepting them. So he considered the possibility that Rett's reaching out to him was a sign that it was time Dwight reconnect with family in general.

Walking into the kitchen to prepare dinner, he notices he'd forgotten to turn the calendar page, the mild disruption of hosting a visitor apparently having caused it to slip his mind. The large squares are mostly empty, Rett's arrival three days ago on the last of May being the only event notated the entire month. As he lifts the page to June the calendar falls, flipping back to February where, again, there is only one appointment. Friday the 11th: "Ms. Devers's class."

Two days before, he had entered Ms. Devers's room post-dismissal to find the words to "Lift Every Voice and Sing" on the chalkboard, obviously related to Black History Month. The second-grade teacher had rushed in. "Don't erase it! I want to keep it up until they've learned it. Hopefully next week."

"Okay." She had noticed Dwight's smile as he gazed at it.

"You know it?"

"Negro National Anthem. We sang it every school day." He began to sweep the floor.

"Did you go to school in the South?"

"Maryland."

"Did you." She searches for the word. "Participate in anything? Sit-ins?"

"Well. I went to the March on Worshinton." Gum stuck hard to the floor. He gets his scraper.

"The *1963* March on Washington? I have a *dream?*" He looked up at Ms. Devers's stunned face.

The next thing Dwight knew, he was lecturing before her class. The children's understanding of the march was solely through Martin Luther King's finale speech, but Dwight informed them there were speakers representing many civil rights organizations, and he patiently described each one, among them James Farmer of the Congress of Racial Equality, John Lewis of the Student Nonviolent Coordinating Committee, Whitney Young of the National Urban League, Roy Wilkins of the National Association for the Advancement of Colored People, and A. Philip Randolph who had been the man to imagine the march way back in 1941, the onetime president of the Brotherhood of Sleeping Car Porters of which Dwight's father had been a member, a man whom Dwight had had the honor of meeting as a child when the famed union organizer was a guest in his family's home. The lecturer also gave much credit to the unsung organizer of the march, Bayard Rustin. Needing very much to keep his job, Dwight knew better than to go on a tangent before the seven-year-olds, albeit a relevant one, in clarifying the irony that after Rustin's well-substantiated commitment to the struggle against prejudice (his astonishingly successful planning and execution of that march of hundreds of thousands being only the most widely known of his many achievements) was undermined by prejudice with*in* the movement regarding his sexual orientation. So Dwight evaded the details while stressing that there would have been no March on Washington without A. Philip Randolph and Bayard Rustin, trusting that the brightest of the students would do further research on their own. The children asked, Were you close to the stage, Mr. Campbell? Closer than most. I had binoculars so I could see well. Who went with you, Mr. Campbell? Well, I still lived near my father then. My mother had died, and my father. My father was having some health problems, so I went alone. Did you meet Martin Luther King Jr., Mr. Campbell? No, but I got to talk briefly to Mr. Randolph. And I met some very nice people in the crowd. That's what the day was all about. Brotherhood, solidarity. Do you know what that means?

When he finished his discourse, Ms. Devers asked the children to thank Mr. Campbell, which they did with enthusiastic applause, and Dwight left the classroom, closing the door behind him, for a moment leaning his back against the wall to catch his breath. The memories stirred up, that brown paper bag wrapped like a present. He would have to write them in his book. He was deciding whether to also chronicle the last hour. The book was intended to document the past rather than the present, but wouldn't he like to *keep* such a fine day as today? Before he resolved the matter, the school nurse approached him to report that a fourth grader had suffered a severe diarrhetic episode so he had better bring his extra-strength cleaners to the cordoned-off second-floor boys' room.

◻ ◻

That brown paper bag wrapped like a present. I opened it.

Aw.

It's nothing.

Aw.

I got it from Goodwill, nothing.

Look out the window with my new binoculars. The trailers.

Don't. Neighbors'll think your spying. But Keith smiling, I give him a kiss. Then beef stew, his specialty. Eating not saying nothing but I feel his eyes, I know where he's going again.

You just leaving from here in the morning? You ain't got to go back to Lewis, pick up nothing?

Just leave from here. On the way.

And come back tomorrow, after?

Figure the crowds make the traffic bad. Probably wait till late, drive in the night, get back early Thursday. My face staring down at my stew whole time. He quiet awhile. Easy, easy.

You ain't even gonna ask me?

I know he wanna know why I ain't asked he wanna come with me. I say nothing. What, I think I say nothing he gonna drop it? Well I knew saying nothing just upset him more, that's the meanness I had them days. But in my head I say I'm being the tolerant. Patient.

It's a historical moment.

That make me laugh.

It is!

For colored people.

For everyone! Whole country!

Tearing apart my buttered bread to dip. Wisht he'd a made his biscuits. Keith got the knack, baking.

Malcolm X called it the Farce on Washington.

Oh now you gonna throw up Malcolm X to me?

No! I don't know why I said that! I was just bringing it up. I was just wondering what you thought about that.

I don't say nothing. That's a black argument, black people, I don't got to discuss that with him.

I make you food. I feed you, I take care of you, you can't even talk to me.

I can just go back to Lewis tonight. I don't got to stay here.

No! Stay.

We don't say nothing else till I finish. I finish but he still eating, he eating slow, know he planning what to say next. I lean back in my chair, toothpick in my mouth. Staring at him.

There's gonna be white people there. Didn't the buttons have a white hand shaking a black hand? Brotherhood.

Twirl my toothpick.

Well. Maybe I'll just go by myself.

Free country. Then I laugh, thinking whole reason we having this march is because it is not.

Silly. Two different trucks leaving the same house going to the same place stead a the people riding together.

You ain't going with me.

Then he gather up the dishes quick like to wash them, used to be we wash them together. How it get to be this? Me some nasty man beating his wife.

Well I look back on it now, it was because of that pain I had, that sad turned to mad. Keith was the bigger person, feeling hurt but he just take it. But them days all I do is look at his face see weakness. All I think is Start your goddam crying I walk out.

Spring before watching the TV, getting a load of Birmingham. Fire hoses, dogs. Sitting close on the couch, but then I pull away. I pull away the days I hate white people. Keith hurt but he just keep his eyes on the TV. Keith so understanding, so understanding them days I hate white and I hate him for being white and I hate him the worst for being so goddam understanding.

That night, night before the march we fuck. Least I owe him, thank him for the binoculars. He try to put loving into it like the old days but to me it's nothing. Morning I leave early, it ain't light out. I don't bother trying not to wake him. I done that before, what happens is he wake anyway and act hurt I was leaving trying not to wake him. He ask do I want coffee and I say thanks and he know I ain't about to sit down with him so he go on put it in the thermos. Thanks. Head out to the truck. Corner of my eye I see him at his window staring out but I never turn to him, I pull the stick shift.

Hours early. Already the crowds! College kids and parents with kids and old people. And white people like Keith said, but mostly this a sea a black faces, coming from Humble Md. and Lewis W.Va. I ain't seen so many black! We are waiting to march because it *was* a march, not just a rally like most young people today think. Some people singing, "Little Light of Mine" and "Eyes on the Prize" I'm feeling good! I can't remember last time feeling good like this, like forgetting all the bad awhile, the world ain't such a terrible place.

Hi, he say to me.

Hi.

Where you from?

Maryland.

Oh, right crost the border.

Well, the Appalachian part. Few hours west.

Oh.

Where you from?

Southeast. Africa. He grin. Got a nice smile.

We at the monument and the march is late, and suddenly the march is going. I'm a fast walker and I find myself moving toward the front. I get a glance of Martin Luther King and I feel my heart flip, like celebrity. But then. Mr. Randolph! Oh he older but I recognize him! Marching—his dream finally realized!

Mr. Randolph! Mr. Randolph!

Yes?

You probably don't remember me. I'm Dwight Campbell. You stayed in our house once, in Humble Md.

Uh-huh.

I was a little boy. You stayed in our house on the way to meet President Roosevelt. About the other March on Washington. You recited Shakespeare in our living room! Winter of discontent!

Uh-huh. Then Bayard Rustin say something to Mr. Randolph. At the time I didn't know who Bayard Rustin was but looking back now, sure it was him. I feel warm in the face, I know Mr. Randolph don't remember me and maybe the people nearby thinks I'm a crank. But I'm glad I said what I said. Everybody looking to Dr. King, I'm glad Mr. Randolph know somebody admired him too.

A few minutes later Mr. Randolph turn around. Hey.

Sir? I say. He talking to me?

You still drawing the pictures?

I wanna bawl right there. He remember that! Yes sir, I lie because lying seem the polite thing.

The rally after, I pull out my binoculars. Notice this little girl, her daddy holding her up to see. She staring at me, my binoculars. I let her see through them she grin ear to ear. Just when I start to worry it be hard to get them back from her her daddy say, Okay, give them back and thank the nice man, which she do even though she don't want to.

When Mr. Randolph speaks I look through the lenses. I see him clear! Now, I have a dream. It was stirring. But I recollect it so well because the news played it over and over, like all them charter trains and planes and 2,000 buses come just to hear one 15-min. speech. But what stayed with me was Mr. Randolph's words, We are the advance guard of a massive moral revolution for jobs and freedom. I have heard that there was people who was disconcerted with the leaders because there was some censorship of SNCC, the part where they wanted to criticize the Kennedy administration. But massive moral revolution sound to me like Mr. Randolph wasn't holding back nothing.

When it's all over, hundreds of thousands and somehow he find me again.

Hello!

Hello.

I'm Lyle. (I don't remember what he said but I feel like he deserve a name so I'm giving him one.)

I'm Dwight.

Dwight. You like to stop in a little after-march party in Anacostia?

I take the bus with Lyle. If the march was black, this neighborhood is ten times blacker! Southeast D.C., Africa like he say and ain't no white men in pith helmets coming in to bother us neither. The party is in the basement of some house. It is packed, people from the march, happy and inspired. Nothing but men. Nothing but black men. And it take me just a little while to figure this out. Nothing but black homosexual men. I ain't *never* been in a place like this!

Dwight, says Lyle. Lyle and I drinking rum and Coke. Dwight, how long you in town?

Oh I'm going back tonight.

Oh. The music is "Heat Wave" and "Up on the Roof" and "Green Onions" and a new song I like. What's that? I ask. "Fingertips" says another man, not Lyle. That harmonica? Some little boy playing it. A little blind boy!

There are men dancing like couples and this is all new to me.

Well, says Lyle, connecting his eyes to mine.

What's that you got there? I ask.

He look down at his ring finger. Yeah, he say, she's a good woman. Four great kids. She got a sister in France, they all there, otherwise she surely be here today, and he turn looking the other direction drinking. Then a friend of Lyle's Noah come up talking about the speeches. I remember Noah, how come I can't remember Lyle's name? We three talk, and after awhile Lyle nod, in tears he so moved. He say he wisht his wife could a been here, his wife's his best friend. He say change is coming, maybe not in our lifetime but. And Noah and me quiet, nodding. Then Noah go to the restroom, and Lyle look at me. No, it'll be our lifetime, I don't want my children to grow old like this, I want my children to see it. New world! Didn't you feel it today? Then Sonny Rollins, saxophone.

Friend of Lyle's (not Noah), his apartment. Lyle hit some tender spot, I don't know. It might seem high and mighty to say about a one-night stand but we did not just fuck we made love. At one point I near cried, turn my face away so Lyle don't see. Even in my ugliness I wasn't never unfaithful to Keith, well who the hell in Humble and Lewis I got to be unfaithful with? And before. Two women before Keith when I was pretending to myself. And a few anonymous men but nothing that meant nothing, this Lyle, something important. I do not remember his name but I remember his smell. Cologne. I can't describe it but when over the years I've catched a similiar whiff I always turn my head fast but it ain't never been him. Still, it always bring me back to that day, which was a very very good day.

I doze a couple hours, Lyle holding me. Lyle's friend whose apartment it is starts work 2 a.m. and he offer give me a lift to where I can walk to my truck. I look one last time at Lyle, sleeping peaceful. He remind me of Sidney Poitier who I heard was at the march and who I always thought was a very beautiful man. Lyle and I did not exchange numbers.

On the highway the city feel gradually go rural. Another scorcher. Deliberate I took my vacation this week so I ain't got to be back to delivering mail today, not till Monday. Turn on the radio there's highlights of the march, and I'm there again, joy again, hope, which I can still taste until two weeks later when four little Birmingham girls be blown to bits.

I could tell Keith about Lyle and he would cry and then forgive me. But what I really need to tell him is goodbye. Set him free. He be a mess awhile, then he be over it. He been talking about moving out to San Francisco, us together. He said there's friendly people out there, after they dishonorably discharged these World War II soldiers for homosexuality and they settled in part of the city there, he said we could have some peace there. I told him I can't go nowhere long as my father's living and I sure am wishing my father longevity. So when Keith pull hisself together he could head on out there on his own, his own self. New world.

Hitting the mountains close to Humble, I think I might pick up some groceries. Sometime my poor daddy don't got none in his house. I see that one place along the road, market and a little dining room for people to sit and have coffee except the sign say BLACK TO GO meaning we can't sit inside though they happy take our money at the window send us on our way. Old white proprietor won't never get no business from me, and even with my upbeat outlook after yesterday my blood boil just bypassing the damn place.

I go to the new grocer, replaced D'Angelo's. Opens early, 7 a.m. Come to think of it my own cupboards could use a little replenish so I end up with two bags full. I get to my daddy's before 8.

He's happy to see me. Well, happy in the relative. His eyes always full these last three years, constant state of mourning. I visit him often and still can't get used to my mother gone, every room I walk in empty, empty. I cook us sausage and eggs and fried potatoes and onions. We sit and eat and he asks about the march and I tell him every detail that don't involve Lyle and he smiles.

I had planned to drive straight back to Lewis. But I got to take Old Mill Road to get there, right by the trailer park. And what I got to say to him. Better get it overwith. Keith ought a be at the office supply store now, stocking and cashiering, but bet my life he took the day off, hoping I stop by. And when I pull in there he is, come running out to greet me.

I saw it on TV! I cried! You was right. If you just wanted to be with other colored people you was right to have that.

I look at him, his eyes shining, hopeful. On another day anything he said would a pissed me off. Blubbering. Trying to get back on my good side. But today. It ain't even his words, I don't half hear what he says. What I'm remembering's what he done for Eliot right after our mama died, something I ain't thought about in awhile.

And all at once my confession just feels like more a my hard-heart, my evil side looking forward to letting him have it. But I'd tell myself it was for his own good telling him the truth, I'd get the guilt off of my chest, relief, then walk out forever, leaving him drowning in his sobs.

I bought all this food. Just had breakfast with my daddy and funny, still got the appetite. I fry up some bacon, you whip up your old scrumptious biscuits? And he grin bright like he just hit the number.

5

The first Saturday since his Tuesday arrival, Rett emerges from his room around nine to find his uncle on the couch sketching, a mug of herbal tea on the coffee table.

"Morning," says the younger.

Dwight looks up, closing the pad and smiling. "Well. That's the first time we got to say that to each other. Fix ya some eggs? Juice?"

"Maybe after my shower." Rett sits on the couch, leaving a little space between himself and his uncle. "Can I look?"

Dwight gestures for him to go ahead. Rett picks up the pad, studying each page. Smiles.

"You were at the circus?"

"Assembly at the school. These Chinese acrobats, I keep thinkin about em. You remember the time I took you to the circus?"

Rett nods. "You bought me a candy apple. I'd never had one before."

"I forgot that."

Rett gets to the page Dwight had been working on minutes before. He stares.

"You appreciate your likeness?" asks his uncle.

Around 10:30 Dwight serves them eggs and toast and cantaloupe. He asks Rett if he'd still like to do an outing today.

"Can we see Haight-Ashbury?"

"You missed the hippies. Most of em."

"That's okay. And the Mission?"

"That's a nice walk." He butters his second slice of toast. "Somethin else I wanted to talk to you about. I got a vacation comin up. The Fourth falls on a Monday, so if I took the week prior we'd get the extra day. I was thinkin about doin it then, but really I can take it anytime. Your birthday the followin week, right?"

"The 11th."

"So I'm flexible, but here's the question. Do *you* get any time off."

Rett thinks. "I'll have to ask."

"You drive?"

"Uh-huh."

"We could take some nice little day excursions. Napa Valley, couple hours north. You could do the tastin while I mosey around. Bring a friend ya want. You makin friends at work?"

"Not really."

"Well, jus been three days. Also the redwoods, that we could do on a weekend. And if they do give ya a little time off. One idea: drive down the PCH. Pacific Coast Highway. You know of it?"

"Uh-huh."

"Goes all the way south to San Diego. We can peek in the cities along the way. Monterey. Santa Barbara. L.A. of course. Could keep goin over the border, Tijuana. Taste a Mexico."

Rett considers the offer.

"Now. We decide to do that, longer trip, thing is." Dwight takes a bite of the toast, chews. "The thing is I haven't missed one a my meetins in two years. *But.* It'll be okay, I'll just be checkin in with my sponsor daily."

"Oh we don't have to do that if you'd rather not, Uncle Dwight."

"I done give the matter a lotta thought, and I wouldn't be offerin if I didn't wanna." He smiles. "I haven't seen ya since you were seven, don't know when I'm gonna see ya again. I wanna make the most of it."

After Dwight's meeting they take a bus to the Haight, and Rett smiles upon catching sight of the street signs marking its most famous intersection. He stops in the record stores, poster shops, booksellers, browsing each establishment for a few minutes without buying.

"Where's City Lights Bookstore?"

"North Beach, near Fisherman's Wharf, the other direction. That where you wanna go now?"

"I can wait till the day we get over there."

They walk a few blocks and Rett recognizes another street.

"This is the Castro?"

"Uh-huh." Every house seems to welcome, or ward off, passersby with its sounds. "You know this music?"

"That's Culture Club. That's the Eurythmics," Rett says drily. Then he turns to his uncle, a crooked smile. "I bet you spent some time here."

Dwight looks at him without smiling. "Some."

Rett is shaken. "No offense, Uncle Dwight."

"None taken." Dwight remembers his days in the legendary gay district mainly as a blur of debauchery and white men and debauchery *with* white men. When he got sick of it, he headed out to Oakland.

The music changes completely when they enter the Mission. Mariachi, rumba, popular Latin. They sit in a restaurant, a late lunch of tamales.

"How's your French comin?"

Initially Rett is confused. "Oh. Okay. It's hard. Irregular verbs. And remembering which noun's which gender."

"Uh-huh."

"And any lessons you get, it's France French. Tourist French, how to order in a French restaurant, oh *that*'ll be useful in a Togo rural village. Plus when I get there I'll have to start from scratch. The dialect."

"You'll catch on. Step ahead, you knowin some version a the tongue."

"Too bad Spain didn't colonize more in Africa. I'm better at Spanish."

Dwight laughs. He knows his nephew is being ironic, and yet Rett's face is contorted in a vaguely pained expression as if he wasn't joking at all. He looks around the crowded restaurant before his eyes come back to settle on his uncle. "Why did you move out here?"

"California?" Rett nods. "Well. My daddy had not been doin too well. After the bad days. He died sudden in '64. Stroke."

"How old was he?"

"Sixty-one."

"Your mother died suddenly too, right?"

"Uh-huh. And my friend Keith had been wantin to come out for a long time." He looks at Rett. "You know what I mean by my 'friend.'"

Rett nods. Then Dwight nods.

"I'm a private person but I ain't been in no closets since Humble. So." He sprinkles Tabasco on his tamale. "Keith had been wantin to come out west, but. I always said I couldn't leave because a my daddy, which I guess means I kinda promised I would after he passed on."

"You didn't wanna come out?"

"I did. The adventure. But it was always more Keith's dream. So, couple months after your granddad died, we sold my truck and packed up Keith's. Drove cross-country."

"Was that fun?"

"Well." Dwight chuckles softly. "It was tryin on a relationship that had already been tried. The year before we kept breakin up, gettin back together.

Probably insane to do what we did with the two of us so rocky. But. He was a comfort when my daddy died. So I convinced myself to go."

"Were you sorry after you got here?"

Dwight stares at the bottles of green and red hot sauce on the table. "I think Keith was. It had always been his idea and—" He sighs. "I guess I don't really wanna talk about it."

"Oh. Okay."

"You better bite that tamale before it gets cold."

Rett does. Sirens. Everyone in the restaurant turns to look. Two police cars flashing by.

"What were the Panthers like?"

Dwight laughs. "You heard about that huh."

"If you don't mind talking about it."

"I don't mind talking about it. I joined in. Guess it was '70. The Soledad Brothers. Free Angela. You know about all that?"

Rett shakes his head. Dwight cuts off a piece of tamale with the side of his plastic fork, spears it with the utensil, places it in his mouth, and chews slowly.

"Well. After *too* many times hassled by cops for driving while black, or for walkin while black in the wrong neighborhood. This was before the addiction, I was nothin but a law-abidin mailman those days. It was good havin a relationship with the U.S. Postal Service, snappin up a job soon's I got out here. But them hills. Deliverin on the inclines a San Fran liketa kilt me." He laughs gently. "So all that harassment, and tired a witnessin the police brutality to black, and. Well." Dwight's face lowers, squeezing his napkin. "I'd been thinkin about the Party for some time. You couldn't get around it, livin in the Bay Area those days.

"But what finally tipped me. George Jackson. Teen in trouble. Eighteen when he was convicted of armed robbery, holding up a gas station. Sentenced one year to life."

"One year to *life?*"

"One year to *life,* now who in the hell gets such an arbitrary penalty? eighteen years old. Eleven years later, twenty-nine-year-old George still sittin in jail, no sense a when if ever he be released. Soledad Prison. Becomes a Panther, starts speakin out about penitentiary conditions along with a couple other prison Panthers, call themselves the Soledad Brothers. On the regular, white guards killin black inmates without cause, and in one particular ruckus a white corrections officer gets killed and here troublemaker George and company gets the blame, lookin at the gas chamber. So. Down the coast sits UCLA professor Angela Davis, somebody always on the last nerve a Governor Ronald Reagan. Angela believed the Soledad Brothers were framed, and befriends George and his seventeen-year-old brother Jonathan who loved George and who snapped. Apparently stole Angela's shotgun—she was put on the FBI's Ten Most Wanted, accused a givin him the weapon—and armed Jonathan bursts into a courtroom, frees some prisoners, and kidnaps the judge and some jurors, demandin the release a the Soledad Brothers. They didn't get far before police started shootin and in the end a coupla the prisoners, the judge, and Jonathan were dead. Soon after, big brother George Jackson instigates a prison rebellion, leadin to six more casualties: three guards, two white prisoners, and George himself. These were shots heard round the country, George's death the spark spawned Attica." A baby girl in a stroller starts bawling. She is quieted by a girl of about nine who coos to her little sister in Spanish. "I signed up, wore my Free Angela button. And twenty months after her arrest, indicted for the crimes Jonathan too dead to face, the all-white jury found no evidence of complicity: not guilty."

They're quiet a while against the roar of the other diners' chatter and the music.

"But you stayed with the Panthers. You didn't just quit after Angela was released."

"A time. Helped with the free medical clinics, the sickle cell testin. Drug rehab. This naturally before I found myself with the problem. The Free Breakfast for Children."

"Did you carry an assault rifle?"

"While I was a member. I guess you don't like that tamale the way you been nursin it."

"No, it's good." Rett takes a bite.

"I missed the big actions. The march on the Sacramento statehouse, everyone carryin the firearms. That was '67." He shrugs. "The militancy was mostly just preparation. Drills. Not sayin there was no violence. But it was mostly later and mostly against ourselves, after the FBI infiltration made everyone paranoid." A silent wistful sigh.

"Did you wear the beret? Leather jacket?"

"That was the uniform."

"The drills. Like the army?"

"I think a lotta the ones leadin the exercises was veterans." He laughs. "Funny place for me to end up after considerin the military and rejectin it."

"You thought about enlisting?"

Dwight nods. "My senior year. That February I turned eighteen and it hit home: What I'm gonna do with the resta my life? At the time the army seemed easy."

"Why didn't you?"

"I been doin all the talkin. I think it's your turn a while."

Rett looks at his uncle, then takes another bite, chewing very slowly, silent, thinking. Dwight waits. He is entirely uncertain whether his nephew is refusing to speak or if he honestly is trying to come up with any aspect of his existence worthy of the syllables it would take to convey it.

"When they brought back draft registration," the younger finally says, "I didn't want to register, but I was afraid I'd lose my financial aid. So I just wondered what you thought about it all."

Dwight chuckles to himself. The boy is *good,* cleverly putting the conversation ball back in the uncle's court. "Well." Dwight sips his ginger ale. "Wars. They was especially ugly to black men. In the ole days blacks complained, not bein aloud to fight, jus servin the white soldiers, no chance for promotions. No worries now, they fill *up* the front lines with the colors." He looks at Rett. "Your daddy. Only in the seventh grade then, but he always was a smart one. We was sittin at the dinner table that spring, and my father and me discussin the pros and cons a the various branches. He'd been too young durin the First World War so never served hisself, whatever pearls a wisdom he had for me come from what his older brothers told him. Uncle Leeroy had moved to Harlem, become parta the Harlem Hell Fighters. Famous soldiers *and* musicians, gimme a romantic view a the military and Eliot not sayin nothin, face in his plate like he ain't even interested, he." Dwight twirls his ice with his straw. "I guess we'd gone our separate ways a bit, he hadn't taken much of an interest in any a my goins-on for a while. The next mornin happened to be the first lawn mowin day a the season. I finished the chore and come back in to wash up, go to my room and there on my bed's this paper. Twelve-page term paper of your father's, big fat red

A as usual. I couldn't imagine why Eliot woulda left his school paper for me to see.

"The theme was this true story from 1944, just three years before. Episode happen right close to here. These white navy officers got bored so they started placin bets, which a the colored sailors would be the speediest loadin ammunition. They ordered em to rush, hop to it, and an order not followed was potentially a court-martial. 'Hurry! Hurry! Throw the damn boxes!' them officers wanted to win. Well. Only took one particular tossed box to trigger the rest. Explosion. Three hundred dead, the vast majority black. Nobody prosecuted. I don't know, maybe all the perpetrators died with their victims. That was the first parta the paper. The second part. A few a the survivors was transferred to San Francisco. When they come here, they told their fellow sailors bout the previous incident, and when push come to shove, fifty a the black enlisted charged with mutiny for refusin to load ammunition in a time a war. Thurgood Marshall was among the ones from the NAACP arguin the case before a military court, all white officers claimin there was no racial discrimination in their guilty verdicts against the protestin sailors. But the idea of a retrial come up, and the Powers That Be weren't interested in more publicity nor did they feel like bein subjected to naggin on behalf a the blacks by Eleanor Roosevelt, so the fifty soldiers were released, put back on active duty. I don't know where Eliot got his information cuz apparently they just struck that procedure from the official record, like the whole thing never happened." Dwight chuckles. "All I needed, my military aspirations disappeared then and there. After I graduated I got a job liftin crates for the local market, just before ole Mr. D'Atri retired. Till I made my career with the U.S. Postal Service. A while."

They are quiet. Dwight sees now for the first time something like outrage in his nephew. It had begun with George Jackson's sentence of one to life and had become progressively more severe. He waits to see where it will go, but after a few moments the creases in Rett's face smooth again. Dwight thinks of how their lunch repartee had been less a conversation and more akin to a journalist (Rett) asking simple questions to get long answers from his subject (Dwight). The whole reason the latter had undertaken this frightening risk of allowing the boy to visit was to come to know his brother's only child, and he was learning absolutely nothing.

"Did my father know he wanted to be a lawyer way back then?"

"Seem like the idea come to him somewhere around that time. Maybe that story *was* what activated him."

Rett seems to be considering this.

"What makes *you* wanna be a lawyer? I know it got to be more than just your mama and daddy done it."

"You don't think I can?" More than a hint of defensiveness.

"No. I didn't say that at all."

Rett frowns, a furrowed brow of worry, looking down into his plate. "Lot to live up to," he mutters, his volume so low Dwight presumes he had not intended for his uncle to hear it. Rett takes a bite, and before Dwight can decide on how to speak to what had just occurred the young man smiles. "I used to play this song on my guitar." Now Rett turns to his food with gusto, making it clear that he's finished with the subject of law and, more pointedly, he's finished with the subject of Rett.

After Dwight pays the check, they go to a movie rental outlet. Dwight gets a kick out of the descriptions on the blaxploitation shelf. He is surprised when his nephew comes up to him holding an old silent movie. "I saw it in a film class. It's really funny."

"Okay."

"Well, it's about Confederates. I mean, it's not offensive, it's not *Birth of a Nation*. Except the fact that Buster Keaton tries to be a Confederate soldier, which you kind of forget. Sort of."

"Well, I guess you piqued my curiosity."

Dwight is not at all sure he wants to spend the evening viewing some ancient silent championing the Old South, but Rett is right. He does kind of forget, laughing in spite of himself at the outlandish physical humor. At one point he glances at his quiet nephew. The young man is not even in the ballpark of smiling, staring at the screen with the solemnity of a pacifist who has just been drafted into the Marines and is somberly resigned to serve his time.

6

On Sunday they go to City Lights Bookstore where Dwight purchases *The Color Purple*, a recent bestseller he'd been meaning to read, and Rett, in honor of his first visit to the legendary bookshop, buys *Howl*.

"You need me to pay for that? I imagine you ain't received your first check yet."

"I got it, thanks."

They have a seafood lunch at Fisherman's Wharf, pick up chocolate at Ghirardelli Square, then head to the bus stop. When they get off, Dwight walks to the Presbyterian church and Rett goes back to the apartment. After his meeting Dwight does some grocery shopping, then walks home. Rett is in the living room practicing his guitar when his uncle enters. The younger jumps up to help put the groceries away. After dinner they spend a quiet evening, Dwight on the couch and Rett on the loveseat, reading their new books.

When Dwight gets home from work Monday, Rett is sitting in the living room watching music videos, his favorite treat on the coffee table: a large bowl of barbecue potato chips and a glass of milk. He informs Dwight that he'd asked at work for time off, and was told he could take a week as long as he let them know two weeks in advance. He'd thought about Dwight's offer and decided a trip down the California coast would be fun.

"Then that's what we'll do." The uncle heads to the kitchen. On the counter are a jar of peanut butter and a jar of grape jelly, both opened, a soiled knife, and a saucer from the resulting sandwich, crumbs on and around it.

"Rett?"

"Yes?" His nephew turns away from the image on the screen, white men in designer Western clothing as they sing and traipse around poor Asian cities and jungles.

"You wanna come out here and clean up your mess?"

"Oh. Oh sorry, Uncle Dwight, I forgot!" He runs to the kitchen and puts the victuals away, washes the dishes, and wipes the counter spotless. Not wanting ants, Dwight is meticulous about cleanliness in the kitchen but has not pestered his nephew about the fact that the guest bedroom has come to look as if a cyclone hit it, directly contradicting Rett's claims in his letter to being "neat." The boy seems so cautious in his every breathing moment, Dwight is actually relieved to witness a bit of carelessness in his nephew so long as the disorder is kept behind the closed door.

Saturday Dwight returns from his meeting with news.

"This man, Mervin, I done a little work for him. He travels for his business, and offered me a couple frequent flyer vouchers. So if you want to go someplace else on the vacation, someplace to fly to, we could maybe do that. Course we'd have to stay in the cheap motels."

Rett seems confused by the complication of this new element in his choices. "Oh."

"You think about it. We can still just do the California drive, up to you. Ready to head out?"

They take the BART to Oakland, strolling the streets. Dwight shows his nephew the former Panther headquarters, which Rett regards with a solemn respect. The uncle points out the Mormon Temple, and they stop in the Oakland Museum. As they are coming out, Rett sees flyers posted to a wall and laughs. "Look at that!"

Dwight nods. "I drew it."

Rett stares at his uncle, then turns back to the Shaft/Superfly AIDS PSA. "I should've known. It's totally your style." But as they walk a little further, his smile fades.

"Uncle Dwight?"

"Uh-huh?"

"You're healthy. Right?"

Dwight is touched by his nephew's concern. "I been to the doctor. Negative." One of life's insane ironies. Rett is instantly relieved and even cheered.

On Sunday they take the BART to Berkeley. Walking around the campus, then they have a late lunch in the last hour before they'll need to board the subway again in order to make Dwight's late afternoon meeting.

"You have a good time at college?"

"It was okay."

"You like St. Louis?"

"It was okay."

"I always wanted to go there. Always wanted to see that Gateway Arch, catch the view from up there. What's it like?"

"Oh I never went."

Dwight stares at him. "You were in St. Louis four years and never went up the Gateway Arch?"

"It's for tourists."

"Well. Weren't you a tourist the first day or two?"

Rett bites his burger, not looking at his uncle.

"So what'd you and your friends do for fun?"

"I wasn't there to have fun, I was there to get my degree," an irritation in his voice that Dwight had not previously sensed so the elder drops the subject.

Wednesday is the last day of school, the teachers looking at least as thrilled as the kids. Ms. Lorenzo asks Dwight to come to her office.

"Well, congratulations. You made it through your first year."

He returns the principal's smile.

"I just wanted to talk to you a bit about the summer schedule. You know about the alternate Fridays?"

He shakes his head.

"You have every other Friday off."

He stares. "That a cut in my paycheck?"

"Oh no, no!" She laughs. "Just a little perk during the down season. There are twelve Fridays between now and the resumption of school in September. Pick any six. One will be part of your vacation week."

"Okay."

"I'll give you a list of the more substantial jobs to be accomplished over the summer. Which walls need to be painted, waxing the floors. We've already talked a little about this."

"Yes."

"You also can rearrange your eight-hour day as you see fit. Eight to five, including your lunch hour, or nine to six. But I suppose the regular schedule works well with your eleven o'clock meetings."

"Yes. I like the routine of it."

"Okay! I may pop in a few times here and there, but I won't bother you unless something comes up. And of course you have my home number if you need anything."

"Yes."

"And take it easy! You won't have the pressure of getting things done before the kids come back the next day. It's summer, Dwight! The building's yours."

When his meeting at the church is over, Dwight rushes back to school. Half-day dismissal at noon, and he wants to catch the kids, their beaming faces as they depart for the season. The little children wave. "Bye, Mr. Campbell! Have a good summer, Mr. Campbell!" Stephanie Takahashi who just passed to the third grade says, "Mr. Campbell, thank you for telling us about Mr. A. Philip Randolph!" and Dwight is gratified to tears.

When the kids are all gone, he goes to the shed and pulls out the neatly stacked summer playground equipment. As he gathers the swings, he notices three children across the street observing him in anticipation.

On Thursday Dwight strolls over to the meeting early. He had volunteered to set up today, to bring the cookies (store-bought) and to make the coffee provided by the church. He is also a greeter.

"Hello," he says to a new face.

The white man, reddish-brown hair, around Dwight's age and height, nods, looking around nervously, and Dwight surmises this isn't just his first meeting at this venue but his first meeting. At eleven the door is closed, and it's part of Dwight's duty today to set the ground rules: speaking optional, the three-minute limit. When the circle comes round to the newcomer, he chooses to talk, and the more he does, the more familiar he appears to Dwight.

"My name is Drew and I'm an addict. To drugs, and I guess to sex too. I just got outa rehab, I been clean three months. Well, I'm gay. I've had some real relationships but mostly fleeting. Lately." A long quiet. "Lately I get a little feverish in the night, I haven't been to any doctor, I might." He begins tapping his foot rapidly, silently. "You all don't gotta worry, you can't get it from using the toilet after me, and these days I give up on intercourse and the needles so." He falls quiet again. "Had me this band. Not many people thinka the flute as a rock n roll instrument, it's all over rock! Canned Heat. Van Morrison. Traffic, Chicago. Tull of course. And 'Stairway to Heaven,' it weren't nothin till they added the recorder at the top. War! you ever listen to 'Spill the Wine'?" Against his instincts, Dwight does what he is honor-bound to do: glances at the clock. The gesture was not meant for Drew's eyes, the speaker still has a full thirty seconds left, but he just happened to be looking at Dwight at that moment. "Well," Drew says, and sits back in his chair arms folded, done.

When the meeting is adjourned, Dwight looks to Drew for any signs of recognition. It had come to Dwight where they had met but the newcomer, who had obviously gathered up all his energy to make it through the door an hour before, summons up whatever is left to bolt out at twelve on the dot.

◻ ◻

You like this music? He screaming over it.

Nope.

Let's get outa here.

His place was big and a wreck. We did poppers and sex, poppers and sex, then lying down, look at the ceiling. Mirrors. I don't even look at him in them all I see's myself, and looking at myself I see nothing.

You ever been to that place before?

Nope.

You prefer white men?

I don't say nothing. My in-between life. The Panthers I'm my black self but not gay. The Castro I'm my gay self but not black. Was a black mens club a while. Then one 3 a.m. I leave with Larry Keys and these white boys out of nowhere Fag! Nigger! Fag! Busted my head, left Larry near dead. I never gone back.

You like the flute?

He plays these songs sound good. I got me a band. Then he walk across his place naked, his body nice. When he come back he holding them. The works.

You ever shot up before?

I don't say nothing. I ain't never shot up before. Reefer yeah. Coke one time, a party. Poppers. I ain't never done hard drugs I don't say nothing.

Here, he says. It's nice.

I know it ain't right, everything always come back to the same thing. But those days I was on a treadmill, every bad decision I make I blame the hurt, come out of that one thought: Eliot, Eliot. Wow. *My* blood in that tube?

◻ ◻

Dwight wakes at the regular time. He didn't set his alarm, but even when he does he always wakes a few minutes before. He hadn't decided if he would take this Friday off, today, but maybe he would. He imagines he didn't receive Ms. Lorenzo's news regarding the long weekends with the enthusiasm she'd expected. Time on his hands. Of course he could continue his regular routine, working every Friday, but he had been clean two years. Perhaps he was ready for time to be a reward, not a threat.

Playing tour guide to his nephew the last two Saturdays had meant forgoing his gallery visits. Over his bran cereal he scans the *Chronicle* and is excited to see an exhibit featuring the work of Henry Ossawa Turner, a nineteenth/early twentieth-century black American painter, his work including the stunning *The Banjo Lesson*. The weather looks gorgeous and he decides he will take today for himself, starting with a leisurely stroll, his meeting at eleven, and in the afternoon catching the Ossawa show. He showers, feeds the cats, and heads out into the sunshine.

Dwight stares at the bench. He has walked four miles to here, a beautiful view of the bay. Ages ago he was coming down, his head wildly clear before the inevitable withdrawal. He was living on the street then, and it was morning like now, and he'd looked up and on this bench sat Keith. Their times in San Francisco had not been all bad, but certainly mostly had been. Dwight's rage, then his infidelity, then his swearing off all things white. This started long before the Panthers, who at any rate had friendly relations with white radical organizations though a white homosexual lover definitely would have been pushing it. But Dwight's connection with his first love had by some small thread always remained intact till the drugs. And after all the screaming and tears, here sat Keith whom he hadn't seen in more than a year—and who didn't see Dwight now—Keith with another white man. They talked, and smiled, and occasionally kissed. Something in Keith's face Dwight had not glimpsed since their early days in Humble. Comfort. To Dwight's knowledge, this would be the first time Keith had been with another man since he and Dwight had met. And though his head was telling him to start some crazed junkie tirade, to ruin this whole damn blissful scene, Dwight was paralyzed by the tenderness of the moment, to perceive happiness in Keith after all these years, and he walked away trembling, a rare moment when such convulsions were completely irrelevant to the chemicals in his system or lack thereof.

He sketches an hour until he hears a church bell striking nine. He puts his pad back into his shoulder bag. He would be home by ten, a quiet morning alone as Rett would have left for work. Dwight realizes it will be the first time since his nephew arrived that he would have his apartment to himself. And while Rett is hardly some rowdy teen disrupting the household peace, Dwight still looks forward to a few hours of pure solitude.

He's sitting on his couch and gazing meditatively out the window, a book in his hand, when at 10:25 he's startled to hear a sound from Rett's room. He bolts up. The door opens and Rett emerges, yawning, clearly having just rolled out of bed. He turns to see his uncle and jumps back.

"Oh! Hi, Uncle Dwight."

Dwight stares at him.

"Oh, they're. They asked me to come in later today. They're having these meetings in the morning, they said they don't need their xerox boy in till eleven."

Dwight glances at the clock. "Then you better get goin."

Rett follows Dwight's eyes. "Oh!"

He runs back in his room, throws on yesterday's clothes, then races for the door.

"Don't you need your glasses?"

"Oh!" Rett turns again. For several minutes the sound of items being flung about, a frantic search. Eventually he reappears, bespectacled.

"I've never been late before so guess they'll excuse this once." He doesn't look at his uncle as he says it, laughs nervously and is gone.

Dwight walks to the kitchen to put the teakettle on. He goes to the window, staring far out. He doesn't want to get ahead of things, to jump to conclusions. Still. He sighs. Like the alternative Fridays, another of life's little challenges, and as he's considering this his eyes absently lower and he is taken aback to see Rett on the sidewalk just below, apparently confused, trying to remember which direction the bus stop is.

Dwight is relieved that by the time he leaves for his meeting Rett has found the bus stop, or whatever he was looking for, as it would have been awkward for them to have run into each other on the sidewalk. After the excitement of the morning he barely makes it on time, seeing the door start to close from the church corridor and having to run the last ten steps to make it. On a day where it would seem he'd most need to talk, he can't sort out his feelings, and when the order comes around to him he makes a rare choice to silently pass.

When the meeting is over he walks a few blocks, sits on the front steps of a residential building, and tries to figure out what to do. He seriously considers going to Morrison & Foerster to see if an Everett Meyers works there. But maybe interns wouldn't be part of the general employee roster. Then he thinks of going to the firm and waiting outside to see if Rett would eventually exit. But beyond the logistical complications, the possibility that there might be a back door, is the uncomfortable sense that Dwight would be reducing himself to something like a stalker, a covert element of himself too reminiscent of his active junkie days. Some voice of reason insists that he simply wait for the boy to come home and confront him. No. *Speak* with him. He wants to go home now. And what. Count to ten thousand waiting for Rett to walk through the door? He forces himself to go to the museum as originally planned. But try as he might, he cannot let go of his domestic concerns enough to give himself over to the work, and promises to come back another day, that Henry Ossawa Turner deserves his full emotional attention.

He's home by 4:15. Knowing Rett was always here when Dwight would return from work by 5:30, the uncle begins to be concerned at 6:15 and is a little sick with worry an hour later when he finally hears the key in the lock. "Hey Uncle Dwight. They made me stay late to make up for this morning." Rett seems tired. "I'll be back. I'm just gonna change." He goes into his room. When thirty minutes pass and he hasn't returned, his room quiet, Dwight gently knocks and calls, then peeks in. Rett is dead asleep on top of his unmade bed. It had been a strange day, one in which the behavior of his mysterious nephew had hinted at even bigger secrets than Dwight had imagined so, just to be sure, Dwight stands in the doorway until he clearly detects the rise and fall of Rett's chest.

He waits in the living room, paying scant attention to the television, the volume on low. By ten Dwight finds it hard to keep his eyes open, and turns out all the lights in the apartment. In the middle of the night he hears creeping in the kitchen. Dwight glances at his bedtable alarm, 1:30, and closes his eyes again.

When he emerges in his bathrobe four hours later he cries out, seeing a man standing in the living room.

"Oh sorry to scare you, Uncle Dwight! I just wanted to apologize for yesterday."

Dwight takes a breath, trying to put his morning head together. "You want some tea? Coffee?"

"Whatever you're having."

Dwight puts the kettle on. It had not occurred to him that Rett would be up first, before Dwight had a chance to get himself fully awake and ready for this conversation.

"You probably think it's weird."

"What." Dwight speaks over the kitchen half-wall to his nephew, who still stands in the living room.

"That every time you come home from your work I'm already home from my work, and then the one time you're home that I definitely should have been at work I was still home."

Dwight's a bit discombobulated by Rett's summary of the situation but he gets the gist.

"It won't happen again, Uncle Dwight. It was just a weird coincidence, the one day I'm told to come in late you—" Rett doesn't complete the sentence.

"I was lookin out the winda. I didn't mean to be spyin on ya, but I happened to look out the winda. I thought you were gone. But there you were on the sidewalk below, like you ain't never been to the bus stop before and didn't know which way to go."

Rett's brow furrows, trying to understand. Then he laughs. "Oh! That happens every morning. Cuz whenever we've taken the bus for sightseeing, it's that other bus stop so I always get confused—" Again Rett stops mid-sentence. The teakettle whistles and Dwight pours two mugs, bringing them to the dining table. They sit. Rett takes a sip, then lowers his cup. "You don't believe me."

"It just seemed odd, two and a half weeks workin at the place and you didn't appear to know how to get there. I just want you to know if there's anything wrong you can come to me. If you're ever in any trouble. I ain't gonna get mad."

"Oh I'm not in any trouble."

"Well if you ever get in any. Cuz I know trouble well and no matter how bad it might seem to you, it can only get worst if ya don't ask for help. And I want you to know no matter what it is you can tell me and I promise I'll help ya so it don't become worst."

"Oh I'm not in any trouble."

"*I want you to stop sayin that.* Hear? I want you to just promise if anything comes up you'll tell me. I can only help ya if ya let me know. Okay?"

Rett stares, not sure whether he should answer. Then he nods.

"Okay. Now yesterday. What happened was I found out I'm gonna have every other Friday off over the summer. That's why I wasn't at work. I took this Friday off, and I'll work next Friday."

Rett nods again.

"Okay." Dwight takes a sip. "Now. Anything special you wanna do today?"

Rett looks at his cup. "I should probably work on my French lessons. I've kind of been neglecting them."

"Okay. How about tonight? Go to a movie?"

"If. If you want to."

"I'd kinda like to. There, look in the paper and see what's playin."

Since they're up early, breakfast is early. And Dwight gets fancy: homemade banana walnut pancakes. Afterward Rett goes to his room and, though his uncle hasn't asked, begins to clean it, leaving the door cracked open as if to show Dwight he has nothing to hide. Dwight washes the dishes, and after his shower he walks by a clean guestroom, Rett sitting on a made bed wearing his headphones and softly repeating: *Je voudrais commander le coq au vin et les escargots.* In the evening they go out for pizza and then to see *War Games,* a film they both enjoy and discuss all the way home.

Sunday afternoon Dwight heads to the grocery store for his weekly shopping before his 4 p.m. meeting while Rett vacuums the apartment. Hardly accurate to call it "weekly" anymore; with his nephew on hand he seems to stop by the market every other day. Dwight had felt inspired to bake his peanut blossom cookies—peanut butter with the chocolate kiss pressed in the center—but after walking two blocks from the house he realizes he'd forgotten to jot down the ingredients. He turns to go home and retrieve the recipe, but as he enters his apartment he is startled to glimpse a movement in his bedroom. He hurries to his door. Rett stands staring at him, frozen.

"What are you doing in my room?"

The silence interminable.

"A mouse. I thought I saw a mouse in here. You get mice, Uncle Dwight?"

"Never."

"I thought I saw a mouse in here. Sorry, tonight I wouldn't be able to sleep if I knew there was a mouse in the house. I had to look for it." He goes back to his own bedroom, sits on his bed looking at nothing, his head hung in juvenile shame.

Dwight goes to the market and when he returns carrying two bags of groceries, he taps lightly on his nephew's closed door. "Rett. You wanna come out and help me put this stuff away?"

Rett appears and quietly does as his uncle has asked. Dwight finally breaks the silence. "I'm sorry about before. I probably overreacted. Just. I been alone for so long. Private."

"It's okay, Uncle Dwight. I never would've gone in there if I hadn't seen that mouse."

On Monday Dwight dials the telephone company from work, asking for a record of recent calls to and from his home. He breathes easier when he hears that the only two he didn't make himself were both to the number Dwight recognizes in Indianapolis: Rett calling home.

No doubt owing to the domestic stress, for the first time in his ten months on the job Dwight has forgotten his lunch. He'd packed it this morning and left the house without it. He sighs, dreading walking into his apartment to find Rett there. He strolls home, and to his enormous relief his nephew is gone. Rett had even made his bed, though the rest of the room is already finding its way back to its occupant's natural disarray. Dwight sniffs. Lately he'd noticed an odor, and now he realizes it seems to be originating in this room. He opens the window, then picks up his lunch and returns to work.

That evening as well as Tuesday and Wednesday are mercifully uneventful, a simple dinner and light conversation. Dwight is surprised that Rett has so quickly recovered from the events of the weekend. If anything he seems strangely more at ease, showing Dwight a California guidebook he'd picked up, expressing his enthusiasm about the forthcoming excursion, how much he loves driving and his eagerness to go rolling down alongside the great Pacific.

On Thursday Dwight comes home from work to find Rett on the couch, MTV turned on, munching on chips with a large glass of milk next to the bowl. He wears his pajamas. Dwight goes to the kitchen to see what he will cook for dinner but is once again distracted by the odor, now seeming to flood the entire apartment. He walks into the living room.

"Rett?"

"Yes? Oh hi, Uncle Dwight." He had not looked up when his uncle entered the apartment and even now his eyes remain glued to Michael Jackson stepping on sidewalk squares and lighting them up.

"Did you go to work today?"

Rett turns to look at his uncle, momentarily confused. Then he looks down at his attire.

"Oh. Sure! I just changed when I got home. More comfortable." And he turns back to the television. Dwight opens the refrigerator, looks in, and closes the door.

"Rett?"

"Hmm?"

"I just bought two large bags of potato chips and a gallon of milk last night, and now they're all gone."

"Oh. Oh wow, I'm such a pig! Sorry, I'll replace em for you."

"Thank you. You know, it might be good if you started chippin in with the groceries a bit. Since you're earnin a paycheck."

"Sure, Uncle Dwight."

Dwight pauses. "Rett?"

"Yeah? I mean, Yes?"

"You're starting to smell."

Now Rett turns to stare at his elder.

"You have very strong body odor. When's the last time you had a shower?"

Rett considers the question. "Oh wow!" he laughs. "Funny how you forget those things," and he turns back to the screen.

"No one at work has mentioned anything to you about this?"

"No, they're pretty laid back. I mean, in a corporate law firm sort of way." Rett still facing away from his uncle.

"Okay. So I would appreciate it if you would bring a couple bags fulla groceries home after work tomorrow?"

"Yes, I will."

"And take a nice thorough shower tonight? Wash your hair?"

"Uh-huh."

"And clean the tub when you're through?"

"Gotcha," and with that word Dwight for the first time glimpses a bit of Eliot in his grown nephew.

Friday morning Dwight applies the second and final coat of paint to the south hall of the school, finishing just in time to run to his meeting. When it's over he is aware of being utterly exhausted. He goes back to work but finds it just too much, and remembers Ms. Lorenzo's advice to take it easy. He calls it a day at one, four hours of work, deciding to make it up by taking one of his future Fridays off and turning it into another half-day. Although he'd asked Rett to pick up a few things at the market he hadn't given him a list, and he remembers now that he needs garlic and onions for his tomato sauce, having planned spaghetti for dinner. At the grocery he puts the vegetables in his small basket, and as long as he's here he picks up a box of cereal, and he could use some eggs, and butter, are they running low on salt? And he should get lettuce, and seven-grain or garlic bread? Italian dressing or Catalina? and as he's struggling over all these dire questions it dawns on him that he's avoiding going back to his apartment early for fear of finding Rett there when the boy should be at work. He'd told him he would be at the school all day today so Rett would not expect his uncle to appear until after five. Dwight adds nothing to the cart, walks to the cashier to pay, and heads home.

When he enters he immediately sees that Rett is indeed there, in his room. The door is ajar, and Rett sits on the floor facing away from it, headphones on. Dwight sighs. He puts the groceries into the kitchen trying to stay calm, *At least the boy is dressed,* and he walks to his nephew's room, pushing the door open wider. Dwight hears the tinny sound from the headphones, the volume must be earsplitting. Rett still isn't aware that anyone is behind him, and now Dwight notices his nephew is reading something. He takes a step in for a better look, and when Dwight sees what is in Rett's hands he cries out in horror.

Rett leaps up and across the room, inadvertently pulling the phones out of the stereo, the room suddenly flooded and pounding with men declaring and demanding *We want the funk! Give up the funk!* Rett quickly turns the stereo off.

"What are you doing reading my journal?"

Rett stares at his uncle, mute, wanting to answer, searching wildly for an answer. Dwight snatches it from his nephew, the composition book wherein he has stored his memories. It was the second of two volumes thus far, and Dwight now notices the first on the floor, apparently already perused. He seizes it and storms into his own bedroom, slamming the door. He paces, catching his breath before making the call. Why had he waited? Until last week he would have been the harbinger of only good news. Two years clean, and he and his nephew getting along well. But now. He picks up the receiver. In all these years the number hasn't changed, and he hasn't forgotten it.

"Hello?"

"Andi! It's Dwight."

A pause. "Dwight? Dwight! What a surprise. How *are* you?"

In spite of everything it's good to hear her voice after so long, and he is oddly catapulted back to their first meeting after his mother had died. The affection in her eyes when she gazed at Eliot, how much her arrival had meant to him. And Dwight had appreciated the warmth in her smile when she looked at him as well, Eliot's brother, in spite of Eliot's orneriness those days.

"Everything alright?" In regard to the silence.

"Well." He looks in the direction of Rett's room, not knowing where to begin. And wondering if Rett is hearing every word. "Well."

"Dwight?"

"He's great, you know I love my nephew, but—" He sighs, lowering his voice. "Andi, I'm not gonna beat aroun the bush. It's obvious he hasn't been going to his job. I have to practically beg him to take a bath, and today—"

Now she sighs heavily, which signals to Dwight that, unfortunately, she is not surprised, that her son's behavior is nothing new. He braces himself for whatever she's going to tell him about Rett.

"Dwight, what have you taken?"

He nearly drops the phone. *"What?"*

"Rett told me in the letter you sent with his graduation gift that you'd really gone clean this time. And I hoped. I hoped—"

"I *am* clean! Two years!"

"Then what are you talking about?"

"Your son! He came here to do this internship, and now he—"

"Rett's *there?*"

"He's been here all month!" She gasps. "You didn't *know?*"

When Dwight comes to Rett's door, his nephew, sitting on his bed, looks up in terror. "Pick up the phone. Your mother wants to talk to you."

Rett lets out a heavy breath, a condemned man about to face his executioner. He walks to the extension.

"Hi."

The screeching tirade emanating from the receiver causes Rett to keep pulling it away from his head, though given the decibel level of the music the boy was blasting into his ears a short while ago, Dwight finds Rett's sudden care for his hearing unconvincing. The uncle quietly closes the door. He goes to work at his drafting table but when he begins to hear Rett's impassioned responses, he turns on the television in an effort not to unwittingly eavesdrop.

Rett is on the line a good hour. When he finally surfaces, he walks quietly to the couch where his uncle sits. Dwight clicks off the set with the remote and looks up at his nephew. "I'm sorry about your journal, Uncle Dwight."

He can't look at Dwight but his uncle, silently, studies him.

"I'm also sorry about. About lying about the internship."

"There never was an internship?"

Rett shakes his head.

"Rett. I've been clean two years. I don't have any drugs stashed here."

Now Rett stares at him, flummoxed.

"I'n't that what you were lookin for in my room that day? Is that why you came here?"

"*No!*"

"Maybe not the only reason, but part of it? Easy access?" Rett wildly shakes his head.

They are still a few moments, then Rett says, "She wants to talk to you again."

"Your mother's still on the phone?" Dwight rushes back to his room to pick up the receiver.

"Sorry, Andi! I didn't know you were still there."

"That's alright. I'm going to pay you back for this call."

"You don't have to."

"Well I am." A silence. "I'm sorry, Dwight. Accusing you like that."

"Well. Until recently you'da had a good reason to." He takes a moment. "I shoulda called you when he got here. Never occurred to me he didn't tell you. And then I checked my phone bill. Your number come up a couple times."

"Yeah, he called and said he was still in St. Louis doing an internship. After he flunked out." She breaks into sobs. "I don't know what I'm gonna do with that boy! *Man,* he's a *man* now! Doing *well,* three point six average, then the last semester he decides to lock himself into his damn room and not come out." Dwight hears her wiping her face. "He doesn't have any friends, wouldn't *make* any friends. Guess I was in some kind of denial. When he said he'd gotten a graduation gift from you, I was so relieved, thinking—" Her breathing. "It wasn't until I told him I'd made the flight reservations that he leveled with me, told me there would be no closing exercises for him, now how stupid was I to then believe that cockamamie story about the St. Louis internship?"

Dwight takes a moment. Then, "Usually. I never woulda guessed. But now."

"Drugs?"

"I wonder."

"What do *you* think?"

He laughs. "My expert opinion. Well I ain't seen no physical signs. But his behavior. He been so solemn. Then lately, all the sudden excited. Well we was plannin a little road trip. Down the coast."

"Yes, he can get like that. New project." She is quiet. "Well. Unless he's started using there, he wasn't before. Trust me, I thoroughly investigated." A silence.

"What he *do* seem addicted to," Dwight finally says, "is sad."

"I know. I *know!*" He has the sense she's pacing. "Sent him to a counselor. He wouldn't talk. The counselor suggested *family* counseling so *we* went to the counselor. He wouldn't talk!" She sighs heavily. "He gets insomnia a lot.

Uses this over-the-counter sleep medication. Last year in the dorm he took too many. The school called, I was in court that day, the school called I had to—" Suddenly crying again, then just as abruptly stops. "We're hoping it was an accident."

When Dwight comes out of his room, he is surprised to find Rett standing in the exact same spot, in the exact same position, his shoulders tense, his back to his uncle. Upon hearing Dwight he quickly wipes his face and turns around.

"You like garlic in your spaghetti?"

"I'm not really hungry."

"Come on out to the kitchen anyway." Rett follows his uncle. Dwight fills the pot with water, snaps the pasta in half, drops it in. This takes a few minutes and he doesn't speak, not sure what to say. He puts the food on the burner, turns on the fire, and indicates for Rett to follow him to the dining table. They sit.

"You know you worry her."

"Well I'm sure The *Judge*'ll get over it."

"Don't talk about your mother like that."

Rett stares at the table. Dwight decides that Rett will be the next to speak if he has to wait all night. After an excruciating silence, Rett begins bawling. "If you're wondering about the hundred dollars you sent for my graduation I used it for my plane ticket here, and. I'm sorry about your journal, Uncle Dwight!" He tries wiping his face but the tears are falling too quickly. "I didn't mean to be spying! I only read the parts that said 'Eliot.'"

Dwight catches his breath. He stares at his nephew, and it's suddenly all so obvious. Why he came here, why he was in Dwight's room last weekend, reading Dwight's personal written history today, why he'd asked about photos of Dwight and Eliot as children. Rett was searching for something but it wasn't drugs. Dwight knew this, had always known this in some sense but perhaps hadn't allowed himself to see the desperate degree of Rett's hunger. "Oh," says the elder, the fog of the last month lifting so quickly. "Oh," he says again, nodding. The purple tint of sunset bathes the room. Rett's sobs gradually subside.

"Steada the California trip. Why on't we head on out to Humble."

Rett's face snaps up, staring at Dwight.

"You ain't never been. Right?"

Rett shakes his head.

"I can call my friend. He be at the meetin tomarra, I can ask him to bring his flight vouchers. This late we probably have to go standby. We can't make it this week, there's always next. My vacation time's flexible." He smiles. "And so's yours."

Rett continues staring at his uncle, then his moist eyes lower, considering it all.

"Now the house got sold. After your granddad died. So we wouldn't be able to go in. I ain't been back since '64, nineteen years, for all I know it coulda got tore down. Doubt it though. When I left things was already startin to go downhill, the economy, so can't imagine no big developers come to buy up blocks and redo em. I could show ya whatever's still there. The neighborhood, where your daddy and me run around. Banneker School where your daddy and me went."

"Miss Onnie's house?"

Dwight smiles. The confused terror in Rett's eyes starts to soften.

"Okay. I'd like— I'd like to see where you and my father grew up for my vacation. If that's okay with you."

"It's okay with me."

That night they sit in the living room watching the Bootsy Collins performance for what seems like the fiftieth time, but instead of their usual joyful bouncing they both quietly gaze at the screen. When the tape gets stuck in the machine and then breaks as they try to pull it out, Rett moans and starts to cry, and Dwight cries a little too.

8

The next morning Dwight calls the travel agent, who suggests a red-eye departing 10 p.m. Monday and arriving at Dulles 7 a.m. Tuesday, then returning on a 6:30 a.m. out of Dulles Thursday, those particular flights showing a few open seats before the holiday rush. As Dwight predicted, they'll be on standby.

"Allowin three hours for the drive outa D.C. up through Maryland, everything on time we oughta be in Humble 10:30, eleven Tuesday mornin."

He wonders if he should be in touch with anyone, to let them know he's coming. Nineteen years. He would be fine not to run into any familiar faces but chances are he would. Sunday morning he reaches for a box in the back of a closet, ancient stuff. He's rather relieved, should the need arise, to honestly be able to say over the years he lost all his old contact information. What he does find, tattered and dusty, is his senior yearbook.

Half an hour later Rett comes busting through the door, back from the errand Dwight sent him on.

"Sorry, Uncle Dwight! There were these jugglers in the street, they were really good! I got distracted."

"That's alright." He knows his nephew is worried that Dwight can no longer trust his word, but this time he does.

"And they didn't have the seedless so I got the regular. Okay?"

"I grew up spittin watermelon seeds, spose I can handle it now. Put it in the kitchen and sit down a second."

They are at the dining table. The uncle opens the yearbook to the seventeen seniors, including Dwight Campbell. Rett laughs out loud, delighted. Then the elder flips back to another section headlined "7th Grade." Rett is mesmerized, his fingertips gingerly grazing the page.

"Your daddy and me was pretty handsome huh." Rett can't speak. "I'll take it to the photo place, maybe they find a way a makin a nice copy for you."

At dinner that evening Dwight serves himself a healthy portion of kale.

"I'm guessin Togo ain't happenin neither."

Rett shakes his head without looking up. "I do know somebody in the Peace Corps there. He was kinda my only friend, but maybe that's just cuz he was the R.A. and had to be."

Dwight seasons his greens with vinegar, watching his nephew.

"He invited me when I was a junior and he was about to graduate and head on over. He gave me his mailing address. I was excited. So this spring I wrote him, then I went out and got the French lessons. I never heard back. Guess he was just inviting me to be nice, he didn't really mean for me to come. Or changed his mind."

"Not nice at all to invite somebody you don't mean it."

Rett picks at his meatloaf.

"What about this lass semester a school you dropped out?"

Rett sighs silently.

"I ain't naggin atcha. I jus like to know whatchu thinkin about. The future."

He shrugs. "I could go back to Indianapolis."

"Might be good. Clear your head, figure out whatchu wanna do."

Rett looks up. "What about the resta the summer?" His voice is small.

"Thought you were spendin it with me. Wa'n't that the plan?"

Rett smiles, sadness and shame and gratitude.

At Narcotics Anonymous on Monday, Dwight makes a quiet joke about his "addiction" to these meetings which he is about to break cold turkey. "But I'll be back, fallin off the wagon by Friday." That evening he and his nephew take the bus to the airport. Fortunately the flight still has open seats and they are given boarding passes. They stop by a bookshop, and Dwight peruses the fiction a few minutes before deciding instead to purchase a book of puzzles, imagining such brain teasers would be good for keeping his mind sharp. Rett has brought his Walkman for the long flight, though his uncle cautions him to get some sleep overnight so as to be alert for the drive tomorrow.

They sit in the waiting area at the gate, Rett lost in his music, Dwight frowning in concentration at a logic problem. He has made strides toward the complicated solution when he becomes aware that Rett is staring at him, and looks up. Rett quickly looks away.

"What?"

Rett shakes his head. Dwight continues gazing at his nephew. Rett turns to him. "Keith died of AIDS?"

Dwight is quiet a moment. "We didn't know what to call it back then. But, yes."

Rett looks down, nodding.

"What else?"

"Were you ever scared?"

"For him?"

"For you."

"That I was gonna die?"

Rett nods.

"Yes." Dwight sits back. "No justice in it. I sure was not particular who I slept with them days. And then the needle. Keith and I came out West together and he stomached a lotta my shenanigans. But not the drugs." He shakes his head. "Clean. Selective. Sixties and seventies nobody else worried about nothin. But Keith jus wa'n't really interested in bein with anyone less he loved em."

"How did you meet?"

Dwight closes his book. "I worked in Lewis, West Virginia, forty miles outside a Humble. February 1st, which was the night before my birthday, I gone to the colored pub for a drink. Sittin on the barstool feelin sorry for myself, lonely, bout to turn. What. Thirty-one, I guess. Quiet, not too many frequentin the place on a Monday. And damn if two a them middle-agers don't get into an out n out brawl over whether nex day the groundhog see his shadow or not. I left, got in my truck. And it was a bit icy, and I was a bit tipsy, and nex thing I know my fender's French-kissin the guardrail. Big drop down the mountain jus beyond it and in that terrible near-death moment I see my mama, and my daddy, and your daddy. And it come back to me, Christmas we jus had. Your granddaddy's sister, Aunt Beck visitin over the holiday, railin bout me and Eliot not married yet." He smiles. "She always had to have somethin to pick on. Now there was a woman, my route. Made it clear she was *very* interested. By then I'd had a few fleetin experiences with men, none of em meanin much, most the men married to women anyhow. So I thought. Maybe time to grow up. Start a family. I'd often entertained the idea a bein a father, how else? Big decision cuz I told myself I was not gonna be like them men, if I committed to a woman and children I'd stick with it, no strayin.

"So, nex mornin. My birthday. *Cold* day. I'm deliverin, ain't yet got to the woman's place, she was the afternoon. And I pull out the mail for 613 Oak Place, bills and circulars and a digest. The digest is covered in brown paper but somehow the brown paper got ripped, the title showin: *Jonathan.*

"I start to put the mail in the box and this young blond man come runnin out on the porch, throwin a coat on. Wantin to know about forwardin his mail, he's movin to Humble. I tell him the procedure, then I mention I'm from Humble and we get to talkin. He say he bought a place out at the new trailer park jus put up along Ole Mill Road. He got a nice smile, a soft, friendly way. Then I hand him his mail. I look at *Jonathan,* and I look at him. And he start to stammerin, Yeah, he's a artist, he like that comic for the art of it. Then I say, I'm a artist too. I've drawn for *Jonathan.*

"Now I knew what Keith was first time I seen him on my route. But he hadn't been around the block s'much. He weren't no baby, twenty-seven, but out there in the sticks he just ain't had much learnin, ain't yet found the inroads I did. So he didn't know yet, about me. Not for sure. And not for sure them days, well. That kinda mistake easily getcha fired, cost ya your livelihood. Or your life. So when I said I drew for *Jonathan,* which was a biblical reference even though wa'n't nunna the characters in the cartoon biblical nor named Jonathan, when I said I drew for that underground gay comic he turned to me, like searchin my face, see if I'm tellin the truth. And then he know I am."

They're quiet a few moments, the silence filled with flight announcements and beeping airport carts. Dwight is not looking at Rett.

"Nineteen eighty-one. There I am in the hospital, beaten, robbed while I was loaded. Gettin my wounds patched up by some disgusted nurse won't look me in the face and the thousandth time I'm makin the promises to myself, goin straight this time, goin clean. And I'm released and as I'm walkin out I happen to pass this room and there's Keith." He takes a quiet breath. "I can't remember ever seein him look so alone before. Scared. His eyes confused. I got this urge, got this yearnin to go to him, put my arms around him, but I been so evil for so long what kinda comfort I be?" He falls silent several seconds. "'Keith?'

"He look up. Starin wild like I'm some stranger, I shudder thinkin maybe after all the junk I done I become unrecognizable. Then he said, 'He died.' Now it was all new at that time, there weren't even a name for it, I don't even recall rumors about it then. Not yet, but soon. I said, 'Who died?' He said, 'Nicholas.' The boyfriend he got after finally givin up on me years after he shoulda. 'What happened?' I didn't understand, probably a year since I glimpsed em but last I seen that Nicholas he was young, healthy. And Keith said, 'Kaposi's sarcoma,' and I said, 'What's that?' and Keith said 'Cancer.' Then he said, 'I got it too,' and I said, 'Naw, Keith, ya can't catch cancer,' but my voice. Shakin. And he looked at me, like finally seein me. 'I wasn't done mournin. He jus died, I barely got started mournin and now I'm scared for myself,' and I say, 'Ya can't catch cancer,' my voice a little stronger and he lower the neck of his hospital gown and there they are. Lesions.

"So. I'm Keith's nursemaid to the death, which turned out not much longer. Few months. Moved into his place. He'd had a good job for years, art director, ad agency. Money. Saved, so I didn't have to get no job, I was full-time there with him. In and out the hospital with him. He talked about Nicholas plenty. I never knew him really but hearin about him now, seem like he was a nice fella. When it got close, he said he wanted to be home. What he said. 'I wanna be home with you.' Like it was our home, like we was never apart." Dwight stares at the floor a long time. "I didn't want the apartment. How'd I earn that apartment? way I treated him all them years. But he insisted, kep talkin about how happy he was I'd gone clean, really gone clean. Which I had. Takin care a Keith." He sighs. "When he was real young, there was a Jake. Both of em babies, twenty. Besides that, and me, and Nicholas, I swear to God Keith never had nobody else. And far as I knew never so much as smoked a joint. I on the other hand did everything to kill myself one way or the other and look who end up with all the god-damn luck. Took my bess friend dyin to save my own life."

After a full minute of silence, Rett gathers Dwight is finished. "He died at home?"

Dwight nods. "Jus turned fifty. Till recently he still looked like a healthy thirty-somethin, but that year aged him." A stir-crazy little white boy throws a tantrum. His mother seizes him, whispering something threatening. "His lass day. We got happy all the sudden, couldn't stop laughin, which was a struggle for him by then. I started tellin jokes. And postman stories. Even junkie stories, some of em *was* funny. And Humble stories, cuz we always had that between us: history. There was a time back home, I was always the one with the anecdotes, everyone come to me for the amusement. And in the middle a one a the laughin bouts, Keith said, 'Now I remember. These lass years I forgot, it jus went outa my head. Now I remember why I love you.'" Dwight swallows, waits until he can speak again. "We talked a little more that evenin, I don't remember what about. And then he went to sleep.

And the nex mornin I tried wakin him, but." He falls quiet, and Rett asks no more questions.

The stewardess at the gate announces their flight will be ready for boarding momentarily. Dwight puts his book in his overnight bag. "Well. What about you? Anybody ever make your heart flutter?"

Rett, his complexion just a shade lighter than Eliot's, blushes. "Doesn't matter. Just when my generation comes into sex, sex equals death." He runs his finger along the embossed letters on his Walkman.

"Not safe sex."

Rett doesn't look up.

"Hey." No response. *"Hey."*

Rett raises his face.

"Not safe sex."

"They don't like me!" He turns away, struggling to keep his voice low. "Girls."

"There's time."

Rett says nothing.

"I can tell you somethin but you won't believe me. You gotta love yourself first before anybody else'll love ya. And if they still don't, it won't matter cuz you'll have yourself lovin you, which is more than most people have anyway."

Rett considers this. "Do you?"

"Love you? You got to ask that?"

"Love yourself."

Though it's a reasonable question in light of the advice Dwight had just bestowed, the uncle is caught off guard. He gives the matter consideration. "Hmm. Guess I'm still workin on it."

"*Oh* so it's all theoretical, you don't really know if it works." A little smile.

"I stand by it as a good lesson to learn. That, and if you're gonna read somebody else's diary, make sure not to wear headphones so you can hear em when they walk through the door." Rett laughs out loud, a heartier sound than Dwight has heard from him since the day he'd arrived at this airport four weeks ago.

"Well." The uncle smiles as he speaks. "I was sad and then I was mad. Guess onliest place to go from there is glad."

"That's what you are now?"

"I don't know. You been livin with me a month, *you* tell me what I am."

Rett's face is suddenly serious. "Really, really, *really* sad."

Dwight's lips part. It had never occurred to him that the perpetual affliction he sees in his nephew might be exactly what Rett is reading in him. But before he has a chance to fully register this, the flight attendant announces the boarding of the back of the plane, which is precisely where Dwight's and Rett's free voucher seats are.

9

The overnight flight arrives ten minutes early, the lease of the Pontiac goes smoothly, and they are on the road by 7:30. Rett is upbeat and chatty, and for a while would comment on his surroundings with Dwight politely responding, but eventually the driver realizes his uncle needs space to absorb the impact of his sudden déjà vu, and they fall to a meditative silence for most of the two-and-a-half-hour drive. The first freeway sign mentioning Humble, still sixty miles away, causes each of them to catch his breath. At last the exit into town comes into view, and Rett turns off. Dwight glances at the Roman numeral clock on the big Episcopalian church. 10:10. "Too early to check in at the hotel. May as well go straight to the house."

As he guides Rett through the winding streets of his hometown, Dwight remembers the intense scene back in San Francisco and steels himself for whatever new emotions this trip might stir up for his nephew. A street sign: ROCK HILL ROAD. "Turn right." Their hearts pounding.

Halfway up the block Rett parks, and they cross the street to 124. When the Campbells were the occupants the house was white, the area below the front porch bricks of various earth colors. Now the building is all siding, a strange Halloween orange.

"The windas off the porch is the livin room. Was. There on the second floor was our parents' room, behind that the guestroom, behind that the room your daddy and me shared. First the double bed, then the twins."

Rett is mesmerized. Smiling, imagining it all.

"Your daddy. He had some appetite. Little as he was, ate everything! And talked! Quiet after he grew up, but when he was small. Sharin that bed useta drive me nuts, I'm tryin to sleep and he would not stop babblin."

Rett laughs. "Why didn't you move out? The guestroom?"

Dwight is quiet a moment. "Your daddy finally did. Seven. Goin on eight." The event a relatively recent entry into the memory book. Rett hadn't gotten that far.

"And that was Miss Onnie's?"

"That was Miss Onnie's, your daddy's buddy. Useta be bushes all along the border here." Gone, replaced by a cheap green wire fence. "That yard was like a cat farm. After she died some family with little girls moved in. That's the lass I knew a the place."

Rett studies the environs, correlating it with the information he has. Then looks beyond to the next yard. "That was Carl's?"

Though Dwight knows Carl's name appears in the journal, it startles him to hear it from Rett's lips. And now the uncle realizes that something within himself had kept him from seeing beyond Miss Onnie's. He raises his eyes to the neighboring house.

"Yep. That was the Talleys." From where they stand, Dwight can view the backyard and front porch. The incident with Parker the Cat was finally the death knell of his friendship with Carl. Dwight had run home to find Eliot hysterical on their mother's lap, she looking up at Dwight with a helplessness and terror he'd never seen in her, the first parental challenge she was not at all equipped to handle. Then Eliot became aware of his brother's presence, waving wildly. "Get outa here, Dwight! Get outa here, Dwight!" The older brother ran sobbing upstairs to his bed. He could hear his mother crying with Eliot, and then her voice on the telephone. "Hello Miss— Missus Talley?" He never knew the upshot of that call, and for months after he would walk around the block, taking the long way home rather than pass by the Talleys. A year later when he did accidentally run into Carl, the latter had just glowered at his former friend. Only once does Dwight remember exchanging glances with Carl's father after that, who then rotated his face slightly in a pretense that he hadn't seen Dwight, and another time with Carl's mother, who had stared at Dwight, a strange look as if she were trying to remember something, and then she did, a pain crossing her face, and she turned and disappeared into her house.

And now as he gazes at the Talley front porch, Dwight's last memory of the family was when he was walking home from school in the eleventh grade. It was spring, and Carl sat on his front porch swing not swinging, his feet propped on the balustrade, ankles crossed, reading a comic book. He had been a cute boy, and had grown into a handsome young man. By this time his mother had had both her mastectomies, which had done little good, and had been brought home to die. As Dwight neared the home, he could hear Mrs. Talley calling out. "Carl. Could you get me a glass of water please?" The rented hospital bed was pushed next to the open and screened living room windows, the venetian blinds drawn. "Carl?" Her voice weak but loud enough for Dwight to hear on the street. Without thinking, Dwight had stopped in front of the house, staring, waiting for Carl to come to his dying mother's aid. Carl, absorbed in *Captain America*, had not batted an eyelash. Then he looked up, only his eyes, glaring at Dwight. After a few moments Carl brought his focus back to the comic, turning the page.

"Dwight!"

The uncle and nephew turn to see an obese white woman running toward them.

"Oh my God, I can't believe it's you!"

Dwight smiles, but his confused frown belies him.

"You don't reckonize me? Well! Guess I have put on a few pounds since you was here. Lucy! Lucy Barton!"

"Lucy!"

"Well, Lucy Winthrop."

"How *are* you?"

"Aw, can't complain. When'dja get back?"

"Jus this mornin, we only here for overnight. This my nephew, Rett."

"Oh my God, I shoulda known *that,* ain't he Eliot all over! Well, what brung yaw home?"

"He wanted to see where his daddy grew up."

"Aw."

"You still livin up the street?"

"Naw, moved over to north end wunst I got married, but after Daddy died my son Josh took over the house, keepin it in the family. Course Mommy died not long after we was outa school."

"I remember."

"So Josh jus had a new baby. My daughter-in-law still recoverin from the cesarean so I'm staying here a while helpin out. I'm only forty-four an a grammaw eleven times over!" She beams. "Now how about you? Wife? Kids?"

"Neither."

"Good. If it ain't one headache it's the other."

"I didn't go to no goddamn race tracks!"

The screen door to the Campbells' former home slams open. A thin black man rushes out, charging by Dwight, Rett, and Lucy, storming down the street. The door flies open again and an equally thin white woman steps onto the porch.

"You ever get in my fuckin bread n butter money again, I'll break your ugly neck!" He is far down the street. *"You hear?"* He turns the corner. She doesn't look at the three people on the sidewalk just feet away from her house any more than the man did, blind beyond their own rage. She goes back inside, banging the door behind her. After a few moments' silence, Lucy shakes her head.

"Whole neighborhood's changed."

She notices Dwight glancing in the direction of the Talleys' former home. "He was there by hisself a long time after the wife died. Well, that Carl, guess he there with his daddy for senior year but then gone away to college firs chance. Don't think he even come back for the holidays. An then wunst the ole man passed, him an the sister fightin over the property. Neither of em wanted it, jus the money to sell it. So I heard anyway." She lowers her voice, though no one else is on the street. "I also heard that Carl drinks too much. Well, you know them businessmen." She brightens. "Oh, Dwight, you gotta see Florida!"

They follow her up and across the street. The Barton house, incredibly, is even more of a shambles than Dwight remembers. The porch is at a precarious angle with a huge hole, big enough for a small child to fall through. A good third of its roof slats are gone, the gutter broken in half and hanging. The dirty toys in the yard have increased exponentially, and a glimpse through a window reveals a vertigo-inducing chaos in the living room. A few feet up from the chimney, which had been sealed and never used as far as Dwight can recall, stands a satellite dish. "They get a hundred n eight channels!" Lucy says. "Wait here."

She runs to the screen door, which is torn. As she opens it, several kittens scamper out. "Them are Miss Onnie's people," says Lucy.

Her guests look at her, confused.

"Member when she died, left all them cats? I knew the city was jus gonna take em, put em all to sleep. So I grabbed a couple. These are the grankids. Or great-great-grans, who knows." And she dashes inside. A little girl and little boy come to the window, gawking at the visitors. A few minutes later Lucy returns holding a newborn, the child and its blankets immaculately clean as if her grandmother had just taken her from some protective bubble in the house. Dwight smiles and looks at Rett, who also smiles politely but seems distracted by the cats.

"Wake up, Florida Jean," Lucy coos. "Come on, little girl. Dontchu wanna say hi to Uncle Dwight?"

"She's a doll baby."

"Ain't she?" The children from the window run out, stopping in their tracks next to Lucy.

"This is Ashley. An this is Woody."

"Hello." But they just stare, half hiding behind their grandmother's legs. Lucy tenderly plays with the baby's lower lip, then looks up. "Hey Dwight. If you got the time, whyn't you go see Roof in the hospital?"

Dwight tenses. When he regains his voice: "Roof's in the hospital?"

"He got the black lung. God, been out there to Marion since he was thirteen. Had to quit a few years ago. Well he couldn't hardly breathe, guess it a miracle he survived this long. Visitin hours two to four, seven to nine."

"It bad?"

"It's bad."

"You like kitties?" Ashley asks Rett. She and the boy have moved closer to the young man, who is stooping, playing with a tan kitten.

"I wouldn't wanna upset him, Lucy. Been a long time. Since we was kids."

"All the more reason."

"Can I have a kitten?"

Rett had blurted it out. He and the children are sitting in a circle playing with two kittens between them. The little ones look up at Dwight, their eyes pleading in Rett's defense as if he were their age.

"I tell ya what," says Lucy, "I'd be fine gettin ridda one of em. Look at this zoo!"

"I know we'd need a carrier for the plane. I'll pay you back, Uncle Dwight."

The elder shakes his head. "Too risky. You know I got my two cats. They was brother and sister, but a new baby? Jealous, they might kill the little thing."

"Oh." Rett looks down, childlike. His ally Ashley stares at Dwight, pouty lips, shining eyes.

"Well. We better get ta goin."

"Well I am so tickled I run into you, Dwight. Where yaw stayin?"

"The Holiday Inn."

Lucy shakes her head, her disapproval that he has wasted his money with all the friends who could have taken him in. "Listen. They got the phone book there?"

"I imagine they do."

"Well I'm listed. The phone here, look under 'Joshua Barton.' Or 'Floyd Winthrop' for home."

"I will. It sure was good to see you, Lucy."

"Wa'n't that luck? I jus happen to be stayin over my ole house the day yaw come by. We're some lucky people!"

Dwight and Rett walk around, the uncle showing him the ghosts. Where D'Angelo's used to be, where the old Messengill house had stood, the empty lot where the beautiful old segregated movie house had been. They stand on the bridge, the creek below flanked by the cement levies.

"When I was a kid the backyards come all the way down, meet the crick, and every coupla years a flood. So they put up the flood-control walls. Ugly, ain't they."

"The tire swing?"

"Up that way. Gone, the dock gone." They gaze at the rushing rivulet. "Musta rained a few days. Water pretty high on the walls, movin swift."

Upstream a white man and boy stand with fishing rods, water to their shins, hopeful in the post-storm gush.

They have lunch at the hotel, barely half-capacity, then check in to their room. Dwight finds the slim county phone directory in a drawer.

"I'ma go ahead and call the florist, put in the order."

In the afternoon they walk to the Banneker School, which with integration had gone through several transformations, conversions to offices and at some point a Head Start, though at present it seems to have been vacant for years. "That was the auditorium slash gym. The principal's office there. Here was the first-grade room. I had ole Miss Thurman but your daddy got Miss McAfee, fresh outa college." They are in the empty gravel parking lot. Rett walks around the grounds. "The cafeteria below. Useta hear the white kids complainin bout their lunch. Not us, our ladies give us good home cookin."

There's a narrow overhang, and Rett leans against the building under it, a modicum of shade to counteract the oppressive mid-afternoon sun.

"Remember all that fightin up in Boston a few years ago? All the fuss over bussin kids to integrate the schools? Funny, I remember this big family, Browns, bussed way down off the mountain, passin all the white schools along the way. Nunna the white people complained *those* days, bussin to *se*gregate." Dwight stares at the steps to the main entrance, remembering Eliot running down them, excited about another second-grade perfect spelling test.

"Was Benjamin Banneker gay?"

Dwight turns to his nephew. "I don't know. I never heard that."

Rett says nothing, wipes his brow with his forearm.

"Why?"

"Well. Your cats."

Dwight frowns, then laughs out loud. "You think I named my cats after gay people?"

"George Washington Carver was, right?"

"The evidence points to it." Dwight stoops, plays with the gravel. "I was jus namin em after black geniuses, I wasn't really thinkin about sexual orientation." He looks at his nephew. "I didn't know you were such a cat lover. Wantin a kitten."

"I thought it might be a descendant of Parker."

Dwight stiffens, reminded again that Rett has perused his most private thoughts. "Parker never had no litters."

"All the cats Miss Onnie had, she couldn't've got *all* the females fixed."

Dwight looks at Rett. Then turns away, staring into the street.

"Uncle Dwight. I didn't read everything, only when I saw 'Eliot.' But I sure noticed the word 'Parker' popped up a lot." He uses his hand to shield his eyes from the sun. "You were just a kid. You gotta forgive yourself."

Dwight turns to his nephew, then looks at the ground, his breath coming quickly.

"You brought your swim trunks like I toldja?" He doesn't look up but presumes Rett is nodding. "Maybe we go back to the hotel, you take a dip. I gotta make a phone call."

Dwight indulges a moment in the air-conditioning of their room before pulling out his address book. He really should have the number memorized in case of emergencies, but truthfully he takes pride in the fact that he hasn't had to call his sponsor often enough to have learned the contact information by heart. In his wallet, he finds the long-distance calling card he'd purchased back in San Francisco.

He's off the phone by the time Rett walks in from his swim looking like a zombie, the lack of sleep from the flight coupled with the harsh sunrays.

"I could use a little nap before dinner too," his uncle remarks.

They each have a double bed and have lain on them only a minute when Dwight speaks. "I called my sponsor."

"Hmm."

"Miguel. Very nice man." Dwight had closed the curtains, a narrow stream of light seeping through. "He said if ya want. He'll hold your kitten for the summer."

It takes a moment for this to sink in. Rett pushes up on his elbow. "Really?"

"I never went to college. I ain't never said no one *has* to go to college, but I do think if ya start somethin, specially that close to finishin, ya oughta go on and do it. So all I ask, in return for this, is you at lease *consider* finishin."

There's a pause in the dimness. "I wanna tell you I'm gonna finish, Uncle Dwight. But I'm afraid to, cuz you'd probably just think I'm lying again. But if I wasn't afraid to tell you, that's what I'd say." Moments later, Dwight hears the even breathing of his nephew's sleep.

It's after seven when they wake and get on the road to a steakhouse at the edge of the county. "When I was livin here, they wouldn't serve black. Always heard they was the best steaks in Maryland."

Near the city limits of Humble, Dwight instructs his nephew to pull over. They stand outside the car, looking at a crowded trailer park in the twilight.

"It sure got extended since Keith was here." Some children playing hide-and-seek among the mobile homes. "And before that, this was the sticks. Boy in my school, Richard lived out here with his mother and sisters. Good painter. Turned a ole chicken coop into a studio."

Half an hour later they are seated in the restaurant. The steaks are good, though Dwight would be less inclined to characterize the place with the superlative reputation that preceded it. On the drive back, the outskirts of town, Rett stops the car. "Look at that!" They lean against the sedan, admiring the numerous twinkling lights.

"All I know's the Big Dipper."

"Well," says his uncle, "that's Pleiades, Seven Sisters. And Orion's Belt. You know the story of Orion and the Seven Sisters?"

"Oooh! See that?"

Dwight grins. "Shootin star."

"Meteor showers!" They're silent several minutes, but observe no more streaks in the sky.

"You going to see Roof?"

Dwight gazes at the star with the orange tint. Mars.

"I don't know. You think I should? Since you read the whole story."

"I don't know."

A wind ruffling the nearby trees.

"You know all my secrets now, read the manual on em. Seem like your turn, share at lease one a yours."

Another shooting star, and minutes later a third. Enough time elapses that Dwight assumes his nephew has decided to ignore his suggestion of a fair trade.

"You ever read this book, *A Clockwork Orange*?" Rett's voice is soft.

Dwight shakes his head. Then, seeing his nephew isn't looking at him: "No."

"This guy. This violent teenager. They do this experiment, fix it so violence makes him sick. Physically ill." He lowers his eyes to the ground. "I think. Because of my father, I think I kind of inherited that. When I was a kid and boys would pick on me, I couldn't fight. If they'd hit me, I'd draw my fists but then my body would get shaky, I couldn't—" His thumb gently rubbing his fingertips. "So I just looked down while they punched me, when they poured milk over my head in front of the girl I liked, she laughed so hard she was crying." He laughs softly.

"Two years before *Roe* my mother defends this old black woman, performed hundreds of abortions starting when she was a teenager. Abortion still illegal and there's my mother, bold! And my father." He swallows. "The case with the little boys. And the. The voter registration." A firefly circles in front of him, then vanishes. "So there I am, poli-sci, pre-law. Junior year I'm like: Do I need my *head* examined? I'm not my parents! I couldn't even defend my*self* against a *bully,* how I think I'm gonna—" A car passes on the lonely road.

"Freshman year I went to IUPUI, remember?" Dwight trying to think.

"State college, people outside of Indiana call it 'Purdue.' So. *Big.*" His eyes seeming to see the campus, to be stunned by its vastness still. "Never understood the other students. Getting drunk and getting laid. And getting rich after they graduated, they didn't care about anything else! And the few who *did* care about the world would get so. *Appalled,* like I was some moron if I wasn't completely up on every single issue." His lower lip curling under. "Sophomore year transferred, moved to St. Louis, maybe I'd do better in a private school, I got scholarships." He shakes his head. "No different. What did I think would be different?" Sighs. "Didn't matter. I studied, kept to myself. I wasn't there to have fun, I was there to get my degree. There was one phone for every eight dorm rooms but when it rang I never answered except Sunday mornings when my mother would call. It was never for me except when my mother would call, she— Worried." He considers elaborating, then doesn't.

"Not long after school started senior year, I saw this news report. These refugee camps and this. *Massacre.* Hundreds, or thousands, I just saw all these bodies, families, *toddlers.* I heard the story, I saw the pictures. Then it disappeared. All these civilians slaughtered! and it was news for maybe a day. And no one talking about it. So I researched. Took effort but I found pictures. I photocopied the pictures and I took them around and I started talking about it. Me, who never had anything to say!" Sweat beads appearing on his brow. "*No one cared!* Or if they did, it was just to get mad cuz I brought it up. The more I had to say, the madder they got." He falls silent.

"Where all that happen?"

"Lebanon. A Palestinian refugee camp in Lebanon. These Lebanese Christian murderers that the Israeli army let loose. Bloodbath!" He briefly shoots a look to the heavens in disbelief. "I never had anything to say before, then I couldn't stop. I wrote to the school paper, I wouldn't shut up!" A dog barking in the distance. "Got some nasty responses. In print. Rachel Miller, another senior, Robert Cohen a junior. I didn't know what I was talking about, or, Some appreciation after all the Jews did for blacks in the sixties." Turning to his uncle for the first time, his eyes glistening. "Well what if it were the Klan, wiping out some black settlement? Or some Southern cracker fire department hosing down a peaceful march? Or a *lynching,* bunch of whites burning a black man, would they say, 'Well it's all so complicated,' 'Well there *are* two sides'?"

They stare at each other, then both look away. A few moments later, Rett calmly pushes his glasses back up his nose, behind his ears, the eyewear having slipped in the fresh perspiration.

"It got— Personal. About me being quiet, no friends. Was I some kind of pervert? They never said what they meant by that, they just threw the word out vague, like since I wasn't a partier, since I actually spent my time *studying* there must be something wrong with me, like everyone who keeps to himself must be some—" He shudders. "A couple strangers came up to me, said they liked what I wrote but they never defended it publicly." Dwight glances at his nephew from the corner of his eye, the latter's face emanating worry, then just as abruptly the weight of it all appearing to fade.

"Felt like a lifetime but guess the war only lasted two weeks. I couldn't fight anymore, I just went to class and to work. My old job: the cafeteria slop line." A pebble at his shoe turns out to be a ball of dirt, and he flattens it. "In the slop line we had to scrape and rinse the cookware before it went into the big dishwasher, so I scraped and rinsed the pots and the pans and the spatulas and the sieves and the butcher knives and the cleavers and one cleaver I slipped under my shirt. I left the cafeteria walking home, it was evening and clear and when I got to my dorm I went up to the second floor where I lived and I went to the bathroom. Took the cleaver out from under my shirt, and I washed it and carried it to my room and shut my door and I took out the campus directory and I saw exactly which room in which dorm Rachel Miller lived and Robert Cohen lived.

"I took out the cloth I used to polish my good shoes. I shined the blade and shined the blade and by accident I cut my thumb and then the clock struck 4 a.m. time to go." His voice has lowered. "It was Monday night and Tuesday morning so even the party students were asleep. Crickets. I walked to Rachel's dorm. No air-conditioning and it was humid so the window to the first-floor lobby had been left open, I slipped through. Quiet dark all dark. I walked through the hall, up the stairs to Rachel's room, 232. I stood outside staring at the door, 232, Rachel I knew from a history class sophomore year. Always with her friends, always with a boyfriend, her latest boyfriend was this rich guy, Patrick Murphy, I stood outside Rachel's room and pulled out my cleaver and in my head I saw Rachel talking on the phone, laughing on the phone to Patrick Murphy, talking about their combined income when they graduated, eighty K, a *hundred* K, and that's when I did what I came there to do."

A small creature scurries across the road. It looks like a squirrel but Rett thought squirrels slept at night. Even as it disappears into the darkness he tries to identify it.

"*What did you do!*"

Rett is startled by Dwight's outburst, the younger having momentarily forgotten his story. He tries to remember his place.

"So then I did what I came there to do. I turned around and I cut the cord on Rachel's hall phone. Dead. Then I left her dorm and I went to Robert's dorm and I cut the cord on his hall phone. It was after five and the campus still asleep by the time I got back home, and on a sudden inspiration I cut the cord on every single phone in my dorm. Then I went to my room and I shut my door and I got into bed and I slept really well, which was unusual. I slept very deep until 7:30 when this screaming starts in my hall, Who got into the dorm and cut the phone lines! It occurs to me that Rachel and Robert must have woken up screaming too, and I found this comforting, and then I was asleep again, I slept a few more hours. My classes that day didn't start until eleven." The animal runs across the road again and quickly vanishes. "The violence, cutting the cords. It didn't make me sick. It made me sad. I guess I was already pretty sad, except before was like being at the bottom of a very deep dark well and looking way up at the light, the tiny distant light. But *this* sad: no light." His left arm reaches to hold his right elbow, right arm hanging. "On Wednesday I had slop line duty again, and I put the cleaver under my shirt, and I went to my early dinner because the slop line eats early, and after dinner I walked back to the kitchen to work and I scraped the plates and the bowls and when it was time for the cooking stuff, the pots and the ladles and the pans and the tongs and the butcher knives and the cleavers I slipped my cleaver out from under my shirt and I put it in the dishwasher to be cleaned with the rest." The wind picks up again, branches swaying. "I didn't miss a class but my grades dropped, A's were now B's, B's: C's. Went home for winter break and I came back and I walked into my dorm room and I shut my door and I stayed. I didn't come out for classes or work and I would hold going to the bathroom till the hall was empty. Sometimes in the middle of the night I'd walk down to the basement television, but I started spending less time with *MacNeil/Lehrer* and more with MTV." For several minutes only the crickets, a creek frog. Then Rett gently breaks the silence. "Do you think I'm crazy, Uncle Dwight." A melancholy but also a resignation, as if he is calmly prepared for whatever honest answer his uncle might offer.

Dwight considers the question a good forty-five seconds before responding, his words soft. "In 1960 I pondered some violence a lot deeper n cuttin a phone cord. Guess we all got our crazy moments, nephew." They stare into the darkness twenty minutes more before Dwight gently touches Rett's arm, and they turn to get back into the car.

Between the jet lag and their naps, they have trouble falling asleep in the hotel. Rett turns on the TV and is delighted to catch an old *Twilight Zone*, but the viewers' anticipatory smiles fade as they come to understand the plot. A white man accused of killing a brutal Klansman is about to be hanged. While all this is happening, the sun refuses to rise. The teleplay features a monologue about hate by a black preacher, and hate seems to be directly related to the 9:30 a.m. pitch-blackness. Rett and Dwight wait wordlessly to see what event will finally bring back the light but they are surprised by the end: the world just gets darker.

◻ ◻

The next morning Rett sleeps while Dwight writes in his memory book. The phone rings. It's Cousin Liddie, excited. Turns out she works at the Kmart with Lucy so heard all about Dwight's visit with Eliot's boy. They chat a while, Rett putting his pillow over his head. Ten minutes later another ring. "Jeanine! Liddie called you *already*?" As Dwight is hanging up, Rett drags himself out of bed.

"Jeanine was your daddy's friend, they was the same grade. She'd like to have us over for breakfast. Liddie's our cousin, around the same age as your daddy. She'd like to have us over for lunch. I told em we have a few things to do today, I'd check in with you."

"Yes, yes," Rett mutters as he closes the bathroom door.

Jeanine still lives in the house where she grew up. She'd never married, and two years ago had to put her mother into a nursing home. Sausage and eggs and fried potatoes and onions and fried apples and cantaloupe and pulpy orange juice from the carton, the type of feast Jeanine clearly rarely indulges in as she's quite slim.

"Your uncle tell you we useta call this Colored Street? An him an your daddy lived on Mixed Street?" She's a jovial sort, and her reminiscences bring out a cheerfulness in Dwight that Rett didn't know existed: panting as they climbed up to the colored tier of the old movie house, the white driver who nearly hit Jeanine in the snow and got a taste of colored kids' sass from Mokie the twin. And she turns to Rett and tells him about playing jump-rope with Eliot, about the day Eliot picked Parker out of her cat's litter.

"You know your daddy was the smartest in our class, firs grade on up."

As they're leaving, she can't take her eyes off Rett. "God, I can't believe how much he's Eliot!" Then to his uncle: "You know, I often think about your mother's funeral. The lass time I seen him. I hope you don't take this the wrong way, but I guess, cuz the only other funeral we'd both been to was my uncle's, I was half expectin Eliot to tell me your mama weren't dead. Was a rabbit in that box!" She laughs and wipes a tear.

Dwight and Rett drive around, the elder continuing to tour-guide his past, and at 12:30 they knock on Liddie's door. Their cousin answers with a huge grin, giving each of them a bear hug. She's nearly as round as Lucy.

"That damn Jeanine tole me she was invitin yaw to breakfast, I suppose she done filled ya up before ya got here."

It's true. Dwight was bracing himself to politely force down more food but, mercifully, lunch is simply gazpacho, a new recipe Liddie's trying for the hot weather, with watermelon for dessert. The concept of cold soup was insane to her, but the dish turned out pretty good she thinks, "Delicious" according to Dwight. They sit outside, her backyard patio under a tree.

"Walter Joe got on at the textiles, that's why we moved back here from Bear. Bear, West Virginia," she clarifies for Rett. "Then it closed like all the rest of em. The mill, the tires, brewery. Glass where your daddy worked. *Any*way." Sighs. "Jus wish my husband coulda been here to see ya but he's out at the Kmart too, workin today." She sucks on a piece of watermelon. "You remember that bike I stole for me an Eliot?"

"No!"

"Borrowed, borrowed!" She turns to Rett. "Me an your father was aroun third grade. My family over for Thanksgivin, an some neighbor white family gone for the holiday. I didn't see the harm in takin one a their damn bikes jus for a few hours, teach ourselves to ride. Your daddy refused, we hadn't asked permission. Well I recalled visitin weeks before when we *did* ask permission, just to share it with the boy, ride it when he took a break. 'No!' that stingy brat said, so Thanksgivin I took his ugly ole bike, an by enda the day I could ride! Eliot watchin the whole time, eyes drippin the envy, but he never joined in. He waited till I finished an watched me put that cycle back where I found it, then he gone inside, quiet. I felt bad, your daddy's sad eyes sure whipped the conscience into me. Him goin into law didn't surprise me a bit, from the beginning he always seemed to have that sense: right an wrong."

After lunch, she takes them into her living room. Pictures of her parents ("That's your great-aunt Peg-Peg," Dwight inserts), of her brother Mitch and his wife and kids ("Yeah that rascal finally settled down," Liddie remarks), of Liddie's own five grown children and plentiful grandchildren. Dwight remembers Liddie's oldests when they were small themselves, the twins Felicia and Fiona.

"Do you have any of my father when he was little?"

She thinks. "You know, Rett, I don't believe I do. But I'll ask my mama. She was the keeper a *all* the pictures."

They're driving again, and Rett pulls into a convenience store lot. When he comes out sipping a gargantuan caffeinated soft drink, Dwight is standing next to the car.

"I don't wanna do this if you rather keep explorin around. But I was thinkin. Maybe I go on and visit Roof."

"Okay."

"Visitin hours jus startin. Two. Maybe you drop me off at the hospital? I'll call a cab to bring me back to the hotel when I'm done."

"Okay. Or. You just want me to come with you? Stay in the waiting room?"

"Dontchu wanna look around Humble some more?"

"Well. What do *you* want?"

Dwight gazes at his nephew.

"You know what? Maybe I'll jus keep showin you around, that's what we come here for, right?"

"You came here too, Uncle Dwight. You have stuff you need to do."

Had Rett said *want to do,* Dwight might have been able to talk himself out of this task.

"Okay. You drop me off, then keep the car. I'll call a cab later. Meetcha back at the hotel lobby."

"Okay. What time?"

"Well. Ferguson's closes at five, so we need to leave the hotel no later n 4:30."

"Okay."

"No later n 4:30."

"No later n 4:30."

At the hospital information desk, Dwight is directed to the third floor. He passes the room twice before seeing the name in the slot outside the door. The space is a double but only the bed near the door is occupied. And the very old man, wrinkled and white hair and colorless skin with the breathing apparatus and numerous other machines, Dwight now comprehends, is Roof. He walks through the doorway, approaching slowly. Roof breathes loud and uneven through his mouth. He's asleep but at one point his eyes open wide, fixing on Dwight, but seeming to register nothing before they close again. And Dwight wonders if this is all a terrible idea, a *selfish* idea. Why's he here? He prays not to upset Roof, and if he doesn't, what does that mean? Absolution for himself? He takes a step backward toward the door.

"Whoa! Careful there. You can go on in."

Dwight, startled, turns around to stare at a fortyish black man in a nurse's uniform, a combination he has *never* before seen in Humble, standing at the room entrance. The man enters, checking on the various mechanisms of life extension. After a few moments, noticing Dwight still hasn't moved: "Please come in. He seems to do better with company." He indicates the visitor's chair next to the bed, and Dwight warily takes it. "If you talk to him he might hear you, even if he doesn't appear to respond."

Dwight stares at Roof, says nothing. The nurse marks on a clipboard. "Your first time visiting?"

"We knew each other, kids. I moved away a long time ago."

The RN nods, not looking up. When he finishes with the chart, he hangs it back on the foot of the bed. "Talk to him." He smiles and leaves.

Dwight sits for a very long time, Roof's heavy, labored breathing the only sound. Finally the visitor quietly walks out. The nurses' station is right across from Roof's room, and the surprised RN looks up.

"He's not. Is he in a coma?"

"No. He's just asleep."

"Oh. Because you said. About he might hear me but not respond."

"Sometimes when he's very tired it's hard for him to open his eyes. But other times he does."

"Oh."

A public-address system request for Dr. Mukherjee to come to the ICU.

"I couldn't really talk to him, not knowin whether he's seein me. Knowin me. Too many years."

"Well. He might wake soon."

"My nephew and I jus happened to be in town. We gotta go back to D.C. this evenin, catch a plane. So I have a few minutes, but."

The nurse nods.

"I live in San Francisco, my nephew's visitin me this summer."

The nurse smiles politely before going back to his paperwork. After a few minutes he notices Dwight looking at a display of several photographs above his work area. Children.

"She died. Dysentery." Dwight is disconcerted, then aware that his eyes had settled on one particular child. "Spent a couple of years working in Ethiopia. They're orphans." He picks up the picture of the little girl. "I'm gonna adopt one of those kids. It's complicated, taking them out of their own country, Americanizing them. But I don't think as complicated as needless juvenile death. I'd do my best, make sure my child knew where she came from. Or where he came from." He's quiet a moment. "Other obstacles too. Prejudice."

"Lem. You doin a double today?" Another nurse standing at the station, this one white and female.

Lem nods. "Be here till eleven."

"Okay." She walks off.

"You ain't from here."

Lem laughs. "Detroit."

"So how you end up in Humble?"

"I go where there's need. Ethiopia, Uruguay. Small-town America. Thinking about New York after the end of the year." He looks at Dwight with meaning. "AIDS is cleaning us out."

Whether by "us" Lem is referring to black men or the black community, or to black *gay* men—because the visitor had discerned a certain vibe from the nurse—Dwight cannot be sure, and before he can ponder on it, Lem says, "Look."

Dwight turns around to see Roof's eyes open, staring directly at him. He cautiously enters the room.

"Hey Roof." His voice is quiet.

The patient's mouth open, allowing for more oxygen to enter his lungs.

"Remember me? Dwight? From kids?"

Roof continues staring, not blinking an eye. Dwight could interpret the expression as Roof remembering him and hating him, or Roof utterly baffled as to who stands before him. Finally, between breaths: "Whatever. Happen ta. The Architeck Club?"

At first Dwight thinks Roof is confused, dreaming awake or mistaking Dwight for someone else. Then he remembers their boyhood clubs, and laughs. "I don't think we quite made our membership quotas."

And then they're talking. And in the talking Roof seems to start breathing easier, and so does Dwight. Tarzan movies and exploring the old Messengill house and Roof's father dropping them off at the fair, Dwight's father letting them on the train that time. Roof had married at seventeen, the girl the same age. "Yeah, I remember hearin about that. Gloria her name?" Thirty-seven years they'd been together. Eleven kids and he's lost track of all the grands, and a couple of the *next* generation. Dwight's mind is boggled by his contemporary speaking of great-grandchildren. No, Dwight didn't marry, been living in California nineteen years. They never mention Carl.

When there's a brief lull Roof, grinning, says, "I done you wrong. Time or two. The movie thee-ater."

It takes a moment for Dwight to realize Roof is referring to the instances when he would come to the pictures with Dwight, then exercise his right as a Caucasian to abandon his colored friend and sit in the floor seats. "Yep. You sure did."

Then Roof's eyes narrow. "An a time *you* done *me* wrong."

Dwight stares at him. Their eyes are frozen on one another, Dwight not knowing what to say, Roof not helping. Finally Roof looks away, trying to make himself more comfortable on his pillows. "But guess what. Useta picnic. Roslyn County. My wife n kids. They wanna swim the river." He goes into a coughing fit. Every time it seems about to stop, it becomes more severe. Dwight looks at the nurses' station but no one's there. He stands, about to run out to look for someone, but Roof raises his hand, waving him to stay, and finally the bout ceases. "I cain't keep em from swimmin. I ain't swum myself since." The rest of the story, which Roof doesn't finish, is part of Dwight's most catastrophic childhood memory. But he sees Roof remembering it, and he beholds Roof's thoughtful calm. "Well I think. I had to, I *could* save em. Any of em drownin. I oughta thank you for that."

Dwight says nothing, his eyes soft, gazing at his old friend. Roof, lying against his raised pillow, turns to look out the window. "Eliot an that ole cat." Roof laughs softly, his eyelids getting heavy. "Eliot, Eliot." Minutes pass, both of them silent, and Dwight realizes Roof is asleep.

It's four when Dwight walks into the hotel. He and Rett have already checked out of their room, their bags in the rental car. Just off the lobby is a phone booth. Dwight, grateful for the privacy, closes the folded door and pulls out his address book. It has been a *lot,* the last twenty-four, but his second call in as many days to his sponsor is as composed as the first. He'd been concerned for his nephew on this trip, but only now is he aware with great relief the miracle that he didn't fall apart himself. Toward the end of the chat he becomes remotely worried Rett may not be here at 4:30, that he may have gotten distracted or lost, and Dwight starts devising backup plans but his nervousness is for naught: when he slides open the door, he immediately sees Rett from behind sitting on the lobby couch, wearing his headphones and perusing hotel flyers for local state parks. Dwight walks over and gently taps his nephew's shoulder.

They go to Ferguson's Flowers, pick up their orders, and put them in the backseat of the car. Then head over to Lucy's. She's delighted they stopped by again, thrilled they're taking a kitten, and elated to hear Dwight visited Roof. Dwight would like to be kept apprised of Roof's progress. It's the word he uses though he's thinking deterioration.

"You can call me anytime. An you can call Roof! Jus phone the hospital, the third-floor nurses' station. Then ask for Lem. He's my favorite."

"I met him."

"Ain't he nice! First I thought it was weird, male nurse, but then I really come to like him. Anyways, jus tell him who you are, I'll put your name on the list. An he'll stand there an hold the receiver to Roof's ear." She turns to Rett. "Now, Eliot Junior, you said you wanted that tan one?"

"Yes, please."

"I'll fix ya up a little box with newspapers, hold on." Lucy goes inside.

Three children stare at them from the second-floor window, none of them Ashley and Woody of the day before. Lucy returns with the carton. "I didn't see the kitty you want. *Ashley!*" She gives Ashley a few moments to reply before yelling for her again.

"*What!*"

"*Bring out that little tan tabby! I know you got her up there!*" Lucy waits, as if expecting another verbal response, but none comes. "Yaw plannin somethin special for the Fourth?"

Dwight and Rett, surprised, exchange glances. "I guess we ain't looked that far ahead."

"We prolly goin on up to the park. Cookout, watch the farworks." Ashley comes out with the tan kitten, and Lucy puts it into the box. "Don't let her run loose in your car," she warns. "She'll tear it up."

"Thank you," Rett says to Lucy and her granddaughter.

"That was Mo, she was my favorite one," whines Ashley.

"Oh whichever one he'da picked you'da said that."

"*I know!*" Ashley, laughing, runs back into the house.

Dwight and Rett get into the car. As Rett pulls out down the street, he slows in front of 124 Rock Hill Road, both of them gazing, silent.

The cemetery is at the edge of town, on their way out. The box is in the front at Dwight's feet, and they fold it closed, leaving a healthy breathing hole for the kitten, take the flowers out of the backseat, and walk to the Campbell family plot. They place the three arrangements on the three graves. They don't speak for many minutes.

"Where's Keith buried?"

"San Francisco."

"Was his family from Lewis?"

"Near Lewis."

"He didn't wanna be buried near his family?"

"He hadn't been in touch with his family since they disowned him when he was twenty. No."

Another silence.

"You gonna be buried in San Francisco? Or here."

Dwight considers. "Tell you the truth. I hadn't really thought about it."

"Good."

They fill up the gas tank, then get on the road. The plan is to drive back to D.C. now and spend the night in an airport hotel before the crack-of-dawn flight tomorrow. Fifteen miles outside of town, Dwight indicates a roadside truckstop. "Twenty years ago this place had a sign: BLACK TO GO. Never thought I'd set foot inside even if I could. Well. Dinnertime and ain't nothin else around."

The music playing through the speakers is country, but they're not the only black patrons, and the waitress, surprising to Dwight, is a middle-aged black woman. She recommends the chili.

"I keep thinkin about what you said. Those refugee camps. I didn't know about nunna that."

Rett sips his lemonade. "Don't think I exactly inherited my parents' drive. Injustice, they *did* something about it. All I ever did was talk, and when people didn't listen I hid away."

"Think you still got a few years left in ya to figure out whatcha wanna do, Twenty-one." Then he remembers. "Sorry, almost Twenty-*two*. July 11th right around the corner." Rett smiles. "Thought about what you want for your big day?"

Rett mulls it over, then shakes his head. "Right this second I can't think of anything I'm in want of."

The next song coming out of the restaurant speakers is "Sixteen Tons," and because Dwight does take stock in a certain philosophy that not everything in the universe is so easily explained, he believes the old miners' tune is Roof sending him a So Long.

As they get back on the road, dusk descends. They don't speak, Dwight gently stroking the kitten on his lap, and driving through the Appalachians he gazes out on the valley, the stunning pink-purple sky. As a child growing up in the mountains, he'd never noticed their beauty. He had to leave and come back to see it. He thinks of the trip they *should* have made down this road all those years ago, or down the old route before the new freeway came through, the trip to the March on Washington in 1941 that little Eliot had so looked forward to and was devastated to find out would not take place, they should have come driving down here counting the cows and Eliot, tiny as he was but ingrained with such a sense of justice already, Eliot would have appreciated the March, would have remembered it but it didn't happen, it wouldn't happen until 1963, too late for Eliot and suddenly Dwight is bawling uncontrollably, huge and hysterical, the kitten jumping, staring at him, frightened, and Rett pulls over on the shoulder of the road and takes the kitten, not looking at his uncle, holding the animal on his lap as Dwight weeps and weeps and neither of them says a word. When Dwight's sobs finally subside, the exquisite afterglow has reached its peak. They both stare straight ahead, and finally Rett speaks quietly as he gently strokes his infant pet.

"You know what, Parker? Next time I come to Humble, it's gonna be October, autumn. These trees." Then Venus appears twinkling, ushering in the night.

1960 REDUX

Last Christmas, when the issue of possible war with Indochina arose at the table, Claris decided her meticulously crafted dinner was not going to be ruined by the grim discourse. So she announced she had a joke.

"The saloonkeeper's goin on vacation an he tells the man relievin him, 'Listen. If Big John comes to town, he's the biggest, meanest thing goin. Pack up! Run for the hills!' The substitute saloonkeeper's shakin in his boots! But the week goes by an no sign a Big John, so he relaxes. Then, on the seventh day somebody runs in. 'Big John's in town!' Well the substitute saloonkeeper *tries* to hightail it but with all the customers runnin an a-pushin he gets knocked down, an by the time he's back up ain't nobody else left an in walks this man. Seven feet tall an lookin *mean. 'Pour me a beer!'* The saloonkeeper does, an the big man guzzles it, then slams down the mug. 'Want another?' The saloonkeeper shakin. 'No,' says the big man, 'I gotta be gettin outa town!'" and Claris had nearly busted a gut laughing. Till she noticed everyone staring at her, confused. Her eyes searched the ceiling for whatever she missed.

"'Big John's comin!'" Claris had blurted. "The big man says, 'No, I gotta be gettin outa town. Big John's comin!'"

This memory, of his mother's perpetual inability to get a joke right, was what little Leona had triggered for Eliot a half-hour ago with her jumbled riddle as he was bidding goodbye to her grandparents Martha and Jeremiah, and why Eliot still can't stop laughing, pulling into Rosie's yard. He sees Beau at the window waving, and Eliot waves back, shifts the car to park, and steps outside. It occurs to him that he should call the colored hospital to inquire as to the condition of Mr. Yancey, the elder who had been arrested and beaten after trying to register to vote yesterday, and he is about to go into Rosie's to do so when Beau comes rushing out. "Roy's dying!"

Eliot gapes at Beau as if whatever he just heard could not possibly have been English. Then an agonizing keening from inside. Beau runs back in, Eliot on his heels.

Beau's sister Rosie sits on the living room floor holding her legless husband Roy in her arms. His eyes are wild, his body violently trembling.

"I think he had a stroke!" Rosie wails. "He was fine five minutes ago, then I went to check on my turnips boilin—"

"Where's the hospital?"

"The colored hospital's hour an a half away," she tells Eliot, "other side a Prayer Ridge."

Looking at Roy, Eliot fears the man doesn't have an hour and a half left in him. "Let's go."

Beau carries Roy to the car and sits in the back with Rosie as she holds her husband. Eliot accelerates.

"Don't speed," Beau warns.

"We gotta get him there!" Eliot is shaking.

"He's goin nowhere you give the Prayer Ridge police a good excuse to arrest that Northern nigger lawyer."

A vague memory of Winston's ten rules for Dixie comes back to Eliot, but the thing about going as fast as your (g)as can carry you, he thinks, applied to driving at night and leaving town. Eliot still exceeds the limit, though not so appreciably as before. They pass the Nathan clinic, then further down the road the Prayer Ridge Hospital, both institutions servicing only whites, and after a drive of about forty minutes, having finally made it to the other side of Prayer Ridge, Rosie says, "He's dead."

Eliot instinctively swerves around to look back, the car still in motion. Roy's eyes remain wide open, his body frozen. "You feel a heartbeat, Beau?" Her voice flat.

Beau feels Roy's chest, then his neck. He shakes his head.

"Then I guess he's dead." She sighs. "My husband's dead, Eliot, we can turn on aroun."

"Maybe—"

"He been like this ten minutes," she tells the driver, "ain't no maybes. Turn back the other direction. The Prayer Ridge Hospital don't accept colored but the Prayer Ridge Morgue do."

For several minutes there is silence on the slow drive back. Then suddenly Rosie is howling, causing Beau to sob holding her, their hands on Roy. Eliot wipes his eyes.

The white man at the morgue is frosty but efficient. Rosie, Beau, and Eliot leave the building, standing outside.

"I'm gonna stay with my sister a few days, help her get situated. You tell Winston?"

Eliot nods.

"You got to get on the road."

Eliot had peeked at his watch just a minute before—11:05. To allow the hour leeway to get to his overnight in Memphis before sunset he was supposed to have left by eleven. He drives the siblings back to Rosie's. As he lets them off, it begins to drizzle. "Thank you. You were very kind to my sister and me," and Beau surprises Eliot with a quick, awkward embrace. Rosie also hugs Eliot, though the gesture is mechanical, her mind worlds away. As he pulls off Eliot waves and they, zombies, wave back.

An hour down the road, the rain comes down in buckets. When Eliot can see nothing, he pulls off and waits. The torrent seems to have no intention of subsiding, and he is too spent to be actively impatient.

When the cloudburst finally abates to a gentle shower, it's half past noon: no leeway for making it to Memphis before dark. Eliot is tempted to try but, a bit of superstition related to the fact that the day had begun so morosely, he turns the car around. It's wasted gas, but he's in the middle of nowhere, and he certainly isn't going to knock on any of these rural Alabama doors, a black stranger with a Northern dialect looking for accommodations. He'll have to call the car owner to explain the situation, to apologize but he'll need the station wagon another night. He heads back to the Coatses', figuring on the way he'll stop in Nathan to see if he can do anything for Rosie and Beau.

Without warning the sun emerges, bright through the soft rain. Eliot sees it forming and pulls over, stepping out. A clear, crisp rainbow and above it a second taking shape, longer and more elliptical, a mother protecting her child.

◻ ◻

Randall wakes every hour from a dream in which he is part of the inferno, a small figure in Henry Lee's miniature train world that Randall had set ablaze at the junkyard last night. He opens his eyes. 10:20. He doesn't ever remember sleeping this late.

His sister's right. He never wanted to be a damn salesman. He ought to celebrate getting fired, breaking ties with that blamed shoe store but my God, Benja was nearly *killed* the night before last by her good-for-nothing better half and Martin had *no* sympathy? Yesterday slowly coming back to him, his fists clenching, *Stop thinking.* He picks up yesterday's clothes from the floor, throws them on, and descends the stairs.

Pacing the kitchen, wiping her eyes.

"I couldn't sleep at all. I can't believe you could sleep after everything!"

How the hell you know I slept since you moved your ass into the guestroom? he thinks. Reaches for the coffee canister. Second thought he opens the refrigerator and pulls out a beer. *Snap.*

"It's cold." Erma wears a shawl. "Chilly in here, drafty ole house." She stares at him. "Well? Whatchu plannin on doin for a new job?"

"Since it barely been twenty-four hours since I lost the previous one I really ain't had time to ponder on the matter."

"Well you *better* ponder! What we sposed to do for food?"

Randall sips his beer. She lets out a helpless cry, then picks up the medicine bottle from the middle of the table. The prescription sedatives the doctor gave her after her most recent miscarriage. She squints at the label as if it were Chinese, then twists it open, her trembling right hand pouring into her left. A pill slips through her fingers, vanishing under the stove. "*Oh!* He only gay me ten! He only gay me ten an I jus lost one. I think he's worried I might try n do somethin foolish."

"I'll pour em."

"You gotta mash em up. You know I cain't swallow no pills whole!"

"I'll fix em."

"Only two at a time, he said! Only two." Randall picks up the bottle, tapping it. "I guess I ain't never gettin to Paris France, am I!" He slowly raises his eyes to her. "You don't know what I'm talkin about. *Paris France!* That little girl's book, when B.J. was teachin me to read! In a ole house in Paris that was covered with vines *I always wanted to go to Paris France!*" Randall lowers his eyes back to his palm, tapping, the bottle stubbornly clinging to the tiny tablets. "You don't care! I ain't never had a day a happiness in this marriage, an you—" The phone. "Oh that's Mama, I called her this mornin an Daddy said she was down volunteerin for the hungry children." *Ring.* "I didn't wanna worry Daddy but I told him to tell Mama to call me right away, soon's she got home. I needta tell her what's goin on." *Ring.* Erma starts to exit the kitchen, then suddenly hurls behind her, *"Don't forget my milk!"* She rushes out of the room and up the stairs to the bedroom extension.

Randall opens the drawer that serves as his toolbox and pulls out a hammer. He grabs a saucer and places one of the minute yellow pills on it, then begins gently hammering it into powder.

"Mama!" Bawling so loudly he can hear her all the way downstairs. "It's awful, it's jus awful! He lost his job!"

Randall takes a second pill, gently hammering it into the powder.

"No! The shoe store, that *nice* job. Well he started throwin shoes at his boss, actin like a *maniac!"*

Randall takes a third pill, gently hammering it into the powder.

"He was in *jail!* I had to go down an bail him out, it was so humiliatin!"

Randall takes a fourth pill, gently hammering it into the powder.

"An then we're walkin home through the streets, everyone lookin at us, I jus know they all heard!"

Randall takes a fifth pill, gently hammering it into the powder. He contemplates the size of the mound, which is starting to look suspicious.

"RANDALL! Are you ready yet? God, I jus need some *sleep,* I cain't sleep!"

"Just a minute." Randall takes two more pills, hammering them into the powder. He pours the powder into a teacup, softly blowing to make sure no granule is wasted. He brings the cup to the faucet, a modicum of water to absorb the particles. He pours a glass of milk, then brings the cup and glass up to his wife. He's surprised to see she's still on the phone since he hadn't heard her voice in a while. Her mother must have plenty to say.

"I should get off now, Mama." She hangs up, wipes her eyes, and takes the cup. Randall wonders if she might be at all curious as to how those two tiny little pills made the water turn so yellow, but as always she closes her eyes tight, scrunching up her face, and throws the contents down her throat, immediately followed by the milk to cut the taste. "So bitter," she mutters, sliding herself under the blankets and wiping residual moisture from the dark circles under her eyes. Randall looks at the clock. 11:05.

He goes outside to the shed. Heavy gray, like the sky might open up any minute. Still he pulls out the mower. The old manual. Slow as it is, he prefers its tranquil quiet to the goddamn motor machine. Erma feels the modern model does a cleaner job and naturally will complain. Well. Not this time.

As Randall rolls the blades over the lawn, he deliberates on the suicide note. He imagines realistically she would use it as a final nag session regarding his general inadequacies as husband and provider. On the other hand the thousandth miscarriage would have more likely tipped her over the edge, maybe he should focus on her devastation in wanting so badly to be a mother and to have had the opportunity denied her yet again. But perhaps it would be most poignant if in her final moments she was at peace, forgiving all. He likes that. Erma the virtuous.

He finishes the job at 11:55. He'd promised himself he'd wait a full hour before he went back and checked. He smokes a cigarette and wonders if there's any bacon left. When ten minutes later a few raindrops quickly transform into a drenching thunderclapper, he calmly pushes the mower back into the shed and walks into the house, strolling up to the guestroom.

He stands staring at her, the rain beating hard against the windows. Her eyes are closed. She makes no sound, he notices no rise and fall of her chest. He sits in the chair.

I hope you're dead.

Then his lips move, mouthing it. *I hope you're dead.*

Then he whispers it. "I hope you're dead."

Then very much aloud so she would hear, if she could hear: "I hope. You're. *Dead.*"

A sudden ring and Randall leaps out of the chair. He fixes his eyes on her again, she who would come sprinting from down the street if she thought she heard their phone. Stillness. He imagines touching her, feeling her flesh cold. Hard. The phone rings ten times before stopping. He allows several moments of silence before placing his right hand on her chest. Warm, some faint beating. He's not sure what that means as he isn't certain how long these things are supposed to take. He walks to the kitchen to make breakfast.

Bacon and eggs and toast. He washes his meal down with beer, staring at the rain letting up. It's incredible to him, *miraculous* how quiet the house is. He glimpses something. Walks to the door, steps out. Double rainbow. Too bad Erma isn't here for it. These small joys of life meant a lot to her. Then the phone. After the eighth ring he sighs and goes inside.

"Hello?"

"Hel*lo!* Figured I called enough I'd catch ya, Randall. This here's Francis Veter."

Randall has to do some major sifting through his mind files before he comes up with it: his high school "fan" from the voter registration yesterday. The one who was so impressed with Randall's little performance at the school anti-integration back in September, the one who remembered Randall was the eighth-grade valedictorian, remembered Randall on the eighth-grade debate team. And still excited about it. These would be the kind of friends Randall attracts.

"Okay?"

"Listen. I don't mean to be in your business but I heard about you losin your job. That's a goddamn shame."

Randall imagines himself undressing unconscious Erma and carrying her naked body into a tub half full of water. How long would it take for her to naturally slip under, or would she need some help? Twenty minutes below the surface would certainly bring clarity to the present ambiguity of her existence.

"He*llo?*"

"Hi."

"Listen. I'm a manager out at Oldham's. You know, hardware."

"Uh-huh."

"We needin some help with the inventory in the immediate. Whaddya say?"

Randall's mouth falls open. For a dazed moment he pulls the receiver from his ear, staring at it as if it were playing a cruel trick on him.

"You offerin me a *job?*"

"Temporary for sure. But my boss come to like ya, good chance it go permanent."

He holds his breath. Luck? For *him?* "Oh. Oh I gotta tell ya, I been goin through a little bit of a bad time, this the firs kind thing I heard in days!"

"Happy to oblige! Toldja, you're my hero, Randall. Listen, I get off at three today. Might I take you out for a drink after?"

□ □

Eliot creeps to the Coatses' in the bright sun. They will have gone to work but no one around here locks doors. As he gets closer, a flood from the earlier monsoon materializes, in some places water halfway up his tires. His windows are open in the post-storm humidity so he hears, "Welcome to The Bowl."

A young neighbor woman smiling at him as she hangs her laundry. Her property is on a slight incline, so while her bare feet squish in the mud, she is otherwise protected from the newly formed pond.

"The dip out here. Floods practically every rain. You that voter registration lawyer, right?"

"One of them."

"I thought yaw went back North this mornin."

"Well." He tells her about Roy's death, and her smile fades. He'd stopped by Rosie's but no one was home.

"Hunter's on Clark Street." She sighs. "Only colored funerals in the county."

The office at Hunter's Funeral Home is just off the entrance parlor, so as soon as Eliot walks in, Beau and Rosie, seated and talking to the funeral director, see him.

"Got stuck in the rain?" Beau asks. Eliot nods. "I wondered."

"Well come on in," says Rosie. "We pickin out the casket. Maybe you got some thoughts."

It has only been seventeen days since he sat in their place next to Dwight making arrangements for his mother. Eliot is willing to offer any help he can, unhappily feeling experienced. But the elderly Negro director seems honest, and Rosie and Beau old hands at dealing with the loss of loved ones.

Eliot is not sure how word got around already, but by the time they walk through Rosie's door at two, several sympathy plates have been left on the kitchen table: baked chicken, pigs' feet, potato salad. Knowing she's about to become inundated with visitors, Rosie begins tidying up, accepting brother Beau's offer of assistance but refusing guest Eliot's. The younger gazes at the photographs on the living room wall, his eyes resting on one in particular—Roy in his sergeant's uniform, about as high a rank as a Negro could get. Eliot calculates that Roy's service was somewhere between the world wars. The U.S. occupation of Haiti? of the Dominican Republic? of Nicaragua? Or were his amputations some home-front mishap like his childhood friend Jeanine's uncle Ramonlee?

"Handsome, wa'n't he?" Eliot turns to see Rosie smiling beside him, her shining eyes on the portrait. Though it's only head and shoulders, the image gives the impression of a large, commanding presence tempered by forbearance.

People start coming around three. Eliot is just about to call the Coatses to let them know what's going on when the family walks through the door. After they pay their respects to Rosie and Beau, Martha walks up to him.

"Looks like we get our houseguest back sooner n we thought."

"If you don't mind."

"*Mind?* The ride over Leona tole me she got three new jokes she need to try out on you."

Twenty minutes later Eliot walks outside, gazing at the lowering afternoon sun in the autumn sky.

"So whatchu plannin on doin tonight?" Rosie suddenly beside him.

"Martha said I can stay with them again."

"Uh-huh. I was jus talkin to Martha. You know they live in The Bowl."

"I found that out earlier."

"So if the rain start up, you could get stuck there."

"It looks pretty clear now."

"Can change fass these parts. What I'm thinkin is maybe you should stay here. Then you be able to get out in the mornin, no matter."

Eliot glances into the crowded house. Earlier he'd overheard Rosie on the phone with far-flung relatives who would be arriving. Given that she refused to let him help clean earlier, he's pretty certain his presence would be just one more burden.

"Dontchu worry, we'll find a place for ya, even if it's on the floor a Beau's room. You don't mind the floor, do ya?"

"I don't. But the storm seems to have passed. I think I'll be fine at the Coatses."

"Well the invitation stands. If yaw get down the road an the rain starts, you can always turn aroun."

"Thank you."

"Course you always could jus stay another day. But I guess with the overnight drive that mean you wouldn't get to Indianapolis till late Friday, not back in your office till nex week."

"That's the problem."

"Awright," she sighs, "you all hardworkin people."

It's just past four when they get into their cars, Eliot to follow the Coatses. Leona is in the backseat but as soon as her grandparents are seated, she opens her door and runs to Eliot behind his wheel.

"Whaddya call a cat suckin on a lemon? A *sourpuss!*"

"That's a good one."

"Girl!" her grandmother calls. "Get in this car!"

Leona runs back. The Coatses pull out, and just before Eliot follows suit he glimpses through the picture window Beau and Rosie among the throng, the siblings holding up but their faces swathed in exhaustion and sorrow. He wonders what Beau must be thinking, having not seen Rosie and Roy in twenty-four years and within twenty-four hours of reuniting with them, this: death. Does he feel he brought bad luck? Or was it on the contrary a divine blessing—that he was able to see Roy one last time, that the brother Rosie adored was here for her in her hour of greatest need. Eliot is certain the latter is what Rosie is telling her guests, and what she believes.

◻ ◻

Randall's bad mood is somewhat mitigated by the job offer. Still, the more he thinks about the events of yesterday—Benja's battered face, Benja and his mother nagging him in the hospital, the uncaring cop outside her room, the humiliation of B.J. having to rescue him from Benja's bastard husband, the humiliation of getting fired, the humiliation of jail, the humiliation of his humiliated wife calling the jail—the more beer he consumes.

He's supposed to meet Francis Veter at the bar at four, so at 3:30 he heads up to the guestroom. He thinks she may have moved slightly from her previous position but he isn't certain. He touches her chest. Her heartbeat seems remotely stronger. He walks down to the kitchen, fills a pitcher with water. Back up, standing over her again, he sticks a couple of fingers into the water and flicks the drops at her eyes. She remains still as stone. He flicks more. Nothing. He takes the jug and pitches its entire contents into her face, soaking her hair, pillow. Now a stir, a little coughing. So she survived. He's neither especially relieved nor disappointed. Well, tomorrow he'd probably realize he wasn't quite ready for widowerhood anyway, tomorrow the anger would dissipate and he'd be back to his usual state of being: ennui. He descends the stairs and out the door.

He walks into the tavern five minutes early. Francis Veter, sitting on a barstool facing the entrance, holds up his drink. "Hello, Randall Evans!"

Randall stares at the gold rim of the shot glass in front of him. Francis Veter has been chattering nonstop since he arrived.

"They musta been outa their fuckin minds! They really think jus cuz they gather theirselves up in droves, suddenly we gonna say, 'Oh in *that* case you *can* vote!'" Francis Veter laughs.

"You figure the job gonna be effective immediate?"

"Oh it's effective immediate. Seein em all lined up like that, I didn't know there was so many aroun here. Whatta ya call em? Flock? Herd? A bevy. A bevy a niggers!"

"So I start tomarra?"

"Tomarra I'm off, an since I gotta bring ya in, introduce ya, it'd be nex day, Thursday, Thursday you can start. Sound good?"

"Sounds great." Randall lifts his glass and downs it. The place is half full, the jukebox asserting *Every puppy has his day, Everybody has to pay, Everybody has to meet his Waterloo.*

"Strickly inventory."

"Mostly inventory. But you also might be called on to do a little a this, little a that."

"Uh-huh."

"Looks like you empty there. Pour him another!"

"Listen. I ain't s'good with sales."

"This ain't shoes, Randall, it's hardware. Somebody come in to buy a Philips screwdriver he *needs* a Philips screwdriver. Ain't no sales pitchin involved."

"Okay."

"Somebody come in to buy 16d nails it's cuz they need 16d nails."

"You know Martin's ain't gonna gimme no good recommendation."

"*I'm* givin ya a good recommendation an I am definitely an employee in good standin. Awright?"

"Awright." Randall relaxes. "Thank ya. Thank ya!"

The door opens and in walk twins. Randall's vision has started to become impaired but he didn't know he'd already graduated to seeing double.

"Over here!" Francis Veter grinning. "These are my nephews. This one's Reggie, that's Louis. Twenty and nineteen."

"Hi," they say in unison. Blond and blonder.

"This is Mr. Evans. Member I toldja bout Mr. Evans?'

"Uh-huh."

"There, have a seat. Told yaw, drinks on me." The only two seats left at the bar are on the other side of Randall, and the boys take them. "My sister's boys, in town a couple weeks. Helpin me build a pool out back."

"Uncle Francis pays nice," says one of them.

Francis Veter laughs. "Well."

Randall stares at the boys. He turns to Francis Veter. "Pool?"

"Oh yeah. Cool things off in the summer."

"That ain't a cheap proposition."

Francis Veter laughs. "Well." Francis Veter is not a guffawer. His gentle chuckles seem to be half for the listener, and half some private internal narrative.

"I take it you boys is twenty-one," says the bartender. He's brought their drinks so it doesn't seem to matter much to him, but the nephews scramble to pull out their fake driver's licenses.

"I got seven kids an I'll definitely be bringin in a little slave labor on that account," Francis Veter laughs. "But the oldest is only eleven, they can only do so much."

"Edna Jo told us she's goin to Catholic school."

"Uh-huh. Well, St. Mary's, I think they get a better education there. So once they reach the seventh grade, that was always the plan. *Double* the plan now, I sure ain't havin my girls go through puberty sittin next to some lecherous nigger."

"I *hate* em," says the blonder boy, his eyes suddenly glowering. "Stinkin, nappy niggers."

"Yeah," says the other.

"They got their own schools!" says the first. "Well I guess they figure how much learnin's a nigger get if his teacher's a nigger. But how much learnin they need anyway? To be a maid. Shine goddamn shoes."

"Yeah!"

"Ain't Catholic school expensive?" Randall asks Francis Veter. "If you ain't Catholic. I'm guessin you're not."

"Not as expensive as havin one a my girls come home with some black bun in the oven."

Out of the blue flash-crash, everything going dark, silent. Then the downpour, and a few moments later the lights pop back on. The patrons laugh, like God was just pulling their leg there.

"But you said you planned it before. You were all set to send your kids to the Catholic before the colored invasion."

"Like I said. Good education."

"Why you plan that? Why they need such a fine education?" Francis Veter looks at him, and Randall's voice hollows as he continues his train of thought. "College?" Francis Veter smiles.

"You know what they'd read in our schools?" says Blonder. "'Othello was a nigger.' Hemingway wrote that. 'Othello was a nigger!'" Both boys crack up.

"Who's Hemingway?" says Less Blond.

"You said you mentioned me to your boss?" Randall asks Francis Veter.

"Boss?" gasps the Othello-was-a-nigger one.

"It's all taken care of, Randall, you got nothin to worry about."

Uncle Francis pays nice.

"Lemme ask you somethin. You *own* the hardware store?"

Francis Veter laughs. "Well."

"We can order another, Uncle Francis?"

"Go on."

"Whyn't you jus tell me?"

"Oh. I guess I didn't know if you'd feel funny about it."

"Why? Cuz *I* don't own a hardware store?"

"Well you was the smart one. An anyway. I didn't wantchu to think it was charity."

"Is it?"

"You need a job, Randall, I need a worker, I don't call that charity."

"Cuz the thing is. The only reason I got that shoe store job was connections. Klan connections, an you see how well *that* panned out."

"You ain't no damn salesman! *I'm* hirin you for what you can do. That you an I also have a philosophical meetin a minds, that's just a plus."

"Well I ain't that interested in the Klan no more. I ain't been to a meetin in I don't know when an can't say ever was a time I was a member in good standin."

"You were at the high school an the voter registration. Far as I'm concerned that speaks a lot louder n just a lotta hogwash secret societin without no action behind it."

Randall doesn't believe it. Every time he thinks his luck might finally be turning around it just transforms into some new backhanded degradation. He'd thought this Francis Veter might have been the *one* person not looking down on him.

"Hey Randall."

"I want the job. I appreciate the offer, I need the job, I want the job." Francis Veter smiles and holds out his hand. They shake.

"I'm glad. I know you don't like to hear this, but I always admired ya. Means a lot to have someone I respect in my employ."

"Hey, Uncle Francis, Grandaddy ever show you that nigger ear?" The boys start giggling.

"What chaw laughin about."

"When we was over there this summer he takes out this little black hard thing claims it's a nigger ear."

"You think it ain't true?"

"I think Grandaddy's full of it."

"Me too."

Here he goes, plunging into some new enterprise. Well he didn't have much choice in the matter, he needs a blamed job. And he sees Martin's face, his goddamn superior attitude, the day he took Randall aside to show him the graph chart, like his poor salesmanship made him less a man. *I'll kill that son of a bitch.* Randall throws back the shot and slams the glass down. "Another."

"Those days they chartered trains for the events."

"No!"

"Course his family couldn't afford that, eleven kids. Still, they had the horse an the wagon."

"Horse an the wagon!" The boys squealing.

"Thousands. My daddy's family in the back but little as he was, he remembers. The cryin out a the big ape coward as they're dippin him in an outa the fire. His daddy had to pay a pretty penny, but bought every one a his sons somethin. Course their sisters disappointed they got no souvenirs. My uncles given chips a the kidney or intestine, but that charcoal ear my daddy got. *That* was the prize."

He sees Aaron kicking the shit out of Benja, their kids staring wild-eyed. One of the little boys trying to help his mother, and his daddy hurling him aside, punching Benja in the face, punching Benja till she's out, dead for all he knew. *I'll kill that goddamn bastard.* Randall throws back the shot and slams the glass down. "Another."

"Uncle Francis, we ever tell you bout that nigger we knocked out cold?"

"What?" Francis Veter smiles.

"Some outa-town nigger, I don't know what his business was, all in this fancy suit. So he got out his car, lookin aroun all perplexed. An me an Louis seen him, I whisper the plan. Louis go up to him, 'You lost? I help ya?' An he ask Louis for directions, and Louis give em to him, an he smile all grateful, then I come up from behind. 'Hello.' He turn aroun confused *Pow!* I sock him, he lyin on the ground out, one blow! Then all the kids comin up, 'What's that nigger doin on the ground?' When he come to he look at us scared, then stagger on back to his car." The three of them hooting, slapping their thighs. "Wonder he ever found where he was goin? Louis give him some good directions."

He sees that nigger lawyer, thinking he's bringing all his precious generosity to the poor white charity case, his shoes, his goddamn *used* medium-quality shoes. And his *arrogance* to just toss his head in Randall's direction, *I brought these in case some Negro needed em, but then.* In the blur Randall needs to bring the glass close to his eyes before aiming for his mouth, *I'll kill that black nigger.* He throws back the shot and slams the glass down. "Another."

Francis Veter slips off the barstool and swings the outside door open wide. The pounding shower, everyone in the establishment turning to it except Randall. "God I love the smell a the rain!" Francis Veter turns back to his party. "Yaw want somethin to eat?"

"Yeah!" But Randall hears neither the question nor the nephews' enthusiastic response, throwing back his shot and slamming the glass down. "Another."

"No other. I got this," Francis Veter tells the bartender, pulling out his wallet. "Come on, Randall, we need to put some substance in our bellies fore we come staggerin home, have the wives shoot us." Randall tries to stand but has considerable trouble. Francis Veter laughs and gives him a hand. "This is exactly why I planned on takin off tomarra. Well, guess your wife won't be too miffed once you tell her boutcher new gainful employment." They move toward the door, Francis Veter's arm around an unsteady Randall. "We got the whole night together, buddy," and they walk out into the dusk.

During the drive back to the Coatses', Eliot's mind drifts to the little boys. He and Diana and Steven had immediately petitioned for an appeal and are awaiting a reply. They're quite hopeful their request will be granted, and if not are ready to petition to higher courts until it is. Meanwhile little Max and Jordan have remained incarcerated, and it sickens him to imagine the horrors they may be undergoing even at this very moment. It's been over a month since the hearing. How'd that *happen?* He sighs, anxious to get back to his files in the office Friday.

They walk into the house, Martha heading straight to the kitchen to prepare dinner. Eliot and Jeremiah sit in the living room, lost in their own thoughts. When Leona keeps chattily interrupting these meditations, her grandmother comes to the doorway, softly instructing her to come help with supper, and the girl grudgingly obeys. Eliot hears Martha murmuring that when someone dies you have to respect other people's quiet, and after that only cooking sounds emanate from the kitchen. Without looking at Eliot, Jeremiah remarks, "Sure wish we coulda met Roy."

"I only met him briefly. He seemed like a very nice man."

And Eliot remembers that he forgot to call about Mr. Yancey. The voter registration, the elder's arrest and beating in police custody—hard to believe it all had happened just yesterday. This reminds him about the other call, to the car owner about the delayed return of the borrowed vehicle. Eliot asks Jeremiah if he might use their telephone, attached to the kitchen wall.

Eliot contacts Warren, the local NAACP rep, to ascertain the gentleman's condition. He is relieved to learn that Mr. Yancey has improved and is expected to be released from the hospital in two to three days. Just as he is dialing the second number, the sky abruptly darkens, and a streak crashes loud followed immediately by a cloudburst, leaving the house in darkness, the phone dead. Jeremiah comes out to the kitchen. "Gonna flood. Might clear up by mornin, might not. You absolutely welcome to stay with us, but goin on 5:30. If you plannin on travelin back to Rosie's tonight, you gotta leave now, before dark."

As Eliot grabs his suitcase, Jeremiah says, "Soon's you get outa Prayer Ridge might be all clear. Our weather got nothin to do with Nathan's."

"Wish I could call Rosie, let em know to expect ya," says Martha, handing

Eliot a bowl of chicken she just fried. "We seem to get the phone knocked out every storm, might last a hour, might last a week." She sighs. "Oh well, be a pleasant surprise. I could tell she really wanted you to stay."

Low beams in the blinding rain, Eliot drives through the fresh flood in The Bowl, then moves slowly through the shallow mud road, intermittently slick. Gradually the sheets moderate to a drizzle. Eliot remembers how much he enjoyed occasional floods as a child, having never experienced a devastating one. Sneaking out into the new river in the street before his mother caught him, the squishing of his loafers, the cool between his toes.

□ □

Randall's old Chevy truck is parked across the small lot from Francis Veter's new Ford. In the downpour, the boys run to get in the bed of their uncle's vehicle, covering themselves in a large piece of blue tarpaulin. After Randall tries thrice unsuccessfully to put his key into his lock, Francis Veter leads him to the passenger side of the Ford.

"You ain't gettin behine *no* wheel till you start seein one key steada three."

Francis Veter drives to the Chik 2 Go and orders two buckets of barbecued wings, two coffees, and two Coca-Colas. The rain lets up and he pulls over, everyone sitting in the back of the truck. Around them are a multitude of bricks tied with rope, shovels, buckets, and trowels, as well as assorted bottles of alcohol: six-packs of beer and Jack Daniel's.

"Mention I'm buildin a outdoor grill beside the pool?" says Francis Veter by way of explanation. Other than that they eat in silence till Blonder says, "I gotta piss," then the other, "Me too." They go off into the nearby weeds.

"I'll be doin that soon myself," says Randall, "but I won't be needin me no buddy."

Francis Veter laughs. "I could never figure you out, Randall."

Randall drops a wing on his pants. He picks it up, wipes up the red-orange sauce with his finger, licks his finger, then goes back to eating.

"Tonight's been kinda your job interview."

"Has it."

"Well, jus to see if we got along."

Randall takes a rest from the gluttony, leaning back against the truck side. He hadn't realized he was so hungry.

"I always wondered why you didn't go on to high school. College."

"Sometimes we don't get to choose, the choice come to us ready made."

"Oh yeah, your daddy. That was a shame."

"Say how come you know so much about me?"

"I don't know. Guess in school I always looked up to the smart ones." He laughs. "An then to see ya when we was kids at the Klan rally, an, what? Month later at the debate? I jus thought you was goin places."

Randall sighs and looks into the distance. Getting real goddamn sober.

"I ain't no stalker," Francis Veter laughs, "an I ain't no pervert. My wife an me was high school sweethearts an still is. Before her there was a couple rolls in the hay with my cousin Vickie Jean. Only one marriage infraction, long ago, barmaid out in Wally so jus to be clear, my taste is strickly toward the female gender. But, like I said, my admiration for the ones got a head on their shoulders. An every so often I'd wonder about that debate kid, did he ever amount to anything. Then I see you at the school demonstration. Yep. He damn sure did."

"Can we go now, Uncle Francis?" The boys returning. "We're ready to go."

"Yeah!"

Randall sips his coffee. "Guess I'm ready too, wife be wondrin. Soon's I piss."

"Tell ya what. Gimme half-hour more? I made a promise to the boys to take em out along the road there for a minute."

Randall pees in the weeds. Dark falling, be just his luck to discover later this fine flora was poison ivy. He looks at the truck in the distance, the three standing around it. He'd like to walk away. The alcohol's got him yearning for his bed, and this Francis Veter's odd. Then again why's he so damn suspicious that someone actually admires him. Martin hired him but had him on probation from the beginning and never let him off. This job on the other hand, this position with someone who trusts him from the get-go. He zips his fly.

"Just a half-hour. Right?"

Francis Veter grins. "Glad you comin along, Randall, glad you made that choice." He laughs. "See, guess we disagree a bit. You said some choices come ready made. Well, true, you *was* a kid when your daddy passed, but by the time we adults I feel choices ain't just handed to us, I believe we always got some say in the matter."

"I hope we get a rabbit!" says one of them.

"Or a squirrel!"

"Night huntin. Ever done it?" Randall, who has done no hunting, shakes his head. "This eerie quality. You the hunter but you can't see, gotta go by sound. Then: whites a the eyes." The boys have pulled out rifles. "Don't worry," their uncle chuckles, "I had it in mind all along to invite ya, brung you a shotgun too."

"Or a polecat!" the less blond boy says. The brothers crack their rifles, and load them.

□ □

Seven miles outside town, halfway between Prayer Ridge and Nathan, the sky has completely cleared but to be safe Eliot continues driving slowly on the damp road. It will add ten minutes to his half-hour drive so he'll pull into Rosie's just at nightfall.

Eliot had loathed the racist reasoning in Steven's summation, yet he presumed it would have had some impact on that cracker judge. It seems the defense team had vastly underestimated the depth of the bench's bigoted resolve, to be willing without batting an eyelash to maintain this vicious severance of two little boys from all their loved ones in order to teach them, and by proxy all colored children, some lesson in the sacred Southern Code of Ethics. When it was all over, Eliot had wondered whether he had made a fatal mistake that last night in Diana's basement by not even bringing to the table the notes he'd been scribbling in the corner. What if, the judge would have been queried, every teacher in every school who caught students kissing be placed under legal obligation to report the incident as an attempted rape to the authorities? Little Jordan had testified that his kissing playmate Ginny Dodgson was just imitating her big brother Beeber and his girlfriend. Shouldn't then Beeber be arrested? Charged with a felony? At the time Eliot had capitulated to Steven, and while he didn't regret that choice per se, he wonders now whether Steven's argument might have been fortified by Eliot's notions.

A tan cat out of nowhere and he swerves wildly in the suddenly slick mud to miss it. The car flips three times off the road before landing upside down in the weeds. He pants heavily, and it takes a few minutes before it registers that he's not dead. The windshield is shattered, sprayed in blood. Eliot's right leg is stuck between crushed metal, and after several attempts he manages to extricate it. He punches out what glass is left in the side window and pulls himself through. Outside, he endeavors three times to stand and three times falls, the leg broken. Can he crawl the six miles to Rosie's? His breath is fast, he tries to calm down, to think. He's landed in a large grassy clearing, thick woods twenty yards to his right, the road thirty yards to the left. That he can see it so clearly, even with dusk settling quickly, leads him to deduce that, miraculously, his glasses are still intact and on his face. The feline is nowhere in view so he assumes it survived. That cat looked just like Parker, he muses.

◘ ◘

In the truck bed, the boys pass a bottle of Jack between them. Randall, sleepy, stares at the stars. He notices clouds returning in the distance.

"Guess you detected one's the leader, one's the follower," says Francis Veter. "Well the oldest is the follower! That Louis. If he walkin in the shadow of his little brother in the *family,* what that say bout the way he deals with the *resta* the world?"

Randall is feeling a little sick about what happened this morning. Erma's a goddamn nag but Jesus Christ she doesn't deserve the death penalty for it. What's *wrong* with him?

"*Or a polecat,* blamed idiot! Louis don't even know polecat's a skunk! I like this song!" Francis Veter turns up the radio.

> *As their hands touched and their lips met*
> *The ragin river pulled them down*
> *Now they'll always be together*
> *In that happy huntin ground*

"Well that's between my sister an her husband. Spose the boy's just slow. Then, guess you was kinda the older brother in your family too? The other deaf?"

His goddamn brother-in-law's who he *should* be killing! And Aaron only the first in line. Randall swigs his beer.

"Barely a sliver of a moon and that gettin clouded out, won't be able to see our hans fronta our face. Good night huntin!" Francis Veter bangs the heels of his hands on the steering wheel in time with the music. "Hey Randall, you ever think about fate? Like maybe there's some divine reason I run into you yesterday at the nigger voter registration? Wa'n't jus chance. I mean you happnin to need a job an me needin to hire Oh my God."

Randall turns to look where Francis Veter is staring. Off the side of the road, a station wagon lies upside down. Francis Veter pulls over. He grabs his flashlight and gets out, followed by Randall and the boys, the latter still holding their shotguns. They walk to the car, Francis Veter inspecting the exterior, holding the light over the license plate for several seconds, then thoroughly examining the inside. "Blood," he mutters needlessly. He shines the light around the nearby weeds. The boys walk around investigating the vehicle, and in glimpses from the intermittent flashlight beam Randall perceives a contained excitement in their smiles. He turns to Francis Veter and sees that the uncle is grinning, illuminating the near distance. Randall's eyes follow the light.

An injured man. A smallish man like Randall, though slimmer, lying in high weeds. Randall has the darkness and his alcohol content against him, but from what he gleans the man appears to be a Negro. And something in the twinkle of Francis Veter's eye confirms this.

"Come on," says Randall's future employer. "I think we're the rescue party."

□ □

Eliot had dragged himself into taller grasses so as to remain hidden. As soon as Martha's phone is fixed she'll call Rosie, and when they realize Eliot never made it someone will come looking for him. They'll see the car, come to the car, and he'll call them. He hoped anyone else who might notice the vehicle, anyone who he might *not* want to find him, would assume the driver must have been rescued or was able to walk away.

Eliot feels tired, and he's heard that falling asleep is dangerous for someone with a concussion, which he may have. He needs to stay awake, he concentrates on the fireflies. Zillions of fireflies. When he and Dwight were kids, they saw a cartoon at the movies about a firefly.

Light. Bright in his eyes.

"Hey buddy. How's it goin?"

They stand looking at him, on all sides of him. The light is blinding. When it momentarily flashes beyond his face, he glimpses them. White men. One. Two. Three. Four.

"Hey." The tallest, dark brown hair. He stoops, close to Eliot. "Seem like you had a little trouble over there."

Two are younger. Blond teenagers. Skinny, almost tall as the brown hair. They grin. There's another, shorter, but he's beyond the light, Eliot can't make him out.

Not *all* Southern white men. Diana's father would help you. Steven would help you, *don't panic*. With considerable effort, he manages to pull himself up onto his elbows. "I was just. I was driving along the road and—" He laughs. "This cat. This cat, I swerved." He laughs, and catches his breath.

"Aw, that's so kinda you. Ain't he a Good Samaritan, boys?"

"Oh yeah," says one of them.

"Sound like you traveled a long way just to save that cat." Eliot stares at him, confused. "Your car say Alabama plates, but I don't hear nothin but North in your voice."

"Oh no I was." Eliot stops.

"What was that?"

Eliot considers how to answer. "I—" He hopes something will follow but it doesn't.

"Cuz no sense tryin to pull my leg, I know you ain't nowheres near local. And I am just very curious what a Northern colored gentleman like yourself's doin all the hell way down in Bamy."

"Funeral." A whisper.

"Sorry, didn't quite catch that?" The man cups his palm around his ear. Scent of whiskey.

"I'm here. For a funeral."

"He's says he's here for a funeral," the man reports to the others.

"I like his glasses," says one of the young men.

"Yeah," says the other.

"Well who died?" asks Brown Hair. "Some little colored boy run aroun the tree an turn to butter?"

"That ain't how the story goes, Uncle Francis!" Giggling.

"Well how's it go?"

"The *tiger* turns to butter. An the mammy uses the tiger butter for her pancakes."

"Oh yeah! I always did mix that story up. The mammy. Aunt Jemima."

"No!" The blonds cracking up. In the moving light, Eliot finally glimpses the smaller man. Older like the tall one, reddish-blond hair. He doesn't smile.

"Well too bad that cat didn't stick by ya," says the dark one. "Ya look s' sad out here by your lonesome, good thing we come along."

"Oh my friends are coming for me."

"Your *friends* comin for ya? Huh. Ya know, friend, that seems highly unlikely given what kinda predicament you done found yourself in. I mean, I don't see no phone booth you coulda called your friends from."

"They were here. They're coming back."

The big man laughs softly. "Son, you are a *bad* liar," gently tapping Eliot on the nose with his whiskey bottle, a teacher affectionately scolding a naughty child.

○ ○

Randall racks his alcohol-saturated brain. He sure does sound Northern but he knows he's seen this one before. He stoops to wipe some of the blood from the Negro's face with his fingertips. The initial touch terrifies the injured man, sending him into convulsions. Randall, startled, snatches his hand back. Francis Veter and his nephews howl, delighted.

"Do that again, Randall," says Francis Veter, as if Randall had pushed some button that had activated a mechanical toy.

○ ○

Calm down. Take a breath, this is not as bad as it looks. The short one, the one who touched his cheek, who stares at him. Something familiar. Eliot sees no kindness in this one's face, but neither the foreboding he senses from the others.

"Well listen. This is *my* friend, an these're my nephews. We was jus gonna do a little night huntin when we come upon your automobile over there. Ain't that lucky? This road can get deserted, you mighta been here all night alone we hadn't happened by. Your prayers been answered, boy. Whatta ya thinka that?"

Eliot starts to speak but is surprised by the taste of blood. Yet his mouth feels dry. He opens it. Nothing comes out. Again. Nothing.

"He looks like a feesh," says a young one, then shuts his eyes and begins opening and closing his mouth fish-like, placing his hands against his torso sides and moving them: fins.

▢ ▢

"Look at his suit." Reggie grins. Since Francis Veter identified him as the leader, Randall has been better able to tell them apart. "What's a nigger doin in a suit like that?"

"Prolly some Yankee N-A-A-C-P," replies his uncle. "Or a goddamn lawyer. *Or* a N-A-A-C-P lawyer. You a N-A-A-C-P lawyer, boy?"

"Yeah. The National Association for the Advancement a Coon People!" says Reggie.

"Yeah!" says Louis. Then frowns. "I gotta piss again."

"The Nigger Association for the Advancement a Coon People! No! The Nigger Association for the—" Reggie is stumped, trying to come up with a better *A*.

"I gotta piss, Reggie."

"Me too," says Reggie, unzipping his fly. "An he looks thirsty. You thirsty, coon?"

▢ ▢

Eliot closes his mouth, closes his eyes, and still it burns, he tastes it. He thinks, I can't believe this is happening to me, I can't believe this is happening to me. Why? Did he think an education would protect him? A loving family? A job he thinks is important?

He's a lawyer, *Where's his reasoning?*

They would be patriots. They would respect a soldier.

"The funeral. He was a veteran. He lost his legs in combat," and Eliot is instantly flooded with shame to have desecrated Roy's memory by bringing him up to these. To these.

"He ain't had no legs?" one of the young ones says. "Well how'd he get aroun?"

"Like one a those monkeys on the *National Geographic*," says the other, and stoops, making chimp sounds, putting his hands on the ground and hopping his legs through. The other imitates this, the two of them moving rapidly around Eliot in opposite directions, concentric circles.

◻ ◻

"Well whaddya think?" Francis Veter is grinning at Randall, the chimp-boys circling. "Will it live?"

Randall looks at Francis Veter, then turns to the Negro, giving the question a few seconds' serious consideration. The Negro's eyes fix on Randall, the Negro's face mildly quivering. "Sure. Get him to the colored hospital, nothin but a few broken bones."

"Thank you, Dr. Evans." Francis Veter swigs, then hurls his bottle, *crash*. "An now, for a second opinion." Francis Veter lifts his right knee and brings his boot down hard on the Negro's face, smashing his glasses into his eyes, before proceeding to kick the shit out of him. The nephews whoop it up. Suddenly the Negro grabs Francis Veter's leg, tripping the man, causing him to fall.

"You ugly black ape!" says Reggie, then he and Louis are on him, their boots and their fists, and Francis Veter, after he gets up, kicking harder than ever. Although Louis follows his younger brother's lead in the bashing, a vague competitive spirit seems to have been unleashed as he tries to land every blow more violently than Reggie, who in turn one-ups Louis with the next wallop. The strikes are coming so quickly now and from so many different directions the confused Negro can no longer protect himself, let alone fight back, his body flung wildly to and fro. Eventually Francis Veter steps out of the pummeling, lighting a cigarette, to allow more space for the boys. A few of the Negro's teeth fly surprisingly high into the air.

◻ ◻

The woods flash by, the road flash by, the car flash by, another bone: *crack*. Eliot stops trying to fight it, he relaxes, calm. When this is over he will have to have his broken arm set into a cast. He will have to go to a nephrologist and see about the damage to his kidneys, he will have to call Diana and Steven to share his thoughts about the appeal, do they have any new ideas? He will have to find those teeth and bring them to a dentist to put them back.

▫ ▫

Francis Veter studies the Negro, his mouth twisted to the side as if calculating what to do next. His nephews, exhausted, have taken a break from the beating. "Boys. Go back to the truck and bring those bricks."

"Okay!" They run off. The Negro has landed on his back, his face turned away from the two white men. Francis Veter stoops, turns the Negro's chin so that they are looking at each other. Copious blood on the face, one eye swollen shut.

"I bet you're thinkin you shoulda jus run over that damn cat." Francis Veter laughs. The Negro pants heavily.

"You don't like this, do ya." Francis Veter's eyes still on the Negro. Then he looks at Randall.

"*Me?*"

"You don't seem to be enjoyin yourself."

"Well you asked my opinion an I said get him to the hospital but since you ignored that, guess my opinion don't count."

Francis Veter laughs, turns back to the Negro.

"I'm takin him to the hospital."

"Long way to the nigger facility."

"I'm takin him."

"Go on."

Randall stares at him. "It'd mean drivin your truck."

"Naturally. Jus promise to come back for us later."

"I understand this means I flunked the job interview."

"Naw, you passed the interview." He is smiling, stands and turns to him. "I didn't plan on us runnin acrost this nigger, Randall, it jus happened. Tell ya the truth, I'm sprised a man intelligent as you are's still here. When I saw you at that rally when we was young, I jus took regular interest cuz you was another kid. What happened was. That debate. Damn! he ain't no dummy. Smart, an no hypocrite. I *hate* the professional men, support the Klan in finance but not want their name on it. Mosta the doctors and lawyers jus fine with what we got here, long's they never get their own hans dirty. Bloody."

"As you know I ain't no professional man, nor a Klan regular."

Francis Veter laughs. "Look at that."

The Negro on his back has subtly moved himself a couple of yards away. Francis Veter walks to stand over him. The Negro seems to have no idea Francis Veter is there until he tries to move again and the top of his head is blocked by Francis Veter's boots. Francis Veter smiles, he and the Negro facing each other upside down. "Ain'tchu cute. Thinkin jus Randall an me here talkin, you could crawl away we wouldn't notice." Francis Veter shakes his head. "You're the guest a honor." He places his boot on the Negro's face, holding him in place without putting any weight on it. "Well you *should*a been a professional. Like this nigger in his fine suit." He speaks softer. "I hate em worst than you do, I guess. Wish we was clear of em, wish the country give back to the white man. But spose that ain't gonna happen so at the very least I'd like to maintain the segregation a the species."

"We got em, Uncle Francis!" The boys have brought the bricks tied with rope. They each hold a freshly opened bottle of Jack.

"I think Mr. Evans would like to take our friend to the hospital."

"*What!*"

"I respect his input an I wantchu to respect it too, so shut up."

Randall looks at them, then looks at the man on the ground, who seems to be staring back at Randall. Hyperventilating, his leg twisted into some insane position, face swollen, How the hell'd it happen? One second Francis Veter and his nephews were playing around, the next they went nuts. He walks over, stoops next to the Negro. Randall takes a breath, then hoists the body over his shoulder. The Negro lets out a great moan of pain, then falls back to panting. Randall starts moving toward the truck. The Negro is heavy. As Randall plods further away from the others his path becomes darker, only the residual light from Francis Veter's flashlight. Then Francis Veter clicks the light off. Randall gropes in the utter blackness for several steps then down, he slips in the mud and falls with a thud, dropping the Negro who emits another moan of anguish. Randall sits up and tries lifting the burden while getting himself back up to standing, but keeps slipping, falling flat out as if he were on ice. The light clicks back on, spotlighting his clumsiness momentarily and Randall sits up catching his breath, gathering his strength and his wits to try again when the boys come running and laughing, Francis Veter strolling behind. He slaps Randall on the back.

"Knew ya couldn't do it!" The Negro is slumped in an odd position, trying to move himself. Reggie harshly throws him onto his back, again eliciting an agonizing groan. The brothers stoop on either side of the supine man, grinning into his face. Francis Veter lowers his voice. "If you prefer, go on back to the truck, Randall. We'll be done here in a little while."

"This little piggie went to market." The Negro screams. "This little piggie stayed home."

Reggie has a knife, and with each piggie he slices off another of the Negro's fingers. The process takes a while with each digit as it's not a clean slice, Reggie needing to saw through. Louis places his knees on the Negro's shoulders, the boy's weight keeping him in place. With Reggie holding his hand, Randall registers the odd image of a manicure, and something snaps, the lunacy of it all, and Randall the consummate failure trying to be all heroic and here a damn slip in the mud foils that, his grand rescue effort turning into some Three Stooges shtick and Randall starts laughing uncontrollably, holding his stomach and his companions join in, everyone sidesplitting which makes Reggie's little amputations sloppier. When he's finally finished with the right hand, he puts the fingers into his front dungaree pocket and hands the knife to his brother to start the left.

"Naw," says Francis Veter, walking over. "That's too goddamn redundant." The uncle takes the knife, holds it up to the Negro's eyes, then begins to slowly unzip the Negro's pants. The Negro's scream is bloodcurdling, his entire body shuddering so violently that it seems he will fly out of there. Francis Veter takes his time slicing off the left testicle, his eyes on the Negro's petrified face the entire time. Randall is frozen, chalk white. The boys display a pulling-the-light-out-of-the-firefly glee on their faces, though sporadically wincing, unconsciously taking their hands to protect their own genitals. Then, suddenly, the shrieking Negro is silent, falling slowly into a stillness. Francis Veter frowns. "Oh no ya don't," he says softly. He takes his fingers, trying to force the Negro's eye open. Then gently slaps the Negro's cheek. When there is no response he waves Reggie over, takes the boy's bottle and begins to pour it, a steady stream, onto the Negro's face. Finally his eyelid, heavy, slowly rises. Francis Veter smiles. "There ya go. You gonna stay conscious for us. Hear?"

○ ▢

Eliot remembers the lynching photos men laughing men grin, kill The men grin at Eliot. The white men, white faces one two three four want my mama. Eliot has one eye, Mr. Daughtery had one eye, Cyclops, Eliot sees blood, the woods red, grass red sky Where's my mama? the man. Eliot remembers the man from jail he gave him shoes, Mr. Daughtery in his wheelchair Eliot gets his wheelchair, Eliot will live Eliot will roll on his cart like Roy How was school today, jumpin bean? A-plus! A-plus! A-plus *I don't wanna die*

○ ▢

"Aw look at him," says Francis Veter. He tenderly touches the tears rolling down the Negro's face. The Negro is trying to catch his breath, short breaths. "What. You fraid a dyin all alone without your family an friends? Well that's why you gotta think of us as your friends, buddy. Cuz we gonna stick by ya, right till the end."

In seventh grade, Mrs. Robbins brought in a wooden skeleton complete with organs. Randall looks at the Negro and imagines the skeleton model but with the leg and arm bones in pieces, several ribs crushed to powder, the kidneys and intestines mangled, skull busted, brain mashed. Randall got A's in anatomy Randall should have been a doctor.

A Buick driving by on the road. Francis Veter clicks off the flashlight. The car slows, having noticed the overturned vehicle. It pulls over. A white man gets out of the driver's seat. White family. The father stands staring, hands on his hips. Francis Veter sets down his flashlight and starts to walk over, followed by his nephews. In the distance Randall can see the man backing up at the sight of them appearing out of the darkness. Francis Veter waves, friendly. An owl hoots.

"Listen you." Randall grabs the back of the Negro's head, brings his face close. "You know me?" Randall picks up the flashlight, illuminating their features. "I seen you before. Where?"

The Negro's lips move. Nothing comes out.

"They gonna kill ya." Randall sighs. "They gonna kill ya, I see that now, they gonna kill ya nothin you can do *nothin*. Jus say your name. Say your name so's we know how to mark your grave."

The Negro's lips move, no sound. Then Randall catches a glimmer near by. Puddle. A cry escapes Randall: the mercy of it. He gently lets the Negro's head down, rolling his face into the shallow pool. The Negro tries to move but can't. Bubbles. Then gradually less bubbles. In the distance the car drives away. The bubbles are gone. Randall exhales. It's over. He remembers a spring day when he was little, walking through the woods with B.J. and finding a dead bird, anonymous as the body before him now. The Evans brothers had buried the creature, Randall had said a prayer, and now he and Francis Veter and his nephews would bury the Negro and Randall would say a prayer, Wasn't there a shovel in the back of Francis Veter's truck? Relief, even joy, Randall feels it, for himself, for the soul before him at last released from his misery.

And with an enormous heave the Negro flips himself out of the puddle, coughing.

Randall gawks. He didn't drown. Randall can't believe it. He didn't drown! By the grace of God he'd been offered a compassionate death and instead he saves himself. For what. More *torture?* Blamed *fool!* Goddamn fool nigger!

"*Well,*" says Francis Veter laughing, returning with his nephews. "Those were some Pennsylvania plates. I told em we didn't know about that upturned station wagon but we been out night huntin. Hence the blood all over us."

"An he believed that." Randall's enraged eyes still on the Negro.

"I'm inclined to say he didn't, but the way Yankee Doodle Daddy was shakin, I don't think we need to be worryin bout the family makin a return visit to Dixie anytime soon."

◘ ◘

When Eliot goes to the dentist about the gaps the dentist is going to say Well where's the teeth? The teeth flying! Eliot needs those teeth. Tooth fairy came, Mama! I got a penny! Look at that shiny new penny, big boy This morning my mother was alive and now she died This morning I was alive I got a penny, Mama! I can buy nigger babies! Heads is good luck, says Andi and she gives it to him.

"Bring those bricks over here," Francis Veter tells his nephews. Randall is sitting next to the Negro. A dramatic streak of lightning. The boys, mesmerized, stare where it flashed. Francis Veter sits on a large rock. "Whew! Guess we're in for more storms." He lights a cigarette.

"Fool fuckin nigger." Randall's furious eyes on the Negro.

"So whatcha think? One a them lawyers come to town? There was some nigger lawyers at the voter registration. I saw em but, well." He shrugs, smiling. "They all look alike to me."

Randall turns to Francis Veter. "So when you figure we done here."

"Fire!" says Louis as he hurls a brick at the Negro's head. "Bull's-eye!"

"Goddamn you, boy!" snaps his uncle, going to the Negro. "If he's dead, you're dead!"

Louis, chagrined after his first show of initiative, stammers. "I wasn't tryin ta. But ain't we—"

"I ain't finished with him yet." Francis Veter's palm hovers over the Negro's mouth. "Okay there's a little somethin goin on here." He lifts the eyelid, checks the pupil. "In answer to your question, Randall. Look like the sand near run outa this hourglass." He sits back on the rock to finish his cigarette. "I jus wanna make sure he's with us till the end. Wouldn't be right kill a man, not let him experience every feel of it."

They are silent, watching the Negro's chest rise and fall. It doesn't rise very high. Reggie starts laying out the fingers, admiring them, like another boy would lay out baseball cards. Maybe he *was* one of those lawyers at the voter registration. That must've been where he'd seen him. Randall thinks about Roger, Roger the successful Chicago nigger attorney, Roger's dismissive look to Randall. After Randall'd loaned him his goddamn schoolbooks.

"Uncle Francis, can I go ahead an cut off his left fingers? I'd like to have some fingers."

Francis Veter puffs, doesn't take his eyes off the Negro. "Naw. I like the right fingers left ball gone. I was never a fan a symmetry."

"But then I don't get any fingers."

"I'll give ya one a mine," Reggie offers.

"I don't *want* one a yours! I can't say I earned it if *you* cut if off, I want my own!"

"Boy?" Francis Veter warns.

"We gonna burn him, Uncle Francis?" asks Reggie.

"We'll see." Francis Veter, waiting for the Negro to regain consciousness, seems relaxed, patient. The owl in the woods hoots.

"Look what I done, Uncle Francis. I used the rope from the bricks."

"That ain't how you make a noose. Here." Reggie takes Louis's rope and demonstrates. Randall knows how to make a noose. Randall made a noose long ago, a kid, hard to remember the circumstances now. Then out the blue B.J.s favorite story: *In an old house in Paris / that was covered with vines / lived twelve little girls in two straight lines*

"We got it, Uncle Francis!" says Louis, holding up the coiled rope.

Francis Veter inspects it from where he sits. "Then go fine me a good tree." The boys, cheering and romping, scamper into the forest. Francis Veter allows the quiet to settle before he speaks.

"He's ours, Randall."

Randall turns to Francis Veter, who still gazes upon the Negro, content.

"Our kill. Guess I been waitin my whole life for this. The opportunity. Justification."

"Justification."

"Stranger in a suit from outa town. An he had a nice way a talkin fore we shut him up. Educated. Gotta be one a them damn voter registration lawyers. An then for him to jus happen to have this accident, us happen to be drivin by. Meant to be."

Randall has a splitting headache. He turns back to the Negro.

"So this what you had in mind? From the start?"

"From the start a findin him?" Francis Veter ponders. "Probly not. When I first spied him, jus thought we have a little fun. An then. I don't know, some line we crost. An I knew no turnin back." The wind picking up, blowing the trees. "Wish I could take a picture nex to him. You ever see them ole photos?" He sighs. "Well. Them days are gone. Least *we* know it happened. An now that it did, I don't never have to do it again. All the elements in the universe made it come together for tonight."

"Bad luck for him."

Francis Veter laughs. "Bad luck for him."

Every few minutes the Negro's shallow breathing seems to stop, giving Randall hope. But moments later the chest resumes rising ever so slightly, life stubbornly holding on. A few hours ago this was a whole man, a healthy man. Randall should have stayed home, to make sure Erma was alright. He should have told Francis Veter he couldn't have a drink tonight, how about tomorrow? And Francis Veter would have delayed the night hunting twenty-four hours, the Negro would've been found by his people, right now having his leg cast set at the colored hospital. Or after the chicken dinner Randall could have told Francis Veter I'm tired, can I take a rain check? Or after things got out of hand here Randall could have walked away, We make our choices, Francis Veter said. B.J. said that too not long ago, then hit Randall with a pillow.

"You shoulda been a lawyer."

Randall glowers at Francis Veter.

"You been more n fair here, some uppity Yank coon. You were kinda the attorney for the defense."

"I tried to drown him while you all went to the car."

Francis Veter smiles, surprised. "That a fact?"

"Make no mistake. I ain't no better n you." The Negro murmurs.

"Reggie's gonna be disappointed when I take those fingers from him. We gonna have to burn em to ashes with the rest."

"We hangin him or burnin him?"

"Burn him. I jus sent em off, get em outa my hair a minute. Nope, all hangin do is leave the body more identifiable." He takes a swig from the bottle he'd all but forgotten. "The river. Burn it, dump it. With the rains oughta be carried miles downstream, he might be swimmin on out to the Gulf a Mexico." Frances Veter looks at the Negro's vehicle. "He gonna come up a missin person. But can't charge nobody for murder if there ain't a corpse. Even if they assume dead the crashed car proves it was an accident. By the time they find the body, *if* they find the body be so disfigured, so far away from the scene a the so-called crime ain't no one gonna make the connection, whatever they pull from the river headed straight to Potter's Field, anonymous." The Negro utters something incomprehensible. "Well. Guess the party's almost over." Francis Veter stands. He takes what's left of the whiskey, which isn't much, and pours it liberally over the body, then crashes the bottle by the head. The Negro barely flinches, the reaction delayed. Then Francis Veter drops his cigarette onto the torso and for a second it sparks a huge flame encompassing some of the Negro's face as well, the burning man mumbling inscrutable sounds while trying to roll over and douse the fire. "Look at him wiggle!" Francis Veter seems tickled pink. Randall's pyromaniac fantasies flash, he hopes the Negro and Francis Veter and the nephews and himself and the whole goddamn forest catch, end it all. But the fuel is minimal, and the fire dies out rapidly.

"This spade refuses to die!" Francis Veter laughs. "Gotta hand it to him, another spook been in nigger heaven hours ago." He walks over and stoops, picks up the Negro's head to face himself. The eye that is open, blood-caked, stares blankly in the general direction of Francis Veter's chin. "Listen, since you ain't usin your car, you mind we siphon some a your gas? There's an object we need to burn. I'd use my own, but we bout to take ya on a little excursion in my truck." The Negro doesn't respond. "I will take that as a yes. Thanks a lot, buddy." Francis Veter lays the Negro's head down, and stands. "I gotta go find those knuckleheads, tell em they can stop searchin for a tree now." He walks into the woods.

□ □

Crash! glass Eliot's ear, brownhair walk into woods. Eliot sees glass rise. Eliot's mind glass rise floating, glass rise from the earth floating, brownhair come out of the woods glass slash brownhair throat blood, blood.

□ □

Randall sits near the Negro, gingerly placing the misshapen head on his lap, maternal. The world lighting up every few seconds, low rumble of thunder, and in the periodic light Randall takes his fingertips to wipe some of the blood from the Negro's burnt face. Eventually a flicker of life in the Negro's eye, appearing to see Randall.

"Sorry bout all this, fella. But it's almost over now, you gonna get to rest soon. An I'm bettin you been a righteous man, heaven awaits ya." The Negro breathing softly, gazing at Randall. "Funny how life works out huh. We didn't even know each other till today an look how our destinies got all hooked." And he leans over to give the Negro a gentle kiss on the cheek goodbye.

□ □

Eliot has seen the man before. Eliot sees two men, *Why your eye doin at?* asks Miss Onnie, *I'm cross-eyeded* Eliot has done this man a kindness, Eliot gave him the shoes. If he can get his mouth to tell him this white man can save him, then Eliot can go find the dentist and bring him back here and they can look for his teeth. He tries to speak but blood in his mouth like drowning. He puts his lips around the word, what teeth he has left, he pushes. He puts his lips around the word, he pushes: "Shoes."

□ □

The tenderness in Randall's face starts to fade. It's coming back to him. The lawyer from the jail. The goddamn nigger lawyer from the jail who treated him like trash! Randall drops the nigger and stands, takes a step back. *This* is who he's been trying to help all night, spare the torment? And why's he bring the fucking shoes up *now?* One final Fuck you? Randall's breath is heavy and slow and then he is bellowing, "Bastard! Fuckin arrogant nigger, you think I *needed* your shoes? Goddamn used shoes from a filthy, smelly nigger, fuck you!" Randall kicks the Negro in the face, his body sailing a few feet into the air, more teeth flying. After he lands Randall snatches him by the shoulders, face to face, Randall shaking in fury, shaking the Negro. "Listen you. I shouldn't be kickin a man when he's down, but other people's got a right to exist too. Lawyer!"

And with a shard of glass from the bottle crashed near his head, the Negro slashes Randall, a diagonal starting at the base of his ear, down his cheek, and across his throat. Randall drops the body, grabs his own neck. Blood.

"Oh my God." Randall speaks quietly. The man's near dead, the cut shallow, and yet. "Oh my God, now you tryin to kill me." Randall stares at him incredulous. "Oh my God, I been strivin to help you all night one way or the other and *I'm* the one you—" He stares at the Negro's left hand that assaulted him, *hates* the Negro's left hand Why didn't Francis Veter let Louis amputate those fingers too? And, just beyond the left hand, Randall sees Louis's shotgun. Randall walks over, snatches it, and brings the barrel against the Negro's temple. "Nothin I done tonight been anything but merciful to you, I was your *only friend*." Tears flowing down Randall's cheeks.

◧ ◨

Daddy's a Porter Daddy carries the peoples' suitcases, Eliot steps into the train, see little Jordan walking up to his attorney: "How do you do!" Mr. A. Philip Randolph walking out of the barn the Dream Man walking in, Mr. Randolph points his finger at Dwight and Eliot in the hay: "Uncle Sam wants *you*." Andi tells a joke in Didi's ear, Didi cracking up doubling over, "No more! You're *killin* me!" There's a rabbit in the coffin! says Jeanine, the little coffin flies open and Roy jumps up, arms spread all showman: "Pencil-VANIA!" Miss Onnie feeding the birds Miss Onnie saved Parker's life, "Sweatin like a nigger in court," says Beau in the passenger seat Eliot and Mama in the coal mountain they grin black teeth Hahahaha Steven basketball-shoots his paper lands on Eliot's hand Aunt Amy's orange hand *Praise the Lord and pass the ammunition* "Useful Tips When Confronted by Southern Hospitality" by Winston Douglas, Esq. Dwight and Eliot and Parker make the snow angels Diana sleds down the hill, "Optimism, Eliot! Optimism!"

And suddenly Eliot's mind is perfectly clear. A month from now, and he is setting the table with Dwight, this first Thanksgiving since their mother died, he and Dwight promised to be with their father. Eliot gazes at Dwight, remembering how good Dwight was to their mother, always staying close to home. Remembering how much Dwight always wanted Eliot to love him, all he ever wanted from his little brother, and Eliot wants to talk to Dwight. Dwight his brother, Eliot *will* talk to him, Dwight is placing the fork and the knife on the table and even if it hurts to speak with just a few teeth Eliot will enunciate and Dwight will understand, his brother will understand Eliot will talk to his brother and now Dwight senses Eliot's eyes on him and Dwight looks up.

◧ ◨

"Oh my God."

Randall slowly turns to the voice. A deadening silence. Francis Veter and the boys have come out of the woods The world has no sound Vacuum Nothing.

"Oh my God," Francis Veter repeats, "you blew his fuckin brains out!"

Randall turns back to Eliot. "I didn't hear it."

"You didn't *hear* it? KA-BOOM!" Francis Veter laughs. "We come back just in time, caught his lass word." Francis Veter affects a tiny, mocking voice. "'Why?' and you answered: KA-BOOM! Shook the whole damn countryside!" The boys stare, awestruck. Randall looks at Francis Veter, considers what he has said, then turns back to Eliot.

"I think he said 'Dwight.'"

"Dwight? Who's Dwight?"

A moment. "Somebody he knows."

Francis Veter scratches his head. "No, I think he said 'Why.' Unless. Maybe he was callin on the president. That's it, askin ole Ike for a stay a execution!" Francis Veter cracks up, a hearty laugh Randall had not previously heard from him. Fireflies everywhere, dancing to the beat of the crickets. Why hadn't Randall noticed them till now?

"Maybe he said 'Die,'" Reggie proposes. "Like he was tryin to put some voodoo hex on ya. '*Die*, white man, *die!*'"

Randall hears more laughter, Randall's eyes on the lightning bugs fluttering around what's left of Eliot's head. "I think he said 'Dwight.'"

"Well whatever he said, time to go on a little trip now. Boys? Everything we come with, put it back in the truck. I don't care if it's a eensy bit a brick got loose, *every*thing." Francis Veter begins picking up items with the nephews.

"What if he's not dead?" Randall puts his right hand on Eliot's chest. Nothing.

"Not *dead?* You blew half his face off!" Francis Veter laughs. The boys giggle. "Louis, lee me that rope, we gonna need it. Reggie, take this pile to the truck an bring back a coupla them burlap potata sacks." Randall sits cross-legged next to Eliot.

"Hey Uncle Francis, I found a tooth. Can I keep it? Souvenir?"

"Why ontchu start strippin him?" Francis Veter suggests to Randall. "Don't think we need to burn the body now since ain't much face left, but still gotta destroy the clothes an easier gettin em off now before he go stiff."

"Can I keep the tooth, Uncle Francis?"

Francis Veter shakes his head. "Sorry, Louis, it ain'tcher granddaddy's day no more. That tooth ain't no souvenir, it's evidence."

"But Reggie gets to keep the fingers!"

"Yeah I gotta talk to him about that. You missed a brick over there."

"What if he's not dead?" Randall puts his right hand on Eliot's chest. Nothing.

"Uncle Francis." Louis swallows, grasping for the words. "Tonight. It's like a dream. I feel like I'll wake up tomarra it won't seem real, I want somethin to keep it real."

Francis Veter is moved by his older nephew's earnestness. "Listen. You take that tooth, this what we do. We gonna bury it deep in a secret place later tonight, the fingers too, you, me an Reggie. An you boys jus gotta remember where we put em. For the future. Think you can handle that?" Louis smiles through his glistening eyes.

Eliot's corpse is drenched in blood, mind-boggling to think a body could ever hold so much blood. Randall unbuttons his own flannel shirt. He puts his right hand on Eliot's chest, his fingers spread. Then brings his palm onto his own bare chest, a red imprint of his hand in Eliot's blood.

Francis Veter, sensitive that this may all seem strange to Randall, rips Eliot's garments off himself. What's left under the clothing seems negligibly human.

"Here's the sacks, Uncle Francis." Reggie is startled momentarily by the shape on the ground.

Francis Veter pulls one burlap bag over Eliot's upper body, the other over his lower. "Wish I had a saw. Be easier to dispose of, piece by piece."

"Hey Uncle Veter I found his ball. You wannit?"

"Jus drop it in here." He opens the sack, and Louis drops Eliot's testicle in with the rest of his body. Francis Veter takes the rope and ties it tight around the sacks, then flings Eliot's shroud over his shoulder and trudges toward the truck. The boys follow. Randall is last. Francis Veter throws Eliot in the bed of the truck, covering the corpse completely with bricks, then gets behind the wheel, the nephews hopping in the back with Eliot. Before getting in, Randall shines the flashlight on the spot where he, Francis Veter,

Louis, Reggie, and Eliot spent the last three hours. The owl from the woods has already swooped down to pick at the remains of the body and the blood and the brains. Then several owls appear out of nowhere. They're usually territorial birds, but occasionally form colonies. A parliament of owls, Randall remembers that from sixth grade. A herd of cattle, a flock of geese, a tribe of monkeys, a murder of crows. A bevy of niggers, Francis Veter said.

Two minutes down the road the rain starts pounding. The boys get under the tarpaulin. Francis Veter turns on the windshield wipers, lights a cigarette, and glances at his watch.

"Only ten. Still plenty hours a dark." He lets out an exhausted sigh. "Tie some bricks to it. Give it the right weight, we can send it floatin downriver without surfacin for miles. Or ever." Randall remembers carp. Randall's brother-in-law fished in that river, shared the catch of the day with him and Erma, carp. "Well, like I said, no workin tomarra. I figured we'd be a little hungover." A few moments pass before this last comment strikes Randall as outrageously funny. He starts laughing and can't stop. It becomes infectious, Francis Veter hooting as well. When the mirth finally subsides, Randall looks back at the truck bed, toward Eliot.

"We shoulda found out his name at least."

"Ned the Nigger," replies Francis Veter and they are roaring, splitting their sides, then Randall pukes out his window. He wipes his mouth. "Oooh, too much liquor." Fifteen miles later the rain lets up, the sky clears. Randall looks back at Eliot. It occurs to him that they're driving in the wrong direction, getting further and further from the colored hospital. What if he's still alive? Randall turns around to face front, picking up a half-empty bottle of Jack near his feet. Twists off the top, lifts it, but as soon as the alcohol touches his lips he's puking out the window again, this time for a good ten minutes, every time the retching appearing it will stop it becomes heavier. When it's over he says, "I'll clean your door."

"You damn sure will," says Francis Veter, and it's his seriousness that sends them into gales again, Randall laughing and wiping tears and laughing and wiping tears and Randall is still wiping tears long after Francis Veter has gone quiet as they pull up along the banks of the river, the waters high and swiftly rushing after a long day and night of intermittent storms.

It's nearly seven, just before daybreak, when Randall arrives home. All the lights in the house are on. He comes in through the kitchen. Erma and B.J. are there, both of them gaping at him. He is momentarily taken aback, then remembers he must look a sight, filthy and smelly, not to mention blood everywhere. Later she will tell him how frightened she was, waking up in a drenched bed (just a drenched pillow, Randall will think but not say), and she couldn't imagine where Randall could be so she called over to Benja's, where B.J. has been staying, to ask if her brother-in-law could come and wait with her.

Now Randall smiles and holds up a big, dead rabbit. "Hi, beautiful," he says to Erma and drops the fresh game on the table. She's too shocked to utter a word (definitely a first), but Randall answers the question in her eyes, "Night huntin," not bothering to sign it, which is to say he is ignoring B.J.'s presence. Without stopping, he walks through the house and up to the bathroom. When Erma regains her senses, he hears a blubbering tirade of "drunken fool" and "barroom brawl" but he is somewhere far away. He fills the tub and gets undressed. For a few minutes he gazes into the mirror at the blood handprint on his chest, then steps into the bath. As he washes himself, he looks at his clothing and shoes. He'll have to send Erma out on an errand today while he throws them into the furnace. Too bad he didn't buy an extra pair of Martin's on the discount when he had the chance. He'd shot four rabbits but gave the others to Francis Veter since he has all those kids, Randall who'd never before gone hunting was never interested in hunting went trigger-happy, everything that moved. The water is quickly saturated, grime and the red, so after cleaning himself thoroughly he drains the tub, scrubs it, draws another bath and scours himself again. When he steps out, another mirror inspection. The slash from his ear to his throat is still there, but shallow enough he anticipates it will heal soon enough. He descends the stairs wearing clean clothes, his washed hair combed and slicked back, teeth brushed. An hour since his homecoming and there Erma and B.J. still stand in the kitchen, Erma sobbing on B.J.'s shoulders. Though B.J. holds her comfortingly his mind is elsewhere, and he is staring straight at Randall when the latter enters. Erma hears something behind her and swerves around, but before she can lay into him again Randall goes to her, takes her hands, gently kisses each of her fingers and asks forgiveness for all the time he's been a bad husband, and she stares at him in disbelief as tears roll down her cheeks, and he tells her how much he loves her and has always loved her and he's never been the best mate but from now on he'll try, he'll really try and he wants to make a good life for her and he wants to make a baby and he wants to start now and she throws her arms around him and cries in joy and they walk off to the bedroom, arms around each other. B.J. stares after them, then quietly leaves.

The next day a picture appears in the local paper. A handsome young Negro leaning against an interior doorway, a closed-mouth but content smile. Indianapolis lawyer, he had been reported missing and the car he had been driving, a Plymouth station wagon, had been found upturned seven miles north of Prayer Ridge. The day after, Friday, the same picture is run again, but the implications of the accompanying article are much more sinister: a few teeth had been found fifty yards from the car. The distance renders unlikely the possibility that the injuries were incurred during the vehicular accident, and the notion that the injured man had managed to walk away now seems chillingly doubtful. B.J., just home from work, reads the item. His mother taps him, tells him Erma called asking if she could borrow a few eggs, could he run them over?

On Erma's coffee table, B.J. notices their copy of the paper, but is surprised to see that the article and photo regarding the missing Negro have been cut out. Erma says she has no idea why Randall had mutilated page five just as he had done yesterday. B.J. stares at the daily, something slowly dawning on him: that the night the man disappeared coincides with the morning Randall arrived home in his blood-soaked clothes, the morning Randall exhibited his bizarre behavior—and suddenly B.J. is nauseated. As if on cue Randall walks through the door, returning from his second day at Oldham's Hardware. He stops short upon seeing B.J. with the paper, his eyes slowly dropping to the dismembered page then back up again at his brother's bewildered face, and Randall turns green. He looks to the floor, having trouble catching his breath, turns around, and walks back out.

Eight days later, Erma sits at Benja's kitchen table having coffee. "It's like everything I prayed for, like God brought it all at once. He been so lovin, an I think it's a really good job, he doin real good an. I think I'm expectin!"

"Aw."

"I know that don't mean nothin, I been down at road *too* many times. But this one. I donno, like all the sudden our marriage is blessed, so this little one be welcomed into a happy home. I think that's what God was waitin for, I think this one gonna pull through!"

"Well I'm sure gonna pray for you all." A commotion from the second floor. "YAW DON'T STOP FIGHTIN OVER IT I'LL GODDAMN COME UP AN TAKE IT FROM YA BOTH!" Silence.

"You want another cup?"

"I can get it."

"Benja, you jus got out the hospital five days ago, you sit there an relax."

Erma walks over to the stove, noticing the newspaper on the counter. "Ugh! How could they print that thing!"

"Tacky."

"*Terrifyin!* Sickenin! you cain't even tell what it is. Monster."

"They figger it been in the water ten days. Parently they set the time a death the day his people filed the Missin Persons report."

"I was terrified when I picked up the paper this mornin! Some dream woke me middle a the night I couldn't go back, so sittin there in the kitchen when the paper hits the door. Got to grab it fore Randall gone scissors-crazy again, well now I know why he done it—tryin to protect me." She shudders. "I thought some psycho was on the loose! You cain't even tell it's a nigger, firs glance I didn't know it was a lynchin."

"Uh-huh."

"I thought it was some psycho!"

"That's a mess though. You know where I stand regardin innegration but *that* is *uncalled* for."

"So's comin down here where they don't belong," says Erma, filling her cup with more milk than coffee.

B.J. has been living with his sister since she was released from the hospital, keeping a watch should her brutal husband show up. When he gets home from work at the sawmill, he walks up to the bathroom to wash before going into the kitchen to see if Benja needs any help with dinner. She waves him off. He picks up the newspaper. Two photographs, side by side. The previous picture of the smiling attorney, and to its right the ghastly disfigured remains just dredged from the river twenty miles south. The positive identification was made based on the remaining teeth of the corpse, which, like those found near the flipped station wagon, were determined to be those of Eliot Campbell. B.J. cannot tear his eyes away from the images, and Benja has to tap him three times before he notices.

"Erma was here. She left a note." Benja hands it to him, then dumps an entire stick of butter into a small pot of peas.

> Dear B.J.,
>
> I'm sorry I haff to rite but you got to no how happy me and you're brother are love eachother dearly. He been so good. He ses you keep bothren him about that night he tell you hunting rabits by hisself say numa you're bisness well for truth too proud to say he hunting with Francis Veter and neffews like job innerview thas how he got that job I tell you so you no all now <u>PLEAS LEAVE IT BE</u> you're brothers need lernt to love eachother that job good for him you should appologize.
>
> Love,
> You're sister-in-law
> Erma.

Had he been subpoenaed, perhaps his mother, sister, and even Randall would have understood, or tried to. But with not the remotest legal suspicion cast upon his brother, B.J. walks into the police station that evening and hands the dispatcher a note.

> Dear Law Enforcement Officer,
>
> I have very strong reason to believe my brother Randall Evans of 102 Poplar Avenue murdered the Negro Eliot Campbell, and that Francis Veter of 78 Roland Drive as well as Francis Veter's nephews were his accomplices. I am deaf.
>
> Sincerely,
> Benjamin Evans, Jr.

The specimens are so tiny as to have been missed even with meticulous cleaning by the suspects, but a bit of Eliot's blood is found in both Frances Veter's and Randall's trucks. Still, District Attorney Dylan O'Connor finds the case to be flimsy. In an already volatile atmosphere with the town enraged by the invasion of Northern lawyers stirring up local Negroes, he is now expected to prosecute local white men for the killing of one such intruder based on the minuscule samples of the victim's blood (a common type) coupled with the hunch of a deaf man with what is presumed to be a vendetta against his own brother. Yet under the pressure of the local NAACP backed by its umbrella national establishment, not to mention the fervent threats of the victim's Indianapolis law firm, O'Connor grudgingly indicts the accused, hoping to avoid another circus like the one that erupted around that Chicago boy killed in Mississippi five years ago. The court decides, given that Reginald Norris and Louis Norris are both under twenty-one, that they would be tried separately in a more lenient juvenile facility, though obviously a guilty verdict there would be contemplated only if the two adult defendants were found as such.

Respecting the constitutional right to a speedy trial, the jury of eleven white men and a white woman are selected the following week and the proceedings commencing the week after, Monday, November 14th. The key witness for the prosecution is Benjamin Evans Jr. Despite his initial reticence, the district attorney has professional integrity and, having brought the charges, plans to the best of his abilities to see them through to a verdict of guilty. So it's over his profound objections that the judge rules, for expediency, to bring in a sign-language interpreter to court rather than to have B.J. write notes. As he sits on the stand describing his brother's strange state of mind the morning after the murder, his clothing drenched in blood, something seems to be getting lost in the translation, partly because of the Evans brothers' raw version of the sign language and partly because the interpreter is a poor one. The only person in the room who fully understands what B.J. is trying to say is the one who taught him to sign, his brother, who sits next to Francis Veter behind the defense table, and at one point without thinking a desperately frustrated B.J. instinctively looks to Randall, as if his younger brother will translate as he always has done. Randall glares at his brother during the entirety of his testimony, not a blink. He wears his shirt buttoned to the top concealing the fresh wound B.J. had recently glimpsed and which, under oath, Randall will claim was a scratch from one of his night-hunting victim rabbits that was not quite dead. In trying to correct the interpreter's distortions, B.J. wildly waves his arms, and as it gradually becomes clear to everyone in the room, most of all to himself, that he will be dismissed as a mental defective, he points to Randall and cries loud enough and with such exaggerated enunciation that even the Negroes in the balcony clearly hear, *"I know he did it!"* Still, his deaf pronunciation causes titters from some of the whites and further clarifies that he is an unfit witness. At any rate his testimony is all circumstantial, as are the blood samples, claims the defense, reiterating O'Connor's concerns that the Negro's blood was hardly atypical.

It quickly becomes apparent that the judge and defense attorneys wish to have the trial over before the Thanksgiving break. So on Tuesday the 22nd the jury is excused to deliberate, and B.J. packs his suitcase. When the police came to arrest Randall two hours after his brother betrayed him, their sister and their mother flew into hysterics, begging the firstborn to recant. He could never bring himself to believe they would condone such an act, and yet they neither seemed anxious for justice to be served once the act was committed. *You have no proof!* and *What good would it do, ruin another life?* and *He's your brother!* What they never said because, B.J. believes, they didn't want to face the truth of it themselves, was *He didn't do it!* When he offered no reply to their beseeching other than to shake his head, his eyes barely, wistfully meeting theirs, they finally threw him out into the street.

Since then, two and a half weeks ago, he has been renting a room from an elderly woman near the center of town. He looks at the space one last time, the bed he made this morning that had afforded him barely a wink of rest since his arrival, the first time in his heavy-sleeper life he had ever struggled with insomnia. He clicks shut his valise, full of the few possessions he will take with him, and brings it, along with the two letters, downstairs to his landlady's kitchen, the wood-burning stove she would sometimes ask him to help her light. The first missive was from the Klan, or so it claimed, guaranteeing a swift end to his life should he testify. There had been one incident that had put that threat into action. B.J. would go to court every day, enduring the anonymous shoves and sporadic punches on his way to sitting in the front row far right, close enough, as best he could, to read the lips of the witnesses. It had been an especially bleak day for the prosecution when a physician claimed that it was possible Eliot Campbell had committed suicide—the burns, amputations, castration self-inflicted, the broken bones and comprehensive organ damage the result of the body slamming against rocks after the man flung himself into the river—the motivation of which, the doctor speculated, could have been personal depression or some mad kamikaze effort to vilify Southerners by making his death *look* like a lynching. The lunatic's proposition was met by gratified applause from most of the white spectators, and this was about all B.J. could take. At the lunch recess he found himself walking alone in a deserted alley, away from any sign of loathsome humanity. Someone with a crowbar running up from behind, apparently having assumed a deaf man would be an easy ambush but having not factored in the angle of the sun at that time of day nor anticipated the magnitude of his victim's boiling inner rage. B.J. had glimpsed the shadow and turned around, seizing the weapon and with his bare fist struck the man down with one blow, instantly poising himself for the next. The goon-turned-target gathered his wits rapidly and sprinted away with a bloodied and likely broken nose.

Having lost his entire family, B.J. found the Klan-endorsed warning a dog with minimal bite. He'd been determined to live long enough to testify, and now there was nothing else left. Which isn't to say he would wait around for those fools to come after him, especially if they were to send that incompetent crowbar clown again who would probably not kill but merely maim his victim in some irritating way that B.J. would then have to lug around for the rest of his days. He tosses the note in the fire.

The other note, like the Klan memorandum, had not come via the post but rather had been placed through the front door mail slot, no return information.

> A brother offended is harder to be won than a strong
> city: and their contentions are like the bars of a castle.
> (Proverbs 18:19)

He would have known it was from his mother even if it weren't so obviously her distinctive cursive. He'd planned to incinerate it as well, but for now, he slips it into the inside top pocket of his suitcase. Glancing out the window he notices people racing back in the direction of the municipal building, just two hours after deliberations began.

In the overflowing courtroom, B.J. stands downstairs against the right wall, nearest the door. It's on the other side of the room from the jury but he wants to be able to leave quickly and, anyway, he will easily be able to tell from the crowd reaction what the verdict is. From where he's situated he can see up into the colored balcony. He glimpses the man named Douglas and the other lawyer from the victim's firm sitting next to three local NAACP men and two round middle-aged women. In the second row are the only whites, a young man and woman from Georgia with whom Eliot Campbell had been working, and directly in front of them in the first row center are the father and brother of the deceased as well as two women friends. B.J. remembers it being briefly mentioned in the paper that the young attorney's mother had died just two and a half weeks before he had. He beholds the staggering exhaustion and horror in the faces of the survivors, especially those in the front, looking as though they have been through grief ten times over. When the foreman stands to read the verdict, they as one lean forward.

B.J.'s coach to Birmingham to Atlanta to Washington to New York City is not scheduled to depart until 8:33 tonight, and the bus terminal's enormous round Roman numeral clock reads 4:16. The proceeds from the sale of his truck had covered his ticket and then some. Most of the surplus cash he had left in an envelope in his mother's mailbox, no note. He's brought with him *Go Tell It on the Mountain,* which he hears is a story of New York, but he can't bring himself to take it out yet. He worries about Benja. The day after she tossed him out Aaron had materialized, moved back in. He remembers how his mother would hold him and sing to him and in his head he would hear her. He remembers walking around the yard holding Randall's hand, little Randall grinning up at his twelve-year old big brother and suddenly B.J. is sick, races to the water fountain. After he has taken several drinks to clear his head, he stands up straight to read WHITE ONLY. He wants to rip the fountain out of the wall. He tells himself from here on out he will only drink from the colored fountain, but he doesn't see any.

A Negro who had been sweeping comes up to him, looking right into his face and enunciating clearly. How does he know I'm deaf? "You alright?" B.J. nods. Then the janitor hands him a note. B.J. looks at it, then up at the man. "We all knew it be 'not guilty.' You did your best." B.J. stares, and the man speaks again. *"Thank you,"* shaking B.J.'s hand before walking away.

He walks back to the bench near his luggage and sits. He reads the note a second time, then opens his suitcase, placing the paper safely into the pocket. In doing so he glimpses the message from his mother and, for reasons he's unsure of, takes the Bible quote out and subtly leaves it folded on another bench, away from him, for someone else to find and ponder. His chest begins to rise and fall heavily. He takes out the New York novel, the book trembling violently in his hands as he glances at the mercilessly slow hands of the station clock.

2010

I am wide awake.

The heavy nurse with the honey-tinted hair pops her head in. "Everything okay, papi?" I hold out the drawing I have made of her, and she's surprised and delighted. In my five days here I've sketched all the nurses and orderlies who have attended me, even the grouches, and when I hand them their portraits they are all touched.

I was not in any denial regarding the risks of surgery at my advanced age—even the simple removal of my kidney stones exposing me to perilous complications—nor was I afraid. Others may lament *If only I had more time!* and I'll certainly take it if it's offered, but I have been very happy for twenty-four years! so when my day comes: no regrets. Having said that, I'll admit that in the past the various procedures of my senior citizenry— the hip replacement, the bladder tumor mercifully caught early, the triple bypass—have engendered something of a panic in me: not the fear of death, but of painkillers. The junkie's nightmare! But by being up-front that I am an addict and demanding the bare minimal dosage (and often taking less), I have never become attached to any prescription medication. I still go to meetings though only on Wednesdays, and if I'm tired I skip them, no longer feeling undying commitment is my thin thread barrier between sobriety and the gutter. And many years ago I finally took the Twelfth Step: I'm a sponsor. Ira, the most troubled of my sponsees, has been clean six months now. Milestone.

Three days post-op, a crisp beautiful mid-October Thursday, I'm feeling like my old self and eager for my release this afternoon. I glance at the journal on my table. Book 102: a lot of words since my first composition book back in '82! I've been reflecting on my life since I woke this morning and, feeling rather contentedly lazy, have not been in the mood to write it down. Besides, these memories I needn't document to keep.

After that trip back to Humble, I did phone Roof three times over the next month. Nurse Lem was there for the first two calls to hold the receiver up to the patient's ear. I couldn't help but be aware of how my heart pounded in the brief moments I spoke with the RN before and after my conversations with Roof, and my disappointment when he wasn't there for the third call, though the female attendant was very courteous. The fourth, in early August, was from Lem to me, to let me know that the best friend of my boyhood had passed. I told Lem how much I appreciated his kindness. He replied that he had met many lovely people in Humble, myself included, but that it was time he was moving on: in September he would begin a nine-month commitment to Médecins Sans Frontières in Sudan. At the time I hadn't heard of the organization and, as a matter of fact, since official U.S. participation didn't commence until 1990 (when the NGO became known in English as Doctors Without Borders), Lem was an early-birder. I told him how I frequently had longed to see Africa and that I remembered his photographs of the Ethiopian orphans and asked him if he had specifically requested Sudan and if he would work in other African nations and what had inspired him to become a health provider and before I knew it we had been on the phone an hour, then two, and I gradually came to realize that this was not an official business call, that Lem was speaking to me from his home and that, though I shuddered to imagine something so miraculous, he was being generous with his time not merely because he was a sympathetic nurse but because he *wanted* to talk to me. And when three hours had passed and it had become late on the East Coast (I would have to wait until the next day to call Roof's sister Lucy with my condolences) and I could hear Lem fading a bit—in that moment I quietly took a breath before asking if he would write me from Africa. He said Yes.

That summer was good for Rett and me. Eventually we did see the redwoods, did take a drive down the Coast. Three months after his May 31st arrival, I accompanied him back to the airport, and we checked in the kitten in her kennel. He and his mother would have a lot of time to talk over the fall, and in January he'd begin his full load at IUPUI in Indianapolis, living at home this time, receiving his B.A. at the end of the year. But on that late August afternoon, just before he boarded the plane, I kissed my brother's son, fighting tears, and he smiled and surprised me by saying, "Hope it works out with Lem." How did he know? Well. I suppose I had casually brought up the nurse's name a few times. This would have to be the explanation as Rett had promised me the days of his eavesdropping on my handwritten innermost thoughts were over and, at any rate, Lem would not be suitable in my memory book as he was not a memory. Living in the present was something I had not done in a very long time.

The first letter came in late September, after Lem was settled and, I presumed, he had deemed an appropriate number of days so as not to appear overeager. I wrote back the same day, setting a precedent so that from then on our exchanges were frequent and increasingly longer. Following the stint in Sudan, Lem did some continent-hopping, fulfilling his duties as a nurse in one place for a few months before moving on: Cambodia, Bangladesh, Sierra Leone, Colombia, Ethiopia. He elegantly described to me the places and the people. And eventually he told me about growing up in Detroit, the fourth of five children. His father was an autoworker and Sunday lay preacher: Bathsheba, Abraham, Isaac, Jerusalem, Rebecka. Lem never understood why he was the only child named for a city but he never questioned it, appreciating both his given name and its diminutive. The classic story: Lem's expulsion from the family on the grounds of his sexual orientation, his mother and sister Sheba continuing to exchange letters with him on the sly. And eventually I told Lem about Keith, and about my mother and father, and about my addictions, and about Eliot.

I used to wonder if my own loving parents, like Lem's, like Keith's, would have disowned me had they been aware. And one day it occurred to me: They *must* have known, even if they never spoke it. It would explain why I was in my thirties and my mother never asked me about marriage, never questioned my preference for male friends. It would explain why my father was so accepting of Keith as a pallbearer for Mom, and then for Eliot. My dearest friend wasn't sure when I'd broached him about my brother's casket, if it was something Eliot would have wanted, and then I wasn't sure myself, as I wasn't sure of anything in those awful, awful days after that horrifying thing that was once Eliot had been dredged from that Alabama river. I finally called Andi over at the colored hotel near Benjamin Banneker School—she and Didi, in town for the funeral, were sharing a room there—and she said through a choked voice that in his last days Eliot had expressed to her how utterly grateful he was to Keith for granting him the privilege of his goodbye to our mother, that she believed if Eliot were here he would *insist* on Keith as one of his pallbearers. And so it was.

After four years of correspondence, of Lem living outside the country, one day I received a letter informing me that when his current assignment concluded at the end of the year he would be ready to settle in one place. Despite the very personal revelations in our missives, we'd never expressed any romantic attachment to one another, and of course had met only the one time at the hospital in Humble. But in reading this announcement, his desire at last to root himself, I wondered where in the world that might occur, on what continent, and how far from San Francisco, my heart beating a bit faster. As I read further, I garnered the answer was New York City, and then: "Would you consider living there?"

He met me at JFK. It was the spring of '88, and he had been living in the city a few months. I was fifty-nine, seven years clean, he a fit forty-seven. I was there for a visit. I may have nurtured all manner of fantasies but I was no naïve kid, to think this was for keeps. It was in fact our first date. We were both nervous, initially shaking each other's hands, then he effecting an awkward hug. Reticent in the taxi after the loquaciousness of our letters that would sometimes run on to twenty pages. Then the cabbie dropped us off in his quiet Brooklyn neighborhood. His home was the third floor of a four-story brick townhouse he called a "brownstone." There were many of these on his street, and although they reminded me of the undesirable row houses of Baltimore, I came quickly to learn that in New York they were quite coveted. He paused a few moments before going inside, then said softly, "I brought something back with me from Ethiopia."

We entered, climbing the stairs. A very dark woman in her thirties sat in Lem's living room reading a book. She looked up at us and smiled. For a moment I thought I'd misinterpreted everything! That he had brought back a wife from Africa, and had asked me about living in New York because, what. He had wanted a little something on the side?

"This is my friend Grace. She lives downstairs. And this is my friend Dwight." It was strange to hear him introduce me this way, we who barely knew each other and who knew *everything* about each other.

"He's sleeping," Grace said. I detected no accent but perhaps a little Brooklynese. We quietly stepped into a bedroom. An infant of about a year old lay asleep in his crib. "This," said Lem, "is Dawit. My son."

It was my first true glimpse of Lem the Negotiator, Lem the Tactician. How he, a single middle-aged gay man, somehow managed to talk his way into the authorization of this legal adoption by both countries. His committed work certainly must have proved a factor with the African documentation. The baby woke then, staring up at us, especially at Lem, and began waving his arms and legs, his dark eyes twinkling, wonder and pleasure.

I was welcome to stay as long as I liked, and two weeks later I moved from the guestroom to Lem's room, and three months after that, throwing all mature caution to the wind, he asked me to stay and I said yes. The toddler called us both "Daddy" from the start, but it took seven years to make Dawit legally *our* son.

Though I was conflicted in a thousand ways, I decided without consulting Lem to sell Keith's wonderful San Francisco apartment. We flew to the Bay Area where I rented a van, and as Lem and I were filling it I became emotional, as if I were saying goodbye to my first love again. Then I got behind the wheel of the vehicle, seated next to my second love, and was suddenly nervous that the cross-country drive back might reveal that we weren't quite so compatible after all. On the contrary: the trip sealed the deal.

So we had money in the bank, and Lem continued working in a Brooklyn clinic. And how would I spend my days? Soon I found myself on the corner of 55th and Madison or 125th and Malcolm X sketching the Statue of Liberty, the Empire State Building, the Apollo Theater, Times Square. But usually, and most gratifying for me, my clients, strolling folks impulsively drawn to a street artist, ask me to portray themselves. Their nervousness, wondering how I may caricature them, then their relief and delight in seeing how I could create something that is both flattering and true. Allowing them to see their own beauty.

In thinking of this, I can't help but gaze upon my roommate here in the hospital. Asleep, as he often is, breathing uneasily. A very old white man in such bad shape that I don't know how I could illustrate him in any way that would be both pleasing and honest. Too weak to walk to the bathroom, the nurses having to change his bedpans. He pushes the button often for this service, and the responses aren't always prompt. His liver spots are multitudinous, only two or three white hairs left on his pink scalp. What teeth he still has are mostly rotten, and he is blind from age. A couple of times he's cried out for relief, and once when the nurse came with "Feelin some pain now?" he replied, "I feel pain constant, jus now it's unbearable." Moreover he seems to be prone to elder confusion. Two days ago when my friends from the senior swim stopped by, we all laughed so heartily once that we startled him awake. I apologized. He had barely uttered a word to me before and I assumed he would be irritable, but he surprised me by saying, "No, go ahead. Yaw seem to be havin a good ole time." He has a down-home quality to his voice that I like, much like my own before the decades with my educated and well-traveled spouse prompted the colorful character of my dialect to recede. I mention all this to say that, after seventeen years as a professional junkie, when I look at him I feel I've narrowly escaped looking in the mirror. I wasted my youth as an old man, and as an oldster I am finally young.

At three on the nose, I hear Lem greeting the staff at the nurses' station. Regular visiting hours are 3 to 5 and 7 to 9, and my husband (if not yet recognized by law then by all else) doesn't miss a minute. But I'm surprised to see Dawit walk in with him! "Hi, Dad." Kissing me on the cheek.

"How'd you get off work so early?" He's had a 9-to-5 in the East 60s on and off since earning his B.A. a year and a half ago, a state college three hours' north. His major was French with independent study in Swahili, Somali, and of course Ethiopian Amharic, his sights set on extensive visits to his birth continent.

"I *took* off." It's good to see them both beaming, my first day fully "back." I remember their shining frightened eyes the night before the procedure, but wanting to keep up my spirits. And I tried to convey to them, My spirits *are* up! What*ever* happens tomorrow, the two of you have made the last quarter-century heaven on earth for me!

"But you already took off the day of my surgery."

"Dad, it's a temp job. I'm not risking my dream career here."

"How're ya feeling?" asks Lem, kissing me on the lips, and in reply I smile and nod. Sometimes I ponder whether this would bother my neighbor if he could see us. On the other hand, when Lem and I have been alone it would be clear by our intimate talk what the score is, and I've sensed no distaste from the bed near the window.

"So. Ready for your homecoming dinner tonight?"

"Yes," I tell my partner, "a quiet evening at *home*."

He grins. "Maybe not so quiet," and in walks my nephew, holding the hand of a little girl.

"Rett!"

"Hey, Uncle Dwight." Another kiss on my cheek.

"What are you doing back already? You already visited this summer!" I'm grinning ear to ear.

"What, I'm not welcome?"

"You know you're always welcome."

The nephew I held in my arms as an infant will be fifty next year. I know this well because he mentions it every time he calls. We grew close after that summer of '83, him visiting a week every summer thereafter while I was in San Francisco, and twice a year since I moved to New York both because he loves the city and because he has always treated my son like the kid brother he never had, with little Dawit equally crazy about his cousin Rett. Soon after receiving his B.A. my nephew landed some administrative government job in Indianapolis and has been there since, bored and lonely.

He met Imani there. They'd known each other only a year before making their vows, which worried me but given my hasty courtship with Lem and ludicrously ever-after happiness, my nephew could not take my warnings seriously. Too soon after the ceremony the only conversations he and his wife were having were conducted at the top of their lungs, and their second anniversary had just passed when they found themselves in the disastrous position of her being pregnant and wanting to keep the baby while simultaneously filing for divorce. The decree, with the stipulation that he would have their future child on weekends, went through the same day she went into labor. Months after the dissolution of his marriage, Rett suffered another aching loss with the death of the kitten he had adopted from Humble, which he had indeed dubbed "Parker" and spoiled rotten, perhaps contributing to the animal's incredible longevity (twenty-two years).

My nephew adores his daughter and worries that she will one day resent that he was not a daily presence in her life. He worries that Imani was his only chance for happiness. He worries that, with no such role model, how could he possibly be a good father? I tell him he worries too much. That he *has* happiness with his child. That his romantic life need not be over and even if it is, he needn't be unhappy. Remember his parents' old friend Didi? She'd never married nor had children but did have many, many good friends, and that doesn't count her enormous fan base from her novel writing, so numerous most had to stand on the street, not fitting into the large church for her funeral back in '06. She was seventy-two. From my perspective now that seems so young, struck in her prime. When I would speak of these things my nephew would become quiet and nod, unsmiling. He'd met Didi a few times and like everyone else was always charmed by her infectious joie de vivre, but was skeptical that such bliss could ever be a part of his own existence.

And what happens to an eight-year-old boy who accidentally comes across the newspaper photograph of his father, the gruesome mass that was discovered by those teenagers—beaten, blinded, burned, bloated by days in the river? Rett knew of Eliot's work, but as of yet hadn't asked how he died. Andi had planned to tell him the truth when she deemed him old enough. What her son had been looking for when he stood on that chair, going through things at the top of her closet, no one ever found out. And there, in the hatbox. Clippings from the local papers of Humble, Prayer Ridge, and Indianapolis: the half-smiling photo of Eliot next to the monster into which those monsters had transformed him. Little Rett began screaming, and petrified Andi came running, and when she saw what he held in his hands she began sobbing. It seemed, she told me, that her son cried incessantly for months, had nightmares for years.

I imagine he occasionally has them still, as do I. The terror had begun the day after—*our* terror, as Eliot had been through his own a thousand times over the night before—when the Coatses' phone service had been restored, and Martha called Rosie to ask if Eliot had gotten on his way back to Indianapolis alright that morning, and Rosie had nearly dropped the receiver. Beau had instantly gotten into his car, driven the road between Nathan and Prayer Ridge and found the upturned station wagon. He notified the local police and phoned Andi at the office, who immediately phoned my father. Until that moment we didn't even know Eliot was in Alabama. When Dad called me he sounded delirious, this so soon after my mother's death, and from what he reported I prayed he *was* delirious, some symptom of widower's grief. I spoke to him in a calm voice, telling him that he must have misunderstood, that everything will be fine, there's an explanation, and I hung up to call Andi at Winston Douglas and Associates, my fingers trembling in the rotary. Every day of the next nine was increasingly terrifying, as each of our desperate logical rationalizations, even after the discovery of the teeth, fell by the wayside with no word from Eliot, and I happened to be with my father on that fateful tenth day when the call from the Prayer Ridge police came through. He was bawling, hysterical, I had no idea what they were telling him and yet I knew exactly what they were telling him, and I fell silent, staring into space. He got off the phone, still sobbing, saying nothing, and me saying nothing, an hour or more passing before his tears had subsided and he finally spoke: "Well. Guess we have to make arrangements," and then I was the one hysterical, and my father came to me and we held each other, shaking and crying. And we hadn't yet even seen the dreaded photo, nor read the coroner's report with the grisly details. The dental identification rendered our positive ID unnecessary, and still we went: We needed to bring him home. Parked outside the Prayer Ridge Morgue we wept for an hour, then gathered our strength to see Eliot. When we were at last looking down at him our horror strangely seemed to fade, and we were overcome with our relief to finally be with him, my father holding his left hand and I holding what was left of his right.

And now, in my hospital room, as I'm speaking to my nephew I cannot take my eyes off the child with him. Eliot's granddaughter. Two plaits, curved like parentheses around her head, in red plastic barrettes. A red jumper, high-top sneakers. Her complexion very dark, her eyes a medium brown with gold specks. She and I have met only once before. Her mother's fundamentalist Christian family is homophobic, and Imani had refused permission for Rett to bring their daughter with him to see me. (That Lem and I frequently attend a diverse, gay-friendly church was not even worth mentioning.) And then we came to Indianapolis: Andi's funeral.

Eliot's dear friend and lover had lived to ninety-two, active till the end, dying peacefully in her sleep. She'd had two husbands but with Eliot, her son's father, she considered herself widowed thrice. She didn't remarry until Rett was twenty-five, living on his own, and she was sixty-seven. Hal Frome, a recently retired college history professor, proved to be a wonderful partner to Andi and confidant to Rett for the next fourteen years until 1999, his own quiet death at home.

The little girl, who had adored her paternal grandmother, had heard the words, *passed on, left us, died,* but Eloise was too young to comprehend that Granmama would not be coming back in a few days, that death is forever. When a week later she was told she couldn't visit her grandmother, she had apparently thrown an irrepressible tantrum. She wasn't at the funeral but I glimpsed her at the dinner. Rett introduced Lem and me to Imani, who was cool but polite. Still, we must not have made a bad impression, or else the loss of Andi in the lives of her daughter and ex-husband had softened her, or both. When Rett visited in June, he said he thought Imani was on the verge of relaxing the New York travel ban on the child.

"Remember Great-uncle Dwight? From Granmama's funeral?" The girl shyly holds onto her father's leg, half turning her face away while keeping her watchful pupils on me.

"Hey Mr. Campbell." We look up. Dawit's latest girlfriend entering, the one who came to dinner the other night. Perhaps she stopped off to go to the bathroom.

"Oh hello there uh—"

"Safiya," they both say. Dark hair, eyes. My son is a good-looking boy and well aware of it. He has had all varieties, and races, of girls. But if this one's white it will be, to my knowledge, a first.

"How are you?" she asks.

"Feeling pretty good for eighty-one."

"Eighty-*one*?" Her mouth hangs open, revealing a wad of gum she'd previously concealed.

"Dawit's geriatric daddy," I say and smile.

"I thought you were in your fifties," and I know she's not lying because the hospital personnel have said the same. I can't help but wonder what they would have thought had they seen the skeleton of me thirty years ago, for nourishment begging for a needle before a noodle.

"I brought you a welcome home present, Uncle Dwight." All these years it seems Rett has kept the same dark spectacles frames. He hands me the offering and I unwrap it.

"How old is she?" asks Safiya.

"Be five November," says Rett. "Kindergarten next year."

The gift is a pile of about ten old magazines.

"Some stuff I found going through Mom's old things. It was the world the year my father died. I thought you might be interested."

This is Rett, his mind. The quirkiest gift, no one else would think of such a thing. "I love it," I say, and mean it.

"Can I see?" says Dawit, already coming over.

"Careful," admonishes Rett, big-brothering Dawit as always.

"You know who you're named after?" I ask my great-niece. She stares at me.

"*You* know," says Rett. Her eyes flash at her father, as if his pressuring her to speak were a betrayal.

"*Life. Time. Look. Look*?" Dawit stares at the logo.

"I remember *Look,*" Lem tells our son. "*Long* time ago."

"*The Saturday Evening Post*!" Safiya peering over Dawit's shoulder. "That a Rockwell?"

"*Eliot!*" The baby, aware of having lost a captive audience, now pipes up.

"That's right!" I smile. "Your grandfather Eliot." Eloise grins, and in her dimples I see a little of him.

Rett gingerly blows dust from an ancient *Newsweek* as his cousin picks up the next item on the pile. "Oh this is all about the Greensboro Woolworth's sit-in!" And Dawit instantly sets down the journal and reaches for an *Ebony,* his smile of anticipation having transformed into his signature smirk. "I think *this* might get a little closer to the truth," as he begins perusing the pages. I am reminded of a summer when his fervent ambition was to become a rap star after high school graduation, and though Lem's and my fervent ambitions for him involved college, we had to admit he was pretty good: cleverly rhyming *Ebony* and "seventy" as part of some astute meditation on being young and black in the new millennium. My husband and I did not want to be colonialists—taking a child from a developing nation and erasing his background—and thus we taught him as much as we could about Ethiopia, it being among the first words he could speak, and still: the boy is all African American, with emphasis on the noun.

Eloise and Rett are whispering. Eloise doesn't look happy.

"What's going on there?"

Rett shakes his head. "I always promised her one day I'd take her to New York and we'd see the Statue of Liberty. But I just told her next time."

"Why next time?"

"When you're well enough to come with us."

"You can take her tomorrow, I can spare you a few minutes."

"A few minutes?" Dawit looking up. "You know lines'll be a mile long."

"Take the Staten Island Ferry," Safiya suggests. "You get a close look, and it's free."

"*Or,*" inserts Lem, "the Central Park Zoo."

"*Zoo!*" Eloise jumps up, clapping her hands.

But Rett frowns. "Are the animals treated well?"

"The zoo, the zoo!" I'm glancing at my roommate to make sure our chatter isn't bothering him, but his unseeing eyes are directed toward *Wheel of Fortune,* a vague smile on his contented lips.

"Yeah, it's progressive," Dawit states, though he wears that expression he gets when he's not quite sure what he's talking about. "I mean, the Bronx has big space for the animals, and it's all part of the same system. Right?"

"And Central Park has the petting zoo," Safiya adds.

"Petting zoo!"

"Okay, I guess *that*'s exploitative." Dawit catching Rett's eye. "But I read where they have to do that entertainment crap, to get funding. Then they can do the stuff they *need* to do: protect endangered species. Which they have."

"My mom and dad used to take me," says Safiya.

"My dads used to take me," Dawit smiles at us. "Long time ago."

"Not so long," I say, gazing at my son, remembering like yesterday his five-year-old curiosity, petting the llama.

"I don't know. I saw this documentary recently," Rett begins, and perhaps because the word is immediately repeated on the television we are all drawn to it. My channel-surfing roommate had just settled on a local news report about a Muslim immigrant taxi driver stabbed by a white male passenger, a student documentary filmmaker. The victim survived. For a moment we're quiet, watching. Lem shakes his head. "Some world."

"Nutcases," Dawit mutters.

"What about all the fuss over the Islamic Cultural Center?" Safiya asks her boyfriend.

"They're building it near Ground Zero," Dawit informs his cousin.

"I heard," Rett murmurs.

"Muslims were in the Towers too!" cries Safiya.

"Muslims were among the rescuing firemen," Dawit remarks.

"But the picketers don't wanna hear that," says Safiya.

"Les crétins," Dawit says.

"Remember that Sikh man in Arizona shot to death after 9/11? Whoops, they mistook him for Muslim, *God,* why don't they just lynch us all!"

The room goes suddenly silent, with only the low-volume TV noise, and now I remember: our dinner table last week, Safiya and Dawit in a discussion over something and the mention that she and her family are Palestinian. Her face snaps to me now, the tears of a mortifying faux pas in her eyes, and I know Dawit has told her. "Sorry!"

A few moments pass, and then I say quietly, "I think you chose the right word there, Safiya."

A nurse enters, walking to my roommate. "Feeling a little discomfort?" She holds a needle.

"Daddy, we going to the zoo tomorrow?"

"Well." Noncommittal Rett looks down smiling, stroking his daughter's hair.

"Penguins at the zoo," Lem tells her.

"Elephants at the zoo!" she proclaims.

"No," says Dawit. "The Central Park is a mini-zoo. You gotta go to the Bronx for the elephants."

"Monkeys though," says Lem.

"Monkeys!" Eloise's eyes dance.

"Red pandas," Safiya contributes.

"Pandas!"

"Snow leopards," says Dawit.

"*No,*" Safiya says.

"Yeah," Dawit affirms.

"Cows?"

"*Cows?*" all but me query the child. I can't speak, just looking at them all. My family. What did I ever do to deserve this?

"Cows!" grins Eloise. "Moo moo moo moo." She makes no attempt to sound like a cow.

"Cows on a *farm,*" says Rett.

"I used to wonder," Dawit muses, "is there anywhere in the world cows would be exotic enough to be in the zoo? When do *they* get to be the stars?"

"Cows!" says my wide-eyed spoiled great-niece, the star of the room and happy to be it. "Moo moo moo moo."

⊡ ⊡

My roommate got the chattiest people, chatter chatter. I don't mind, cuts through the quiet, somethin beside *Wheel a Fortune*. Nice colored family, nice be aroun happy people. One time he hushed one a his for givin away the TV answer, stealin that opportunity from me. I'm blind! I cain't see the puzzle! I had me a little chuckle over that.

I don't mind leavin, I been ready a while. What's to stay for? my mine half gone. Sometime I repeat myself. You already said that! somebody say an I wanna slug em, but eventually enough people claimin it I come to see muss be true. But ain't it disconcertin, this story weighin heavy on you, need to get it outcher system but everyone snappin You jus said that, ole man! Only one who missed the story you told was you.

I don't mind leavin, I been ready a while. What's to stay for? Erma gone. Benja gone. B.J. gone. An Randy gone too soon. Nineteen years ole, wa'n't nothin but the whole future ahead a him. Wrote to Leslie Jo years back, Benja's oldest, try to make some family connection but no reply. Did let me know bout Benja's funeral but after that guess she figgered our relationship was done. When I come here they ast bout next a kin, I didn't know nobody else so put her name an number down. She might jus leave em to Potter's Field me, well. I prolly be in good company.

Oh gimme that remote, I hate the damn commercials, soap for the dishwasher. They had dishwashers at Oldham's. Hardware store but they carried a few appliances. Funny I remember it, hardly worked there a week fore it all ended but I sure had the expertise: planks an plungers, paint at long last a job I fit in so shoulda known be over quick. That thing. That thing what happened, don't even recall what all the fuss was about no more. B.J.'s hans flyin on the witness stan, oh I like this show! That Tavis Smiley, he cares about poor people!

Lookit at boy go! How he run like that, Monique? Sure didn't get no athletics from me. Maybe from my pa, he was the All-American, *I'm a chess man in a checkers town,* Ma wail: *It woulda been my first baby! That's jus why women shouldn't go into the military* The War to End All Wars model Sopwith only 98¢!

"You think I can maybe have a little more a that medicine? Oh. Well when you think I can? I'm hurtin. All over. All over!" Why they gotta hole back that morphine? My liver cancer done spread head to toe, think gettin addicted bout least a my worries now.

I sure am sorry to tell ya this, Randall. You wouldn't believe what the niggers done to my sales, their goddamn boycott. An even some a the damn coward white folks, actin goddamn *embarrassed.* This never woulda happened my daddy's day *Resolved, that the territory of Hawaii should be granted statehood* I'm jus gonna lay low a while. I'm gonna put a ad in the paper sayin Oldham's been sold to new management, that'll fool em! Watch em come runnin back, so happy thinkin they got ridda me. Francis Veter laughs. I'll be a fine reference for ya, Randall.

"His people gone, ain't they? Then maybe you wouldn't mind changin this bedpan again? Sorry for the trouble."

Awake now. Sometime out the blue my mine come back sharp, clear. I recall was a hullabaloo but still it escape me, what the whole damn thing was about. Erma even more a mess than usual, cryin, cryin. No more employment I was gonna get local so off to Texas we go, Texas where she got about a dozen-dozen people, one cousin sayin we could stay in their basement till we get on our feet. Ma couldn't even speak to me without bawlin, seem half relieved when I come tell her the plans. Sell what we can, pack resta the furniture in the pickup, fourteen-hour drive an Erma sayin nothin. We'd leff four in the mornin, she'd fried chicken we ate in the truck. Roun five that evenin we finally pull off to a diner an even then only words come outa her mouth was the order to the waitress. Not till near enda the meal do Erma finally speak. *I wanna whole new start. I know now we ain't never gettin to Paris France like I wisht so I'ma be Paris France. My name is Monique.* An that's how I got my second wife.

'Eighty-nine I'm sixty-one, her fifty-nine. Down to Galveston, firs vacation we ever took our whole life together you don't count visitin her sisters an cousins. Quick learner, got my boatin license right before the trip. So we rent us a little cabin cruiser, feel like we livin high! Middle a the Gulf she drinkin peena coladas like they goin outa style an my wife don't drink. We on vacation! she keep sayin an I agree. Her sunnin on the deck high noon. I go down below in the cool, readin the paper, fall asleep. Half-hour later come back up: no Monique. Runnin all over! down, up but this a tiny little boat, nowhere for her to go, she ain't here! Pantin, I holler to the waves: Monique! Monique! *Erma!*

Shakin, the police questionin. I'm a wreck, don't care if they lock me up, come close to smartassin em: I tried to kill her wunst an it didn't take so I ain't bothered with it since, but keep my mouth shut. Back in Shelbourne it haunt me: She jus pass out, slip off? Or dove in an too drunk to resurface? Maybe she decide she gonna swim to Paris an keep goin, goin. On the third week she wash up some shore. I go down, identify the body. Bloated, but her. This all déjà vu, another time I recollect a picture, somebody all water-deformed but at the time rack my brain I couldn't come up with who it was. Jus shock I guess, Mr. Alzheimer hadn't taken occupation a my mind yet.

After she leff me I weren't much good for a long while. I don't mean the fendin for myself, cookin n cleanin. I missed *her*. Erma had been a clingy thing, not to me but to appearances. Always tryin to keep up, feelin like she's hearin the whispers behine her back. But soon's we crossed over into Texas, that Monique. Different person. Acceptin. Of me, of herself, of the life been laid out for us. Hard times, but on the regular: no complaints. She was a good friend to me.

Lass couple years at the factory things gettin darker, the peripheral went first, gradually movin the blackness all over. Too many tiny pieces, too much close work. Shoulda made retirement '94 but it all folded '91, disappeared, no pension, nothin. My landlord says, You know the blind industries? Makin the nurses' uniforms, they put me in the cuttin, the threadin, liftin boxes a fabric fifty, sixty pounds. Part a my job description was keep a steady walkin pace which tired me out sometimes. An the crazy overtime. Flip side, as my vision losin all light they gimme a nice walkin cane, learnt me to use it.

Got the bad diagnosis couple weeks ago. What I wanna go through chemo for? It's time. Still, the days I got leff, what I'ma do with em? I decide: see my brother. I know he died, I ain't holdin onto that no more. Jus wanna be close to him again, for a day. So I hop a bus like that other time, I remember the address, 53rd Street. Stan outside. Some a the people comin out, I say, My brother B.J. Evans lived here. You knew him? Deaf? Nobody did. Cheap hotel tonight, tomarra I'll head for Prayer Ridge, figger that be final destination this life, die home. But then I feel some big pain I cry out, fall. Wake up here. I don't mind leavin, but. Guess I jus wisht it wa'n't *all* alone. Heard my neighbor say he checkin out today. Thought for sure I be gone before him, jus sleep it away. Well guess long as I got these machines, don't know why I don't jus say turn em off, now I gotta go with nothin but the damn TV for company? Eighty-two years come to *that*?

I know I made mistakes. That thing. Don't quite recall what that thing was but sometimes I think. Sometimes I wonder when Erma finally conceived somethin carried to term. Was it that very mornin after? And if so that mean Randy's life cursed from the start? If there is a God I can't believe he be that cruel. Whatever sins I committed was mine, that boy nineteen years ole nothin but the whole future ahead a him I don't mine leavin Erma gone, B.J. gone *pain!* Oh the pain, *nurse!* Where the button be? *God! Oh help me, God!*

"Thank you. Oh thank you so much, this shot. This shot"

You my big boy. You like this bunny, Randall? You want Ma leave it in your crib? Ma loves you! Ma loves you! Model train go roun the bend *And now for a very tragic accident* Margaret Laherty knocked up big as a house Randall! B.J. teachin me to read! Deb Ellen crash that jar the fireflies flutter We live in a time of war. As we eighth-grade graduates of Prayer Ridge School chiken make bj deaf Until we are all free none of us is free Moo moo moo moo.

▫ ▫

Dawit has volunteered to cook my welcome home dinner, an Ethiopian meal, enlisting Safiya as vegetable-chopper. He learned the technique three years ago, during his first return since infancy to his birth country. When he announced to his fathers his planned destination for his college junior year abroad, we were hardly shocked, though any foresight did not mitigate our terror. Reports at the time indicated the region was not exactly stable, to which Dawit easily countered with all the countries wherein Lem had worked that weren't exactly stable: checkmate. So we became addicted to Skype, helpless pawns to the vagaries of international telecommunication. I gaze at him now, frowning in concentration at the batter he just poured into the skillet, and I remember his many stories from that year. His mission was to assist impoverished communities as they improved infrastructural living standards, while Lem and I observed his own rapid personal growth before our eyes. Our son: an exemplary product of the New York City public school and New York state college systems. We certainly had our battles: the ridiculous standardized test obsession, the charter school that moved into the fourth floor and proceeded to usurp his high school's supplies and space. But I am overwhelmingly grateful that *these* were our struggles with our millennial child, as I am acutely aware of his hairsbreadth miss of the last decade of the twentieth in the Big Apple and its prevalent gang violence. I don't think I could have survived another brutal death of a loved one. There was a time when I questioned the selfishness of adopting so late in life, risking my child losing a parent while he was still very young, but we've brought up a fine young man and whatever regrets I have in life, fatherhood is not among them. It took way too long for me to learn that while it's a beautiful and remarkable thing to live by our consciences as my younger brother always did, it's pointless and indulgent to live by our guilt.

The meal is vegetarian as are Lem and Dawit, and me nearly so. It's lovely sharing the same platter in the Ethiopian style (Eloise sticks with her macaroni and cheese) and all's fine until Dawit, typically, picks a political fight. Rett dares to comment that he feels encouraged by some recent announcement of the president and my son is all over him: the sixteen percent black unemployment rate which is vastly underestimated by not counting the forty-four percent of prison inmates who are black and let's not even go into the racially lopsided death penalty and racially motivated police killings and then his snide "I guess you think with a black president we live in a post-racial era." "Al*right*," Lem says and our cynical son grudgingly backs off. Orneriness: Dawit knows damn well that the perpetual and unjustified prosecution and persecution of African Americans is hardly a controversial subject in our home. When the meal is finished we assure self-critical Dawit that the food was just as delicious as at the Ethiopian restaurant, Rett being the most appreciative, and while my grown child knows we're all lying he nods his gratitude, smiling sheepishly at the cousin he'd attacked a half-hour before.

After dinner Rett, Eloise, and I sit on the couch and enjoy *Babe,* a movie Dawit adored growing up and that Lem and I still love. Toward the end she's yawning, and as Rett is putting her to bed, Dawit's old room, I glance in on them. He tells her a story, acting out the parts, her smile broad in anticipation of a tale that has obviously been relayed to her a thousand times. Rett portraying a playful bear begins to tease and tickle his child, she squealing in delight, and I'm moved to finally witness such carefree happiness in my ever heavyhearted nephew.

When he emerges twenty minutes later, Dawit instantly hits him with a proposal: they will go to Africa together, a plan he has just been outlining to his parents. Rett stares, seeming as confused and unsure as that twenty-one-year-old who came to stay with me in San Francisco so long ago.

Dawit is as spontaneous as Rett is reticent. Finally my nephew speaks. "I can't. My daughter."

Dawit frowns, having not considered this obvious factor. "But you can visit me for a couple of weeks. Togo?"

Rett quickly turns to me, and I'm not sure if he's feeling betrayed. Clearly I've told Dawit how his cousin's youthful desire to travel to that particular West African nation has as yet remain unfulfilled. But before my nephew can say anything, Dawit is chattering excitedly about the mud architecture, the markets, riding a camel, and Rett can't help but be drawn in, daring to imagine. For better or worse, Dawit is a boy who makes things happen.

This morning, after a nice breakfast with Rett and Eloise (my son and girlfriend having departed last night to return to their separate apartments of multiple roommates), my nephew and great-niece head off to the Brooklyn Children's Museum (as a dinner debate about the zoo proved inconclusive), thus lunch is a quiet affair with just my husband and me. Yesterday evening Lem had calmly offered Dawit whatever advice he needed with regard to his prospective trip, but as always in private he confides his concerns to me.

"He has to keep his wits about him, you know how his mind can wander. Of course he did fine in Ethiopia. Still."

I'm nodding my agreement. A tiny chip on the edge of my dish. We've been together twenty-four years, there must be a chip in every plate. A daisy engraved into my fork, I never noticed that before. The spoon's design matches but the knife is plain. Lem's left hand suddenly on my right, holding it firm. "What is it?" and I realize my hand is a clenched fist.

"I guess. I hadn't time to think about it. With everyone here." I put down my fork. "Remember yesterday, when the nurse came in to shoo you out?"

He nods.

"The doctor didn't come right away, and I dozed."

"Yes. You told me there was a delay."

"I dozed and when I woke. When I woke a man was standing at the foot of my bed. An old white man. Plenty of hair on his head, gray, white. He stood very straight. Distinguished. He had a cane, and was holding the hand of a little black boy. The man stared at me. Then he looked at my water pitcher. My name. Then he looked back at me. He saw then that I was awake and he was startled. Embarrassed. The nurse came in and said, 'He's right over there,' turning the man to show him. As if the man had come to visit my roommate but was confused." I'm quiet a moment.

"Maybe he *was* confused," Lem suggests. "Old man."

"The only visitor my neighbor had. He walked over and sat in the far corner near the window. He kept his eyes fixed on my roommate, who was asleep. The little boy sat on the floor, took out some coloring books and crayons and began to work quietly. The boy and man said nothing, but were clearly very familiar with one another."

I fall silent again. Then, "You saw him! As we were leaving, when you came to take me out in the wheelchair. A tall man, though perhaps you couldn't tell with him seated."

Lem shrugs. "I suppose. I didn't really pay attention, love. All I was thinking about was bringing you home." But he must see the frustration on my face because he goes on. "What does it matter?"

"He was not confused! He stared at me because he *does* know me! I know *him!* I just can't remember how. As a younger man I knew him." I look up at my husband. "Before you."

A frown crosses my life partner's face. It's the first time I've ever glimpsed anything like jealousy in his eyes. He's always known about Keith and never felt threatened by his memory. But now I see worry. I'm sure he's unaware that his hand is clutching my fist tighter, uncomfortably so, and he repeats: "What does it matter?"

"If I could remember that," I say softly, "I could remember him."

We're silent a moment. Then Lem collects himself, reining in the emotion that had surprisingly manifested, loosens his grip and taps my hand affectionately before retracting his own to pick up his fork.

"Please eat, D. Your quiche is getting cold."

◻ ◻

Year since I lost all light an still I ain't use to wakin up the dark, no matter what time, 7 a.m. or noon, no matter how wide I stretch my eyes, dark.

Scratchin. What's at? Somebody writin? Nurse?

"Who's air?"

It stop. I heard it close, my neighbor gone, I heard it close to *me, my* side.

"Who's air!"

Breathin. Swear I hear—

"Ernest."

A child? "Ernest?"

Nothin.

"Who's Ernest?"

Nothin. My throat tight.

"Ernest? You come visit me? Somebody with ya?" My heart risin an a fallin.

"Paw-Paw."

"*Paw*-Paw? Mean your granpaw?"

"Uh-huh."

"Your paw-paw got a name?"

Nothin.

"*Ernest!*"

"B.J."

Oh! cry outa me. "*B.J.?*" Breath my breath heart so fast. "That *you*, brother?" An like automatic my hans movin with the words. "You gotta get over here, I cain't see! I did the close work all them years, it turn me bline, you gotta get close to me, brother, lemme feel ya!"

Nothinness. I wonder: I'm dead? If B.J. dead, that make me dead. Right? I'm fine with dead but I jus like clarification on the matter.

Then the chair scrapin, movin close. Beside me. An oh God: his right han touchin mine! I clutch it!

"B.J.! B.J.!" My tears streamin.

But gentle he loose my grip, start to move his hans, lemme feel my han on his: the words.

I'm here.

"I thought you was gone, brother! I thought I lost ya!"

No. I'm here.

"Oh my God. Oh my God sweet Jesus!" Gotta catch my voice fore I go on. "I was gonna be the donor. I was gonna give ya my bone marrow but we moved. I didn't get the letter your wife sent till a year later, it said you don't have the bone marrow soon you be gone. I thought. I tried to reach ya, I called but they said nobody your family at your apartment no more, I thought."

He study on it fore he answer.

My recuperation took a long time. They had to replace me with another super. We had to leave.

"Aw, sorry to hear that." When he bring his hans close to his face for the signs I feel his cheek, lips, yeah. My brother. My brother! "Where yaw go?"

Harlem.

"Harlem?" I cain't help but grin. "Well how yaw like it down air?"

Up there. One hundred Twenty-seventh Street.

"It nice?"

He wait again, thinkin fore he reply. Guess I jus have to get use to the hesitations.

It was. Too many white people moving in now.

I gotta laugh out loud! In a single lifetime my brother gone from Klan to colored! But wait a minute.

"Brother, I called. Your buildin, somebody tole me they heard you died. Now who gonna start a rumor like that?"

Again he wait.

They said the super died?

"That's what he heard."

He must have been talking about Lloyd. The super before me. After I recovered, news came that Lloyd who'd retired a few years before had passed on. The person you spoke to must have confused the supers.

I grin. "Guess so, Who's on first. B.J. *B.J.!*" I jus like sayin his name! "But hold on. How you survive without that bone marrow?"

He spell it out. Deb Ellen.

"Deb Ellen?" I gotta rack my brain for that, some file a whole *pile* a decades old. *"Deb Ellen?* Our cousin?"

His han don't move. Why he bringin *her* up. Then I get it.

"Deb Ellen donated the bone marrow?"

Yes.

"Oh my God. You still been in touch?"

I'd been in touch with Leslie Jo, Benja's oldest. When I got sick, my wife wrote to Leslie Jo, asking if anyone in the family could help.

"An ole Deb Ellen stepped up huh. Well! How's *she?* An all them badass kids God, they muss have their own *gran*-brats by now!"

She lives with a woman. Joyce.

"A woman?" My forehead furrowin. "You mean she ain't with Calvin no more? She got herself a roommate?"

I mean she's not with Calvin and she lives with a woman.

It take me a sec. Then I get it! "Deb Ellen! Why didn't I figure that out before?" I gotta chuckle over that! "Now tell me boutcher daughter, that Iona. See, I remember her name! April sent me her little kindergarten picture, it been settin on the mantelpiece all these years with resta the family. What she doin? You turned out to be the bookworm a the Evanses, bet you sent your daughter on to college."

Now his hans take to flyin.

"Slow down!" I say, laughin. "This is new, brother, feelin your hans, not seein em. An been a long while since I engaged in a signin conversation, take it easy on me." But I'm happy! I'm happy!

She graduated from her public high school with honors. She went to college in Atlanta and majored in music composition. She sings and plays the piano and the guitar and the accordion and various African flutes and harps and drums and assorted percussions. She spent six months in Vienna on a fellowship. She's married with children and still composes and occasionally performs.

"Well whadda ya thinka that." I'm all wonder, what B.J. the head saw operator from the mill done brought out into the world.

"B.J. He Iona's? Your granbaby?"

His hans don't move at firs.

Yes, this is Ernest. He's seven.

"Ernest! You gonna come say hi to your great-uncle Randall?"

Somethin goin on, I know Ernest an his granpaw signin back an forth. Arguin, I guess. Finally the boy, "Hello" from where he standin.

"You gotta come closer! I'm a ole bline man, I got to touch you."

Their hans goin wild.

Then B.J. come back to me. He doesn't want to.

The water in my eyes. "Please, B.J.?"

I shouldn't have brought him. He's staying with me tonight because he has a dentist appointment tomorrow, his dentist is in Harlem.

"Jus this once! Promise I won't never ask again."

Somethin goin on. Then I hear the boy sigh, drag hisself near me, but leanin his body gainst his granddaddy for protection.

"Well hello there, Ernest. You gonna lemme touch your face?" I reach out for it. I feel him turn away, not obstinate but like he lookin up at his granpaw, This okay? I reach, get a good feel. I see him.

You said his face, not his hair.

"I know, I jus wanted—"

Yes, he's black.

"I don't care, I love him! He's my blood. All the same."

Ernest signin to B.J., pretty sure he askin can he go now. "Ernest, you go on back to playin." He still don't move, guess seein if it okay with his granpaw. Then he quick run off. "What *are* ya doin? Drawin?"

"Colorin."

Well! He answer me without checkin in with his grandfather firs. "I used to like doin at! Your age." An it occur to me I ain't feelin no pain, an painless is somethin I ain't felt in months. An happy like this somethin I don't remember since my Randy a little boy, *great day!*

"Hey B.J. How you find out I'm here? New York?"

Leslie Jo texted me.

I sigh, hospital musta called her after I give em her name. And guess she did care, a little. Now I feel his han lettin go, maybe he afraid I gone to sleep, I snatch it back!

"You ain't said. How's that wife a yers?" He don't answer. "Well. I loss my Erma. 'Eighty-nine. And Randy, my boy. He was jus nineteen, he died in the military trainin exercises."

I didn't know. I'm sorry, Randall.

"Yeah, well." I sigh. But also I notice B.J. signed my name for the firs time. I swallow, I cain't say nothin for a little bit, an jus when I think B.J. no intention a ever sharin any pain with me, he do.

She's gone. My wife. Seven years ago.

"Oh. Oh I'm sorry too, brother, I truly am. Lord, she musta been young?"

Fifty-seven. His hans still a while. Diabetes. Her family.

"Aw. Your little girl. How ole was she then?"

Twenty-one.

"Well. Guess if it ain't one thing it's the other. Our family, we had the cancer curse. Cep Pa. That damn head saw blade."

Somethin distractin him.

The nurse says I have to go.

"What? What! You jus got here!"

You were asleep a long time. She'd come in with a note saying she needed to examine you when visiting hours were over, that I would have to leave, that she would let me know when.

"But cain'tcha stay till after she done?"

Visiting hours are over.

"I bet they make an exception I ask em! B.J.! You the onliest visitor I ever had!"

His hans is still a second.

I have to go.

I hear him bringin his chair back to the corner, I hear the boy puttin his crayons together, movin toward the door.

"B.J.!" My hans wild. "Please come back tomarra! Please come back see me!" Nothin. "*Ernest!* Ernest, your granpaw don't hear me, turn him roun! I'm beggin he come back, turn him roun so he can see me, see I'm talkin to him. Please! I need to tell him Come back tomarra!"

"He's lookin right atcha," says Ernest. Then their footsteppin away.

▫ ▫

I place the freshly printed photos neatly into the album: Dawit and Safiya preparing the Ethiopian meal; Eloise on Rett's lap, both beaming. I don't touch computers of any kind, which is just as well given the arthritis in my hands, but Lem went picture-crazy after acquiring that digital camera. Christmases and birthdays and Pride Weekends and of course our world tour. We'd been saving and last year, after Dawit graduated from college and moved out, and with Lem retired, my husband and I spent six months traveling the globe. The first order of business had been to get me a passport. Eighty years old and I'd never been out of the country.

Rett left this morning, his usual Friday-to-Sunday visitation with his daughter adjusted to Thursday-to-Saturday so he could be here for my homecoming. I'm tired, an old man recovering from surgery, and thus my adieus to Eliot's son and granddaughter aroused in me mixed feelings of melancholy and relief. Lem just left on a few shopping errands, which means for an hour I have the quiet apartment to myself. It's nearly two and, as the Saturday postman should have come by now, for a little exercise I walk down the steps to retrieve the mail.

Three handwritten envelopes addressed to me. I've received so many well-wishes, Lem must've called everyone in my address book! The first is a card from the household of my old San Francisco sponsor Miguel. We stayed in communication twenty-two years until his death in '03, and I'm touched that his widow still sends an annual Christmas card, and now this.

After all the time and distance, it takes me only a moment to recognize the name in the return address of the second item. My cousin Liddie! A get-well card, and slipped inside an old black-and-white, she and Eliot standing next to each other, grinning, he holding Parker the Cat. On the back: "August 1942." It must've been their visit for Ramonlee's funeral, shortly before Parker's death. It's a copy, a scan, but clean and clear. I stare at it a very long time before realizing the tissue paper beneath was separating it from another photo from the same time: me at thirteen and a half, a touch of the pubescent complications I was going through afflicting my expression, standing next to seven-and-a-half-year-old Eliot, my baby brother's smile brighter than the sun. When at last I can turn my eyes away, to see through my blurred vision, I pick up the Hallmark, reading the note beneath the store-bought sentiment.

> Remember when Rett asked me for a picture of little Eliot?
> Found these in Mommy's things after she died. Lost your
> address but then Lem called. God bless you, cousin!

I need a rest, a glass of water, and then I remember the third envelope. I don't recognize the return though it's local, uptown Manhattan, postmarked yesterday. I can tell it's a letter rather than a card, and I take it out. The printing is very neat.

> Dear Mr. Campbell,
>   Please forgive me if this is any intrusion. I saw
> you at the hospital today, and when I came home I
> found your name and address in a web directory. In
> 1960 I testified against my brother at the trial for the
> murder of your brother. I left Prayer Ridge immediately
> afterward, moving to New York and never returning to
> my hometown. (My brother moved to Texas and, before
> today, I had only seen him once in the past fifty years.)
> At the Prayer Ridge bus station, an African-American
> man handed me the note I have enclosed regarding your
> brother. I thought you might like to have it.

I remember you well from the courthouse; you have not changed much in all these years. A half-century too late I wish to apologize with all my being on behalf of my family for the atrocity and suffering my brother wreaked upon your family, and I send my long overdue condolences.

Sincerely yours,
Benjamin Evans, Jr.

The note is crackling old and yellow. I unfold it gingerly.

> Thank you for what you did. Eliot stayed with us when he was in Prayer Ridge. He was a good, good, brave man. We are proud he was our guest.
>
> Jeremiah and
> Martha Coats

Steady. Yes, now I remember the visitor. But the two words I keep staring at, what has me closing my eyes: *before today*. Because that would mean. *That* would mean my *roommate*, my breath coming deep, fast, fast.

A shriveled-up old man, nothing of his former self, unlike his brother who still carried something of his youth, enough for me to find him familiar. And yet: *How could I not have known?* Why hadn't I *sensed* it? Smelled the stench of him? the *monster*

The particulars of Eliot's gruesome and torturous demise as repeatedly detailed by the prosecutor to the jurors (the latter eventually crossing their arms and frowning in their determined desensitization) began to play out in a loop in my head, and after the verdict my former dreams of legal justice had metamorphosed into visions of fierce revenge: inflicting every pain Eliot had suffered onto Randall Evans Francis Veter, those four words incessant in my head Randall Evans Francis Veter. I'm a bull, murder now in *my* heart, I vow to destroy Randall Evans Francis Veter I would consider the fate of Veter's nephews later *plans*. I visualize their dying breaths their mutilated corpses and dare not speak which might dilute my rage, I strategize and tell no one. I go through the motions of caring for my grieving father, staying with him at the house but my head elsewhere *plans*, if Eliot no longer walked this earth then neither do Randall Evans Francis Veter I am methodical. Days after returning to Humble that lump of wrath in me growing, hardening I call the Prayer Ridge phone company. I inform the woman I've just moved, all my family and friends still there, it would be useful to have a phone book to stay in touch, I make sure my voice is white white. She's politely efficient, writing my address on the directory herself, she might have recognized *Humble, Maryland* from the newspaper but *Lewis, West Virginia* would mean nothing to her, I change my name but I'll take care of that when the package arrives, I'm a goddamn mailman after all. "Oh Mr. Perkins, I went to school with Lenora Perkins, she relation to you?" "Distant." I receive the directory five days later, the street addresses I need, then a week goes by. Three. This is good, I think, all this time since the trial they'll never suspect me I purchase a gun I purchase a dagger, I *will* do to them everything that was done to Eliot *no mercy.*

I've plotted everything but the when, like Nat Turner I wait for a sign from God and it comes. Dad tells me Aunt Beck called. She'd like to stay with him through the Christmas holidays. I'd just gone back to Lewis but still phoning my father every day, seeing him every other day I tell him Aunt Beck's visit has come at a good time as I have some out-of-town business with the post office. I'd never had any business trips before and in his right mind my father would have questioned this, but he'd lost much of himself after my mother's death and what happened to Eliot left him barely the shell of a man, nodding, agreeing.

So two days after Christmas, five weeks to the day that Randall Evans Francis Veter are pronounced not guilty I'm crossing into Alabama, the revolver within easy reach in the glove compartment in case there's trouble early on. I'd debated, pistol versus the shotgun, the latter being more precise eye-for-an-eye. But I could be tempted then to shoot from afar. A pistol is up close and personal and would provide many options for maiming, then torturing, *then* killing. I'm careful not to take unnecessary risks, to die before my mission is complete. I devise a two-day journey, staying overnight on the way in a North Carolina colored hotel, paying cash so there will be no record of my stay should it come up in a court of law later. This is how I cover my tracks, even while knowing I'll never get out of this alive. How my father will survive the third and last family member gone all in the course of two and a half months I selfishly don't think about I'm focused Randall Evans Francis Veter

Half-moon. Light, but Francis Veter's house is in a wooded area, I'm concealed by the trees. Voices. I'm shaking and this catches me unawares. I never once reconsidered, why tremble now? Bunch of kids running around. They're out late, I think, carrying little guns and shooting at small animals. Well why should I be surprised that piece of trash lets his offspring run wild? His wife comes out, yells for them, bedtime. They groan and she yells more and they come in. I circle the house, nearly fall in a trench, my mind thinks my grave's already dug for me. Then see the ditch is dug for an out-door pool, though seems the workmen gave up halfway through the job. The window. Him and her in the living room, eating something, watching the news. Finally they turn in, lights out. A long dead quiet. I pick up a pebble. Throw it at the wall near the bedroom window. Nothing. Another. She wakes first, saying something to him. He clutches the pillow, waves her off. I hurl a bunch of stones and he snaps up, comes to the glass, looks out, the pitch-black. Must've woken up one of their brats, I hear crying from another room. Puts on his pants, snatches his rifle. I cock my pistol. He moves toward the back door and so do I. Francis Veter comes out of his house. I stand ten yards in front of him. This would be the moment for a clean, accurate shot, but unless I just want to kill him and run, if I want to follow through with the plan to make him know me, feel me, beg for the mercy he won't get, then I can't kill just yet. I have to get him into the woods. How? I could shoot to wound but I don't have a silencer, his wife would get on the phone to the police and the gig would be up fast. I can't die yet, not until I get to Randall Evans's to also make him beg for his life in vain. I study Francis Veter. Well. If I'm meant to die now, I'll take him with me. And he *will* see me, he's not going to think I'm just some damn burglar. I want to say my name. And who my brother was, there will be no confusion. I'm just about to step into his line of vision when a blond child comes running out of the house and into her father's arms. She's crying, and he speaks to her softly, comforting. She's a baby, no more than three. Why's she *out* here? Why didn't she just go to her mother? Francis Veter holds that shotgun in his right hand, moderately vigilant to any sign of an intruder, his left arm around his clinging daughter, her back to me, arms clamped around his neck. Eventually he'll send her back to bed, I'm patient, patient.

Wait. Francis Veter's asleep! Out in the chill December night holding his girl, dozing. Both of them still, dreaming.

I creep closer. When I look back on it, I guess this was the moment I was most pleading for suicide, for Francis Veter to help me to it, end the hurt. I get right up on Francis Veter. He doesn't budge, his mouth slightly open. And I smell it. Goddamn whiskey, the piece of trash bastard passed out! I could slice his throat. I could rip open his white neck while his child sleeps on his chest and no one would know till morning.

And then she lifts her head and looks at me. Oh my God! she wasn't asleep at all. Might she scream? Oh sweet Jesus I did *not* plan on killing a child!

But she doesn't scream. She smiles and speaks, all Alabama rural. "You Birdy's brother?"

I wait for her father to stir awake now but Francis Veter hasn't batted an eyelash. Who the hell's Birdy? The *maid?* I shake my head.

"You know Birdy?"

I shake my head.

"What's your name?"

If I speak Francis Veter's subconscious may register the voice he doesn't recognize and he would wake. If I don't answer she might get louder. I could kill them both now and run, save myself.

But I can't. Him, yes. But a child. If only she hadn't come out! if only

I wave goodbye, hoping that it will make her stop talking, and I creep away. She keeps staring at me and my teeth start chattering so violently I fear they'll be the element to finally wake Francis Veter. Or that the girl will call out to me. But she just watches as I leave. I wonder what she'll tell her father tomorrow. I pray he'll assume she dreamt it. I don't want any local coloreds to be falsely accused since local justice for colored I'd guess is accusation equals execution.

Walking. I'm walking what happened with Francis Veter will *not* happen with Randall Evans, I distinctly remember from the trial that Randall Evans is childless. No one else in his house but his stupid wife and if she gets in the way, well. She should have thought of that when she married the beast.

Randall Evans's house is not isolated like Francis Veter's but rather on a tree-lined street of other homes, so killing him will be a little more complicated. I park my truck a few blocks away and stroll, step lightly. Three in the morning, all the houses dark. Wake up anyone they see a nigger on the street I'm fairly certain they'd shoot first ask questions later. Poplar Avenue. I find it: 102. A sign on the lawn.

I walk around the back, look in a window. Empty. Not a picture on the wall, not a chair.

I am calm keeping this information at a distance, I stay calm because the only alternative, when reality fully hits, will be to *scream* and that will not do right now I stroll step lightly seven blocks to my truck. I slip into my truck and quietly drive to the outskirts and it comes. I waited too long. Randall Evans is gone, Francis Veter I couldn't, couldn't, *Why'd I wait so long?* My baby brother was tortured and torn and blown to bits by strangers killing a nigger just for the hell of it and they'll scot-free get away with it. There's no justice no mother fucking justice in the whole goddamn world Eliot, Eliot.

It takes a good hour for my wailing to subside. Then I pull out, heading north. I shouldn't be driving at night, a Northern nigger at night well I have bullets, I'll take a few of them before they take me. But naturally nothing happens. I tempt fate, taunt fate, *pray* fate makes its appearance but there's no God because I'm safe, the entire twenty-two-hour drive home I don't stop to eat or sleep, only once to piss and I'm untouched.

At five in the morning I pull into Keith's trailer park. He's stunned to see me. We've not been in contact since I went down for the trial. I know the phone calls I didn't answer were his, the knocks at the door I ignored. I sit in his place silent, staring into space. The ghost I will more or less be for the coming two decades.

If that toothless ugly old man in the hospital is not dead yet I could go now. I would tell him who I am, then hold his pillow over his face. Or I would tell him who I am, then press my fingers against his throat. His near-lifeless body would surely squirm, fight. Full up with cancer or whatever he has he could go any second, but isn't it instinct to struggle against murder? I'd probably be sent to prison for the rest of my life, which at this point would mean a very light sentence.

But how pathetic, two old geezers throwing it down fifty years too late. I've seen a few of those cracker savages being tried now—ancient, frail. Throw away the key! I say. But Randall Evans and Francis Veter were already tried, you can't try a man twice for the same crime. And if you could, if that near-dead thing in the hospital was finally locked up in a cell, would I feel gratified? If justice is not served swiftly, can it ever be?

I don't realize I'm bawling until the phone rings. I let the machine get it, though I know it's Lem calling from the supermarket to ask if we need this or that but really to check that I'm alright, his post-op elderly husband. If I don't answer he'll be petrified that I've dropped dead so finally I pick up, interrupting the message he's leaving, his voice attempting casual but clearly shaky. "I'm here." I can't speak much as I'm holding back the sobs, and he knows something's wrong and asks and I snap that I'm fine, I have to go, and he says Okay, he's at the checkout and will be home soon and I know he'll rush.

Perhaps I just need to go to the hospital and look at him one more time, knowing who he is. And to tell him who I am. To witness just a little of the terror in his eyes that he thrust upon my little brother.

But in the end, I simply pull out stationery and sit at the dining room table to write a note to Mr. Benjamin Evans Jr. I realize I have much to say though I jot just a few sentences. That in the hospital I recognized his face too but couldn't quite place from where, that I also never had a chance to thank him for his courage, for what he had done for my family, for what he had done in the name of, in the hope of, justice. I'm just peeling off one of these self-adhesive Forever stamps, a new innovation that I as an old postal carrier have admired, when I hear Lem's keys in the door.

□ □

Movin my han oer my body. Skeleton, days I ain't ate or ain't kept it down, IV only thing between me an gone. Thursday after B.J. leave I give the order: DNR, shut off the damn machines. My brother come see me, all the gratification I'ma get this side a life, time to head on.

But here it be Saturday, still my breath goin. What I'm waitin for?
That don't sound like the nurse. Chair scrapin close!
"B.J.?"
He pick up my han.
"Thank you! Oh thank you so much, brother, I didn't think ya be back!"
His hans don't move.

"Never bought Ernest with ya this time?"

I came alone.

"Oh. I cain't tell ya how glad I am ya here again! That Ernest. Now seem like he a good boy."

His hans don't move a while. Then start to turnin slow, like he wanna make sure I understand.

I almost didn't come back. There's something I need to ask you.

He wait. I don't know what it could be but I get the feelin it ain't gonna be somethin I wanna talk about. I also get the feelin I say I ain't interested then he jus gonna stan, walk out the door.

"Go on, brother."

His hans still. Then, Do you know who the other patient was? The bed next to you?

I frown. *That* question I didn't expect. Then I get it.

"I know he was a colored man, it don't matter to me." I laugh. "Mighta had my moments but never like I flat out hated the whole race. Remember Roger from Henry Lee's? An his ma? Sally?"

What black man?

What black man?

"B.J., I muss be confusin your signs. You say '*What* black man?'"

Yes.

"What black man I shared this room with?"

Yes.

"Now how would I. Whatchu *mean?*"

His name is Dwight Campbell.

That don't ring an exack bell, but it's ringin in the ballpark, somewhere I don't wanna go.

His brother was Eliot Campbell.

My lungs! losin my breath "Whatchu sayin?" No answer. "*You* don't know! Why you come in here, make stuff up? *Lie* like that. Huh? Lie like that!"

His hans move away.

"Uh-uh, dontchu do it! Drop that bombshell then go away, *no!*" Me swingin all directions, searchin crazy for him. "How you know? How you know?" I cain't find him. He still here? "B.J.?" My voice small.

When he good n ready he come back, scarcely touch back a my han with his an I grab em, seize his hans fore he try take em away from me again. Catch my breath, calm, calm. Then I sign with jus my leff han, I ain't lettin go a his in my right.

"So whatchu want? Me say I'm sorry? That what you come back for?" His han don't move. "That stuff happened fifty years ago, B.J.! Why you gotta bring it up now?" His han don't move.

Then he say, You never admitted it before.

Antlers scratch my face Pa wearin the pink Klan hood *People think deer all gentle, nothin but prey. Well ain't nothin more dangerous than prey on the defense* an their little grinnin heads pop out the antler points: Mr. Holliman the mill boss what fired me, Mr. Martin the shoeman what fired me, Dr. Earl Mattingly thirteen years old copied my test crushed my Sopwith, Jesse the jail deputy, Francis Veter smilin through the blood *I* was the prey, Pa! *I* was the prey!

Wake up, "B.J.! You still there?"

He put his han nex to mine. I relax.

"Few years ago, the news. World War II decorated, Purple Heart, he come home to Mississippi, Klan. Nineteen sixty-three shot dead some important colored man. Convicted the nineties, *forty years later.* Ole man, liver spots, walkin with a walker they make him stan trial, they send him to prison! His lass days! You think at's right? They didn't condemn him back *then,* you think it's right doin it *now?* Sick ole man?"

There's no statute of limitations on murder.

"I didn't ask that! I asked, You think it's right, treat the elderly like that? *I ain't had nothin my whole life, B.J.!* An Francis Veter lost his business, I heard half his kids grown up to be drunkards or drug addicts, that one girl kilt herself in her twenties, ain't that punishment enough? I lost my son! I lost my son to the U.S. Armed Forces, now you think jail me too?" I'm feelin no answer. "B.J.—"

You were my brother.

An I hear somethin. Snifflin. Tears. Then jus as fast he plug it up. I'm quiet a while.

"I guess I letcha down huh."

That's not the point.

"That's *some* a the point." I sigh. Then I chuckle sad. "At neck scar still there?"

Yes. Barely.

I nod. "So. Ya think he knew? My roommate?"

Not while he was here.

I gotta teeheehee cuz I know what that mean. "My honest brother, my upright brother. Whadja do, write a letter to him?"

Yes.

"An lemme guess. Apologized for me?"

I apologized on behalf of our family.

"Yeah, you would. Not your place to, nunna your business to, but you would." I take to dry heavin, pick up that metal pan spit up in it, lie back down. "Well, there go my pain pills." I rest a second. "Hey B.J. Wa'n't I married? Coulda swore I was married but don't recall no wife."

Erma.

"*Erma?*" Rack my brain. "Don't recollect no Erma."

She changed her name to Monique.

"Now why would she do that?" I feel for my cup a ice water, sip through the straw. "We stayed in Prayer Ridge?"

Texas.

"Oh yeah! That's familiar, we moved after. After that thing. What the hell *was* that thing?"

You know.

At first I don't. Then I do. "Oh yeah." I chuckle but no joy. "Hey brother, I'm picturin you from 1972 but occurs to me you musta changed a bit. You still slim? Still gotcher hair *Aw!*" Swallowin. "B.J., I jus had a little accident. You get the nurse? Tell her, tell her the bedpan, you please get the nurse?" His footsteps scurryin off.

Pa cuttin the log at the sawmill. In walk slender Ole Bruce, sixty-year-ole shoeshine boy, walkin tall, strollin like a easy, kick-a-stone day. Pa look up an the head saw cut him in half, scalp to privates.

Pa's leff han point down to that shoe, right han to *that* shoe. *Think I could use a shine,* both halves a Pa says.

Ole Bruce reply, *In 1863 the slaves was set free.*

What's funny?

"*B.J.!* Brother, I thought you left. I called for the bedpan an thought you gone."

That was yesterday.

"Yesterday?"

I went for the nurse, and she helped you and you talked some more but it didn't make sense.

"Oh Lord, I don't even remember that. So what it now? Sunday?"

Yes.

I sure hope you're considering law school, says Mr. Hickory. Ma an Benja an B.J. an the trophy: Randall Evans/Best Speech/Prayer Ridge Debate Competition/Feb. 20, 1942.

"B.J. You call up Monique, tell her I'm in the hospital? Fraid she'll worry."

Henry Lee an me an Roger runnin the train in the basement, then we hear somethin an Roger look up. Emily on the steps cryin, cryin.

"B.J.! B.J., somethin in my eye! B.J., hard to liff my hans up to my face, you blow in my eye like Ma useta?"

He lean into me.

"Other eye! Other eye!"

His breath cool, gentle.

"That's it, that's it. Thank you, brother." On the sidewalk I walk right pass Martin's Shoes in my new used wingtips an Mr. Martin an Brenda Jean an Diane stand in the door admirin my footwear admirin me. I smile, I ain't tellin em my secret, who give em to me. Strut on down the sidewalk an come upon my ole friend grinnin at me. His suit clean an pressed, standin in his stockin feet.

Fitcha good, Randall? he ask.

Oh yeah, Eliot, like walkin on air.

"He gay me them shoes!" I laugh out loud.

Who?

"It was a kindness. Aw, he never meant nothin mean by it."

An here I am starin through the Pearly Gates an Eliot on the inside, like this is the jail you *wanna* be in but to me the sign say No Trespassing. Eliot typin on a ole typewriter, his face all concentration, the lawyer work.

"Hey there, Eliot! I jus figured it out. Looks like I owe you a heck of an apology."

But Eliot don't seem to hear. Keep typin, typin.

Awake. My throat take to catchin, B.J. put a tissue to my face, tears soakin it soppin, he gotta bring another tissue, nother. Then the gulpin stop. Startin not to feel my body. Like maybe I already done left it, no pain.

"Well, big brother," I smile, "looks like ya outlived me."

Backa his han against backa mine say nothin.

"B.J.? When you said, 'You were my brother.' What else?" I rest fore I go on. "Didja mean, 'You were my brother, an I loved you'? Cuz I still love you. I never stopped lovin you, B.J."

His han against mine shakin, shakin. I'm in the tree. I done my eighth-grade graduation speech I'm way up in the tree, I got the world. Nobody see me but I see them, Roger an Emily on a picnic. They kiss. *Crazy?* That could get em kilt! him for sure. All I gotta do is holler! But I don't. I like em. I like Roger an Emily.

"Roger an Emily! It's okay! It's okay, yaw look happy. It's okay, I jus hope yaw're happy." Then I say it softer, all smilin to myself. "Roger an Emily. I jus hope"

⬚ ⬚

Today, Sunday October 17th, is Eliot's seventy-sixth birthday. Every year I wonder about the man he would have become. I imagine him having stern talks with Rett about his defeatism, I see him walking with Eloise through a park, much like he'd walked Liddie's twin little girls around the block that Christmas way back when.

I woke up feeling strong, renewed. I told Lem I'd like to stroll through the Botanic Gardens. He looked at me skeptically and I assured him I'd take it easy, calling out for rests when necessary. I want to breathe in the fresh autumnal air, to walk among the vibrant colored leaves. New York is a city of only two seasons unless you make the extra effort: the parks and gardens hold the equinoxes.

October was once a month of despair, but it has transformed into one of reflection. My mother died on the seventh. We don't know for certain what she went through, those moments her weak heart gripped her for the last time, but the evidence, that she was found simply slumped over in her chair, has led us to the comforting conclusion that she died peacefully. I still miss her. But the bittersweetness that accompanies the anniversary of her death differs infinitely from my complicated feelings every October 25th. This is the month Eliot came into the world and the month he was viciously torn from it.

Lem could see I didn't want to talk when he came home with the groceries yesterday afternoon. He didn't push me, just went to the kitchen to cook. Last night we sat up in bed to read as usual, my paperback open on my lap but my mind elsewhere. Finally he closed his book to look at me. And I told him. The letter I'd received and what it had revealed about the stranger with whom I had shared a room for five days. Our son was already ten before I divulged to my husband, on the anniversary of my brother's passing, the story of my journey South for the aborted kill mission, and last night I told him how I'd seriously considered going to the hospital and at long last finishing the job. He was quiet a long time.

"What's left of him, D? A lump of ugly, diseased flesh, inside and out."

I turned to him. "So?"

He was silent.

"That's justice?"

"In a sense."

He could be like that. Karma. "You're saying every terminally ill patient just got what they deserved."

"No. I'm saying this one did."

"He's an old man! Everyone dies of something, for all we know his life up until now's been one long party."

"How many people came to visit him? And this only the second time in fifty years his own brother's seen him? Something tells me his life up until now's been nothing."

I shake my head, eyes filling. "We don't know."

"We *don't* know, we'll never know." He's quiet again. "It was an apology. He's felt shame for his brother for half a century. What's that tell you?"

I swallow. "Eliot felt shame for me."

"Eliot was twenty-six in 1960. And Eliot was coming around at the end, you've said that. Andi told you about his wholehearted gratitude to Keith."

I nod, look away. He shakes his head.

"Nothing I can say to make you feel better. What happened to your family, to Eliot. I wouldn't wish it on anyone." Several sirens dashing by. "And those decades the only Campbell left was lost. But how long you been clean now. Twenty-nine years? And what you've meant to Eliot's son the last twenty-seven? And now starting a relationship with his grandchild, Eliot looking down sure must be relieved you're here taking care of things, proud of his big brother."

I stared at my partner. His words had never occurred to me, and yet they suddenly felt so blatantly, undeniably true. And then the tears in my eyes flowing hard, and we held each other a very, very long time.

At sixty-nine Lem still does a little running every morning, and while he's out Dawit stops in briefly with Safiya to see how I'm feeling, the both of them off to some demonstration, his sign saying "Close Guantánamo Now!" and hers "WikiLeaks Don't Lie!" I realize I'd forgotten to tell him about the play Lem and I saw a few weeks ago, an off-off-Broadway production written by a friend and focusing on a young gay soldier in Afghanistan, a gung-ho American boy who comes to see the dismal pointlessness of it all after some confrontations with local civilians. I expect my son to reassert his well-established own low opinion of the war but instead he grins: "Oh, so you all had a *date* night."

Lem returns in time for a quick hug as they're leaving, then makes us an omelet brunch before going to our bedroom to check his email. In the living room we have a few extra picture frames in a drawer, and I find one for the note from the Coatses, among the last friendly faces Eliot ever saw, and two more for the photos Liddie sent, of Eliot and me in our precious boyhood, which Lem has already scanned on his machine—the copies I'll send to Rett. I place the newly framed portraits on the coffee table next to one of Rett as a child, the resemblance between father and son astonishing. My solemn nephew Everett, conceived just days before his father's unimaginable end.

I hang the note near the framed sketch I'd sent to Didi in '85, six years after the promise I'd made at Max Williams's law school graduation to send her a work of mine. There are no photographs of her and Eliot together so I imagined one, drawing them both smiling, nearly laughing, him seated and looking down at a document he holds, her just behind him and looking over his shoulder. I still have her thank-you letter somewhere. She said when she opened the package, she had to quickly move away to prevent marring the sketch with her tears. It was in her will that the illustration be sent back to the artist upon her death.

The living room wall is also graced by the two paintings of Keith's from my San Francisco apartment, Keith's apartment. Those shattering days when my beloved companion had been such a comfort in my harrowing grief, and later transformed into the scapegoat for all my unleashed fury.

My brother's senseless death set in motion a slow killing of myself for twenty-one years, and it took my best friend's senseless death to resurrect me.

"Chilly out, D," Lem says, coming out of the bedroom. "Grab your jacket." He goes into the bathroom, brushing his teeth. As much as I may scoff at the determinism of Lem the preacher's son, I must admit to my own moments of embracing something like destiny. Did my mother plan it? Could something in her being have arranged it so Eliot and I would have to come together for her funeral? So that, when Eliot's grief broke, we would have that one night of brotherly reconciliation before he was abruptly and terribly gone?

The problem with this theory would be the implication that Eliot's death was inevitable. It most certainly was not. But too many decades I've wasted in screaming at the universe, demanding answers. My profound bitterness was justified, but what good did it do? In my old age I ponder: What if, instead of focusing on the potential of a life of greatness and graciousness being so appallingly cut short, I could have beheld the greatness and graciousness Eliot had already given the world? Winning the case for Mr. Daughtery, the police brutality victim. Laying the groundwork for the release of the little boys. And all the lives he'd touched personally: Andi, Didi, Beau, Winston Douglas, the other gentleman from his office who'd sent that lovely condolence card, lonely old Miss Onnie, little Jeanine and cousin Liddie and Parker the Cat and the Coatses and Rosie from Alabama in the brief time he knew them. And my mother, father, and me. My book-smart, hyperactive, aloof, annoying, mysterious, justice-seeking, huge-hearted baby brother.

Lem goes back into the bedroom to grab something before our stroll. I gaze at the pictures on the table once more, the gallery of our history. A baby shot of Dawit, a studio sitting of the three of us when our son was an adolescent. The picture of Eliot smiling that last year, the one we were fortunate to have after my mother made him stand still for it on Christmas, the one my father and I sent to the police during the investigation and which appeared in the papers. Hard to believe half a century since my brother has walked this earth, since I've seen him, held him. I'm blessed to have had the family I was born into and to have the family I made. And now I glimpse the photo of the four Campbells at Eliot's law school graduation, him beaming in cap and gown, and I'm catapulted back to that spring evening of '58, our family celebratory restaurant dinner. Mom had recently taken up Aunt Beck's habit of scolding Dad for his salt intake—his perennial high blood pressure leading us all to believe he would be the family member we'd lose first—and Dad grumpy about the chastening, and as they lightly bicker my brother and I exchange glances, secret smiles, as if we'd never had a conflict between us in all our lives. Eliot, Eliot. Forever twenty-six.

◨ ◧

My brother is dead. His right hand clutching my left has gone weak, and now his left hand feeling my right for the signs has slowly slipped away. I lay it down next to him.

I don't understand his last words. I don't know who Emily was, or Roger, though the latter seems to ring a distant bell, from when we were both very, very young. I gaze at his blind eyes. After my first visit three days ago, I found on my shelves my old book of Helen Keller writings, the one Abigail the librarian had recommended to me so long ago and which I eventually purchased. "I, who had thought blindness a misfortune beyond human control, found that too much of it was traceable to wrong industrial conditions, often caused by the selfishness and greed of the employer." Now, as in the minutes Randall spoke his last words, his eyes have settled into a soft contentment. I gently close them.

And an ancient memory comes flooding back, something I haven't thought of in decades. My little brother, a thirteen-year-old child teaching me the manual alphabet. Teaching me to read. Introducing me to the library. There were signs I'd created to communicate my basic needs to my family, but even the most rudimentary complex thought was out of reach until I learned language. Once there was a shoe, and a stove, and a brother, but Randall walked me through a door and on the other side was integrity, and logic, and justice. My mother gave me life, and when I was eighteen my little brother Randall gave me the world. I realize now, looking down at the empty corporeality of him, I never thanked him for that. I lean over and kiss his forehead, and I stay here a very long time. When I lift my face, I wipe my tears from his eyes, his cheeks.

I walk out into the corridor. I should probably tell someone at the nurses' station that my brother has passed, but I imagine that will activate all sorts of complications and I want to leave the hospital *now*. He's not going anywhere. They'll find him and get in touch with Leslie Jo who will get in touch with me and I'll cross that bridge then.

Outside I put on my reading glasses to text Iona. She had some shopping errands to do in Manhattan and told me to let her know when I was finished with my visit so she could pick me up. We take turns every Sunday. Last week she and her family had dinner with me in Harlem, and today I'll ride with her to the 'burbs.

My brother's confusion regarding my mortality brought me back to a spring night in '81. April May June and I had been invited to the birthday party of her old Gallaudet friend Marielle. I never became comfortable at parties and my wife had long stopped cajoling me on such matters, so as always she went alone. I helped my eight-year-old daughter with her homework and after I put her to bed, I thought I'd catch up on some bills but had trouble locating a pen. In my search I opened April May June's desk drawer, found a ballpoint and inadvertently noticed near the back a ragged composition book. How I'd missed her sharing her stories with me! In the three years since my near-death, I noticed my wife had ceased to write. When I mentioned it once she became defensive—her time consumed by the need for her to work outside the home since my hospitalization (only part-time), having to take Iona to her musical events (a task we shared), helping Iona with homework (ditto)—so I dropped the subject for the time being. But this evening I sat rereading the narratives, indulging once again in her words and her worlds. The latter tales became wildly creative, her earlier concerns about not having the imagination to craft anything but autobiography having long been put to rest. "Deaf Baptist Revival," among my favorites, was followed by one final work, a lengthy untitled piece I'd never seen before. It was the chronicle of a deaf couple, a black woman named Paulina and a white man named Orville. They met on a subway platform.

When April May June returned close to midnight, all lights were out in the apartment save the small lamp near my chair in the living room. She walked in smiling and tired. Then she spied the notebook on my lap, and froze. She came to me, falling on her knees, putting her face into her hands and on my lap, weeping. After a few moments, I began stroking her many braids which had grown halfway down her back. She looked up, her forty-three-year-old face still so young, and she saw that my eyes were soft.

It was after the dream. The dream I wrote about in the story, I was sitting in your hospital room and I fell asleep and I dreamed you were reading *Madeline* to Iona. When I woke, I thought you were gone. Your chest wasn't rising anymore. I thought you were gone.

She waits for me to respond. I don't, but my gaze encourages her to continue.

I brought the notebook with me to the hospital that day. I don't know why, I had a feeling. I woke up that morning with the feeling that it would be your last day. *Our* last day. I wanted to bring it.

But I didn't die.

I thought I'd lost you. But then you began to breathe, shallow breaths. And I sat down and wrote it. Our lives. I wrote everything, up to my dream. And then, I guess. I guess I needed to go through it. Your passing. I needed to go through it so I would be ready when it happened. So I imagined it. I imagined it and I'd just finished writing it when I looked up. A woman standing in the doorway. A strong-looking woman, staring at you. Then she turned to me. She walked in the room and handed me a note: I'm Deb Ellen, B.J.'s cousin.

For a moment our hands were still.

You need to submit it. It's a good story, my love. You need to send it out.

She was agape. I never intended to submit it! I just. I wrote it because. Because—

My right fingers softly touching her hair.

You need to submit it.

She looked down, unsure.

Just please, please, don't write about Randall and Mr. Campbell. You have a wondrous imagination. You can invent something else.

Of course! she had said, upset I would suggest such a thing, I would *never*. She didn't finish the sentence, but gently repeated: Of course. A tear rolling down her lovely cheek.

We were living in the church then. It took a long time for me to convalesce after my leukemia, the rigors of tending to the needs of a six-floor walk-up and all its residents beyond my capacity for quite some time, so we weren't surprised when the president of the co-op board came to our door, delicately expressing the necessity to replace me. By the greatest stroke of luck, an old Gallaudet acquaintance of my wife's told her he had an uncle in Harlem, the minister of a Baptist congregation, and connected to the pastor's church was a two-bedroom apartment reserved for the church's caretaker: once again a janitorial position in exchange for free rent! I'd just started getting up and around by then, and the three of us went to be interviewed by the preacher. He seemed most interested in having people he liked living in the church, my experience as a superintendent merely being a plus. As an employee of a nonprofit organization my pay was minimal, as was the workload: no longer constantly on-call as in a residential building. April May June continued with her part-time proofreading during Iona's school days, and when I grew stonger I contacted Joy, the principal from the private school, to ask if I might have my old job back. She was delighted, and while her curtailed budget allowed for only one class, within two years finances had been restored and I was able to teach a second.

In our interview with Reverend Shriver, he admitted that our deafness was an advantage: previous custodians had trouble adjusting to the noise— choir practice, Wednesday evening services and twice on Sundays. He was concerned about Iona, however, as were her mother and I, but our daughter loved the apartment (as we did) as well as the enticing idea of living in some hidden cranny of a church, and she begged us to accept the position. Mercifully the worship activities neither disturbed her sleep nor her homework. On the contrary, the sweet sounds she absorbed sparked my child's love of music. For a while she sang with the children's choir, and April May June and I would attend services when they performed, sitting close to observe the joy in our daughter as her mouth made huge forms around the words. By her teenage years she'd quit, not being about to reconcile her love of the hymns with her doubts regarding the church's political conservatism, but ever-generous Reverend Shriver allowed her access to a piano when it was not employed by the congregants. She taught herself to play.

My daughter was gifted, and this is not just her father's opinion. She was giving a full scholarship, all expenses covered, to Spelman College. And she excelled until her last semester, her mother passing on two months shy of her graduation. She was given incompletes in all her courses, ultimately passing her exams in the fall, but she declined to participate in the closing exercises the following spring, having missed the chance to walk with her own classmates and feeling heartbroken that her mother would not be there. I respected her wishes but my own heart was broken, not to see the dean hand her that degree. I, with not a day of former schooling and my daughter a college graduate! So for me she rented the cap and gown, and when I came to Atlanta to pick her up I took photos of her all over campus. I snapped dozens, and this before the days of digital cameras.

I was fond of Dex Ryland, whom she'd been dating since she was a sophomore and he a Morehouse junior. Dex had grown up in the Georgia countryside but was committed enough to their relationship to move with her back to New York. An economics major, he landed a job at the United Nations that he loved while Iona struggled with temp jobs. When she became pregnant at twenty-three, I worried whether it was the right choice to have the baby as they were barely making rent on their tiny Queens studio, then I worried about their choice to jump into marriage, so many huge life decisions at once! But they did it, a courthouse ceremony with me as sole witness in the tradition of her mother's and my wedding (though, at the insistence of Dex's family, they wound up flying to Georgia for a second more elaborate observance). Fifteen years later my daughter and son-in-law are still very good friends, the only displeasure I ever hear from Iona related to the bit of weight she gained with the babies, and even then she usually laughs about it, occasionally starting a day with a diet that lasts until after-dinner dessert.

When Fela April was two, the family moved out to the grass of New Jersey. Iona began teaching music part-time in the secondary schools, and she still composes and occasionally performs in small venues. Her vocal specialty is jazz, and I can see it in the way she forms her lips around the notes, though she likes to play around with traditional African rhythms as well, and has experimented with all sorts of indigenous sounds, Mayan flutes and Tuvan throat singing. She sees how I've aged—so much weight of a tall man on these old bones (I take the bus now rather than attempt those subway steps), a bit of arthritis in the legs (but mercifully not the hands, my language) as well as the backaches after decades of leaning over to converse with the shorter rest of the population—and she's told me she would happily present for me private recitals in my home but I haven't yet been able to give in to this, not when I see her face beaming at me with every public performance. She's recorded four CDs with a small independent label and I play them frequently, my hands on the speaker to feel the beautiful vibrations of my daughter's creativity.

In 1993 as I was turning seventy and April May June was just beginning to take ill, I decided it was time to retire, to stay home full-time to care for my wife, to nurse her back to health. I'd been lucky so many times in my life: the superintendent job, the teaching job, the church caretaker position, and now a couple at the church who'd always been fond of us offered a one-bedroom at the top of their Harlem brownstone at a very reduced rent. Of course most lucky of all was my running into April May June on the subway platform so long ago, and her choosing to ask *me* for directions! So perhaps I'd gotten cocky about my fortune and heartily believed my wife would kick the diabetes, even as it had already claimed the lives of her father and three siblings, including Ramona, the sister she most cherished. A year later when Iona was twenty-one, the amputation of her mother's right leg still very fresh for all of us, April May June's condition suddenly took a crucial turn and she was gone. It was without a doubt the most devastating day of my life, and it had had some pretty stiff competition for that inimitable spot. I was fourteen years older than my wife. How could she possibly have gone before me? *I should have died in '78!* I bitterly cried, *If only Deb Ellen hadn't come through with the bone marrow!* The thought of enduring life without April May June was unbearable, and I seriously and selfishly considered not. Then I looked into the eyes of my barely grown daughter and was reminded that I wasn't the only one broken. And joylessly forced myself to carry on.

At the funeral one of April May June's longtime Gallaudet friends took me aside to express her condolences. I remembered the woman had had her own share of grief: three weeks after her teenage son earned his driver's license, he was killed in a head-on collision with a drunk driver. The woman wanted to express that she understood what I was going through, the utter pain of their absence from this earth, the frightening mystery of where they are now, if anywhere. I nodded my empathy, but in truth I was perplexed by her feelings of some sort of limbo regarding her son's essence, or his complete oblivion. Other than Iona's children's choir concerts, I haven't sat through a church service since I was expelled after singing too loudly and too deafly as a child, yet I've always believed in an afterlife, this Christian conviction reinforced by April May June's readings on traditional African spirituality, the faith that our ancestors are active, watching over us. In that respect my young wife is now my ancestor. I speak with her often.

Standing outside the hospital this bright, crisp October Sunday, I'm surprised to see the van pull up as I'd expected Iona would have come alone in her Prius. The doors open and the gang pours out. Nine-year-old Maurie and seven-year-old Ernest running to me, "Paw-Paw!" on their lips, their hands moving rapidly, each of them telling me so much I can't keep up. Next to my grandson is his best buddy Vincent Cho, moving his own hands in wild imitation and desperately hoping they might mean something. Vincent has taught Ernest a few Korean words he learned from his grand-parents, so perhaps I'll suggest to Ernest that he return the favor in ASL. Fela walks over too, smiling broadly but hanging back with Scott, her fif-teen-year-old boyfriend. They've been together a few months. What does a fourteen-year-old girl need with a boyfriend? I'd asked Iona as she folded laundry one afternoon. Oh, they're not doing anything, Dad. Yet! I coun-tered. She put the clean towels into a pile. I watched her, debating whether I should continue with what was really on my mind. And then I did: And *must* he be a *white* boy? I had had to put my hands in her eyeview as she was bent over away from me, and then I witnessed her entire body shaking in response. What? I demanded, *What's so funny!* And now the hearing boy nervously signs his respectful greetings, trying to impress me. Well I do remember a few Sundays ago, when the younger children dragged him away from an NFL game on which he and Dex had been intently focused so he could play Chutes and Ladders with them. I was in the kitchen, Iona washing the dishes and me drying, and Scott didn't know I was watching. Hard as it was to pull himself away from the fourth-quarter action, I could see he was willing to make the sacrifice because it made the children happy. I was touched, this white boy. Guess I'm getting liberal in my old age.

Now Maurie takes my cane and grabs my right arm while Ernest clutches my left, marching me to the van, Vincent skipping beside us. Fela's yelling something about not pulling too hard on Paw-Paw. Iona is outside the front passenger side of the vehicle, clearing the space for me, the inside always chaotic with the various discarded items of four kids. My daughter looks up and smiles, kisses her father. I'm a lucky, lucky man.

We cross town, Iona expertly navigating the capricious Manhattan traffic. Just behind me Ernest and Vincent wrestle and laugh, I imagine a hearing person would say *squeal,* Iona periodically hollering at them to stop, which they always do for several seconds, a look of shock on their faces as if they had no idea they were being disruptive, before resuming the brawl. Next to them and behind Iona, Maurie reads a book. No one will ever know, but of the three older children she's my favorite. A darker complexion, and she wears glasses while Iona never did, but otherwise the spitting image of her mother at her age. She comes to me often, initiating long manual conversations, but with verbal speech she's reticent. She reads a children's novel I gave her, *The Watsons Go to Birmingham—1963,* a wonderful story about a black family from Michigan who eventually travel to my birth state in a volatile era. There was a time when I didn't even want to talk about where I came from, but those days are long past. While Iona was still small, I'd even started accompanying my wife and daughter on their trips South to April May June's family, having finally decided there was nothing healthy in my holding a grudge against my home region forever.

Now my granddaughter looks up and, seeing me smiling at her, grins ear to ear. Someday I'll take her to the Civil Rights Institute in Birmingham which we visited after one of those South Carolina visits, a stunning museum built right across from the Sixteenth Street Baptist Church where the four little girls died in the bombing. I was overcome with emotion. Yes, Alabama has changed, and perhaps, in a small way, redeemed itself. I've never been back to Prayer Ridge.

In the far backseat, Fela and Scott pass an MP3 player back and forth, discussing the songs and giggling. And I am reminded of when I first held her, a tiny infant in my hands, her mother telling me she shared her name with a Nigerian recording artist. And then Iona granting me the privilege of giving my firstborn grandchild her sign name: a variation of the sign for "music" with my moving right hand an *F.*

Now Fela turns to affectionately touch the nose of her youngest brother in the baby seat next to her. The fourth pregnancy was a surprise to everyone, especially Dex and Iona, and she swears he's her last. When the amniocentesis revealed the child's gender, this one, my daughter informed me, would be Benjamin. What the amnio didn't divulge, or perhaps the doctor missed it, is that, like his namesake, Benny would be deaf, a product of his genetic history. I sign now to the two-year-old who grins and replies. Babies, deaf or hearing, pick up manual language quicker than verbal, and my toddler grandchild already has quite an extensive vocabulary. I wish he could have met April May June. Well, I wish they all could have. When I show him her pictures he signs "Grandmother."

Early in the baby's first year, I tentatively broached the subject of cochlear implants with Iona, the surgery that could cause Benny to hear and thus speak. She said that she and Dex had already had this discussion and that she categorically refused to put her perfectly healthy child through any major medical procedure, Dex more ambivalently coming to agree. While I'm sensitive to parents who struggle with this question and may choose differently, I couldn't have been more pleased with Iona's decision and knew April May June would have felt the same. In my wife's last years she'd become quite apprehensive about the Human Genome Project. At a meeting in a city deaf school auditorium, April May June in her beautiful dreadlocks nervously stood and wrote "**Deaf**" on the board before signing her speech. There's a reason when referencing the culture that "Deaf" is now capitalized, she began. How can we help hearing scientists resolved toward the elimination of deafness as a universal good—How can we make them understand that sign language and Deaf culture, Deaf *people,* should always exist? They talk of hearing as life-changing, and they're right. If they could have made me hear as a child—and then I was startled when my wife turned to me in the audience. If they could have made *you* hear as a child, my husband, it would have affected you, your entire being. It would have made you a different person, the B.J. we know never would have existed. And what a loss to the world that would have been.

On the van floor behind me, I notice the copy of *Madeline* I'd given my firstborn grandchild when she was very small, opened to the inside front cover: "To Fela April Ryland-Evans, Love, Paw-Paw." Maurie and Ernest had adopted it later and there are scribbles throughout the pages, all of them knowing the story by heart. Their hyphenated surname is the legal appellation of the entire family, including Dex. There was a time when I would have been fine to have had the name Evans vanish with my generation, my family shame. But as I've grown older, I've come to realize how reductive it is to define an entire clan by one event, even if that event was a cataclysm of the first order. Or perhaps I *just* discovered that in the hospital, remembering how much my baby brother Randall had meant to me in our beautiful, innocent youth. Yes, we are never, ever too old to learn.

Up to the West 40s and under the mighty Hudson, the Lincoln Tunnel. Ernest taps me and signs that he wants to look through my wallet. They've all loved going through my many pictures, especially of themselves at different ages. But this time, while showing the photos to Vincent beside him, Ernest asks, Is this your brother from the hospital? The eighth-grade picture of Randall with Pa. Yes, I tell him, it is. Then my grandson says, Paw-Paw, the picture of Mr. Campbell's falling apart. Maurie says, Let me see Mr. Campbell!

The *Prayer Ridge Times* photo of Eliot Campbell, October 1960, a handsome likeness of the young lawyer. I did *not* keep the image of his mutilated corpse. My daughter and, with the exception of the baby, all my grandchildren know who he was, though Iona and I have been ginger with the details for the smaller ones. When Fela began asking more incisive questions at twelve, we filled in the truth for her, and now I see the sadness in her eyes at the mention of his name.

In 1960 Alabama my brother and Francis Veter and his nephews never would have been sentenced to death for killing a black man. I've always been opposed to the death penalty, and I've sometimes wondered if I could have testified had I thought my brother might possibly been handed any reprimand harsher than life imprisonment. (More likely single-digit years.) I suppose we all spend too much time considering the *what if*s. I gently take the photo from Ernest. It's been a long time since I gazed at it.

I'll get it laminated, Iona says. Or I bet I can google it, old newspaper, print a new copy. For the moment she ends her plans there because she knows not to speak at length to me while driving. Her unconscious lifelong habit of interpreting everyone's utterance used to terrify me when she was at the wheel, barely touching it while both her hands fluttered rapidly. My wife had grown up in a deaf family and would have been unfazed, the Junes having always driven this way, but by the time I met April May June I was a public transportation New Yorker so I never became used to the practice, and I finally warned Iona if she kept it up I wouldn't ride with her anymore. What I didn't mention was that I appreciate the solitude, the time alone with my thoughts.

We emerge from the tunnel, and now we are at my favorite part of the route. The panoramic view of Manhattan. The city I journeyed to fifty years ago, the city I have adopted as home. Iona frequently reminds me that when I'm ready there will be a room for me with her and Dex, and Dex has always enthusiastically seconded the invitation. But my daughter knows I love my apartment in Harlem, the neighborhood where I raised a child with my wife and partner. I'm still quite self-sufficient, so Iona doesn't push the issue.

I've never been a man of goals. Whatever life handed me I went with: the sawmill, the diner, the high-rise window cleaning, the superintendent job, the museum docent, the teaching, the church caretaker. But now at my advanced age I've decided on an objective. I plan to live to be a hundred. This is not so easily attainable as it may seem: as a babe of eighty-seven, I still have thirteen years to go. But I've made it my private ambition to be a part of that elite club I've dubbed The Centenarian Society. The beauty of this plan is if I achieve my aspiration, I will have seen three of my grand-children graduate from high school and the fourth well on his way, per-haps even witness the birth of a great-grand. And if I fall short, well. All the sooner to be with April May June again.

Win win.

ACKNOWLEDGMENTS

First and foremost, I owe my undying gratitude to all the people who read my novel in an early draft—when it was even bigger than it is now!—and provided invaluable initial feedback, both in offering their thoughts and in patiently and readily answering all my questions. That list includes my sister (and fellow writer) Kara Lee Corthron, and my friends Jacqueline Kelly, Cori Thomas, Michael John Garcés, Marina Shron, Lisa Leaverton, Molly Porter, and Adam Kraar, whom I also would like to thank for introducing me to my terrific agent Malaga Baldi. Also, thanks to the email introduction by Maggie Sherrerd, I would like to express my huge gratitude to Iris Kinley, someone who didn't know me at all and yet generously agreed to read my tome—my first Deaf reader *and* the first time I was able to hear thoughts from a complete stranger (though we are now certainly friends), both these perspectives proving beneficial beyond words.

Two other early readers and respondents: Garrett Wright, an attorney with the Urban Justice Center and a member of the National Lawyers Guild, who provided both literary and vital legal feedback, and who accompanied me to court to observe; and Tomas Medina, another lawyer friend who answered questions about legal education and career, and who also was a wonderful firsthand source regarding 1983 gay San Francisco. And I want to thank my friend, lawyer and writer Cynthia L. Cooper, for advising me on the history of juvenile law, and for bringing me to the chambers of the Honorable Emily Jane Goodman, New York State Supreme Court Justice (since retired), who, along with her astute clerk Andrea Field, Esq., provided superb insights into the mid-twentieth-century legal world.

I am grateful to my friend Joanne Jacobson for opening her home to me as a quiet space to write when the novel was the germ of an idea; and to my friend Naomi Wallace, another of my early readers and responders, who likewise invited me to work at the home she shares with her husband Bruce McLeod—and thanks to Caitlin McLeod for her room.

A responder who came later in the process was Cory Silverberg, a friend who has been outrageously supportive of the book since he read it, and who brought it to the attention of his own publisher, Seven Stories Press.

Much gratitude for the generosity of their time and advice with regard to the medical references to physician's assistant Florentino Reyes on an early draft, and to Dr. Lucy Painter on a late draft.

I must mention two other crucial guides: Michael Mejias, who read the long(er) form of the manuscript and shared his thoughts, as well as provided me with my first lessons regarding the profession of publishing; and editor Susan Dalsimer, who on a barter (I read her play and she read my novel) provided insightful impressions of a later draft.

In Indianapolis, I'd like to thank Katharine Springer, State Data Center Coordinator, Reference and Government Services, Indiana State Library, as well as a young male librarian whose name I unfortunately didn't get at the Indianapolis Public Library, Central Library branch. And by email, the IUPUI University Archives Specialists Greg Mobley and Mindy Marie Cooper.

Over the time I worked on the novel I was very fortunate to have been awarded focused time at several outstanding artist residencies: the Virginia Center for the Creative Arts via its Wachtmeister Award(where the writing truly began in earnest), the Hermitage Artist Retreat, Dora Maar House (France), and three different stints at the MacDowell Colony, one of which resulted in my eternal gratitude to Blake Tewksbury for driving me to the computer shop in Keene after my laptop died on *my very first day!* I'd also like to acknowledge my month as Visiting Artist at the Siena Art Institute (Italy) where I was able for the first time to read a chapter in a public event, Hawthornden Castle (Scotland) for late-stage tweaking, and Bogliasco Foundation (Italy) where I received the ARC for the final proof.

I would like to thank Amy Robbins for being a fabulous copy-editor. And I want to thank everyone at Seven Stories Press, in particular my wonderful editor Veronica Liu, someone who believed in the book from the start in all its massiveness, and whose thoughts expressed a deep understanding of everything I was trying to do. For a first novel, I couldn't have been luckier.

As a work of historical fiction, *The Castle Cross the Magnet Carter* is a product of my imagination founded in documented reality. My imagination is a product of my upbringing, so lastly I must acknowledge my immediate and extended family, and my hometown Cumberland, Maryland. A heck of a lot of my own memories, as well as recollections of the previous generation that have been handed down to me, appear herein, consciously and, probably much more frequently, not.

REFERENCES

The Castle Cross the Magnet Carter is a fictional narrative steeped in twentieth-century American history. I utilized numerous sources, some to garner
specific information, some inspiring in other ways. Below is an abridged list.

Allen, James, ed. *Without Sanctuary: Lynching Photography in America.* Santa Fe, NM:
Twin Palms Publishers, 2000.

Apel, Dora, and Shawn Michelle Smith. *Lynching Photographs.* Berkeley: University of California Press, 2008

Aretha, David. *The Trial of the Scottsboro Boys.* Civil Rights Movement Series. Greensboro,
NC: Morgan Reynolds Publishing, 2007.

Aronson, Josh, dir. *Sound and Fury,* documentary. Aronson Film Associates et al., 2000.

Bemelmans, Ludwig. *Madeline.* New York: The Viking Press, 1939.

Berryman, Clifford Kennedy. "Oh, the old gray mare, she ain't what she used to be."
Cartoon, published December 26, 1943.

Bullard, Douglas. T. *Islay.* Dallas, TX: TJ Publishers, Inc., 1986.

Cameron, James. *A Time of Terror: A Survivor's Story.* Baltimore, MD: Black Classic Press,
1982.

Campbell, James. *Talking at the Gates: A Life of James Baldwin.* Berkeley and Los Angeles:
University of California Press, 1991.

Clinton, George, et al. "Tear the Roof off the Sucker (Give Up the Funk)," as recorded by
Parliament. Casablanca records, 1976.

The Code of Georgia of 1933. Adopted March 24, 1933; effective January 1, 1935. Prepared
under the direction of the Code Commission by Orville A. Park and Harry S. Strozier.
Atlanta, GA: Harrison Company, 1935.

Collins, Bootsy, performing "Stretchin' Out" on *Night Music,* NBC, episode 204, 1989.

Davis, Angela. *Angela Davis: An Autobiography.* New York: International Publishers, 1989.

DeBruyne, Nese F. and Anne Leland. *Congressional Research Service: American War and Military
Operations Casualties: Lists and Statistics.* January 2, 2015.

Ellison, Ralph. *Invisible Man.* New York: Random House, 1952.

Feldstein, Albert L. *Allegany County.* Postcard History Series. Charleston, SC: Arcadia Publishing, 2006.

Foner, Philip S., ed. *Helen Keller: Her Socialist Years.* New York: International Publishers,
1967.

"The Freedman's Bureau! An agency to keep the Negro in idleness at the expense of the white man. Twice vetoed by the President, and made a law by Congress. Support Congress & you support the Negro Sustain the President and you protect the white man." Cartoon. 1866.

Garey, Diane, and Lawrence R. Hott. *Through Deaf Eyes*, documentary. PBS, 2007.

Gibbs, Wilma L., ed. *Indiana's African-American Heritage: Esssays from Black History News & Notes*. Indianapolis: Indiana Historical Society, 1993.

Giddings, Paula J. *When and Where I Enter: The Impact of Black Women on Race and Sex in America*. New York: William Morrow, 1984.

Golladay, Loy E. *A is for Alice: Poems of Love and Laughter that Reflect Life Behind the "Plate-Glass Curtain" of Deafness*. 1992.

Good, Benjamin. "A Child's Right to Counsel in Removal Proceedings." *Stanford Journal of Civil Rights & Civil Liberties*. January 2014.

Hairston, Ernest and Linwood Smith. *Black and Deaf in America*. Dallas, TX: TJ Publishers, Inc., 1983.

Harper, Timothy. *The Complete Idiot's Guide to the U.S. Constitution*. New York: Alpha Books, 2007.

Heard, Alex. *The Eyes of Willie McGee: A Tragedy of Race, Sex, and Secrets in the Jim Crow South*. New York: HarperCollins, 2010.

Hemingway, Ernest. *A Farewell to Arms*. New York: Scribner, 1929.

Hidden Stories, Discovered Voices: A History of African Americans in Cumberland, Maryland. Cumberland: Allegany County (Maryland) Board of Education, 2010.

Holcomb, Roy K., Samuel K. Holcomb, and Thomas K. Holcomb. *Deaf Culture Our Way: Anecdotes from the Deaf Community*. 3rd ed. San Diego, CA: DawnSignPress, 1994.

Keller, Helen. *The Story of My Life*. New York: W.W. Norton & Co., 2003. (originally 1903)

Kelley, Robin D.G. *Hammer and Hoe: Alabama Communists During the Great Depression*. Chapel Hill: University of North Carolina Press, 1990.

Kersten, Andrew E. *A. Philip Randolph: A Life in the Vanguard*. Lanham, MD: Rowman & Littlefield Publishers, 2006.

King: A Filmed Record . . . Montgomery to Memphis. Conceived and produced by Ely Landau. Kino Classics. Martin Luther King Project, 1970.

Lazarus, Emma. "The New Colossus" (poem), 1883.

letter about Benjamin Banneker in the *George-town Weekly Ledger*, 1791.

Lewis, Anthony. *Gideon's Trumpet*. New York: Vintage Books, 1989.

Lief, Michael S., Ben Bycel and H. Mitchell Caldwell. *Ladies and Gentlemen of the Jury: Greatest Closing Arguments in Modern Law*. New York: Touchstone, 1998.

Loesser, Frank. "Praise the Lord and Pass the Ammunition." Sony/ATV Music Publishing LLC, 1942.

Loudermilk, John D., et al. "Waterloo," as recorded by Stonewall Jackson. Columbia records, 1959.

Marable, Manning. *Malcolm X: A Life of Reinvention.* New York: Viking Penguin, 2011.

McCaskill, Carolyn, Ceil Lucas, Robert Bayley, and Joseph Hill. *The Hidden Treasure of Black ASL.* Washington, D.C.: Gallaudet University Press, 2011.

Minnesota Research Society. *Duluth Lynchings Online Resource.* http://collections.mnhs.org/duluthlynchings/

Montgomery, Ben, Waveney Ann Moore, Edmund D. Fountain, and Kelley Benham. *For Their Own Good.* Six-part series revealing conditions at Florida's oldest reform school during the 1950s and 1960s. *St. Petersburg Times,* debuting April 17, 2009, and running through December 2009.

Mulrooney, Kristin. *American Sign Language Demystified.* New York: McGraw-Hill Companies, Inc., 2010.

Musgrove, George McCoy. *Competitive Debate Rules and Techniques.* 3rd ed. New York: H. W. Wilson Co., 1957.

Narcotics Anonymous. Van Nuys, CA: World Service Office, Inc., 1982.

National Public Radio staff. "'The Kissing Case' and the Lives It Shattered." NPR, April 29, 2011.

National WWII Museum, New Orleans, Louisiana.

"Oh My Darling, Clementine." Folk ballad, usually credited to Percy Montrose (1884), or sometimes to Barker Bradford.

Padden, Carol, and Tom Humphries. *Inside Deaf Culture.* Cambridge, MA: Harvard University Press, 2005.

Rada, James, Jr. *Looking Back: True Stories of Mountain Maryland.* Gettysburg, PA: Legacy Publishing, 2009.

Richardson, J.P. "Running Bear," as recorded by Johnny Preston. Mercury records, 1959.

Ridley, Thomas Howard, Jr. *From the Avenue: A Memoir.* Indianapolis, IN: self-published, 2012.

Robinson, Plater, producer. "The Murder of Emmett Till." *Soundprint,* National Public Radio, 1995.

Dr. Seuss Collection. "Don't let them carve THOSE faces on our mountains. Cartoon. *PM* magazine, December 12, 1941.

"Stagger Lee," folk song as recorded by Lloyd Price, ABC records, 1959.

Stone, Sly. "Thank You (Falettinme Be Mice Elf Agin)," as recorded by Sly and the Family Stone. Epic records, 1969.

Stremlau, Tonya M., ed. *The Deaf Way II Anthology: A Literary Collection by Deaf and Hard of Hearing Writers.* Washington, D.C.: Gallaudet University Press, 2002.

Takaki, Ronald. *Double Victory: A Multicultural History of America in World War II*. New York: Little, Brown, 2000.

Terkel, Studs. *"The Good War": An Oral History of World War II*. New York: The New Press, 1984.

Thompson, James G. Letter to the editor, *Pittsburgh Courier*, Jan. 31, 1942.

Thornbrough, Emma Lou. *Indiana Blacks in the Twentieth Century*. Bloomington: Indiana University Press, 2001.

The Twilight Zone. "I Am the Night—Color Me Black." Episode 146. CBS Television Distribution, 1964.

Waldrep, Christopher. *Lynching in America: A History in Documents*. New York: NYU Press, 2006.

Williams, Juan. *Thurgood Marshall: American Revolutionary*. New York: Times Books, 1998.

Wright, Mary Herring. *Sounds Like Home: Growing Up Black and Deaf in the South*. Washington, D.C.: Gallaudet University Press, 1999.

Wynn, Neil A. *The African American Experience During World War II*. The African American History Series. Lanham, MD: Rowman & Littlefield Publishers, Inc., 2010.

NOTE: In chapter 4 of the 1941-42 Prayer Ridge section, I mention *A Handbook of the Sign Language of the Deaf: Prepared Especially for Ministers, Sunday School Workers, Theological Students and Friends of the Deaf* by J. W. Michaels, and then I proceed to refer to excerpts from it. The book was published in Atlanta, 1923, by the Home Mission Board, Southern Baptist Convention. However, I have never seen it so, while the book exists, my references are purely fictional.

ABOUT THE AUTHOR

Kia Corthron has written many plays, fifteen of which have been produced nationally and internationally. For her body of work for the stage, she has garnered the Windham Campbell Prize for Drama, the Simon Great Plains Playwright Award, the United States Artists Jane Addams Fellowship, the Lee Reynolds Award, and the Otto Award. She has also written a bit of television (Edgar and Writers Guild Outstanding Series awards for *The Wire*). *The Castle Cross the Magnet Carter* is her first novel. She grew up in Cumberland, Maryland, and lives in Harlem, New York City.

JAN 2 6 2016

Sayville, NY 11782
88 Greene Avenue
Sayville Library